Praise for *Our Lady of the Islands*

~

"This satisfying feminist tale ... features an empathetic middle-aged, middle-class protagonist managing the roles of businesswoman, mother and grand-mother, fugitive, and unwilling savior with realism and grace ... The second half of the book [is] ... a celebration of female friendship and cooperation. Page has done a phenomenal job of completing Lake's work after his death, honoring his contributions and vision while giving the novel an emotionally authentic, coherent voice."

— *Publishers Weekly* (starred review)

"When a dead giant — a god, perhaps? — washes up on Alizar's shore, the ruler orders it butchered and fed to the poor. (As one does.) That choice sets the stage for ... a powerful, thoughtful tale that stays with you long after you turn the final page."

—Jim C. Hines, Hugo-winning author of *Libriomancer*

"... A tale of political and religious intrigue in the midst of changing times. Page and Lake's voices blend perfectly, with her eye for character and his eye for setting, making *Our Lady of the Islands* a great, fast, and meaningful read."

— Ken Scholes, author of the *Psalms of Isaak* saga

"A gorgeous tale of courage and friendship, with appealing characters and an epic sweep."

— Tina Connolly, author of *Ironskin*

~

OUR LADY
of the ISLANDS

SHANNON PAGE
∼ JAY LAKE ∼

per Aspera

OUR LADY OF THE ISLANDS. Copyright © 2014 by Shannon Page and Joseph E. Lake, Jr.

Edited by Jak Koke
Cover illustration & map by Mark J. Ferrari
Design & interior illustration by Karawynn Long

Published by Per Aspera Press
www.perasperapress.com

Our Lady of the Islands
ISBN: 978–1–941662–07–6 (tradepaper)

Library of Congress Cataloging-in-Publication Data

Page, Shannon, author.
  Our Lady of the Islands / by Shannon Page & Jay Lake.
    pages cm. — (The Butchered God ; Book One)
    ISBN 978-1-941662-06-9 (hardcover) — ISBN 978-1-941662-07-6 (tradepaper) — ISBN 978-1-941662-08-3 (ebook)
    1. Fantasy fiction. I. Lake, Jay, author. II. Title.
    PS3616.A337624O96 2014
    813'.6—dc23
                          2014035911

First printing: December 2014

For Jay

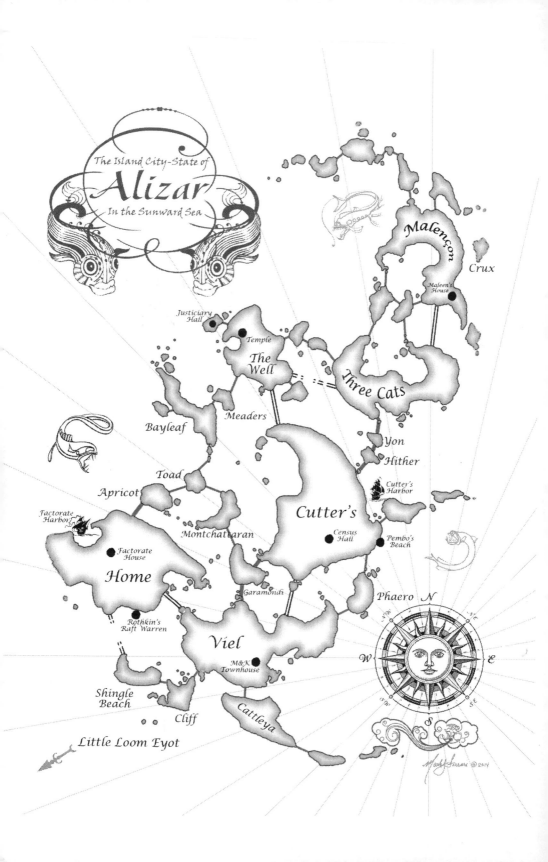

The Island City-State of
Alizar
In the Sunward Sea

Malençon

Crux

Maleen's House

Justiciary Hall

Temple

The Well

Three Cats

Meaders

Bayleaf

Yon

Hither

Toad

Cutter's Harbor

Apricot

Factorate Harbor

Cutter's

Census Hall

Pembo's Beach

Montchattaran

Factorate House

Home

Garamondi

Phaero

Rothkin's Raft Warren

Viel

M&K Townhouse

Shingle Beach

Cliff

Cattleya

Little Loom Eyot

N

W   E

S

AUTHOR'S NOTE

In 2009, Jay Lake and I decided to write a novel together. We'd already enjoyed collaborating on stories; this was the natural progression.

It was also a natural decision to make it a fantasy novel. We decided to set it in a remote corner of the world he'd already built in his *Green* and *Flowers* novels (Alizar is mentioned in passing at the very end of *Kalimpura*). And who would be the main character? "A young woman —" Jay started, but I was having none of that. "No more coming-of-age novels. Let's write someone who's already OF age. Someone who thinks her story is, if not over, then at least comfortably established."

Thus was born Sian Kattë, a respectable middle-aged businesswoman whose life is upended by an unlooked-for magical 'gift'.

The process of writing *Our Lady of the Islands* was initially smooth. Jay wrote a complex, detailed outline; I quibbled with it until we got something we were both happy with. (The one thing I remember really putting my foot down about was the tired old 'she cuts her hair to disguise herself' trope. Honestly, would that ever actually work?) Then I wrote the first draft, leaving a few 'Jay to fill in here' blanks, mostly about nautical details.

From there, Jay took the manuscript, filling in those blanks, and adding lots of nuance, detail, and flavor. We passed it back and forth several times, then sent it out to a few first readers … and then life interrupted, and all progress stopped. The book sat, trunked, until early 2013, when Jak Koke, managing editor of Per Aspera Press, asked me, "Whatever happened to that book you wrote with Jay? Can I read it?"

By this time, Jay was valiantly struggling with metastatic colon cancer. He was happy to see the book marketed, but made it clear that he would not be able to work on any revisions. So I agreed to take that on, and soon Jak made us an offer … contingent on some major reworking.

I began that reworking in early 2014, with crucial and generous editorial input from Mark Ferrari. We were hoping to finish by June, for Jay's birthday, but it needed more work than that deadline permitted.

Jay entered hospice on May 21, and died on June 1.

I think Jay would like this version of the novel, though it diverges from the draft we worked on in a number of places. His world and his characters remain; the story is still the one we set out to write. I am deeply sad that he won't be able to read it. This book quite literally wouldn't exist without Jay Lake. I hope it does honor to his memory.

But even a collaborative novel isn't the product of its two authors alone. I've already mentioned Mark Ferrari: his insights and creative contributions enriched the story greatly, and he kept me honest whenever I tried to rush through the revisions (hyper-focused on the deadlines as I tend to be). Mark also drew the gorgeous cover and the beautiful map. Jak Koke provided several iterations of insightful, sharp editorial advice. Any remaining flaws are entirely my own. Early readers Aaron Spielman and Michael Curry provided much valuable input; Michael's detailed dissection of the novel is part of what made everyone realize how much work it still needed, though I know he didn't mean for us to trunk it! I thank Ken Scholes for years of love and encouragement in general and for his lovely blurb now. Holly King listened to parts of the story as Mark read them aloud; that process was invaluable for me, both in her feedback and in just hearing the book brought to life. Karawynn Long not only copyedited the manuscript, but finalized and improved the cover and designed a beautiful interior, including the bone flower illustration.

And I thank you, dear reader, for joining us in this journey — a story is nothing without an audience. Welcome to the world of Alizar. I hope you have a lovely time here.

Shannon Page
Portland, Oregon
July 26, 2014

PROLOGUE

A century and a half after the island nation of Alizar had freed itself from continental rule, in the seventeenth year of Viktor Morrentian Alkattha's troubled reign as Factor, a giant corpse washed up onto the eastern shore of Cutter's, at the island cluster's very center. The greatest typhoon in generations had blown spume for three days over the walls of even the mightiest houses on the highest hills, swamping the rotting, coastal boat-towns altogether, drowning legions of the poor, and flushing every darkest alleyway and sewer tunnel with a boil of cold, salty rage.

On the storm's fourth day, dawn was accompanied by a peculiar pearl-escence to the east, as if the clouds were loathe to release their clammy grip. Those first few to venture out onto the streets of Cutter's — guards, priests, looters, the desperate — found on the shingles of Pembo's Beach a body so large and long that all agreed it couldn't possibly have been a man. And yet, it had the form of one.

Its pale complexion was, by then at least, the color of a Smagadine, that unhealthy tone indicative of life lived underground, or solely under moon-light, far from any sunlight's benediction. Its wrinkled fingers were the size of longboats. Its gelid, unseeing eyes as large as the wine tuns stored beneath the Factorate House. The cock across its thigh, a toppled watchtower.

The corpse was an instant nine-days' wonder, and a panic. Nearly two hundred years earlier, gods had returned to faraway Copper Downs. Had they at last come to Alizar? The nation's streets were flooded for the second time in days, this time with rumor, prophecy, and hushed prognostication. Had the storm birthed this monster or slain it? Would it rise to lay waste to the city, vanish back into sea like a dream half-remembered, or just putrefy, poisoning Cutter's scenic bay and vast commercial port as it rotted on the beach? Might it be an omen of some even greater calamity in store?

While the Mishrah-Khote, Alizar's ancient priesthood of physicians, maintained a careful silence in regard to their position on the corpse, the nation's Factor did not find the unexpected arrival of a 'dead god' convenient in the least. Already struggling to navigate his country's growing pains, he had no need of ominous portents inciting the poor and ignorant to erratic imaginings and potentially volatile assessments of his governance. He just wanted the great body gone! Though not in any manner that might make him look defensive or afraid, of course.

Fortunately for him, Alizar was virtually swimming in very poor and hungry citizens after such a devastating storm. His advisors assured him that the giant carcass was still at least as sound as many others hanging in that tropic nation's butcher shops on any given day. Why not address two problems with a single cure? Thus, the Factor demonstrated his consideration for the city's starving masses by ordering the inconvenient corpse butchered quickly, before it started rotting, and distributed — for free — to all and any wishing to fill their bellies with its meat. Since animals alone — never people, much less *gods* — were ever butchered and consumed, he asserted dubiously, the corpse's fate must somehow prove its nature. Whatever superficial form it might have borne, this creature had been "nothing but a great sea monster of some sort."

Huge crowds rushed to Cutter's bloody shingle to accept their portion of this windfall, by which their desperate families were kept fed for some weeks after. Despite this fact — or perhaps because of it — memory of the giant corpse did not fade as hoped. If anything, the common folks' awe of this *dead god* increased. New tales began to circulate, of teeth and bones extracted, giant fingernails pared, and god-meat scraped from long, pale flanks not just to feed the desperate, but to bless and heal them as well. From the furtive repetition of these stories, a new cult emerged around the *Butchered God*, if at first just in cautious whispers and anonymous graffiti.

After a while, as no other evidence of returning gods appeared, the wealthy and the comfortable middle class put the event aside. Life went on.

New urgencies seized attention — new wonders, scandals, and attendant gossip.

Old storms are eventually forgotten. Old flotsam always drifts back out to sea.

As long as what is buried stays that way, and its memory is left unstirred.

PART 1

ONE

Domina Sian Kattë hummed quietly as she poured two glasses of *kiesh*, worked the cork back into the stout little bottle, then brought the drinks to the sitting room.

Captain Reikos smiled up at her from his seat on the rattan sofa; he moved to rise, but she waved him back down. His pale eyes were as warm as the early-evening air fluttering the curtains at the front windows of her Viel townhouse. Sian could hear the murmurs of street noise from below — the cries of cart runners, the sound of dishes in the tavern's kitchen three doors over, at the head of Meander Way. "I thank you, my lady." Reikos lifted his glass in a formal toast.

Sian laughed and took a seat in the armchair, arranging her golden silks comfortably about her. "None of that, Konstantin; when we come upstairs, we are friends."

"Friends." He tasted the word, then the sweet liquor, before setting his small amber glass on the delicate table between them. "Domina Kattë, I had imagined us more than that. Please forgive my presumption." But now his courtliness was a tease. He went on before she could reach over and give him the gentle swat he so clearly deserved. "Ah, Sian, it is good to see you."

"Yes. It's been too long. What news of the wider world?"

"Well, much of it is still covered in salt water. And little of it is as warm and lovely as these islands are." Reikos leaned back and stretched a bit, without seeming to fill any additional space. He was a trim, agile man able to live comfortably aboard his ship for months on end; entirely at home in a cabin only four or five paces wide in any direction, with its narrow little bunk. He looked quite natural on her small sofa, she thought. "We spent half the voyage here pushing through squalls to make a sailor think seriously about buying a plow. Lost Port's upstart new vineyards have suffered a blight for their impertinence. Some little fly, they are saying, has come by boat from the City Imperishable and developed a liking for grape leaves. The price of wine has soared there now, and every ship that comes to port is treated like a threat."

"That's unfortunate," Sian said. "I've been enjoying the Stone Coast wines."

"Many folk have. I am certain the vintners will do all they can to rescue their investments." He took another sip. "Beyond all that, though, I've seen nothing half so interesting as what I find in Alizar. And not merely because you are here."

She smiled again at this. "I'll bet you say that to all your women."

"Only the best ones." He grew serious. "But tell me: is everything all right here?"

"What do you mean?"

Reikos waved an arm vaguely in the direction of Cutter's, the next major island in the chain, where foreign traders docked. "I almost couldn't find a berth for *Fair Passage*. Ships just aren't leaving — though not because trade is lively; quite the opposite. Yorgen told me he's waited a month or more to fill even half his capacity. The Kenner brothers have lost a good number of their crew to desertion. And I find the streets filled with rabble now, marching around and chanting."

"Oh, the prayer lines." Sian sighed. She thought she could hear one now, in fact, out beyond the end of Meander Way — the leader's call and the crowd's mumbled response. "They follow the so-called Butchered God."

"So-called? You don't believe it was a god, then?"

"I don't believe it was a sea monster, no matter what the Factor would have us think. But a god? Do gods die?"

He shrugged. "I am not a religious man."

"I have little use for priests myself. But if there were gods anywhere near Alizar — and if one should die — I can hardly believe they would allow their bodies just to wash up on a beach somewhere, much less be carved up to feed the poor."

"What a bizarre gesture that was. Your cousin is a … an interesting man."

"You speak as though I know him." Sian shrugged. "Even so, I can't imagine a god's appearance was convenient for him."

Reikos smiled as he finished his drink. "I expect the Temple Mishrah-Khote was pleased."

"Perhaps," Sian said. "Though one must wonder whether the arrival of a god was any more convenient for them. They do not seem to embrace the new cult."

"Such interesting times, as I say." Reikos toyed with his empty glass. "You live amidst these giant ruins. Does no one wonder at the coincidence — or worry that whoever built them might be coming back?"

"From the age of legends?" She took a sip of wine, and sighed. "The Factor may ask himself that question every night. But I don't have to. We've had no Green Woman here, that I'm aware of. And the thing was dead, which is *very* convenient for everyone. Will you have another before dinner?"

"Yes, I will — delicious. I believe I recognize this vintage?"

"Indeed you do. A certain well-traveled sea captain brought me a case on his last visit. I hope he's brought more; my stores could use restocking."

"It's eminently possible that he has."

After checking to see that their bouillabaisse from the tavern was still warm, Sian brought the bottle to the table. "You're right, though: matters here aren't what they should be, and not just on the docks. I can't retain my workers either — I need new weavers, and probably a new dyer, if I can find anyone suitable. I've been to the hiring hall four times this season already." She smiled wryly. "Not that anyone is happy to see me there these days."

"I cannot imagine who would not be pleased to see your lovely face at his doorstep. Show me these ungrateful men!"

Sian laughed. "Ah, flatterer, you warm an old woman's bones."

Reikos gave a half-bow, elegant even from his seated position. "Always happy to be of service. Though you are *not* old."

Sian raised an eyebrow. "Nor am I young."

"You are ageless, a creature of great and abiding beauty."

Sian gave him a long look calculated to wither.

Reikos cleared his throat. "So, what are these marches, then? Some sort of protest?"

"Our work force abandons honest labor now to roam the streets in prayer, begging their Butchered God for a more equitable distribution of wealth. As if coins might just fall on them with the rains!" She shook her head. "I don't know what they hope to achieve. But they seem reasonably peaceful. Enough of this gloomy talk. You must be famished — shall we dine?"

"Eager as I am for fish soup, my lady, I find myself in the grasp of a ... different hunger at the moment ..." He glanced beyond the small kitchen to the daybed behind its gauze curtain at the back of the townhouse. The fabric around the bed stirred gently in the fragrant evening breeze. "I was a long time at sea, far from the comforts of shore."

Laughing, Sian got to her feet and gave Reikos a hand up. "A man after my own heart. So we shall have dessert first, and dine afterwards."

～

The bouillabaisse had kept perfectly, making a fine late supper. Sian found a bottle of Stone Coast claret to accompany it, hoping indeed that Lost Port's blight should pass. When the meal was done, Reikos carried his dishes to the sideboard, then took the empty wine bottle downstairs and set it outside the back door for the glass-scavengers.

It was not his custom to stay the night when he visited. A ship's captain had responsibilities early in the morning that required a well-rested body and an alert mind. This equally suited Sian, being well past the age when sleeping like piled pups in the townhouse's small daybed would leave her refreshed at dawn. And though the place was no storefront, clients and associates did happen by with some frequency when she was in town; it was just easier, and more professional, for her to rise alone there.

When he returned from the alley, Reikos nuzzled the back of Sian's neck, planting a few small kisses on the tender skin there. "When shall we dine again?"

"How long are you in port this time?" Sian scraped the soup-bowl into the covered scrap container, lest she encourage the islands' large roaches, and set it aside for return to the tavern. A bright green gecko climbed the wall behind the sideboard, ever alert for mosquitoes.

"A fortnight, perhaps; until I can turn over my cargo. I have you down for one case of *kiesh*, at the very least."

"I thank you." Sian thought a moment. "I need to go to Little Loom Eyot tomorrow, but business will bring me back to Viel within three or four days."

"I look forward to it." He kissed her again, pulling her close. "Such a brief respite this was from the desolation of my days. Will you not come with me this time?"

Sian smiled, turning around in his arms to face him. "My dear, your shipboard bed is even smaller than mine."

"No, not just tonight. Sail with me when I leave. I will show you the world!"

"And what will all your other women think when I show up?"

"There will be no one but you, Sian."

Laughing, she said, "Now that is going a bit far, even for you." She gave him a gentle push. "Go on, get back to *Fair Passage*. I shall see you in a few days."

Reikos let go of her and took up his jacket and satchel. "I hope your husband knows what a lucky man he is."

Sian looked up at him, a little surprised. "Of course he does. As I know how lucky I am. Comfort, and freedom, and interesting work — I have it all."

"Yes, you do." Reikos gazed at her. "He truly does not mind your ... independence?"

"We have long since passed the time of caring about such things. Our arrangement is clear: he runs the manufactory, and I manage the business in town. Our free time is our own." She frowned at her lover. "As I believe I have explained to you."

"Yes, you have." Then he grinned, the mischievous glint returned. "May your dreams be filled with delightful adventures involving dashing sea captains."

"You sleep well too." She walked him down to the front door, then kissed him farewell as he slipped quietly into the night.

She watched his trim form retreat down Meander Way, then bolted the door.

~

Sian spent a productive morning visiting a new dye-seller on Three Cats, buying several sacks each of ochre and indigo and putting in an order for some rare carmine at a decent price. At least *some* businesses were still thriving. After closing up the townhouse, Sian walked through Viel's crowded streets to the public dock, looking around for Pino, finally spotting him near the end of the wharf, waving madly at her. She and Arouf had hired the young man just a few years back, but he was proving to be a very dedicated worker, cheerfully filling in anywhere the firm of Monde & Katté required — from hauling supplies to the storehouse, to general repair and maintenance, to fetching whatever Sian acquired in town, as well as ferrying her back and forth between home and Alizar Main.

Resting her feet on the dye-sacks piled in the bottom of the boat, she let herself daydream during the hour-long passage across the smooth waters of Alizar Bay to their private island — perhaps she had had less sleep than she'd realized — only noticing their approach when the boat bumped against the dock at Little Loom Eyot. "Thank you, Pino," Sian said, alighting. Unencumbered, as usual. No matter that she managed fine in town; Pino would never let her carry her own bags when he was there.

"Happy to have you home, my lady," the boy answered, pushing his dark brown hair out of his eyes and grinning at her.

After a perfunctory glance around the lush grounds, she went to her little office upstairs in the loom house to file and sort the documents, orders, and purchase receipts she'd brought from town. Always so much paperwork! Once again, she resolved to hire clerical help.

When the bell chimed for change of shift, she looked up, startled to see the afternoon entirely passed. She straightened her desk, then began the short walk up the hill. She passed alongside the loom house and in front of the dye works, the two largest buildings on the island. Blue-and-red macaws shrieked and hopped about in the chinaberry trees above her head, scolding her for disturbing their evening congress — without offering food.

"Peace, you little beggars," she chuckled at them as she turned beside the unmarried women's dormitory, nestled in a riot of blooming lacuina vines next to the refectory for her workers. Beyond that came the cottages of the older, married employees, and the few bachelor couples of whom she did not inquire so much.

Her own house stood on the highest part of the island, an often cloud-capped bluff situated on the rain-shadowed western face of the peak. Like the compound's cottages, it was built raised on poles in the traditional Alizari style, albeit with the modern conveniences of plumbing and a decent indoor kitchen. Its sweeping teak gables were pierced with tall windows and wide, elaborately carved lattice shutters to close against ocean storms or open to the sun's benediction.

The walk might be short — the entire island was little more than a thousand paces north to south — but the rise was of a steepness, and Sian was of an age (no matter what Reikos might say), as to leave her half out of breath by the time she'd passed the stand of bony Dragon's Blood trees outside their gate, and slid aside the soft peg that held the front door closed. No need for guards or even locks when you owned your own bridgeless island.

Inside, a warm glow came from the kitchen, bearing with it the welcoming aroma of food on the stove. "That you, wife?"

"Yes, Arouf, it is I." Sian unwrapped her elaborately patterned silk shawl and hung it on a hook by the door, next to its many mates. Today's had been blue, with the spectacular image of an iridescent morpho butterfly picked out along its length.

In the kitchen, she found her husband standing over a large pot, a long wooden spoon in his hand. Bela was nowhere to be seen; Arouf must have given their cook-housekeeper the evening off. "That smells good," she said, going to kiss him on his damp and bristly beard.

"It's cold enough out for a spicy sweetprawn stew, I should think." He gave her an affectionate pat on the arm, his attention still on the pot.

"Cold?" She lifted an eyebrow, smiling as she went to the cool box to find an open jug of tart white wine. She poured herself a glass, then refilled Arouf's. "Only a man from the farthest reach of Malençon could possibly call this weather cold."

"Or perhaps one who had a particular craving for spicy sweetprawn stew." Arouf sipped his wine. "It should be ready soon, don't wander far."

"I won't."

Without mentioning any names, she began to tell Arouf about conversations she'd had with 'several trading partners' — news of the Stone Coast grape blight, the increasing labor shortage, the stagnation at the harbor at Cutter's. "And the city feels … less civilized all the time. Jamino Fanti tells me that his runner-cart was ambushed by a mob of angry vagrants last week, demanding money from him."

"Or what?" Arouf asked.

"Or they'd push the cart over and break its wheels, they said. That's what he told me."

"Did he give in to this? Where was his runner while all this happened?"

"There were too many of them for the runner to fend off, apparently."

Arouf shook his head, his dark eyes flashing. "I do not like you going there."

"Oh?" She gave him a wry smile. "Does that mean *you* will go next time?"

He scowled at her. "That is your world, down there, wife. This is mine."

Such a powerful-looking man, Sian mused, *and yet such a child, to be so upset by even a mention of the outside world.* She bit her lip and went to set the table, refraining from telling him that someone in the crowd had flung a fistful of mud at her as she had left the townhouse in Viel to meet Pino that afternoon. They had missed. So what did it matter?

"Did you do any entertaining while you were in town?"

Sian looked up at him. "No. Why do you ask?"

Arouf shrugged, not looking up from the cutting board where he was dicing firefruit. "Why doesn't the Factor *do* something about all this unrest?"

"I don't know." She thought a moment. "He might be too distracted. I hear his son is not recovering quite as quickly as they'd hoped."

"That's unfortunate." He dropped the peppers into the stew and stirred vigorously. Then he lifted the spoon to his lips, frowned, and returned to the board to dice another.

"Indeed." Sian thought about their own daughters, with the mingled love and fear that fills any mother when she hears of a child's illness. Because they would always be her babies, no matter that they were grown and gone. Maleen, at least, still lived in Alizar; Sian had been meaning to visit her and the grandchildren for far too long. Life just seemed to crowd out every space she tried to clear for such things lately. She shook her head and resolved more fiercely to do it — soon.

"Well, supper is ready," Arouf said, ladling stew into a serving bowl. A good measure remained steaming on the stove when he brought the filled bowl to the table.

She dipped her bread in the fragrant broth as the first bite seared pleasantly down her throat. "Your best yet."

Arouf patted his belly and swallowed his own generous spoonful. "A little bland." Tears leaked from the corners of his eyes and his cheeks flushed slightly. "But, it was the best I could do with these poor ingredients."

"Any better and this old body could simply not stand it."

"Well, then. It must be exactly good enough."

"Exactly."

As they ate, Sian asked Arouf about matters in the dye works. He had nothing much to report, beyond complaining of being short-staffed, and soon enough they were passing their supper in silence.

"I'll take the sacks out to the shed, if you'll see to the dishes," Arouf said, pushing back from the table with a contented sigh.

"Of course. Go ahead." Sian rose and gathered the bowls, carrying them to the washbasin. "A one-pot meal shouldn't be much trouble." *Though if you wouldn't keep sending Bela home early, I wouldn't have to do even this*, Sian thought. It had been a long day, and she had more to do before bed.

Her husband pulled his boots on and went out the kitchen door. He hefted the sacks of dye two at a time, which made Sian cringe in sympathetic pain. Small as they appeared, they were dense and weighty. Arouf must not be feeling arthritis in his joints, like she was.

Or maybe it was all the spicy meals he ate. Sian felt her insides burning as she scraped the bowls into the bin for the flamingos and tamarins. Not an unpleasant burn, exactly; but she couldn't make three meals a day of the peppers as Arouf could.

The dishes done, she moved to the sitting room and lit a lantern by her reading chair, batting off a Luna moth that fluttered toward it through the window. After going to pull the shutters closed, she sat down, took a report from the large stack on her side table, and began to read, making occasional notes on a small sheet of paper as she went. The reports were gathered from everywhere Sian could acquire informants, and spoke, in one way or another, of the future of the market for silks and other luxuries. Unfortunately, this general topic was the first and last thing they had in common. It seemed nobody knew what was going to happen: demand would increase; it would most certainly decrease; unrest would interrupt the supply channels, or facilitate them as nervous investors dumped inventory; no two reports could agree.

Some time later, she had filled her sheet with notes and marked up a handful of other documents, putting several aside to keep. She looked up as she started to ask, "I wonder whether we should —" but her husband wasn't in his chair as usual. Come to think of it, she hadn't even heard him come in from the shed. She stretched and rubbed her eyes, glancing down the hallway that led to their sleeping chambers. Arouf's door was closed, and no light burned under it.

Extinguishing the lantern, she went back into the kitchen and checked that the shutters were pulled down there as well against invading night-tamarins, then plodded down the hall to her own room. It was, in theory, the marital suite, though Arouf had not made this bed his home since Rubya, their younger daughter, was born. He did tourist here on occasion, sometimes by entreaty, sometimes in a burst of drunken ardor, and once for a long, sweet passage of nearly six months, during which time Sian had let herself believe that their distance had passed. But, eventually, he had complained of his head, and of her shifting while she slept, and of her cold feet, and returned to his own chamber.

Sian let down her hair and rummaged through her overnight bag for her brush and sleeping shift, wondering just when, and why, their desire for one another had cooled. Their nights had once been as passionate as any she now shared with Reikos. Would she and Reikos drift apart someday as well? She shook her head with a wry smile. No. More likely she would just lose him sooner and more quickly to some younger woman — or some dozen of them. These were not questions to be pondering just before sleep. If ever.

She climbed into the tall, mosquito-netted bed, stretching her legs out across the cool, soft sheets. It did feel good to get into bed of a night.

She thought about reading a while — there were always more reports — but instead extinguished the lamp, and was asleep before she'd had a chance to reconsider.

~

Arouf lay awake, listening to his wife move around her bedroom, unpacking from her trip. Sian did so love her journeys to town, enjoyed dressing up in her fine silks, being the social and business face of Monde & Kattë. Arouf was more than happy to cede her the responsibility. He had no taste for mingling with the traders and merchants; it was an unwelcome change of pace, as far as he was concerned. It was very convenient that she had been willing, even eager, to take this task on. And she was very good at it, better than he'd ever been. The smartest thing he had done was to promote her to the counting house.

No: the smartest thing he had ever done had been marrying Sian Kattë in the first place, followed closely by agreeing that she should keep her own name. As Sian Monde, she would have vanished into obscurity; as Monde & Katté, their dye works claimed an undeniable family connection to the ruling Alkattha house, which had hardly hurt the business.

That wasn't why he had married her. Of course he loved her, and their two magnificent daughters perhaps even more. Arouf was still taken by surprise at times by his wife's beauty — her long dark hair, still thick and glossy even as it grew streaked with gray; her smooth copper skin; and those startling eyes, so dark as to seem almost black, until lamplight lit them up, revealing the amber glow within. And when she laughed, she became a girl of twenty again, her cheeks rosy and glowing, her whole face shining.

That she didn't laugh so often these days — that was simply a matter of the inevitable aches and weariness of growing older. Arouf understood growing older; he didn't fight against it as so many men of his generation did with dyes and perfumes, and squeezing into confining clothes to hide the evidence of a healthy appetite. Youth had been lovely. It was over now.

Fighting the inevitable was a foolish waste of time. He did the best he could to remain active, for he knew that the longest-lived men in his home village on the eastern shores of Malençon were the ones who chopped wood and dug post-holes to the very end of their days, refusing to let the younger men take these tasks from them.

So all was as it should be.

Even if he had not made the success that he had dreamed of in his youth, Arouf was satisfied enough with the enterprise he and Sian had built. They employed almost three dozen weavers, dyers, and other hands; they had built and furnished this fine, comfortable home; Maleen had made a good marriage match, and Rubya was pursuing her education far away in Dun Cranmoor, on the mainland. And the grandchildren! Arouf smiled in the dark at the thought of them. If only Maleen would bring them to visit more often. Arouf did not like to leave Little Loom Eyot. So much to do here. The older he got, the more daunting travel became. After all the years he'd given to raising his children, why could they not take just few days now and then to come back and see their father? And their mother too — though it was hard these days to catch Sian at home. Or anywhere else, he supposed.

Soon the sounds of Sian in her chamber grew quiet. She would have gone to bed, and quickly to sleep, tired from her work in Alizar Main. Well, he supposed it must be exhausting, though she seemed to thrive on it.

He did sometimes find himself wondering what went on in that town-house she'd chosen and retrofitted. He'd seen the renovations, shortly after they had bought it for use as an in-town *office* — the addition of sleeping quarters, for when business kept her overnight. The curtained-off upstairs rooms. For additional privacy from the street.

Ever since they'd moved to separate bedrooms, Arouf had wondered if she were … satisfying certain needs elsewhere. They had never spoken of such things openly, not in so many words. Speaking of it would make it real, somehow. He hadn't even wanted to think of it.

And he despised himself for thinking of it now.

One could not run a successful business entirely from afar. Sian needed to go to town periodically. And the dyes she'd brought home today were certainly fine; Arouf would likely have never heard of the new dye-seller from here.

Arouf shifted in the bed, arranging his pillow more comfortably beneath his head, listening to the kakapos calling one another in the night, and whatever might be rustling through the hisbiscus under his shuttered window. His sleeplessness had grown worse of late, but there was nothing to be done for that. More wine, less wine; a change of diet; being weary or well rested at bedtime; powders from Viel or farther; nothing made any difference. Sleep would find him when it chose to, and not a moment before.

He was almost ready to rise from bed and find something to relieve his wakefulness when he realized that it was in fact morning. He had slept after all, even if his body believed otherwise.

"Ah, me." He sat on the edge of the bed and rubbed the grit from the corners of his eyes. Kava: that's what he needed. He heard Bela's uneven steps in the kitchen as she shuffled around, probably rewashing the dishes Sian had cleaned last night, and putting them where they actually belonged. Yes, his wife's strengths most decidedly lay on the business side of things.

Pulling on his trousers, he tugged his long tangled hair back into a tail, capturing it with a stretchy band. Clever stuff, this tree sap which expanded and contracted. Idly wondering if it could be put to use in textiles, he walked down the hall and poked his nose into Sian's room.

It was vacant: she must already be in her office over the loom house.

Time for kava. He followed the aroma to the kitchen.

TWO

A few days later, Sian prepared to return to Viel. She packed a small overnight bag, along with a satchel of reports, inventory lists, and instructions for their two bankers. Today she wore yellow silks: the color of commerce. And of romance.

Arouf was already busy in the loom house when Pino appeared at the house shortly after breakfast, his brown hair neatly combed and slicked down with water. "Are you ready, my lady?"

"Yes, thank you." Sian followed him down to the little boat and settled herself comfortably aboard.

He rowed them out into the open waters that separated Little Loom Eyot from Alizar Main. Sian peered down over the boat's edge to see what jeweled fish might be dancing about the coral underneath their boat this morning, until the reefs began to fall away and vanish into deeper, bluer water. Then she gazed out at the placid sea under turquoise skies lined with puffs of cloud at the horizon, grateful for this time of enforced inactivity. She so seldom just rested.

It was a breezy day, less humid than usual, and Alizar sparkled in the tropical sunlight. As they drew closer to the central cluster of islands, she gazed through the straits, up to the graceful, monumental bridge connecting The Well and Three Cats, and the half-sunken ruins of the City of Giants that surrounded it. In the opposite direction, the island of Home was dominated by the grand Factorate House, rising atop its hill above clouds of fan palm and flowering Keelash trees. Another immense stub of once-mighty pillar, left from ancient times, rose from Home's small harbor.

"Who do you think built such things, Pino?" she said, thinking of Reikos's questions the other day.

"My lady?" The boy looked up, startled from his rhythm; one oar smacked flat against the water, juddering the boat. He recovered quickly and had them moving smoothly again.

"The old ruins."

He blinked. "The ancients built them, my lady."

"But who were the ancients?" Pino looked so worried that Sian smiled at him. "I mean, they were giants, clearly. Were they gods, though, or just great big people?"

Pino rowed a few more strokes before venturing, "I've only ever heard that they were ancients, and that they left long ago." He glanced over his shoulder at the pillar stub off Home with an uncomfortable shrug. "Before ... you know, two years ago, I never thought about it."

Nobody did, she thought. *Until a giant washed up on our shores.* "Was the Butchered God one of these ancients, do you think?"

"I don't know, my lady," Pino answered at once. "Some people say ... they say the Butchered God came to heal the city. At least, that's what I hear."

"Yes, yes ..." she mused. "I have heard that too. I do wonder how much healing a dead god can do for us."

The boy leaned forward, eagerly. "Would you like me to go into town, to ask around?"

"No. It was just idle curiosity — I'm sure Arouf needs you back on the Eyot." She did not want to think about it, really — as she remembered every time she did. Gods returning. These were thoughts too big. Too strange and frightening. What was one to do with them? She knew the tales of Copper Downs, of course; how the gods there had been released from their long captivity. Who didn't? The undying Duke's demise, and the chaos that followed, had helped catalyze Alizar's successful bid for independence, after all. But that was Copper Downs, and centuries ago. If there had ever been gods in Alizar, they'd been gone since long before the memory of anyone's historians. Surely, the Cutter's giant had just been some kind of freak. Dead, doubtless, of its very size. Let it rest, she told herself. Let it go. She had plenty of *real* troubles to contend with, just keeping their small business in good working order.

They approached the landing at Shingle Beach. The name was apropos, for the flat, arid island had little to recommend it save for this wide beach of coral rubble on its western shore, and the first bridge on Sian's way from Little Loom Eyot into the inner island cluster that made up central Alizar. Such bridges had proliferated under continental rule, engendered by a foreign ruling class less comfortable with traveling by boat than the native population was. The widely varied structures had transformed a scattershot gathering of rocks, low hills, coral atolls and long-dead volcanic peaks into a coherent city-state; Sian took a special, almost patriotic pride in walking them.

Which was why she usually preferred to have Pino drop her here, though Viel was two bridges further on. She rarely hired runner-carts and water-taxis unless she had too much to carry or too far to go, savoring any chance to walk across the smaller islands and their bridges, and ever conscious of the need for thrift, of course.

"Thank you, Pino." Sian gathered her bags. "Tomorrow afternoon, then?"

"Yes, my lady. Four bells after the midday."

The servant boy stayed and watched as Sian made her way up the rough-planked pathway that served as a floating pier when the tide was in. She had never been able to make him leave until she was out of sight, so she had stopped trying. He was charged to see his mistress safely to Alizar Main, and he would do so, until he could see her no longer.

He would also return as arranged, without fail. So she could hardly complain.

Sian walked into Shingle Beach's sole tiny village, through narrow streets crowded with hovels and cottages on short stilts against the tide. Like many of the lesser islands, Shingle Beach had its own flavor of taverns, markets, even household gardens. The rocky soil here did not support lush vegetation. Tall wild grasses, and a range of lovely succulents, delicately lavender or red, filled border rows and window boxes. Thorny heart's blood vine, with its mass of scarlet flowers and sweet, blood-red berries, covered many roofs and porches.

She was through the built-up area in minutes, walking past a waving stretch of orange stargrass, then onto the bridge to Cliff, where she always paused to catch her breath. She leaned against the rail, admiring the lofty Factorate House across the water on Home. It had been built not long after Alizar won its independence from continental rule, to replace the continental Factor's palace on Cutter's — which was now the Census Taker's Hall. This shining hub of Alizari industry and trade was a monument to the nation's independence, wealth, and power; and, for Sian, a symbol of family connection and prestige. The Factor himself, who lived there with his consort and their son, was her very distant cousin. She had never actually met them, of course, and her errands rarely took her to its busy marble halls, but from time to time she went there to arrange for necessary licenses, or charm one of its many resident officials into granting her some important tariff exemption or regulatory concession.

She soon walked on, passing across Cliff, an island about half the size of Shingle Beach, mostly covered with hutments and shanties, and barely a business district of its own. The only reason it was connected even by a rough bridge to anything was because of its proximity to Viel. Cliff itself was a nothing of a place, dusty and barren nearly to its jutting eastern shoreline, teeming with a seemingly endless crop of poor. The island's unusual weather was defined by winds that whipped relentlessly through the channel between Home and Viel.

The Cliff-Viel bridge was a far more substantial affair than the Shingle Beach-Cliff span. Its strong iron stanchions held up a roadbed paved with flat white stones salvaged from the broken buildings of the City of Giants. Some said that many of the islands themselves were nothing more than the rubble of those fallen structures, dust-covered and overgrown millennia ago.

Nobody slowed across the bridge today. Merchants, traders, and other folk out on their daily business, dodging runner-carts and the occasional larger oxcart, pushed past Sian without even glancing at the lovely structure. Capuchin monkeys climbed through the bridge's ornate grillwork overhead, chattering to one another, ever alert for the chance to pilfer some tasty morsel from an open cart.

Sian kept moving too, passing over onto Viel, through increasingly crowded streets towards the townhouse, nodding at faces she knew. She paused for a moment to talk with Mother Whinn at the corner tavern and bakery which stood at the base of Meander Way, a blade-straight street, artifact of the sense of humor of Viel's ancient designers. Or of their delicate grasp of reality.

At 45 Meander Way, Sian stuck her large brass key into the thick wooden door, jiggled it left and right, then turned it. The lock slid free, and she went in.

"Ooh," she muttered as stale air greeted her in the commercial front room. It had only been a few days; unfortunate that she had to keep the place sealed tight when she was away. She laid her bag and satchel down and set about opening shades and windows, letting in not only the perfumed tropical air but a good deal of light. The front room immediately became far more cheerful, and a whole lot hotter.

"Small price to pay." Sian never talked aloud to herself at home on Little Loom Eyot, but here, she often found herself doing so.

She bustled about the room, opening the smaller windows at the back and on the half-floor upstairs, propping the shutters open as wide as they would go, checking the levels of oil in the lamp wells, bringing in the flyers, notes and letters from the postal lockbox out front, sweeping the small front porch. Then she rested a bit, with a glass of tepid water from the townhouse's supply; a cool drink would have to come later, when she was out.

Her first errand today would be visiting the large Hiring Hall in the center of Viel's business district, though not for another hour or two. Business associates from the continent often had a hard time adjusting to Alizar's more languid tropic pace. In the meantime, she would work on her correspondence here — or perhaps find a comfortable café along the way. Yes, that was a much better idea. A small cup of kava was just what she wanted.

She stood by her open back door, letting the somewhat cooler air of the jacaranda-shaded alleyway filter in, then pulled the door closed again, and bolted it. The windows and shutters could stay open while she was out; they were fitted with narrow bars and net screens against invasion — human or insect.

Before she left, she took a moment to sort through the notes and messages that had been left. Most of them were routine, though she did find a notice about the upcoming Census. It included a little 'personal' note from another of her cousins: the Census Taker himself, though obviously dictated to a secretary. "Escotte, ever the politician," Sian muttered, setting it aside on her 'keep' pile. Then she came across a more important note: the Hanchu silk merchants she'd been trying so hard to pin down were inviting her to dinner this very evening, at their trading house on Malençon. Sian felt a mixture of annoyance and relief at this: what if she'd been on the Eyot today and missed this invitation! Well, thank goodness she wasn't, and double thanks that she kept a closet stocked with appropriate clothing here.

At the bottom of the stack, she found the item she'd been looking for: a small, tri-folded piece of manila-colored paper.

Unfolded, it revealed a short yet flowery note, labeled with today's date and written in a man's blocky hand; the slightly uncertain scrawl of someone who'd learned both the Alizari language and its flowing script as an adult:

Domina Sian Kattë:

Greetings and most felicitous welcome upon your return to civilization. (A joke, lady, if you please.)

I am most graciously anticipating the resumption of our negotiations on the subject of the northern silks I have in my stores, the afore-mentioned case of wine, and any other matters which may interest you. I trust our previously arranged appointment for this evening remains convenient. Please respond as to your pleasure in this matter as to the particulars of the time; I am assuming the place is to be the usual?

Looking forward to our continued negotiations, I am, as ever, your faithful servant:

Konstantin Reikos of Lost Port, Commanding, *Fair Passage*

Sian smiled as she read the note, then frowned, realizing that their rendezvous was now in conflict with her invitation from the Hanchu syndicate. She refolded it and tucked it into the purse hidden within the folds of her yellow silk.

Locking the door behind her, Sian headed out, intending to stop by her favorite kava house, the Green Island. But the day had now grown steaming-hot, and the streets unusually crowded with a strangely cranky assortment of people. After being run up against a wall by some scowling fellow on a runner-cart, then jabbed in the ribs — for a second time — by someone's wayward elbow, she decided the Green Island was rather out of her way, and stepped into the fenced-off area of the next sidewalk café she came to. She sank into a chair under the shade of a crape myrtle, and shooed a pair of small blue skinks off of the table.

"Lady?" A thin girl in rough cotton, with the pale skin of a northerner, stood above her.

"Hot kava, and a glass of cold water, please," Sian said. The girl nodded and ambled back to the tiny kitchen.

Sian sat, watching the flood of humanity passing by. People of every color and shape and age. Many of them were the proper dark-skinned folk of Alizar and the southern extents of the Sunward Sea, but strange pale folk from Copper Downs and the City Imperishable passed as well. Across the busy lane, she noticed a rather grimy local man in ragged clothing, leaning idly against a wall. He seemed to be staring, none too happily, at *her*, for what reason she could not imagine. Recalling Jamino's ambushed runner-cart, she turned away from the street to glance casually through her stack of papers until the girl returned with her kava and water.

"Anything else?"

"Thank you, no." Sian dug out her purse. "How much?"

"Three."

She paid, and was left to her correspondence. The first note was to the Hanchu merchants, graciously accepting their dinner invitation. Then came the more routine letters and replies. She glanced casually back across the street, relieved to find the unpleasant stranger gone. Really, what was wrong with people these days that one couldn't even sit down in an open café without being scowled at by some vagrant? Her stack of finished notes grew as she sipped the cooling kava and warming water, and came at last to Reikos's note.

She imagined him writing it out. He was so different from the huge, golden-bronze expanse of Arouf, or indeed most men in Alizar. Smagadine, with hair of pale brown, sea-green eyes, a clean-shaven face, and a lithe, corded body that would get a local boy laughed at and beaten. An unusual man, a considerate paramour, and so different.

But, alas, she would be all the way over on Malençon at dinner time. She had no choice but to cancel her meeting with Reikos — unless …

Sipping the last of the tepid kava, she pulled out a piece of blank paper.

Reikos,

Greetings and felicitations on this fine day.

I too warmly anticipate the resumption of our negotiations and am eager to view the cloths and other items of which you speak. Sadly, a last-minute business engagement has presented itself, and I shall not be available this evening before the twelfth bell of night.

I am terribly sorry for the late notice and the imposition on your no doubt busy schedule. If the revised hour is at all feasible, we could meet at my offices. I do hope to see you, though of course I will understand if you must reschedule.

Please let me know by return note if I should expect you this evening.

Yours,

Domina Sian Kattë

Sian read the note over once, then folded it up. Tucking the whole stack of finished correspondence into her satchel, she set out into the streets to find an errand boy.

∽

Her messages dispatched, Sian joined Viel Road, the island's largest thoroughfare. The streets seemed even more crowded now, and surlier; people bumped into one another with cross words and frowns. She took a deep breath and pressed forward. Perhaps she had been spending too much time on Little Loom Eyot; she felt unused to the pace of central Alizar.

She passed by the grander houses and shops of the wide street, then nearly tripped over some large obstruction, just catching herself by thrusting an arm against the adjacent building. "Oh!" She sucked in a breath as pain shot through her arthritic shoulder, and looked down to see what in the world had caught her feet.

A beggar woman sat below her, soiled, scarred, with bruised legs splayed into the cobbled walking border of the road. The creature gazed up at Sian with dull, red-rimmed eyes, but made no move to escape or protest, or even to get out of the path.

"I beg your pardon, I did not see you there." Though Sian's words were apologetic, her tone was sharp, which she instantly regretted. But really, who sprawled into a crowded street with so little regard for their own safety? Her shoulder pain eased slightly as she rubbed it, but she knew it would go on smarting for some time.

The beggar woman blinked, staring up at her sullenly.

"You should take more care. You're lucky I didn't injure you. You ... aren't injured, I hope?"

"Butchered God say I be safe wherever I lay me head."

Sian stared down at the woman, at a loss for words. So now the 'god' was suspending the rules of the physical world as well as those of economics? Where would this end? With the poor flying off to live in the stars? She shook her head and stepped over the beggar woman's legs, continuing on her way.

Soon the Hiring Hall loomed before her. She nodded at the old men as she went inside, then smiled as she walked up to a booth run by the Brownrock brothers — Gord, the elder, and Ellevan, the younger, yet smarter of the pair. Not that either of them could be called particularly young; they'd long been in business even when Sian was a girl. She always enjoyed passing the time with them, even to the point of sitting down for a game or two of bone-match.

Today Ellevan was there, leaning spindly elbows against the hard countertop of his meet-table. The board behind him was heavily chalked with men's names, nearly all of them crossed out with a thin white line, indicating that they were working, but might be available at the right price. Erasure only happened with men who were hired out to distant islands on long-term contracts. Or dead. And even then, sometimes the brothers didn't erase a name till a month or more had passed.

"Greetings, Ellevan." Sian walked up to the high counter and leaned her elbows opposite the frail fellow's. She looked for the usual answering light in his eyes, yet it was a long moment before he yielded to her charm.

"Greetings, Domina Kattë."

"How is your brother?"

"He passes fair well, I suppose."

"And your mother?"

"Still eating broth."

Sian nodded. The woman was rumored to be over one hundred years old, and seemed bound to outlive everyone in Alizar. Good thing she was sweet; being so helpless, and with her sons so businesslike, they might have poisoned her soup decades ago if they'd had a mind to.

"Excellent."

There was the usual pause as Sian and Ellevan regarded one another. In earlier days, Sian would have jumped right into whatever negotiation she was here about. By now, she had learned better. As with all other business in the islands, there was a pace and order to these things.

Continuing his part of their ritual, Ellevan said, "Arouf, he passes well?"

"Fair well."

"Your lovely daughters?"

"The same. And Maleen's children never stop growing."

"Your business is not in trouble?"

Sian snapped into focus, looking into the man's eyes. What an odd question. Quite outside the usual run of the thing. Was his mind slipping, or was he trying to maneuver her in some way? "No," she said, barely missing a beat. "In fact: I have need of two more weavers. I need men of good strength yet short stature, to work the great loom. Young, late in their second decade at the most, but full-grown. Who do you have for me?"

Ellevan shook his head as she spoke. "Might have one fellow for you, might not. A bit simple in the head, but he follows directions well."

"I need two good men — not some great oaf who can't read a pattern." Sian looked at the board behind Ellevan with a rising sense of desperation. "Are all those men working? The crossed-out ones?"

He gazed back at her. "Might be. Might be roaming the streets. I don't hear for certain, I leaves them put." Shrugging, he added, "I don't get the renewal fee, then I know."

There were three or four men not crossed out. "What about them?" Sian pointed.

Ellevan paused another half-beat, then hoisted himself up and went to the board behind him. His shoulders were hunched as he ran his finger over the columns of names, muttering to himself. "These fellows, you don't want them." His hand hesitated over two unfamiliar names; they looked foreign. Or maybe that was just Ellevan's crabbed handwriting. "No, I only got Frico. He got the strength of two men."

"I need *two* strong men," Sian repeated, but without much force.

"I give you one," Ellevan said, with a note of finality. "And you lucky to get that. Good customer, these years."

"Yes." She bit back her disappointment. "I thank you." She didn't doubt he was doing the best he could for her, however irritable he might seem about it. "How soon can he make his way to Little Loom Eyot?"

Ellevan grumbled again, carrying on a complex conversation with himself as he made a series of elaborate check marks and notations in a tattered notebook. "Three days, he should turn up. Check back with me if it's been a week." He turned away to get the necessary paperwork.

"I shall. And perhaps you'll have more men in a week?"

"Might could."

Sian pulled a small handful of silver from her purse as Ellevan set the contract on the table. She signed it, then passed him the coins, which disappeared into his grubby robe.

"I thank you."

"Aye."

Sian sighed. Well, at least she had secured one new laborer, for whatever he might be worth. She would check other booths; Ellevan could hardly object. She had, after all, come to him first. "Well, I'll see you next time.

Please give my best to your brother and your mother."

"Will do, lady Kattë."

Sian departed his table and started to make her way through the large room. But nobody was behind the counter at the Longstrand booth. Capri Lotello avoided her gaze, turning to see to boxes in the back room as she approached; his chalk board told an even more dismal tale than the Brownrocks' had. Down at the end of the hall, a loud, angry argument at House Mars discouraged her from approaching the counter at all.

The anxious energy in here finally wore her down altogether. Sian left the Hiring Hall and stepped back out into the sweaty, crowded street.

The whole city was in a foul temper today, she decided. It might be better just to return to the townhouse and prepare for her dinner meeting in peace and solitude. She must be both sharp and calm to negotiate with the Hanchu. They were notoriously difficult trading partners, but their silks were unique and exquisite; the effort would be worth it.

THREE

*S*unset promised to be glorious as Sian set out for her dinner meeting. Towering thunderheads far out at sea, limned in molten gold, threw pale streamers up across the powder-yellow sky. Sian was dressed in thicker silks now, close-cut and midnight blue. After careful consideration, she had discarded the yellow: its dual messages muddied the waters, and not in any advantageous way. This fabric, screamingly expensive but subtle enough that only sophisticated textile experts would recognize the fact, would convey her message to the traders much more satisfactorily.

Mindful of Jamino's tale of the attack on his runner-cart, and still uneasy about that ragged stranger who had stared at her at the café, she had decided to carry no bag or satchel. Even her small purse had been stripped down to its tiny inner coin-pouch and tucked into a pocket of her undertrousers. Nothing flowed or dangled as she moved. Her long hair was tied in a black ribbon and braided into a queue hanging down her back.

Sian glanced at her reflection in the dark panes of her front windows as she stepped into the street. Yes: she looked exactly right, confident and strong. And there would be plenty of time to change into something more … comfortable … before Reikos's visit at midnight. His return note had made clear his eagerness to be there.

She passed out of Meander Way onto Viel Street, looking for one of the runner-carts normally ubiquitous in this part of town. She liked to walk to such meetings when she could. Such gentle exertion always left her more alert and energized upon arrival at these contests — which had paid off handsomely on numerous occasions. But Malençon was at the other end of

Alizar; hours away, even by cart. Lady Suba-Tien of Crux had married into the Hanchu Tien family three years before, and after moving into the Suba estate, her new husband had since moved his family's Alizari trading house to the closest island with a major port — to everybody *else's* inconvenience. Such were the privileges of success. So, a runner-cart was needed, though Sian supposed she might even splurge on a water-taxi coming home, if things went very well.

Tonight, however, a cart was nowhere to be seen. Business must be strangely brisk for such an hour, she thought with irritation. Or had this strange new unwillingness to work in Alizar spread even to cart runners now? What were all these work-resistant people doing to feed themselves, she wondered.

She crossed the bridge to tiny Phaero, still looking for a cart. The only ones she'd seen so far had been at a distance, and already occupied. The narrower streets felt even more crowded than Viel's had been, making her glad that she had changed into more close-fitting garb — and that the day's muggy heat had subsided. Processions and prayer lines were everywhere, in far greater profusion this evening than she'd ever seen them. Muttering, chanting devotees of the so-called Butchered God surged past around her without looking at their own footfalls, pushed along by sheer force of numbers. It occurred to her that perhaps the runner-carts were just avoiding all this congestion.

"A curse, a curse upon the city." The sudden wail, practically at her shoulder, gave Sian a start. She drew back against a spindly guava tree and let the latest procession wend past her, all weeping and praying. "A curse … a curse …"

Sian reached out and caught the arm of a young boy, perhaps thirteen summers old. "What is happening? What is wrong?"

The boy stared at her with tear-stained eyes. "I… Lady, please!" He yanked his arm out of her grip and ran to join the rest of his procession.

"It's Konrad, the Factor's boy," said a quiet voice behind her.

Sian turned to see a middle-aged man standing in an open doorway, a greengrocer's apron tied around his ample midsection. His face was grim, but his eyes were kindly enough.

"What about him?" she asked, taking a step towards the man.

"They're saying his illness has become much worse. The rumor is that he will die now. And the Factor and his Consort are too old to bear another heir, of course. These fanatics claim it's a sign that Alizar is doomed to barrenness as well."

"I had heard that Konrad was improving, if slowly." Sian did not mention, of course, that she was related to the Factor. "What has changed?"

"Crab disease, or so they say."

"Oh no." A likely death sentence, certainly. The poor boy. And very bad news for House Alkattha. Still … "How does that suggest a curse on Alizar? The crab disease strikes where it will, and often, sadly."

The man shrugged. "All I know is what these fanatics say as they whip and reel throughout the city." Sian raised her eyes at his artful language. Grocer by day, poet by night? "If the priest of the Butchered God proclaims the heir's illness a curse: then it is a curse." He nodded her good-evening, and stepped back into his shop.

The Butchered God again. Sian stared at the receding prayer line even as her ears picked up the ecstatic calls and wild mutters of yet another somewhere near. Why would any god smite the Factor's child? It would only distract the man from tending to his people's needs. Did this Butchered God of theirs *wish* trouble on Alizar?

Sian shook her head, walking on. This kind of unrest was bad news indeed for the average small business owner. Particularly a business dealing in luxury items, whatever the more optimistic of her many reports might have her believe.

Sian found herself following in the rambling prayer line's wake now, and hung back, careful not to seem a part of it. The lines were not, strictly speaking, illegal, but they were unambiguously disapproved of by both the Factorate and the Mishrah-Khote, and clearly nothing a respectable businesswoman would want to seem connected with. She glanced around, reconsidering her decision to walk, but still saw no ready conveyances. She began to look down each cross street she passed, and, to her great relief, soon saw an empty cart parked just a block away. She all but ran to flag its runner down before someone else could rob her of his services.

The lean, bare-chested man turned as she called out, smiling from underneath his bowl-shaped hat.

"Where have you all been?" she asked, nearly out of breath.

"Lady?" he said, puzzled. "I am being right here." He flashed her a winning smile. "Waiting for pretty lady to come hire me."

"Aren't you charming," she said dryly. "Can you take me all the way to Malençon?"

His smile became a furrowed expression of concern. "Oh, crowds very bad tonight. That take a long time more than you want, maybe. Maybe cost a lot."

She looked back at the mob-choked street she'd left. She was clearly going to be late. There seemed no help for that now. She turned to the runner. "Can you not find some way around all this?"

"Sure, lady." He shrugged. "On the islands, yes. But there no way around the bridges. They clog all them. At the bridges, nothing I can do."

"Well, I don't seem to have much choice," she sighed, climbing into the open wicker cart. "Do the best you can, please. I will tip you handsomely if you can get me there by two hours after sunset."

He nodded, hunching his shoulders to concede the possibility of failure, but hurried to pull on his harness and haul the cart into motion.

They dodged one way then another across the rest of Phaero, keeping to the edges of Lady Nissa Phaero's large east-shore estate where the prayer marchers seemed least in evidence, but, as her runner had predicted, the bridge to Cutter's was a solid mass of shuffling, chanting cultists. *Whatever are they doing?* she thought, exasperated. Was something special happening tonight?

Half an hour later, they were still not even past the Census Taker's lush grounds. The prayer lines were right there in front of them, no matter which street the runner dodged to next, it seemed. *Are they off to meet the Hanchu traders too?* she wondered. Not until they'd made their sluggish way across the densely packed bridge to the twin atolls of Hither and Yon did the press of worshippers finally abate. By then, the sun had nearly touched the sea, the screech of gulls and terns had given way to the rolling trill of nightjars, and the sky was all ablaze in orange and crimson fire. Sian began to hope she might not miss the meeting altogether. Perhaps her hosts had even heard by now about the unprecedented congregation of so many marchers, and were anticipating her delay. She could only hope so.

They made very decent time across the larger island of Three Cats. Her runner was clearly trying to earn that tip she'd promised him. But then they reached the bridge to Malençon, and Sian threw her hands up with a loud sigh.

The island's entire shoreline, as well as the bridge itself, was packed to overflowing with chanting cultists who seemed more prayer meanderers now than marchers. They bobbed and swayed almost in place, clear across the channel.

Sian's runner turned in his harness to look up at her. "You maybe get there faster walking now," he said, shaking his head. "Sorry, lady. Nothing I can do here. Not for long time, I thinking."

This was beyond ridiculous. Sian had little choice but to agree with him. She would have to get out and try to push her way across the bridge, which would take another hour at the very least, she estimated, and would likely leave her décolletage drenched in sweat. But missing such a meeting altogether would send even less desirable messages to her Hanchu associates.

A curse upon the city, indeed. Did this Butchered God of theirs have some grudge against her personally?

Discreetly, Sian reached between the folds of her dress and slipped out her coin purse. Straightening her garment, she stood and climbed down from the cart, pulling out enough to pay the runner more than double the usual rate. None of this was his fault, and he, at least, was working still. For that alone, she wanted to reward him. He saw what she had handed him, and looked up to beam at her. "Pretty lady very generous! Thank you, thank you. You want me wait, I stay here all night long to take you back when you are finish, yes?"

She smiled and shook her head. "I have a daughter on the other shore. It's long past time I visited her. Thank you for getting me this far."

He bobbed his head, gave her a grateful wave, and turned his cart around to head back toward Alizar Main.

Well, there's nothing gained by waiting, she thought, and started down the dusty road into the crowd. The press grew ever tighter as she neared the bridge. Once on the span itself, she was forced to barge her way quite physically through the endless throng of worshippers, knowing now that this was going to take far too long.

She pressed on, keeping to the bridge's railing, where the crowd was thinnest. Perhaps a third of the way across, one of the marchers — a man in his twenties, broad of shoulder and dull of eye — bumped her nearly hard enough to knock her off her feet.

"Sorry," Sian said, though surely it was he who should have been apologizing. The young man just continued on his way, lost in mutterings, as she tried to step even further back, though there was almost no room left between herself and a long drop into the bay.

Such fanatic faith puzzled Sian. She had been raised in the usual manner: temple on the feast days, a small dusty altar in the corner of the kitchen, remembrances to the ancestors when her mother took the family out to their memorial shrines. But there had been no particular passion behind the rites: no ecstasy, no terror. It was just something one did, like the weekly laundering, or repairing the roof — though with less obvious reason. Alizar's gods were nowhere in evidence, nor had they been for as long as anyone could remember. Worship had no more relevance than did Popa Chinnai, who brought woven grass sandals and ylang-ylang incense for the youngest children at the turn of the year.

Any vestige of faith she might have retained had left Sian for good after increasingly complex and costly rites prescribed by Mishrah-Khote priests had failed to save her mother's life from bloodpox. The order's endless demands for "donations" had produced nothing; her mother had died in agony, coughing up more blood than a body should hold. After declaring her demise "the will of the gods," the self-important priests had left young Sian to care for her bereft father all alone. Only one gentle-faced acolyte had shown any kindness to Sian at all, whispering furtive apologies for their failure, and offering to counsel and comfort her if she should wish to come see him at the temple, before he was whisked away by his superiors.

All these muttering, sweating folk around Sian now were clearly tapping into something she could not perceive. She could not fathom what drew them. What were they hoping to find?

Perhaps an hour later, as she neared the darkened bridge's other end at last, the way became slightly less crowded. Sian seized this opportunity, weaving faster through the massive prayer line's margins toward what appeared to be the front of it.

At last! she thought, putting on a final burst of speed. But as she broached the procession's leading edge, she drew up short in new amazement. There, a very familiar figure danced and chanted, holding high a whale's tooth, his face suffused with religious ecstasy. Young, strong but slight, light brown hair — she could not believe her eyes.

"Pino!" Sian shouted, moving towards him. He did not reply, but danced on, brandishing the whale's tooth before him. As Sian continued to approach him, stepping through the tangled enthusiasts, she realized the others about him were gazing at the tooth reverently. As if it were some kind of a relic.

Was it the tooth of a whale? It had an oddly human look to it … Surely it was not … Oh, surely not.

"Pino!" she called again, stepping closer, pushing past a hefty woman in a gauzy blue wrap who carried a large cloth bag rattling with unknown objects. "What are you *doing* here?"

The boy finally turned his head and looked at Sian, a mixture of joy and fear on his face. But still he didn't speak; he only kept dancing and brandishing the filthy tooth.

"Pino — talk to me!" Sian tugged on his arm, trying to yank him from the line.

Pino resisted, his eyes glittering with something — feral, almost. A look Sian had certainly never seen in him before. Suddenly he grinned, and stopped, seeming only then to see her through his ecstasy. "My lady! You have found us! Just as he predicted!"

"I …" Sian was at a loss for words. "As who predicted? What are you doing with these people? Why are you not back on Little Loom Eyot with Arouf?"

"The Butchered God's priest — he said that you would find us!" Pino ignored her other questions, if he'd heard them at all. "He wants to speak with you, my lady!"

"With me? Whatever in the world for?"

"You had questions — on the boat — and he can give you answers! It is such a gift, my lady. I will take you to him!" Pino reached for Sian's hand, then hesitated, recalling his place perhaps, reticent, even through his religious frenzy, to touch her without permission.

"Impossible," Sian said. "I'm already late for a very important meeting. And you have no business here, Pino. I insist that you return home. Does Arouf know where you are?"

"But … No, my lady. Really. You must come! Now!" The line had continued to surge and flow around them for some time now, and grown thicker too. They found themselves squeezed against a building. Pino again moved to take her hand, clearly wanting to compel her along.

"No," Sian said, pulling back, but keeping her voice gentle, trying to mollify him. Had someone given the boy powders? "Perhaps I will speak with him tomorrow." Suddenly the prayer line seemed less obnoxious and more sinister. "Go home to the Eyot now; meet me at the townhouse in the morning, and you can take me to the priest then."

Pino stared at her with pleading eyes. "No!" he shouted. His gaze seemed oddly unfocused, or was he looking at someone behind her?

Before she could turn to see, a strong blow at the back of her head sent her sprawling to the ground. She could find no voice to scream. No air. She struggled to rise, but the darkness took her.

✌

Factora-Consort Arian des Chances watched her husband pace, until he stopped at last before the conference chamber's great round window to stand gazing down at Home's distant harbor, where his family's fleet of cargo ships sat uncharacteristically idle, though the streets around it would doubtless be clogged with marchers now. Hivat, Viktor's chief of security — which was to say, his top spy — had been by just before this meeting to inform them of the evening's sudden but as yet indecipherable outburst of cultist presence in the city's streets. He was back out there now somewhere, trying to find out why.

"They are surely here on your father's behalf, my dear," said Viktor. "You must know better than I what will appease them."

"My *father?*" Arian said, astonished. "Whatever makes you —" Then she realized that he was, of course, not speaking of the cultists, but of the trade delegation, just arrived in time to see this massive display of unrest.

"They are sent by the Trade Authority in Copper Downs, are they not?" said Viktor. "Which means —"

"Of which my father is merely one member among many," she interjected.

" — that they are sent by your father," he continued as if she had not interrupted. "*First* of many members. Who has better cause than we to know it?" He turned from the view to gaze at her. "They are here because your family is not enjoying the bride-price they had counted on."

Arian made no further effort to hide her incredulity. "What an absurd assumption, Viktor! We've been married nearly twenty years. This union has been worth my family's trouble many times over by now." Her husband's paranoia still surprised her sometimes. "Has Hivat provided you any scrap at all of evidence to support such a suspicion?"

Viktor shook his head.

"Then this delegation has come for the same reasons such officials have always visited important trading partners: to gather first-hand information and to strategize. That is all."

He responded with an impatient humph, and came back to sit across from her at the room's long, polished ebony table. "What can they expect me to tell them that they don't already know? Does being Factor endow me with power over every vicissitude of life? Can I control the weather?"

"The weather is not our problem." Arian sighed. Her husband lost himself so easily in such useless theater.

"Then what *is* our problem? If you know, please tell me. A nation filled with labor-hungry businesses, yet suddenly the poor choose not to work.

How am I to deal with such a thing? How am I to understand it? How do they even feed themselves now?"

"The sea is full of food. As is the jungle," said Arian, as baffled as her husband by this senseless protest movement — if that's what it even was. The 'Butchered God' cult responsible for all of this had made no demands of any kind yet; given no clear indication of what all this marching was supposed to mean at all — that she'd been told about, at least. "But those supplies of food cannot last forever under such a strain. These marchers will return to the hiring houses soon. When the monsoon season returns, at the very least. They'll have to."

"This delegation requests *clarification* of my *plans*," Viktor said, very nearly whining. "I have no plan. They want *financial forecasts*. Does that not sound like weather to you? It might as well be, for all the sense it makes to me. They want my *head*, Arian. They and half the leading families in Alizar. That is what they've come here to 'strategize.' On behalf of your unhappy father and his bankers. I am certain of it."

Arian swallowed her impatience. At such times, her husband needed propping up, not dressing down. "Viktor, any Factor would feel as you do in times like these. But none of what's happening out there is your fault. Everyone knows that. I married you because I trust and believe in you. My father let me do it because he trusts and respects you too — as do these trade representatives. Trust *me* in this. I grew up among them. They are greedy savages sometimes, but they are not fools. Seeing you deposed would only double Alizar's unrest and further undermine the very productivity and commerce they want bolstered, not to mention end the considerable trade benefits my family has enjoyed here since we married. What possible gain could any of that bring them?"

"Perhaps they've made some better arrangement with another family." He leaned toward her conspiratorially. "Orlon has had several cannons made this year. Hivat did tell me that much. And Gentia Suba-Tien seems to be burning through a rather astonishing amount of her husband's money suddenly, for someone without greater prospects than any Hivat or I are *aware* of."

"*Viktor.*" She gave him the look, perfected over many years: one-third pleading, one-third maternal fierceness, and one-third puppy love. Her masterpiece.

He glanced away, then looked down to fiddle with the embroidered lapels of his brocade robe before raising his hands in apology. "This is all that damned corpse's fault. And the Mishrah-Khote's. Don't tell me I am wrong in this as well."

"The Mishrah-Khote is even less fond of the Butchered God's cult than we are, husband. You know that."

"But it didn't hurt them any to have a god wash up on our doorstep, did it? These priests never cease craving their old prominence, and whatever that great slab of meat really was, it plays far better in support of their claim to authority than it does to mine. There is nothing to prevent them from denouncing this new cult, while stirring the ignorant masses under their sway against the *discredited secular authority* I wield too. How am I to compete with a tangible god? Even a dead one." He looked bleakly at the ceiling, as if petitioning some divinity himself. "You were right, though. I should never have insisted it was some kind of sea monster. That … was just desperate stupidity."

Arian composed her elaborately painted face in sympathy and remained silent, having long ago learned that feeding his shame only damaged her tenuous power to steer him. Her husband was as good-hearted and honest a Factor as Alizar had known in many generations. But he was not a man well made to rule. Perhaps the two qualities were incompatible. She had often wondered since coming here from Copper Downs to be his bride.

Her husband looked away. "Do you think it *was* a god? Could the gods be coming back to Alizar too, now … from … wherever they have been all these ages?"

She gave him a smile designed to reassure. "If there are gods in Alizar, I know less of them than you do, love. But whatever that giant was, we are fortunate that it was dead." She shrugged. "Its appearance has been followed by no further miracle of any kind, has it? Let it go, love. We've more pressing questions to address tonight."

"But, what if —"

"Listen to me now," she interjected. "These men tomorrow will want nothing from you but some marginally credible report for their superiors, who, in turn, want nothing but some vaguely plausible justification to leave everything just as it is. Any serious effort to *fix things* would be an egregious affront to my country's chronically over-extended bureaucracy. Just tell the delegation that we are developing a new array of programs and incentives to appease the labor force here and persuade them back to work. That's all they'll want to hear."

"Programs and incentives like what?" Viktor asked, frowning.

Arian rolled her eyes. "Renovation of slums, improved distribution of staple foods through work-assistance programs, state-subsidized access to a greater share of the Mishrah-Khote's services."

"Since when? With what funds? Our tax revenues are plummeting, Arian. Now is hardly the time to start —"

"Do you suppose for a minute," she cut in, "that this delegation will go crawl around the raft warrens or down into Hell's Arch or Alm's Crib to ascertain the truth? I am trying to tell you that all they want is some passable way to claim they're working on solutions to the world's unmanageable problems *without* incurring any actual responsibility to do so in earnest. Give them that, and they will leave us in peace." She paused, then added, "We might even consider some of the options I've just mentioned. Could it hurt to discuss them? Quietly? Why should this 'Butchered God's' priest be allowed sole claim to concern for Alizar's poor? Even in times like these, haven't we resources to do at least as much as he can about any of this?"

"You're telling me to lie to the delegation?" Viktor blinked, seeming to have heard nothing else she'd said. "That seems most unlike you."

Arian drew a deep breath and shoved her frustration down once more. "It is not a lie if we are looking into it." She could not solve all the problems of their nation's poor tonight. She was just trying to help her husband find some breathing room. Was he too dull to see even that? "So let us just look into it, all right? I promise you, this delegation will not come back to check on our progress. And these current troubles *will* get better, Viktor, precisely *because* you are *not* to blame for them. Just buy us time to get there."

He continued to gaze at her curiously, then shrugged. "It is as good as any other plan at my disposal. I thank you for the council, wife. It is a great help to have someone so much wiser in the ways of this game at my side."

"There are many kinds of wisdom, husband. Yours are no fewer than mine, just of a different nature."

"If you say so." He gave her a rueful smile.

She rose and went to kiss him on the cheek. "I do. And on this occasion, I am right. Now, I must go to see our son. It is getting late. He will be sleeping soon." *I hope*, she added silently. The more Konrad needed sleep, the further off his fever seemed to keep it.

Only when she'd stepped into the hallway and closed the door behind her did she allow herself a huff of exasperation. The very idea that her father would wish his own daughter's husband toppled … Viktor was not a stupid man by any stretch. How he managed to arrive at such bizarre conclusions, she was unable to imagine.

As she continued through the Factorate House's labyrinthine hallways, silent at this time of day but for the soft rustling of her silken robes and the ever-present calls of this fecund country's strange wildlife, Arian considered the baroque columns, continental embellishments, diamond-tiled floors, and mosaic ceilings around her. Marble, malachite, alabaster and stained glass. Viktor and his family had brought all of this from the mainland, entirely remodeling the island nation's modest palace at unimaginable expense, as a wedding gift for her. *To make you feel at home*, Viktor had told her grandly the first time he had shown it to her. She'd never had the heart to tell him that this great fantasy of 'continental architecture' was as oddly out of step with anything she'd known in Copper Downs as it was with her adopted country's culture or native architecture. The grandest expression to date of her husband's … impressive … imagination.

As she approached her son's chambers, she met her younger brother, Aros, coming the other way.

"Factora-Consort," he said, sweeping his pale hair back and giving her a courtly little bow, as mocking, somehow, as it was technically correct.

"What brings you here so late, Aros?"

"Just keeping my poor nephew company, of course, as any doting uncle should. Was your conference with the Factor fruitful?"

"I suppose," she said, a bit annoyed that he had been allowed her son's company while she, his own mother, had been denied the privilege. "How is he tonight?"

"The same." Aros's brow furrowed in concern. "I worry for him, Arian. He was recovering so nicely. Now … Is there nothing more the Mishrah-Khote priests can do?"

"Is there ever? They mumble new prognostications every day. Each as vague and ineffective as the last."

"Now, sister. Have some faith," he said, his words laced with sarcasm.

"I've come to see my son, Aros. I must go."

"Did you speak with him?" her brother asked as she swept by him.

"With who?" She turned back.

"The Factor."

"Did I not just say so?"

"I mean about the matter I discussed with you," he said. "*Two weeks* ago."

So that's what he'd been doing here. Waiting for her. "I believe I made it clear, *two weeks ago,* that I could do you no such favor."

"Why not?" he said, all pretense of courtly manners abandoned. "In all these years, you've granted not a single favor I have ever asked."

"Might that have anything to do with the recklessly inappropriate things you always seem to ask for?" She offered him a smile, hoping to cast the rebuke as a mere sisterly tease.

"There's nothing inappropriate about it," he snapped. "Those taxes just go to support the government, which is *us.* Why should I pay fees to some bureaucracy just so that they can skim two-thirds of it away before returning my money to me? Waiving that absurdity would only save your subjects added cost. Can't you see that?"

Arian shook her head in disbelief, struggling not to laugh.

"What good is having a queen for a sister if I may ask nothing of her? The Factor listens to you, Arian. You rule these islands through him. Everybody knows that. You could do anything for me if you wished to."

"I am not a queen, Aros, as you know very well," she said less patiently. "We are not on the continent anymore. I am but Factora-Consort. My husband is the Factor here, and in this nation we may be legally replaced by any of a dozen other families at a moment's notice, should the people insist on it. I can think of few better ways to precipitate such a catastrophe — especially at a time like this — than to have the whole nation watch him excuse his self-indulgent brother-in-law from fees and licenses by which everyone else is bound. He would never consider it. Nor would he respect me for suggesting it. He cares about integrity. That's why I married him."

"You married him because Father told you to," Aros said.

"I refused the first three men Father tried to wed me to. I could as easily have refused Viktor." They glared at one another for a moment. "When did you become such a little prick?" she asked him. "You were so sweet once. We were friends, remember?"

"Yes. We were," he said petulantly. "You were less high and mighty then."

Arian released a pent-up sigh. "If you want to own an island, Aros, I wish you every success. But you will have to acquire it in accordance with the same rules governing everyone else here — including Viktor and myself. If you need financial help, why not ask Father? He's got gold to spare, and there'd be no scandal at all in seeking his help."

"Men like Father do not invest in *younger sons*, remember?" Aros said. "Father's favors are for Alexandros. *Younger* sons must go off and prove themselves. Alone. That's why I came to this benighted country, trusting my beloved sister to understand, and help, at least a little."

"Stop it," she said, shaking her head. "Such whining is unworthy of you. Come to me with any *ethical* request, Aros, and I will do all I can for you. You've got everything it takes to be whatever you wish if you'll just grow up a bit and embrace the cost of achieving it."

"Well," he said. "That does cast everything in quite a different light. Thanks so much." He turned and stalked away without waiting for any response.

She watched him go with real sadness, wondering when and how all of them had become so … lost. Then she shook her head and continued toward her son's bedchamber.

Upon arriving, her quiet knock was answered by Maronne, one of Arian's two personal attendants. Maronne and Lucia were cousins who had come to Alizar with Arian from Copper Downs. Two decades later, they were still her closest and most trusted friends, and, as Konrad's illness had grown more serious, Arian had insisted that one or the other of them watch over him both night and day.

"Is he awake?" Arian whispered.

Maronne nodded, her long grey-streaked hair picking up a glimmer of candlelight. "Your brother only just now left."

"I know," sighed Arian. "I ran into him."

Maronne stood aside, and Arian went to sit at her son's bedside. "Hello, my darling," she said softly, reaching out to stroke his once-glossy raven hair. His forehead felt far too warm — as always lately. "Are you feeling sleepy?"

He smiled at her, and nodded, though whether truthfully or just to please her, she could not be sure. Like his father, Konrad was at times a bit too eager to please. It worried her. Or it had, until this illness had made all such lesser worries seem ridiculous. "Did you have a pleasant visit with your uncle Aros?"

Konrad nodded again — more vigorously this time. "We talked of Copper Downs. He told me about winter there, Mama. I would very much like to see snow someday. It must be wonderful and strange to see ice fall from the sky. As soft as feathers, Uncle Aros says. May I go to visit Copper Downs someday, Mama? In winter?"

"It is a very, very long ways off," she said. "But when you are older, you may go anywhere you wish, my love." *If you are ever older*, she could not keep herself from thinking. *Oh, all the gods, I beg you. Please let my son grow older.* She caught Maronne's sympathetic look, and shoved such thoughts away for fear that Konrad might see them in her face as well.

"Uncle Aros says the harbor there could hold a hundred fleets like Father's," Konrad said, clearly skeptical. "Do you think he's right?"

She nodded. "Possibly. Or something near that. What other fascinating things has Uncle Aros been telling you?"

Konrad gazed at her uncertainly, as if unsure whether to answer. "He told me he is worried," he said quietly. "About Father."

"*What?* Why ever would he — Worried why?" She could not believe that even her feckless younger brother could have decided to say such a thing to Konrad — under any circumstances, much less now.

"He said people expect Father to fix problems here in Alizar that can't be fixed by anyone. Because Father is the Factor." Konrad paused, as if trying to gauge her reaction before going on. "I said it wasn't fair, and he said I was right, but that some people do not care about being fair, and that they might ask Father to step down and let somebody else be Factor. Is it true, Mama?"

Struggling to master her anger, Arian turned to fix Maronne with an incredulous glare, as if there had been any way for a mere lady-in-waiting to control her brother's behavior. Arian herself had been unable to do that for some time now. Maronne gave her a helpless gesture, and Arian turned back to her son. "Uncle Aros worries far too much sometimes, my dear," she said as lightly as she could manage. "And imagines troubles that are just not there. Your father is Factor precisely because he is so good at dealing with such things. He's just fine, and will be fine still when you are old and married with grandchildren of your own."

Konrad looked up at her. "I don't know if I can be Factor," he said at last. "Even when I'm grown. I don't know if I'll be … smart enough to beat such people who don't care about being fair."

"Oh, Konrad, love." Arian held back a sigh. "You will be more than wise enough, but you're only twelve. You need worry about none of this for many, many years yet. And you don't have to be a Factor ever. Not if you don't want to. If you're still not interested when you are grown, you can just say so, and any number of others will be happy to serve in your stead. All you need to do right now is rest until you're well enough again to go outside and play. Will you do that for me?"

"Yes, Mama." He tried to smile for her, but failed.

"What is it, love?" She saw that something more was weighing on him. "You can tell me anything, you know."

"Is Uncle Aros …?" Konrad seemed to lose his breath, or perhaps the words themselves.

"Is Uncle Aros what?" she pressed, contriving an encouraging smile.

"Father … told me once …"

Arian waited, trying not to let her unease show. What could *Viktor* have said now, that her son would be so afraid to repeat in her hearing?

"Father said that I must not always trust Uncle Aros too much …" Again, he paused, clearly trying to decipher her reaction. She barely managed not to drop her face into her hands. Was there no rock in all her world now that it was still safe to look under?

"I thought he just meant that some of Uncle Aros's stories are not … completely true," said Konrad. "Like snow, or the size of Copper Downs' harbor. But, now … sometimes …"

"Shhhh," she said, not wanting him to guess at such things yet, much less think about them. "Your father worries too much sometimes too, but there is nothing wrong with either of them, Konrad. I've been married to your father almost twice as long as you have been alive, and have known your Uncle Aros since the day he was born. They are both good men at heart. The very best of men. Which doesn't mean they're perfect. But they do both love you very much, and you may trust them both completely. This I promise." She leaned in to kiss his glistening forehead. Much, much too warm. "Now sleep." She offered him a tender smile. "And dream of being well." She caressed his cheek, and stood. "I'll see you in the morning."

"Good night, Mama." Konrad closed his eyes obediently.

"Good night. I love you," she said, then walked to the chamber doorway, beckoning Maronne to follow her into the hallway.

When they had closed the door behind them, Maronne said, "I am sorry, my lady. I too was appalled, but there was nothing I could —"

"Yes, yes, I understand," Arian assured her. "Aros is a law unto himself these days. You are not to blame. But next time he comes to visit Konrad, tell him I have ordered you to send him to me first. I will have his promise to keep that tongue curbed in my son's presence, or, I swear, I'll forbid him any access here at all."

FOUR

S ian awoke hard, head throbbing. She lay on a rough surface; a stone dug into her back. Everything was bright and noisy and confusing; it took her a minute to focus enough to be able to see.

What she saw when her vision cleared made her wish it hadn't.

Folk from the prayer lines had formed a circle around her, too deep to see beyond in any direction. The gathered mass chanted and hummed. A beast with a hundred legs and less than one mind, as the proverb went. There would be no escape for her even if she did manage to get to her feet.

She could see Pino nowhere, but there was a new man standing over her; young, very nearly handsome, with broad shoulders and dark skin — a native of Alizar, clearly. His lettuce-green smock and tight canvas pants looked like naval regalia, though if he'd been a serviceman, he clearly wasn't any longer. His dark eyes held her with terrible intensity.

"She awakens!" he cried, as Sian's gaze met his. He bent over her, holding a long bone stripped clean, almost bleached. A thigh bone, maybe — but from what? Not ox or cow; no wild animal so large roamed any of Alizar's islands.

"What — who are you?" Sian cringed away from the massive bone, still on her back, only managing a crablike movement of a few inches. Everything hurt, her head worst of all.

The man straightened up and gazed out at the assembled masses, then looked down again at Sian and said in a quiet voice, "I am the Priest of the Butchered God."

The crowd murmured louder — a benediction, a ritual response. Then their noise died back once more into a low chanting growl.

However ambivalent her own religious convictions, she could not imagine honoring this man with such a title. "Do you have a name?" she asked, wondering at her own temerity. He could strike her again — no doubt he would.

The man leaned forward; Sian cringed. "I have cast off my secular name. I exist now only to serve the Butchered God." Again, the answering murmur as the crowd pressed closer.

Only then did Sian notice they were all men. Where were the women who had been in the prayer line? And their eyes...she recognized their shared expression. It was the look of men who think themselves released from the ordinary rules that bind society. The look of a feral mob.

"What do you want from me?" she cried. "Release me. I mean you no harm."

"We mean you no harm either, lady, though we must harm you anyway, I fear." The priest touched the long bone to her face. His cheeks and forehead were beaded with sweat and his eyes were shot with blooded veins. He had the air of a madman, and all these mad people followed him. Where was Pino? He would never have ... but then, what *had* he done?

Sian could smell her own fear even as she smelled the violent intent of the men around her. Still she struggled to keep her strength of will, pushing herself up to a seated position, her elbows scraping against the rough stones of the street. "Then release me at once."

"You are Domina Kattë, are you not?" asked the would-be priest. "Cousin to the Stirpes Alkattha?"

She grew even more frightened as she considered the meaning of this. Had she been attacked because of her distant relation to the ruling family? "Why do you ask?"

"Answer me, woman!" From 'lady' to 'woman' in the twitch of an eye. The crowd pressed a step closer. One man near her feet rested a hand at his belt as he looked her up and down.

"I am cousin to the Alkatthas, yes." She kept her voice strong, though it threatened to break. Would they rape a member of the ruling family?

The priest loomed over her. The low torchlight flickering off the nearby buildings carved eerie lines in his young face, gone suddenly sad. "Then you are fit to carry the god's message to those who rule."

Sian breathed a sigh. They wouldn't rape a *messenger* they were sending to the rulers, surely. As she drew breath to respond, he smacked her hard in the face with the bone.

Reeling, Sian fell back against the hard stones, her head bouncing on the same spot that had been struck before. Sick and dizzy with the pain, she cringed and curled up, trying to protect her belly as her mouth filled with blood.

The priest stood over her, his face grim. "It is a hard passage, lady. I am … sorry, but you will understand." He raised the bone and dealt her another blow, on her shoulder.

Sian screamed and rolled over, but the priest kept beating her, now on her arms and back. Understand *what?* She kicked out toward his feet, but he merely struck her ankles and knees, forcing her to draw them back, protecting her arthritic joints. She tried to scrabble to her feet, but everywhere she turned, she was struck by the bone, cascades of pain pouring through her. "Why are you doing this?" she choked out, spitting salty blood onto the ground.

He did not reply.

She was trapped by the encircling crowd; he could kill her easily. She fell back down in panic, curling once more into a fetal position, sobbing. All her former pretense to strength dropped away as his blows fell. The beating became everything — would it never stop? The circle of men around her continued to chant; their words and tones falling into a pattern. Would rape follow after all? So much for the protection of high-placed relations.

It was a long while before Sian realized that the blows were coming in time with the chanting. Not only that, but the priest seemed to not be beating her as hard as he had before. Or perhaps she was at last becoming numb. Still, every blow, coming atop some already bruised or bloody part of her body, sent even more excruciating waves of pain through her. She drew her arms over her head more tightly, trying to protect herself, to make it stop, even as she struggled to retain consciousness.

She lost all sense of time as the beating continued. And then the priest stopped. "That is enough." She heard his footsteps on the gravel, moving away. "Truly. I am sorry."

Sian lay trembling on the stone, bleeding, sobbing. A moment later, strong arms picked her up, and she was tossed roughly over a large, sweaty shoulder. She tried to open her eyes, but they were swollen shut. So she merely felt and smelled and heard that she was being taken to the waterfront. No one answered the disjointed questions she managed to stammer out.

Eventually, she was roughly tumbled into the bottom of a boat, judging from the feel of boards beneath her, their gentle, creaking motion. Quiet voices around her murmured words she could not make out, and then the boat was cast off.

Was she alone in the vessel? Where were they sending her? Would she drift out to sea? Sian struggled to sit up, to open her eyes, but they would not budge. "Hello?" she whispered, but there was no answer. "Is anyone here?" She felt around the small boat for oars, or anything that she could use to take charge of her journey, but there was nothing. The searing pain in her arms and legs and belly and back and head and neck and *everywhere* was almost numbing, but never numbing enough.

And what be-damned *message* was she meant to carry? The priest had merely beaten her bloody, then walked away.

She tried again to pull herself up the short side of the boat, but succeeded only in making it rock dangerously. Sian rolled back to the center and began to cry once more. She could not see, she could do nothing to save herself. She was at the mercy of the elements, of the night.

Handing her fate over to the long-vanished gods, she lay down again and sobbed herself to sleep.

~

Captain Konstantin Reikos stood in front of the Monde & Katté townhouse, wondering whether to knock gently once more. It seemed clear that no one was within, but he could not understand why Sian would miss their appointment. Her note had been quite specific. And, beneath the veil of the language of commerce, quite enthusiastic. Or so it had seemed.

Where would she be, in the middle of the night? What business dinner could run *this* late — or preclude even the sending of another note? The townhouse certainly felt vacant, though the shutters were propped wide, letting in the cool (well, cooler) night air. Could she have returned earlier and thought to nap before their appointment, then overslept? He knocked again, slightly louder this time, though mindful not to advertise his presence to the close-knit neighborhood. Domina Kattë did entertain clients with some frequency and often at late hours, but she did so discreetly, as befitted a respectable businesswoman.

Still no answer.

He shifted the ditty bag to his other hand and sighed quietly. The satchel was filled with silk and dye samples, and a small bottle of *kiesh*. He'd considered the Sunward wine he had picked up recently, but rejected it; the vintage was too thick and heavy for a warm night. Too cloying. He knew Sian would prefer the *kiesh*.

Reikos was neither young, nor foolish; he did not deceive himself that he was in love. For one thing, no matter what marital arrangements might obtain, Sian's husband would certainly object. She had made that much clear the first time their negotiations had moved to the daybed, three years past: her time on Viel was her own business, but it stayed here, in this townhouse.

Which suited Reikos as well. In choosing the seafaring life, Reikos had given up the notion of wife and family and home — and with very little hesitation. A lifetime of such broad travel had brought many fine mares into his stable. It was all lovely, but not love. Still, he had come to favor his time with Sian more than most.

Even a seafaring man likes *some* routine and comfort in his life. The intensity of his disappointment at finding her gone surprised him. It was not just the physical need, though certainly he'd looked forward to satisfying that. There were a dozen establishments on his path back to *Fair Passage* that would all too happily supply that service. No. This was ...

Where could she be?

Reikos waited at the doorway, watching a spotted civet nose around the yards, until an armed patrol had passed by the end of the street twice more. If he were still here the third time they passed, they would likely come and ask him unwanted questions.

He was not going to get an explanation tonight. He would speak with Sian on the morrow. For now, there was nothing left to do but sigh and begin the long walk back to his ship.

FIVE

S ian woke to the blinding light of morning. She could open her eyes. With that realization came a rush of dread and anger as she remembered the events of last night.

She sat up gingerly in the boat, cringing in anticipation of pain … which did not come. Straightening further, she blinked and looked around. A flight of graceful white pelicans flew by in single file just off shore. The tiny, weather-beaten vessel had clearly drifted during the night, washing up on the flat, muddy beach of an island densely overgrown with mangrove and scrub palm. The tide, it seemed, was out; the boat leaned against a mussel-covered boulder.

Still nothing hurt. She looked down again, examining her arms, then her legs. Though her once-elegant silks were ruined — filthy, bloodied and torn — her body was clear of any injury. Where had the wounds gone? The cuts and abrasions? The massive bruises that should certainly have been there? She reached up with both hands to touch her face, but again found no pain, no scabs or swellings. Yet she remembered with such dreadful clarity …

Shaking her head in confusion, Sian rose carefully and stepped out of the boat, grimacing as her feet sunk ankle-deep into the mud. She stretched her legs, turning her head this way and that. Still no pain; not even any stiffness. She took a few steps, looking around to get her bearings. In the distance, she picked out the telltale Age of Giants stumps and the tall bridge between The Well and Three Cats. She had drifted quite a ways in the night. It would take a while to get back to …

Oh no! She had missed her dinner with the Hanchu traders!

She laughed aloud. She had also been kidnapped, beaten severely and set adrift, escaping, somehow, with her life — and she was worried about a *business* meeting?

Then she recalled the other meeting she had missed. Reikos must be beside himself.

"Damnation," she muttered, wondering how everything might be re-scheduled, her mind turning reflexively to practicalities, despite all that had happened.

Or was *still* happening ... wasn't it? Why did she not ache?

In fact, her neck and lower back felt better than they had in years of sleeping in soft beds. Perhaps something in her head had been damaged, and she could no longer register the pain that must certainly be there? But she wasn't numb: all her joints and muscles felt ... well, good, actually. She could feel the sun's warmth, and the suck of the mud under her bare feet. And what about the wounds? She looked down at herself again. Could her terror of what was happening have so altered her perceptions that she had just imagined such injuries? Could she have been *that* unhinged?

But no. She had been desperate to see what was happening when they'd dragged her to this boat, yet her eyes had been too swollen to open, no matter how she'd tried. That could not have been imaginary, surely. Yet, such injuries did not just vanish in a night.

How long has it been, then? she wondered with a chill. Had she been lying unconscious long enough to heal like this? How long would that have taken? Days? Weeks? Would she not have perished of thirst or starvation by now?

She left the mud for higher ground, then walked more urgently down the beach, searching for any signs of habitation. She found none. Countless unpopulated sandbars and coral rubble piles peppered the channels and bays of Alizar; it was just her luck, washing ashore on one of them. She gazed at the nearby islands, calculating how far she would have to go to find someone who could help her — or at least help her understand what had happened. It would be a hard row, even if she *did* have oars; probably an hour or more to the Main, farther still to Little Loom Eyot on the other side. But the islands of Alizar Main might not be safe for her now. What if this so-called priest and his crazed followers were still watching for her there?

A few steps further, nearly to the edge of the mangrove-hemmed beach, and the palm-studded shores of Malençon came into view. *Maleen!* If the islands were unsafe for Sian, her daughter — her *grandchildren* — would be in danger as well. This madman had known who Sian was, after all, and to whom she was related! Thank goodness Rubya was far enough away to be out of danger. But she must get to Malençon immediately, collect Maleen and her family if it wasn't already too late, and flee with them at least to the Eyot.

Sian turned and strode back to the boat. Now that she could see, she easily found oars tucked away under the small lip of the gunwale, fastened in place with a slender rope.

She leaned over to unship them, still disbelieving of her absent aches and pains. Her wrists and fingers felt none of the incipient arthritis that had been plaguing her of late; she felt no stiffness from her passage in the boat; even the twinge in her uterus, a near-constant companion since the birth of Rubya, was gone. It was as if she had shed two decades of age overnight.

Perhaps she had indeed been beaten senseless; perhaps she was not even awake now. Though the world around her did not seem like a dream.

If it was, she dreaded waking up.

None of it made any sense.

As soon as Maleen was safe, Sian should go straight to the Justiciary, crying kidnap and attempted murder … but what would she say? *They beat me, but I have no bruises or cuts. And nobody holds me captive; I do not even have a name for my attacker.* No. Not much imagination was required to play out that scene.

Brushing at her clothes in a vain attempt to remove the worst of their filth, she found her small purse, still full of coin. They hadn't even robbed her! This made less sense all the time. Though her sandals had clearly gotten lost in the beating.

She went to wash her hands, arms, and legs in the shallow surf, then rinsed her skirts and blouse. She could hardly go back among people looking as she did. Crusted blood moistened, staining the water and drawing the notice of tiny minnows. At least the silks were dark. Not much she could do about the rips, though. Still, she might pass now, if no one looked too closely.

She put the wet clothes back on, thankful at least for the sultry morning.

Sian took a deep breath and got behind the boat, pushing it towards the water, then jumping in when it was afloat. Even this was less difficult than it should have been, even before her ordeal. The oars came easily into her hands, and pulling them through the water felt invigorating. There was no ache or stiffness in her now loose, strong shoulder muscles. Sian smiled briefly, leaning into the work. But bewilderment quickly returned.

It was an hour's hard work to reach Malençon, yet, though quite hungry now, she was barely more weary than she would have been after walking the few hundred yards from her house on the Eyot to the dye works. In fact, she felt ready to do it all again. She dragged the little boat up onto shore a few hundred yards south of Anglers Wharf, then paused to wonder whether she should try to secure it somehow. It wasn't *her* boat; they could take Maleen's family's larger craft to the Eyot. Still, one didn't just walk away from boats ... except, yes, she *would*. If this dreadful priest wanted it back, he could damn well come and find it.

Sian strode up the beach to a long wooden staircase that led to street level. She was hardly surprised that the climb merely invigorated her further, as did the short walk across this end of the island to her daughter's house. If this were just the energy one felt after a near miss, she supposed it would fade soon enough. Then she would feel all that had happened. Surely.

Maleen lived in a small but comfortable house of carved and gabled teak, raised above the yard's dense foliage on poles behind her husband's smithy. Haron worked in fine copper and brass, and the occasional silver plating, producing household goods for those who could afford more than tin or iron but less than solid silver (or, the gods forefend, gold). He did delicate, lovely work; Maleen was slowly learning the trade by his side, in the rare moments when her children didn't need her.

It always made Sian smile to visit them, to see what latest bit of decorative scrollwork Maleen had etched onto a serving platter, or the elegant curve of her spoons. As she approached the house's bougainvillea-covered wrought-iron gate, she tried to remember when she had last been here. Far too long ago. That much was certain.

Haron, thick gloves up to his elbows, was melting a great ingot of copper, clutched in long iron grips. His son Biri, with his pet mongoose on his shoulder as usual, watched closely by Haron's side, forbidden to touch the equipment until he was older. Haron glanced over at her as Sian walked in, nodding briefly. Sian waved but did not slow down as she walked through the garden; he and Biri would likely come back to the house when the dangerous work was at a point where Haron could set it down without ruining anything.

She climbed the short flight of steps to their front porch, and knocked twice before Maleen answered with a squalling baby on her hip. Sian almost didn't recognize little Jila — how she had grown!

"Mother? What are you doing here?"

"Can't a mother decide to visit her daughter?" Sian laughed. It sounded forced, even to herself. *What are you doing here?*... Far too long indeed.

"Of course," Maleen rushed to answer. "I just meant..." She frowned as she shifted the howling child to her other hip, looking Sian up and down. "What have you done with your — Oh! Look at your *clothes!* What *happened?*" She reached out to touch the long tear in Sian's skirt. "You're all wet! Are you all right? Where are your sandals?"

Sian discovered that she did not know how to begin the story, much less tell it here on her daughter's stoop. "I just ... had a bit of a fall on some stairs down at the docks — quite clumsy of me! I am unharmed, but I'd love to borrow some clothes, if I may."

"You look..." Maleen stared at her, trying to work something out. "You're not hurt?"

"I am not, no. May I come in?"

"Yes, yes." Maleen stepped aside. "I was just brewing some kava — I'll add more water."

Sian followed her daughter into the small, bright kitchen at the back of the house, Jila leaving an audible trail of angry wails. "Here, let me take her," Sian said.

"Oh, thank you." The baby gasped and sobbed even louder as Maleen handed her over. "It's the colic, they tell me; nothing to do but wait it out." Maleen's smile could not disguise the exhaustion in her young eyes.

"There, there," Sian cooed to her granddaughter, jiggling the child gently against her hip before sitting down at the table and nuzzling the top of the baby's head. That marvelous smell of baby ... and ginger? Maleen must be feeding her ginger tea for her tummy troubles. Sian's own stomach gave an uncomfortable turn. From hunger, she supposed, hoping it was only that, and not some internal injury. She was quite hungry, come to think of it.

Jila hiccuped once and abruptly stopped crying, gazing up at Sian with wide dark eyes. Sian kissed her tiny, reddened nose. "There you go! Who's a sweet girl!"

"Oh, blessed silence!" Maleen said, adding a small jug of water to the pot already bubbling on the stove, then giving it a stir.

"A grandmother's touch." Sian smiled as Maleen came to the table with two steaming mugs. "Thank you. If you've some bread as well, I'd love a slice or two."

"Of course." Maleen went to the cupboard. "Have you not breakfasted?"

"Er, no — nor dinner last night either."

Her daughter brought out two rounds of jolada rotti, plus butter and some fig preserves that Sian had given her last fall. She sat down and gave Sian a long, wary look. "What *is* going on, Mother? Are you sure you're all right?"

"Well, there is more to tell ... but this is marvelous." She tore off a thick chunk of rotti and slathered butter on it, then took a big bite.

"Is that your Selistani silk?" Maleen was looking more closely at Sian's poor garments. "Have you been out all night?"

"I ... did sleep," Sian ventured, looking down at the baby, now babbling happily while reaching for her grandmother's long hair. *Dark* hair, with far less gray than yesterday, it seemed. Sian covered this further surprise by occupying herself with a second piece of rotti. Eventually, she said, "I do not entirely understand what happened to me."

Maleen glanced toward the front of the house. From Haron's shop, both women could hear the steady sound of pounding as he shaped whatever he was forging today. "Tell me."

"Well ..." Where to begin? "You're aware of this 'Butchered God' religion?"

Maleen snorted, but looked even more worried. "*Mother.* Even I get out of the house once in a great while. Are you telling me ... are you a follower?"

"By no means. Yet ... I appear to have come to their attention in an unfortunate way — and I'm afraid that you — that my whole family may ... be in danger."

From there, the story tumbled out, as best as Sian could relate it, over Maleen's anxious interruptions and many questions.

"I feel certain that I was badly beaten," Sian said at last, increasingly unsure of her own memories, despite their clarity, "though I can see as well as you can that, despite my clothes, my body shows no signs of it."

"Yes. You do not look beaten." Maleen's voice was quiet, wary. "Your clothes have obviously been through ... something. But you ..."

"I feel fine as well. More energy than I can remember having in years."

"You do have the appetite of a youth." Maleen glanced at the empty bread-board, then bit her lip. "And your face, and hair — you could be my younger sister."

"Well, I thank you ..." Sian demurred.

"No, I mean it. Come, look in the glass." Maleen stood up and walked to the sitting room, where there was a fine framed mirror — a wedding gift from Sian and Arouf. "You see?"

Sian followed Maleen, hoping not to upset the finally-quiet Jila. The child remained happy and quiet in her arms as she carried her over to the glass.

What Sian saw was undeniable: she looked bright and well rested, quite undamaged. She was still herself, a woman of nearly fifty summers; but one with lush, dark hair, no worry lines between her eyes, and supple skin. It was as though a long-parched plant had been watered; everything had perked up and filled out. And the baby in her arms felt light as a feather.

Sian shook her head. "Very strange."

"What does Father make of this?"

"I came to you first." It had not occurred to her to go to Arouf. "He will be more ... complicated, I fear." Sian turned to look at her daughter, standing behind her, her face drawn with concern.

"Why?"

Sian sank into Haron's plush chair, adjusting the still-happy baby into her lap once more. Why *did* she cringe at the thought of speaking to Arouf?

They had long since ceased discussing difficult things; *impossible* things would be ... quite beyond the pale. "I ... he just ... he would not understand."

"I don't understand either, Mother. Are you truly certain this all ... happened?"

"I know that it did! Do you not believe me?"

"I ... you just don't look beaten! I'm sorry — but, can't you see? Other than your clothes, you look as though you've spent two weeks at the Auglentine Baths!"

"I *was* beaten! I know I was. And I know we're in danger — all of us. Won't you please come with me, to safety? We can speak to your father together."

Maleen shook her head. "Mother, I ... this is just not making sense. Why are you not wounded?"

"I cannot explain it!"

"So ... why should we all flee with you?"

"Were you not listening?! That madman knew our family name — all my relations!"

Maleen sighed, struggling. Sian could see the disbelief on her face. How could she make her daughter understand? "It is not such an unknown name ..." Maleen started.

"That's not the point — something is very wrong here. Please, bring Haron and the children now — just for a week, until we know ..."

"Mother, we can't just pick up our children and leave our home. We're busier than ever — Haron is working on two orders that are already overdue." Maleen gave an unhappy smile. "Yes, they knew your name — because your own employee led you to this priest. That is not about *us*; that sounds more like a complaint about Monde & Kattë."

Sian frowned. "No, I was supposed to take a message to 'those who rule'."

"*What* message?" Maleen shook her head.

"I ... I do not know."

"Mother, even if you did manage to convince Haron of this — this unknown danger, whatever it is — he would just insist on staying, to protect our home and smithy. This is everything we own — abandoning it would ruin us."

"Then *you* come with me — you and the children. Haron is strong, he can ..." Sian faltered; Maleen's face was set. "What should I do?" She bit back tears.

Maleen leaned over the arm of the chair, hugging her mother. "I don't know. I can see that ... something ... very strange has happened to you. Maybe you should just go home to Father, stay off the islands for a few days? Let things settle down?"

Don't patronize me, Sian wanted to snap, but she could hardly blame Maleen; at least she was being kind. Would Sian have believed such a story, if it had not happened to her? She hardly did believe it, even now.

"May I borrow some clean clothes?" Sian asked instead. "And a pair of sandals?"

⌒

After a quick bath, and a promise from Maleen to be careful and to stay in touch, Sian left. She walked through the palm and philodendron-lined streets of Malençon, watching for prayer lines or any other unusual activity. But the island was quiet; just the usual passage of commerce and the raucous calls of jungle birds.

At the Hanchu trade hall where she was to have had dinner the night before, Sian inquired about the meeting she had missed, hoping to send immediate apologies, and perhaps reschedule, but was astonished when the porter informed her that no such delegation had reserved a room there at all. When she insisted that they had invited her to dinner there just last night, he informed her only that there had been no message left for her. Sian could do nothing but shake her head and leave, bewildered. Had this been some kind of subtle reproach for having missed the appointment, or just the porter's overzealous regard for a client's confidentiality? Or ...

She thought again of the massive prayer lines she had worked so fruitlessly to get past. Always in her path, as if ... Could they have gone to that much trouble just to ... what? Bring her to their priest? Could such aimless, mumbling wanderers have planned anything remotely that elaborate? Had Pino helped them? The very idea seemed ridiculous ... and in other ways, even more terrifying. What *was* all this about? How long had they been planning this?

Lost in such unnerving thoughts, she headed back to see if the rowboat was still where she'd left it, wondering whether to go to the townhouse or to Little Loom Eyot. Halfway there, however, a sudden commotion in the street ahead made her startle, then cower into a jasmine-shadowed doorway.

But it was no prayer line or angry priest this time. A street urchin had simply made the wrong decision about whom to rob, it seemed. He lay wailing on the cobblestones. Sian glimpsed a well-dressed back disappearing into the gathering crowd as she hurried toward the child almost without having decided to.

He was a small boy, not more than five or six summers. His intended victim must have slashed him with a sharp knife, deep into the right forearm. Blood flowed from the long, gaping wound as the boy screamed. Pushing past a ring of frozen onlookers, Sian grabbed the child, lifting him easily as she clutched her fingers tightly around the wound to hold its edges together.

"Get help!" she yelled, to no one in particular. "He'll bleed to death!"

The boy shrieked louder, struggling in Sian's grasp. She felt a sharp pain in her own right forearm — *there's my arthritis after all* — then noticed a pungent smell of ginger in the air, disregarded as she held tight to the boy. Some of the bystanders simply left. The remaining few still seemed immobilized by indecision. "Call the Mishrah-Khote, get someone!" Sian cried.

Finally, a sturdy-looking carter bent over the boy. "It be all right, then, boy. We have you right, soon. Let me see." The carter's assistant, a gawky youth only a few years older than the boy, stood nearby, nervous and unsure.

Sian released her grip just a bit so the carter could see. He leaned in for a closer look, then glanced up at Sian, confused. "Where be the wound?"

"What are you talking about? He's badly cut. Right there across his arm."

"I see the blood," he answered, shaking his head. "But the cut… That nothing but an old scar. Perhaps he scrape himself somewhere. Scrapes, they seep a lot of blood sometime. There no call for temple healers." He rose and turned to leave.

"They have their charity allotment," Sian said scornfully, disgusted at his callousness. "They won't charge you just for calling them." This child might be an urchin and a thief, but death was no just penalty for petty theft.

"If I call 'em, it be to come and heal your eyes," the man scoffed. "Come on, boy." He beckoned his assistant to follow. "Ain't paying you to gawk at thieves and imbeciles."

The urchin whimpered. "It's all right," Sian whispered, forcing down her fury at the carter. "Let me bind this up, and I'll go call the priests myself." She began daubing away the blood with the hem of Maleen's nice clean silks. Two dresses ruined in a day. But as the blood came off, she leaned back in surprise.

The carter had been right. The gash was closed completely.

"La-lady," the boy stammered, staring white-faced at his arm, then up at Sian.

Sian wiped more blood away, as if the wound might be there after all, just misplaced somehow under the mess. But she found nothing but a thin white scar; something long-healed, a wound from infancy. "Oh," Sian managed, letting go of him.

He scrambled to his feet, gave her a frightened look, then turned and bolted.

Trembling, Sian got up as well. Her hands were covered with blood. The diminished crowd backed slowly away from her, seeming nearly as terrified as the boy had been.

Except for one middle-aged woman dressed in ruddy coarse linen, gazing at her in astonishment. "I saw what you did," she whispered. "Who *are* you?"

"I'm nobody," Sian said. "Just a person, passing by ..." She could not stop shaking.

"You healed him," the woman said, more loudly. "Does the Mishrah-Khote anoint women now?"

Sian shook her head in urgent denial as the implications washed over her. The priests-hospitalars of the Mishrah-Khote looked very harshly upon 'false' healers. They barely tolerated old women growing medicinal herbs in their gardens. "No, no. The boy — I must have misunderstood, it must have been just a scratch ..."

"I saw you! The blood is still on you!"

"I did nothing!" Sian yelled, as the crowd pressed in once more. "Leave me be!" She pushed past the gathered folk and broke into a run, as desperate to get away as the stricken boy had been.

"My lady!" a man cried, but she kept running, as if the Sea-Serpent of Pennlet itself were after her.

SIX

The priest's boat wasn't where Sian had left it. She wasn't surprised.

She was hungrier than ever, despite her small meal at Maleen's, but she just wanted to get as far away from here as fast as possible. Though no one seemed to be pursuing her, she knew she must keep moving. The crowd's attention had been ... unnerving.

After washing her arms and hands off in the shallow, lapping surf, she hurried on toward the bridge to Three Cats. There, she found the usual cluster of cart runners waiting for those in need of transport off the island. *Where were you all last night?* she wondered, walking toward them. "Where to, lady?" asked the nearest runner, a far younger and more muscular young man than last night's fellow, if noticeably less flirtatious; his long black hair was elaborately knotted up with strings of terracotta beads.

Where to? That was the question. She drew breath to give him the address of her townhouse on Viel. But no. They had known who she was last night. They might be waiting there now. A public dock, where she could hire passage to Little Loom Eyot? But ... she was still not ready to face Arouf with this. Not alone.

Then it came to her. So obvious. "The port on Cutter's," she told him.

He nodded. "I have you there in no time, lady." He nodded at his bright red wicker cart. "I help you up?"

"I can manage," Sian said, already reaching for the step rail.

The road was empty now. They were across the bridge and onto Three Cats in hardly any time at all. Where had all those marchers vanished back to? What *had* they been doing here last night? Despite the warm and windless day, a chill ran up the length of her as she looked up to watch a flock of egrets glide through the steamy sky above her, still trying to understand what had just happened with the boy on Malençon.

Why did she keep imagining wounds that weren't there? But ... there had been blood. Again. There was always so much blood. And she had seen the wound. So clearly. She had pressed it shut. The boy was screaming, he'd fallen to the street. Was she crazy? Maleen clearly thought so ... Could she be right?

～

The *Fair Passage* was a two-masted brig of the latest Stone Coast design, with an oversized gaff sail and a lean, elegant prow. Sian breathed a sigh of relief as she approached the ship. Its gangplank was down, indicating it was open for business.

"Hello the ship!" she called up.

A young seaman on the deck leaned over. "Who calls?"

"A visitor for Captain Reikos. Is he aboard?"

"Your name?"

Though she seemed not to have been followed here, Sian did *not* want to be shouting her name across Cutter's wharf. "Tell him it's the lady about the wine."

The sailor looked dubious, but nodded and went below.

Reikos appeared a short time later. A broad grin, and a look of great relief, crossed his face. "Sian!" he cried, then clearly remembered where they were. "Er, Domina Kattë. Such a pleasure to see you!"

"Permission to come aboard?"

"Of course!" He dashed over to the gangway, appearing ready to rush down and carry her up himself.

Sian forestalled this by hurrying up the gangway herself. "I thank you," she said, as she stepped on board.

"Come, come, my cabin — we must discussion," he said, losing all semblance of his usual Alizari fluency in his excitement.

A minute later, they were in his tidy stateroom. Reikos bolted the door, then began unfolding two wooden chairs from their wall niches. A porthole window behind Sian let in a moist but gentle breeze. In an airy cage beside it, his golden-crowned cockatiel tilted its head at Sian.

"I was so worried to not find you last night," Reikos said. "And I am so glad you are here — and looking so well!"

"I'm sorry, I was detained — something awful has happened." Sian sank into the cunning little chair. "I didn't know where else to go."

"Of course I am delighted that you came here! You must tell me everything."

"I…" Once again, she could not think quite how to begin. "Yes. That's … why I've come. But first, I have not yet had much breakfast. Would you happen to have —"

"Oh! Yes, of course." He leapt up, already starting toward the door. "I've had them purchase many fine things in the galley now, since we have docked. What do you wish?"

"Anything," she said. "Whatever strikes your fancy. Thank you."

"I will be not a minute, then." He grinned and hurried out the door.

What *was* she going to tell him?

Her own daughter had clearly thought her mad. What would Reikos make of such a story? How well did they really know each other? Well enough to trade intimacies in the dark, of course, but … Well enough for this? Had she been a fool to come here?

No. No, he was a sophisticated traveler, who'd surely seen all kinds of things far stranger than she could imagine. Did they have gods in Smagadis, his homeland? He had never told her, but perhaps miracles were nothing unusual for him … She hoped.

"*Pretty lady! Pretty lady! Kiss me, pretty lady!*"

Sian looked up at the cockatiel, startled. She knew it could talk, of course. This was hardly the first time she'd been in Reikos's cabin. But she had not heard this before.

"*Kiss me, pretty lady!*"

A second later, the door opened and Reikos returned, bearing a platter piled with fresh oysters, flaky frosted pastries and sliced green starfruit. He grinned at her. "The oysters are in a very pleasant citrus sauce. I hope you like them." He set the platter down on his small folding table by her chair. "Such things are necessary after three weeks of hardtack and salted meat, no?"

"Your bird's been talking to me," Sian said. "It said, 'Kiss me, pretty lady.'"

Reikos looked with raised brows at the cockatiel.

"*Damn bird! Damn bird!*" it squawked.

She *had* heard that one before. She gave him an arch smile. "It must hear a thing quite a few times to learn it, mustn't it? That's what I've been told, at least."

Reikos turned to her, looking even more surprised, then burst out laughing. "You know Matilda is a lady bird, Sian! That is what I always say to her, while we are at sea together." He walked over to the cage, bent down until his face almost touched the bars, and cooed, "Pretty lady, yes. Pretty lady." He puckered his lips comically. "Kiss me, pretty lady. Kiss me." The bird thrust its head toward the bars, opening its beak, as Reikos darted back before it bit his lip off. "Damn bird," he muttered softly, then turned back to Sian. "You see? My heart belongs to no one but yourself."

"All right, I believe you now. About the bird," she conceded, reaching out to pluck an oyster shell from the platter and tip it into her mouth. "Mmmmm," she said, reaching for another.

She very quickly polished off the plate as Reikos watched in guarded amazement, then wiped delicately at her lips with a corner of her sleeve, not quite meeting his eyes.

"You are very hungry, to have had such a late dinner last night, perhaps?" Reikos asked, his voice hesitant.

"I had no dinner."

"What has happened?"

"I . . . don't really understand it." There was no easy way into any of this. "I fear I may be going mad. Or perhaps I have been given some horrible power. But why?" Sian shook her head, still trying to make sense of what had happened with the street urchin.

"My lady, surely I would know by now if you were capable of madness."

"Konstantin, I touched a badly wounded boy ... and *healed* him. I think."

Reikos shook his head, bemused, still smiling. "What do you mean? You helped a boy?"

"I mean I healed a gaping wound. Just by touching it." Sian shivered. "I'm terrified."

"Healing is a good thing, is it not?" He was not understanding her; that much was obvious.

"Of course it is. But this isn't — natural! I don't know what's going on, why it's happening."

"Tell me everything," he said again, clearly confused. "From the start. Something happened last night?"

"Well, it started then. I was on my way to the business dinner I wrote you about. But I never got there." She told him the whole story, just as she had explained to Maleen, adding the new element of the healing, and the crowd's frightening attention immediately afterwards.

"I don't know what any of this means," she said, when she had finished. "It's obviously connected. But there was no message! This madman just beat me, set me adrift, and ... here I am, unwounded, but with this terrible curse."

"I would like to see this ... curse."

"What do you mean?"

"Can you heal this?" Reikos held up his left thumb, blackened halfway up the nail. Sian remembered him complaining of the injury; he'd hit it with a hammer, repairing some rigging. He would likely lose the nail.

"I don't really know how this works," Sian protested, suddenly reluctant.

"Then what is the harm?" He held his hand toward her. Behind him, the cockatiel *quark*ed at her, then shuffled about its cage, tossing seeds. "*Damn bird.*"

More afraid than she was willing to admit to herself, Sian gently grasped his thumb, thinking about the old injury, how much it must still hurt him. An answering pain appeared in her own left thumb, accompanied once more by the smell of ginger — more subtle than it had been in the street, but still unmistakable, as if ginger tea were brewing nearby. Startled, she let go of his thumb.

He gazed at it, mouth slightly open, eyes wide with wonder. There was no purplish stain, no unevenness on the nail bed. In a moment, her own thumb stopped hurting as well.

"Oh, my," he murmured. Then he looked at Sian, eyes still wide, now bright and excited. "Sian, this is amazing! Think of what good you can do!"

"No, Konstantin, you don't understand! I cannot be doing this! No one can know."

"Why ever not?"

"The priests-hospitalars would have my hide. The penalty for fraudulent healers is severe — I could be jailed until my grandchildren are married. Or worse."

"But you are clearly not fraudulent!" He waved his thumb at her, pink and healthy. "You have been given a power, an amazing gift!"

"If you are not an anointed Mishrah-Khote priest, you are by definition a fraud — and they do *not* anoint women."

Reikos shook his head. "They would never deny a true miracle!"

"They care nothing for truth, nor for miracles. They only want to protect their own position, their *wealth*. I've known that since my mother died horribly, under their care." Angry tears crowded her eyes; she turned away, staring unseeing out the porthole. "I know you are not from here, but you *must* know how things are."

"Sian, Sian." Reikos put his arm around her shoulder, his voice gentle. "Don't be sad. It will be all right. It is a large and confusing thing, I can see that. But it is still a *good* thing."

She shrugged him off. "It is certainly *not*. That man is targeting my family — he knew me by name. And I can't even get Maleen to leave the islands. Everyone has gone mad." Reikos continued to look at her, excited but stymied. "You as well — are you listening to me at all? How can you not see how threatening this is?"

Reikos spread his arms out in a gesture of helplessness. "Who am I to question a gift from the gods?"

"But the gods don't *give* gifts! Not here! There have been no gods in Alizar for ... ever!"

"Did one not wash up on your shores a year or two ago? We talked of this, remember? Sian, where else could such a gift have come from? What else can it mean? You have been chosen. You cannot withhold this gift from those who need you! Think of all the folk who suffer in this world. Think of all the children!"

Sian could not ignore the eager gleam in his eyes. He wasn't concerned about sick children or suffering folk … he was too excited. Scheming already. A sensational new commodity fallen into his hands literally from heaven …

"What would you have me do?" Sian asked, her voice quiet.

"Mansur, of the *Valiant,* two berths down — a very wealthy man! — he has a crewman with the bloodpox…"

"No!" Sian surged to her feet. Wealth! She'd known it. "I thought you'd help me — I see I was wrong." Eyes blurred with tears, she struggled with the door-latch, then wrestled it open.

"I want nothing more than to help you!" Reikos protested.

Sian ignored him as she stumbled to the gangway, nearly tripping as she hurried down to the street below. Reikos followed her as far as the rail, beseeching her to come back and just listen — but she had heard enough. He would sell her curse to the highest bidder! If she'd known how, she'd have given him his purple thumb back again, and twice as hard.

～

Sian was almost more angry with herself than at Reikos. She had badly misjudged him, blinded by the sweetness of their private relationship. Well, and his *previously* honest business dealings with her over the years.

How could he think to profit from her misfortune!

It was quite clear to her now why he had never married. He obviously had no understanding of women, beyond the gentle game of occasional dalliance. He certainly did not know how to listen.

No one did, it seemed. Not her daughter. Or her lover …

Madness. Everything had become madness. She had no choice left but to go home to the Eyot — to face Arouf alone. And why not? Really, why not? He was her husband! Her business partner all these years. Father of her daughters. Why should he, if anyone, not help her? Why should she so fear asking him to? Madness! Everywhere. Even in herself. Half the day remained. She should have gone there to begin with.

There was a boat yard nearby — Jennian's. They had done repair work on her skiff not long ago, competently and at a fair price. She put her back to *Fair Passage* and headed off to rent a sailboat.

Jennian's son, a strapping boy of twenty, was in the boat yard, sanding the boards of a small rowboat which sat up on blocks by the main warehouse. Sian thought his name was Andian, or was it Anther?

He looked up from his work at her approach. "Domina Kattë! What can I do for you?"

"I need to hire a skiff. What have you?"

"Is yours not fixed then?"

"It's fine — just not here." She was already glancing down at their dock as she spoke. There, a little red one, with clean enough lines, near the end of the pier. She couldn't see the condition of its mast from here, but the Jennians were honest traders. They wouldn't rent her a rotten boat.

The boy followed her look. "That one's here for repair — I can't let it. But I've a little sloop that one man could sail, just there." He pointed to a weathered green boat rocking gently in the breeze.

"Or one woman?" Sian walked down to inspect the boat. Yes, it was sound enough; needed more than a splash of new paint, but its structure was tight. "How much, for a week?"

"Sixteen."

"I'll give you twelve, and you'll change this jib for a new one." She pointed to the sail: it looked to have been recently scraped clean of mildew, making the tiny cracks and tears along its fold-lines apparent.

"Fifteen," the boy mumbled, obviously embarrassed at the condition of the jib.

"Thirteen, in advance," Sian said, producing her purse and counting out the coins. "And give my regards to your father."

The boy took the coins, still flustered, tucking them into a pocket of his worn trousers, then ducked into the warehouse and emerged with a new jib a minute later.

After helping Sian aboard, he untied the boat, and watched her sail out into the harbor.

〜

Though she had been here only the day before, it felt as though a thousand years had passed since Sian had seen Little Loom Eyot. Bringing the little sloop in to their dock, she looked for Pino's boat, but it wasn't here.

She tied off the rented sloop, then started walking up the hill, through the tree ferns, toward the house. Arouf met her on the path before she'd gotten halfway there.

"What has happened?" he asked, concern etching lines on his sundarkened face. "Pino never returned yesterday — what is that boat?" Several workers stepped out of the dye house to see what was going on.

"Husband, I have some things to tell you — in private. Come to the house."

Arouf frowned again at the sloop, then turned to follow Sian.

They passed Bela in the kitchen, limping about as she washed pots and prepared adzuki and cherimoya for the evening meal. Closing the door to the sitting room, Sian sat down. Arouf took his customary rattan chair, then peered at her. "Have you done something with your hair?"

"It goes deeper than that." She gave him a sad smile. "Something has happened to me — it defies explanation, but I need you to believe me."

Arouf, still frowning, nodded. "You have never given me any reason to doubt you," he said, with a notable emphasis.

Sian took a deep breath. "Good." *Let that remain true.* "Last night, on my way to meet a delegation of Hanchu silk traders, I was attacked by a prayer line. Our Pino was in it, but he vanished before the beating started in earnest."

"You were *beaten*? By *Pino*?"

"Quite badly. But not by Pino, no. I just told you ..." She checked the impulse to argue. She needed him to listen, for once. To stop just reacting with such instinctive dread to anything out of the ordinary. "He ... disappeared when all the trouble started. When they were done, they set me adrift in a small boat, too wounded to move, or even open my eyes. I woke this morning on a deserted islet as you see me now —" she spread her arms, showing her lack of bruises or cuts " — and feeling no pain."

"Are you sure? Let me see." He got up and came to her, reaching for her arm, taking it gently in his large hands. *More intimacy than we've had in months*, she thought. "Where did they hit you?"

"Everywhere. But I have no mark."

He peered at the exposed skin along her arms, touching her oddly smooth skin. "Yes, you seem quite unharmed." He gave her a puzzled, skeptical look. "Nothing pains you?"

"Nothing, no."

"But you say they beat you 'til you could not move or see ... Then where —?"

"I did not imagine this, Arouf! My clothing was quite ruined. Still covered in my own blood when I awoke this morning. Maleen loaned me this."

"Maleen was involved?"

"No, I went to her — Malençon was the closest inhabited island. And besides, I feared for her — I fear for us all. Before they set me adrift, a man calling himself the 'Priest of the Butchered God' made a point of our family's connection to the Alkatthas."

"This all makes no sense! And now the Alkatthas are involved?" Arouf glanced around in growing agitation. She could almost hear his thoughts: *Say it is all a terrible joke. Tell me it was nothing.*

"I have no idea. But then, on my way from Maleen's to rent a boat, I encountered a wounded boy in the street ... and I healed him, just by putting a hand on him."

"You ... what?"

"Later, I realized I had likely done the same with baby Jila — she'd been screaming with the colic, yet she quieted at my touch."

Arouf sank back into his chair, still staring at Sian. "Coincidence. Children love their grandmothers."

"That may be — but the boy in the street —"

"What was his wound? Also colic?"

Sian leaned forward, trying to manage her frustration. "A knife wound, quite deep and bloody. I touched it. The skin knit back together."

"No, such things are impossible! Even the priests-hospitalars do not work such miracles!"

"I promise you —"

The door from the kitchen opened, and Bela poked in her head. "Domni, Domina? Do you require anything before I go see to the laundry?"

Arouf started to answer, but Sian interrupted him. "Yes, please, Bela, would you come in here a moment?" The cook-housekeeper shuffled into the room, hampered, as always, by the twisted leg she had nearly lost in a childhood accident. "You seem to be walking with more difficulty lately. Is that leg giving you more pain?"

"Sian, I don't see —" Arouf started, but Sian silenced him with a gesture.

Puzzled, the housekeeper said, "Yes, my lady. Some. But not enough to bother with. Are you ... I hope you do not feel it's interfering with my work here?"

"No, no. Of course not. May I touch it?"

Even more mystified, Bela nodded, then drew her skirts up to just above the knee.

I hope this works on very old *injuries,* Sian thought, reaching for Bela's thigh. She had her answer as soon as her own thigh throbbed, and ginger filled the air. Ginger. *Why ginger?* she wondered.

"Oh!" Bela shrieked, drawing back in fear, then astonishment. "Oh! The pain, it is gone!"

Arouf got up and rushed to Bela, taking her arm. "Sit down! Are you all right?"

"I am quite well!" She gazed at Sian, wonder in her eyes. "My lady, it is mended!" She straightened her leg, then took a few tentative steps. "It is a miracle!"

Arouf turned on Sian as she rubbed her own thigh, the pain still ebbing away. His face was filled with naked terror. "What have you *done*, woman?!"

"I have shown you that I am telling the truth!"

"You are a saint!" Bela cried, now hopping from leg to leg.

"No! What have you done to gain this terrible power?" Arouf shouted. "You will ruin us!" He turned to Bela. "You may not tell *anyone* of this! Go, now!"

Crestfallen, Bela slunk from the room.

"Don't you yell at her!" Sian shouted, getting to her feet. "She's done nothing to deserve that."

Arouf took a deep breath, visibly gathering himself, though he still shuddered. "Fine," he said more quietly. "She has not. I still want to know what *you* have done."

"I have done nothing!" Sian said. "Were you not listening to me? This was done *to* me, I did not ask for it!"

"If the Mishrah-Khote hears of this, they will have our charter revoked — we will never sell another bolt!"

"Do you think I don't *know* this? Why do you think I'm asking for your help?! We are being targeted, and I don't know why."

"*You* are being targeted. *I* am no relation to those Alkatthas."

Stunned, Sian stared at Arouf, his stony face, the grim line of his mouth under his thick beard. He would so coldly cut her loose — and their daughters too? — in his worry for the health of their *business*?

She had misjudged her lover. Did she know her own husband even less? No. She had known she could not bring this to him from the start. Had she not said so to Maleen?

And it wasn't even rational: it was a response born of fear. Denouncing Sian now wouldn't save him *or* their business, if it came to that. He simply had no courage; he hadn't for many years. Had he ever?

Sian shook her head, then turned and left the room, not stopping until she'd reached the little sloop. There, she looked back at the house. Arouf had made no effort to follow her.

"So I am alone," she whispered, and got back into the boat. She had always known.

SEVEN

A storm was clearly blowing in from the Sunward Sea. Late afternoon sunlight still shone like silver on the choppy water, but the coming front's capricious winds fought Sian from every side as she returned to Alizar Main. No matter how the sails were trimmed, they soon luffed again, only to snap taut seconds later with a crack, causing the small craft to jibe or heel alarmingly as she struggled with the rudder. It all reminded her, quite forcefully, why she had always let Pino row her here — back when Pino had been here to do so. Not that she gave any thought to turning back.

It had been naïve of her to think she could hide on Little Loom Eyot — from the Mishrah-Khote or anybody else — even if Arouf had been willing to help. The first time one of their weavers or dye pit workers suffered an injury, Sian would have felt compelled to heal them, even if she had decided to hide this talent. If she could not avoid rushing to the assistance of an urchin in the street, could she stand by while someone she knew suffered? So she would do it, and of course word would have spread. The only way to avoid using this power would be to stay locked in her room, seeing no one, touching no one, hearing nothing from outside its four walls — for the rest of her days? Even if she were mad enough to try such a thing, it was too late for that now, given what she'd just done for Bela.

As Shingle Beach approached, Sian tacked the boat, avoiding her usual landing. She'd rent a day-berth at the public dock on Viel, then begin her search. Her fear of this Butchered God's mad-eyed priest had, little by little, given way to a full, fuming anger. Who *was* this man, to dance in and destroy Sian's life, mumbling his meaningless apologies as he beat her bloody?

In the space of a night and a day, he had upended her life. He had broken her ties to daughter, husband, and lover. And Arouf, cowardly though he may be, was right about one thing: how was she to run a business with this curse? Even if the Mishrah-Khote let her be, the mob of sick and injured at her door never would. She would heal everyone — and perish her own self.

The mad priest's powers were certainly real. Her curse proved that. But surely, one with power to give would have power to take as well. She needed to find this man and make him fix what he had broken.

She struggled to shore at last as evening fell. Loose-tailed bats had started fluttering about the Sinyan coral trees, gobbling up the evening insects as she secured her rented sloop to the dock, then headed for her townhouse. She *hoped* now that he would be waiting for her there. But all she found was the usual pile of mail, including a note from Reikos:

Lady Domina Kattë:

I deeply regret the interruption of our recent negotiation. The fault was entirely mine. An unfortunate presumption, based on erroneous market information, which I have since rectified. If you are still willing to do business with this humble soul, I have just come into possession of some rare and high quality Sircussian cloth that I can only imagine, nay, hope, you might not find utterly odious.

If you can countenance the possibility of reopening trade with such a careless, worthless bumbler, send word to me on the *Fair Passage*. I would be more than pleased to arrange a time that I may show you these fine examples of cunning workmanship.

I remain, forever your servant,
Konstantin Reikos

Sian set the note on her desk and frowned. *Sircussian cloth, indeed!* Well, the apology was nice, she supposed; but his use of one of their saucier code words only demonstrated that he still did not understand the least bit of the problem. This was no mere lover's spat.

Taking out a clean sheet of paper, she composed a terse, business-like reply, informing him — in both plain language and underlying code — that, due to unexpected circumstances, of which he was well aware, she would be unavailable to *negotiate* for the foreseeable future.

That done, she rose to wash her face at the townhouse's small sink, then ate every scrap of food left in the house. After that, she shed Maleen's gauzy silks in favor of a plain, dark outfit of coarser fabric, suitable for weathering the imminent rain. It was time to go out looking for prayer lines.

~

It amused her grimly that just last night she had been unable to travel five steps without tripping over a prayer line, while today it seemed the islands were devoid of them. Perhaps it was the coming storm. Or … had they truly been put there just to trap her? She still could not believe it. Whatever the case, Sian had walked, then resorted to faster travel by runner-cart across Viel, Cutter's, and Three Cats over the span of four hours, and seen not a single line.

And she was starving again. *I've eaten more yesterday and today than I have in the last three weeks put together,* she thought, passing up a kava house in favor of a tavern. It was coming on evening; she needed some more substantial meal.

She had no sooner been served her fisherman's pie, however, than she heard the telltale chanting and drumming of a prayer line. "Damnation!" she whispered, taking several hurried bites before leaving coin on the table and rushing out.

It was a short, disorganized line, which she caught up with easily, scanning it but seeing no priest, no Pino. She followed it a few blocks, hanging back as she had done the other night, as it meandered in the usual way, losing members to each tavern and wine-bar it passed. She was considering whether to approach one of the stragglers when the line reached an open plaza and fell apart altogether. A large bonfire whipped and danced in the strong winds, sending smoke into the overhanging banyan trees. Most of the line joined the folk around the blaze.

Sian walked up too, warming her hands beside a young erstwhile line-member with the scraggly start of a beard. Though the storm had clearly not yet fully broken, a few drops were starting to fall. "Rough night ahead," she said.

The young man looked over at her. "Yep. They say this one'll last a day, maybe two."

"Smells like it."

He gave her a few more glances, no doubt thinking himself stealthy. Well, it made conversation easier.

"Do you follow the Butchered God?" she ventured.

"Oh, yes; we all do." He smiled and opened his arms, indicating the circle around the bonfire. "It's exciting, don't you think?"

"Mmm," Sian said, noncommittally. "And his priest?"

The boy's eyes shone. "A saint among men. When he speaks ..." He gestured again, helpless, beaming.

"He's not ... here now, is he?" In the shadows around the fire, Sian could not make out much in the way of individual features on anyone.

"No. You would know — the crowd would be enormous. You have not met him then?"

She shook her head. "How does one find him?"

The boy shrugged. "One doesn't. He shows up when he has something to tell us."

"I've not had the pleasure of hearing him speak yet. Do you think he'll come tonight?"

"Who can say?" The boy sidled closer to Sian. "At least we have a fire."

"Yes."

Well, this was worthless. She waited a polite minute more, then said, "I must get home," and slipped into the darkness before he could answer.

∿

Sian finally got a decent meal into herself, then went back to traveling the islands until she found a larger, more purposeful line. It was now full dark and raining in earnest. That, and her inconspicuous attire, emboldened her to join the marchers this time.

As she shambled along with the chanting, muddy crowd, she asked several people about the priest, but no one could tell her any more than the boy had. This new religion was an odd one indeed: its adherents walked the streets day and night; its priest could turn up anywhere, at any time, or could vanish for weeks. Yet everyone spoke of him, and his message, with radiant awe. Whatever he was telling them, it was something they were desperate to hear.

Unless he was merely god-spelling them as well. But to what end?

Frustrated, and soaking wet, Sian kept deciding to abandon the search for the night, then following one more prayer line, across one more bridge, sustained by her strange, newfound strength and stamina.

Somewhere near the night's twelfth bell, shouts suddenly rang out as four huge men boiled from a narrow alley, armed with heavy lengths of wood. A man in front of Sian shrieked and fell under a great blow; his attacker then turned to smash a woman in the face with his fist, breaking her nose, even as he spun to smack another youth with his stick. Chaos erupted around Sian as the four thugs laid waste to the panicked prayer line, as skillful as they were dispassionate.

Sian cried out as she dodged the backswing of one man's bludgeon, then ducked and rolled toward the edge of the melee — toward the woman with the broken nose, who lay screaming in the mud. "Lady, here," Sian said. Without any time to think, she put her hand on the bloody mess. Her own nose ached and swelled; if there was ginger in the air, she couldn't detect it — and here came another injured woman, barely more than a girl, bleeding from a torn ear — which Sian healed too, just grabbed it and let it go before turning to another victim.

It was over in minutes, though those minutes seemed like hours as Sian healed at least a dozen brutal injuries, enduring the echoing pain of each one. The thugs vanished into the downpour as quickly as they had arrived.

There was only a shocked silence now, as the people around her realized what had happened. "You ... healed me," said the woman with the formerly broken nose. She reached up and slowly wiped away rainwashed blood. "You *healed* me."

"Don't tell ..." Sian begged. "Please!" But it was hopeless. She scrambled to her feet and started running, before the crowd could find any coherent will to follow her.

Must I always be running away? Sian thought helplessly. *Is this my life now?* But she ran on, mud spattering up the backs of her legs, slowing only when she reached Viel.

Walking through the last streets before the townhouse, she began to ponder what had happened. She had not heard of prayer lines being attacked before; was the Factorate cracking down? Or the Justiciary, or even the Mishrah-Khote? The thugs had worn no uniforms or insignia, but they were clearly professionals. This was no private grudge, nor youth pushing a drunken dare too far.

She reached Meander Way with a sigh of relief. She had no idea what time it was, but it would feel good to get out of these sodden clothes, clean up, and get at least a few hours rest before dawn came. She could resume her search for the priest tomorrow.

"Domina Kattë?"

The words were spoken as a firm hand came from behind to grasp her upper arm. Sian gasped, and turned to find two black-robed men flanking her; the taller wore a priest-hospitalar medallion on his collar.

So the Mishrah-Khote had found her. So quickly.

～

Reikos sat in the Eighth Sea Tavern at the end of Meander Way, waiting for his meal. He hadn't chosen this place in hopes that Sian might pass by: no, it was simply that their bouillabaisse was the best in Alizar — not that he was having stew for breakfast, but Sian had introduced him to the place; and of course he had many happy memories of eating here with her, just a few doors down the road from her townhouse ... so ... yes, perhaps he did hope to see her pass by. Tangentially.

He sipped his lager and glowered across the nearly-empty common room, then back through the window. It was more crowded than ever out in the streets, but the flood of humanity wasn't translating into more business in here, at least. This tavern had been busy at all times of day, once, even in the mornings, with workmen come for hot kava or a warm meal before setting to their labor for the day. Alizar was troubled, to be sure. Trade had come almost to a halt. Which was all right, he thought wryly; for if he had sold anything, he might have trouble finding men to unload and deliver the crates now.

Another cursed prayer line wandered past, its leader's hoarse ritual cries making no sense at all. Not that the followers seemed to care as they murmured their responses. Not bad enough that they had ruined this formerly delightful city; now they had stolen his Sian as well. He heard the prayer line's rhythm interrupted, then an exchange of angry voices. "Go to work, you fools," he muttered under his breath.

The barmaid arrived with his sausage and hash, and a chunk of fragrant amaranth bread. Delicious, as always.

As he ate, he thought again of love, and freedom, and adventure. He had once fancied himself in love, as one does, in his early youth; but the girl's father had forbidden the match, betrothing her instead to one of Lost Port's borough captains. Konstantin Reikos had been unable to compete with a man of such position. So he had taken to the sea, working his way from indentured seaman on a trading galleon, to crew-partner on a smaller barquentine, then finally saving enough to buy his own little cutter. Now he had a fine brigantine, and toyed with the idea of buying a second, if he could find a trustworthy captain to sail her. Perhaps Kyrios, in a year or two …

Freedom. The giddy joy of it — the open seas, loving arms in every port. Which was why, no doubt, he was sitting glumly in an empty tavern, in a tiny, squabbling island nation at the end of the world, mooning over a married woman.

A married woman with a sudden, inexplicable magical power. What more could any man want?

Reikos looked at his healed thumb. It remained unblemished, the pain gone entirely.

Yes, he had handled that quite poorly. But, damn it all, why would she not let him apologize? Her cold, unyielding note had left him no way to make it up to her, to help her handle a situation which was clearly distressing her.

He wiped the last grease from the bottom of his bowl with bread, washed down with the last of his lager. The barmaid approached as he noticed a new shift in the noise from outside. "Another, sir?"

"No, I am finished," he said, digging in his pockets for the strange, hard-edged coins they used here as he peered past her out the large front window.

The prayer line outside had become a jumble of folk crowding the narrow street. Reikos saw two young, strong men in a quiet argument at their center. Had two lines run afoul of one another? More strong men flanked them, listening, as the gentler folk faded toward the edges of the group, or left altogether. It didn't take instincts honed in a life spent traveling the world to sense trouble. Reikos got to his feet, about to ask the barmaid to show him to the tavern's back exit, when one of the men outside turned and spotted him in the window.

"Foreigner!" the man cried, pointing. "Parasite!"

The agitated heart of the combined prayer lines turned at once. Then half a dozen burly men poured into the Eighth Sea. "Get out of here!" the barmaid screamed, but no one heeded her. She ran to the back of the common room, disappearing through the kitchen door.

"Stop, you fool!" Reikos heard someone shout, as the man who'd called him a parasite knocked over chairs in his haste to get to him. "The god abhors violence! Our quarrel is not with foreigners!"

Reikos pulled out his short knife and gave his first attacker a poke in the gut — not enough to kill him, but sufficient to get his attention. The man screamed and fell back against a table, knocking it over into the man behind him. Shouts filled the room, as the men who'd barged inside began attacking each other as well as Reikos, who swiped at another sweating young man, scoring his face. As blood flew, a third man nearly got Reikos in the throat with a long knife, but he fell to the floor and rolled under a table, scrabbling to his feet on the other side.

"We betray the god!" the other man cried again, but Reikos didn't wait to hear them resolve their differences. He burst through the kitchen door, where the terrified barmaid cowered against the back wall.

"Door?" Reikos demanded, his breath short.

She pointed; he dashed out into the alley and turned right. His way took him past the back entrance of number 45. Sian's shutters were closed, though the torrential rains of last night had given way to a pleasantly warm day. He ran on, not slowing until he reached a crowded market five or six streets away. From there, he donned an attitude of casual unconcern, and made his way back to the safety of his ship.

～

Sian fumed in her damp limestone cell, somewhere deep in the warren that was the Temple Mishrah-Khote. After hauling her across the long bridge to The Well, her captors had deposited her here just before dawn, without a word of explanation or even accusation, and no more than a bucket of questionable water and a moldy straw mattress. She had been brought a trencher of thin gruel for breakfast, and again for dinner tonight, with no kava or even tea. And still, no one had come to question or accuse her. Her cell's high slit of window had gone dark many hours ago. It must be near twelve bells already, but sleep eluded her. Was anybody ever going to come explain what she was doing here, or would she just be left to rot forever, unremembered?

Last night, she had tried repeatedly to talk with the priests who'd brought her here, but once they'd had her in their custody, they'd treated her as if she were invisible. Her apparent jailer, Father Lod, had been the very essence of cold officiousness. No, he could not tell her what the charge against her was; yes, someone would be back to speak with her as soon as possible, things were so very busy at the moment, surely she understood.

Little worm, she thought for perhaps the hundredth time, drifting toward sleep at last.

She was awakened some time later by the soft clank of keys and the jarring rasp of hinges as her cell door opened with a wincing flare of torch light. Father Lod walked in, with two robed underlings she hadn't seen before.

"You will come with me, Domina Kattë," Lod said, unlocking the cell door. Sian came out gladly enough, but he dug his hand painfully into her arm as he led her out of the cell block and along a series of corridors. They climbed a flight of stairs, then bypassed a puzzle box of forecourts, gates and offertory halls leading into cloistered precincts deeper within.

Their path took them unexpectedly back into the public spaces, across a torchlit healing hall. Sian had been here once before, when Biri was born. Maleen had married young, and, in a fit of piousness, requested a Temple Blessing for the boy. This uncharacteristic devotion had passed by the time Jila arrived nearly six years later; perhaps the miscarriages had dampened her fervor. Sian's gaze swept the large room as she was hustled through. Square-cut pillars painted red and blue held up a stepped ceiling where gilded images of the Seven Vile Humors and the Seven Sacred Essences were in glorious ritual array. Altar nooks around the walls offered sacrifice to the unnamed, indeed often faceless, gods of healing.

The scattering of ill and infirm present in this lovely room lay in sickbeds suspiciously well-appointed with cloth-of-gold and Hanchu silks.

Sian was yanked roughly onward toward a nondescript doorway at the room's far side. "I am not resisting you," she hissed.

Lod eased up the pressure a fraction. The other two priests walked close behind as she was led into dimly lamplit space barely larger than a closet in a tradesman's home. One of the silent priests locked the door behind them.

"Sit there." Father Lod pushed her toward a wooden hold-chair on one side of the tiny room. As she complied, the second priest threw one of its crude iron latches into place around her waist.

"We have news of you which disturbs us," Lod said, coming to loom over her.

"What news is that, Father?" Sian asked, struggling to keep her voice polite and obedient. It would not serve her to show impertinence to these men, though having never ventured on the wrong side of official powers, she was uncertain of how to behave — or what they might do.

"We have heard that you are masquerading as a healer," Lod replied, "claiming that your mere touch erases injury and illness." The priests behind him stood silent.

"It is the truth, Father. But I did not choose this curse; I do not want it. It was done to me, against my will. I want nothing more than to be relieved of this burden and go back to my —"

"You *lie*," Lod snapped. "You pretend penitence now because you have been caught, but half of Alizar is talking of your fraudulent performances.

They call you a new goddess. I am told you are a successful businesswoman. Was that not enough for you?"

Sian leaned as far forward as she could within the confines of the hold-chair, looking up at Lod beseechingly. "I have no wish to be a goddess. I don't *want* this power. You are healers — cure me of this thing!"

"There is nothing to cure! Lying is a *sin*, not an affliction!"

"I am not lying. The curse imposed on me is real, as is my desire to be rid of it!"

Lod's face blanched nearly white with anger. He slapped Sian hard across the face. Astonished, her eyes filled with tears as her cheek stung. He slapped her other cheek so hard her head snapped to the right and her ears rang. Almost too quickly for her eyes to follow, he whipped a small knife from his belt, and reached up to slice her left earlobe. "*Heal that!*" he shouted. As Sian cried out, reaching for her ear, Lod grabbed her hand away, crushing her fingers in his iron grip.

She stared at him in shock, pain cascading through her. "What do you *want* from me?"

"I want the truth," he hissed, bending several of her fingers back painfully. "Admit that you are *no healer.*"

"Please!" Sian cried, trying in vain to yield to his grasp, prevented by the chair's embrace. "Please, stop!"

"I will stop when you stop *lying*." Lod shoved her fingers further back with a violent twist. She heard the thin bones snap an instant before new agony filled her. "This is what comes of fraud!" She hardly heard his words through her own screams. "Your pain is nothing next to that of all the suffering, vulnerable souls whom you *pretend* to heal."

Sian clutched her broken fingers, struggling to contain the agony. "Heal, oh please heal," she whimpered to the shattered bones.

And ... they did. She could feel her injuries begin to knit together. The sensation nearly made her faint as the shadow pain she felt with every healing now joined the awful pain of her bones recombining. The scent of ginger in the air was sickening, overpowering. She would *never* eat ginger again.

Sobbing, Sian lost herself for a time. When she returned to her senses, she held her right hand out, flexing the formerly broken fingers. They felt stiff and sore, but they were whole. And the pain itself was fast slipping away.

Sian touched her ear and found it slick with blood, but the once-parted flesh was already joined again as well. Exhausted, she leaned back in the hold-chair, panting, and closed her eyes. "Are you satisfied?" she breathed.

"If I hadn't seen it with my own eyes..." murmured the priest closest to the door.

"It is ... not possible," Lod growled, clearly shaken as well. "An illusion. Group hypnosis of some kind ... I have seen such vile tricks before." His voice regained its strength as he convinced himself. "Or something even worse, perhaps. What djinnis have you dared commune with, woman? To what demonic abominations have you sold yourself?"

Sian opened her eyes again, fearing further torture. "I commune with nothing," she said, trembling. "I told you the truth. This was done to me by the Butchered God's mad priest! I want no part of it! I just want it gone! What must I do to make you believe me?"

"The *Butchered God*," Lod spat. "His would-be priest is the greatest fraud in all of Alizar. If that slippery eel had any power to bestow such gifts, why should he need to hide from us? And why single you out anyway, if you sought nothing from him?"

"He said it was because of my relation to the ruling family. He said I was to carry some kind of message to them from his god. Though he never told me what it was," she added, fearing they would call her a liar yet again when she could not elaborate.

For a moment, no one spoke, then Lod asked skeptically, "What relation to the ruling family?"

"I am of House Alkattha," she replied. "The Census Taker is my cousin; the Factor also, though more distant."

A palpable stillness fell over the room. Lod actually took a step away from her.

"All the gods protect us!" the second priest gasped softly.

"*Silence*," Lod hissed, glaring at the man. "It's doubtless just another lie."

"You did not know this?" Sian asked, nearly as astonished as they seemed to be. "You have called me several times by name. You seem to know my business." What kind of bumbling functionaries could have tracked her down without learning such a crucial fact? She did not ask this aloud, of course, hardly wanting to goad Lod into some new display of umbrage.

"If she is cousin to the Census Taker —" began the second priest.

"I said *silence!*" Lod shouted, whirling on the man. "This is precisely what she wants: to have us eating from her hand. Maybe she imagines she can get a fool like you to let her go." He turned back to face Sian. "If you are lying to us, you had best tell me now, before I go to check your claim. It will be far, far worse for you once I've been put to all the trouble of exposing your lie myself."

These morons must really not get out much, Sian thought with rising disgust at all the needless suffering she had just been put through. "Please feel free to go ask Escotte yourself, Father Lod," she replied. "I hope you will convey my greetings while you're there, and tell him I'll be by to thank him personally for helping to rectify this small misunderstanding."

Lod had grown noticeably paler now, but not in anger this time, she suspected. "Very well," he said stiffly. "I fear we must continue to detain you while this claim is verified, Domina Kattë. I trust you understand."

"Of course," she replied.

"Return her to her cell," he told the priest behind him.

"The same one, sir?" he asked. "If her claim is true —"

"I *said*, return her to her cell. Question me again, and you may join her there."

Obviously flustered, the man responded with a clipped bow and came forward to remove the latch around Sian's waist, glancing up with an apologetic expression.

"I feel bound to remind you," Lod said as she was led back toward the door, "that political connections, however lofty, are still no defense against a valid charge of spiritual fraud. That question remains to be resolved, regardless of your family."

"I am no fraud," Sian said, turning to look him calmly in the eyes. "As you saw yourself. And I mean the Mishrah-Khote no harm nor disrespect. I remain eager to see this unwanted burden lifted. If you can cure me of it, I will cooperate enthusiastically."

He gave her a nod, looking more weary than offended for the first time since they'd met.

As she was led through the Healing Hall once more, Sian touched her restored fingers, then her ear — not in a healing-power way, but simply in the manner that one does a bruise or injury. Though she doubted there would be any trace remaining by the time she was returned to unfettered possession of her own body.

Despite the air of seeming calm she had retrieved, she was still struggling to catch her breath and steady her pounding heart when they arrived back at her dark cell.

Such things should not be happening to a grandmother.

EIGHT

Arian des Chances swept through the Factorate House's pillared
maze. Her clothing, hair, and cosmetic mask this morning were all
designed to project maximum status and power. Unfortunately, the dress
she had chosen was proving more confining than she'd realized. Too late to
change that now. She took deep measured breaths as she walked, cultivating
as much calm as she was able to. For all the years of effort she had made to
play nice with Alizar's self-important priesthood, the Mishrah-Khote had
never liked their Factor's foreign bride. But, oh, she was sick with worry for
her son. She had heard about the stories being passed on Alizar's streets:
that Konrad was dying of the crab disease. But that was not what these
damned priests were telling her. *It might be this, my lady. It could be that. A
little longer, and we should be able to determine… His condition is quite grave,
of course, but we are sure that with the proper treatment…* Every day, Konrad
seemed further from this world, and she was tired of waiting for answers.

Arriving at the Frangipani Conference Chamber, she nodded to the
uniformed Manor Escort waiting there. "He is inside?"

"Just as you requested, my lady," he replied, pulling the door open for her.

As she strode into the sunlit room, the Mishrah-Khote's most senior
priest rose to greet her with hands outstretched and an obsequious smile,
his heavy robes gleaming with ornamentation and smelling faintly of san-
dalwood. "My Lady Factora-Consort, how may I be of service?"

"Thank you for coming, Father Superior," she said coolly, then took a seat
in one of the large carved teakwood chairs by the marble fireplace.

"If it pleases you, my lady, 'Father Duon' would be entirely sufficient."

The father returned to his chair, facing her across a small table. He was a substantial man — not fat, precisely, but with none of the ascetic leanness Arian had noted in the more junior priests.

"Very well then, Father Duon." She was well acquainted with this game. If he were not 'Father Superior' here, it would be easier for him to sidestep the fact that she was 'Factora-Consort,' officially his superior. But such trivialities hardly mattered in the absence of any audience, and perhaps the man would be more helpful if indulged a bit. "I've asked you here because I wish to know your opinion of my son's current condition." Though Duon had not been treating Konrad personally, all of her son's actual practitioners would have been reporting to this man. Meeting with him should be tantamount to speaking with them all at once, and better still because, unlike them, he would not be able to put her questions off by claiming need to consult *superiors* first.

"My lady," Duon said, "I assure you, there is no matter of greater concern to me — or to anyone in Alizar — than that of your son's health. Any smallest development in regard to his care or treatment is brought immediately to my attention. But I must confess that without having examined the boy myself, I feel unequipped to tell you much more than I'm sure the healers attending him have already conveyed. If you would like me to go see him now, I might be more able to —"

"Father Duon," she interrupted, already losing patience despite herself, "in your expert opinion, from all that is reported to you, does Konrad seem headed toward recovery or not?"

Father Duon spread his elaborately beringed hands, as if to ask how such a question could be answered. "From what our finest healers have reported to me, my lady, he is a boy of exceptionally strong constitution, admirable persistence, and powerful will, who seems, at present, to be stable at the very least. I have every hope that he will turn the corner soon, and —"

"Every hope founded in *what precisely*?" she snapped, unable to stand even one more word of such vague reassurance. She and her husband had been paying this flock of holy charlatans a fortune for months now. Where were these unnamed gods they charged so steeply to intercede with? Where were all these miracles they peddled so smugly? "Every day his fever is a little higher, his color a little grayer, his voice thinner, his weight lower. He looks like a bundle of sticks. He's started losing hair! Have they reported this to you? Where in all of this, *exactly*, do you find cause for hope? I *need* some clear, specific answer to this question, yet your *finest healers* give me only the same thin gruel of seemingly gratuitous optimism that you offer me now. If you possess some better answer, please tell me what it is. If you do not, then stop patronizing me and just tell me that ... he's ... going to die."

She fell silent, needing all her remaining strength and focus just to keep from bursting into tears. So much for veils of diplomatic calm. All her discipline was failing; a rare and terrifying event in itself. After so many years of false cordiality and careful political waltz, she and Duon gazed at each other now like two scorpions in a bottle. She wondered just how candid things might finally get here, and found herself suddenly unable to care anymore.

"My Lady Consort," Duon said, shifting in his chair, "your distress is entirely understandable. What mother would not feel as you do? But the healing powers we possess come not from ourselves, but from the gods. We give our entire lives to service as their conduits, but we may dictate outcomes no more than you can. I have faith in the gods, and in your son's eventual recovery, but I must wait, as must we all, to learn what they will do."

"Have you ever spoken with these gods of yours?" Arian asked. "Face to face, I mean? I would pay a great deal more than we've already given you to speak with one of them myself. Can they be summoned?"

The priest looked shocked. "Lady, surely ... You are overwrought."

"Am I?" She felt helpless to staunch the flood of rage rising within her. "Where I come from, Father, the gods are no longer hidden behind mortal conduits. They appear in person, to exercise their will — for better or for worse — out in the light where all can see. If your shy gods can do nothing more to heal my son, perhaps I should use our remaining funds to petition one of my own nation's more *visible* deities for help."

It was a ridiculous, even childish thing to say. Initially drawn, somehow, by the mad girl Green, the gods of the Stone Coast appeared when they would, intervened as they chose, and vanished again just as abruptly — though not before leaving great swaths of turmoil and destruction in their wake, as often as not. Arian had spoken, in her youth, with people who had seen it happen with their own eyes, but she knew as well as they would that no amount of wealth or prayer could bend a god to someone else's bidding. Still, she was so deathly tired of humoring these impotent thieves and liars. The giant ruins scattered all about her husband's island kingdom might suggest that there had once been gods in Alizar, but she felt certain that if even one such still remained here, it would have stricken all like this oily priest dead centuries ago for such empty presumption.

"That would be most unwise, my lady," said Duon. "For yourself, your husband, *and* your son."

"Do you threaten me, priest?" Arian hissed, certain there was nothing left to save between them now. "Will you produce one of these gods who cannot be moved to save a child's life then after all, just to punish his mother?" Whatever she and Duon had agreed to call themselves at the beginning of this meeting, he knew as well as she did that her power and authority exceeded his considerably, and for all these years of polite pretending, would dislike her no more after this encounter than he had all along. They'd just be able to admit it finally, which might even make him easier to manage.

"I threaten nothing," Duon grated. "I but *warn* you, Lady Consort, that challenging a thousand years of Alizar's spiritual tradition and conviction will not endear you to your husband's people — especially in such times as these. You are surely as aware as I of the growing discontent already brewing in this city's streets. I would not stir that ant's nest carelessly."

"That unrest has not sent our people running to your priesthood either, has it, Father?" she parried, unwilling to let him think her so easily cowed. "I'm told the marchers answer to this so-called Butchered God's priest these days — not to you and yours. *His* god was visible, at least. How do you suppose our people might react to the arrival of a *living* god, summoned by their Factor rather than by the Mishrah-Khote? A god that could be seen and heard without such costly intercessors." *Let him wonder if it could be done,* she thought with bitter satisfaction. A man like this could know nothing of gods anywhere, and still have so little fear of them.

"Our gods have never stooped to idle show as yours do, it would seem, but I think you'll find that they protect Alizar and her people quite effectively from *outsiders*, as the dead god recently washed ashore here may well have learned, to his dismay. You may wish to ponder that before attempting to summon any more vainglorious tulpas from your homeland."

So, he did suppose it possible. The ignorant fool. She just managed not to spoil things by laughing. Not that she had anything to laugh about, of course. She hardly dared imagine how Viktor would react when she confessed her dreadful conduct here to him. Shying from such thoughts, Arian noticed an uncertain, calculating look cross Duon's face, as if he too, perhaps, weighed the possible consequences of this exchange.

"As chance would have it," he added in a slightly more conciliatory tone, "I was informed, just last night, of a rather remarkable new healer recently emerged among us. I have not had time to evaluate this new prodigy myself, and have unavoidable business on Home for the remainder of the day. Tonight, as you surely know, I am dining with the Factor, here. But I will make that assessment my first priority upon returning to the temple afterward. Who can say, my lady? Perhaps the gods we serve have already addressed your concern by sending such a talent to us at this moment. If you wish, I will send a messenger to you in the morning with the results of my inquiry."

"I would appreciate that, Father Duon. Immensely." She could not prevent the tiny pang of hope that leapt up in her breast, though she was highly skeptical of this suddenly produced, and absurdly convenient, bit of news. To hide her own confusion, she rose from her chair and walked to one of the room's elaborate, teak-framed windows, pretending to gaze at the manicured grounds below. A peacock strutted across the lawn, tail flared in preening display. "Thank you for your understanding, Father. I'll not keep you any longer, then." With that, she glided from the room without waiting to hear what if anything else he might have to say.

Stupid, stupid, stupid! she berated herself silently as she fled the room. It was all she could manage not to break into a run. Away from what she had just done. Away from the Factorate House itself, from her hopelessly unwelcomed and isolated existence here, from Konrad's dreadful illness, and her husband's insoluble problems — let alone Alizar's. Only when she'd reached her private chambers and slammed two sets of doors behind her did she allow herself to breathe again — to *gasp*, in fact — for air.

Drawn, clearly, by the sounds of Arian's arrival, Lucia appeared from within her own small quarters there. At first sight of Arian's obvious distress, her blue eyes went wide and she came rushing forward. By the time she arrived to take Arian's hand, there were tears leaking from Arian's eyes.

"Is it … Has Konrad …?" Lucia whispered.

Arian shook her head, further angered with herself for this self-indulgent little scene — added to all her other lapses of the past half-hour. "I've just been the biggest fool, Lucia!" she groaned, still weeping reprehensibly.

"Oh! Certainly not," Lucia cooed, putting an arm gently around Arian's waist, and guiding her toward a set of chairs beside the windows. "There is no less foolish person in all these islands than yourself, my lady."

At that moment, it hurt Arian just to hear *my lady* from Lucia's lips. They had been practically sisters since childhood. That was why Lucia had agreed to come here all those years ago when Arian had left Copper Downs to wed Viktor. As had Maronne, off, at this moment, watching over Konrad. This place had put *my lady* even between herself and such close friends. "Why did I ever think I could be happy here?" she asked as they sat down together.

"Oh, now, my lady —"

"Please! No more *my lady*, Lucia. Not here in my own chambers. Not now. Can no one ever just call me Arian anymore? Am I no longer allowed a *name*?"

Lucia gazed at her quizzically. "Very well then, Arian, my love. Since I am invited to be forward, I would remind you that you *have* been happy here. I have seen it with my own eyes. Many times. Watching you look after Viktor. We both know you love him. I've seen the delight you take in your son's inquisitive mind and tender heart. I have watched you throw yourself with something very like gleeful abandon into caring for the people of these islands — in ways no one else I've known here seems to do. And I've no doubt you will be happy here many times more in years to come. The air in Copper Downs never smelled of flowers like this, even in spring, did it? In how many other lands does summer rule eternal, and winter never come?"

"I do not care how the air smells, Lucia," Arian said wearily. "There are troubles which cannot be covered with perfume."

"What has happened to put you in such a state?"

"I have just openly declared war on the Mishrah-Khote — to the Father Superior's face — and at the very moment when my son's life may depend on their good graces."

Lucia's comical expression of astonishment might have made Arian laugh if there'd been any room left for laughter in her world just then. "Surely ... you exaggerate."

Arian shook her head. "I called him and his priesthood frauds — or as close as makes no difference." She realized she needed this rehearsal before going to confess it all to Viktor.

Lucia shook her head. "Well, it's long past time *someone* said it, I suppose. A dose of truth can only do those pompous mummers good."

"Oh, Lucia, no, it can't," Arian protested. "Open conflict with the Mishrah-Khote is all Viktor needs right now. I'm supposed to help him — not hasten his demise!" Knowing that she mustn't stop until she'd said all of it aloud, Arian took one more deep breath. "I threatened to divert the funds we're paying them to summon gods from Copper Downs instead ... Since their gods can't seem to help Konrad."

Lucia almost laughed. Arian saw it come and go, just before her face went slack with realization that her mistress wasn't joking. "Oh my," Lucia murmured. "That ... may have been somewhat ... overplayed."

"I think he believes it may be possible." Arian sighed. "Which means there will be even more loss of face involved — for both of us — before all this is over." She stood up, feeling short of breath again. "I must go speak with Viktor before any of this reaches him some other way. Before he dines with Duon tonight, we must decide how best to distance him from what I've done. Please, Lucia, find me something looser to wear. Something more modest — that I can breathe in." She took a swipe at her drying tears, and the hand came away smudged with kohl. "And help me remake my face. Any chance that Viktor might still listen to me now will vanish altogether if I go there looking this deranged."

NINE

The cell which had seemed so incommodious her first night there now felt quite comfortable — almost peaceful, even. Amazing what a difference the absence of torture made.

Sian sat on her rough mattress and smiled ruefully at the thought.

Exhausted after her ordeal, she had collapsed onto the thin mattress and lost consciousness almost as soon as they had dumped her back into the cell. It had taken her until well into the morning to recover her equilibrium and start thinking coherently again. Though her wounds were healed, her body and mind — her very spirit — was still carved with the memory of injury. She'd cringed each time she'd turned over in the night, anticipating pain that was no longer there. The fear, the helplessness at such wanton cruelty — these things would surely leave scars in places beyond the flesh. For a very long time.

Beyond simple relief, Sian now felt no small amount of chagrin at herself for not thinking to mention her family connections sooner. She had never been the sort to think that way, but clearly she would do better to remember such advantages in the future, and to use them.

All that mattered to her now, however, was knowing that Lod's superiors would finally realize what a horrible mistake they had made, and …

And what, exactly?

Release her, with apologies and monetary reparations and an emerald brooch for her troubles? Perhaps a ride home in a golden dhow, with bannermen and criers proclaiming to the world how badly the Mishrah-Khote had blundered?

Certainly not.

The Mishrah-Khote would not want the ruling family, much less the general public, to learn that they had hastily tortured even a minor member of House Alkattha. How could they turn her loose now, even quietly, without fearing that Sian might announce their misstep wherever she chose?

No, they would need to assure themselves, somehow, of her silence.

Sian shivered in the dimly lit cell.

Might these *healing priests* kill her to protect themselves? Or would they merely keep her locked up here forever? On some pretext of guilt, of course. As Lod himself had pointed out, the Mishrah-Khote could still very easily prosecute her for 'spiritual fraud' … never mind that her powers were real. In fact, far worse that they were.

Was her guilty verdict inevitable then — because of their mistake?

And how much did her family connections *really* matter anyway? Her cousin Escotte, the all-powerful Census Taker, had been friendly enough whenever they had met, but such encounters had been more and more infrequent as he had become more powerful. It had been several years since she had last seen him. Would he even notice if she vanished from the world? She had never even met the Factor, or seen him close up, except once, at the crowded reception following his installment as Factor two decades past now.

Arouf, at least, would certainly raise an inquiry …

Or would he?

They had parted very badly. He had not come after her. He had been angry and frightened, and … quite clear in his disdain for these very family connections — as soon as they had seemed more liability than advantage to him and their business.

Could nearly thirty years of marriage be worth so little?

No. Surely he would calm down eventually and begin searching for her. Even if he no longer cared for her at all, they were legally and financially entangled. At the very least, he would require her to help settle up their business holdings, their property. Their home.

Sian bit back tears at the thought of losing … everything. She did love Arouf. Yes, she did. But it struck her that her grief came most keenly when she thought of leaving her house.

She lay back on the prickly mattress, trying not to surrender to despair.

～

Morning crept toward early afternoon, and still no one came to feed her — or for any other reason — leaving her ever more certain that the reprieve she had so briefly assumed was not coming after all. And she was so hungry again. This power, god-given though it may be, certainly consumed an awful lot of energy.

It was at least another hour before Sian at last heard footsteps outside her door. *Food at last*, she thought.

There was a quiet jingle, and her cell door opened, revealing only one priest this time — a fellow she had never seen before. Save for the keys in his hand, however, he carried nothing.

Sian rose to her feet. "No *gruel*, even? Am I ever to eat again?"

The priest gave her an embarrassed look, then, oddly, stepped inside the small cell and closed the door behind him. He glanced around, perhaps searching for a place to sit, though there was only Sian's mattress.

He sighed and shook his head. "Domina Kattë, I am so very sorry."

Sian trembled with sudden fear. "What do you mean?" Was he here to quietly dispatch her? Was this how they were going to solve the problem she presented?

"I mean … I just … You have been treated very poorly by us. Now, and in the past." He glanced around again — reluctant to look her in the face, it seemed. "I … do not suppose that you remember me."

"I do not. Were you one of those who brought me here last night?"

"No." He looked abashed. "We met when you were just a girl. Your mother was ill … I was still in training when she came, with you, to the temple. Hers was the first Benevolent Healing ritual I had ever attended."

"Oh, well then perhaps you also recall that there was no 'healing' — benevolent or otherwise." Sian was startled at her own sudden vehemence — the amount of pain such memories could still arouse in her. "We did all your foolish rituals and paid all that money, and she died anyway. Terribly."

"I know." He had the grace, at least, to look very sad. "It was … I have never forgotten that experience. Or your grief that day. I felt … We failed you all so badly, and I couldn't understand ..." He fumbled into silence for a moment, then said, "It was that experience which awakened me. And broke me as well. My faith in our gods remains absolute. But since that awful day, my faith in the fallible men who intercede with them has been ... much less so."

Sian glared him, still struggling with her anger. He was roughly her age; so, too young to have been one of the pompous old asses who had tended her mother. If he was in training ... then it came to her. "The acolyte!"

"Ah. You do remember."

"You were ... kind to me." Now it was her turn to look abashed as she recalled the awkward boy — hardly more than a child — who had tried to comfort her that day. "I'm sorry," she said. "I don't recall your name."

"I am called Het now. Father Het."

"Well, thank you, Father Het." Sian sat back down on the mattress, calming a bit, but not enough to offer him a seat beside her. "For your apology. Even now."

"We are not all so monstrous as you must believe. I have always wished there were some way to make amends for our failure with your mother."

"Well, if you are looking for some way to help me, I *am* awfully hungry — they've given me nothing since breakfast."

He looked pained. "I will see what I can do. Though, from what I've heard, your case is ... complicated."

Sian snorted. "I imagine it is. I've been sitting here thinking about some of those very complications." *He seems a decent sort. How much more harm can it do me just to ask?* "Are they going to kill me, do you think? Or just lock me up forever as a heretic?"

"I am not in the innermost circles of power. Nor even those adjacent to them. But I can scarce believe that they would ..." He fell silent and looked at the stone floor. "I do not know, Domina Kattë."

"An honest answer — from a priest." Sian felt her heart fall. "Now there's a miracle." She studied him again. "You've been in the temple since boyhood, yet still achieved no rank? How long does it take to rise here?"

"My path has not been smooth." He gave her a rueful smile. "They tell me I am stubborn, and excessively inquisitive. I am slower than most to truly understand the mysteries of our gods, yes? But, as my faith is pure, my superiors promise I will amount to something some day."

Is your faith pure? she wondered. "Will you be in trouble for speaking with me?"

Het sighed. "Oh, very likely."

"Then what are you doing here?"

He leaned back against the wall. "There is whispered talk of you throughout the temple, Domina. It is said that you are a heretic, and guilty of spiritual fraud."

"My healing power is real, you know."

"That is also being said."

"So, what do *you* think?"

"I try not to think anything without gathering what evidence I can on which to base my judgments." He gave her a wry smile. "One of the many failings that has slowed my rise to rank here, no doubt. I have simply come to offer a long-overdue apology, and to learn the truth. For myself rather than from others."

"I see." She sighed. "How much more will it take to convince you all?" She got to her feet. "Have you some injury or affliction that requires healing, Father Het?"

He looked startled.

"Is that not what you've come for? Like all the others? *Proof?*"

"Lady, I did not mean ..." He shook his head, almost frantically. "I am fortunate to be in very fine health at present. I just —"

"What sort of evidence am I to give you, then?" Sian asked. "Have you come here to examine my spiritual scholarship — my *creed*? If so, I might as well confess right now that I have none at all. I have always been a simple woman without any spiritual ambition. As I've been telling everyone I've met here, I never wanted this power. I do not want it now. Yet, somehow, my touch heals, Father Het. That is my apparent crime, and all the evidence I have to offer you." She was so tired of explaining this. Of having to.

"Well, I guess I do have ... a bruise of sorts," he said. "From stacking lumber near the refectory. The temple is in constant need of renovation. I often help with —"

She waved him silent and beckoned him closer, wanting to have it done. "Show me."

Awkwardly, he lifted the hem of his robe to expose his shins, one of which was heavily abraded, stained dark purple and green across a patch of seven or eight inches.

"A bruise of sorts?" she asked in grim amusement. "That must have hurt."

"A stack of timber fell. On me."

"Well then." She bent and reached toward his leg. "May I?"

He nodded.

Sian barely registered the smell of ginger anymore. And after all she'd been through here, the dull ache that now throbbed through her own right shin seemed hardly worth notice either.

A moment later, she took her hand from his leg, and stood up to find him staring down, open-mouthed, at his now all but unblemished shin. He looked up at her with an expression of intense dismay, stepping backward to lean against her cell door, as if the leg she had just healed could no longer be trusted to hold him up.

"Are you well?" she asked.

"It is as I feared," he murmured.

"That's an odd sort of thanks." She went back to sink onto her humble mattress. "Does my *evidence* displease you for some reason? Did you hope I was a fraud?"

"No, my lady," he replied. "My displeasure is not with you." He gave her a searching look. "Please understand, my whole life has been defined by a deep desire to be of service to the gods. But with every passing year, I find myself in greater fear of what new crime we may commit against them next. In you — in *this* — I find all such fears confirmed. I am truly sorry, Domina. For all that you have suffered at our hands. For all you may yet suffer. Rest assured, I will beseech the gods on your behalf." He turned to go, grappling the ring of keys back out of the pocket of his robe.

"Wait!" Sian leapt to her feet. "What do you mean? What further suffering do you expect for me?"

Het stood gazing at the keys in his hand. Finally, he bowed his head, his shoulders slumped, and he turned around to face her with a look of such exhausted resignation that she found herself wrestling with an urge to comfort *him.*

"Domina Kattë, do you have any idea what a dilemma you pose for the Mishrah-Khote just now?"

"Some," she said. "They were careless enough to torture an old woman without first bothering to find out who she was related to. I've already realized how difficult it may be to keep that mistake a secret now."

Het shook his head. "That is the least part of it, my lady."

Sian arched an eyebrow. It got worse?

"Our order has been losing power and prestige ever since we failed to support Alizar's move to independence," Het continued. "The gods we serve here have not chosen, for many centuries at least, to make themselves known so dramatically as some do now on the mainland. We are more and more dismissed here as a quaint sideshow, yes?" He issued a quiet humph that might have been grim laughter. "This problem has grown much worse for us since the Factor's son fell ill. We healed him very handily at first. He was all but recovered when he suddenly relapsed, and worse. Now, we have no real idea what ails him, and nothing we can do has much effect, though none of us knows why."

"I have heard the rumors," Sian said.

Het sat down at last, on the grimy flagstones by the cell door, with his back against the wall. "I know you have ample cause to doubt us, my lady. But, truly, we are often quite able to heal even very serious afflictions. None of us can understand why that power has failed us so mysteriously with Konrad. Yet we are all badly tainted by the failure."

"Wait," said Sian, as the realization hit her. "Might this not be the very reason I have been given such a gift just now? To save the Factor's son?" She threw her hands up in frustration. "What am I doing here, like this, when I might have the power to —"

"Power given you by whom?" Het interjected wearily.

"I don't know. Perhaps it really did come from the gods. Does that matter? I can do what I can do. Have I not proven that sufficiently?"

"I misspoke," Het said. "I doubt that such a power can have come from anywhere *except* the gods — whatever some of us might rather believe. But what I should have asked you was, *through* whom was this power given?"

"The Butchered God's ..." Sian fell silent as the rest of the understanding dawned. "Are you priests really all so petty that you'd let the Factor's son die just because the gift I bear has come sealed with someone else's *brand?*"

"Not *all* of us, no," Het replied, looking miserable. "But I do suspect it would be very hard for those entrusted with the preservation of our order and its ancient legacy to send a *woman*, un-anointed and un-anointable by the Mishrah-Khote, to the Factor, ostensibly blessed with healing power by a god the temple has tacitly disavowed, through a fugitive priest we have publicly accused of fraud, to succeed at what all the Mishrah-Khote's best healers have been unable to do." He gazed up at her. "Surely, you can see as well as I, Domina, how many nails such an event would likely pound into our already closing coffin — all at once."

"So I am being kept here *because* I might be able to heal the Factor's son?"

"I ... have no idea what will happen, my lady." Het rose to his feet and pulled the door open without turning back to look at her. "I have lost all faith in my ability to predict what other men may do. Even my own brothers. And I have no power here in any case. I'm sorry, but I must go now. I will do my best to see that you get a meal, as soon as possible." He pulled the door shut behind him. "And some more comfortable accommodation, if I can," he called softly through the door as keys jingled once more in the lock.

None of that will matter now, she thought, listening to the hasty pat of Het's receding footsteps. *Not if what you say is true.*

~

The light through Sian's tiny window had begun to pink toward evening before she heard keys in the lock again. Her cell was quite dark, the hallway nearly as dim as her door swung open to reveal yet another monk — a bit more portly than the last. She hung back, wary, until she saw the tray of food he carried.

"Finally!" Sian exclaimed, just holding herself from rushing to the door.

"Sadly, none of this is for you," the monk whispered, managing to close the door behind him with one foot as he entered. "Your food will be provided soon, though."

"Father Het?" Sian asked, trying to reconcile the voice she recognized with the plump figure she did not.

"Keep your voice down," he said, coming to set the tray down on her straw mattress. "In fact, don't speak at all." Before she could think of what to say to this, he straightened and lifted his robe to tug at something heavy underneath it. It took her another moment to recognize the second robe he'd wrapped around himself under his garments. "Put this on." He held the robe out to her as it came free. "Pull the hood as far down as you can and still see where you're going."

"Why? What is happening?"

"Did you not hear the bells? It is the temple's dinner hour. There's no other time of day or night when everyone is likely to be more distracted."

"But … What are we doing?"

"First, we are going down the hall together to serve the guard on duty his dinner." Het rearranged something else he'd stashed under his robe. "Motuque is an old friend of mine. Let me do all the talking there. *You* have taken a vow of silence. Understand?"

"No," she said. "I mean, yes, but —"

"Do you want to leave here?" he asked, sharply. "Or would you stay and throw yourself upon the mercy of our brotherhood?"

She began fumbling into the heavy robe. "But why am *I* going to serve dinner to the guard, of all people?"

"Because it's the last thing he'd expect an escaping prisoner to do. When he and I have exchanged the usual pleasantries, and his meal has been eaten, you and I will head back to the refectory — or someplace very near it — with the empty tray. If all goes well, you'll have been fed and gone for hours before anybody here thinks to check on *Domina Kattë.*"

"Why are you doing this?"

"Some of us still care about what the gods must think of us. The worst of us still have a conscience, even." She realized that he was grinning. "Have I not also mentioned that I am something of a disappointment here?"

Heart pounding, Sian managed to get the robe over her head and find its other sleeve with her left arm. "Will they not punish you for this?"

"Perhaps. Though they may merely pity me when I stagger out of your cell later in my underclothes, and tell them how you used your heretical magic to rob me of both consciousness and robe before stealing away. That is my robe you're wearing, by the way. Sorry it's not cleaner. I've had no opportunity to visit the laundry since we last spoke."

"I have no such power," she protested, pulling the oversized hood down as instructed. "My touch cannot hurt. It only heals."

"You know this? Have you tried it to find out, or do you simply leap to untested assumptions like everyone else?"

"Of course I have not tried to hurt anyone," she said, scandalized.

"It doesn't matter. The people I will answer to have less idea than you do what such power is capable of. All they know is that your power is real, and can affect the body in profound ways. That will be more than enough to make my story credible."

"It will be enough to make me seem a criminal — and dangerous."

He turned to her in the dimness. "Domina Kattë, let us be quite clear: you are already both of those things in the minds of many here. Of political necessity. You leave this temple a wanted fugitive — no matter what you've really done, or would do. Your life depends on understanding that, yes? If I were you, I would leave these islands as quickly as possible."

"Leave *Alizar?*"

"It is but a suggestion, my lady. Alizar is a very small place to stay well hidden in for long, but what you do is yours to decide — or will be very soon. Right now, however, we must go." He put one hand lightly on her shoulder, and gave her a gentle push toward the door.

Her heart was in her throat. "I thank you, Father Het."

"Now we are even, yes?" He retrieved the meal tray from her bed. "My failure of your mother is forgiven?"

"It was not your failure, Father Het. Were more priests like yourself, the Mishrah-Khote would not be languishing, I think."

"Vow of silence," he said gruffly, handing her the tray. "Starting now."

～

Moments later, Sian stood just inside the guardroom doorway, clutching the now-empty dinner tray with both hands in breathless fear. Her cowled head remained bowed to hide her face as Het stood just before her, chatting amiably with her guard about the disappointing quality of temple food these days.

"Ah well," Het sighed. "Revenues are not what they were before the current economic troubles, are they? We must all make concessions until such things improve, I suppose."

"If by *all* you do not mean to include our illustrious leaders," the guard corrected him with a sardonic grin. "The platters sent to our Father Superior's chambers are as sumptuous as ever, I am told. If I'm not mistaken, *he* is dining at the Factorate House tonight. I doubt *they* are being served stale bread and boiled skate fin in such tasteless broth."

"Oh, cheer up, Motuque. I suspect your latest *guest* would not complain so much about the meal before you."

Motuque looked down uncomfortably at his wooden bowl and platter.

"How long will they go on starving her like this, do you suppose?" Het asked casually.

"It is the only way she can be hurt," Motuque said, avoiding Het's gaze. "More than temporarily, at least. You must have heard of her power to heal."

"Of course," said Het. "And of her ties to House Alkattha too. Bad enough that she was tortured, yes? Why compound our troubles by starving her as well?"

"They want her rendered more compliant." Motuque shoved his meal aside as if he'd lost all appetite. "Het, you know very well I'm not the sort who likes inflicting pain — especially on a woman old enough to be my mother. Whoever her family might be. But what am I to do? This is my job. My orders are clear. She is still too defiant to be managed, and —"

"I can scarce imagine why," Het interrupted with a smirk.

To Sian's intense discomfort, the guard looked past Het then, to her. "Is this a conversation to be having in front of... Exactly who are you again?"

"Brother Pavri," Het quickly answered for her. "One of our newest acolytes. It seems he has been ordered by his mentor to assume a vow of silence until he learns greater wisdom — having already proven even more prone to question his superiors than I was at his age."

"That bad?" Motuque sounded impressed.

"Oh yes," Het said cheerfully, turning to grin at Sian. "I think we must have recognized some kindred spirit in each other, for he was reckless enough to *explain* all this to me — despite his vow — almost as soon as I met him on his way here with your dinner." Het turned back to the guard. "So you see, Motuque, I hold this disobedient pup's fate in my hands now. *He* will not be telling any tales on us. You can be sure of that."

Motuque gave Sian a grim smile. "You are lucky it was this old reprobate you ran into, lad. Any other priest here would have marched you right back to your mentor after such an infraction, for far more unpleasant discipline, I'm sure. Repeat a word said here to anyone, however, and, as Het just said, we'll make life very hard for you indeed. Do not doubt me."

Sian bowed her head more deeply, wondering again why this was necessary. Could they not just have left her cell and fled?

"So, old friend," Het said lightly, "you were about to enlighten me, I believe, as to why we are now in the business of torturing old women?"

"Stop tormenting me, Het," Motuque complained. "You know as well as I do what they'll have to do now. But that will still involve a trial, at which she must be present — and cooperative. If she hasn't learned to fear us, who knows what she'll do or say there?"

Het shook his head. "Tell me you are merely parroting your superiors, or I must fear for your very soul — oh *healing* priest."

"You were always a soft-hearted fool, Het. Ideals are well and good. The gods know I admire yours. But the world works as it does, not as we wish it to. I cannot have been here, doing this, for so many years without coming to accept that." Motuque took up his spoon again, and stirred his bowl of thin broth idly. "I am sorry for her too. But the world is much too large for me — or you — to fix, old friend."

Het regarded Motuque sadly. "There could be little harm in offering her that bit of crust you've left there, surely," he said at last. "I'll do it. On my way out. Who will ever know?" Motuque opened his mouth, but Het rushed on before he could object. "If they do find out somehow, I'll just tell them I said it was for myself, then decided to offer it to her on a whim as I was leaving. I have not been given any order to starve her, and you won't have knowingly disobeyed the order you were given. Come, Motuque. For the sake of both our souls. It's just a crust of bread — and stale, yes? You said so yourself."

Sian's heart had climbed back into her mouth. Was Het mad? What if the man was persuaded to go down right now and give it to her himself?

But Motuque just shook his head, gazing up at Het. "You really are … How have you remained such an innocent all these years? You set a terrible example for this boy, you know." He looked past Het at Sian again. "Imitate nothing that you see this old fool do, lad," he told her. "His life is just an endless cautionary tale."

She had no idea how to respond, except to cringe even further into her heavy robe.

"There, Motuque," Het said. "He is terrified of both of us. He'll do very well here, yes?"

The guard's smile soured. "Fine." He took the crust off of his plate and held it up to Het. "*You* take the risk then, Father Het. For both our souls."

"You see, Pavri?" Het asked Sian over his shoulder as he took the bread. "Motuque is almost as reckless as I. And a better man than he pretends." Het shoved the crust into his pocket and bowed to the guard in thanks. "May I borrow your key?"

"If a whisper of this ever surfaces, Het, I will contrive whatever lies are needed to protect myself — and make life hell for *both* of you," said the guard, wrestling the key to Sian's cell off of his ring. "Just so there's no misunderstanding, friend."

"I loathe misunderstandings," Het agreed. "I'll return this in a moment, and we'll all forget this ever happened." He turned to Sian. "Come, Pavri. Let's dig you even further into trouble, yes?" As Het ushered Sian back out of the guardroom ahead of him, he turned back to Motuque, smiling. "And you should eat that soup before it gets even colder, friend. If not for its fine taste, then from respect for your starving prisoner."

"Don't test my patience further, *Father Better Than Most*," Motuque retorted. But as Het closed the door behind them, Sian heard the scrape of his spoon against the wooden bowl.

A moment later, they were back outside the door to her cell, where, to her astonishment, Het used the key he'd borrowed from Motuque to open up the door and usher her back inside it.

"What now?" Sian whispered in frustration when he had followed her inside and closed the door behind them. "You said we were leaving!"

"Why, we must feed Domina Kattë her crust of bread."

Sian suppressed an urge to pull her hair and scream. "What are you talking about? I don't want his crust. I want to leave!"

"Patience, Pavri," Het said quietly, listening at the closed door. "Our timing here is somewhat delicate. We must not return with Motuque's key too quickly."

"Why return to him at all?" she hissed as softly as her mounting panic would allow. "With all respect, Father Het, if you have really come to help me escape, should we not actually try fleeing at some point?"

Het took his ear from the door, then reached beneath his robes again, this time pulling out a burlap sack which he held out to Sian. "Eat this as quickly as you can, Domina. We must not wait here too long either."

Sure he must be mad, she took the sack and opened it to find a large chunk of pale cheese, three slices of parrot fruit wrapped in cotton, and a handful of fatty candlenuts.

"Just to keep your strength up," Het said, returning to listen at the door. "There will be more food later."

She still had no idea what Het was up to, but her hunger now eclipsed all else. She sat down on her mattress in the all-but-darkness and started tearing chunks off of the cheese, which she stuffed into her mouth and swallowed almost whole. The parrot fruit and candlenuts followed quickly after.

"How did you get in here before?" She licked traces of the fruit juice from her fingers when everything was gone.

"What?" he asked, still focused on whatever he was listening for.

"You borrowed Motuque's key just now to open my cell door, but you'd just been in here to get me without it."

"I have acquired copies of most of his keys," said Het. "Not that he can ever be allowed to know that, of course. I've collected quite an assortment of keys from all around the temple, in fact. They prove very useful on occasion, as you see." He took his ear from the door again, and turned to her. "I think sufficient time has passed. Bring the sack, and follow me, but remain as silent as before — no matter what may happen, yes?"

She shrugged helplessly, pulling her cowl down again as Het opened her cell door and beckoned her outside.

At the guardroom door, Het knocked lightly. When no reply was given, he called softly, "Motuque? We're back with your key." Still no reply. Nodding to himself, Het pushed the door open and walked in.

Sian just managed not to gasp aloud as she followed him to find Motuque lying face down beside his overturned soup bowl.

"Excellent," Het said. "It was truly such poor soup, I feared he might not eat it."

"What happened to him?" Sian asked, forgetting her vow of silence.

"A healer's knowledge and skill may be applied in many ways, for many purposes." Het took the empty sack from her and stuffed it into his pocket. "On this occasion, I applied it to his meal."

"You *poisoned* him?"

"No, no. Of course not. He is among my closest friends. I've just encouraged him to sleep a while. He will be fine in very little time. Physically, at least. We'd best be on our way now."

"But, why do any of this?" she asked as he led her back into the hallway. "Why did we not just flee? Won't you be in far more trouble now — for what you've done to Motuque?"

"I?" Het said without slowing or turning to face her. "I did not bring Motuque that meal. Pavri did. I but met him on his way here."

"But … there is no Pavri. Motuque will learn that as soon as he tells anyone what happened."

"Oh, yes," Het said. "And I will be as shocked as Motuque to learn that harmless, frightened young Pavri was a wicked imposter."

Sian shook her head in confusion. "I do not —"

"Might not a heretic with such power, in league with the Butchered God's cleverly elusive priest, have confederates? It will go far easier for poor Motuque to have been overwhelmed by means of poison than to have allowed your escape while he sat eating his dinner down the hall. My own position and credibility will be strengthened too, if I was not the only one taken in by you and your accomplice. Everyone is better off now, yes?"

Only then did Sian realize how skillfully Het had just arranged his answers to at least half a dozen inevitable questions later on, including what he had been doing in her cell to start with. No fool after all, she thought with chagrin.

"Now," Het said, turning back to her as they approached a stairwell at the hallway's end, "it is time that you recall your vow of silence, Pavri, and exert some real discipline. Stay right behind me at all times. Keep your head down, and, please, make no sound of any kind — no matter who or what we should encounter, yes?"

Sian nodded meekly inside her cowl, tucking her chin down against her chest as they began to climb the stairs.

Het's evident cleverness was still dreadfully little comfort as she followed him through the temple's crowded hallways with their empty tray. Even less comfort as they pressed together through the refectory's dinner lines, shoulder to shoulder with other priests. Het bantered with those around them as if there were nothing in the world to worry him, occasionally making dismissive references to the troublesome acolyte with whom he had been saddled for the evening. Not until Het had gathered a tray of food for himself and his ostensible charge, then managed to steer them inconspicuously even farther back into the currently deserted renovation site that Het had mentioned to her earlier, did Sian find herself truly able to breathe again.

"There, you see?" Het uttered brightly after making certain they were finally alone. "The best place to hide things is in plain sight."

"You've taken a lot of horrifying gambles tonight," she replied, still trembling.

"As any *living* person does." He took the burlap sack she'd eaten from before out of his pocket and quickly refilled it with the items on his own newly filled dinner tray. "Take this with you. For after your escape."

"We're leaving now?" Sian asked.

"*You* are leaving now. I must go get out of this robe, and back into your cell before Motuque awakens."

Her gaze darted in renewed alarm around the still half-dismantled chamber. "You're leaving me? Here? I have no idea where we are, or how to —"

"I will show you," he said. "Do not panic, and you will be fine." He guided her even further from the refectory, through another doorway into a second chamber, where they walked around behind a tall, precariously stacked pile of lumber, tools and containers to a ragged hole that seemed recently bashed through the plastered wall.

"This is where I acquired my bruise. The falling timbers opened this wall." He offered her a wry shrug. "Being the excessively inquisitive fellow I am, I have since explored the passages beyond it some. They will lead you safely to an exit well beyond the temple grounds, by a fairly simple route which I'll explain. From there, Domina, you will have to proceed as best you can alone."

She gazed through the hole into an inky darkness. Before she could protest again, Het rummaged beneath his robe once more, pulling out a small leather purse, from which he drew a blown glass globe of clear liquid. Het shook it vigorously before handing it to her.

"What is this?" she asked, marveling at the dim light it now emitted.

"Have you never seen the surf glow blue and green on warmer nights?"

"Of course. But how —"

"The water on those evenings is filled with tiny creatures — much too small to see — that do the glowing when they are disturbed."

"Is that so?" She had never known, or even wondered, really. She had just taken the ocean's occasional glow at night for granted, as she did so many other things about the vast and omnipresent sea.

"This float is filled with them. We make them here to use when we must work or travel in the dark. And to awe our patients with at times," he added somewhat sheepishly. "Shake it periodically, and it should last you more than long enough. Its light is dim, but your eyes will adjust." He handed her the leather purse as well. "Sadly, I have no power to retrieve any of the possessions taken from you when you were imprisoned here. But what money I have is in this purse, to see you through at least a day or two if you are frugal. I wish it were more, but I am not a wealthy man, I fear. Even for a priest."

"I owe you too much already," Sian said. "I cannot take your money."

"You must. You will have to eat. And it may be difficult to access your own funds in whatever ways are usual." He pressed the purse further toward her. "They will be looking for you everywhere, my lady. And having been so careless once, they *will* know where to look this time. You must trust no one, Domina Kattë. Not even those you care about, if you would spare them danger. Please take the purse — and use it sparingly."

Sian accepted his gift. "You are far too generous, I fear. Will you be safe here now?"

"Having been careful to play the fool here for so long, I am unlikely to be credited with sufficient cleverness to be blamed for anything beyond stupidity in this affair." He gave her the ghost of a smile. "Now, listen carefully. The route is simple, really. Just a couple of turns. Have you an agile memory, or should I write them down?"

TEN

*S*ian woke with a groan to find morning arrived. The bed of surf-worn stones and pebbles on which she lay made her moldy straw mattress in the temple's dungeon seem luxurious by comparison. She turned stiffly to peer out from beneath the skiff under which she had taken shelter the night before. Up and down Pembo's Beach she saw others emerging from abandoned hulls much like her own, or from shelters fashioned out of cast-off cargo containers, or just haphazard piles of flotsam. Here and there morning fires had been lit, and cooking pots set to boil above them. These were the kind of people the Butchered God's priest seemed to favor. The god's body had washed up here, after all. If she could gain their trust, perhaps they would help her finally find the priest. He seemed more than ever her only hope now.

Sian had passed this unsightly shantytown — no more, really, than a vast graveyard for abandoned craft and other refuse from Cutter's nearby commercial port — any number of times while going about her business for Monde & Kattë, or for the occasional shipboard meeting or more private rendezvous with Reikos. Never could she have imagined that she would find herself living here among Alizar's poorest and most dispossessed. With another groan, she rolled onto her back again to stare at the overturned hull above her.

As Het had promised, her route through the temple's abandoned service tunnels had been simple, and the little light had lasted long enough to see her to a long-eroded doorway — more a cave mouth now — beneath a rugged cliffside on an abandoned beach somewhere on The Well's west shore.

She had left Het's coarse robe inside the tunnel mouth for fear the streets might already be filled with temple guards looking for a false monk. Then, rejecting travel by runner-cart as both too expensive and too dangerous, she had begun to make her stealthy way across The Well.

Keeping to the darkest, least populated streets and paths, she had struggled in vain to think of any plan or destination that made sense. The townhouse was out of the question, of course. She had not dared go back to Arouf or Maleen. If Het's warning were true — and she had no cause to doubt him — the Mishrah-Khote might already be lying in wait for her at either of those places. They had certainly found her the first time quickly enough. And even if they weren't waiting, and her family could be made to take her fears seriously now, how much might they be endangered by her mere presence? The thought of Arouf, much less her daughter, wasting in a temple prison cell because of her was more than Sian could bear.

She had briefly considered asking Reikos to take her to her younger daughter on the continent. Had he not half begged her to go with him when he sailed? Even if he hadn't been entirely serious, he would probably not say no ... But, she did not really trust him. Not now, not after his ... mercenary reaction to her troubles. And recalling Maleen's reaction to her plight mere days ago, Sian had no sure idea what reception she might get from Rubya either. If Rubya proved unprepared to take her in, Sian would just be left penniless in some foreign land to be ... what, exactly? Not a captain's wife, surely. Reikos was not the marrying kind — even if she could imagine wanting that from him now. In any case, if her new healing powers followed her from Alizar, her troubles would surely follow as well. No. Leaving Alizar made no more sense than staying did.

More ravenous than ever, it had seemed, Sian had finished the last of Het's bagged meal before she'd even reached the long bridge back to Cutter's, and could easily have eaten six more like it in a blink. She'd made her way across the island yearning for the bouillabaisse served by the Eighth Sea, though there was no question of showing herself at any such place now, even if she'd possessed the money anymore to pay for such luxuries.

Upon reaching the eastern end of the island at gods knew what hour of the night, exhausted and weak with hunger, she had found herself heading, perhaps by force of habit, toward the docks where Reikos doubtless dreamed peacefully in his narrow shipboard bunk. Looking down from the harbor road at the beachside shantytown she'd passed so many times without concern, she had realized that this, at least, was nowhere the Mishrah-Khote or anyone else would think to look for Sian Kattë. Her pride had been no match by then for her fatigue or her despair. It had not taken long to find an overturned hull under which nobody else already lay. It had taken even less time to fall fast asleep.

Now even sleep had left her, with nothing but the few coins Het had given her and the ragged, badly soiled clothes she wore. In all likelihood, she was the poorest person on this miserable beach. They, at least, had knowledge she lacked of how one navigated such a life.

As so often seemed the case these days, it was hunger that impelled her forward. Het's largess would be at least sufficient to buy her a chicken at the harbor market. She supposed someone here would lend her a flaming twig with which to light a driftwood fire of her own to cook it on. There. A plan at last.

Gathering her resolve, Sian crawled out from underneath her rotting hull, adjusted her rumpled veil, and stood to stretch her stone-ground muscles in the early light. Her emergence startled a flock of sandpipers, who started *weet-weet*ing at her in alarm as they fled down the beach. Several of the shantytown's human denizens looked up at the disturbance, then glared at her suspiciously. She summoned a small smile and waved at one of them, a gaunt-looking woman half her age with a ragged child of uncertain gender clinging to her knees. The woman turned away as if Sian's wave had rendered her invisible. But the child continued staring, its dark eyes like two holes burned through a dirty blanket, framed in a raven's nest of tangled, coal-black hair. Flinching from the accusation in those eyes, Sian wished suddenly to look away, just as the child's mother had, but found herself unable to disengage. *My mother is a woman too*, the child's smoldering gaze seemed to say. *Raising a child just like your own. But here, beneath a pile of wreckage. Without hope of ever* —

Sian wrenched her gaze away, breathless with the effort it had taken to break whatever power inhabited those dreadful eyes. She turned, unsteadily, to head for the market, feeling the child's stare still fastened on her back, though she dared not even glance over her shoulder to see, for fear of being recaptured. The power that child's eyes possessed ... had seemed unnatural. Or, she thought with a sudden shiver, had some power possessed the child?

The memory of Het's voice came unbidden to her mind: ... *that such a power could have come from anywhere* except *the gods*...

It wasn't a new idea, of course. What she could do now with her hands was certainly miraculous. Yet not until this moment had the implications truly reached through her cloud of dismay and confusion. She had just gone on thinking of her new power as something done to her by a crazy, would-be priest — imagining she had the power, or the right, to make him, or the Mishrah-Khote perhaps, take it from her again. But if this power had actually been given by a *god* ... to *her* specifically, for some unimaginable reason ...

She shook her head in stunned denial as she pushed through the dense scrub palm and thorny vine which lay between the shantytown and the harbor road, reconsidering the child's disturbing power to immobilize her with its gaze. The accusation in its eyes. Were others on the islands being seized and used by this so-called Butchered God as well? Did it peer out at Alizar from all sorts of little portals, working its will through whatever tools were handy at the moment? Had Sian any power left at all to make *plans* of her own? Or would this god steer her as it wished now, regardless of her own intentions? Might the eyes or tongue of any stray bystander be commandeered to reproach her if she began to drift off whatever course it willed for her? Had it just done so through that strange, unnatural child?

And what course *did* it will for her, anyway? Why choose her rather than some more significant member of the ruling family? What was this *message* she'd been so roughly conscripted to carry to them? She still had no idea — and this god, if god it was, was taking no pains she could see to help her deliver it. Had she been transformed like this to heal the Factor's child? Or was there some greater concern at stake here; something that only a god might have sufficient vision to foresee?

None of these were questions she had any wish to ask, much less be used to answer. Yet now that this unnerving child — or whatever had made use of it — had uncorked their bottle, more such questions just kept pouring out inside her.

What could a *dead* god want anyway, of anyone, much less of her? Was all this really being driven by the god whose body had washed up here two years ago, as the priest who had inflicted this *gift* of hers obviously believed? Or might some other god simply have elected to work through the dead one's shadow? Perhaps its killer? What besides a god could kill another god?

Such maddening questions!

Finding her hands pressed to the sides of her head as she walked up the narrow lane, she quickly let them drop. She must be as invisible as possible now. Just one more of Alizar's teeming, irrelevant poor.

The possibility that she really might have been chosen for this fate by some deity did nothing at all to make her a more willing vessel. More desperate than ever for some path toward escape, she finally conceded that, after she'd obtained some food, there was no option but to swallow her pride and turn to Reikos. He could help access her money somehow, or convey messages, or run necessary errands for her with at least as much safety as anyone else now. And he could get her off the islands altogether, if it really came to that. Might whatever god had seized her be outdistanced after all? She had heard stories of the continent's more active gods and godlings all her life, yet, to her knowledge, none of them had ever shown up here in Alizar. Might gods be as regionally bound as people were? Perhaps her unwanted power would vanish too, if she could cross beyond the borders of this new god's influence. And even if her power remained, she might still find refuge where no *healing priesthood* felt threatened by her. Might she not be able to do some good with such a power, if she were allowed to — even make a living with it?

Ugh! Now I sound just like Reikos.

Her stomach rumbled fiercely, bringing her back to ground. All she needed to be thinking of right now was a chicken. And a messenger, perhaps. Yes. The port market would be full of messengers to hire for just a few of her precious coins, and without attracting any notice at all amidst the usual hubbub there.

She began mentally composing a carefully phrased invitation to Reikos. One that he would understand without leaving anybody else, including her messenger, means to deduce her current whereabouts, or the location of their intended rendezvous. They would have to meet on some other island, of course, so that if her missive fell into the wrong hands it would not lead anyone back to her new home in the harbor shantytown. Fortunately, her long history of clandestine communications with the captain had provided her a well-established code in which to frame such instructions.

As the busy harbor market came into view ahead of her, however, Sian could not help but imagine being waylaid and captured yet again. Recalling Het's suggestion that her power might be used to harm as well as heal, Sian recoiled again from the idea. She doubted any god who wanted her to heal would have given her power to hurt instead. And she wanted no such power anyway. The idea sickened her. This so-called gift had reduced her to many things, but she had no intention of allowing it to make a thug of her as well. She was alert to the full danger of her situation now. If her best precautions proved insufficient, she would not be passively cooperative again. This time, at the slightest sign of trouble, she would flee for her life.

As the market's babble and activity engulfed her, Sian felt increasingly safer. Few people took any notice of another spent woman in rags, as Sian wandered through the press of haggling customers, vendors crying out their wares, and palm-thatched, bamboo food carts with their fragrant, smoky fires. The few who seemed to see her at all offered no more than frowns of distaste before looking away again. Once she might have been offended or ashamed, but now, she was simply reassured. It took her very little time to find her messenger; a boy of perhaps twelve or thirteen summers — clearly new at his profession — who looked far too innocent and eager to be in league with anyone. He had the usual writing implements and paper which they all carried to accommodate the unprepared. In keeping with her appearance, she pretended to be illiterate, dictating her message for Reikos as the boy wrote it out for her.

"You won't forget what I have tell you, or the name of his ship?" she asked, as if untrusting of such magic as writing. "I don't know when it may sail, maybe, so you hurry, eh? Find him quick for me. It's important that we speak. Okay?"

"Yes, my lady," he said earnestly, despite her ragged state. "I go right this minute."

"If you cheat me," she pressed in imitation of other desperate and helpless people she had observed, "I tell everybody at the market here, you cannot be trusted. Don't you doubt I will, boy."

"I would never cheat you!" the lad protested. "I am the best, most honest messenger in all of Alizar."

"I hope you are." Then, more kindly, to encourage him, "I believe you. Find him quick, and I tell everybody that you are the best man to hire."

He smiled at this, and dashed off with a reassuring wave, reminding her so much of Pino that she just managed not to laugh. Back when Pino had been her eager and adoring employee, anyway. This thought sobered her again.

It took little time to do her shopping. After a bit of shrewd bargaining, Sian left the market, balancing a rope sack of mainland potatoes over one arm as her hands gripped an unruly bunch of nearly wilted mustard greens and the ankles of a newly slaughtered chicken. The bird dangled quiescent now, still warm but finished with its gruesome twitching. Inconvenient as it would likely prove to cook over a fire on the beach, she felt confident that this much food would hold her for a couple days. Long enough to work out some better arrangement with Reikos's help, if her messenger proved as effective as he'd claimed.

In the meantime, she *would* still try to find that priest.

"What was your be-damned *message*?" she muttered to herself, continuing the one-sided argument she'd been having with the absent priest for days. "For the love of the Seven Unruly Goddesses and their false riders, what would you have me *do*?"

The cooling chicken in her grip gave a subtle but unmistakable twitch.

Flooded with horror, Sian flung the bird against the mud-brown wall of the building next to her. "Don't you dare!" she shrieked at the bird. "I've just had you killed! I'm going to *eat* you now, not raise you from the dead!"

The chicken tumbled limply to the ground, where it lay in an inert heap of feather-covered flesh. Only then did Sian notice that people all along the street had stopped to look at her. Alizar was never a quiet place, but generally speaking, people did not scream at dead poultry.

Sian looked away from the eyes on her and walked over to the bird, studying it for signs of further movement. There were none. She reached down and poked at its body to be sure.

If anything, it was colder than before, just beginning to stiffen, as a dead bird should. She decided that its tiny, puzzled spirit had finally passed on to whatever other shores accepted such creatures.

Sian stooped to pick it up again, very carefully, by the ankles, then rose to her feet, reset her veil, and looked around. She had dropped her bag of potatoes in her panic. She wandered back along the sidepath, gathering strays that had escaped.

A middle-aged woman with an open sore on her narrow face approached her timidly. "Our Lady." She took a step closer to Sian. "Our Lady of the Islands, heal me, I beg you."

People were still staring. More of them, in fact.

Sian tried to still her racing heart, keep her breathing slow. "I have no idea what you mean. I'm no priest."

The woman looked confused. Wounded, even. "I saw …" she said quietly. "We all did. The chicken in your hands. You are —"

"No," snapped Sian. Did she owe her life — her very safety — to everyone she met? Misery was everywhere; it was endless. She could spend herself night and day, and never put a dent in it — she was miserable herself now, homeless and exhausted and starving, all alone in the world. "Please," she whispered. "I am no one. I am nothing more than you. Just leave me be!"

"We beneath your effort then?" This from an older man standing in the shadows of the building she'd flung the chicken at. He took a step forward, limp at the leg, his skin an ugly, mottled color, indicative of an advanced case of the spiderpox. "The God's gift too precious to waste on *lesser people, Domina Kattë?*"

"Of course not…" Sian took a step back, no longer caring about her stray potatoes. He knew who she was. Did everyone? Had her story spread so far — already? How long before the Mishrah-Khote heard of her appearance here? All she wanted was to get back to Pembo's Beach — to the safety of her boat. "I didn't mean … I never said —"

"Bitch," the man said softly. "I've heard how you run off whenever people ask your help. We've all heard. Where you been hiding since the God gave you his treasure, eh?"

Others in the crowd advanced on her now, something harsh and broken in their eyes.

"I … have not been hiding anywhere," she stammered, caught between escalating terror and a flash of outrage. "The Mishrah-Khote. They came for me. I have been —"

"Rushed right into their arms, have you?" sneered a woman who stepped boldly into Sian's path. She had no obvious affliction, beyond the angry gleam in her eyes. Her hair was red and thick, tumbling to her shoulders in exuberant waves, making Sian even more self-conscious of the heavy veil and scarf she wore. "Lady *Special Thing*, rich and fancy. Too good to help us common types when you can join up with the greedy priests and charge more than the lot of them, I'll bet. The god's gift is for *us*, my lady princess. Not for the Mishrah-Khote — and not just to fatten fancy silk merchants like you."

"No…" Sian protested, stepping back further. The woman advanced on her, crushing a tender potato beneath her chunky sandal, sending its juices into the cobblestones. She came another step forward, raising her hands menacingly. In one of them, she held a knife. A poultry knife, of all things. "No, leave me be, please!"

"'*Please*'!" her assailant mocked, then gave an acidic bark of laughter. The sound rubbed at the back of Sian's throat like the taste of too-young wine. "We've been waiting for you. Everywhere. Ready to adore you, *Lady of the Islands*. But he's right. You're just another bitch — no better than the other so-called healers here." She darted forward, thrusting her blade straight for Sian's face.

"No!" Sian raised her arms to fend off the attack, but they were full of burdens. Too late, she thought to drop the vegetables and chicken. The knife bit her cheek, drawing an immediate splash of blood and a gasp from the crowd. Sian screamed.

"There! Not so perfect now, are you!" the woman crowed. "Fix that, Lady Precious!"

Sian felt blood flowing down her face, saw it drop to the stones of the street. As if aroused by the sight, the crazed woman thrust her knife again; Sian flung her hands out against the coming blow, and managed to grab the woman's knife arm just before the blade bit her again. She threw all her strength into the grip and felt something tidal thunder through the contact. Both women gasped as the red-haired woman crumpled suddenly into a heap at Sian's feet.

For a moment everyone froze in stunned silence. Then from well back in the crowd there came a scream. Someone turned to run off, back toward the market.

"What you done to her?" asked an awestruck boy shying backward into the circle that had gathered around their fight.

"Nothing!" Sian was as shocked as any of them. "Look what she did to *me*!" But she could already feel her cut face healing, as if in denial of her claim to victimhood.

"You're no bitch. You are a monster," gasped the older man who'd started all of this, now backing toward the entrance of the building he had come from.

"I did nothing!" Sian cried again, hoping desperately that it was true. Had she done this? Had Father Het's invention been prophetic? She fell to her knees beside the woman, grasping her arm in both her hands.

"Leave her alone!" shouted a young, dark-haired woman who seemed unsure whether or not she dared rush to the red-haired woman's aid.

"I can heal her!" Sian cried. Any hope of concealment was clearly gone. The crowd around her now seemed uncertain whether to be outraged or fascinated.

Awaken. Please awaken! she willed her erstwhile assailant. She had promised herself this would never happen. Had believed it wasn't possible. Was she allowed to decide *anything* now?

Seconds ticked by. The woman lay inert. Sian could almost smell the crowd becoming uglier as they crowded closer in. She had no hope of escape. What would happen if they attacked her? Could she be killed, or would she just heal and heal as they kept tearing her apart?

"Please! Whatever god has chosen me for this," she groaned, "help me."

A ruckus erupted from further back in the crowd. She had run out of time. "Awaken, woman," she murmured, wondering if this was how the gods rewarded instruments who dared resist them, "or I'll be joining you in death."

A man burst through the inner ring of bystanders, pushing everyone aside. "Sian!"

He swept her from the ground into his arms.

Sian's heart gave a disbelieving jump. "Reikos! Oh, thank all the gods there are!"

Just then, the woman she had felled came to with a great gasp. She blinked up at the crowd around her in confusion.

"Look!" somebody yelled. "She lives!"

"The Lady's healed her!" shouted someone else.

The news spread like fire through the crowd, prompting cries of astonishment.

"I knew you couldn't be so wicked," exclaimed the dark-haired girl who, just moments earlier, had told her not to touch the woman.

The red-haired woman staggered to her feet, clutching at her own torso with an expression of incredulous wonder. "She's healed me! The Lady's healed me! Fifteen years of crippling menstrual cramps, and now they're gone! I have no pain. No pain at all!"

"It is a sign of the God's mercy!" a man behind her cried. "Our Lady of the Islands healed the woman who attacked her! As the Butchered God will heal Alizar, though we destroyed his body!"

"Our Lady of the Islands!" someone started chanting, quickly joined by others — their bloodlust transformed suddenly into jubilation as Sian and Reikos looked around, bewildered.

"We have to get out of here," Sian whispered urgently, "before the temple comes! I will never get away from them a second time."

"The temple? ... Is that where you have been?"

"Yes! I will explain it all to you, but not here!"

Reikos turned, still carrying her in his arms, and elbowed his way back through the chanting, ecstatic crowd as forcefully as he had barged through them to reach her.

"Don't drop me," she begged as they were jostled ever more fiercely by admirers reaching out to touch her as they passed.

"Don't worry," Reikos said through clenched teeth. "I haven't finally found you just to lose you to a swarm of lunatics now."

She wondered abstractly what had happened to her chicken. "We can't go to my townhouse …"

"My boat is safe."

"Are you certain? They may know that you and I —"

She felt a hand grasp her arm and cringed, for fear the temple guard had already found them, then gasped as she recognized Pino, of all people. "What…?"

"We'll explain as well," said Reikos. He glanced at Pino, who looked both excited and frightened.

Once free of the crowd, Reikos set her down, and the two men hustled her through the streets without looking back. The noise of celebration faded into the normal sounds of any busy island day, and soon the docks came into view. Reikos and Pino flanked Sian protectively as they approached the *Fair Passage*. When they reached the gangway without being set upon by temple guards, Sian unclenched at last with a deep sigh. It was so comforting to be with men she knew, who didn't seem to mean her any harm, that she half believed things might still turn out all right somehow.

ELEVEN

Safely back in Reikos's cabin, Sian gladly let the two men pamper her. The captain sat her in one of his little fold-down chairs and poured her a stiff, delicious drink, while Pino washed the blood off her healed cheek. In her tidy cage, Matilda chortled and cocked her head at Sian.

"All right," she said, regathering her wits. "What are you two doing together? And how did you find me? The note I sent you said that we should meet tomorrow — on Meaders."

"And you thought I would just wait 'til then?" Reikos asked.

"*Pretty lady! Kiss me!*" squawked the cockatiel.

Pino flushed and glanced first at the bird, then at the older man. "We asked your messenger where he had received this note from you, of course. And when he told us he'd just left you at the market —"

"I tipped him generously to keep closed his mouth," Reikos jumped in, "and we went right away to find you — which I think you must be glad of now. Am I mistaken?"

"No. I am very glad indeed." She must keep her promise someday, she thought, and tell everyone she knew who Alizar's best messenger was. "But what are *you* doing here, Pino? You appear in all the strangest places lately."

Reikos stepped forward, laying a hand on Pino's shoulder. "He came to me yesterday. Said he'd lost his job with you, and asked if I might take him on as crew." Reikos gave the boy a wink. "I was moved to hire him by a sense of fellow feeling, I suppose — having just been fired by you too. We have been searching for you ever since."

Well… she thought. *Coincidence? Or has this also been arranged somehow by my new employer? If so, to what purpose, I wonder?* There seemed no smallest surface she could simply take for granted anymore.

"Can I get you anything else?" Reikos asked. "I bought that *kiesh* just for you."

"I thank you. But, in all honesty, I am far hungrier than thirsty. Another drink, before any food, would be unwise, I fear."

"Of course. Just sit right there." Reikos left the cabin, closing the door gently behind him.

She gazed at Pino: still the same gangling, eager-to-please boy. Young man, really. She saw that now, though he didn't look any more the dangerous conspirator than he had before.

Pino shifted in his chair. "I am … glad to see you well, my lady."

Sian widened her eyes, then laughed, looking down at her ragged, filthy clothes. She hadn't bathed in days, and had just slept on a rocky beach underneath a rotting boat. Then bled all over herself on a dusty street. All after, of course, spending such a delightful passage in a dungeon prison cell. "Oh, Pino. You dear boy. It's all right to speak the truth." *Isn't it? Can we do that? Now?*

"But you do look well!" He pointed to her cheek. "I mean … your cut — already, the mark is gone!"

Sian nodded. Odd, how you could get used to the strangest things. "Yes. That happens now. As I'm sure you know."

He frowned uncomfortably. "I had heard, of course, of your healing power, but …"

"A gift bestowed by your new priest," she said, as lightly as she could. "Or by his Butchered God, I guess. You helped arrange my fate that night, did you not?"

Pino looked down at his knotted hands, blushing nearly the color of Heart's Blood berries.

"I've had time to reflect on things," she went on. "The prayer lines always in my way that evening. The invitation to meet 'Hanchu traders' that do not seem to have existed. *Your* unexpected appearance just in time to usher me into that priest's waiting embrace. None of this was coincidence, was it?"

She had never seen the boy look so forlorn. "I had no idea what was going to happen," Pino murmured. "He told me you were favored by the god." He looked up at last, giving her a nervous smile. "How could that have seemed surprising to me?" His gaze fell again. The smile disappeared. "I thought there was something wonderful in store for you." His eyes brimmed with remorse. "I have not seen him since, my lady. I will never speak to him again."

"Oh, but you must! Pino, I have tried and tried to find him, but —"

The sound of footsteps just outside brought a wave of panic to Pino's face. "I have not told Reikos why I lost my job with you, exactly," he whispered. "Please, don't —"

She silenced him with a reassuring gesture as the cabin door opened.

This time, Reikos carried a plate piled with manchego cheese and oat cakes, artfully surrounded by clusters of tiny purple grapes.

"*Cracker!… Damn bird! Cracker!*" the cockatiel cried.

"Oh, thank you!" Well beyond caring about niceties, Sian rose to snatch an oat cake and a great chunk of cheese before Reikos had time to offer them to her, and bit into each with grateful abandon.

Watching Sian with a half-hidden smile, Reikos pinched off a finger full of oat cake, and went to push it through the cage to Matilda. After that, both men picked at the meal as well, marveling circumspectly at Sian's healthy appetite. She soon felt better than she had in days. She leaned back in her chair, and said to Reikos, "Now I *would* have a touch more of your *kiesh*, if it won't deplete your stores overmuch."

"Not in the least, my lady." Reikos stood to take the bottle from a high shelf, refilling her glass as well as his own and Pino's, then tucked it back onto its shelf behind a stretchy cord clearly designed to hold it fast even during violent storms. "Habit," he said, smiling when he saw that she had noticed. "One never knows when the waters might become rough."

"As they have," she said.

"I suppose they have, at that." Reikos took a long sip of his drink, watching Sian.

He looked happy to see her; the alarming glitter of greed in his eyes was gone. Had he repented of his desire to use her curse for financial gain? "The

Mishrah-Khote had me locked up," she said, feeling it was time to get down to business. "I only escaped with my life because of the generous heart of one of their number. He is probably in great trouble now."

"We are aware that the healing priests seek you," Reikos admitted. "Indeed, we have heard it put around that if you return, all shall be forgiven. They seem quite anxious to assure all and sundry that no harm will come to you."

Sian snorted. "That is quite a different tune than they sang while I was there. They broke my fingers and sliced my earlobe in half."

Pino gaped. Reikos paled as well.

"I healed, of course," Sian added. "But I have no wish to suffer so again."

Reikos shook his head. "Then remove yourself from such danger. We can sail tomorrow morning — I'm already overdue for a spice run up the coast to Pepperell and the Isle of the Gods. We can travel anywhere from there. No one need learn of your strange talents."

Sian sighed. If only that were true. "No, Reikos. To keep that secret, I would never be able to touch another human being." *Even you*, she added silently. "I am not sure my departure would be allowed anyway, even if I wished to go."

"I and my crew could easily protect you," Reikos insisted.

"From a jealous god?" Sian countered. "I doubt this power was thrust upon me just so I could wander off with it unused."

"Gods," Reikos muttered, then set his glass down on the small table with a thud. In her cage, Matilda gave a *chirrup* of protest. "If one believes such things ..."

Sian's power did not extend to mind-reading, but she could guess the trail of his thoughts. She'd entertained them herself for quite a while. "I also used to think this could be fixed somehow. But now, I'm far less sure." She turned to Pino. "I need your help. And to get it, we must all be able to talk freely here. It is time you told my friend the truth."

Pino closed his eyes, looking wounded and betrayed. It hurt Sian to see it, but, well ... Life was harder than any of them had once believed. Had she not felt wounded and betrayed as well — on the night Pino had led *her* into the shark's maw — unwittingly or not?

Reikos frowned, glancing back and forth between them. "What truth?"

"Reikos," Sian said, "if you care for me at all, promise not to punish him in any way for what he is about to tell you. I assure you that, however naïve he may have been, I have never had a better, harder working, or more trustworthy employee. He will make you as fine a crewman as you could ever wish for."

"I must hear this confession now, I think," Reikos said to Pino. "Then I will decide what I can do for you, young man." He looked apologetically at Sian. "More than this, I cannot promise. One does not take such risks with one's choice of crew at sea."

She had known he would respond this way, but she had felt compelled to try. She offered Pino an apologetic look in turn.

"I have been a disciple of the Butchered God's priest," Pino said, meeting no one's eyes. "I helped lure Domina Kattë to him the night she was ... changed."

Reikos's mouth hung slightly open. "You did this to her?"

"No," Sian insisted, well aware of the way anger built to crest before breaking with her onetime lover. "Pino was gone before I was beaten that night. He had been as badly deceived as I was about what the priest intended." She looked back at Pino, who stared stolidly at his own feet. "I believe so, anyway. With all my heart."

"As I have already told Domina Kattë," said Pino, "I left his cult that night. I want never to see that man again. Or any of his followers." He kept gazing downward. "I trusted him."

"So this is how you lost your job?" Reikos asked.

Pino nodded mournfully.

"Well ... I should think so," Reikos said with the ghost of a smile, to Sian's surprise. "We've both been fools then, in one way or another. Just as I've said all along." He turned back to Sian. "And what help do you think this mere boy can offer, which I cannot just as well provide?"

"I need to find this priest," Sian said. "I need desperately to talk with him, but he is like a rumor — always there and gone just hours before I arrive. Can you bring me to him, Pino? Do you know someone who can find him, at least?"

Pino shook his head, still looking at the floor. "He does not stay in one place for long. And I am ... hardly in his confidence anymore."

"But you do know how he operates." She could read it in his hesitation. "Whatever he intended for me, it couldn't have been this — my life in shambles, running and hiding from everyone. Show me where to find him. Let me ask him how to fix this."

Reikos pulled gently at her sleeve. "Sian, do not go to that man."

"I must," she said. "No one else can help me. Whatever else he may be, he must understand what's happened to me — and what his god wants now." She turned back to Pino. "I cannot just go on wandering from threat to threat like this with no idea what I'm even meant to *do*."

Reikos got up, his catlike grace clearer than ever in the confines of the tiny cabin. "Do not do this, Domina. Come away with me. My crew and I will take you to the priests at the Isle of the Gods. They will know the answers to your problem. You will find nothing but trouble here."

Sian shook her head. "It makes no sense to rush off to some far-off priest without even speaking to the one *right here* who did this to me." She turned back to Pino. "You do know how to find him?"

Still staring at his sandals, the young man said, "I have ... heard word of another sermon, at the north beach on Three Cats, this evening." He looked up at last. "But, my lady, I also beg you not to do this thing. Truly, he is no one to be trusted."

"I must." She got to her feet. "We shall go there. Captain Reikos, you are more than welcome to accompany us."

"Sian, please. Listen to the boy," Reikos urged. "He is wise beyond his years!"

"The rumor could be false — they often are," said Pino. "People gather and he doesn't even come. This could be a waste of time. And a big risk, taking you out across so many islands."

"But sometimes he does come?" she pressed.

Pino nodded, reluctantly.

"Well, that's better odds than I've enjoyed so far."

"I shall come with you, then," Reikos said. "You will need what protection we can give."

"I thank you."

"But the boy is right in one thing," Reikos said. "It will be risky just to take you there, after what you've told us — and what happened just now in the market. We must make sure you are well covered. And we'll take a two-man runner-cart, to ensure you are not waylaid this time. You will sit between us, while we do any talking needed. Agreed?"

"Agreed. Of course." Once she would have bridled at the mere suggestion of being handled so like baggage, but after all she'd been through on the streets of late, she was only grateful now for such protection.

"And I think it is unsafe to keep you staying in those clothes you wear," said Reikos, giving her the merest hint of a smile. "These temple men will likely have your description soon, if they do not already. We must find you something better."

"That may take some doing," she said. "Do we have the time?"

"No time is needed, I am thinking." He turned and left them again, with a secretive grin.

Sian turned to Pino as soon as Reikos was gone. "I'm sorry. Truly, Pino. I took no pleasure in exposing you that way. It's just that —"

Pino raised his hands to silence her. "You were right. As always, Domina. I was afraid, but it will be better this way. Living without secrets. I … I thank you, my lady. You always know the right way of things."

Sian reached out to pat his hand. "I most certainly do not. Not these days anyway — if I ever did."

They heard Reikos at the door again, and turned to see him enter with a lovely dress of dusky rose silk, piped in brilliant orange, draped across his arm. Sian managed not to blush — or glance at Pino. She knew every detail of its low cut and feather-light construction before he held it up and shook it out with a dramatic flourish for them both to see.

"Will this do?" he asked Sian, knowing that it would as well as she knew when she'd left it there. "It is a sample from one of the latest Hanchu lines, which I was hoping to show before I was … er, *fired*. I think that it may fit you reasonably well."

Like a glove, she thought, careful not to roll her eyes. *What are you thinking, to drag this out before the boy?* She risked a sidelong glance at Pino, wondering suddenly just how much he knew. Enough to have come seeking Reikos when she'd disappeared. But had he learned somehow that they'd been more than close friends and important business partners? "It is lovely, but hardly seems inconspicuous."

"It will be quite perfectly inconspicuous, I think, to men searching for a woman dressed in rags."

"It is beautiful, my lady," Pino agreed. "I think ... You will look very nice in it."

She could decipher nothing in his guarded expression. *'Fellow feeling,'* indeed, she thought. How much had Reikos been fool enough to tell the boy?

"We may still need to walk some of the way, though," Pino added. "Especially on Three Cats, where ..." He blushed, and looked down again self-consciously. "Where the roads may become clogged with marchers. We should leave by mid-afternoon, I think."

"That will give me enough time to wash up, and change clothes," Sian agreed.

"I will leave you to that, my lady." Pino stood, looking sullen now, for some reason, and went to the door of the small cabin, where he fumbled with the latch before leaving them conveniently alone.

"How much does he know?" she asked Reikos. "Did you brag about us when he came to you?"

"Do I seem *that much* a fool to you now?"

"Then why did he come to you? How did he even know of you?"

"He said he'd heard you speak of me with *trust*. You did once trust me, I believe."

She gazed at him across the tiny cabin, feeling oddly confused. "I trust you still," she said. "Within reason. I owe you a great deal just since this morning."

"You owe me nothing, Sian. Whatever I may do for you is freely given. Always."

"And I am very grateful." She sighed. "I'd best get cleaned up and into that dress now." She glanced at the door. "If you wouldn't mind, Captain? We don't want to give the boy ideas, do we?"

"Indeed not, my lady." He went to the door as well. "I'll bring some water, then leave you in peace."

Reikos returned a minute later with a large basin of warm water, hibiscus-scented soap, and three clean towels — all far nicer than she'd expected from a bachelor on a ship full of sailors. "I thank you."

"We'll await you at your leisure," he said without turning as he left.

ᔐ

Domni Arouf Monde had dismissed Bela for the day, yet again. He could make his own dinner and see to his own washing-up: he was perfectly capable.

Truth be told, he could hardly bear the sight of the old woman. Every normal, unimpaired step she took was a reminder of Sian. Of her terrible new powers. And of what had passed between them just before she'd disappeared.

Yes, he had been angry. But who would not have been? Sian had come to him demonstrating a strange and frightening power, out of nowhere. Where could such power come from but a demon? Yet she'd denied any agency in having acquired it — or responsibility to see it fixed! What should he have said to her — that's very nice, dear? Have some wine, and let us talk about what we should do to live now that we're ruined? For this would certainly destroy their business. It had clearly already destroyed their marriage. Why else would she have stopped responding to him?

It had been days and days now since Sian had done that wicked magic and then stormed off of the island in an unfamiliar boat. Well, two days, but he'd had not a single word from her since then, though he had sent several notes off to their townhouse. Notes of increasing... urgency. He had assumed that she would settle back to normal, that he would hear from her in a day or two. She had always been so level-headed. He had relied on her entirely. It was like missing his right leg, having her gone.

He had half a mind to go down there himself... yet he was afraid of what he might find.

Their marriage, their partnership, had begun with hot passion and intense love, and had mellowed into the clever, comfortable business and child-rearing arrangement of later years, just as any marriage should. Or so he had thought … They'd had their moments of disagreement, of course, but this … This was different. This … was not just about … themselves. He was quite sure of that now.

He got to his feet and began pacing the large room, stepping around overstuffed chairs and delicate side tables without even seeing them.

The boy Pino was still missing, too. That was the problem.

The boy who always eagerly volunteered to row Sian to Alizar Main and back; who carried her bags, though Sian was perfectly capable of doing so. Arouf had noticed his puppy-crush, of course; a man would have to be blind to miss it. But he had given it no great concern. Boys would always be boys. These things happened. Sian was more than old enough to be the boy's mother, so why should he have worried?

And yet … they had both run off at the same moment? What was he to make of that?

He did not know what to believe any more.

Arouf shook his head, pausing at the darkened window to stare out at the empty water below. Stars hung in the sky, and danced on the waves. Farther out, at the horizon, it was hard to be quite certain where one ended and the other began. The tiny surf pushed glowing, pale lines toward the shore of Little Loom Eyot.

She was cheating on him. Probably for some time now. It had to be faced. She had been discreet, at least. The main partnership had remained unchallenged. That was what had really mattered. But now, Sian had violated every boundary of discretion.

It would be one thing for her to pass the occasional quiet night with a fellow trader or a responsible, married man. Sometimes that was business — here in Alizar, as in all other places, he assumed. People strayed from the marriage path. Arouf was no fool, not to understand this. But to run off with a boy half her age? That was quite beyond the pale. That was no discreet arrangement. That was full-blown scandal! An abomination — like these powers she had *contracted* somewhere.

He had heard of women becoming … restless … when they approached their change-of-life. He had never, however, heard of them developing bizarre healing powers in the process.

"Which is not the point!" Arouf growled at his reflection in the darkened window.

The point was that she should come home, *now*. She should relinquish this strange power and resume her rightful place beside her husband's — and *business partner's* — side. This had gone on far too long already. If their clients and trading partners were not talking of it now, they would be soon enough. And then everything Monde & Katté had worked for all these years would be lost.

No, there were times when a husband must stop sending weak entreaties to the townhouse of his faithless wife, and be more forceful. It had been cowardly of him to wait even this long. It was time for the next step. He must bring in the authorities.

Resolved, Arouf went to his writing-desk to begin drawing up a formal complaint.

TWELVE

After a quiet afternoon together aboard *Fair Passage*, and a small early evening meal, Pino went out to hire a two-man runner-cart. When he returned, Sian raised her embroidered hood and fastened its silk veil across her face, then followed her protectors up onto the deck. As Pino led her down the ship's gangway, she was quite conscious of Reikos's strong presence behind her. He did not touch her, but she could feel his nearness as if they were entwined in the most intimate of embraces.

She still had no clear idea what exactly he expected of her now that she'd returned. Nor, for that matter, what she might *want* him to expect. Having Pino underfoot just made things that much harder to navigate.

The two lean runners harnessed to their rented cart gave Sian an appreciative looking-over as she climbed aboard between Reikos and Pino. But after asking where the party wished to go, they spared no further attention for their cargo as they strained to set the vehicle in motion, then jogged off toward the bridge to Yon.

The long ride across several islands and bridges was uneventful. Even pleasant. Pino had chosen their able runners well. They pulled the cart along too quickly for anyone in the streets to catch more than a glimpse of its three passengers, much less cause them any trouble. For the first time in days, Sian felt completely safe: invisible, despite her finery, just as Reikos had predicted. She was no one now. The decorative lady of some foreign man, traveling to who-knew-where with a young servant. What could any of that have to do with the ragged fugitive, Sian Kattë?

Their runners were so fast, they arrived on Three Cats rather earlier than anticipated.

"Maybe we should walk from here," said Pino, when the runners stopped for one of their short breaks to drink and take a bite or two of the food they carried with them. "We're kind of fancy to blend in with the priest's folk." He glanced sheepishly at Sian. "We'll attract even more attention in a runner-cart. I'm sorry, my lady. I should have thought of that."

She shrugged. "I should have known as well. I too have traveled with the prayer lines."

"Then walk we will," said Reikos, going to pay their runners. When they had tucked their meal away with grateful bows and trotted off the way they'd come, Reikos returned, slipping his purse back into some inner pocket of his vest. "Where to now, Pino?"

"Across the island, to the waterfront facing Malençon."

"That far?" asked Reikos. "I wish you'd told me so before I sent our cart away." He turned to Sian. "That dress is hardly made for such a trek."

"I love to walk," she said. "And it has been too long since I could do so without fear. It is a pleasant evening, and with you two to protect me, I can think of nothing more enjoyable." She offered one arm to Reikos, and the other to Pino.

They started down the street together, at a leisurely pace, enjoying the antics of wild squirrel monkeys frolicking in the mangosteen trees overhead. In the distance, Sian watched fruit bats flapping their great wings above jungle canopy as their evening foraging began. Nestled between the two men, Sian felt as if she'd traveled back in time, to another life, where Sian Katté had been a relatively wealthy merchant with no greater worries than an overfull schedule and an unwieldy pile or two of paperwork. What happy days those must have been.

And yet, they hadn't been. Not really. She saw that now as she had not even guessed it then. In fact, she could not recall feeling half as happy then as she did right now.

Half an hour later, Sian's feet were feeling less content, and she was getting hungry again. Reikos and Pino gave each other a look when she told them so.

"Let's buy you another supper then," said Reikos. "That seems a likely tavern over there." He pointed to a door nearly hidden by a riot of bougainvillea.

"All right," said Pino. "I'll wait out here and watch for any signs of trouble."

"You will not," Sian insisted, certain the boy was only trying to hide his lack of money. She gave Reikos a solicitous look. "Pino is on my tab. Agreed?"

"Your *tab*?" he asked. "Since when have you a *tab*, my lady?"

"Surely you don't think I'll simply let you pay for everything while all this gets resolved. I want a full accounting kept of anything you spend on my behalf, Captain. As soon as I am able to access my usual accounts again, you will be repaid every penny, with interest. I insist." She did not smile, wanting to be sure he knew she wasn't joking. She turned back to Pino. "Your meal is on me tonight. There's no need to stand outside keeping watch. No one will trouble us here, for I am no longer the woman they are looking for. In fact, if all goes well tonight, I hope never to be that woman again."

The mood over their meal was light and comfortable. Her two companions laughed and teased each other now, as men do, and Sian enjoyed the half-forgotten luxury of relaxing over fine food and good wine with pleasant company. Even if she did eat most of it herself. Was it her imagination, she wondered, or was Reikos exhibiting an almost paternal enjoyment in Pino's company? She smiled to think of Reikos as a father. The image was both sweet and laughable.

It took them nearly another hour after dinner to reach their destination. They were still quite a distance from the northern shore of Three Cats when they encountered a prayer line heading in the same direction. A few blocks later, a second line appeared, melding with the first. By the time they reached land's end, many prayer lines had converged to become a street-clogging crowd, as Pino had predicted, all trying to pick their way down a short, steep cliff side between themselves and the rocky beach below.

The close proximity of so many marchers, the muffled roar of their shuffling feet and murmured chanting, were rather too reminiscent of that awful night on Malençon for comfort. She began to sweat inside her pretty dress, to cast anxious glances behind her with increasing frequency, and flinch at every unexpected noise. Finally Reikos noticed, his eyes widening in understanding as he pulled closer to his side and gestured to Pino to come take her other arm. Their protective presence helped, but not enough to make her certain this had not been a great mistake, as they had suggested.

Sian wondered how such a mob could fail to attract the attention of authorities eager to find and arrest the renegade priest they'd come to see — Alizar's most notorious 'spiritual fraud,' according to her temple persecutors. Then again, when and where these days did such prayer lines *not* clog Alizar's streets? Perhaps the authorities had grown just as weary of following them all as Sian herself had, not so long ago. If the priest showed up at all here, his appearance would doubtless end before the authorities had time to learn that this crowd had signified anything more than the others did. She almost empathized with their frustration.

Almost.

Pino led her down a makeshift path while Reikos came behind her, as if to demonstrate that no one would be sneaking up on her tonight. Scores of other people preceded and followed them, knocking sand and small rocks loose to shower the beach below. An elderly woman stumbled; the man before her caught her arm, so she did not fall.

As everyone descended to the beach, Sian noticed many around her giving them strange looks, just as Pino had also feared. Her fine silk dress may have worked as a disguise while traveling across the islands, but it stood out very oddly here among the Butchered God's poor and disenfranchised flock. Though she did not think the resentment she sensed was mere imagination, no one gave them any trouble. The priest had many followers, clearly. Who could say that all of them were poor?

The narrow beach was quite crowded by the time they reached it. Sian sought an open place for the three of them to stand, but as more and more folk came, she had to settle for a spot so near the shore that the highest waves sometimes lapped at their toes.

As dusk descended, the humid air grew heavier. Her airy silks wilted and clung to her, as even the gentlest breezes faded into stillness. Soon, Sian noticed that the crowd had grown still too, turning, without any signal she could detect, toward a large pier just south of where she stood. The tide was low; the pier's tall pilings rose in deep gloom, encrusted with barnacles and stinking rot; the rocks from which the pilings rose were wet and slippery with seaweed and exposed sea creatures. This was not a spot likely to attract much of anybody normally, she realized. Likely why it had been chosen.

Sian took Reikos's hand in the fading light; he squeezed hers back as they gazed into the darkness beneath the pier, trying to see what everyone was staring at. Many others had come to stand before her by now, standing knee-deep in the water itself, but she was still able to see the man step out from some even deeper shadows into a small clearing in the gloom.

She had not forgotten his face. She didn't think she ever would: young and handsome with those smoldering eyes, though he seemed far more serene tonight than he had the last time they had met. She gave Pino a grateful nod for having led her, finally, back to the man who'd beaten her into a different life, then set her adrift — in so many ways — cursed with this terrible 'gift'. The priest was robed more traditionally this time, almost as if to pass for a brother of the Mishrah-Khote. Was this disguise, she wondered, or pretension? She tried to step forward, but the crowd had grown too thick, and would not part for her.

Pino grabbed her sleeve. "No, my lady — after he speaks."

She schooled herself to patience, as the crowd around her strained forward too, as eager as she, it seemed, to get closer to this man, if for very different reasons. She tried to listen through the rush of surf, the evening cries of shore birds, the restless humming of the crowd around her, wondering whether she'd be able to hear him when he began to speak — and fearful, suddenly, that he might just slide back into the shadows when he'd finished, before she could reach him. Her throat felt suddenly dry despite the smothering humidity.

When it came at last, his voice was surprisingly full and clear. The crowd gave an appreciative murmur as it carried over them with the soothing cadences and sweet rhythms of a natural-born orator.

"My blessed friends — my spiritual family, welcome." His face was relaxed, smiling and open. "I know you have wandered long and far to be here, and I thank you. I know too that the path ahead still seems unclear. But look around you: more join our numbers day by day. More wise, blessed souls are remembering the way of light, and turning from the dark, destructive path that Alizar has drifted onto in its rush to take what it then finds so little joy in, to rise by shoving others down, to sell all of its tomorrows in a frenzy to engorge itself today. More of our countrymen will join us tomorrow, and the day after tomorrow, and the day after that, until Alizar recalls itself at last, and wakens from the dark dream it's been lost in. That bright day will dawn, not just on our nation's loftiest towers, but on its lowest valleys too. On that morning, none in Alizar will live in fear or shame or anger any longer, for *all* will have their heart's desire, and *none* will need what only others have. This I am empowered to promise you, by the very god who called me out of darkness, as he has called each of you. Him they call the *Butchered God* — who nonetheless comes ever nearer, to set the crooked straight, right what is imbalanced, and heal every inch of poor, lost Alizar!"

His words washed over the crowd like a cool, exhilarating wave. Sian felt its power, despite herself. But she knew firsthand how capable this humble, sunny promiser of peace and harmony was of inexplicable violence. She recalled the crazed and bloodshot face he'd worn just a few nights before, and resolved to resist the seductive power of his oration. Surely there was some incitement to riot and revolution underneath his gentle-seeming words. While those around her closed their eyes and turned their faces toward the sky, already reaching for religious ecstasy, she opened her eyes wider, straining to hear the threads of sly deceit that she felt certain would be woven through this pretty speech.

"I know you thirst for justice," the priest went on. "You desire wages that the humble can feed their families on, not just more wealth for the lucky few who rule you."

Ah. Here it comes, Sian thought with grim satisfaction. The hook of resentment. Permission to punish the successful. Did those around her not realize how they were being used? If this man got his way, he might end up their new king, but they would find themselves impoverished still; *his* laborers instead of someone else's.

"You want more than tents and shacks in which to raise your children. You imagine an end to unpaid apprenticeships to unscrupulous and exploitive manufacturers."

That is not how Arouf and I have ever run our business, Sian thought with rising umbrage. This man painted everyone alike, with whatever brush suited his agenda. She had known he would.

"You long to see the end of different rules for different classes, to enjoy the kind of privilege and education that your masters take for granted, to be free at last of those who deny you access to your own potential. I know all of this, and feel the pain and outrage these inequities fill your hearts with every day. Did I not crawl out of the same bleak slums and shantytowns that you are trapped in, day after weary day?"

Did you? Sian challenged silently. Not this accomplished orator. This charlatan had clearly enjoyed the very privilege and education he now encouraged his audience to resent. She'd have bet her savings on it.

"I will not pretend I do not know what it is like to dream of seeing those above us all cast down and overthrown," he said, as if the admission were painful to him.

Oh, she wanted to reach down, grab two handfuls of wet sand, and hurl them at him, but she was also increasingly conscious of her damned fancy dress. No point in bringing this mob down on herself instead. She wondered how much longer it would be safe for her and Reikos to remain here, if he took this rant where she was now quite sure it must be going.

"But, though many of you surely wish to hear me tell you it is time to rise up in righteous indignation and bring our masters to their knees, burn their palaces, and drag them off in chains to rot in their own dungeons, or better yet, the slums they have created to contain you in, I must disappoint you. The god I serve wants no such thing — for you or for them."

What? Sian looked around, but with very few exceptions, no one around her seemed at all surprised, much less disappointed. They just listened more intently, some nodding as if this were what they'd come to hear. What twist in the old game was this?

"The very masters who torment you today were forged in someone else's torture chambers," the priest said with a slow nod of his own. "They allowed themselves to be consumed by the very anger that tempts all of us here, and told themselves that when they had destroyed all those above them, they'd be free.

"But free for what? That is the question they never thought to ask themselves. Free to rule instead of being ruled? But to rule whom? Free to wield the whip instead of bearing it? Against whose back?" He fell silent, gripping all before him with that burning gaze. "You know the answer, friends," he told them softly. "Better than anyone else.

"*Their* righteous tantrum of destruction freed them to rule *you*. To wield the whip against *your* back. They beat their persecutors down at last by becoming all the very things they'd hated most about them."

Sian shook her head, trying to understand how he would twist this bizarre new sleight of hand to his benefit, but she was at a loss. If he did not approve of beatings, how did he justify what he had done to her?

"Give in to rage, my true and blessed friends, and you will know the truth of all I say — when *you* sit in their places as the world *you* oppress seethes and boils at your feet. You will know what *they* feel now, lying in their privileged beds at night. You will fear what they fear, and hide what they hide, and become as monstrous as so many of your leaders have become, running desperately from what you've taken for yourselves, and from those who want it taken from you in their turn. The god I serve ... did not yield his body up for this. He does not feed you still so that you can rise up to be next year's crop of monsters. No, the god I serve offers all of us on Alizar — high *and* low, rich *and* poor, wicked or innocent — something infinitely better."

Around her, Sian heard the sounds of quiet weeping, the sighs of murmured thanks, breathless affirmations of what the priest was saying, though she could not imagine why.

"If you have heard the message I am chosen to bear, then you already know what the Butchered God offers to us all, and how costly it will be — and has already been — for all of us to gain. If you have not yet heard his message, then listen to me now."

Sian strained forward, struggling to remember that she could not trust this man — that this, surely, was where the trick would be performed somehow, the worm revealed at the center of his lovely oratorical fruit.

"The god who drew me out of my own hell bids me tell you that justice for both high and low, a life together without any cause for fear or shame or anger, a nation without need or inequality, will be ours as soon as every one of you wants such things more than you want what the ones who rule us now possess. Overthrow a thousand governments, and men will still make what they want out of the rubble. If you want what your oppressors have, that is what you'll make — again and again and again. If you want something better than what your oppressors have, you must renounce all that those oppressors have to offer, and give yourselves to *making* a *new* world instead. Making! Not taking. The god I serve wants nothing short of this, my blessed companions: that we withhold nothing we possess — not our minds, our hearts, our bodies or our lives — from the one true task of *making* the new world. The cure we need, the dream we seek, these lie inside each of us, not out there. Inside ourselves is where the battle must be waged. The only place it can be waged. All else is doomed illusion. Set it down, my blessed companions. Set all of it down, and come *make* the world we want instead, together ... out of nothing, if we must.

"The god I serve be with all who hear him," he said very quietly.

Sian waited. For the trick. But nothing happened. Surely there was something more. Where was the final flourish? The impassioned crescendo, cunningly designed to bring this audience roaring to their feet, ready to do anything he bid? She looked around again at all the needy people, swaying, smiling, weeping softly in this eerie silence. What did they imagine they'd received? What had he offered them? He had told them nothing, really. What new world did he mean? He had described it not at all, except in the vaguest generalities. Why did any of them leave their lives and livelihoods to march and march across the islands — for this? And why did they seem so ... *gratified* now?

She turned to Reikos, and found him just as wrapped in unnatural silence as all the others. What did *Reikos* think he'd heard?

She turned to Pino, whose face was washed in tears.

"I cannot understand," Pino whispered roughly. "How can he see what he describes, and yet ..." He looked at Sian hopelessly. "Do you see now? Why I helped him bring you when he asked me to?" *No*, she thought, beginning to feel crazy. *I don't see any of what's doing this to any of you.* "How could I have known, my lady? Nothing in the world fits anymore." He drew a deep breath, then another, wiping at his eyes. "If you want to speak with him, we should do it now. This is ... when it happens."

"When what happens?" she asked, increasingly unnerved.

"He lets us come to him," said Pino. "All who want to. I thought that he just meant to talk with you that night. As he does with us." He gave her a worried look. "I don't know what he will do tonight, though, either. Are you still sure you wish to do this?"

"Yes," she said, turning back to Reikos. "Are you coming?"

He blinked at her as if awakened from some kind of trance. "Of course. I too would like to meet this man." He rushed to add, "And to make certain he has no ideas about hurting you again."

She shook her head, and started for the pier as Reikos and Pino flanked her. The crowd had begun to thin, drifting up and down the beach, or back toward the cliff-side paths. But as she neared the pier she was dismayed to see a long line had already formed between herself and the priest. More waiting.

She joined the line, peering impatiently through the lowering darkness at the priest. He sat on a large rock now, flanked by two leaning pilings and several large, frightening men. Someone had lit a driftwood fire beside him, which was just starting to catch in earnest. His young face still seemed open and serene as he laid hands gently on the heads of follower after follower. Had any of these people been there, she wondered, when he had beaten her? Did they know about his other face? The one he wore when he was wielding his god's heavy bone? Did no one care about such obvious hypocrisy? Such madness?

Several times, after some brief exchange too hushed for her to hear, she saw him slip a fragment of some dark material into the mouth of his petitioner.

This made her shiver. She had heard the rumors. Could what he was feeding them really be cured flakes of the Butchered God's dismembered flesh?

"I am not eating any of whatever that may be," Reikos muttered in her ear, as if he'd read her thoughts.

"Nor am I," Sian replied. "For once, I am not hungry."

From atop the cliffs behind them, chanting floated down as prayer lines re-formed to set out through the darkened islands — with renewed enthusiasm, she supposed.

One by one, those in line before her had their moment with the man before surrendering him to the next in line. Most left with smiles of satisfaction, or what seemed happy tears, though some went looking more perplexed or haunted than relieved by whatever he had told them. Either way, the line grew shorter, until, finally, Sian found herself before the priest.

She let go of Reikos's hand and took a step away from him and Pino to close the gap between herself and the priest. She didn't kneel, as others had. She felt anything but overawed by this young zealot now. Where had the frightening young firebrand she remembered gone? She could see tiny beads of sweat on the soft fuzz of his upper lip in the firelight. How could she have let this veritable schoolboy take such power over her that night?

For a moment, they just gazed at one another in the gloom. Then his brows climbed up a notch, and, to her surprise, he stood. "Our Lady of the Islands," he said softly, astonishing her further with a delighted smile.

"So I'm told," she answered.

She heard murmurs of amazement start to ripple down the line behind her as the news spread. Not what she'd have wished for, if she'd had a choice, but if the priest was safe here, she supposed she must be too.

Beside him, two of his enforcer-bullyboys shifted their stances ever so slightly, their eyes still on the crowd, though Sian was certain they too had turned their attention to her. It suddenly occurred to her to wonder if they saw *her* as the potential threat now. Might they be worried about what her magic touch could do to their young charge? An amusing thought. She kept her posture relaxed, her expression calm, not wanting his guards to think she might be planning something — or afraid.

The priest looked past her at her two companions. "And is that Pino with you?" he asked just as happily. "I am glad to see you, brother."

Pino shook his head, unwilling, or perhaps unable, to reply.

"I have been searching for you," Sian told the priest.

"Am I so hard to find?" He gestured at the dissipating crowd around them.

"When you wish to be, it seems."

"You think I have been hiding from you?" His smile widened. "Why would I do so?"

"Maybe you still have a shred of conscience somewhere in there. Or feared I'd bring the authorities with me to drag you off in chains — as I have been dragged off."

His smile vanished. "That was an awful night. For both of us."

"For *both* of us?" she blurted in disbelief. "I'd say it was far easier for you. For a man who preaches so persuasively against giving in to rage, you wield a bone very convincingly."

The priest's guards no longer pretended to look anywhere but straight at her. His charming face lost some of its youthful buoyancy as well. "I am not fool enough to try and fix what I was made to do to you, Domina Kattë. Some things must be left broken, whatever one might wish. But while it is true that all the physical pain that night was borne by you, do not think that proves I did not suffer too. Nothing I have ever done ... was so ... horrific ..." He seemed to have run out of words at last.

"Then, by all the gods there are, why did you do it?" she demanded.

He sighed and looked away into the darkness. "I am fool enough after all, it seems." He turned back to her in obvious frustration. "My lady, the memory of what I was required to do that night will fill me with remorse forever. But I am no more able to outrun the god that we both serve now than are you."

"You have not answered my question." She gazed at him implacably, realizing, as she had not until now, how many questions she needed him to answer if she was to find any peace. "I asked *why*?"

"Why *you*? I do not know. The god makes his choices known to me. He does not explain his reasons. Why *what was done to you*? That I may be able to explain. Some, at least. For it was done to me as well, once." He turned to the guards behind him. "I must speak with this one privately. We will walk up the beach alone. That way." He pointed north. "Tell the people that I'll be back to see them, if they wish to wait. Then make sure that she and I are not disturbed before we're done."

They nodded, some heading past Sian to spread this doubtless unwelcome news to those still waiting behind her, while others headed north into the darkness, to clear the indicated stretch of beach, she supposed.

"I trust you don't expect *us* just to wait here," Reikos said sternly to both Sian and the priest.

Pino nodded grimly in agreement.

"My friends will remain with me," Sian said, no more comfortable than they were with the thought of heading off into the darkness with this man.

The priest looked at her protectors, then shrugged. "Of course. They are welcome." His gaze lingered on Pino. "It may help my wounded brother here to join in this discussion."

He turned and started up the beach, followed by Sian, Reikos and Pino.

"A bone set badly must sometimes be re-broken before it can be healed," the young priest said to Sian as she came abreast of him. "Many things cannot be healed without being broken first. This is among the first and hardest lessons the god taught me. I know you have no cause to pity me, my lady. And I do not ask you to. But my breaking took far longer than a single night, and far more than a single beating." He turned without slowing, to look her in the face. "I would not change what happened to me now, however. Not for all the wealth in Alizar."

"Why not?" she asked. "What happened to you?"

"You do not seem unwell to me now," the young man said, ignoring her question. "You look quite well, in fact. Far better than you did the night you came to me. Nor, from what I hear, have you been left unrewarded for your suffering."

"*What!*" Sian snorted. "Do you mean this *gift* I am afflicted with?"

"The power to heal — yourself as well as others — with a touch is an *affliction*?"

"When all the world wants you punished for it, yes! I live in hiding now. My whole life is gone. My marriage is failing, my business is threatened; the Mishrah-Khote will likely have me killed. I have nothing left and nowhere to go. I cannot walk down the street to buy myself a chicken in peace. I had to sleep beneath an abandoned boat last night, on stones, for fear of being found — by anybody!"

"Your life was long gone on the night we met," the priest said, sounding half-disgusted. "Your marriage was a farce already, and your business had owned *you* for many years."

Sian opened her mouth but found too many words clogged up there to get any out. How could he know any of this? What business of his was it to judge her? After what he had done?

Not that she could claim his assessment was wrong, however. That was the troubling part. Not even she had known herself so well the night they'd met. So, how could he possibly …

"Perhaps you would not have to live in hiding, Domina Kattë, if you were not so frightened of what you've been given." He looked at her again, less angrily. "It is much harder to chase someone who is not running."

"What do you mean? What exactly *have* I been given? I still have no idea what I am supposed to do with this. You called me a messenger that night — to the ruling family — of which I am barely part, as you must know if you know so much else about me. But you left me not a clue about what message I should take them. Or to whom."

"If you had made any effort to deliver it, you would likely have found out by now."

Without thinking, she balled her hand into a fist and slugged him in the shoulder, hard.

He stumbled to one side, gaping at her, as Reikos and Pino lunged to stand between them, unsure, it seemed, of who needed their protection.

"That is what infuriates me!" Sian shouted. "You talk and talk and talk so cleverly — and never say a thing that anyone can understand! You beat me into being your messenger but will not name the message. I ask you simple questions and you respond without giving me an answer. Your big speech back there was utter nonsense! You offered not a single specific goal to all these followers of yours, not even one clear instruction anyone could act on! Do you *know* you are a bag of worthless air? Or are you so caught up in your own performance that you haven't noticed it is empty?"

He stared at her, blinking. "The god has not sent me to tell them what to do," he said at last, clearly still reluctant to come near her. "They already know. The answers are inside them. They have been all along — and the instructions you request are bound to be different for each one of us. There is no *one instruction* I could give them if I wanted to."

"Then what are you for?" she asked, exasperated.

"I am … just to wake them up," he said with a shrug. "To disturb their sleep before the house burns down around their beds and takes them with it. That is all the god requires of me. The rest is his to do, not mine. I am not a god to give anyone instructions."

"Then, what is this new world you want us all to make?" asked Reikos. "Do you even know?"

"Don't you?" the boy-priest asked in turn. Sian felt herself tensing for another swing. Seeming to sense this, the priest added hurriedly, "What did you see — inside yourself — while I was speaking?"

Reikos looked blank for a moment. Then his mouth parted in surprise.

The young priest nodded. "That is the new world. Your part of it, at least. They all saw something as I spoke. Those who hear the god at all. They all come here knowing what the new world looks like. They've just forgotten it is there inside them. They've been trained, quite harshly — whether rich or poor, powerful or helpless — not to look for it. I am here … to make them think again. That is all. They march to remember. They will march until it becomes clear enough again inside them to be acted on. But it is they who will decide, when that time comes. I just serve the god who wants us free. All of us, not just my friends or followers." He shook his head, wide-eyed, frightened even, Sian thought. "I am no dictator to tell others what they should do."

"But you beat her!" Pino rasped. "I trusted you, and you tricked me into bringing you the finest, most admirable person I've ever known. Then you *beat her* into doing what you wanted! How can you say now that —"

"I *did not want to!*" the young man shouted. "It was the only time since I myself was broken that I resisted what the god was asking of me." He looked desperately at Sian. "I had to drink all day. I took things. Powders I have never wished to use as others do, just to lose myself enough to do what was required of me that night. And even then …" His face began to crumple as he struggled not to cry. He grabbed the neckline of his robe and yanked it down to expose his naked chest. "Oh, lady, heal me!" he sobbed. "Take these scars I bear. It costs us *everything* to make the world new! Can you not understand that — even now? Can you not have pity on me too?" She stared, stunned, as he fell to his knees on the sand. "For I cannot forgive myself. I'm sorry. I am sorry; it was what he bade me do. To awaken what you had inside you. But I cannot forget the blows now." He covered his face with his hands, weeping, and pressed his head almost into the sand. "The bone upon your skin. ... I cannot ... set it down."

Hardly of her own volition, Sian bent down and wrapped him in her arms. She felt his body stiffen as she did, and the air filled with the potent scent of ginger. They remained that way for many minutes. Reikos and Pino remained still and silent. None of the priest's guards came to ask them what was happening. It felt as if the world had simply vanished in the darkness.

Eventually, the young priest's weeping subsided, and he gazed up at her with blank incomprehension. She knew that look. She had seen it on the faces of her daughters, when they were still just infants. This boy had been someone's infant too, she realized, feeling heat rush to her eyes and her chest compress, as tears gathered on her own lashes.

"Oh, my lady," sighed the priest.

She nodded, at a loss again. Nothing here was as she had expected. Nothing ever had been. She saw that very clearly now. All she'd learned here was that she had never known until now how much she didn't know.

"Please," she said, rising, then reaching down to pull him up as well. "Can you tell me nothing of what I am meant to do, or what it is that I am sent to tell ... my family?"

He gave her a helpless look, seeming still half elsewhere. "I have rarely known what I was doing either, since the god came for me. I can tell you only this. Stop trying to hide your gift. Stop fearing it — or what others may think or do to you for being what you are. Just use what you've been given openly, and that will lead you to whomever you've been sent to. When you reach them, I think you'll know what the message is. Or they will, even if you don't." He smiled, and gazed at her. "I am sorry, Domina. But that is what it's like to serve a god. I know you did not ask to serve him. Nor did I. And it will not all be pleasant." A shadow of his earlier grief crossed his youthful face again, even as he offered a crooked smile. "But I do not think you will regret this burden in the end. I do not. ... Even less so now." His smile brightened as the fire came back into his eyes. "You are greater than I, my lady. I am only sent to break what's broken. But you will help to heal it. Somehow. Of this, I am quite certain."

Sian looked back at him, knowing she had received all she would find here. "I should let you return to those who wait, then." She turned to leave, then looked back at him. "How can a dead god be served by anyone? What can a dead god want?"

The young priest's smile became wry. "A god is not his body, Domina, any more than you or I are ours. To make the world new, even bodies may be left behind, if necessary."

"Lady, if you'll let me, I would like to stay," Pino said, staring at the priest. Reikos gave the boy a sharp look, but said nothing. "I would serve you," Pino told the priest, "if you'll have me back."

"Thank you, Pino," he replied. "But you should go with Domina Kattë. Knowing that the god's purpose will be fulfilled does not mean she will have no need of protection on her way. I have my guards, as you must have noticed. I would not last a day without them. She will need hers too." He nodded at Reikos. "You and I may meet again, or maybe not. But either way, I hope you'll not let go of whatever you saw earlier. Good luck. To all of you."

He turned then, to walk down the darkened beach alone, leaving Sian and the others to stare after him.

THIRTEEN

Sian walked behind Reikos as they made their careful way back up the cliff-side path; Pino followed her. As they climbed, a fog rolled in, wrapping the island's palm-and-wild banana-fringed bluffs in its muffling embrace. The weather was well suited to their introspective states of mind, Sian thought. The men appeared as lost in private ruminations as she was as they wandered back along the darkened streets of Three Cats, listening to the night-calls of tree frogs and crickets.

What had Reikos seen inside himself during the priest's speech, Sian wondered. And why had she seen nothing — except suspicions of deceit? She still wasn't sure what she had done to that young man when she had held him in her arms. Though she had felt no echoing 'pain,' the memory of all that ginger told her that her gift had been employed to some effect. But how, exactly? She had never asked him who he was, or where he had really come from, or even what his name was ... She had meant to, but her whole life seemed to steer itself these days. Or it was being steered. Was that not what he had suggested at the end? Not a completely new thought, or a comforting one. She recalled again the frightening, haunted-eyed child she had seen on Pembo's Beach ... had that been just this morning?

"I ... I hate to say this." Sian broke their silence at last. "But I am rather hungry again."

Pino laughed, then pretended he had just been clearing his throat.

"We'll find another tavern," said Reikos, still uncharacteristically withdrawn. "And another runner-cart. If we wish to reach *Fair Passage* before dawn."

"What time is it, do you think?"

"Too late to be walking all the way to Cutter's," Reikos said. "Pino, while I find someplace to feed our lady, would you mind going to see if you can find a cart for hire somewhere at this hour? We will meet you back here in, say, half an hour?"

"Gladly," Pino said, already jogging off.

"So, what did the priest's new world look like?" Sian asked when he was gone. "To you."

Reikos turned to her, surprised, she thought, and gave her a long look. "You were in it. I can tell you that much."

She drew a startled breath, and looked away. So, he did still want her. She had suspected as much. Was that a problem? How big a problem? She was not sure — of anything right now. She shook her head without intending to, feeling exposed. This was not a conversation she was ready for. Not tonight, with everything else she had just been through.

"More than that, I do not know quite how to describe to you," said Reikos, looking off into the misty night as well. "Perhaps we should be looking for that tavern, eh?"

Before she could answer, they heard the sound of running feet. A second later, Pino came dashing toward them out of the swirling fog.

"You've already found a cart?" Reikos called.

Pino shook his head urgently, bringing a finger to his lips to silence them. "There's a squad of soldiers coming," he panted. "Not the temple, but not just some patrol either, my lady. They're searching for something."

Instantly, Sian recalled the murmurs passed behind her when the priest had named her. Or had their cart runners earlier been less disinterested than they'd seemed?

Pino gave Sian a worried look. "I think we better go, and fast."

Reikos grabbed her hand and started pulling her away.

"No, stop." She took her hand back. "You both heard what the god's priest told me." It was perhaps the only clear thing he had said to her all night. "I am done running. I am done following fear. Let us find that tavern, just as we had planned."

"Don't be mad!" said Reikos. "This is not what he meant."

"What did he mean, then?"

"He also asked us to protect you!" Pino pled. "He can't have meant you should just give yourself to them."

"I'm not giving myself to anyone," she answered, wondering if men *ever* learned to listen. "I'm just doing what I had set out to do, and letting them do whatever they are meant to. If that is finding me, and this god allows it, I'll go with them and see if our young prophet was correct."

"Sian, please!" Reikos reached again to take her hand, but she withdrew it from him.

"Which way are they coming from, Pino?"

He pointed back behind him.

"Then we'll start looking for our tavern this way," Sian said, starting off in the opposite direction. "Are you coming, gentlemen?"

"Oh, she is a handful," Reikos sighed.

"Don't I know it," Pino muttered. "I worked for her, remember?"

Sian arched a brow in amusement. The first disparaging words she'd ever heard him speak — about herself, at least. Could the boy be growing up at last?

They had walked hardly more than two blocks before the fog parted in front of them again to reveal a party of five armed men. Not Mishrah-Khote — these wore short leather skirts and body armor, cap helmets, and carried pikes.

Reikos turned to Pino. "I thought you said —"

"This isn't them," Pino said under his breath.

Two patrols? Sian thought. From the Factorate this time, if their unusually fancy armor was any indication. Could she have come to seem this dangerous to everyone already?

"Halt!" shouted their commanding officer, identified by his elegant uniform, lace collar, and feather crested leather helmet.

"My lady, would you be Domina Sian Katë, of Little Loom Eyot?"

Ah well. She only sighed as Reikos pulled her close, almost shoving her behind him while Pino drew in toward her other side.

"What do you want?" Reikos growled.

Sian felt him reach for something underneath his coat, and grabbed his arm to stop him. Weapons were the last thing any of them needed now.

"I am," she told the man. "May I know why the Factorate sees fit to honor me with such a well-armed escort? Have you some cause to be concerned about my safety?"

"I am Prefect-Sergeant Ennias," said the grim-faced young officer. "We've been ordered to find you in regard to a complaint filed by your husband, Arouf Monde."

"*Arouf*? That's ridiculous. What could he possibly ..." But then, what might he *not* do? Now. The Factorate did not serve complaints, however. She knew that much. Could this officer be lying, or were they working with the Mishrah-Khote priests? What a strange union that would be.

"May I know the nature of this complaint?" Sian asked, her heart pounding.

The sergeant reached underneath his surcoat and withdrew a sealed envelope, which he held out to her.

"Don't touch it, Sian," said Reikos. "I'd wager my boat it is a trap of some kind."

"The matter requires immediate attention, I'm afraid," the sergeant said.

"One has five days to answer complaints," she said, ever more alarmed. Nothing about this transaction was at all correct.

"I tell you, do not touch it," Reikos warned again.

"We are three against five," she told him levelly. *Not to mention they are far better armed than we are, whatever you've got concealed in that coat.* She stepped from behind him and reached for the envelope. *Don't hide. Don't fear.* That's what the priest had said. *Even bodies can be left behind, if necessary.* He had said that too, of course ... "Thank you, Sergeant."

She opened the envelope and removed two folded sheets of cream-colored paper.

"I cannot read this in the dark."

Ennias signaled to one of his pikemen, who brought out a small punk-torch and lit it. The glow was irregular and flickering, but sufficient.

She scanned the document, expecting the flowery language of the Mishrah-Khote, but no. "What in the..."

"What is it?" Reikos leaned in.

"It's from Arouf."

"Did he not say so?"

"No, I mean this letter is from him directly, in his own hand." Sian held the papers out to Reikos, whose face darkened as he read.

"That wretched...infidelity and abandonment? Who have you abandoned?"

Sian flushed with anger, and some embarrassment, her mind racing. She knew things were badly broken with Arouf, but ... They'd had an understanding, after all, of sorts. Of course they did.

Prefect-Sergeant Ennias cleared his throat. "You are to come with me, Domina Kattë."

Sian looked up at the man, startled. "Certainly not. I see no arrest warrant here. I will compose my response and answer the complaint in the usual statutory time." She glanced at Reikos and Pino, then took a confident step forward, moving to brush past the armed guards.

Four long pikes were raised to stop her.

"Has the lady not made herself clear?" Reikos growled. "You are outside the law." He took a step toward Sian and two of the raised pikes were turned on him.

Before Sian could draw breath to object, Pino came hurtling past her with a cry of rage and, to her horror, a knife raised in his hand.

"No! Pino, stop!" she shouted.

To his credit, he got close enough to slash the forearm of one disbelieving pikeman before a second whirled to thrust his weapon into Pino's side. The boy crumpled to the ground.

"Pino!" Sian screamed.

She lunged to touch him, but the sergeant grabbed her arm. Reikos pulled, of all things, a hand-cannon from underneath his coat and aimed it at the sergeant's head.

"Are you serious?" asked the astonished sergeant. "You're as likely to kill her as me with that reckless weapon. Or yourself."

"I've had lots of practice with it, lad," Reikos said. "Enough to take the chance, if you insist."

"Stop it!" Sian said. "All of you! I will come with you, Sergeant. Reikos, put that stupid toy away, or I promise you, this is the last time we will ever speak. I mean it."

Reikos gave her a desperate look, then seemed to wilt. No sooner had he lowered his weapon than two of the sergeant's men rushed in to bind his hands behind his back.

"Sergeant, please. I must see to Pino," Sian begged. Pino had begin to writhe and flail, clutching at his wound, his mouth stretched open in a cry of voiceless anguish.

Ennias did not release Sian's arm. For all his effete clothing, the man's grip seemed made of iron. "Is it true that you can heal, then?"

"Yes! Please let me help the boy. Look at how he suffers."

"Heal my man first." Ennias let go and shoved her forward, towards the wounded guard.

The man's arm bled, but it still seemed just a cut. He stood there looking almost unconcerned, if slightly curious as she approached. It made her angry that she should be forced to waste her time on him when Pino's wound was so clearly far more serious. Still, the faster it was done, the sooner she would be allowed to help Pino.

She placed her hands upon the pikeman's arm, weaving her fingers through the slash in his pathetic, ceremonial leather grieve until her fingers touched his skin. She pressed the edges of his shallow laceration together as best she could, and willed it closed. The pain in her own forearm was sharp but brief, the smell of ginger almost too faint to detect. A very minor cut, as she had suspected. Pino had begin to moan aloud now.

The soldier looked down at his arm in wonder. "Gods and little fishes!" he exclaimed. "She did it!" He twisted his wrist to flex the arm experimentally. "I'm fit as ever, Sergeant."

"Good," Ennias said, seeming less surprised than most folk had thus far. "Let's go." He pulled a short span of rope off of his belt, and came to tie Sian's hands.

"Wait!" she protested. "What about Pino?"

"The sooner we get where we're going, without any further trouble," he glared pointedly at Reikos, "the sooner you can see to him as well, my lady."

"Bastard!" Reikos snarled.

"No! Sergeant, look at him! He cannot travel in such condition. Where are you —"

"Joreth, get the cart, please," Ennias said dispassionately, then turned back to Sian. "I've spent time on lots of battlefields, my lady, and seen lots of wounds. The boy will live. He may not be very comfortable, but he should have thought of that before he rushed at my men with a knife."

"Oh, Pino," Sian moaned, twisting to look down at him. "Reckless boy. Don't think of leaving me before I am allowed to touch you." In the distance, she heard heavy wooden wheels rumbling toward them. "I will not forgive you if you die."

∾

Sian sat chained at wrists and ankles to the wall of the cramped and sooty cart. Pino was chained in front of her, tantalizingly out of reach, and mercifully unconscious for some time now. Reikos sat lashed to the opposite wall, staring into space as the cart rumbled along. Half a dozen more soldiers had joined the party after they had been apprehended — the first patrol Pino had spotted, Sian supposed.

"Is *this* your god's path we are on?" Reikos sighed.

Tears stung Sian's eyes. "How am I to know? Maybe I am being brought to heal the Factor's son."

"In chains?" Reikos shook his head, and looked away again. "I am sorry, Sian. I have failed you terribly."

"How? This is in no way your doing."

"If I had not pulled that damned hand-cannon out, well ..." A rueful little smile came, and vanished. "I would still have it, for one thing. And I might still be a free man now, able to help you and Pino somehow. Instead of being chained up like a worthless sack of meat in here."

"Hush," said Sian. "If anyone's at fault, it is the woman who refused to flee when you and Pino told her to." She blinked away her tears and looked at Pino. His wound looked ugly: dark, sluggish blood now saturated patches of his light canvas pants and jacket. He gasped for breath in his unnatural sleep — when he seemed to breathe at all. "They will let me touch you soon," she whispered. *I hope.*

"I will still get us out of this," said Reikos.

"How?"

He turned to gaze out at the dark street receding behind them. "Somehow."

She followed his gaze, trying to calculate how much longer it might take them to reach the Factorate House. Then she looked again more closely. Weren't they going in the wrong direction? Instead of heading toward the bridge to Hither, on their way to Home, the cart seemed pointed back toward the center of Cutter's. "Where are they taking us?"

Her question was answered not ten minutes later, as they pulled through the lavishly scrolled and gilded ironwork gates of the Census Hall's gardens and up the long crushed-shell driveway, finally rumbling to a halt in its paved forecourt. The building's imposing, continental architecture loomed ghostly above them against the moonlit sky, seeming, for all its size and grandeur, somehow huddled nonetheless against the even darker jungle towering around it.

"They've brought us to my cousin Escotte's home," she said, bewildered.

"The Census Taker?" Reikos asked.

She nodded.

Prefect-Sergeant Ennias appeared at the back of their cart, climbing in with keys in hand. "All right then, come along." He bent to unlock Sian's chains from the cart wall.

"May I heal Pino now?"

"Soon enough," he said, as a second guard climbed into the cart to stand over Reikos. "We'll bring him to you just as soon as you're inside with no more trouble, understood?"

"What about me?" Reikos asked.

"You're fine where you are, for now," the sergeant said.

"You told us you were from the Factorate," said Sian.

"Did I?" The sergeant straightened, pulling Sian up beside him. "Let's get going now."

Sian was helped out of the wagon by two more soldiers, much less roughly than she had been loaded in, and marched off toward the elegant hall's wide marble steps, flanked by the sergeant and three other men, rubbing at her chain-chafed wrists.

"If you had simply come with us as asked, my lady," the sergeant told her, sounding abashed now for some reason, "all that could have been avoided. You're not actually in any trouble, I don't think."

"*What?*" She gaped at him.

"Your arrest was just for show, in case anyone was watching." He shook his head and glanced back at the wagon. "Damn shame about the boy. What a stupid thing. Unfortunately, I'm not sure how much I can do for either of them now. They did threaten and assault a Factorate embassy. But I will try, my lady."

"Whatever do you mean?" Sian demanded. "This was some kind of ruse? And yet you will not let me heal Pino? What insanity is this?"

"Sian! My darling cousin!" She whirled about to see Escotte Alkattha, Alizar's second most powerful official after only the Factor himself, beaming down at her from atop the flight of stairs. He'd come to greet her dressed as if for a formal ball, in falls of purple silk shot through with silver thread. The fabric glimmered in the darkness as he started down with arms spread wide in welcome. The elegant effect was somewhat undermined by the golden squirrel monkey perched on his left shoulder, wrapping its tail around his neck as though to strangle him.

Steps away, Escotte stopped, his smile fading. "You look simply wretched."

Sian looked down to discover that her dress had gotten soiled and ripped somewhere during their transport here, probably as she'd been *helped* into or out of that filthy wagon. Another of her best silks ruined. She must stop over-dressing for these beatings.

"Come here, come here. What's happened to you?" Escotte frowned down at the sergeant as Sian came up to stand beside him. The monkey bared its teeth at her and retreated to the opposite shoulder. "Explain her condition, Sergeant."

"There was unexpected trouble, sir." The sergeant stared calmly at nothing as he spoke. He didn't even seem to sweat, despite the sultry night. "We found your cousin in the company of two male companions who mistook our intentions and attacked our men." Escotte put his hands against his hips and tisked in apparent exasperation, though whether with the sergeant or with Sian's companions, she was uncertain. "It was necessary to restrain all three of them, sir — to get them here without further risk."

"You *restrained* my cousin?" Escotte gasped, incredulous.

"It doesn't matter, Escotte," Sian said. "It was clearly just a great misunderstanding, as he has said. But one of my friends is badly injured, and the sergeant ..." She aborted what she'd been about to say, hopeful that the man might really try to help Reikos and Pino if she didn't antagonize him further now. "I have had no chance to heal him yet. May I do so now? Please?"

"Heal him?" Escotte said. "So these dreadful rumors I have heard are true, my dear?" He studied her, then grinned. "How fascinating." He turned back to Ennias. "You heard her, Sergeant. Bring the man to us immediately."

The officer gave Escotte a stiff nod, and went to do as ordered.

"Oh, thank you, cousin," Sian said, washed in relief.

"For what?" he asked, all graciousness again. "This is quite convenient, really. I have been hoping to see a demonstration of this ... new talent you are credited with. Now it will not be necessary to have someone injured." He tittered briefly at her shocked expression. "It would not have been a serious injury, of course. We have known each other all our lives, Sian! You cannot think me such a monster. A pricked finger. Something trivial. That is all I meant." He glanced off toward the forecourt, where several soldiers were hoisting Pino's limp body from the cart. "Oh, *he* does not look well, though, does he."

"Escotte, what is going on here?" Sian struggled to control her resurging anger. "The sergeant says that my arrest was just a ruse. Why would you do such a thing? We were frightened out of our minds. My friends would never have attacked your men if we had simply known that you had sent them!"

"Oh, dear cousin!" He threw his arms into the air and rolled his eyes. The monkey hissed and scrabbled onto his back, clutching at his fine robe. "You can have no idea what a wasps' nest you have stumbled into! None at all. I will explain it all to you, of course. But that will take some time, and they are coming with your friend now." He patted her shoulder and drew back to watch as the guardsmen arrived to lay Pino's body on the steps at Sian's feet.

His pallor was ghastly. She could not tell if he was breathing anymore at all.

She fell to her knees, shoving both hands down onto the awful gash at one side of his stomach, steeling herself for the —

Even braced for it as she was, the pain was astonishing. It was all she could do to keep her hands in place and still hold onto consciousness. An involuntary moan escaped her lips, as if the injured boy were moaning through her, like some carnival ventriloquist. As the stench of ginger became stifling, all strength fled Sian's body, leaving her to sprawl face down across Pino's torso. Her only remaining thought was for keeping her hands on his wound.

"Domina …?" Pino groaned, squinting down at her, then up at all the others, clearly trying to make sense of where he was, and what was happening. "My lady … what …"

"Amazing!" Escotte cried, rushing in to take a closer look. Dark, congealed blood still clung to Pino's clothes and skin, but the wound itself had knit back together as if stitched by expert chirurgeons. Already, just a small white scar remained to mark the spot. "I must admit that I did not believe what I was hearing — but it's true!" He beamed down at Sian, who was only just recovering enough to raise her head again. "Cousin, we have so much to catch up on. And I'm sure you have at least as much to tell me as I have to share with you. Come, come. Oh. Are you unable to rise?" He looked impatiently at all the men still staring down in awe at Pino. "Don't just stand there, you louts! Help my cousin up! She cannot be left here in a pile on my front steps after such a feat. We must take her to her quarters to revive in comfort. Hurry!" Two soldiers came to grasp Sian beneath the arms, and prop her on her feet as best they could. "Sergeant, please find my cousin's two companions suitable quarters as well. I believe you know the ones I mean."

Ennias nodded once again, though Sian thought he looked quite unhappy. Was that because Reikos and Pino weren't to be arrested after all? She could not focus on the question long enough to wonder further. It was all she could do to navigate the spacious marble steps ahead of her — even with two strong men doing more than half the work. "You will … take good care of them," she managed to tell Escotte as she was carried past him. "Won't you?"

"Please don't concern yourself, my dear," Escotte offered her an absent wave. "You will all be quite safe now."

Safe, she thought. *At last.* What a blessed word.

This late at night, the grand receiving room and public offices of the Census Hall were dark, though Sian was unable to pay much attention to her surroundings. They passed through a few more gilded rooms, and several stairways, the first few grander than the later ones. There were glimpses of crystal and flashes of mirror, and soft voices, and soft hands. Somewhere along the way, the scent and stiffness of leather armor and brass studs had been replaced by the swirl and swish of silk dresses trimmed in lace. Finally, the blessed softness of a mattress stuffed with down. The smooth, cool weight of linen sheets. She wanted to thank the people helping her, but she had such trouble keeping her eyes open anymore.

Safe, she thought again as sleep pressed her further into the delightful bedding. What threat could touch her now, tucked safely inside her cousin's home? A man even more powerful than the Mishrah-Khote's highest priests. And all at once the young priest's words came back to her. She would have laughed if she'd possessed the strength to. She had stopped running, just as he'd instructed, and been led straight into the highest circles of Alizar's elite, just as he'd predicted. How clever that boy was. How modest, really. *Now,* she wondered, *whatever will this message I am bearing prove to be…?*

FOURTEEN

Sian awakened in a lovely room, all spun sugar, cream, and gleaming gold. Even the light glowing from beyond the foot of her bed seemed to have a golden cast. And what a delightful bed it was.

Tap tap tap.

Sian raised her head just far enough to glance about. She saw a gilded door. That was what had awakened her; someone knocking at her door. But where was this? Not home; not her townhouse. Then she remembered.

Escotte! She was … "Come in?" Sian drew the covers up around her modestly.

The door cracked gently open, just far enough to admit a pretty face framed in lustrous dark hair pulled back in pearls, and a shoulder draped in pale blue silk. "Domina Kattë? Good morning. I am Cleone, your maid. Would you prefer to sleep a while longer?"

"I … What time is it?"

"Too late for breakfast, and too early for lunch." The woman smiled impishly. "Though I can bring either to your bedside if you wish."

Food! What a *wonderful* idea. "I will have both, I think." Sian gave the maid an impish smile of her own. "If you don't mind."

The maid blinked at her. "Both, my lady?"

"Breakfast *and* lunch, please. I'm feeling … rather peckish."

The young woman brought a graceful hand up to her mouth and giggled, then gave Sian a nod and disappeared again, pulling the door closed without a sound behind her.

Sian grinned in pure delight, stretched luxuriously, then threw back her covers to find herself wrapped in a white silk nightgown woven out of air itself, if she was any judge. And who would be a better judge of fabric than she? She stood up and looked around for the dress she had arrived in. It was nowhere to be seen, which was not surprising, she supposed, given its condition by the time she'd gotten here.

She wandered to the room's great, delicately partitioned windows, and gazed down at a garden full of gorgeous orchids and hibiscus. There was a marble fountain filled with flowering lilies, a graceful stand of carefully manicured date palms, and, in another corner of the courtyard, a fig tree heavy with ripe fruit. Luridly blooming bougainvillea crawled up the opposite wall, almost too bright to look at. A large frilled lizard clung to the wall as well, several stories up.

Safe, she thought again, and sighed.

The gentle tapping came again.

"Come in." She took no care to cover herself this time.

It was the maid, as she'd suspected.

"Would my lady like to dress before her meal, or eat first?"

"I seem to have no clothes," Sian said, gesturing around the room.

"Oh, but no one will have shown you yet! How silly of me. May I enter?"

"Of course," Sian replied, unused to such deference.

The maid swept in and walked briskly to what seemed nothing but one more of many gilded panels on the room's walls. When she pushed this panel with her fingers, however, it issued a soft click, then swung outward to reveal an entire closet full of dresses, which Sian saw instantly were … really rather hideous.

Everything was both far too elaborate and many years behind the times, as if someone had stuffed all the ladies at some dreadful coronation ball into this little space fifteen or twenty years ago, then locked the door and left them until everything had rotted away except their dresses. Where in all of Alizar, Sian wondered, had her cousin acquired these? And why ever had he kept them?"

"I … will eat first, I believe," Sian told the maid.

Clearly perceiving her dismay, the maid said, "These are what your cousin had sent up, my lady. But, if you wish, I am sure he will not mind if I find something … simpler?"

"That would be lovely, if you're sure he wouldn't mind." Sian had no wish to risk insulting her host — at the best of times, much less right now.

"I will bring the food, then," said Cleone, "and go find you something nice to wear while you are eating, if that is acceptable?"

"Thank you. Yes."

The maid smiled, and ducked out of the room again. A moment later she was back, pushing the door wide to drag in a silver cart barely narrow enough to fit through. It was laden with more elaborate confections, more smoked and salted meats and fish, more fresh-baked breads and cunning little rolls, more savory cheeses and delicately sliced and sugared fruits and nuts than Sian had ever seen. And a whole rack of lovely wines and morning cordials, plus — naturally — a silver pot of kava with a matching pitcher of heavy cream. She raised both hands to her face in wonder, and laughed aloud.

"Is anything amiss, my lady?" Cleone asked. "Do you require something more?"

"Oh no." She laughed again. "This will keep me very busy for a while."

"I will go then," Cleone said happily, already moving toward the door with brisk efficiency. "But I will not be long." She turned to point over her shoulder at a velvet pull hanging in the corner. "If you require anything before I'm back, just tug at that."

"I'll be fine, Cleone. Thank you. Very much."

"Your pleasure is my own." And the girl was gone again.

True to her word, Cleone returned not fifteen minutes later. When Sian bade her enter, she walked in with arms full of silk and various other accoutrements, set them on the bed, turned to say something to Sian, and saw the virtually empty meal cart. Her mouth dropped open as she cast a startled glance around the room, as if all that food might merely have been moved for some strange reason.

Sian could not help grinning. "I have a very healthy appetite these days."

Recalling herself, Cleone snapped her mouth closed, and lowered her eyes in chagrin. "Would my lady like to sample something more?" she asked demurely.

Sian shook her head. "Not until it's time for lunch, at least."

Cleone arched her brows, then allowed herself to grin as well. "Shall we see then if the dress I've brought is any more to your liking?"

"Please," Sian said, thinking it could hardly be much worse.

Cleone shook out and held up a simple shift in light green silk with accents and delicate piping in darker emerald.

Sian sighed in relief. "It's perfect. Thank you."

"Very well. Let's get my lady dressed then," Cleone chirruped.

They had hardly finished when a less delicate knock came at Sian's door. "Cousin? Are you decent?" Escotte called. "I am extremely eager to continue last night's conversation."

Sian nodded to Cleone, who went to admit him.

Escotte entered in a robe all stripes and paisleys, mauve and gray and charcoal. Less glimmer but more ruffles than the previous night's attire; it didn't clash as badly with the monkey. "You may leave us," he said to Cleone, who dropped him an unsmiling curtsy and left without a word. "So, my dear Sian. How did you sleep? Well, I hope?"

"Quite well, cousin. Thank you. The bed is marvelous, as is Cleone and every other aspect of the hospitality I've been shown here."

"Good," he said, then paused to examine her with a frown. "You did not find the dresses I had sent to you?"

"Oh! Why ... yes, of course. Cleone showed them to me right away. But they seemed far to nice to waste just wandering around my room here. I assumed they were for some special occasion? Dinner perhaps?" Escotte still looked ... hurt? "I'm honored by your thoughtfulness," Sian rushed to add, "but I asked Cleone to find me something simpler — just to loaf around in. You don't mind, do you?"

He shrugged. "Of course not. Those were just some old things Víolethe left behind."

"Oh." That would explain it. His wife's taste had always run toward excess. "Is Víolethe not here? She is well, I hope?"

"She is fine, and will be pleased to hear that I have seen you looking in such good health as well, despite your, er, clothing and all." Escotte went to pour himself a little glass of morning cordial from one of the un-emptied bottles on her breakfast cart. He studied the decimated cart with interest, then turned to give Sian a curious look as the monkey hopped down and started looking through the empty dishes. "My wife does not so often reside here on the islands anymore," Escotte added, going to sit in the room's most spacious chair, arranging his robes with care, lest some important pleat or panel be crushed. "Víolethe seems to prefer cooler climes now. I suspect it's something to do with the change." He made a dismissive little gesture of distaste.

"The change?" Sian asked, unsure whether this was just a vague reference to Alizar's troubled economic condition, or some part of the 'wasps' nest' he'd referred to last night.

"You know." He laid a hand against his groin. "These sudden spells of heat that overtake her at all hours. I can understand how Alizar's warm climate might exacerbate … all that."

Sian tried not to look too startled — or to laugh. "And how are your children?"

"All well," he said, sipping at his cordial. "Kareen is to be married in a fortnight. I am sorry we were unable to invite you, but, given my position, the guest list is already as horrific as you might imagine, and times being as they are…"

"Of course," she murmured. She had not invited any of her cousins to Maleen's wedding either, if only because they were all so much more important than she was that she had wanted to spare them the discomfort of having to decline.

There was a crash as the monkey toppled a chafing-dish. "Gigi, no," Escotte scolded. The monkey returned to his shoulder — sulking, Sian was sure of it.

"How are Reikos and Pino this morning?" she asked, wondering suddenly why they had not yet come to see her.

"Who?"

"My companions. From last night. Does Pino still seem well?"

"Oh! Yes, his health was really quite remarkable this morning. That was quite a marvel, dear. I, myself, am still recovering, just from the astonish-ment."

"Could I prevail upon you to invite them up to see me when we're done?"

"Sadly, that will not be possible. They are no longer here."

"*What?* Where would they have gone?"

"As I believe I mentioned to you last night, dear, though I well under-stand why you might not remember, we are all embroiled at the moment in a tangle of very delicate dilemmas. Now that he is reassured of your safety, your good captain has agreed to help us *navigate*, if you'll excuse the pun, one of our more urgent peccadilloes. He and his young crewman set sail very early this —"

"No!" she gasped. "That isn't possible! Without even saying goodbye? I can't believe —"

"You were sound asleep, my dear," Escotte calmly interjected. "We all concurred that, given everything you've been through these past few days, it would be best to let you have your rest. They did ask me to convey their deepest affection, of course, and their delight at your newfound security here. I would tell you more about what they have gone to do, but it is all extremely hush-hush. And to be honest, it is almost as important to have them safely off the streets of Alizar right now as it is to keep your presence here a secret. You have acquired enemies, my dear, to my amazement, and until all this can be sorted out, your two friends know far too much about you for their own safety."

"What are all these games about, Escotte?" she demanded. "First it's false arrest. Then Pino nearly dead. Now you're telling me that my two dearest friends have just disappeared mysteriously in the night, without a word to me? I'm sorry, cousin. While I am deeply grateful for your help, I must insist that someone tell me what is really happening."

"But, my dear Sian, that is precisely what I've come to do." He gave her a patient smile. "If you will but allow me to." He sat back and took another sip of cordial, then ruffled the monkey's fur. "I've been waiting half the morning for you to be up and finished with your ... breakfast." He gave her naked cart another glance. "Such an appetite, my dear. Did the temple fail to feed you very well?"

"You knew I was there?"

"Not until your two friends informed us of it. Though we had begun to fear something of the sort. There have been so many disturbing rumors circulating."

"Then I assume they also told you I was tortured there — before they left, I mean?" She had no idea anymore which of her proliferating questions to pursue first.

"Yes," he said, setting his glass down with a grimace. "How absolutely dreadful for you. Clearly we were not a moment too soon in gathering you to safety here."

"But why do it that way, Escotte? I still don't understand. If your men had simply told us they were sent to offer refuge, I'd have thrown myself into their arms, and Pino never would have suffered so for trying to protect me."

"I've been trying to contact you more directly for days, my dear," Escotte protested. "I've sent letters to your home on Little Loom Eyot, your town-house on Viel. I even sent inquiries to your daughter on Malençon. Forgive me, I've suddenly misplaced her name."

"Maleen."

"Yes, of course: Maleen. But when you did not respond, I began to think that you were hiding. From *me*. Your own cousin." He placed a hand against his heart, looking wounded. "With all these nasty stories I've been hearing, what was I to think? I confess, it even crossed my mind to wonder if you really might have fallen into league with that fanatic priest." He gave her a sidelong glance. "The one who leads this new cult of the Butchered God." He seemed to shiver in revulsion at the thought, and got up to pour himself another drink, putting a hand on the monkey's tail as though to keep it in place. "Anything for you, dear?"

"No. Thank you. I am quite satisfied."

"With all due respect for our beleaguered Factor," Escotte said, returning to his chair, "Viktor really stuck his foot in that one. It's the influence of that foreign bride of his." He shook his head again. "Of all the bizarre things to do. I ask you. Cutting up the creature's body, and —"

"From what little I am able to observe, our Factor tends to be a very practical man," Sian interjected, unsure why she suddenly felt so protective of this Factor she had never met. "In a nation with so many hungry people, he may have thought only to demonstrate his concern for the poor by making the best use of a sudden, large supply of edible meat." She shrugged. "They ate it, didn't they? Perhaps they agreed with him." She hoped the dead god would not be irritated with her for speaking of him this way. But his own followers were still eating that flesh, if she was not mistaken.

"I am not so sure what the poor are thinking these days, cousin." Escotte studied her again. "I assume you aren't."

She shook her head in confusion. "You assume I'm not what? Sure what the poor are thinking?"

"In league with that fanatic priest, I mean."

Sian stared at him, caught off guard — again. She had been anything but in league with him, until just last night. This morning … This was nothing she wished to parse right now. Least of all with Escotte. "Please refresh my memory," she said, trying to sound exasperated. "Who was reminding me just last night that we have known each other all our lives? Have I ever seemed the slightest bit religious, *cousin*?"

"You never seemed a miracle worker either, *cousin*. Yet, now …" He raised his hands uncertainly. "I would, of course, be fascinated to hear your version of exactly how this remarkable new skill of yours was acquired. The rumors I have heard, of course, but I've been reserving judgment for this opportunity to ask you directly."

"Well, if you've heard that the fanatic priest you fear I'm in league with beat this power into me somehow with a giant bone, then you know the truth of it as well as I do. But, once again, Escotte, I ask you why you'd think me likely to conspire with someone who had nearly murdered me, and shattered my whole life. Just tell me plainly. Was I really brought here for my own protection, or am I under arrest after all?"

"Cousin, if I wished to arrest you, you'd have been locked up in my dungeon long before the Mishrah-Khote had so much as time to think of throwing you in theirs. You are here because a world of urgent issues seems suddenly to pivot around you, of all people, and it unnerved me greatly to have so lost track of you these past few days. I have no desire to lose track of you again. Does that make me a jailer?" He gave her what was doubtless meant to be an ingratiating smile; Gigi bared her teeth as well, in ghoulish mimicry of her master. "You are here because you matter deeply to myself and to the Factor. And your friends have been sent off to do something useful *elsewhere* as much for their own safety as for any other reason."

Sian paced over to stare out the window, trying to digest all this. "So what is this world of urgent issues you keep alluding to? I am so tired of mysteries and riddles. You have no idea."

"But I do," he said. "Mysteries and riddles are my entire life, dear cousin. I empathize. More profoundly than you might expect. So allow me to lay things out for you."

"Please do," she said, turning to face him again.

"First, there is a longstanding power struggle between the Factorate and the Mishrah-Khote, which is coming to one of its periodic crisis points just now — in part because of the Factor's unfortunate handling of this so-called Butchered God affair."

"I know something about that power struggle," Sian said. "It was brought to my attention in some detail while I was imprisoned at the temple. I understand that I am something of an embarrassment to the Mishrah-Khote — and a threat to their prestige."

"Good!" Escotte said. "That saves us some time. But do you understand that you are also problematic for the Factor?"

"Me? Why?"

"His son is very, very sick, as you have doubtless heard."

"And here I am!" she said. "You've seen what I can do. Take me to him, and I'll heal his son. How is this a problem for him?"

"Oh, dear cousin," he chortled. "How lovely it must be to live in such a simple, sheltered world."

"*Simple? Sheltered?* What part of 'beaten, imprisoned and tortured' seems *sheltered* to you?"

"The part that's free to go on day to day and year to year imagining no threats larger than those leveled at yourself, Sian." He was no longer smiling. "My world, and the Factor's, are both filled with threats aimed not just at us personally, but at an entire nation full of people. Right now, Sian, the Factor's feet are made almost entirely of clay. Was that explained to you at the temple also?"

She shook her head.

"I am relieved to hear it," Escotte said. "Though I'm not innocent enough to hope they do not know it there as well as I do."

"What feet of clay?" She felt suddenly ridiculous, despite all she had been through.

"Our economy is crashing, cousin. Surely you're aware of that much, given your modest but reportedly solid skill at business. This, and Viktor's foolish handling of that giant body on the beach two years ago, has helped accelerate the deterioration of our nation's social fabric as well, which was a fairly rotten cloth already, if you ask me. In such times, the tension between Factorate and temple always rises, but the addition of this Butchered God cult has thrown all the usual stops in that tug-of-war completely out of balance — not to mention drawing more and more of our already faltering labor force away from their constructive employment to go marching 'round the streets all day instead. As you may imagine, dear, neither Alizar's other leading families nor its continental allies are very satisfied with Viktor's performance at the moment." He turned to pin her with his gaze. "And if House Alkattha falls from power, *cousin*, we all fall with it. Had you considered any of that during your little skirts with trouble these past few days?"

Sian had forgotten how good Escotte was at shaming people when he chose to.

"If Viktor should fall while Alizar's economic and social affairs are in such disarray," Escotte continued, "there will be a struggle for dominance between at least half a dozen other leading families here, such as Alizar has not seen since the rebellion. Many of them are already jostling for position at the starting line of that disaster. It is even rumored that Lady Sark is finally considering Patterin Orlon's longstanding marriage proposal, in hopes of strengthening her own position in this race. You think Alizar a quiet, peaceful nation, don't you? Everybody has, for so long now. I doubt that you have any notion just how quickly this could change. And not just for *you*, and *me*, and our small but thus far fortunate little family."

"I had no idea things were so bad," she said.

Escotte drew a deep, unhappy breath. "And you could be the detail that sets match to powder here, Sian, in either of two ways.

"On the one hand, if the Factor's only heir should die, the other Houses — Orlon, Suba, perhaps even Phaero — would almost certainly not wait for Viktor to die too before swooping to displace him, and the chaos I've described would ignite immediately.

"But bringing you openly into the Factorate House to keep the Factor's heir from dying, thereby defying and humiliating the Mishrah-Khote at this already delicate moment in their relations, would be tantamount to declaring war between Factorate and temple, which might also tip the balance far enough to give the other families their excuse to lunge.

"Compounding this is the apparent fact that, willingly or not, your new power seems to be derived from the Butchered God's fanatic cult leader. Any appearance of alignment between the Factorate and that madman, however insubstantial, might well get the Factor and his foreign consort immediately beheaded, for all I know — political process be damned." He leaned back into his chair and smiled at her. "Such a quandary, eh, dear cousin? Damned if he doesn't let you heal his heir, and damned if he does. Can you see now why I couldn't even risk that someone in the shadows last night might have overheard *Our Lady of the Islands* being invited to take refuge with the Census Taker? Even if we are related. The Mishrah-Khote has eyes and ears in every shrub and pillar, as you must understand all too well by now, my dear."

She nodded, though her head still swirled with the complexity of it. "So what can be done? Am I to heal the Factor's son or not?"

"Oh, it is crucial that you heal him, of course. But first, some way must be devised to do it so that the Mishrah-Khote, which has more eyes and ears inside the Factorate House than anywhere in Alizar but their own temple, can never find a shred of evidence that you were ever there, or in any way involved." He leaned forward again. "I fear you must be prepared to absorb yet another indignity, my dear. However all this is arranged, your success in healing young Konrad will almost certainly be credited to the temple priests who have attended him so ineffectually so far. Can you bear it, do you think?"

She snorted, and looked back out at the garden. "Such nonsense is of no concern to me."

"That's the spirit, cousin!" He got up and went to set his glass back on the breakfast cart. The monkey looked down longingly, but stayed put. "All of this will take time to arrange, of course. Bringing you safely back into our possession was but the first of many steps. I fear you may have to be content to stay here for a while, and tolerate more of my hospitality. Can you bear that as well?" He gave her an amused look.

"I am sorry I was so cross with you before," she said. "I hope you can understand how difficult and strange all this —"

"Please! Dear cousin! Do you imagine me able to comprehend the politics of Alizar, but not your own entirely legitimate distress? Really, dear. I do wonder sometimes if we've ever really met at all!" He tittered at his little joke, and came to kiss her on both cheeks, in the continental style; Sian closed her eyes so as not to stare into Gigi's dark gaze. "I shall look forward to your company at dinner. Until then, I shall make sure that you have things to entertain you. Do you like to read?"

"Why … yes. I used to anyway. It's been so long since I've had time to read anything but paperwork and reports …"

Escotte made a face, waving at the air between them as if dispelling some bad odor. "No more reports for you, my dear Sian. You're on holiday now. For a little while at least. Try to enjoy it!" He headed for the door. "I'll send Cleone straight up again. Ta for now, cousin!"

PART II

FIFTEEN

... That this new healer possesses a gift unprecedented in recent temple history seems no longer in question, my lady. I have little doubt that he will be able to heal your son. Unfortunately, his gift is accompanied by an extraordinary cathexis to the spiritual realm, so far beyond our normal experience that its impacts are difficult to anticipate or manage. Hence the current difficulty. I assume the trance state I have described will abate soon, as his current immersion is so profound that he has taken neither food nor water in several days, and must certainly need to soon. Still, as these waters are so uncharted for us all, I can be completely sure of nothing.

I deeply regret this latest delay, My Lady Consort, and understand how much frustration these impediments must cause you. I appreciate your patience immensely, and feel sure that we will be ready to receive you and your son very shortly now. I will, of course, keep you apprised of any and all further developments as they occur.

Respectfully your servant,
Duon, Father Superior, Temple Mishrah-Khote

Arian set the letter down, trembling with anger, and looked up at Viktor. "I am finished putting up with these maneuvers."

"Arian," her husband said warily, "we cannot afford to further antagonize —"

"It's been more than a week, Viktor! Every morning, we are informed again of this extraordinary new healer who is *still* unavailable until tomorrow — or perhaps the day after that — while our son draws nearer death each day. Now the man is in a *trance* — and cannot be disturbed? Do you think Duon truly believes I am so stupid, or are these insults intentional?"

Viktor made a helpless gesture. "What do we know of such matters? If he says the fellow might be harmed by —"

"*This has nothing to do with some medium's delicacy!*" she snapped. "This is a blatant power play, pure and simple. Can't you see that? He is waiting for us to beg. To offer the temple whatever concessions he requests, if only he will condescend to save our child." She rose to pace around the table still laden with remains of their breakfast. "I know I was a fool to launch this battle in the first place, but if he thinks to win our argument this way, then we must end it now — with sufficient force that there can be no further question about who rules Alizar."

Viktor looked alarmed. "Are you deranged? I cannot use force against the temple! I would be deposed by my own government just for suggesting it. You know that as well as —"

"I do not mean physical force, Viktor," she cut him off in exasperation. "Give me some credit, please. I am talking only about the projection of power." She stopped before one of the windows to gaze out over the surrounding jungle canopy at the shore of Apricot across the channel. "The question, of course, is how."

"Arian, listen to me. I am in no way equipped for such a confrontation at this moment. I am fighting just to keep my seat."

"If you allow that pompous temple toad to dangle the life of our son on his leash with impunity, you have lost your seat already. The Mishrah-Khote will *own us*. This is a necessary fight."

"It doesn't matter," he said bleakly. "One cannot fight with both hands chained behind his back." He shook his head and looked away from her. "I am a cripple in the water, and the sharks are circling very closely now. I have failed. Not only Alizar, but you and Konrad, terribly. I'm sorry. Truly. If our son is spared what's coming, that may be a mercy."

"Meaning *what*?" she asked in outraged disbelief. "That you also wish him dead now?"

"Arian, don't —"

"*Do not speak to me!*" she shrieked. "I cannot endure another word of your spineless pessimism. If your hands are chained, then fight with your feet!"

"Spare me the impassioned metaphors, wife!" he shouted, finding sufficient spine to stand and thump the table with both hands. "Is there some obvious solution to this nation's downward spiral that you have not thought to recommend to me? I have tried everything I can. To no avail." He stared down at all the half-empty platters spread around him. "This is why nations appoint leaders: so they'll have someone else to blame when everything goes wrong. A demon close at hand to exorcise at last resort."

"So … We are just to sit here waiting for our dismissal, then? Hoping Konrad *dies* in time to save our *pride*?"

"It may not just be our pride that needs saving when all this collapses, love. People can get very angry when their lives fall apart. When it happens to a lot of people all at once, that anger can be very violently expressed." He gave her a pointed look. "How much that violence costs you and me personally may well hang on whom we have offended, and how badly."

She held his gaze, wondering what had happened to the modest, good-hearted, yet confident and optimistic man she had agreed to leave her own home and country to marry. "Well, my dear," she said, already heading for the door, "if you're so convinced that we're already doomed, you can have no reason to object to whatever I may choose to do about it in the meantime."

He offered no reply as Arian left the breakfast room and stormed toward her chambers, sorting through her options. By the time she got there, her decision had been made. It was the best she could do quickly enough to matter, given Konrad's rapidly deteriorating condition. If it worked, point and game to her. If not … At worst she would appear deranged with grief, as her own husband had just suggested. He could disavow the act and divorce her afterward, if that was what it took to shelter himself from blame. Should his dire predictions turn out to have any merit, it would hardly matter, would it?

"Maronne! Lucia!" she called as she burst into her chambers. "I need you!"

Maronne came rushing from her room, wide-eyed with alarm. "What is wrong, my lady?"

"Where is Lucia?"

"With Konrad, as you requested."

"Of course." She brought a hand up to massage her forehead. Poise would be essential now, and poise required calm. "Run and get her, would you?" she asked more gently. "And find Kafahl as well, please."

Maronne dropped a hurried curtsy and rushed off.

Arian went quickly to the windows and looked down at the great sundial in the courtyard, set within its ring of dazzling plumeria. If she lit sufficient fire underneath the chief of staff, there should be time to do this. Just.

Unwilling to waste precious moments waiting for Maronne's return, Arian walked through her rooms into her wardrobe. Well back to where the most seldom-used items were stored. There, behind dozens of beautiful dresses simply too outdated — or too narrow at the waist and hips — to be worn any longer, she paused before a rack on which just three dresses hung.

The first was a great bell-shaped gown composed entirely of wired jade beads and russet fan-shells, which she had worn to Escotte Alkattha's instillation as Census Taker. It had cost a fortune, and she had given it not another thought since then. The second item was a black and red silk ball gown, edged and accented with hundreds of cut rubies and garnets, as spectacular as it was completely inappropriate for this occasion. The third dress there was sewn from cloth-of-gold, with a high, rigid collar and shoulder ruffles of beaten copper. Hanging with it was a train of the same fabric at least as wide, and twice as long as the dress, covered in mosaic patterns of dangling bronze and copper beads. Arian had worn this dress when she had wedded Viktor — a gift from her father in Copper Downs, worth almost as much as the ship which had brought it and her to Alizar. She had expected never to wear it again until the day of her son's instillation ceremony as Factor.

She tried not to wonder whether that day would ever arrive now, as she stood back to consider the jade and fan-shell gown. Of the two dresses, it would lend her the larger, more imposing profile. But it was as heavy as a suit of armor. She had been required to do little more than sit in it at Escotte's instillation, and still she had been exhausted by the time the ceremony was concluded and she'd been freed to exchange it for a blessedly airy silk reception gown. It was fairly dark as well — which might make her seem formidable from close by, but would likely just render her a shadow at any significant distance. And distance would matter here — briefly.

The cloth-of-gold was not much lighter in weight, but far easier to move in. More important, possibly, it would likely burn like fire in the afternoon light — even from half a league away. Its symbolic value as a reminder of her father's wealth and continental influence — however irksome to Alizari national pride — might lend some pointed perspective to the occasion too. If the tiresome priest happened to recall where he had seen it before, at any rate.

Her decision made, Arian began to take things from shelves and hangers, tossing them in piles for Maronne and Lucia to carry out when they arrived. She was still at it when she heard them calling from the parlor.

"My lady?" called Lucia. "Are you here?"

"In the wardrobe!" Arian called back. "Come help me!"

"Domni Kafahl is here as well," Maronne warned.

"Good. Bring him too. I'm not undressed."

The two women and the Factorate chief of staff arrived a moment later, entering the wardrobe with uncertain glances at each other and at Arian.

When Maronne and Lucia saw the cloth-of-gold and its accouterments lying piled at Arian's feet, they gasped.

"My lady! What has happened here?" Lucia asked, as if fearing the clothing had just fallen there by accident.

"Please carry these things out and lay them on my bed," said Arian. "I will need at least two of my hairpieces as well. The largest ones. And the amber jewelry. All of it, I think."

The women's eyes grew round with astonishment — as did Kafahl's.

"May I ask what occasion is being prepared for, my lady?" asked the chief of staff, clearly puzzled, if not panicked. "Have we some ..." He surveyed the clothing being gathered up and carried out by Maronne and Lucia. "... perhaps unexpected visitor?"

"No, Kafahl. I will be the unexpected visitor. I need the royal barge equipped immediately in full ceremonial regalia suitable to a state occasion. Full crew, formal entourage, and honor guard in dress attire." Kafahl's mouth fell open as Arian went on. "I wish the barge accompanied by a large flotilla as well, outfitted in the same manner, and fitted with as many cannon as may be available. Full ceremonial dress guard aboard every craft."

"My lady," the man sputtered, "may I ask how many craft you wish, exactly?"

"How many of my husband's ships are currently at harbor?"

He blinked at her, clearly stunned. "Many more than we can outfit as described, I fear."

"As many as you can, then," she said pleasantly, brushing past him to go join her maids.

"But ... my — my lady ..." Kafahl stammered, seeming to progress from 'stunned' to 'appalled' as he followed her out of the wardrobe, "to where is this flotilla bound?"

She turned back to face him, realizing instantly that she dared not answer. The temple had too many ears inside her house. That was a long-accepted fact of life. Tell the chief of staff where they were going, and the temple would almost certainly have been informed before they even departed. Surprise was half the substance of this exercise. *Without any warning.* That was a crucial suffix to the message that she wished to send Duon.

"I will tell you when it's time to leave," she said, offering him an apologetic smile.

His eyes grew even rounder, and he began to shake his head — clearly without meaning to. "But, my lady, if am I to provision such an ... an *elaborate* embassy, I must at least know how long it will be gone, and toward what sort of climate, not to mention —"

"It will require no provisions at all," she said, aware that she was torturing the man, and starting to feel somewhat bad about it. "We will all be back here before dinner time."

"Dinner time!" he blurted, forgetting appropriate conversational protocol entirely.

"We will not even be leaving the islands, Kafahl."

"But it will take at least that long just to equip and launch such a flotilla! ... My lady," he rushed to add, ducking his head in embarrassment.

"You have two hours," she told him. "We must be gone before midday."

He stared at her, blanching visibly. Like a man who'd just been told he would be hanged.

"Commandeer whatever staff you need, from anywhere," she said, not wanting him to have a heart attack before anything at all was seen to. "Use the entire grounds and kitchen staff to get this done, if it will help. Just do the best you can, but we must depart on time."

"My lady," Kafahl said with a nervous but respectful nod, and turned to dash out past the wide-eyed maids, who watched him go before turning back to stare at Arian with twin expressions of bewilderment.

"When you two have got me into this dress," she told them, "I will need hair and cosmetics suited to a goddess. A very fierce one. I have some ideas about my headdress. Maronne, we will need the wire, please."

～

"Perhaps my lady would enjoy a trip to the garden this morning?" Cleone asked as Sian finished yet another sumptuous breakfast.

Though as flawlessly deferential as ever, the inquiry grated on Sian a bit. Must Cleone always be guessing what Sian's next want might be before she'd had time to think of it herself? It was the girl's job, she supposed, to anticipate the wishes of others, but after more than a week of being so well managed ... Sian was tempted to refuse, or to propose something else, just to assert herself, but knew that would be peevish. She did enjoy the little courtyard garden — or anything else that got her out of this *lovely* room.

"That sounds quite refreshing. Thank you, dear." Sian grimaced mentally. She was even sounding like the woman now.

They left her fancy room high in the Census Hall's east tower, and made their way down the carpeted back staircase toward the courtyard. Cleone led the way, as always. Sian was allowed to go nowhere unaccompanied, it seemed, even inside the house. For her own protection and convenience, of course. This had been made clear. Repeatedly. But it did leave her feeling five years old again at times.

As they descended, Sian eyed the adorable little leather-bound case clutched in Cleone's slender hand, wondering what the girl would be offering up for their amusement today. She sighed quietly, reminding herself that Cleone had been charged with keeping her entertained, and doubtless felt obliged to fulfill Escotte's expectations. But, oh, this sudden, enforced idleness was awfully challenging after so many years of fruitful, unmanaged productivity. She almost wished at times for the freedom and privacy of her overturned boat back on Pembo's Beach.

Then again, it was much more comfortable here. And she had not been beaten or even arrested by anyone for more than a week now. She'd been attacked by no street mobs; she hadn't even ruined any dresses. Perhaps a little less discontent was called for ...

At the bottom of the stairs, they found Prefect-Sergeant Ennias waiting for them, as he seemed magically to be each time they left the confines of Sian's upper suites. Yet another measure taken for her protection, she'd been told.

"Good morning, Sergeant," Sian said, careful to sound pleasant, though she still had not come entirely to terms with the way he'd handled things the night of their ... *escort* to safety here.

He gave Sian a short bow, then stood back as they entered the garden, doubtless waiting to see where she and Cleone would settle before positioning himself. If Cleone's management had begun to leave Sian feeling rather like a child, Ennias's omnipresence sometimes made her feel a bit like a prisoner.

Still, the courtyard garden *was* outside, and one never knew when Mishrah-Khote priests might start falling from the sky, she supposed. Better safe than sorry, as Escotte so often hastened to remind her. She glanced up at the walls to check for saboteurs, but found only frilled iguanas this morning.

"Would my lady like to sit near the pond, perhaps?" Cleone asked, as if Sian might not be able to decide without her help.

"That sounds very nice," she replied, trying harder to adjust her attitude.

"Marvelous!" Cleone enthused. "The light is perfect there."

Sian raised an eyebrow. "For what?"

The maid blushed prettily. "I thought — if you would like, my lady — that we might read a bit of poetry today."

So that was what the case contained. Well, this seemed an improvement over embroidery, tatting, bead stringing, or painting little figurines — if the poetry was any good, at least. Really, the delightful girl was possessed of the most astonishing array of useless hobbies. How long had it taken her to acquire them all? Was there some school, Sian wondered, at which one trained to be so decorative, or was Cleone some sort of natural prodigy?

Well, Sian knew how to read, at any rate, which should make today's entertainment less embarrassing than the past few. She walked over to the pond, choosing a wicker chair festooned with scarlet silk pillows exactly the same shade as the canopy of bougainvillea blossoms above it. The usual small buffet table had been set unobtrusively nearby, with a glistening carafe, several crystal tumblers, and, as always, two lace fans for further moderation of the day's warmth and humidity — which, as always, Sian ignored, finding them a very continental affectation. A pair of brilliant dragonflies flitted about, inspecting the carafe before moving on to the pond.

Cleone sat in the matching wicker chair beside her, and, as always, picked up a fan and snapped it open expertly to flutter at her chin and breast as she set her case down on the low table between them. "Your cousin has a remarkable library, does he not?"

"Indeed." Sian had spent quite a bit of time in it over the past week. In her opinion, Escotte favored rare bindings and gorgeous calligraphy over literary quality, but then, reading was a subjective thing, wasn't it?

Cleone snapped her fan closed and set it in her lap before reaching out to open the case she'd brought, taking out several slender volumes. Exquisitely bound, of course. "I've brought some folios from the Moulena Era, translated by Daktylos." She looked up at Sian, eyes cautious through her dark lashes. "They have some rather … poignant things to say, if I might be so bold."

"Do they?"

"Of course, my lady might disagree …"

"I wouldn't dream of it," Sian murmured. Across the courtyard, Ennias shifted slightly, placing a hand on the pommel of his short-sword. Did he have some divergent opinion of Moulena Era poetry, she wondered?

"When we've read a few of them," Cleone continued, seeming encouraged, "I thought my lady might wish to try her hand at composing a villanelle or two? It is such an *expressive* form, is it not?" She smiled brightly, already drawing several thick sheets of parchment out of her case as well, and a set of fine pens and ink bottles.

Sian swallowed her largest sigh yet. Reading poetry was one thing, writing it quite another. Was there something wrong with simply sitting in the light here, gazing at the plants for a while, listening to the birds? She couldn't keep doing this. Just couldn't, *couldn't!* What would be next? Glass etching, silver smithing, cabinet making, tanning of hides? Pearl diving, rock quarrying, lion taming? At least those might get her all the way out of this house for a few hours. Even answering business correspondence again began to seem preferable to this endless gauntlet of idle entertainments. "I am suddenly very thirsty," she announced, for lack of any more gracious escape.

"I will pour you a glass of water," the maid said, setting her fan aside and rising at once from her chair to go to the buffet table.

"Might I have some fruit juice instead? Citrus, perhaps?" Sian patted the hollow at the base of her neck. "I often suffer a tightness about the throat that only tart citrus can ease." Cleone glanced uncertainly at Ennias. "The sergeant will be ample company while you're gone, dear," Sian assured her. "You needn't hurry."

"I shall be right back, my lady." Cleone gave her a bright smile, and hurried back into the Census Hall.

Ah! Blessed silence, Sian thought. Then, *What a bitch I've become.*

She turned to gaze down at the pond behind her, where rare and astonishing bloodfish and Graver's carp swam lazily between the floating lilies. A siluva eel at least ten feet long wriggled sinuously in her direction, its violet and turquoise body wreathed in vivid crimson spots. Sian leaned down for a piece of gravel, then tossed it toward the eel, who showed no sign of interest, though half a dozen other fish came racing over to investigate the sound. Finding no edible treat to hold their interest, however, they went back to circling endlessly around the pond. Just as Sian had been doing here all week. From gilded breakfast room to well-appointed library to her feathered nest of a bedroom, accompanied everywhere by servants and guards, with no sight, much less news of the outside world.

It was undeniably good to be safe. Of course it was. But for all the comfort and luxury to be found here, she did feel so … imprisoned.

She glanced up at Ennias. "It must be very tedious to spend so much time watching me feed gravel to the fish."

He smiled slightly, not quite taking his eyes from their ongoing examination of the courtyard and its undoubtedly dangerous geckos. "I've pulled far worse assignments, my lady."

As have I, she thought. "Did you have any further chance to talk with my friends before they were sent off that night, Sergeant?"

"Your friends, my lady?" he asked, still not meeting her gaze.

"Captain Reikos and the young man, Pino." *Whom your men nearly killed,* she added silently. *Can you have forgotten them already?*

"Sadly, no," he said. "I was assigned many other duties that night."

"I don't suppose you've heard any news of them, then?" she tried without much hope. "Or how their mission for my cousin is proceeding?"

"Such things would all be far above my station, Domina."

"Of course."

The courtyard door opened and Cleone sailed through, a brilliant smile on her lovely face and a silver tray in her hands. "Pomara juice, only slightly fermented," she announced, rejoining Sian by the pond. "May I pour for you?"

"Thank you."

Cleone filled a tiny crystal glass and handed it gracefully to Sian.

Sian felt rather bad now about being so difficult before. The girl was only doing what Escotte had told her to, and quite well too. If she wished things changed, she ought to take it up with him, not take it out on her. "Won't you join me, dear?"

The girl's eyes widened as Sian picked up a second glass. "Are you sure, my lady?"

"Of course I'm sure. And then perhaps we'll work on those villanelles."

SIXTEEN

The *Alkattha Swan,* more commonly referred to as the Floating Palace, was essentially a gigantic state luxury barge built to impress important visitors. But the wealth and power announced by this floating building, bristling with undulating oars, could be intimidating as well, especially when its massive decks were lined, as now, with well-armed 'honor guard' — however smartly attired. To Kafahl's credit, the enormous barge now moved ponderously toward The Well surrounded by half a dozen larger sailing ships, all armed with cannon, and twice that many smaller sailing craft, all manned with armed ceremonial guard as well, and extravagantly festooned in bunting, banners, streamers and flags of gold, green and blue: Alizar's state colors. It had taken an hour longer to arrange than Arian had hoped, but Viktor had made no move to stop her, as she'd feared he might, and they had gotten underway in sufficient time to accomplish her purpose and get back to Home in time for dinner.

As the flotilla came around the windward side of Bayleaf, the entrance to The Well's temple harbor came into view across the channel. Two monumental pillars flanked a darkened gap in the island's verdant coastline, where the vast interior sinkhole for which it was named opened to the sea. The Mishrah-Khote's opulent central temple and headquarters was built into the near-vertical rock walls enclosing this perfectly round bay — glorious testimony to the priestly order's once preeminent political and economic power over Alizar.

For over a hundred and fifty years, however, the Mishrah-Khote's authority and influence had been eclipsed by that of the secular Factorate. Ever since they'd made the error of remaining noncommittal during Alizar's uprising against the continental Factor, by which the nation's independance had been won. Arian had come here this afternoon to make sure the order's now secondary relevance and authority in Alizar had not slipped their Father Superior's harried mind.

When the flotilla was less than half a league from the temple harbor's entrance, Arian stood and beckoned her two maids, now dressed almost as impressively as she. "I know we have a while yet, but I want him to wonder what burns so brightly at our prow." She smiled as they made their way sedately to the barge's bowsprit platform. The azure sky was cloudless, the afternoon light perfect. Better even than she'd hoped. Her dress and all the other golden trappings they had contrived around her perch would catch the sun like fire and aim it straight into the temple's eyes.

When they were positioned at the barge's bow, with her luxuriously costumed entourage arrayed behind them, Maronne and Lucia stooped to arrange Arian's train to maximum effect, then stood, erect and grim, beside their mistress as the harbor gates drew nearer.

Far below her, in the barge's deepest galleries, the vessel's hundred oarsmen strained to achieve a final burst of speed, so that the barge and its festive armada all but flew between the harbor's ancient pillars. The sunlight vanished as they passed from open water into The Well's shadowed, vine-draped interior, startling flocks of black cormorants off cliffs and ledges. At that moment, the flotilla's three largest ships, behind and to either side of the *Swan*, fired all their cannons, stuffed with harmless powder, frightening even larger clouds of seabirds into keening, wheeling flight above the bay.

The noise was deafening inside the sinkhole's echoing confines, and doubtless terrifying to anybody not expecting it. That had been Arian's very reason for ordering this 'salute' held until they were inside the harbor. The *Swan's* captain had expressed concerns when she'd informed him of this plan. *My Lady Consort, I feel compelled to comment on the risk of our salute at such close quarters being mistaken for actual attack.* She had thanked him for his candor, and said she rather hoped it would be. *Though it should take no longer than an instant, surely, to see that nothing has exploded. And I will make very certain that my intentions have not been misinterpreted, of course, just as soon as I have disembarked.* Clearly alarmed by this response, the captain had deferentially expressed further concern that, while the temple harbor was certainly no fortified installation, they were not entirely without weapons. *There is some small risk, I fear, that we might be fired upon in return, my lady.* She had allowed herself an open smile then, and said simply, *How very embarrassing for them.*

Whatever the good captain might assume about a lady's knowledge of warcraft, Arian knew very well how long it took to prepare a cannon for firing — especially when its use hadn't been at all anticipated. The fright she hoped Duon felt just now would be long past before anyone here was even capable of doing something so stupid as firing gratuitously on a well-armed fleet of gunboats with whatever lonely cannon or two they might have lying about. He should even have time to change his undergarments before the Floating Palace moored.

By the time their thundering salute had finished echoing off the harbor cliffs, Arian was gratified to see a great deal of frantic arm-waving and rushing-about on the temple docks. The barge was close enough now for her to see amazement on some of the faces of those rushing from inside the temple walls to either side of them, like disturbed ants. Wherever Duon might be in there, Arian felt reasonably sure that she must finally have captured his attention.

That's right, priest, she thought with satisfaction. *The full might of Alizar — at a moment's notice, without a word of warning. Think on that before you trifle with me further.*

Quite a crowd had gathered on the temple wharfs by the time the entire flotilla was assembled within the harbor's confines. Only the barge would actually be docking, of course. What Arian wanted here was alarmed surprise, not utter chaos. Now that she was close enough to be both seen and recognized, she raised her gold-draped arms in regal greeting to all those staring up in astonishment from below. She made no attempt to smile, though, doubting that the gesture would be efficacious, given the fierce mask of kohl, rouge and gold cream with which her face was painted.

By the time the huge boat had been made secure, and its gangway erected, a flock of bewildered, mid-level temple functionaries had assembled, wringing their hands and staring up at her in open-mouthed astonishment as she disembarked amidst a cloud of elegantly dressed attendants and Factorate officials.

"My Lady Factora-Consort," their apparent leader fawned as her crystal-clad feet alighted on the dock, "to what do we owe the, ah, overwhelming honor of this, er, unexpected visitation?"

"I have come to speak with your Father Superior." She gazed calmly past them, then about the suddenly hushed assembly of onlookers. "He is here somewhere, I take it?"

"Indeed I am, My Lady Consort!" Duon called, wading toward her through the crowd, still tugging on the last few of his vestments, if she was not mistaken. He looked askance at his harbor suddenly filled with festively decorated yet heavily armed ships, then turned back to study her own remarkable presentation. "We had not expected you, I fear, in ... quite this manner, or at quite this time. Can some crucial piece of correspondence have been mislaid, perhaps, without ever reaching me?"

"None that I'm aware of," she replied.

He gave her another anxious look. "Then ... I am at something of a loss, my lady ..."

"The last piece of correspondence I am aware of having received from *you*, Father Duon, was this morning's missive informing the Factor and me of your new prodigy's latest affliction."

"Oh, it is no affliction, My Lady Consort. He is merely deep in some extraordinary communion with the gods. If I failed to make that —"

"Wonderful!" she cut him off. "I was so concerned. But now that he is well at last, I would very much like to see him."

"But, my lady, surely, I explained why that —"

"I'm sure you did," she cut him off again. "You have explained so many things to us this past week, as our son lay dying, that I find myself no longer able to keep all those explanations sorted. That is why I thought it best just to simplify things by coming here to see him now." She offered him a smile at last, heedless of its translation through her cosmetic mask. "Would you be so good as to escort me, Father Duon?"

"It would be an honor, My Lady Consort, of course, if not for the fact that —"

"Thank you, Father." She extended her hand, no longer smiling.

"My lady, as I'm certain I explained in my last letter, disturbing him in this condition could —"

"But I have no intention of disturbing him," she said. "I just wish to see him. How can that disturb him?"

"He is ... secluded in a portion of the temple forbidden to all but anointed members of the Mishrah-Khote, my lady, and cannot be moved without risk of trauma to his —"

"Forbidden to the Factora-Consort? Here on behalf of the Factor himself? Why, Father, whatever for? Is something seditious being done in there?" She laughed, just a tad too loudly.

"My Lady Consort," Duon said through half-clenched teeth, "were I to admit *any* un-anointed person, much less a woman, to the inner sanctum of the temple, weeks of costly cleansing ceremonies would be required to —"

"I believe the Factor and I have paid this temple sufficient sums to cover the cost of any such ritual, have we not?" she asked, careful not to let anger taint her voice the way Duon's had. She had no intention of becoming *the hysterical woman* here. Let Duon's discipline be first to fail. "You have repeatedly assured me that this extraordinary new healer of yours is capable of healing the Factor's heir. Yet now, if I understand correctly, I am expected to continue waiting while my barely conscious son drifts ever nearer death, so that this order of *healers* can avoid some costly cleansing ceremonies?"

"I meant no such thing!" he snapped. "How dare you put such words into my —"

"How dare *I*?" she said very quietly. A collective step back was taken by everyone but Duon himself as Arian came further toward him. The silence became absolute. "Do you have some reason to wish our son's healing endlessly delayed this way, Father Duon?" she asked with icy calm. "I have no wish to put words of any kind into your mouth. I merely ask a question so unavoidable by now, that it would voice itself, I think, if I did not."

"My Lady Consort," he replied, struggling in vain to match her calm now, "no one has greater cause than I to wish for your son's swift recovery."

"I would agree," she said almost too softly to be heard by anyone but him.

"But … *why*, my lady?" he blurted awkwardly. "What can merely seeing him accomplish?"

The expression on his face just then was fleeting, but unmistakable, and caught her utterly by surprise. In all the years she had spent dealing with this man, she'd never seen it there before. Not the cunning or calculation, the anger or condescension or arrogance she had come prepared for, but, for one unguarded instant, unadulterated desperation.

She almost stepped back in dismay as the implications started to sink in. Until that moment, she had assumed with complete confidence that Duon *was* withholding access to some great new healer in retaliation for her slights during their earlier argument, or, more likely, in a calculated gambit for control of Viktor and herself. All her own calculations since leaving her husband in the breakfast room this morning had been based on those assumptions. Not until this moment had it ever crossed her mind that Duon might actually …

"Tell me, Father Duon," she said, struggling to conceal her alarm and incredulity until she knew if she was right, "does this healer you've been dangling before us exist at all, or have you simply been too proud to admit that you have nothing left to offer?"

"My lady *jests*?" he sputtered, clearly trying to sound offended. But the truth was written on his face too plainly now for even her innocent young son to have mistaken.

"By all the gods you claim to serve, Duon," she gasped, "what can you possibly have hoped to achieve with such a … moronic ruse?"

"My lady, you misapprehend the entire situation! I have invented nothing! The healer of which we speak is as real as you and I are — and every bit as talented as I have claimed!"

"Then show him to me! Now!" she snapped, abandoning all pretense of restraint.

"I … cannot," he said, plainly struggling to think of some further explanation where all others had failed.

Wasted! This entire spectacle. This ridiculous, horrifically costly charade! All wasted on a phantom. A mirage! She turned in fury to the entourage behind her. "We are leaving!"

"My Lady Consort, *wait!*" Duon called out as she stormed past her own attendants toward the boat. "None of this is as it seems! I swear to you!"

"Have you still not tired of toying with a grieving mother?" she shouted over her shoulder without slowing down. "Betraying your Factor's good faith? Defrauding your entire country in its time of crisis?" Breathing fire — or wishing to, at least — she stopped at last, halfway up the gangway, and turned to glare back down at him. "There are alternatives to your spiritual carnival, Duon. And I'll waste not another moment in pursuit of them. As for this … *travesty* you've perpetrated against us, rest assured that, just as soon as my son's illness is resolved, one way or the other, my husband's government will take whatever measures may be necessary to ensure that your unthinkable lapse of judgment in this matter is revisited. With a vengeance."

～

Reikos blinked awake, staring up at a low ceiling crudely hewn of natural stone. There was a hard, narrow pallet underneath his back. *Ah yes. The Census Taker's 'guest quarters'.* Even after so much time, it still took a while sometimes to remember where he was. A week now? Two, perhaps? He was no longer sure, though Pino had started scratching marks into their cell wall some days back, each time the guard brought them what passed for dinner here. What must his crew think by now? That he had abandoned them — or died somewhere? Was Kyrios keeping their port fees paid? Was his ship even there still? He sighed, and sat up to rub his eyes, dearly hoping that Sian was doing better than himself, wherever she'd been taken.

"You awake?" Pino asked him from the other corner of their little cavern. The boy held up a wooden trencher and an even cruder wooden spoon. "He brought our meal about half an hour ago, but I figured you'd want the sleep."

"Did you save me any?" Reikos asked. It was too old a joke by now to wrest even a grin from the lad. Since Sian had healed him, Pino's already youthful energy had become unnaturally manic, and his appetite seemingly inexhaustible. It must be dreadful, Reikos imagined, to have so much hunger and be forced to settle, day after day, for nothing but stale bread and half an onion every morning, more stale bread and a wooden trencher slopped with thin, cold broth and a few half-rotten vegetables each evening. If evenings they were. Without windows, such distinctions had become purely academic some time back. They had nothing now but the unsteady light of a single torch outside their cell, lit each 'morning' and doused at bedtime every 'night' — not that the boy seemed to need much sleep now.

Pino came and handed him a stale biscuit. Reikos shook his head and gave it back. His own stomach had shrunken pretty thoroughly by now, not that he didn't still lie awake at times, suffering fantasies of the bouillabaisse he had so often shared with Sian back on Meander Way.

"Are you sure?" asked Pino, looking at the extra food with naked desire.

"I am fine. If I'm hungry later, I'll just get up and club a rat."

The boy gave him a brief, uncertain chuckle. They might both have laughed a little harder if the joke had been less plausible. There was no scarcity of rats here, appearing with greatest frequency just after meals to sniff and gnaw at their empty trencher, no matter how thoroughly licked clean it might already seem. Still, he'd eat rats before he'd eat the giant cockroaches this nation seemed to have in such flagrant numbers.

As Pino ate, Reikos listened to the slow but endless drip of water somewhere in their cell block. This part of the Census Hall was clearly lower than the water table. He wondered yet again if the dungeon was well drained, or whether it had just not rained that hard yet since they'd been locked up. He knew how hard it rained here in the islands sometimes, and hoped they wouldn't have to add flooding to their list of woes before this whole ordeal was ended … somehow.

Such were the perils of entanglement in foreign politics, he supposed.

Pino sighed and sat down on the floor, his back against Reikos's pallet. "Do you think they're ever going to let us out of here?" he asked. "Or just kill us, even? Dying wasn't all that bad. Compared to this."

"I know as much as you do, lad," said Reikos, wondering if the boy's remark was just another joke, or … "Were you dead then? Truly?"

Pino shrugged. "I can't remember. But as good as, I suppose." He tossed his head and shifted his legs restlessly. "Isn't there supposed to be a trial, or something?"

"I'm not sure this is that kind of prison," Reikos said, still wondering just how far Sian had reached to bring this boy back into the world. "The Census Taker, from what I've gleaned of your land's politics, is something of a power unto himself."

A silence fell between them, filled only with the drip, drip, drip of water in the distance.

"Do you miss her?" Pino asked at last, his voice strange and melancholy.

"Miss who?" asked Reikos. "Domina Kattë?" Yes, he did. With surprising intensity. Not that he meant to tell that to the boy.

"I miss her," Pino said, ignoring his attempt at subterfuge.

The silence stretched again.

"Were you two lovers?" Pino asked, even more quietly.

Reikos stared down at him, mouth open in surprise. "That's none of … What an impertinent question. Which I will not even dignify by answering."

"I thought so," Pino hardly more than whispered. He sighed deeply without looking up, and shook his head.

By all the gods… thought Reikos, stunned not to have seen it earlier. "Are *you* in love with her?"

Pino nodded, still not looking up. "Desperately. … Stupidly." He shook his head again. "What does it matter now? I'm locked up here, and … she's married. And what chance did I have anyway, against a man like you?"

"Good Anselm's anchor," Reikos exclaimed softly. The boy was more than young enough to be her son. "Did she … Surely she did not return your —"

"*No,*" Pino cut him off petulantly. "Of course not. She doesn't even know."

"Well … I'm sorry. Truly. Love unreturned is no laughing matter."

"You would know?" asked Pino.

"Oh, I've been sent packing by more women than you would imagine, lad. That's just part of the game, I fear. Domina Kattë fired me as well, you know. Have I not told you that?"

"So you *were* lovers then!" Pino slapped the dirt floor with his open hand, scattering a few barely-seen crawly things. "I knew it!"

"But you just said you knew already!" Reikos protested.

"I had hoped you just meant fired," Pino said gruffly. "As in business partners."

Well, that was poorly done, thought Reikos. Sian would surely skin him to the last eyelash now. If she ever got the chance.

"So she was just a *game* to you?" asked Pino, dripping with disgust.

"Well — of course not!" Reikos exclaimed. "What makes you ask such —?"

"You just said that getting fired is 'part of the game.'" Pino stood and stalked off to the farthest corner of their cell, turning there, his back against the wall, to glare at Reikos. "I suppose you've got all kinds of women. One in every port, eh? Do you actually care for *any* of them?"

"Pino, you're bending this all out of shape."

"'Cause I do care," Pino said, his expression fierce. "I think the world of her."

"As do I," said Reikos quietly. "I love that woman dearly. More dearly than even I knew. Until very recently." He hung his head, ashamed to face this boy whose passions, however innocent and doomed, were so much purer than his own. He thought again about Celia, the first girl he had ever loved — until her father had forbidden them to marry. "Oh, lad, you're right. I've been as big a fool as any man alive." He forced himself to look up, straight into Pino's eyes. "I think you'd have stood every chance against a man like me." He dropped his gaze again. "But we're both run out of luck now, aren't we."

They remained that way in silence for a while, until Pino said, "I'm sorry I got us into all this trouble."

"You?" asked Reikos. "How are you at fault in this?"

"If I hadn't tried to stab that soldier, maybe neither of us would be locked up in here."

"If I hadn't pulled out the damned hand-cannon, well... I don't think you can blame yourself for *my* presence here, at least. And I'd not have had a single stitch of respect left for you if you hadn't rushed that bunch of leather-scaled flatfish trying to abduct our Sian."

"To be honest, nor would I," said a quiet voice from outside the bars of their cell door.

Reikos and Pino spun about together to find Sergeant Ennias gazing in at them. Reikos had been too absorbed in his conversation with Pino to notice the man's arrival in the dimly torch-lit passage. "Well," he said, "the dog returns to its vomit, does it?"

"I've never thought of you as vomit, Captain Reikos," Ennias said levelly. "I just wanted to come see how you're being treated down here."

"How do you suppose?" growled Reikos.

"Are they feeding you anything?"

"Do you take pleasure in asking starving men such questions, you sadistic son of a bitch?" Reikos replied.

"I suspected as much." The sergeant loosened a mid-sized leather satchel hung underneath his cloak, and tossed it to them through the bars.

With an untrusting glance at Ennias, Pino bent down and grabbed the satchel off the floor, then opened it and looked inside. Reikos saw the boy's nostrils flare. "It's meat," he moaned, reaching inside to draw out a link of peppered sausage. "And *cheese*."

"Your jailer is a friend of mine," said Ennias. "He knows I'm doing this, but if you value your own hides, much less mine, please do *not* tell Alkattha I was here, should you ever talk with him."

"Oh, you're our friend now, are you?" Reikos said, salivating as the scent of sausage reached him. "Our secret protector?" Pino shoved the link into his mouth, then tossed the bag to Reikos.

"Your presence here brings me no joy," said Ennias. "It's nothing I intended."

"What's happened to Domina Kattë?" Pino demanded.

"She is safe and well, living as the Census Taker's honored guest."

"And she doesn't mind that we are here?" asked Reikos. "I do not believe you."

"She doesn't know that you are here," said Ennias. "And I am not allowed to tell her. The Census Taker tells her lies. She seems under the impression that you've both been sent on some important mission for him. She's been asking about you both, though." He really did sound troubled by what he was telling them.

"What is going on here?" Reikos asked. "How have we offended your employer so?"

"By seeing something he did not want seen, I think." Ennias glanced upward, as if hearing something through the rock-hewn ceiling. "I will see if there is some way to improve your situation, gentlemen, but right now, I'd best be going."

"You've been too kind," said Reikos. "By all means, do not let us keep you."

The officer gave him a grudging nod, as if taking his words seriously, then turned and left as quietly as he had come.

After wolfing down a bit of Ennias's largess, Reikos returned the bag to Pino. "Finish it," he told the boy unnecessarily. "Leave any for the rats or roaches, and they'll just become unmanageable."

Reikos went back to lie down on his pallet. He stared up at the water-stained ceiling and thought about the free and easy life of a sea captain. Sailing wherever he liked at a moment's notice. Slave to no one. A woman in every port. Yes, that had been the life for him. Once.

No more, though. Whether he got out of here some day or not. No more.

SEVENTEEN

By the time the *Alkattha Swan* was docked at Home's commercial port again, Arian's fury with Duon had been overtaken by apprehension about what she would say to Viktor. That the Mishrah-Khote's top priest had been stringing them along was something he must know. That she had responded to this discovery with yet another clear, and this time very public, promise of overt war against the Father Superior himself was something she wished he need never know at all. As she and her entourage disembarked, she was so absorbed in wondering how to frame this news that she failed to see her brother waiting on the dock until she'd practically run into him.

"What an *extraordinary* costume, sister," he said. "Wherever have you been?"

She rolled her eyes, trying to brush past him. "I haven't time for this right now, Aros."

"No, Arian. I didn't mean it that way. Just, please, tell me what is going on."

She drew breath to rebuff him more sternly, then realized that there was none of the usual mockery on his face, or even in his voice.

"I came up after lunch," he said, "and was greeted with the news that you'd run off in high dudgeon with half the family fleet, though no one seemed to know where to, exactly. Is … everything all right?"

Still no hint of his usual sarcasm or smug amusement. His worry seemed sincere. How odd. "I appreciate your concern, Aros, but I really must go speak with Viktor right away. I've barely time to change out of these horrid clothes first. Might we discuss this later?"

"Yes. Of course." He sounded genuinely chastened. "But if there's anything I can do to help, I really do hope you'll let me."

Had that been an apologetic tone? From Aros? She studied him more closely. "Is everything all right with you, brother?"

"You mean, besides the fact that it's been weeks now since you completely cut me off? Arian, I know I've been … well, quite an ass, I guess. But I *am* still your brother, and … if you're in any kind of trouble …"

Would wonders never cease. *Family feeling* from Aros? Better late than never, she supposed, and it was not as if any reduction in the growing bog of conflict she was suddenly entangled in would be unwelcomed. "I appreciate that, Aros. More than you can know. I really must go straight to Viktor now, but let's talk this evening. Over dinner perhaps, in my chambers, say, an hour after dark. Just the two of us." Viktor would likely welcome her absence anyway for a while, once he'd heard what she must tell him. "I would like that, if it is acceptable to you."

"Thank you, sister." He offered her an almost bashful smile. "I look forward to it."

"Until tonight, then."

They exchanged respectful nods, and Arian turned to find most of her party gone on well ahead of her, except for Maronne and Lucia, awaiting their mistress at a respectful distance. "Well, that's an unexpected mercy," she told them as they continued toward the curtained litter waiting beyond the dock to return them to the Factorate House.

"He has pestered me to let him visit Konrad several times this week," Maronne said. "But not half so discourteously as he used to. Perhaps he's finally gotten the message."

"That would be very welcome news indeed," said Arian. "Now, if I can just escape this dress before it crushes me, I'll go see if I can work some miracle with Viktor too."

⮑

When they arrived at Arian's chambers, however, they found Viktor there already, gazing out a window at the distant harbor. He turned as they came in, responding to their startled silence with a sanguine smile. "Would you ladies kindly permit me and the Factora-Consort a private moment?"

Maronne and Lucia dropped quick curtsies to the Factor and retreated back into the hallway.

"Well, my dear," he asked, "how much new trouble have you caused us?"

"Some," she said, dreadfully self-conscious of her bizarre cosmetic mask and overblown attire. "Quite a lot, I suspect."

He nodded, seeming neither much surprised nor even too upset. "Yes, well, we can talk about it later, I suppose. Right now, I am afraid we have much bigger trouble to attend to. Would you come with me, please?"

She gave him a startled look. "Like this?" Was her punishment to start this quickly? "Has someone already told you?" she asked, trying not to sound as frightened as she was.

"About your visit to Duon?" He shook his head, and started for the doorway. "That doesn't matter now. Just come."

She raised a hand to her mouth in alarm as he came abreast of her. "Is it about Konrad?"

"*No,*" he said, beginning, finally, to show some sign of irritation. "Please stop second-guessing me, and just come along now, will you?"

In the hallway, Maronne and Lucia gazed at Arian in obvious concern. Arian glanced questioningly at Viktor, who shook his head. "Go and change," she told them. "Then await me here."

They curtsied and re-entered her apartments.

"Viktor," she said as they began to walk, "won't you just tell me what is —"

"Not until we are in my apartments."

"Oh." It was something that unsafe for discussion then, even though they seemed quite alone here. Her trepidation grew.

As they continued through the house, Viktor turned and took her hand. "I've had much time — and much new cause, I fear — to think about the things you said to me this morning. You were right, my dear. I'm sorry. Truly. If there really is some way left to fight, even with our feet, I will try." He gave her a tender and apologetic smile.

She smiled back, deeply grateful for this reassurance that she might not be in as much trouble as she'd feared — with Viktor, anyway. Then again, he hadn't heard what she had done yet. "Viktor, there is something you should know." She saw no reason to reserve this news for greater privacy. It had all been said quite publicly already. "The Mishrah-Khote has been lying to us. There is no healer in seclusion at the temple. It seems clear there never was. Duon has just been —"

He put a finger to his lips, and shook his head again.

Not even this? she wondered anxiously. *What in all the world can be going on* now?

The entrance to Viktor's apartments was flanked by guards who pulled the double doors open as they arrived. After instructing them to allow no one else entry for any reason, Viktor led Arian through his outer chambers to the sitting room outside his bedchamber, where two men stood waiting. The first she recognized immediately: Nishahl Hivat. The other man was a young copper-skinned military officer in Alkattha house guard livery whom she had never seen before. Hivat showed no surprise at her bizarre attire, probably better apprised of her activities since breakfast than even she herself was. The other man was clearly struggling not to stare.

"My Lady Factora-Consort," said Hivat, giving her a bow, immediately duplicated by the young officer at his side. "Allow me to introduce Prefect-Sergeant Ennias, commander of Escotte Alkattha's house guard."

The sergeant bowed again, unnecessarily, though if he was Escotte's man, Arian supposed he would have learned quite quickly to err on the side of excessive deference.

"This involves the Census Taker?" she asked, wondering just how much more alarming all this could become.

"I fear it does," said Hivat.

Worse and worse. She glanced around, and went to sink into a chair beside the case of exotic maps and charts that Viktor had collected since his boyhood. Hivat and the young officer pivoted to face her as Viktor came to stand beside her. She thought of trying to explain her clothing to their younger guest, but could think of no way to do so that would not just make her seem even more ridiculous.

"Have you by chance, my lady, heard any of the rumors circulating in the city about a new healer commonly referred to as *Our Lady of the Islands?*" asked Hivat.

"A *healer?*" she asked, wondering how they had veered to such a topic from Escotte Alkattha. "I haven't. No. But ..." She turned to Viktor. "This can't be the healer Duon has been pretending to offer us, can it?" She looked back to Hivat. "Duon has always said their healer was a man, and I cannot imagine the Mishrah-Khote would tolerate a woman in their midst, regardless of her talent. I've just been lectured on the costs of such *contamination.*"

"It does appear they had her, briefly," Hivat said. "In their dungeons on charges of spiritual fraud."

"I see," she replied wearily, only conscious of the latest ghost of hope briefly risen up within her as it faded in the inevitable light. "More empty theater. Not that I'm surprised."

"That's what I've assumed as well, my lady," said Hivat. "Until this afternoon, when our young sergeant here very wisely came to see me with some disturbing information." Hivat turned to Sergeant Ennias. "Would you please tell the Factora-Consort the tale you've shared with the Factor and me?"

The sergeant raised his chin a bit, gazing into the air before his face, and began reciting his tale in the dispassionate tones of a military dispatch. "Ten days ago, my lady, my employer, Escotte Alkattha, informed me that a relative of his had been arrested and imprisoned by the Mishrah-Khote on false charges of spiritual fraud."

"This is the healer?" Arian asked in surprise. "This *Lady of the Islands* is a relative of ours?"

"Sian Kattë, it seems," Viktor told her. "A very distant cousin. I have never met her."

Arian shook her head. Stranger and stranger. "Please continue, Sergeant."

Ennias nodded, still meeting no one's eyes. "Lord Alkattha also informed me that this woman had escaped the temple somehow, and had last been seen on Cutter's, involved in some sort of public disturbance there just that morning. He did not explain how he had come by all this information, but ordered me to find her and bring her to him secretly. He was also in possession, somehow, of a marital complaint recently filed by the woman's husband, which he gave to me with instructions to detain her under the pretense of some related investigative matter. Lord Alkattha said I was to do this so that no one witnessing our exchange would learn of his involvement, or of the woman's actual destination."

"But … was that not also false arrest?" Arian interjected, wondering what new trouble Viktor's cousin had gotten them all into now while trying to cover up some petty family scandal.

Ennias nodded, still looking no one in the eye. "In a sense, my lady. But I assumed the woman herself would approve once she understood the reasons for our deception. She was not actually to be arrested or imprisoned, after all. It was just for show, as I have said.

"We tracked her to Three Cats, and overtook her after dark, in the company of two male companions who, unfortunately, assumed that we were part of some temple ruse to recapture her. They attempted to defend her forcibly. One of my men and the younger of her companions were injured in the resulting skirmish; the young man very gravely. Regrettably, this made it necessary to subdue both of Domina Kattë's companions and bring them with her to the Census Hall, where all three were delivered into my employer's keeping." For the first time in his presentation, Ennias looked directly at Arian. "At that time, my lady, I witnessed what I can only describe as a miraculous event. The lady's younger companion had suffered a deep pike wound to his side and stomach. By the time we had reached the Census Hall, I'd have wagered his chances of survival low to nonexistent, though I denied this concern to Domina Kattë for fear she might become hysterical."

As women always do, of course, Arian thought irritably.

"The injured boy was brought and laid out on the steps, unconscious," Ennias continued. "Domina Kattë knelt down and laid her hands over his wound. At first, she appeared to suffer greatly, crying out and seeming near the loss of consciousness. Then the boy revived and started speaking. When Domina Kattë was able to sit again, I saw with my own eyes that his stab wound had closed completely. Not just closed, but healed and scarred already." The sergeant shook his head, clearly still haunted by the wonder of it. "She had healed my injured man as well by then, but his wound had been so minor that I had just suspected trickery of some kind. This second healing, though … My lady, I grew up and served for eight years in Kalimpura before enlisting here. I've seen a lot of things I can't explain, but nothing more impossible than this."

Arian looked in astonishment at Viktor, then at Hivat. "Then … she is *not* a fraud?"

"It begins to seem so," Hivat said. "During the past week, my agents have begun encountering tales of people miraculously healed from all sorts of ailments by this so-called Lady of the Islands. Until Sergeant Ennias appeared this afternoon, however, we had found no one who knew — or would admit to knowing, anyway — who this woman was; and, to be quite candid, my lady, the very suddenness of so many seemingly implausible tales led us to dismiss them out of hand as just one more manifestation of the religious hysteria that has gripped the islands since that would-be priest appeared." His eyes, she noticed, wandered everywhere just then except toward her husband. "The rumors we were hearing just seemed far too overblown to merit serious consideration. This Lady of the Islands seemed to be everywhere at once, and yet never anyone identifiable." He shrugged. "What were we to think?"

"Then, she might really heal Konrad?" Arian exclaimed, hardly daring to believe. "And Escotte has her?"

"So it would seem," Viktor said, looking anything but happy. In fact, everyone looked extremely grim.

"But why is this bad news?" she asked, rising from her chair. "Why have we not —"

"Arian, my love," Viktor said softly, "you are so much smarter at this sort of thing than I am. Can you really still not see it?"

"See what?" she asked. "If there's finally a real healer on these islands, and Escotte has her safely in his …" Then she saw it, and sat down again. "Oh … Oh dear."

Hivat nodded. "He's had her there for nine full days, and not a word to either of you. Or to anybody else we know of. It would seem, my lady, that the Census Taker may want your son to die."

"I've been telling you for months now," Viktor sighed. "They want my head."

"You've been telling me that *my* family wants your head," she replied, trying to untangle the vast new knot of possibilities unfurling in her mind. "But this is *your* family, Viktor. That's what I cannot begin to understand. Escotte is Alkattha too. If Konrad dies, you have no heir and would surely be deposed. Your cousin knows as well as we do that any family replacing us would trade out the Census Taker too. Why slit his own throat that way? It makes no sense."

"Unless he's been assured by someone that in exchange for his help securing the Factorate, they will keep him on," said Viktor. He began fiddling with the bronze latch on his map-case. "The question now, it seems to me, is who, and how many others in our camp might be in league with this conspiracy?"

"If the Census Taker himself is turned against us," said Hivat, "then, beyond the people in this room, I fear there may be absolutely no one we can trust completely."

Arian looked sharply up at Sergeant Ennias. Deception might run in many directions. If someone wanted to drive a wedge just now between the Factorate and the Census Taker, for instance ... "What exactly led you to come betray your own employer, Sergeant?"

He looked her in the eye this time, betraying no sign of nervousness at all. "After the boy had been healed that night, I was told to lock both of Domina Kattë's companions up inside his private detention facility beneath the house — where they remain today. Lord Alkattha clearly did not want his cousin to know what he'd done with them. A chance comment from her just this morning leads me to believe she's been told they're off on some important secret mission on his behalf." He gave Arian a shrug. "They did attack a detachment of duly appointed house guard, I guess, but only in response to the incorrect but well-intentioned assumption that we posed some dire threat to the Census Taker's cousin. I have never understood why Lord Alkattha should want them locked away for that — in secret, even from his cousin — nor why a healer of her obvious power was being held in secret too, when all the world knows of your great need for her services."

"You say held in secret," Arian interjected. "Is she part of this conspiracy? Does she hide there willingly, or is she captive against her will?"

"Not quite either, I would say," said Ennias. "I think she believes she's being hidden there from the temple, but … Lord Alkattha has made it very clear that no one is to know she's there, and I do not think she would be allowed to leave the hall, even if she asked to. She is very closely guarded, even inside the house; always accompanied by her maid during the day, and at least myself or Lord Alkattha at other times. She seems more a prisoner to me, however unwitting, than a guest. Which is why I thought I'd better come make sure I wasn't being made party to some act I would be left to take the blame for later. I did not enlist to be anybody's scapegoat, my lady."

"But why come all the way to Domni Hivat, rather than to some more immediate superior?" Arian asked. This defection still seemed terribly convenient.

"My lady, none of my superiors are higher in the chain of command than the employer I had come to check on, and as there were clearly important secrets being kept at the highest levels here from someone, for some reason, I had no idea what I might spill into the wrong ears, even if Lord Alkattha's motives were legitimate. Especially if they were legitimate." He shrugged again. "I knew who the master of *all* secrets was, and assumed that if even he did not know what I had to tell him, I'd have been right to come."

She nodded, impressed despite herself. "You are a perceptive man, Sergeant. Perhaps you would be better employed as a diplomat than as a soldier."

"Soldiers are the front line of diplomacy, my lady, are they not?"

She could see him suppress a smile, and felt sure that if she were not the Factora-Consort, he'd have winked at her. She was developing a begrudging respect for him, despite his *hysterical woman* remark.

"To our good fortune," said Hivat, "it seems he spoke to no one else before reaching me, my lady. I brought him straight here to the Factor. We may reasonably hope that none of this conspiracy suspects we are the wiser yet."

"Which buys us some time, perhaps," said Viktor. "Now we must decide what we're to do with it — and quickly."

"So, who has more to offer your dear cousin than his own quite powerful family?" Arian asked. "That's what I still want to know."

The room fell silent as everyone grew thoughtful — except for the sergeant, who just stared straight ahead, awaiting further instruction.

"Could Escotte think to make *himself* Factor somehow," asked Arian, "once Viktor was deposed? That, at least, would make a little sense."

"I don't see how he could do it without some other substantial base of political support," Hivat said. "And I can hardly imagine any of the other families supporting an Alkatthan candidate over one of their own house. Maybe House Suba, but ..."

"What about the temple?" Arian parried. "Their support of Escotte might mobilize enough of the general public to overrule the wishes of any single house. Duon had this healer in his possession too, it seems, and said nothing to us either."

Hivat shook his head. "If the Census Taker were in league with the temple, my lady, why not just hand Domina Kattë right back to them, and let her rot there? Far fewer of his fingerprints left on this that way, if it were discovered — as it has been. And why would Duon have spent the past week promising to deliver her to you if their intent were simply to withhold her? No, it seems more likely now that this mysterious healer Duon's been promising was, in fact, Sian Kattë. They were probably planning to disguise her as a priest somehow, just long enough to use her gift to heal Konrad and restore the temple's reputation, then dispatch her somehow. But it seems they lost her before she could be put to their intended use. I would guess Duon's been vamping ever since in hope of finding and arresting her again." He gave her a dry smile. "I'd give a small fortune to know how her escape was managed. That might tell us quite a lot about who else is really playing here."

"Still ..." said Viktor, staring inward. "Might there be members of this conspiracy even inside the temple — unknown perhaps, even to Father Duon?"

"Like whom, sir?" Hivat asked. "Have you some particular suspicion?"

"My son seemed to be healing for a time. Then, suddenly, his illness returned and he's grown worse ever since — no matter what his priestly healers seem to try ..."

Arian felt her jaw go slack as his meaning registered. "Are you suggesting he's been *poisoned*? By the *priests themselves*?"

Hivat looked troubled, his gaze turned inward too now. "We do have reconnaissance suggesting that Duon is not much better liked inside the temple these days than he is here in this room. He is perceived by many of his own priests as ... well, rather pampered and self-serving, apparently. He could be headed toward a coup of his own, I suppose, completely unaware. If the Census Taker promised to throw his own considerable resources into seeing Duon replaced — legitimately or covertly — by one of these conspirators, perhaps, that might explain the temple's strange lack of success — as well as Duon's apparent ineffectuality."

"I want every priest removed from this house, immediately," Viktor growled, turning as if to march to the door and make it so.

"My lord," said Hivat, stopping Viktor with a placating gesture. "If this conspiracy has any reason to believe they've been discovered, they might feel forced to desperate measures. We could bring the coup down on your head this instant without any time to prepare ourselves."

Viktor looked down at Arian. "I believe my wife has given us all the cover we need — for this, at least. How *did* your conversation with Duon turn out, my love?"

"I ... He ... When I realized he had been lying about all of it, I ..." She looked down and shook her head. One more *hysterical woman* for the sergeant's collection. "I told him we would have his head, basically. ... In front of everyone this time."

"There! You see?" Viktor raised his hands triumphantly. "How could we possibly continue to trust priests in Konrad's chambers after such an altercation with their leader? Everyone may wonder if we're crazy, but no one will wonder why we sent them packing so suddenly." He gave Arian a grim smile, which she hadn't the heart just then to return.

"It will be seen to, then," Hivat said, still clearly very dubious.

"But what good will that do now, if Konrad dies anyway?" Arian protested. "There is someone in this city who can heal him, and we know exactly where she is. We *must* get her out of there and bring her to him while there's time!"

"My lady, I see no ready way to do that without alerting the Census Taker that he's been discovered. I can think of no better way to ignite whatever coup may be in the offing. We simply must have time to find out how badly your own household has been infiltrated, and then to formulate a plan for defusing the plot without launching Alizar right into civil war. For that is what's at stake here. Civil war. The stars themselves have seemed aligned against this nation for some time now. All these islands need is one more shock, and the entire fabric could give way. We have no choice but to act more cautiously than ever."

"Which means that I'm to sacrifice my son, our heir, to the slender hope that if we all just sit still enough and hold our breaths, this storm may dissipate?" She looked up at her husband, trembling with frustration. "You just told me that if there was any way to fight, even with our feet, you'd do it. Did you mean for our son, Viktor, or just for Alizar?"

"Arian ... please. Don't cast the difficult decisions before us in such a light. I exist — *we* exist — to care for Alizar. I too love our son. I would do anything within my power to save him, but I cannot plunge the whole nation I am sworn to serve into fiery chaos just to spare myself ... or those I love. That would mean betrayal of all I'm sworn to do and be."

"So you would betray instead the son who loves and trusts you?" Arian surged to her feet once more. "To accommodate a country that would throw you — and me and Konrad — to the sharks without a second thought? You said yourself, this morning, that they only endure us so they'll have a ..." she glanced at Ennias, "a scapegoat to spare themselves responsibility! Well, we've given them our best for half a lifetime, but we owe *no one* the life of our son. If there's a woman out on Cutter's who can save him, then I want that woman here! No matter what it costs this ungrateful nation." She spun to glare at Hivat. "Find a way to get her here immediately. I am done waiting and waiting while he dies."

"Arian," pled Viktor. "If Escotte has the slightest reason to suspect —"

"Tell Escotte he can have the Factorate!" she turned to snap at him. "Tell him we will give it to him — or to whomever he's been plotting with — and good riddance! What joy has it ever brought us?" She turned back to Hivat. "Wouldn't that help even more to ensure an orderly transition? Why let Konrad die, when we can just make plain to these conspirators that there is no one standing in their way?" All three men were staring at her now, in speechless astonishment. The quintessential *hysterical woman*. It made her want to scream at them — as loudly and as incoherently as she was able.

All her life, she had allowed the disciplines of statecraft to define her — first in her father's house, and then in this one. It felt sometimes as if she had spent every minute of every waking day holding her breath in the fearful service of whatever avatar of wealth and power might be looking down and judging her performance. And now they wanted her to hand them Konrad and just look away. For the greater good of Alizar and the Alkattha clan.

Well, she was finished serving at such altars.

"I know what you're all thinking," she said, with glacial calm now, "and I don't care." She looked at Hivat, then at Ennias, and finally at Viktor, holding each man's gaze until it wavered from her own. "You ask me how one child's life can matter more than all these vastly larger things at stake. Is it not possible, gentlemen, that such perspectives are precisely what has led our country to this impasse?" She gestured toward a window at her husband's fraying kingdom. "Ask these threadbare islands what has rotted all the bonds that once welded them into a nation. You say the stars have been aligned against us, Hivat, but I'd say we have simply been aligned against ourselves. If Alizar had not sacrificed so many children over all its centuries, perhaps there would be less discontent seething in its streets today, less ruthlessness driving its most fortunate citizens to betray each other. Less fear of *civil war* to bind our hands."

"What would you have us do then, Arian?" Viktor asked quietly. "I cannot just write Escotte and offer him the Factorate. You know it's not that simple. Especially if he's made a deal with some other house. My own family would as likely have me assassinated, and go to war with him themselves, as allow it. Nothing would be fixed that way."

Now it was her gaze that wavered. In the end, no matter how good one's intentions, there was always that godsdamned insurmountable question. What to *do*. What *could* be done? She turned back to the chief of security. "I do understand the need for caution, Hivat. I too want this crisis defused without calamity. But if Sergeant Ennias is correct, it would take this cousin of ours no more than a touch to heal my son. A single moment of contact. Is there no way this could be arranged? In some manner that Escotte would never be aware of?"

"How, my lady? She is kept imprisoned in his house."

"Perhaps ... we could pay Escotte a visit of some kind. To discuss ... my mishandling of the temple. I don't care. And someone ..." she turned hopefully to Ennias, "could smuggle Konrad very briefly in to see this woman while Viktor and I kept the Census Taker distracted. Do you think you might be able to do that, Sergeant?"

The sergeant cleared his throat, and looked nervously from Hivat to Viktor. "I would need to know more specifically what my lady has in mind ..."

"My lady," Hivat asked carefully, "are you suggesting that you and the Factor show up at the Census Taker's home, for some hastily scheduled meeting, with your unconscious son in tow? That would seem quite strange, to anyone, I should think."

"Well ... of course we would not bring Konrad to the door with us," she said, scrambling to articulate what she did mean, exactly. "He would be hidden in our litter, I suppose, and smuggled inside to the woman by this sergeant, perhaps, while we were in discussion with Escotte elsewhere?"

"An unconscious boy carried into the Census Hall from your litter in the building's unobstructed forecourt," said Hivat, "then through who knows how many corridors, and up any number of stairs, by one man, without being seen by an entire household of serving staff, into the presense of a woman who is, by the sergeant's account, never unaccompanied?" He shook his head. "My lady, I am sorry, but we must come up with some more likely plan. Can we be sure your son would even survive such strenuous transport at this point?"

She did not know. And it was a fair question, she reminded herself sternly, determined neither to allow herself tears right now, nor to snap at him for asking it. "All right then. Might we smuggle her outside to him, somehow, while Viktor and I were with Escotte?"

"My lady," Hivat said, "we've been told that she is always under guard, and I cannot imagine that Escotte would not have her more closely guarded than ever while you and the Factor were in his house. Indeed, he would likely find your very presence there, on such short notice, quite suspicious under these circumstances."

The sergeant cleared his throat again, and said, "If I may, my lady, Domni Hivat?"

"Please," Arian replied, leaning against her chair.

"I believe Domni Hivat may be correct about the Census Taker's unease with your presence there, which means that *I* would likely be the guard assigned to Domina Kattë during your visit. For whatever that is worth."

"Might that not make everything easier?" she asked.

"Some, perhaps," said Ennias. "But there would almost certainly be others with her too. Her maid, at least. Unless you came after Domina Kattë had retired for the evening, and her maid had gone home — which would be a strange time to visit the Census Taker, I assume."

"I see," Arian said. "How much might it take to subvert this maid to our purpose as well, do you think?"

Hivat shook his head before the sergeant could answer. "Much too dangerous, my lady. Even if she could be persuaded somehow, she might lose her nerve at any moment during or after the task, and expose us. Sergeant Ennias is a military man, with all the nerve and discipline implied, I'm sure. But an untempered domestic trained to fear the authority of a man like Escotte Alkattha … I would never trust my back to such a creature."

Hysterical women. Again. Arian turned to Ennias. "What is your opinion, Sergeant? You have actually met her, surely. And, as a commander, you must be a decent judge of character. I will trust your assessment. Is this maid a willing party to Escotte's conspiracy? Does she like or dislike her employer? Might she be persuadable, do you think, and if so, trustworthy, or not?"

Ennias glanced uncomfortably at Hivat, then back to Arian, clearly understanding what an awkward position she had placed him in, which just affirmed her growing trust of his perception. "Cleone seems a decent sort, my lady. She's clearly been instructed not to leave Domina Kattë unsupervised, and to keep her presence at the Hall a secret, but I doubt she has any idea why, or would ever think of asking. She is quite proper — or she would never have been trusted with this task to start with." He fell silent for a moment, looking thoughtful. "In fact, she is so proper that, if she were to learn what her employer was involved in, and involving her in, she might well feel compelled, as I did, to do the right thing."

Arian was careful not to smile in triumph. Not yet, at least. "And what about her nerve, Sergeant? Once persuaded, could she be trusted to keep her head and follow through?"

She saw Ennias suppress another of his little grins. "No one remains in Lord Alkattha's service for very long unless they are equipped with ample nerve and ability to keep their heads and follow through, my lady."

Arian turned back to Hivat and raised her brows.

Hivat sighed deeply, clearly struggling not to roll his eyes. "And what do you think it might take to persuade this woman that betraying her longtime, and frighteningly powerful, employer was the *right thing*, Sergeant? Would *you* be able to do it?"

Ennias thought about it for a moment, then shook his head. "I doubt she would trust my word enough to risk the Census Taker's wrath."

"Whose word might she trust enough, then?" Hivat asked, seeming to suppress a triumphant smile of his own now.

"None I can think of," Ennias conceded. "Except..." He looked uncertainly at Arian. "Cleone respects authority. Unquestioningly, from what I've seen. If she were to be told what's happening by someone whose authority exceeded the Census Taker's, I have little doubt she would comply with whatever they requested. She would see it as the *only* right thing to do."

"Well then," Arian said briskly. "Can we not smuggle her up here somehow? Tonight, after she's gone home from work, perhaps."

Hivat shook his head and sighed again. The game was not going his way after all, it seemed. Poor man. Arian was careful to look sympathetic.

"Do you have any idea, my lady, how difficult it was to bring the sergeant here without being seen by anyone? And now we are to do it twice? In a single day?"

"And yet, you succeeded, Hivat," Arian parried. "In broad daylight, while we will have the cover of night and almost no one about, this time."

"I believe I could get her here, sir," Ennias informed Hivat. "I am given the afternoon and evening off once a week. This is the day. It's why I came to see you now. I could intercept Cleone tonight and bring her here, if you wish."

Hivat nodded, glaring daggers at the sergeant now, to Arian's considerable amusement. "Very well, but I will be accompanying you. We must be certain that you are not seen — at any point along the way — a task I dare not leave to amateurs."

Amateurs! Arian thought. What had happened to all that seasoned 'nerve and discipline' Hivat had credited this military man with just minutes earlier? It was a struggle, suddenly, to keep herself from laughing. She was liking this young sergeant quite a lot by now. Perhaps when this was over, he might better serve in the Factorate house guard — if not some higher post. "Unfortunately, I am having dinner in my chambers with my brother tonight." Viktor gave her a surprised look. "It seems he's tired of being an outcast," she told him. "He met me on the docks this afternoon, an utterly changed man, concerned about my visit to Duon, and offering to help if I was in any trouble — quite sincerely, if you can believe it."

"Pardon me, my dear, if I trust sincerity in your brother even less than I trust his self-serving arrogance," Viktor replied. "His help is the last thing I want, at any time, least of all right now."

"I understand that, Viktor. But, as I've been telling you all along, it does seem he is not the snake in our fruit bowl. I hardly wish to risk discouraging this sudden change of heart, so I will have to see this maid after Aros and I have finished supper." She turned back to Hivat. "Do you think that you could have her here by ... three or four hours after dark?"

Hivat turned an inquisitive, if still quite disgruntled, look at Ennias, who nodded.

"Cleone leaves after Domina Kattë has retired for the evening. That should give us time."

"Good," said Arian. "I'll send Maronne down my private stair to fetch you two and the maid as soon as my brother is gone, if that's acceptable?"

"As you wish, my lady," Hivat said. "But, if I am not mistaken, we have still devised no plan for bringing your son and this healer together. Should we not know what we're asking this woman to do before smuggling her into your presence?"

"Yes, of course," Arian said pleasantly. "By all means, let's devise a plan, then. I have at least another hour or two before dinner. Sergeant, can we not offer you a seat? You too, Hivat. This will doubtless take a while."

EIGHTEEN

S ian followed Cleone up yet another stairway toward this evening's cocktail hour with Escotte, being served tonight, it seemed, in a third-floor sitting room on the building's northwest corner, as opposed to all the other sitting rooms she had been shown to on all the other evenings in who knew how many other wings. She sometimes felt as though she were being taken on an extremely slow tour of the Census Hall, one or two rooms per day.

"Will that be all, my lady?" Cleone asked, hesitating at the doorway when they had arrived.

"Thank you, yes. I can safely find my way inside from here, I think."

The maid curtsied, seemingly oblivious of Sian's attempt at wit. "I hope you pass a pleasant evening, then. I will see you before bed."

Sian did, in fact, navigate the passage from plush hallway to elegant sitting room without incident, to find Escotte waiting for her, seated in a large, well-upholstered chair, clad in magenta and puce like a particularly ill-painted chessman. Gigi was nowhere in evidence tonight. Sian wondered if she should inquire after the monkey's health. Perhaps she had retired to the continent as well.

"Please, refresh yourself," Escotte said as she walked in, waving toward Quatama, his chief butler, who stood stiffly by a sideboard generously laden with bottles and a plate of pastries, ready to serve her. As usual, Sian was hungry. Everyone seemed used to that by now.

When she had accepted an arak-and-soda and a small sterling plate of pumpkin-and-goat-cheese tartelettes from Quatama, she went to settle herself in the large upholstered chair beside Escotte's. The butler followed to refresh Escotte's drink and offer him another tartelette, then bowed low to them, and withdrew.

Her cousin made his usual show of enjoying the snack, as though he'd never dined so sumptuously in all his life. "Have you had a pleasant day?" he asked around a mouthful of pastry.

"Lovely," Sian said, savoring the bitterness of the anise against the sweet soda. "Cleone and I wrote hideous villanelles."

Escotte tittered. "I am sure they were quite capably executed. I should like to see them."

"I am certain you would not, but I'll let you be the judge of that."

"Oh, yes, do send them to me." He watched her eat her second tartelette, making her self-conscious of the crumbs falling on her dress. "You look stunning tonight," Escotte added.

"Why, thank you," Sian said, trying not to laugh as she brushed the crumbs away. The dress she wore was one of Víolethe's, and not much more attractive than Escotte's own appalling robe tonight. She had quickly realized that, whatever Escotte might pretend, showing up for cocktails or dinner in anything other than the clothes he had procured for her caused him disappointment. She'd started working her way through the closet of horrors, wearing the least objectionable first. After more than a week, however, she was left with this tight-bodiced tangerine and scarlet gown with its extravagantly padded sleeves and ruffled peplum. It was almost a cruel parody of her own, more muted dusty rose dress with orange piping, ruined the night of her ... rescue. If these clothes had not been on loan to her, she would have at least torn off the layers of frothy red lace at its neck, wrists, and hemline, but alas ... "It was kind of you to find me all these lovely things to wear."

Escotte waved his hand dismissively. "The pleasure is mine! Truly, cousin, you should wear warm colors more often. They quite suit you."

They quite do not, Sian thought, smiling pleasantly as she cast her eyes about the room in search of something else to talk about among the tapestries or sofa-cushions. The small round table between them caught her eye, its marbled top cunningly inlaid with brightly colored tiles. The pattern was abstract, yet pleasing in some mysterious way. What a fine bolt of cloth it would make, she thought, her business mind already trying to organize its preparation for Monde & Kattë's looms. "Where did you find this lovely table, cousin?"

"I have my sources, dear." Escotte gave her a mischievous smile. "It's from the City Imperishable. An artifact from *before*," he added to be sure she understood the table's mind-bending antiquity. "I relish things of beauty from the past, don't you?"

Sian tried not to gape. If what he said was true, the table alone was worth more than her entire … everything. She looked again at the exquisite jewel-box of a room, the gilded onyx wall lamps, the exquisitely carved teak and mahogany furniture, the crystal decanters and silver-furnished sideboard, the Hanchu silk rug at their feet. How much wealth did this one room contain? How much of Alizar's treasury had it taken to furnish the entire building?

Escotte set his glass down on the priceless table, then ran his hand gently across the tiles before looking up at Sian. "I can guess what you are thinking, cousin."

"Oh! You are a mind reader now?" she said, trying to cover her discomfort with humor. "Strange powers clearly run in our family."

"You think me just a hoarder of wealth."

"You are an utter failure at this skill you boast of, cousin," she teased, unnerved by this evidence of her own transparency.

"Come now," he replied. "Don't deny it. I can see it very plainly in your eyes."

"Don't be ridiculous. What reason could you, of all people, have to care about more wealth, Escotte? But surely you do not suppose that anyone could look around here and be unimpressed." She was careful to smile as she said it, thinking, *A hoarder of prestige, if anything.* "Can even you take so much treasure for granted?"

"I take nothing I possess for granted, dear. Nor, to be candid, am I as unconcerned about more wealth as you claim to suppose. In my experience there is no such thing as enough, let alone too much, especially in troubled times like these. But I fear you do misunderstand me." He looked at her earnestly. "This table, beautiful and rare as it may be, is not just wealth to me. It is *history*. And history tends to be the first thing lost in times of upheaval." He gave her a wistful smile, and stroked the table again. "Whole civilizations come and go, leaving us nothing more than these rare glimpses."

Dear me. Escotte Alkattha, noted preserver of history? A shame your tastes don't equal your ambition, she thought, recalling the absurd contents of his library. Everything about this conversation was rubbing her the wrong way. "So you're just collecting all these lovely things against some future rainy day?" she could not help asking with a teasing smile.

"I've no desire to be disingenuous, cousin." Escotte leaned back into his chair again. "We both know what a crucial resource wealth is. It is my money, at least as much as my position, which enables me to keep you here in safety — not to mention comfort."

"And I'm very grateful for that," she answered automatically. Which she was, of course.

Escotte gave her a look, then said, "Shall we have another tartelette or two? Dinner is an hour off yet."

"Yes, please." She was almost not embarrassed by her hunger now. Almost.

Escotte picked up a tiny crystal bell from the ancient table between them. Its tinkling sound was sweet enough to please the gods. Such a bell, she thought, must surely have been imported from the very stars above, and presented to Escotte Alkattha by winged gremlins on a blanket sewn of albino nighthorse skins. Or some such. She kept this uncharitable thought to herself, of course, as Quatama entered to refresh their drinks and bring them more pastries from the sideboard mere feet away, before withdrawing once again.

"How go your arrangements for my meeting with the Factor's son?" Sian tried, between sips of her refilled drink.

"Laboriously, as you might expect." Escotte shifted in his chair and crossed his legs, revealing a magenta-and-puce-stockinged ankle and a bit of plump calf.

"Anything you can share with me?" she asked.

"Nothing useful or safe for you to know." He sipped his drink without meeting her eyes, clearly wishing for another change of subject.

Sian fought back a sigh, and gazed around the room again, finding no safer topic even there this time.

"Truly, dear, you needn't worry about it," Escotte added, more gently. "Everything will be resolved quite soon, I'm sure. Just relax, and enjoy your holiday here."

"I ..." Sian started, then stopped.

"Yes?"

"I just wonder if there's a way I could relax here in some ... less supervised way?"

"What do you mean?" Escotte's voice sharpened a bit. "Has Cleone's service been less than satisfactory?"

"No, of course not — she is quite capable ... and creative. But she is with me constantly, always trying to amuse me. I have not a moment to myself. If I leave my chambers, Ennias or Wurrit are there standing guard as well. Can I never be alone — even here inside the house?"

"I believe I have explained more than once the dangers involved for you — even here, regrettably."

"Yes, I do understand that ..."

"Is there some further diversion or amenity you desire? Perhaps a favored delicacy that our kitchens are not providing? Just say the word and I shall have it done." His words were kind; his tone somewhat less so.

"No, no — your kitchens are quite astonishing. There is nothing more I want."

Escotte frowned. "Then what *is* the problem, cousin?"

Fighting down frustration that she knew she must not show, she said, "I simply find it quite uncomfortable to be escorted even to the toilet, like a child. Surely you can understand that, Escotte. I cannot visit your innermost courtyards without an armed guard. Are your fish that dangerous? I am used to some amount of freedom." She picked up her cocktail and took an unusually large swig.

Her normally foppish cousin fixed her with a glare more stern than any she had ever seen on his round, soft face. "My dear Sian," he said, his voice cold, "I am sorry that you find my hospitality so offensive. I will happily return you to the Mishrah-Khote at any time; you need only ask."

"I … no! I meant no offense, Escotte. Have I not told you how grateful I am?"

"Ah. Forgive me. I misunderstood then."

"Yes. Of course. I'm sorry to have so poorly expressed my concerns, cousin."

"Let's just consider this unfortunate exchange forgotten, shall we?" He got up to get another pastry for himself — the little bell also forgotten.

After that, an uncomfortable silence fell across the room, settling like a veneer of oily dust on all its lovely furnishings. Sian concentrated on her cocktail, though it no longer tasted half so sweet. When it was finished, she sat wishing desperately for any of Cleone's little bags of sewing or bead-stringing kits with which to fill the awkward vacuum, until, finally, Quatama came to announce their dinner. She leapt up and started for the door, tempted to embrace the man from sheer relief, though, for once, she had no appetite at all.

ᴧ

"Would you like a bit more cake, perhaps?" Arian asked, just a tad frantically, already beckoning Lucia with a glance.

"No, no. I am quite sated," Aros said, setting his fork down and lifting his linen napkin to dab at the corners of his mouth. "Thank you for such a lovely meal, sister. I cannot tell you how relieved, and grateful, I am that we're on speaking terms again. I'm so sorry that things ever came to such a pass between us. But … well, it's been difficult, you know? I've been so … unsure of what to do with myself here. For so long now. One drifts. And becomes a dreadful idiot, it seems, without ever meaning to, or even noticing." He looked down sadly. "Until he hits a wall."

"Oh, dear brother, I understand you all too well," said Arian. "I've felt quite adrift here for some time myself. And look where it has gotten me! I've made such a dreadful mess of things with the Mishrah-Khote, I fear. I've just been so worried for my son. And all the trouble on our streets these days, with this awful Butchered God cult. You would not believe the things I'm told they're saying about Viktor now. And myself, of course." She raised her own napkin to dab yet again at manufactured tears in the corners of her eyes.

Part of the plan hashed out that afternoon would rest on a broadcast fiction that the Factora-Consort had succumbed to pressure and gone into seclusion in her chambers. Hysterical women could be good for something after all, it seemed. That part had been her idea, if inspired by her male companions. She had taken full advantage of this supper to convince her brother she was on the very edge of nervous collapse, lest he become suspicious when her maids began turning away all callers tomorrow, including him. Viktor's paranoia about her family had always been absurd, of course, but even she conceded that she could not trust Aros to keep his mouth shut until all of this was over. So, alas, he must be decieved as well, for the time being.

"I too wonder what I'm doing here," she continued with a sigh, pressing a trembling palm against her forehead. "Every day. I ... I honestly don't know how much longer I can take it, Aros."

"I had no idea you were suffering so," he said tenderly, reaching across the table to lay his hand upon hers. "You've always seemed so calm. So ... in control."

"That's all I *can* do lately. *Seem*. And now I've grown so tired, even of that. The mere idea of any actual control is just ... a cruel jest." She fell silent, as if struggling with herself. "It helps to talk ... with someone I can trust." She looked up at him in feigned desperation. "I can trust you, can't I, brother?"

"Well, yes! Of course," he rushed to reassure her. "I am quite concerned for you. Perhaps you ought to take some rest? The kingdom will not fall apart, I'm sure, if you just take a day or two to get away. Is that not possible?"

"Oh, dear Aros. I suspect you're right. Father's always drummed it in so that withdrawal is weakness, and that weakness is never acceptable. But ..." she breathed a little faster, and forced a few more tears into her eyes. "I do so wish I could just run away. I am so tired of having to perform like this. So tired of all the people. My very skin hurts at the thought of them. I just want to ... to stop all contact sometimes. Retreat into a thick cocoon, and hide. Does that sound awful? Do I seem ... weak?"

"No. No, sister. Not at all. I see now just how strong you've been, for far too long. While I was busy being such a thorn in your side." He looked down again. "It shames me, truly. But *you* have no cause at all to feel ashamed.

Take that time, Arian. Apologize to no one."

She gazed at him. "Viktor says the same. Oh Aros, it makes me so sad that you two do not get on better. He's really such a good man, if you knew him. As are you. Say you'll try to give each other a second chance. Will you do that? For me?"

"I'll do anything for you," he said. "If Viktor is willing to allow it, I will make every effort to repair that misunderstanding too. I promise."

She reached out to grasp his hand. Like a drowning woman. She knew she was performing, but it was also true. The two men she loved best in the world ... and so much distrust and dislike between them. "Oh thank you. That would help me ever so much more than you might guess."

"It is the least I can do. And if there is more, anything at all, just tell me."

"That will be ever so much more than enough, dear brother." She glanced toward the darkened windows of her sitting room and released a weary sigh. "I feel so tired." She looked back at him. "This has been lovely, Aros, but I fear that I am spent."

"Yes, yes. Of course." He rose from his seat. "You need your rest. I'll go now. But thank you, dear. For making this time, and for your understanding. You will not have me to worry about any longer. That much I can promise."

"Thank you for that. We must dine again like this. Soon. Perhaps ... with Viktor even? If you don't think that would be —"

"A pleasure. It would be a pleasure," he assured her, coming round the table. "Now you should go to bed." He helped her up gently. When she was standing, he leaned in and kissed her on the cheek, then turned and headed for the door, arriving just a step or two behind Maronne, who had gone to pull it open for him. "And do think about that day or two of rest, will you?"

"I will." *Though not just yet*, she added silently.

He gave her an encouraging smile, then stepped through the threshold and was gone.

"What a changed man he is!" Lucia said when Maronne had closed the door behind him.

"What a changed man he *was*, you mean," Arian corrected her. "Don't you remember what a sweet boy he used to be? None of us has quite survived this place intact." She gazed through her windows at the darkness once again. "I'm just so glad to see him remembering himself. I feel dire need of such encouragement. Now, quickly, clear these things away, and let's make sure I look as regal as possible. It's time to inform this maid they've brought me of her sudden illness, and convince her to cooperate."

"I still cannot believe they're making you do this?" Lucia said, carrying dishes away from the table with Maronne.

"They're not making me do anything," said Arian. "I made *them* do this. There is no one else in this house we can trust just now, and I'm the only one who can be gone so long without being missed immediately."

"But surely he will recognize you," said Lucia.

"We will dye my hair tonight, of course, as soon as this girl is gone. And tomorrow morning: no cosmetics."

"Oh ..." Lucia murmured. "How dreadful."

"I still say Domni Hivat could have gone instead," Maronne insisted.

"To be a maid?" Arian scoffed. "It is a woman we're in need of, and Hivat would not look inconspicuous in a dress." She glanced up at Maronne. "It is I, not Hivat, who must apologize to you, dear. I'm the one who's placing you at such risk. You may still refuse, of course. I hope I've made that clear."

Maronne turned to face her, as close to haughtily as Arian had ever seen her. "Do I seem afraid to you, my lady? A *cowardly woman*?" She smiled slightly, knowing just where to twist the blade. They'd been friends a very long time.

"All right then," Arian said. "Lucia, please come see that my face has not been ruined by all that dabbing over dinner. Maronne, will you go down and bring them, please?"

"My lady," Maronne said, heading off to Arian's bedchamber where there was, of course, a panel easily opened if one knew the secret of its operation, and a staircase that allowed the Factora-Consort to come and go when needed without risk of being observed.

NINETEEN

"More marmalade, my dear?" Escotte asked Sian. "That toast looks rather dry."

The under-butler serving them this morning started toward the indicated preserve, but Sian shook her head. "No, thank you. I've run out of room, I think. I'll just leave the toast."

"Really!" Escotte said, his brows raised. "But you've hardly eaten anything."

By her new standards, perhaps. She'd still eaten at least two meals worth for any normal woman, surely, though her appetite had still not quite recovered from the effects of last night's unpleasantness. Escotte's carefully cultivated cheer over breakfast seemed dangerously shallow. Of course, that might just be due to his displeasure over Cleone's failure to appear that morning.

Sian was worried for her too. She could not believe the conscientious girl capable of oversleeping. So what had happened to her? Sergeant Ennias had been dispatched immediately to find out, leaving Sian's alternative guard, Wurrit, to escort her down here to Escotte's 'informal' breakfast room. She had yet to see the formal breakfast room, and did not expect to, as it was doubtlessly reserved for functions to which her cousin's *secret guest* would never be invited.

Quatama entered in what, for him, seemed quite a rush, and bent to whisper something into Escotte's ear. Gigi, apparently recovered from last night's indisposition, began searching through the butler's hair, as if for fleas.

"What sort of illness?" Escotte asked, drawing back as if Quatama himself might be infected. Keeping a wary eye on the monkey, the butler bent again to whisper his reply, but Escotte shooed him back in irritation. "Just speak up, man. There is no one to be keeping secrets from in here. It's her maid we are discussing, after all."

The head butler straightened almost convulsively, blushing visibly, though his expression remained calm as ever. "Sergeant Ennias did describe some of her symptoms to me, sir, but … I am hesitant to relay them too specifically while you are still enjoying breakfast."

"Is it contagious, do you think?" Escotte asked. "Should I be concerned?"

"It seems a common fever, sir, accompanied by severe, but not unusual … excrescences."

"Yes, yes. I see. Well, that is quite enough, just as you say." Escotte cast his eyes around the room impatiently. "Now what are we to do? This is very inconvenient."

It would be a simple thing just to go heal the girl, Sian thought. But she was not about to suggest that she be let out of the building after last night's quiet row. Cleone could be brought to the Census Hall for healing — Sian opened her mouth to mention this, but Quatama spoke up first.

"I beg your pardon, sir, but I was just about to say that Sergeant Ennias has brought a lady with him to replace her. Someone Cleone referred him to, it seems."

"*What?*" Escotte exclaimed. "The head of my house guard is procuring maids now, without a word to me? Who is this woman? What can he be thinking to bring some stranger here, sight unseen?" He glanced warily at Sian. "My cousin is not just any guest to take potluck off the streets."

"I shall send her off, of course," Quatama said, already turning to leave.

"No, no. We need someone to look after my dear cousin's needs until Cleone recovers." Escotte leaned back and rolled his eyes; the monkey dropped into his lap and began inspecting his plate. "I suppose it cannot hurt to find out who this woman is. You say Cleone recommended her?"

"Quite highly, according to the sergeant," said Quatama.

"Well, Cleone would know what I expect of such a person. Bring her in, I guess. Let's have this over with."

"Bring her … now, sir?" Quatama asked. "While you're still at breakfast?"

"Yes!" Escotte said, clearly verging on exasperation. "You don't imagine I would leave my cousin here to eat alone while I go out there to interview her, do you?"

"No, sir. I shall bring her right away, sir." He turned back at the doorway and asked, "Shall I bring the sergeant too, sir?"

Escotte drew a deep breath, and said, softly, "I am not interviewing the sergeant, am I, Quatama. I've already hired him, and plan to keep him on a while. Most likely."

"Yes, of course, sir. Thank you." He was gone before his murmured thanks had faded.

Gigi sidled up onto the table and began poking through the serving dishes, moving slowly, as though that made her invisible.

Escotte turned to Sian and shook his head. "Do you have any household staff, my dear?"

"Just a housekeeper," she said, wishing she were home with Bela now.

"I envy you," said Escotte. "Just one is likely still too many, but an entire household of them …" He piffed and made a helpless gesture. "What a chore they are to manage. It's a wonder I get anything done at all with so much *help*."

Sian was spared having to invent some safe response to this by Quatama's return with a nicely, if conservatively, dressed woman in tow. She was middle-aged and somewhat haggard looking, despite her tidy décolletage, with dark hair, well but clearly dyed, if one knew how to look for such things. *Poor woman*, Sian thought. Still struggling to look young and pretty, in a business where that could make the difference in finding employment — at houses such as this one, anyway. A closer look at this woman's face told Sian all she wished to know about how hard a maid's life must really be. Would Cleone look like that, she wondered, in another ten or twenty years? Sian felt truly awful, suddenly, about the uncharitable view she'd taken of the girl's efforts all this time.

"My Lord Census Taker," Quatama intoned, bowing deeply to his master in this woman's presence, "this is Freda Machen, of whom we have been speaking."

The woman curtsied as well now, very deeply, with striking grace and self-possession, pretending not even to notice the monkey now making quite free with the unfinished smoked langoustine frittata. This was clearly not the first fine house that she had worked in, Sian thought.

"Freda Machen. You are foreign then," said Escotte. "How long since you arrived in Alizar?"

"Several decades, my lord," she replied without any trace of accent or sign of nervousness. "I married an Alizari seaman, who unfortunately died shortly after bringing me to these lovely islands."

"How sad," said Escotte, sounding more bored than sympathetic.

The maid responded with a graceful shrug. "Everyone is dealt a blow or two, my lord. So are we made stronger and wiser."

"I admire your stoicism," Escotte said, somewhat more sincerely. "I have no need of weak or whiny staff here. Where else have you worked?"

"I have worked as a domestic maid ever since my husband's death, my lord, in some very fine houses, including the Factorate itself. I have no doubt they will refer me highly there." She showed no fear at all of Escotte, nor any trace of umbrage at his callous remarks. She might not be as pretty as Cleone, Sian thought with admiration, but she seemed far more poised.

Escotte waved dismissively. "There is no need for that. I expect your tenure here, if any, to be over in no more than a few days. Have you any hobbies?"

At this, Freda raised an eyebrow slightly, then calmly rattled off a list of decorative arts that put poor Cleone's supply to shame.

"The guest you would be serving here is under my protection," Escotte said, "and entangled in a very sensitive and potentially dangerous diplomatic situation. Her presence must be held in strictest secrecy. Are you capable of keeping such a secret, Freda — even from those closest to you?"

Well, I'm already sitting here in front of her, Sian thought dryly. *What are you going to do if she says no, throw her in your dungeon?* Only then did it occur to her to wonder if he really might. Her cousin surely hadn't risen this high without being capable of ruthlessness. She felt the axe swing over her own head again, and suppressed a tremble, hoping that he really was concerned for her well-being, and not just for her concealment.

"The officer who brought me here explained that discretion would be called for, my lord. As I mentioned, I have served at the Factorate itself, and can be trusted to forget whatever I have seen or heard here, at the doorway of your household every evening. If you wish, I believe the Factor himself will attest to my propriety."

"That will certainly not be necessary," said Escotte. "I'll be keeping my own eyes and ears on you, and will know very quickly if you've failed in this respect. But tell me, please; I am not entirely a stranger to the Factorate myself. How is it that I've never seen you there, or heard of someone that, if your claim is to be credited, the Factor himself would vouch for?"

"It is not a servant's purpose to be memorable, my lord. It is a servant's job to be invisible. If you have never heard of me, perhaps I've done my job to satisfaction."

"Well ..." Escotte said, smiling for the first time. "I could hardly have provided any better answer myself. I am impressed, my dear. I will admit it. And I had not expected to be." He turned to Sian. "What do you think, cousin? Will she do for a few days until Cleone is fit to rejoin you?"

Freda turned to Sian and curtsied, less deeply than she had to Escotte, but still more than low enough to make Sian understand how much she hoped for an affirmative answer. Sian felt rather worried for Cleone, actually, wondering if this seasoned veteran might not end up displacing her here altogether. But she felt sympathy for this woman too. "I am more than satisfied," Sian said, offering Freda a reassuring smile.

"Very well, then," Escotte said happily. "Freda Machen, allow me to present my cousin, Domina Sian Kattë, your charge until Cleone returns. Quatama will explain your duties to you. When he is done, you may return, and I will leave you to enjoy each other's company. You and Quatama may leave us now."

Freda dropped another deep and graceful curtsy to her new employer, a second, slighter one to Sian, then turned to follow Quatama from the room.

"Well, that was not as bad as I had feared," said Escotte, lifting a small piece of fruit from plate to mouth, then calling Gigi back to his lap once more. The monkey obeyed, reluctantly, scattering frittata crumbs across the lace tablecloth as she went. "I guess the sergeant is forgiven." He chuckled as he chewed and swallowed. "Which is a rather great relief, actually. *He* would not have been so easy to replace."

～

As it turned out, Escotte did leave Sian behind in the breakfast room after all, though not alone. The under-butler still stood woodenly beside the doorway, ready to serve her more breakfast, should her appetite return — or, more likely, to prevent her unaccompanied departure.

Hardly a moment later, however, Freda flowed back in, offering Sian a gracious smile. "I'm sorry to keep you waiting, my lady. It seems I am to take you to your quarters now, but the butler's directions were ... not entirely comprehensible. This is such a very large house. Would it be dreadful of me to ask if you might lead the way?"

"Goodness no," Sian replied. How refreshing to be the one escorting rather than escorted for once.

As they made their way from hallway to staircase to hallway again, Sian could see Freda making careful mental notes as to their course, and the position of particular landmarks. She was certainly not dull, nor inattentive.

"And here we are at last," Sian said as they arrived outside her bedroom.

"Thank you, my lady." Freda moved gracefully around Sian to open the door for her, then followed Sian in, but stopped almost immediately with an ill-concealed expression of dismay. "Oh, but it is just this room? I had thought ... Where would my lady like me to wait when you desire privacy?"

Privacy? Had Quatama explained Freda's duties to her that poorly? "I've no need of privacy when you are with me," Sian replied, not knowing what else to say. "When you arrive each morning, or if you're called away for any reason during the day, I would appreciate a knock before you re-enter my room. That is my arrangement with Cleone, and it seems to work well enough."

Freda blinked at her. "And ... when my lady has need to ... refresh herself?"

"Oh! My bath and toilet is just down the hall," Sian explained. "Cleone accompanies me there, but waits outside, of course. In case I find myself in some need I had not anticipated. But there is a door." She laughed softly at Freda's incredulous expression. "We're allowed at least that much privacy. As for the rest, we will be like sisters. And if you promise not to tell Cleone," she added, wanting to put this poor woman with her dyed hair more at ease, "I confess it will be very nice to have a sister closer to my own age than dear Cleone is, if only for a couple days."

"I ... Thank you, my lady. Rest assured I will respect such confidences." Freda gazed around the room again. "So, what do you and Cleone do here in this lovely room all day?"

"Well, the girl does have a great many hobbies, which she seems determined to involve me in at every moment, for fear I might grow bored and run crying to my cousin. But I'd be just as happy to sit and read a book from time to time, or gaze out at the garden, or even nap," she said, wishing she had known enough to say so when Cleone had first arrived. "You need not entertain me round the clock, whatever Quatama may have led you to believe."

"I see." Freda considered her strangely. "I beg my lady's pardon if this seems too forward ..."

"Oh, ask anything you like," Sian assured her.

"Then, if my lady will forgive the question, do I detect some small hint of ... *dissatisfaction* with your cousin's hospitality?"

Sian leaned back slightly in surprise. What an odd question. Especially from a maid. Freda *was* brand new, of course. And it was refreshing to be asked. Sian had seen this woman's performance with Escotte at breakfast. She would certainly know better than to carry anything they said back to her cousin. ... Unless ... Could this whole sudden illness of Cleone's just be another of his ruses? Was Freda actually some agent of his, sent in after last night's altercation to find out what Sian really thought about him and the rest of this?

"Please forgive me," Freda said when Sian's hesitation stretched. She ducked her head in embarrassment, if not alarm even. "That was a dreadful thing to ask. I just ..."

"No!" Sian cut in, still fearing some trap, but not wanting to chase off what might be the first honest person she had been allowed to speak with here. "There is no need to apologize. It's just that ... Cleone is not ... so frank, and I've grown so used to being circumspect since coming here. But, please, feel free to speak your mind — with me at least. It would be so nice to have the company of anyone who does. I will keep your confidences, if you promise to keep mine."

Freda nodded, as if still not completely sure of her position either.

They gazed at one another for a moment. Then, seeming to have reached her decision, Freda reached for Sian's hand and said, "You seem afraid of him. Your cousin."

"I am extremely grateful for his protection," Sian said at once, still terrified of what might happen should she turn out to be wrong in trusting Freda. "As he told you, I have stumbled, quite unwittingly, into a great deal of trouble that I still hardly understand. In the past few weeks, I have gone from living a quiet, normal life to being … subjected to terrible attentions, from all sorts of people who should have no cause to know that I exist. All that stopped as soon as Escotte took me in."

"And yet …?" Freda prompted her.

Sian gave her a helpless shrug. "You have already guessed, I think; to judge by your questions. When Quatama was explaining your new duties here, he must have explained about how much privacy you were to allow me?"

Freda nodded, gravely. "I thought he must be exaggerating, until we walked in here. But yes. He said that I was not to allow you out of my sight."

"For my protection. Is that what you were told?"

"Yes." She looked at Sian uncertainly.

"Do you believe it?" Sian asked.

"Do you?" Freda replied.

Sian could not find quite the courage to say 'no' aloud. She pulled loose of Freda's hand, and went to stand beside the windows, gazing down at all the flowers growing silently in Escotte's walled-in garden. "The Census Taker and I are family," she said at last. "I have no idea what is really happening here, but … I cannot believe he means me harm." She turned back to find Freda looking at her with the kind of intensity she had seen Reikos direct at tangled knots, or shipboard instruments in need of some repair.

Freda turned and went to stick her head out of the door, glancing briefly up and down the hallway. When she pulled the door closed again and turned back to Sian, her eyes shone with some new resolve.

"Sian Kattë," she said, coming to stand before her by the windows. "I am going to put my life and the lives of those I love into your hands. If I am wrong… But I don't believe I am, and there is very little time. My name is not Freda Machen."

"What?" Sian took a step away, confused and frightened. "Who —"

"My name is Arian des Chances. Though I can hardly expect you to believe it, I am the Factora-Consort."

Sian's mouth fell open. Then, suddenly, she understood, and breathed again. "So it is finally happening!" She suppressed an urge to laugh for sheer relief. "But, if this is how we're doing it, why did you and Escotte put on that little play at breakfast? Was that just to fool the butlers?"

Now Freda, or the Factora-Consort, rather, took a step back, looking puzzled. "I'm sorry. I don't… How we're doing what? What's finally happening?"

Sian's uncertainty returned. Could this haggard woman with dyed hair really be the Factora-Consort, she now thought to wonder, or had she just fallen into some even more elaborate trap than she had feared? "Haven't you come to take me to your son?"

"Well… yes," the other woman said in obvious astonishment. "How can you know that?"

If this was a trap, Sian supposed, then she was doomed already. "Escotte explained your situation to me on the day I first arrived," she told the woman. "Your trouble with the Mishrah-Khote. The need to set things up so that I could heal your son without their ever knowing I had been involved. He's been hiding me here until he could arrange all this with you. Is that not why you've come?"

The other woman brought a hand up to her cheek, then shook her head and closed her eyes. "Oh my poor, dear woman. How you have been tossed about." She reopened her eyes and went to sit down on the edge of Sian's feather bed. "There have been no negotiations or plans of any kind arranged between your cousin and ourselves. I am sorry to be the bearer of yet more bad news, my dear, but Escotte has no idea I am in this house. Civil war might break out if he did, or so I'm told. He has been hiding you, yes. But *from* us, Domina Kattë. Not *for* us. The Factor and I have reason to believe he is complicit in a plot to overthrow my husband's government, and seize the Factorate for some third party."

Sian stared at her in disbelief, shaking her head, and groping toward a chair to sit on before her legs gave way. "That … is not possible." She collapsed onto a gilded stool beside the windows. "They are cousins. What you're saying … Escotte would never … It makes no sense." She looked more sharply at Freda, Arian, whoever she might really be. "How do I know you're not the one who's lying? You're asking me to believe they sent the *Factora-Consort* herself on some … secret mission to infiltrate my cousin's house? That the Census Taker just talked for who knows how long downstairs with his own cousin's wife, and didn't recognize her? The third most powerful public figure in Alizar?" Sian snorted at the idea's sheer lunacy. "Who are you? Really. That's what I will want know as soon as I have called my cousin's guards." She stood up, but so did the other woman, stepping out to block her path.

"Have you ever even seen the Factora-Consort?" the woman asked.

"Only from a distance," Sian said through gritted teeth, "but she looked nothing like you."

"I'm sure she didn't," said the woman. "Nor have I looked anything like her for many years now. You cannot imagine how many hours it takes each morning, not to mention what a fortune in cosmetics, to make me look like the Factora-Consort. I doubt that anyone besides my maids has seen my real face in ten or fifteen years. Possibly not even Viktor."

Sian stared at her, trying to sort through what she'd just heard.

"Viktor is my husband. The Factor."

"I know what the Factor's name is," Sian growled. "He's my cousin too, though I doubt he knows it, much less cares. What are you trying to say to me? Speak plainly, or I'll just scream for help if you won't let me by."

"Oh, *for all the sand in Alizar!*" the woman spat in sheer frustration. "I've dyed my hair and gone into the light without the mask my ladies paint on me each morning. That is all it takes for the Factora-Consort to go almost anywhere unrecognized by those who aren't looking for her. *She* is a political invention. *I* am exactly who I've claimed to be: a mother, fighting for her son, who is days, perhaps just hours, from dying. It seems that there are people who would like him dead, and if Escotte has any notion that we've discovered he is one of them, it may drive this conspiracy he's working with to who knows what disastrous acts of violence. So I and the tiny handful of others we can still trust have managed to sneak me in here to beg you, please, to help us save my son." Sian saw tears gathering in her reddening eyes. "And to save my husband — and the nation he is trying so hard to care for. Viktor is your cousin too, Sian Katë, and he is well aware of you, and of how very much you matter. To everyone in Alizar, it seems. Not just to us." She was struggling very hard by now to rescue her composure. "Please, tell me how I can convince you."

Sian stared at her, no longer knowing what to think. The desperation in this woman's face and voice seemed very real. This was how Sian supposed she'd look and sound, if Maleen's or Rubya's lives were threatened.

"I chose to tell you the truth because I saw that you too fear your cousin," the woman said, more calmly now. "Was I mistaken? Do your own instincts really tell you that the things I have accused him of cannot be true?"

Sian did fear Escotte. She had for some time now. That much was true.

"Don't you wonder where your two friends really are?" Arian asked. "They are not on any 'secret mission' for Escotte. They're in his dungeon, right here, below the Census Hall."

"How do you know … about any of that?" Sian asked, already certain it was true. She had never believed they would just have left her here without so much as a note in their own hands to explain and say goodbye. She'd just been too afraid to face it. More and more afraid with every passing day here. Her cousin *was* a monster. And she'd known it, all along.

"I know this because one of *our* conspirators is here in Escotte's house," said Arian. "It was Sergeant Ennias who came to tell us what Escotte was doing."

"The same officer who arrested us?"

"The very one," the other woman said. "Now I've handed all our lives to you." She stood aside, and waved Sian toward the door. "If you still mean to call for help, I doubt very much that I could stop you anyway. I'm at least as old as you are, dear, and in far worse condition, if the healthy glow you wear is any indication."

"So you just came here without face paint," said Sian, still reeling in confusion. "That was … brave."

The Factora-Consort responded with a nearly silent humph of swallowed laughter, but remained otherwise silent, still waiting to learn what her fate would be, it seemed.

"What will he do with them?" Sian asked her.

"With who? Your friends?"

Sian nodded, her heart breaking to think of Reikos and Pino languishing down there in the dark, for all this time, while she'd been up here stuffing herself with pastry. "Will he kill them, do you think?"

"I do not know," the Factora-Consort said. "But if I and my husband are defeated here, there will be nothing we can do to help them, or you."

Sian nodded, believing at last that her new maid really was who she claimed to be. She dropped immediately into the best curtsy she could manage.

"Whatever are you doing?" the Factora-Consort asked.

"I have just spent quite a while threatening the Factora-Consort of Alizar," Sian said meekly. "It seems wise to show you more respect, now that I am convinced you're —"

"Oh, don't be silly," said the other woman, coming to pull her up. "And I'd prefer that you continue to call me Freda, please. We can't risk slipping up in front of others. While I am here, it's crucial that I be nothing but your maid, in every respect. Which means no deference of any kind. Is that clear? None at all."

"As you wish, my lady."

The Factora-Consort glared at her. "Did you hear anything I just said, *my lady*?"

"My apologies … Freda," Sian said, still trying to come to grips with it all. "So, what is to happen now? Is your son nearby somewhere, or has some plan been arranged to sneak me out of here with you?"

"The latter. But first we must convince your cousin that you absolutely need to have a new dress sewn. Your maid has led me to believe that this request might not be too hard to justify?"

"My maid?" Sian asked, confused. "You mean, Cleone? You've talked with her?"

"Of course, my dear. Who do you suppose convinced her to fall so conveniently ill this morning? We had a long chat just last night. She was extremely helpful and informative."

"Are your lives always filled with such intrigue?" Sian asked, aborting the *My Lady Consort* just in time.

"Not quite this much," the Factora-Consort sighed. "Mostly it's just piles of correspondence and dull paperwork."

"My life as well!" exclaimed Sian. "Who would have thought it?"

"So, can you convince him that you need a seamstress — rather quickly?"

"That I need a *seamstress*?" Sian was no longer able to stop her laughter. "I will let you be the judge of that, my — Freda." She walked over to the hidden closet's panel-door, and gave its latch a shove. "Behold the wardrobe my dear cousin has supplied for me."

As the door swung open, the Factora-Consort gasped, both hands flying to her mouth in undisguised dismay. "Oh, my dear. How simply ... ghastly!" Her eyes grew even wider. "I remember that one!" She turned to Sian. "Víolethe! She wore it to a Factorate diplomatic ball. Two years after I was wed to Viktor, I believe!"

"These are all Víolethe's," Sian sighed. "Left behind. Some time ago, it would seem. I can't imagine why. I do believe that I could use a seamstress, yes. If my cousin can be persuaded to part with what it costs to pay her, knowing, as he does, that there's no one but you to see me in it here. May I ask why I need this dress right now?"

"Oh yes, my dear. We have a great deal to discuss. But, let's go sit by the windows." She glanced again into the closet with a shudder. "I much prefer the view there."

⟶

Her feet sinking nearly to the ankles in the plush hall carpeting, Arian reached up to tap upon the healer's door. She could only hope that Sian was equipped to execute her part of their necessarily vague plans, and be convincing about it. "My lady? I have brought Lord Alkattha, as you requested."

"Thank you, Freda," Sian answered from inside. "Please bring him in."

With a glance back at the Census Taker, and the absurd monkey on his shoulder, Arian pushed the door open and stood aside to let him pass.

"You wished to see me?" Escotte said as Arian followed him inside.

"Yes, dear cousin. Thank you very much for coming." Sian sat before the windows looking as calm as a mid-summer tide pool now.

"Of course, my dear. I have few greater concerns at present than ensuring your comfort here. Is there some further problem to address?" He looked pointedly back at Freda.

"Oh, no. Quite the opposite. Freda is just wonderful, and I am … Well, I have been thinking, actually. Quite a lot. I wish to apologize for having been such an ungrateful guest. I think I had begun to confuse the strain of all this turmoil in my life for some vague discontent with your extraordinary hospitality. I feel terrible about that. Now that it's so clear."

"Oh, cousin." He gave her an indulgent smile. "You need hardly have concerned yourself. I understand completely." He glanced back at Freda briefly, then gave a little shrug and turned to face Sian again. "I understood all that last night, in fact. As soon as my own little fit of pique had passed. I really must apologize as well, for having answered you so sharply. We are both under quite a bit more strain than usual these days. Please, don't give it any further thought."

"Thank you," Sian said, slumping visibly in relief. Arian relaxed some too. The woman clearly had some acting ability. They might pull this off. "But … there is one other little thing?"

Escotte raised an eyebrow, and waited.

"You asked, last night, if there was anything more I might desire … I hope I am not wrong to presume that this was intended as an invitation to ask you if —"

"Yes, yes, of course," he said preemptively. "Have you thought of something?"

"Well … I have." She smiled shyly at him, like a little girl before an indulgent uncle. "I have also come to realize that what I miss most these days is really my work. The fabrics and the dyes. The patterns and designs; these have been my life, cousin. And suddenly, they're gone. It feels as if … my very hands are withering for lack of use."

Oh, very good, thought Arian. *What a fine embellishment.* Her optimism rose further.

"Cleone has done a marvelous job of finding diversions to keep me occupied, of course, but what I'd really like to do, dear cousin — what would truly make me happy — is to create some dresses."

"Dresses?" Escotte glanced toward Sian's hidden closet, his brows rising another notch.

"Oh, you have been so much more than generous to provide me such a wealth of lovely things," Sian rushed to assure him, "but it's not more clothes I'm wanting, really. It is the creative task of making them. The fabric in my hands again, envisioning design and cut, working out the best approaches to construction. These dresses are all lovely, but they aren't *mine.* Someone else has done the best part. I am left no greater role to play than letting someone put them on me. Do you see? To design a dress or two myself, to see those designs realized … Oh, dear Escotte. Such a task would bring me back to life here. I am sure of it. Might I have a seamstress to come work with me, right here in my room? Freda says she knows a very good one. Here on Cutter's."

Escotte turned to Arian, who looked down modestly. "My guards procure my maids, and now my maids procure my seamstresses?" Happily, he seemed more amused than irritated. The monkey scrambled up to the top of his head and peered about the room. "Perhaps I should just go join Víolethe up on the continent and let the staff run my affairs without me."

"She is an extraordinarily fine seamstress, my lord," said Arian, eyes still cast down respectfully, "and quite inexpensive."

"Humph," he grunted. "Money is not an issue where my dear cousin is concerned." He turned back to Sian, considering her thoughtfully.

"I have worn all these by now," Sian said, looking bashfully toward the hidden closet door. "Will a man of your refined tastes not grow tired of seeing me in the same things every night? Would you not be curious to see what sort of things I would create?"

Escotte humphed at her again, but with a crooked smile this time. "I would certainly not have said this to you under any other circumstances, dear, but there have been occasions when seeing you across the table wearing Víolethe's old dresses did remind me of my wife in … somewhat unsettling ways." His expression grew more wry. "I had actually already considered having some new things made for you."

"Then you will let me have this seamstress?" Sian asked with an excited smile. "Could we start today, dear cousin?" She put a hand across her mouth as if to take the question back. "Is that asking too much?"

"This would make you happy here?" he asked.

"Oh, you cannot imagine how happy," she all but gushed.

Arian had trouble keeping a straight face. Who'd have guessed the woman was this good? Then again, she *was* a self-made success at business, from what Hivat had been able to tell them about her. She'd have to know a fair amount about maneuvering others to have accomplished that.

"Your happiness means everything to me, dear cousin. Of course, you cannot let her know who you are. For your continued safety." Escotte turned to Arian. "You are able to give me an address for this seamstress, I presume?"

"Oh, I could have her back here in a trice, my lord. Her house is hardly blocks away."

He shook his head. "I would not want my cousin deprived of company for even that long, I'm afraid."

Damn! she thought, struggling to let nothing reach her face. *There goes the entire plan.*

"I'll have Sergeant Ennias get her," Escotte said. "He seems to be my new procurer of such persons these days. Can you tell him where to find her?"

Aplologies to all the gods I've just been damning. "Of course, sir. Shall I await him here?"

"I'm here already." Escotte shrugged. "I might as well just take the address to him."

"My stationery kit is over there," Sian told her with an uncertain look, pointing to a miniature cabinet of drawers beside the bed.

Arian went to find it, mentally reviewing her knowledge of the immediate neighborhood. Escotte was surely well aware of everything around the Census Hall, and if the address she gave him made no sense, he'd know it. Were he not a man who'd had no female family members in his house for quite a while — except Sian, of course — Arian would have worried that Escotte would find it strange he hadn't heard of such a fine seamstress so nearby. Or might even have one on staff. Fortunately, though most of Cutter's was a virtual blank to Arian, the neighborhood around the Census Hall was somewhat more familiar, as she'd had occasion to come here a few times. As she found the right drawer at last, and pulled out Sian's supply of writing instruments and paper, she searched her memory for any street name in a residential quarter near enough, then bent to write one that she hoped would pass.

She straightened, and brought the note to Escotte. "It's just a house, my lord. Assidua has no storefront — and needs none, if you take my meaning."

"I shall pass that fact along to Sergeant Ennias," he said. "It's good that she is accustomed to discretion." He turned back to Sian. "Have we anything more to discuss, my dear?"

She shook her head, beaming delight at him. "Thank you so very, very much, Escotte. You can have no idea how much this kindness means to me."

He smiled back at her. "Have I not just explained to you, yet again, how much your happiness matters to me?" He turned and started toward the door. "I look forward to being ravished by these stunning new creations of yours over many dinners in the coming week." He wiggled his fat fingers at her. "Ta!"

Arian closed the door behind him, then turned to grin at Sian. "Oh, well done, my dear! Well done! You'd be a natural at any continental court I know of. I believe this will work beautifully."

"But what address did you give him?"

"Oh, I just made up a number on a residential street nearby. It won't matter to the sergeant. He knows this plan as well as I do, and will understand what must be done. Relax now. You did your part just wonderfully. We've nothing left to do but wait until he brings Maronne."

"You really think we look enough alike to make this work?" Sian asked, all the confidence she had just been wearing laid aside as quickly as she had seemed to take it up.

"She is not that far from your build and coloring. And the silks and veil she's wearing cover her hair and much of her face. She'll be buried behind piles of fabric and supplies as well, of course. No one's likely to have much idea what she looks like, or what you look like either, as we leave."

"But what if someone comes —"

"Into your room? In the middle of the night? Does that happen often here?"

Sian shook her head. "Never that I know of, though I'd have been sleeping, so how would I know if I am checked on?"

"There is a guard at your door all night. Is that correct?"

Sian nodded.

"Then unless they fear you'll climb out these windows and shimmy down the trellis all the way into the garden far below, I cannot see why they should feel any need to check on you in here before your maid comes in the morning. I will certainly find *you* sleeping peacefully when I arrive. And as the *seamstress* is returning so early with the first of your new dresses, we'll have you back up here and dressed in ample time to ravish Escotte over breakfast."

"You keep making it all sound so easy," Sian sighed.

"Cleone will be recovered from her fever by tomorrow evening. I'll be gone by the next day, and Escotte will have no idea anything at all has ever happened. Except that you will look a great deal better over meals, and my son will have suddenly recovered despite the Census Taker's best-laid plans — all praise to the Mishrah-Khote, of course. The hardest part of this was getting Escotte to agree to let Maronne come see you up here in the first place. Now that's done, thank the elusive gods of Alizar."

Sian still didn't look entirely convinced. "And your maids will not mind giving me so many of their dresses?"

"In exchange for new ones?" Arian laughed. "Oh my dear, they'll be blessing you before the mirror for months to come. I'll make sure of that. They'll have more than earned it by the time all this is over."

TWENTY

Sian fidgeted as the minutes ticked by. Half an hour became an hour, and still no one arrived. She and the Factora-Consort had fallen rather quickly into thoughtful silence after their initial burst of self-congratulations. For all her reassurances, Arian seemed no more inclined to chatter now than Sian felt.

"Do I hear something?" Sian asked, glancing from the windows toward the vague suggestion of a footfall from beyond her door.

Arian rose immediately and rushed to check. She cracked the door and stuck her head out, then pulled back into the room and closed the door again. "No one there. Perhaps it took Escotte some time to find the sergeant, or he was distracted by some other matter, and forgot about us. Would you like me to go inquire with someone?"

Sian shook her head, fearful of trying Escotte's patience any further than she must surely have already done. Or of raising his suspicions. "What will you do to Escotte, when all of this is over?" she asked, wondering how much more the world might change before she was returned to it.

"Assuming we are able to determine who else is involved this conspiracy, and defuse it before it can succeed," the Factora-Consort said, "a lot of heads will doubtless roll. For your cousin, I assume it will mean exile at the very least. For others, likely even graver consequences. The least powerful conspirators will doubtless suffer most. That is usually the way of things. You and Sergeant Ennias, however, will likely find your fortunes vastly enhanced."

Would Arouf want her back then? Sian wondered. Once she was an *asset* again ... Would she want him to?

This time the sound of footfalls was unmistakable.

"Thank the gods," said Arian, rising to head for the door again.

She pulled it open to reveal someone bent back under such a load of bolts and skeins and bags of ribbon that it was difficult at first to be sure it was even a woman, much less guess at her appearance. The poor creature came wobbling in beneath her load, followed by Sergeant Ennias carrying a trunk upon his back half as big as Sian herself. With a groan, the woman dumped her tower of fabrics on Sian's bed, while the sergeant squatted almost gracefully to let his burden slide gently between his hands onto the floor at the bed's foot.

"I am glad they sent a man to fetch me," said the woman. "We'd just have had to ask for one if you had come as planned, my —"

"Shhhh!" The Factora-Consort rushed to close the door.

"Thank you, *Freda*," said the sergeant, giving Maronne a gentle nudge.

"This may not be quite so easy as I thought," Maronne said, twisting to stretch out her back. "Old habits die hard, dear Freda."

"You are here now," said the Factora-Consort. "That is what matters. Most of these things can remain where they are tonight, until the dress-maker returns in the morning for Sian's final fitting." She looked at Ennias. "Was there some trouble? You were longer than expected."

"If you wished us back here sooner, *Freda*, you should have given him an address that wasn't two miles away. We had to hang around the wagon long enough so that Lord Alkattha would believe I'd gone that far, found this woman, helped her gather all these things, and gotten them back here. Had I come dashing back much sooner, he'd have thrown us all in prison at the door, I'm pretty sure."

"I'm sorry," Arian said. "I had not thought the street was that far off. It's been quite a while since I was here, and I had very little time to invent an address for him."

"As you said, we're here now," Ennias replied. "Unless there's anything else I ought to know, I'll leave you ladies to your work. Guards don't usually hang about to gab with guests." He started for the door.

"Sergeant," Sian said.

He turned to face her.

"Thank you. I've misjudged you. Clearly. Would you tell Captain Reikos, and my Pino, that … I am deeply sorry for what they suffer, and that they never leave my mind, or my heart?"

"I will, my lady. Just as soon as I can do so without risking notice. They are well, all things considered, and quite concerned for you too. I'm sorry I wasn't free to tell you earlier."

"You have nothing to apologize to me for, Sergeant," Sian said. "My profound thanks go with you."

He offered her a nod, and vanished through the door.

"Well, then," Arian said with satisfaction. "Maronne, it's my pleasure to present Domina Sian Kattë. Sian Kattë, my maid Maronne, hereafter to be addressed as 'Assidua, the seamstress' just as I must continue to be Freda." She gazed pointedly at Maronne. "Are we all clear on that now?"

"Quite clear, dear Freda," Maronne said, blushing. "It's a pleasure doing business with you once again."

"Good." Arian spread her arms. "Let the fittings begin."

"What kind of dress should we be making?" Sian asked.

"Does it matter?" the Factora-Consort asked. "The dresses are already made. And anyone who comes to check on us — in this household, at least — is going to be a man, who won't have any notion what he's looking at in here." She went to Maronne's pile of quite breathtaking silks and airy brocades, and began to toss them here and there around the room. "Let's just make things look like we're working hard, and pin some of these fabrics onto you, gracefully enough, of course, so that if anyone should knock we can stand you up and let them have a glimpse before we shoo them off again."

While Arian went on draping gorgeous fabrics over furniture around the room, Maronne came to start pinning lengths of shimmering violet silk and mouthwatering gold brocade onto Sian.

"So what are we to do for all these hours until we leave tonight?" Sian asked.

"I brought cards," Maronne said, smiling. "And chocolates, of course. No seamstress of any quality would come to a home as fine as this one without chocolates."

"And wine, I hope," Arian chimed in.

"To the home of Escotte Alkattha?" Maronne scoffed. "Surely we can send down for far better wines here than any I'd have brought. The Factorate's neglected cellars have grown quite disappointing lately, have you not noticed, Freda?"

"I may have been distracted by some larger issues," Arian said. "It's just as well, though. Given the brilliant exchange Sian conducted with her cousin earlier, I suspect we'll want to call the servants up from time to time so that they can report to him what tremendous girlish fun we're having. Which reminds me, you should send me downstairs in an hour or two, my lady, to request that your meal be sent up here tonight, due to such extended fittings. If your cousin objects to being deprived of your company at dinner, we may have to stage another audience with him up here so you can wheedle his permission. It is crucial that the dressmaker not be asked to leave before the maid goes home as well. And they would never let Assidua just sit up here while you were in the dining room."

"I trust you will remember, Freda, to convey the lady's wishes that we be fed as well," said Maronne.

"I am a maid, dear Assidua, not a moron," the Factora-Consort said with a smile.

Listening to this banter, the *Factora-Consort* began to fade in Sian's mind into … well, Arian des Chances. A woman made of flesh rather than of mere power and politics. Capable of friendship. And of feelings … Feelings as real and immediate as Sian's. *Arian.* Sian had known what the Factora-Consort's name was just as well as she knew cousin Viktor's. But never until now had she connected it this way with the woman herself. *Arian.* It was a lovely name. Like music. *I'm so glad I did not call the guards on you, Arian,* she thought with a shudder.

As Maronne continued covering Sian in fabrics such as she would likely never see again — even in her line of work — Sian studied this woman's appearance more closely too. Though clearly of an age with Arian, Maronne's skin was far lovelier, if several shades lighter than Sian's. Probably a benefit of having had to slather far less cosmetic paint across it than the Factora-Consort did each day, if her claims were not exaggerated. Maronne's dark hair was long and delicately curled, though heavily streaked with gray, as Sian's own hair had been just weeks ago. Maronne's eyes were green, not fire-spattered black like Sian's.

Noticing her scrutiny, Maronne looked up and smiled. "Of course, we will spend some time with the cosmetics case I've brought as well, Domina Kattë. Do not worry. By the time you are ready to leave me here, I will be a darker, younger-looking woman, while you, alas, will look a great deal more like me."

But I am not a younger woman, Sian almost said, having briefly forgotten, even now, the effects this god's gift had worked upon her thrice-healed body.

The time flew by. Twice they sent Freda down for wine, then laughed and japed as Sian posed for the servants who brought it up to them, to reassure Escotte that he need have no further worries about Sian's discontent. Then they sat playing Five Birds, Picapenny, and Spar with Maronne's cards until the time came to send Freda back down with Sian's request that she and her attendants be allowed to eat dinner in her room that night.

A new, more careful simulation of real fitted drapery was pinned to Sian just beforehand, in shimmering silver and peacock blue silks even more breathtaking than the ones before, just in case Escotte himself should come to debate this latest request in person — which, as they had feared, he did.

Freda had been gone for hardly any time at all when the knock came. Sian and Maronne rushed into position, Sian's arms held out, Maronne's clenched teeth filled with pins as she adjusted pleats. "Come in!" Sian called out.

"You are decent then, cousin?" Escotte asked, already through the door, just steps ahead of Arian. "What marvelous colors, my dear!" He brushed past Maronne as if she weren't there, to finger Sian's nascent dress appreciatively. "What truly lovely fabric!" His surprise seemed quite genuine. "My congratulations! Your creations promise as much elegance as I had hoped." He looked down at the seamstress finally, and said, "I am impressed with your selection, woman. Perhaps we should have a word downstairs before you go. Several of my sitting rooms are in need of drapes." He gazed around at the textile treasure-trove thrown over half the furnishings. "These luscious fabrics fill me with ideas."

"It would be my great honor, lord," said Maronne, neither rising from her crouch at Sian's hem, nor raising her green eyes to meet his gaze, which was quick thinking, Sian realized.

"Very good. Very good," Escotte purred, smiling back up at Sian. "So what is this I hear about our dinner, cousin? I am to eat alone?"

"Oh, dear Escotte," she said, bringing both hands to her mouth as if just realizing he might be disappointed. "I am so sorry. I did not mean to hurt your feelings; it is just that I am having *such* a wonderful time, and there is still so much more to do." She let her eyes grow wide. "I know! Why don't you bring your dinner up here too, and join the fun!" She spread her arms wider to gesture at the fabrics he had just been praising. "I am sure you would have wonderful ideas to contribute to some of my designs. We could make dresses together!"

He did not disappoint her. His expression grew just a little queasy, his smile a bit less certain. Even Gigi looked dubious, burying her face in his fleshy neck with a low whine. "I am honored and delighted by your invitation." His joviality seemed hardly forced at all. "And were my attention not required by so many other tasks tonight, I would accept enthusiastically, of course. But alas, the burdens of my position often curtail my freedom. I have come to enjoy our evening conversations so, but, if you must go on without me here, I will simply look forward all the more to your company in one of these fabulous new dresses tomorrow evening. If that would be acceptable to you, my dear?"

It was getting almost too easy to pull his strings by now. "You are so kind, dear cousin. Thank you for understanding. I shall make it up to you, I promise. And, please, don't put the kitchen to any more trouble than necessary. We require nothing fancy here. A plate of sandwiches or something will do very nicely."

"I would not hear of such a thing," he said with mock severity. "I'll make sure personally that they send up something worthy of all this beauty." He had the grace to gesture at all three women as he said this, not just at Sian.

As soon as he was gone again, Maronne started giggling. "Oh my," she said. "You *are* a genius. I would never have thought to ask him to come join us."

Blushing at such praise from this sophisticated woman, Sian turned to Arian, only to discover that she seemed far less amused.

"Unfortunately, we have a problem," said Arian. "Now he wants to speak with the seamstress before she leaves."

Maronne's laughter fled instantly. "Oh. I did not think." She looked up at her mistress, horrified. "I am so sorry."

"What for? You did not offer. He asked, and Assidua could hardly have refused. But while merely escorting Sian from the house would not have been too hard, allowing her to sit and talk with Escotte about drapes for any length of time … I am not sure that can be managed."

"Perhaps … if we stay here late enough," Sian tried, "he will have gone to bed?"

Arian shook her head. "Staying here through dinner has already pushed credible convention much too far. We cannot risk more such attention."

Maronne looked up suddenly, the light of an idea in her eyes. "He clearly intends to send us something unusual for dinner. Did you see him take our lady's bait? *Sandwiches*, indeed." She shot Sian another appreciative smile. "A second brilliant stroke, my lady. Escotte Alkattha's pride would never allow a supper of sandwiches to be served in his house, even delivered to a room of working women. Which means that there will surely be something in tonight's meal which poor Assidua's tender stomach has never encountered and cannot begin to handle."

"Oh! I am surrounded by genius," Arian crowed. "We would have to cut our labors short then, wouldn't we? Sian will order me to accompany poor, sick Assidua home just as soon as I have asked Sergeant Ennias to call the runner-cart for us — and tucked my exhausted mistress into bed early for the night, of course. We will make our escape all the sooner!"

"I doubt my cousin will even wish to say goodnight to her if she is ill," Sian said. "When the butler informed him of Cleone's illness, he just seemed terrified that she might have been contagious. This could work very well indeed."

"As soon as they have brought up dinner," Arian said, "we must close the door and begin work on the exchange."

Maronne had not guessed wrong. The meal they received was as exotic as it was sumptuous. Cockles and trumpet snails in a spicy sauce of coconut, curry and powdered firefruit. Spade fish poached in curdled cream with tarragon and leeks. Saubot root mashed with truffle oil and honey imported from the continent ... The list ran on for half a dozen courses, accompanied by three different wines, one spiced, and one almost too sweet to drink without pinched noses. Who could have sampled all these dishes and not risked growing ill?

Sadly, the women had little time to do much more than nibble at the feast as all three worked to darken and straighten Maronne's hair while curling and streaking Sian's with gray. Paints and creams Sian had never even heard of made Maronne's complexion darker while engorging whatever skin it touched to make all but the deepest wrinkles disappear. Sian's face, neck and hands, which were all Assidua's concealing silk ensemble revealed, were swabbed with some astringent rinse that made her skin dry and pucker, wrinkling like leather, before being painted in a clinging cream to lighten her tone.

"I hope this is reversible," she murmured as Maronne and Arian applied their wicked magic to her wrists and fingers.

"It washes off far more easily than it goes on," said Arian. "Regrettably, in my case. What I wouldn't give to be free of the ordeal I must go through every morning."

By the time their meal might reasonably have been finished, Sian could well believe that anyone might mistake Maronne for her, or vice versa, as long as they didn't look too closely. Assidua would be bent over in illness as well, clutching at the veil across her face in distress and embarrassment as any common woman might, leaving a grand house in such condition after so fine a meal. It should work, Sian assured herself again. It really should.

As soon as Maronne had been tucked in bed, the lights turned low, and everyone felt satisfied that the two women should pass reasonable inspection, even if Escotte came up himself, Arian went down to inform the butler of the seamstress's distress, and Sian's wishes in the matter.

Not long later, she was back. Alone this time, to everyone's relief. "Quatama has assured me that Sergeant Ennias will be sent to engage a two-man runner-cart," she said, closing the door behind her. "I saw no sign of Escotte down there. So, hopefully, he really was required elsewhere tonight and will not hear of any of this until it's long over."

Sian crouched in one of the room's more shadowed corners, clutching her silk robes around her, waiting breathlessly for Escotte to show up, demanding explanations. Maronne's dress fit her a bit loosely, and her sandals too tightly, but nearly all of her was covered, which was what mattered most. Eventually, they heard footsteps coming down the hall, followed by a knock at the door. "Come in," Sian said. It was important that whoever was outside the door hear *her* voice.

To her deep relief, it was just Quatama. He glanced briefly at the woman lying in Sian's bed, then looked rapidly away, as if unsure that even one look at a sleeping female guest was not some violation of propriety. Next he peered at Sian, bent over in the corner wearing Assidua's clothes and coloration now. "I am informed the runner-cart you requested is … pulling through the gate, my ladies," he intoned uncomfortably. "Do you require my assistance to convey the seamstress downstairs?"

"Thank you, no, Quatama." Arian offered him a grateful smile. "I can take her. My lady has requested that I escort the woman home, however. So I will be departing a bit earlier than usual. As you see, my lady is abed, and retired for the night. You may send up her guard at any time."

He glanced again at Maronne, who nodded her dark head without turning to look at him.

"Very well, then," said Quatama. "I shall go to fetch him now."

Without further comment, he turned and started back down the hallway, leaving the door open for Arian and Sian.

"Goodnight, dear," Arian said very softly to Maronne. "Sleep well. We will see you early in the morning. I'm sure Assidua will be quite recovered. And … I will not cease to think of you until then."

"Thank you, Freda," said Maronne. "Good luck, Assidua. I can hardly wait to see my new dress." She gave them a pale smile. "Travel safely."

Arian led Sian out the door, and turned to close it softly before they started down the hallway toward the first flight of stairs. Sian clutched at her arm, bent in obvious discomfort, face turned toward the floor. Only now did what they were about to do truly reach her. It was suddenly not hard at all to feign weakness and a sour stomach.

They traveled through the house without encountering anyone except a couple stray domestics, none of whom seemed to pay them any attention. As they approached the grand entrance hall, Sian again braced herself to find her cousin waiting with a thousand questions. But no one was there either except Quatama. He stood by the huge front door, watching them come as if they might be ghostly specters rather than women.

"Lord Alkattha bids me extend his apologies for not being here to see you off. He is unavoidably detained, but asked me to assure you that he would still like to discuss those draperies with the seamstress if she is well enough to return as scheduled in the morning."

Sian could well imagine Escotte quaking in some other room until the contagious seamstress was safely gone. Not that she was anything but grateful for such cowardice just then.

"Thank you, Quatama," Arian said as they reached the door. "I fear she is too ill to speak just now. But I am sure she will be better before morning, and would be delighted to accept Lord Alkattha's invitation then. Please thank him for the lovely dinner."

"Very good … Freda. I will convey that to him." He pushed one of the two grand doors open for them. "Farewell, then. I wish you both safe journeys home, a pleasant night … and a quick recovery."

Sian nodded slightly, as if in gratitude, wondering if the man ever smiled.

Then, despite all her fears, they were outside! The Hall's great forecourt seemed more open space than she had seen in years, though she'd been confined here not even two weeks.

Arian supported her down the steps, then stopped and looked around. "That's odd. I don't see the runner-cart. Did Quatama not say it was pulling through the gates some time ago?"

While Arian peered around the forecourt, Sian remained crouched and looking down, in case anyone inside should be observing them.

"Perhaps we took too long to get here," Arian said. "Could they have left again when we did not appear as soon as they expected?"

What were they to do now? Sian wondered. Not go back inside, surely.

"Well, this is irritating," Arian said. "Let's walk down the drive a ways and see if they've just gone to wait somewhere else."

They began to make their slow way across the forecourt, Sian still shuffling at Arian's side in pretended illness — and because Maronne's too-small sandals were pinching her feet rather painfully. Even so, she was more than willing to walk all the way to the Factorate House. Just as long as they weren't forced to go back inside the house behind her. Ever again.

⟋

Reikos shoveled the last spoonful of this evening's 'dinner' into his mouth, scorning the sergeant's empty promises. They'd received the same watery broth and rotten vegetables last night and tonight as they'd been given every other night so far. If there'd been any *improvements* made in their *situation* here, he had yet to detect them. "Probably hasn't given us a thought since he stepped back into the light," Reikos muttered to himself.

"What?" asked Pino, finishing his own slops across the room.

Reikos shook his head. "Wasn't talking to you, lad."

He was doing that more often now, talking aloud, but not to Pino. How much longer, he wondered, before he too preferred dying to rotting slowly in the bug-infested dark like this?

"What's that?" asked Pino.

"I didn't say anything… Did I?" Reikos turned to find the boy staring through their bars, head cocked uncertainly.

"Listen." Pino set his trencher down and went to peer through the bars, down the rough-hewn passage toward the staircase. "Someone's coming. Lots of them, I think."

Reikos heard it too now. Boots on stone, echoing loudly down the long staircase above them. He went to join the boy. Clearly not just their jailer coming back for some reason. Were they to be hung at last? He dared not hope they might finally be freed. In such hopes lay madness.

The footfalls grew louder, joined by the soft clink of armor — or chains perhaps — and a voice he recalled almost at once, and did not think he wanted to be hearing again now.

"I can still make this easier for you, Sergeant," came the Census Taker's foppish whine. "Just tell me who those ladies really are."

"I've already told you, sir. A dressmaker and a maid, as far as I know. If you'll tell me what makes you think otherwise, perhaps I can be of more help."

And that was Ennias's voice. Was he coming to *improve their situation* finally, Reikos wondered, or to bring them some new grief?

"Stop being obstinate," growled the Census Taker. "I am to believe that Cleone fell ill just in time for you to find such a distinguished and *convenient* replacement for her — and then a wealthy, discreet dressmaker I've never heard of either, practically waiting at my gates?"

"Cleone steered me to Freda, sir; and you sent me to get the dressmaker."

"Who *also* falls suddenly too ill to speak with me before she leaves? And who my cousin, the famous healer, somehow neglects to cure of this affliction? If I were as stupid as you seem to think me, Sergeant, perhaps you would be the Census Taker now, and *I* would be the mercenary soldier on his way into a prison cell."

"Well I'll be a little purple sea monkey ..." Reikos murmured in astonishment.

Pino turned to him, wide-eyed. "They're arresting *him* now?"

Reikos shook his head, unsure, as torch-cast shadows filled the staircase landing.

"Do as you feel you must, of course, my lord," said Ennias. "But when you've had a chance to check this out, I believe you'll find you've been mistaken."

The first person to come into view was Sarit, their jailer, looking even more morose than usual. The second was Sergeant Ennias, now lacking most of his house guard armor, and chained at wrists and ankles. Behind him came two more house guards, herding the sergeant. Last of all came the Census Taker, with a squirrel monkey clinging to his left shoulder.

"I was certainly mistaken when I entrusted this affair to you." The

Census Taker peered past his grim entourage. "Captain Reikos? Ah yes, there you are. And I am sorry, but I have forgotten your name, boy."

"Pino," Reikos said, before the rash youngster could say something to get them in even greater trouble. They did not need to be aggravating this man further, now especially, it seemed.

"Pino, yes, of course. Well, I imagine it must get somewhat lonely here, so I have brought you company." The Census Taker nodded at Sarit, who stepped forward with his ring of keys to open their cell door. "I believe you've already had the pleasure of Sergeant Ennias's acquaintance. Sergeant?" He thrust his double chin at Ennias, who, with a look of stolid resignation, shuffled into the cell. Sarit followed to unchain him, then stepped back outside to close and lock the cell door behind him.

"What have you done with Domina Kattë?" Pino demanded fiercely.

Reikos grimaced, wondering why the gift of youth was wasted on such witless people.

"Why, I have lavished every luxury at my disposal on her, boy." The Census Taker frowned at Sergeant Ennias for some reason. "And warned her very clearly about the consequences of ingratitude." He shook his head sadly, then turned to smile at them again. "I wish you all a splendid get-together, gentlemen. May the best man win." He beckoned his two house guards to follow, and started for the stairs. Just before he turned the corner, he turned back and said, "If you decide to tear each other into pieces, please try not to make too big a mess. I don't get anyone down here to clean that often."

"My lord, why are we being kept here?" Reikos tried in desperation.

The Census Taker looked back in apparent surprise. "What? Has no one told you?"

"No, my lord. How ... long are we to stay?"

"Well," the Census Taker sighed, "I'd love nothing better than to stay and answer all these questions, but I have too many bigger messes to clean up at present. I will let Sergeant Ennias explain it to you."

Then he was gone, leaving Ennias and Sarit to stare after him and his guards, then up at the ceiling as the sounds of their departure grew fainter. Ennias rubbed his chafed wrists.

When it seemed clear that they were well outside of hearing, Sarit lowered his eyes to gaze balefully at Sergeant Ennias. "I'm truly sorry, sir. Seen a lot of sad things down here, but I never half imagined seeing this. Not in my darkest dreams."

"Thank you, Sarit," said the sergeant without any sign of emotion. "I'd been meaning to discuss this with you, and hope it won't seem too self-indulgent now, but … if there's any way to get the three of us something of a bit more substance by way of provisions — from time to time, even — I would be deeply obliged."

"Well now," Reikos said, "that's rich." He turned to glare at Ennias. "Your concern for our well-being does take on a whole new urgency, doesn't it?" He was sorely tempted to haul off and punch the man, but Ennias still looked a formidable fighter and had at least of foot of height on him, while Reikos's own strength was paper-thin after all this time without food or light.

"Did he not bring you extra food just yesterday?" the jailer asked.

"No need to defend me, Sarit," Ennias said gently. "I thank you, but if Alkattha should return for some reason, you ought not to be found down here with me, eh?"

The man grimaced, but nodded at the sense of this and headed up the stairs as well.

When he was gone, Ennias looked back to Reikos. "I arrested you two for attacking me and my men while I was doing nothing but what I *thought* was a good thing for your friend, Domina Kattë. I've already told you that I have no beef with either of you personally, nor feel anything but worse and worse about where all this has landed you since then."

"Or where it's landed *you*, huh?" Pino said, his lip curled in disgust. "So, who did you rush to get thrown in here?"

"I'm in here for the same reason you two are." Ennias sighed, reaching up to run a hand through his thick, dark hair. "Trying to protect a woman. Several of them, actually."

"What women?" Reikos asked in alarm. "Is Domina Kattë in danger now?"

Ennias raised his eyes toward the rough rock ceiling, betraying the first real signs of distress — or any other emotion — Reikos had ever seen in him show. "Somewhere up there, right now, Domina Kattë, a Factorate maid, and the Factora-Consort herself are waiting for me to help get them safely out of this building." He dropped his gaze and gripped his head into his hands. "And there's not a godsdamned thing that I can do to let them know we're all in trouble."

Reikos's eyes were now as wide as Pino's. "The Factora-Consort is *here*? With Domina Kattë? Does she not outrank the Census Taker? Can she not just order him to —"

"Alkattha doesn't know that's who she is," Ennias cut in. "She's pretending to be Domina Kattë's maid."

"The *Factora-Consort*?" Pino blurted in disbelief.

"Sian's maid?" Reikos shook his head, wondering if maybe this confinement had already driven him mad. Could he be asleep? Was this just a dream? "How … Why on earth would —"

"It's complicated!" Ennias barked, losing his infuriating cool at last.

"No, it is *insane!*" Reikos protested. "What in hell is going on up there?"

"I wish to all the gods I knew," sighed Ennias, his frustration seeming to evaporate as quickly as it had boiled up. He gazed around, looking for somewhere to sit, it appeared, only now seeming to realize that there were just two pallets for the three of them. He went to sit on Reikos's, though the captain hardly cared at that moment. "The Census Taker is apparently involved in some kind of plot to overthrow the Factor and his government," Ennias explained, as dispassionate as ever once again. "Domina Kattë is involved now, because of her ability to heal the Factor's son. Because there's no one they can trust, the Factora-Consort and her maid are here themselves, trying to sneak Domina Kattë away without giving the Census Taker any reason to suspect she's gone — although I'm pretty sure that plan is broken past repair now." He shook his head and sighed. "They fear that if Lord Alkattha knows they've discovered his involvement, this conspiracy might just launch an all-out civil war."

Reikos and Pino were both gaping at him now.

"Civil war?" gasped Pino. "There is going to be a *war*? Over *Domina Kattë*?"

"Not over Domina Kattë, son." The sergeant bowed his head again, looking very tired. "She's not the cause of this. She's just stuck in the middle of it — along with all the rest of us."

"Is the Census Taker not your Factor's cousin, though?" asked Reikos, wondering if his understanding of Alizari politics was even more muddled than he'd thought. "Why would he wish to wage war against his own family?"

"The Factor's government has been teetering for some time now, and the Alkattha family's prospects with it. The Census Taker may just have decided to flee his family's burning ship before it goes down anyway — as any rat will do."

Reikos began to pace around their cage, rubbing at his stubbled beard, and trying to absorb these mind-numbing revelations. His Sian was at the mercy of her clearly deadly cousin, at the center of an unimaginable catastrophe. How had the whole world come to such an edge in just the few short weeks since he had docked his ship here in such placid-seeming waters? His *ship!* It was anchored in what might soon be a war zone! His ship and Sian ... They were all he had. And there was nothing he could do for either of them. "Is there no way to get us out of here, Sergeant?" Reikos pled. "The jailer, he is clearly liking you quite well, it seems. Can you not explain to him what is at stake here — just as you have done with us? Surely, he would see ... There might still be something we could do if we were not stuck here."

"I have thought about it, Captain, I assure you. But though these women are in danger now, Lord Alkattha does not seem to have recognized the Factora-Consort or her maid yet. I don't know whether they would be in more danger or less if he found out. If I tell Sarit what I've just told you ..." Ennias raised his hands and shrugged. "He's clearly very sorry for me, but you'll notice he hasn't offered to let me go. He's as afraid of Lord Alkattha as everyone else here is — with good reason, obviously. I have little doubt he'll find some way to feed us better now. Whether he would do more if he knew the rest, or just run fearfully to his master and make everything worse for the Factora-Consort and Domina Kattë, I have no way of knowing."

"He'll hurt her, if he figures it out," said Pino, as much to himself as to anyone else. "And there's nothing I can do now. Nothing ..."

Reikos didn't need to ask which 'her' the boy meant. It wounded him to watch Pino still clinging to this hopeless love of his. There seemed nothing left in all the world that didn't hurt to look at now.

TWENTY-ONE

Arian led the healer from the Census Hall's forecourt out into the darkened drive, glancing up and down, but there was still no runner-cart in sight. "Well, something has gone amiss. But we are out, at least, and the harbor is not so far away. Our boat to Home should be waiting there. We can just walk."

Sian nodded, limping after her.

"You can stop pretending now," Arian said after a minute. "We're no longer visible from the house."

"It's these sandals," said Sian. "They're too tight."

Arian looked down at Sian's feet, frowning. "Why did you not say so?"

"I didn't think we'd be walking." Sian gave her a reassuring smile, trying to walk more naturally, though it was obvious the sandals pained her pretty badly. "I'll be fine."

"Perhaps we'll find a runner-cart along the way," Arian said hopefully, though they would have to walk beyond the Census Hall's jungle-covered grounds before reaching populated streets. There would be very few people out at such an hour, though she heard the faint echoes of a prayer-line in the distance.

Despite the minor setback of their absent cart, Arian felt more exhilaration with every step they took away from the Census Hall. They had done it! Sian was out of Escotte Alkattha's clutches! Konrad would be healed at last. Arian blinked back tears, recalling Sergeant Ennias's tale. "Does it truly happen all at once?" she asked Sian. "This healing you do?"

Sian glanced up at her, surprised, perhaps, at the change of subject. "Very nearly."

"It must feel strange to wield such power."

"To be honest, it feels … quite uncomfortable. If it's a wounded arm, my own arm aches. If it's colic, my stomach hurts along with the child's."

"So you *can* cure illness then — not just injury? I mean … you have no doubt, do you, that you will be able to heal Konrad?"

"My lady, you have risked so much to come for me, and were not sure of this?"

Arian fell silent a moment. "I didn't have much choice, really. Sergeant Ennias was most convincing, but the truth is, I have exhausted every other option." She gave Sian a pointed look. "And, I'm still *Freda*, please, till we're safely at the Factorate."

"Of course. I am sorry." Sian smiled at her sheepishly. "I feel quite certain I am meant to heal your son. Perhaps I'll find some peace again when this is done."

"What do you mean?"

Sian stumbled over a loose cobblestone; Arian reached back to steady her. "When this power was first … given to me," Sian said, "I wanted only to be rid of it. Now, I've come to understand that there are forces much, much larger than myself at work here, though I still don't know why *this*, why *me*." Sian looked at Arian and shrugged. "I'm a mother too. That alone is reason for me to come with you — whatever other reasons the gods may have."

"Is this power truly given you by some god then?" Arian asked. Was it this 'Butchered God' after all? Was Sian able to communicate with it somehow? Sian looked at her strangely, clearly uncomfortable with the question. "You needn't answer," Arian added hastily, having no desire to alienate this woman on whom so much depended now. "I have no wish to pry. It's just … I really did not think there were gods in Alizar … Until I heard of you." *Do they resent me for such disbelief?* she wondered. *I'm truly sorry if I've seemed disrespectful,* she silently assured whichever of them might be listening to her now — or walking right beside her even, within the body of its avatar. *You have simply been so quiet. For so long.* Arian smiled at Sian, and gave her arm a gentle squeeze. "I thank you, cousin, for all this must have cost you."

"I do wonder, sometimes, if the power will leave me after I have healed him." The healer sounded pensive. "Or if this will always be my life now."

By the time they emerged from the Census Taker's wild estate and returned to streets lined in shuttered shopfronts and dark houses, Sian's limping had grown noticeably worse. Arian wondered why she hadn't just healed herself of this small pain. She was trying to decide whether it would be rude to ask her this when three black-robed priests stepped into their path from an alley just ahead of them.

"Halt!" the foremost of them commanded.

Fright coursed like lightning through Arian's entire body, freezing her in place. Sian yanked at her from behind, trying to pull her into flight, but the priests were too fast. The leader reached out and grabbed Arian's arm, pulling it so hard she feared it might be injured, while the two behind him dashed past her to catch Sian as she turned to flee. Arian began to struggle now, unable to believe that this was happening — after all they had come through — but her captor just clamped down even harder on her wrist, wrenching her off balance with a single hand.

"Let us go!" Arian yelled, pulling against his grip. "What right have you to —"

With his other hand, the priest cuffed her sharply across the face, knocking her to the cobblestones. Arian reeled with shock; never, in all her life had she imagined … had anybody dared … It took a moment for the pain even to register.

"Stop it!" Sian yelled, thrashing in the arms of her own captors. *"Don't hurt her!"* She kicked her sandals off and twisted around, jabbing her bare foot at the shin of one of the priests. He howled, and must have loosened his grip on her arm, for she spun and thrust the heel of her hand against his chin with a wordless cry.

The priest opened his mouth in silent astonishment, and fell to the ground, gasping and clutching at his chest for some reason.

Sian's remaining captor threw her face-down on the ground with terrible force, crushing one of her hands against the gravel with his booted foot, while falling atop her back and trying to pin her other hand beneath his knee. "Father Lod, it's her!" he shouted. "I think she's killed Poden!"

Ridiculous, Arian thought in half-abstracted rage. *Anyone can see he's moving still.*

The sound of running steps drew nearer. Arian turned her head to see an older priest coming toward them from somewhere nearby — *Father Lod?* — flanked by two younger, stronger priests — initiates, perhaps. *Do they always come in threes?* Arian wondered, struggling to regain possession of herself through her still-rebounding shock, and dawning despair.

"He's not dead!" Sian yelled. "I have killed no one!"

"Bind her hands, fool!" snarled the older priest. "Don't let them touch your flesh!"

Donning gloves as they ran, the two young priests with Lod raced to grab Sian's arms while the first man kept her pinned in place, then deftly tied her hands behind her back with rope.

"Don't let this one get away either," Lod said, casting a sidelong glance at Arian as he strode by. "She may be useful."

Arian's attacker yanked her to her feet, holding her tightly by both wrists now.

The priests tying Sian brought out more rope to truss her with, eyeing her warily, clearly aware of the power her hands could wield.

"Sian Kattë, at last," Lod spat, glaring down at her. He nodded toward Arian. "Is she another fraud like you? Some disciple of yours perhaps?"

"No!" Sian cried. "Leave her alone, she's done nothing! She is no one."

Lod gave Sian an ugly smile. "I think not." He turned to the priests. "Bind her as well. Better safe than sorry, as we've learned to our great cost."

"Let her go!" Sian screamed. "Take me — just let her go!"

Do they know me too? Arian wondered fearfully. *Is Duon to have his revenge here on this darkened street, un-witnessed?* They had shown no sign they knew her, so far. Their attention seemed focused on Sian Kattë. "My lady," Arian choked out in the deferential tones of a terrified maid. "Oh, please, my lady ..." *Please don't lose your head and give me away now, healer,* she thought, as the priests tied her own hands behind her back.

"Be strong, Freda," Sian said, still glaring at Lod.

Thank all the gods. Again, Arian thought. Sian understood. But how had they been found like this? Had someone betrayed them, or had they just been impossibly unlucky? Did the gods of Alizar hate her after all for her disbelief? Where *had* their runner-cart gone? When, exactly, had all this fallen so terribly apart?

"Well, well. *Domina Kattë*," Lod growled when they had both been bound, "what a lot of trouble and embarrassment you have caused our order." Arian could see him struggling to retrieve an air of icy calm. "And for what? Did you think you could elude us forever?"

"When my cousin, the Census Taker, hears of this —" Sian started, but Lod cut her off.

"Your *dear cousin* is the one who warned us, just this afternoon, that you might be found nearby his hall this evening," Lod answered with clear satisfaction. "It seems your distinguished family has cut you loose. And who could blame them, really?"

Maronne! Arian thought, biting her lip to keep from crying out. She'd left her dearest friend locked in the serpent's lair, with no way out now. *Oh, Viktor, what have I done?* Her husband and Hivat had warned her, but she had refused to listen. Yet should she not have tried to save her son? *Oh, Maronne. I'm sorry. I'm so sorry…*

"But don't think that's going to make me over-confident again," Lod continued, all his satisfaction seeming vanished now. "I know the threat of pain or injury means nothing to you. Not even starvation was intimidating, was it? But I've a hunch that you have other weaknesses." He lurched over to grab Arian's hair, yanking her head around by it.

Arian yelped, more in surprise than pain, stumbling in a tenuous attempt to stay upright. Only Lod's fist in her hair kept her from falling.

"Stop it, stop it!" shouted Sian. "I'll go with you, just don't hurt her!"

"That's what I thought." Lod smiled unpleasantly. "And what I mean to make quite sure of, this time." He let go of Arian's hair and elbowed her hard, in the ribs. She buckled and fell to the ground with an *oof*, unable to use her bound hands to catch herself. Her face had hardly hit the stones before Lod kicked her in the side. Arian heard a rib snap just before the pain hit. She screamed; Lod stepped away, beckoning to his young companions. "Nothing fatal, please."

The first priest leaned down to punch her in the face, slamming her head back onto the cobblestones. Arian felt blood begin to fill her nose and mouth, choking her screams as a second priest joined in, paying particular attention to her broken rib. Soon it had siblings. She heard Sian screaming too now, but only faintly as all sensation grew remote, and Arian … fell away. Inside.

She found herself detached somehow, watching the whole scene from high above. On a nearby rooftop, maybe? Oh look, those priests are beating some poor woman in the street. How terrible. Why is no one helping? … all that screaming …

She was still in her body too — remotely. It wasn't really hers, though. Not anymore. Her face felt made of bone, unfeeling even as she felt it pummeled mercilessly. Her hands were tied; her legs did not obey her, though she still struggled with some vague notion of defending herself, or of fleeing. Ultimately, though, there was nothing she could do, except bear the blows.

And then they stopped. Arian came back to herself sobbing in a ball on the ground. Pain filled her, everywhere; every breath a stab wound in her sides. Blood flowed into the mud.

Sian still screamed, somewhere nearby. "*Stop! Stop!*" She had been screaming the whole time. How could such things happen on a public street, and no one come to save them, or even to investigate? Was Alizar that broken? … *Yes*, she thought. *Clearly*. As broken as herself. It must have been for some time now. How had she failed to notice sooner …?

As Arian lay gasping for each painful breath, struggling for coherent thought, a righteous anger began boiling up inside her to displace the stunned disbelief, wrapping around the pain like a fiery lover. *These gods-damned priests … who feel entitled to beat me on the street; to kill my son!* If they let her live; if they made that mistake; she would see their temple burned to the ground, every last offertory hall and stained-glass window and shred of altar cloth … If she could but live!

"All right, then," she heard a disembodied voice say somewhere above her. A voice she intended to remember — and to silence utterly. Someday. Somehow. "Heal her, if you wish to."

Arian recoiled at the touch of someone's hands on her broken body, though they seemed soft and gentle now. She could not abide the thought of being touched again. By anyone.

"It's all right, it's all right," Sian crooned, even as she gathered Arian up closer.

Arian gasped, flooded with sensations for which she had no language. She cried out as her cracked bones began to throb and shift. Her cries were echoed by Sian, who gripped her tighter now. Convulsively. It wasn't pain, exactly. Nothing like the pain she had just known, at least, but neither was it pleasure. It was ... disintegration. Disassembly. Both stretching and compression; an earthquake through her body, and the tearing of a cloud. And then, as suddenly, it became euphoric! Disorienting ecstasy! A wave of pure, erotic pleasure rolled through her body as the healer's touch brought first upheaval, then relief to all her wounds at once. Arian wanted to weep and laugh and scream. She buried her face in the other woman's lush silks, wishing she could put her arms around her ... kiss her, reach past the clothes to run her hands across Sian's skin ... Then this vast erotic urge winked out as suddenly, and Arian fell back, resting on the ground as Sian collapsed beside her.

"Oh," Arian whispered, sensing something just beyond her reach — a glimpse — elusive. A shadow veering toward her, too large to encompass — and something else sprang loose inside her, falling away like the ruptured fragments of some suffocating corset. A voice, almost too small to hear. Her mind nearly caught it, like a dream half-remembered. Her heart swelled with joy, then clenched with frustration as it eluded her again. Arian sighed deeply at the loss, then realized it hadn't hurt to do so. Incredulous, she rolled gingerly, one way, then the other, testing her ribs; but no, the pain was gone. *She has healed me,* Arian thought. *She has really done it. I am mended. I am whole!*

And not just physically. She knew this now, as she knew Sian was there beside her.

"Get them up," snapped Lod's voice above her. Arian cringed anew, but the young priest bending over her just jerked her to her feet this time, then pulled Sian up to stand, trembling, beside her.

"You will come quietly now?" Lod asked Sian. "No tricks this time?"

"Yes," Sian whispered, tears streaming down her face. "There was no call for that."

"Oh, but there was. You had to understand that we are not the helpless fools we were before. I have allowed you to soothe your friend's discomfort. I am not unkind. But, should there be *any hint* of trouble, whatsoever — here or after we've returned you to the temple — we will not hesitate to beat her again. And again, if necessary. We'll even kill her if we must."

Sian just glared at him.

"Bind her again," Lod ordered. "And bring the cart."

A minute later, Lod's two priests returned, leading a small ox-cart. The priests frog-marched Sian over to it, lifted her in, then tied the loose end of her rope leash firmly to its side, forcing her into a half-reclined position that looked torturous to Arian. Then they came for her, and did the same, tying her bound hands to the cart's opposite side before setting off.

As the cart rumbled away, leaving the nearly attained waterfront behind, Sian caught Arian's eye. "Are you all right?" she whispered. "Physically, I mean."

Arian nodded. "Changed, I think. Somehow. But ... less afraid, if that does not sound ..."

"No. That's how it feels to me as well."

The cart rolled on through Cutter's dark and empty streets, priests arrayed around them, keeping lookout. Arian kept marveling at the sensations inside her, as the truth continued to sink in. ... *This healer's power is real. There is at least one god left in Alizar.* And ... it did not hate her, Arian knew now.

"I am sorry, Arian," Sian whispered.

"*Freda,*" Arian whispered back. "And I ... am not so sorry now. Not anymore."

❦

The all-too-familiar dungeon of Temple Mishrah-Khote was quite a step down from Escotte's gilded cage. Not that Sian wanted to go back there, even now. Not really. Going forward might have been quite nice … *Not all of it pleasant*, the young priest of her new god had warned. *And right you are again*, she thought grimly.

"I'm hungry," Arian said, sitting beside her in near darkness on their single pallet of moldy straw. "Quite extraordinarily hungry. I wish we'd eaten more of that delicious food your cousin sent up."

Sian turned to look at Arian curiously. "You sound a lot like me now. It's always worst after I heal someone." She had never really stayed with anyone she'd healed after it was done. Did they … *catch* some of whatever burned in her? "Perhaps they'll feed you," she added, trying to ignore her the growing protests of her own stomach. "Me, they like to starve, here. It's the only way they've found to hurt me. For very long at least."

"But why should they so want to?" Arian asked. "That's what I cannot understand. It would make perfect sense for them to hate me — if they found out who I was." She had informed Sian by now of all the trouble she'd been making for the temple's leaders recently, revealing one more reason why no one must realize who she was if it could be avoided. "But what can you have done to them — or anyone — to justify hatred like Lod's?"

Sian shrugged. "I am a spiritual fraud, of course. The worst of all crimes, it seems."

"But you are so clearly not!" Arian protested. "From all I've seen, you are the only one here who is not!"

"Well, that might be the problem then," Sian said dryly. "Ugly women never like a mirror, do they?"

Arian was silent for a moment. "Not even pretty women sometimes," she said quietly. "I have no great wish to look too closely just now."

Sian wondered what she meant by that, exactly, but just couldn't find the energy to ask. Lod and his anointed thugs had dumped them here nearly an hour ago. They had whispered back and forth since then, about what might happen next, and what exactly might have gone wrong at her cousin's house. Escotte had so often seemed such a self-absorbed and rather silly man to Sian, but Arian had told her frightening tales of the man that confirmed the true intelligence and ruthless power he hid behind that mask.

"I wonder how long he'd suspected," Sian said.

"I still can't see where we went wrong."

"Well, I know one thing we did wrong. I would have healed Assidua, not sent her home with an upset stomach."

Arian groaned. "How could we have been so dense?" She shook her head. "But that can't have been the reason, if he informed the temple this afternoon." She gave a quiet laugh. "Perhaps that third bottle of wine was ... premature."

Sian remained impressed with Arian's calm and poise, wondering if such qualities were inborn or just trained into those raised to rule. She doubted she'd have been so calm herself if she had come so suddenly to this from such a lofty place in life. Not with a dying child waiting somewhere just beyond her reach ...

"How sick is Konrad?" Sian asked. "Will he ... survive this delay?"

"He's been ill for months," Arian sighed. "And grown far worse in just the past few weeks. I have no sure way of knowing whether he's still living now." She drew a trembling breath. "When Viktor and I discovered the plot against us, we began to suspect these 'healing' priests of poisoning our son ..."

Sian turned to gape at her. "Surely, not even these —"

"We've just thrown them all out of the Factorate House," Arian went on. "So, perhaps he'll have a better chance now, or even improve a little ... But I cannot know." She turned to Sian in the gloom. "You do see why I must remain 'Freda' until we get out of here." She looked down at her knotted hands. "If we ever do."

"We may not be as helpless as we seem," Sian murmured very softly. "Not all the priests here are so ... unsympathetic."

"Is that how you escaped, the last time? Did someone here help you?"

Sian bit her lower lip, realizing that she might already have said more than was wise. "It is better, maybe, that you don't know." She did not say, *in case you're tortured again, and forced to tell,* but Arian's sudden stillness in the dark beside her made it clear she didn't have to.

The sound of a heavy door opening and closing again echoed down the hallway. "Maybe that's food," Sian said, not quite convincingly, she feared.

The familiar clink of keys outside their door was followed by the screech of rusty hinges, and a wincing flare of firelight from the hallway, through which came several large, well-armored men bearing torches to light up their cell. Behind them came a tall, stern priest, in black robes made of shimmering brocade rather than the normal rough-spun hemp and cotton. Heavy ropes of polished jet and alabaster bead hung elegantly from around his neck and shoulders. There was a belt of silver links around his waist, with opals set into its buckle. Arian turned instantly away to cower behind her hood, playing the humble, frightened maid, Sian assumed.

The burly guards closed ranks before the priest, clearly there to safeguard this important person from such a dangerous grandmother. Then again, Sian had just used her gift to disable one of their henchmen, so perhaps she couldn't fault their caution.

The tall priest gazed at both of them, then settled on Sian. "You are Sian Kattë, I presume?"

Sian stood up, if only to prevent him from looming over her, and nodded. Arian remained seated, clutching her robes around her in apparent terror.

"I am Father Superior Duon," the priest announced, clearly expecting her to be overawed. "Head of the entire Mishrah-Khote."

Sian just kept herself from glancing back at Arian in alarm. No wonder she was trying to conceal herself. This was the very prelate Arian had spoken about. Would he see through Arian's disguise, Sian wondered, even if she looked right at him? Escotte hadn't seemed to.

"I do not usually come down to speak with prisoners in the middle of the night," he said severely. "I do not normally concern myself with prisoners at all, but you are not just any reprobate. You are a problem of unique concern — to me personally. Were you aware of this?"

"I have never even met you," Sian said.

"And yet, you have wreaked havoc not only on the good name of the entire order I am sworn to guide and care for, but on my own once-smooth relationship with the Factorate of Alizar itself. Does this fill you with pride, Domina Kattë? Does it leave you feeling smug now?" He looked pointedly around her cell. "Perhaps not, after all."

"I had no wish to —" Sian started, but Duon preempted her reply with an upraised hand.

"I have no interest in the explanations or excuses of a confirmed heretic. I've come only to explain how, even now, you might earn our forgiveness."

Sian felt her face flaming, but she held her tongue.

"That your powers were obtained by wicked and entirely illegitimate means is beyond dispute. But we are a *healing* order, and among the core convictions of our faith is a firm belief that no beginning is too bent to be made straight with skill and discipline. That no disease is beyond at least the possibility of cure. Thus, I offer you this one chance at redemption. After much heated debate, the brotherhood has decided that your powers, however sordid their origins, may yet be put to beneficial use. If you submit to our authority and guidance, it is possible that you may yet expunge the lethal stain upon your soul." He raised his brows inquisitively. "Is this of any interest to you, Domina?"

"Are you offering to make a priest of me?" she asked.

"Don't be absurd."

"Then, what —"

"We have a task for you," he said impatiently. "One that even you should not find too distasteful. Our Factor's heir is badly ill. Help us heal him, and the gods might be sufficiently appeased to countenance your continued existence."

Behind her, Sian heard silks rustle sharply, and turned to find Arian peering desperately at them from underneath her hood. "Oh, my lady, please do what they ask!" There were tears in her eyes. One might have thought she was just concerned about her mistress's head, or her own … if Sian had not known better. "Anything to make them let us go, my lady."

Sian turned back to Duon. "If I do this, will you let us go?"

"Alas, that much forgiveness is beyond my power to bestow," he said. "You have demonstrated, several times now, how capable you are of wounding with this power of yours. One of our priests lies at this very moment in the care of his brother healers, still struggling to recover from your last assault. The islands are in a terrified uproar over the threat you pose to everyone. We exist to protect as well as heal, Domina Kattë, and could never think of leaving Alizar at the mercy of such an abomination. Do as we require, however, and you will be allowed to live here, as our permanent guest, in far more dignity and comfort than this." He gestured at the cell around them. "That much I can promise."

"And if I refuse these terms?" asked Sian, struggling not to weep as she imagined a whole lifetime of Escotte's sort of *hospitality*, only much, much worse.

"Then, I fear we'd have no choice but to find out if it's possible to kill you, Domina," he said with nearly convincing regret. "I imagine beheading would be a difficult thing even for you to heal."

"Oh, my lady, listen to him. Please," pled Arian. "Do as he asks."

Duon glanced at Arian, distastefully. "One of you, at least, is not devoid of wisdom."

"I have always wished to heal the Factor's son," said Sian. "I've been trying to reach him ever since I left your little inn here, last time."

"Oh?" Duon asked, clearly unconvinced. "Then you were twice the fool, for that's precisely what we wanted for you then as well. You'd have known that if you'd given us a chance to tell you."

You imperious monster. Sian struggled with an urge to spit at his self-satisfied face. "Whatever could have scared me off, I wonder? Could it have had anything to do with being beaten, do you think? Or starved?"

"Had you just cooperated with us, Domina, none of those tactics would have been required. Cooperate this time, and you will see that, I believe."

"So, you don't mind then, if the Factor sees his son healed by an abomination — and a female one at that?"

"Oh, they won't ever know that you're involved," he said. "The Factor's heir will be brought here to the temple for his healing. No one will see what happens then, of course. Such great works always require focus and seclusion."

Careful not to sneer openly, Sian gave him a nod. "I'll gladly do as you request. For the boy's sake." *Not for fear of you,* she was too wise to add, though she had no doubt they understood each other all too clearly. She had been given this power to save Konrad. Whatever came of her life after that … well, perhaps the Mishrah-Khote had a better library than Escotte did.

"Very good." Duon nodded, unsmiling. He turned and motioned to one of the priests beside him, who stepped past Sian to take Arian firmly by the arm, pulling her to her feet.

"What are you doing?" Sian asked in alarm.

"I'm afraid it's far too risky to leave witnesses around," Duon said. "And much too expensive to support a second permanent guest here." He seemed not quite able to disguise his satisfaction at her horror. "Do not worry, Domina. We will get you another attendant, one at least as suitable to your station here, just as soon as you've been settled into your new … quarters."

"No!" Sian raised her hand, then yanked it back again, horrified at how quickly — how unthinkingly — she thought to harm rather than heal with her power now. "Please, Father Duon! Freda is completely innocent of any crime, she will never speak a word!"

"My lady, do not concern yourself for me," Arian said in dull resignation, as Duon's guard hauled her toward the door. "Just save the poor boy, and yourself."

You can't mean that! Sian thought, frantically. But she knew better, deep inside. Arian would sacrifice herself to save her son's life, just as Sian would have done to save her daughters.

Blinking back tears, Sian cried, "Freda, I am sorry!" *I will heal him! He will live! You won't have died in vain.* But Sian could not say such things aloud. Not if Arian herself still cared so much about maintaining her disguise.

"I will leave you to compose yourself," Duon said, then turned and left, followed by his guards. The light followed them out, leaving Sian nothing but the jingle of their keys in her cell door, and then silence, for company in the darkness.

TWENTY-TWO

Arian's new cell was even smaller and shabbier than the one she'd shared so briefly with Sian. It smelled of septic damp and pungent fungal growth, and didn't even have a pallet. She lay in darkness now, upon the floor, reviewing all the things she'd gotten wrong in life — beginning with this doomed attempt to do Hivat's work for him. Not that Hivat had ever offered to try rescuing Sian himself. Only warned against it — as had Viktor. Should she have listened to them?

She still wasn't sure.

She knew very well that telling Duon who she was might avert her execution. But she had no way of knowing what use he might make of her instead, against Viktor and the Factorate. There was also some slim hope that Escotte had betrayed Sian and her 'maid' without realizing, even then, who that maid had been. If so, this secretive surrender of her life might still purchase Viktor and his nation time to bypass an instant plunge into civil war. She might get *one* thing right, at least, before the end.

The soft glow through a slit of window, high up in her cell wall, told her dawn had come. Maronne would be waking soon, expecting their return, if she had not already been discovered. Arian closed her eyes against the scenes that followed, though there was no real light to see by anyway. She worried for Viktor without her — not just this morning, but for all the years of mornings she hoped he still had ahead of him. Had he realized yet that she was lost? He must have, she supposed. And Konrad. Her poor Konrad. If they allowed Sian to heal him — *oh, please, any god that may be listening to me still, let them get her to him soon* — she dared hope against all hope that he, at least, might still live long enough to be Factor in his turn someday … Or, better yet, something much less terrible than Factor.

This thought led her back to Viktor. She had ruined him, of course. She saw that now. Not during these past few awful weeks, but years and years ago. She shook her head, letting tears fall freely. Who was there to see now? What would it matter anymore if someone did? The exercise of power had never come easily to Viktor, as it had to her. She could have helped him learn it. But she had been no more willing to allow him the risk of error, or its consequences, than she had ever allowed them to herself. Instead, she'd spent their years together making sure he never made mistakes … or learned … or dared to try to learn.

She'd kept her husband sealed inside his fear of failing her — and thus, infantilized him.

Arian had come to see this not long after being healed by Sian. Something inside of her had shifted in those awful, wondrous moments of transformation. She'd been left rearranged, in all sorts of ways that she was still just starting to sift through. Most of which would have to go un-sifted altogether, she supposed, if she was to die soon. All she knew so far was that some lifelong … *rigidity* … had melted beneath whatever touch had mended all those broken bones and lacerations. Had that touch been Sian's? The Butchered God's? She had no idea. But in some way she still could not name, it had left her less afraid — of everything. Even death.

She'd always thought she knew so much. Now she knew how much she'd never known. With only hours left, if that, to apply the insight. How could any god so kind have timed his gift so cruelly?

She heard something in the darkness. An intermittent, grinding sound so soft, she thought it might have been imagined. She sat up and listened, straining her eyes against the dark, suddenly imagining rats, or who knew what other crawly horrors snuffling toward her. There was a footfall to her left. She twisted round to look that way, quite sure she hadn't made it up. "Who's there?"

"A friend," somebody whispered.

Her gaze swiveled toward the sound. "I have no friends here. Show yourself."

"You must be much more quiet, please." A patch of shadow moved against the other shadows. "I am a friend of Sian Kattë's. Perhaps she mentioned me, yes?"

"She may have," Arian said more quietly, recalling Sian's allusion to more sympathetic priests. "She did not give me a name, though."

"No?" the whisper answered. "Clever woman. I am reassured to hear it." The darker patch of shadow came a little further into what scant light now drifted from the slit of window high above. "Can I trust you to be as circumspect?"

"If you knew me, you would have no need to ask. But yes."

"Then my name is Het," the shadow said, its form rustling suddenly and shifting in the darkness. A moment later, a small orb of pale blue light erupted less than five feet off, revealing a face both lined with age and youthful, topped in thinning, light brown hair under a priest's hood drawn halfway back. "*Father* Het, my lady. At your service, it would seem."

"Why call me 'my lady'?" Arian asked in alarm.

Het looked nonplussed, then shrugged. "It is a courtesy. What would you prefer?"

"Freda. That is all the name I need."

"Very well then, Freda. Shall we go to see if we can find Sian, now?"

"*What?* Go where?" She saw him smile, seeming to enjoy confusing her. "How did you get in here?"

"I am a passionate collector of the temple's lost places and hidden ways." He grinned. "It is knowledge any renegade as troublesome as me has frequent cause to need, yes?"

"Then … you'll help Sian and me escape again?" She hardly dared rekindle hope.

"Not escape, no, sadly." His smile became apologetic. "The temple is too closely watched these days for that. My fault, I fear — in part, at least. But you and Domina Katté can easily be hidden here inside our grounds until news of your latest escape grows stale enough to allow for relaxation of our current vigilance. Then I'll help you all the way to freedom."

Arian heaved a disappointed sigh. "How long might that take, do you suppose?"

He shrugged again. "From what I hear in certain circles, the alternatives are hardly thinkable, dear Freda. Especially for you. Am I misinformed?"

She shook her head. "I do not mean to sound unappreciative. It's just …" She sighed again, and gestured at the tiny cell — all the smaller for his light to see it with. "You have some way to get me out of here?"

"Of course. The same way I got in." He beckoned her to follow him, all of six or seven steps, into the lowest, farthest corner of her little chamber. There she saw a large block of perforated stone grating lying beside the darkened gap it had been removed from.

"You moved this so quietly?" Arian asked, astonished. "I can't believe it's here at all! Has no one else discovered it and escaped?"

"It is much easier to lift from below," he said. "And even if you could have pried it out yourself, it would have done you very little good to crawl down there without this too." He held up a blackened key. "There is a sturdy gate at each end of the drainage this leads into." He beckoned her to follow, scrunching his arms and shoulders inward as he slipped the rest of the way through.

All Arian could see now was a ghostly suggestion of the hole itself, where Het's pale light still shone a little from below. Groping toward it, she too wound her robes more closely around her legs, and lowered them into the gap. She felt nothing beneath her feet.

"Come further," she heard Het urge softly from below.

Bracing her hands against either lip of the opening, she lowered herself almost to the waist, and still felt only air beneath her. Then Het's hands grabbed her feet, and steered them toward a narrow bar. There was a ladder, though it was positioned awkwardly. With his help, she found the next rung, and the next, and after just a bit more squirming and yet another rip or two in Freda's once-neat dress, Arian was through and standing next to Het in several inches of revolting, smelly water. She managed not to gag as he climbed back up to retrieve the grate and set it back in place above his head, then came back down, with his little light, and beckoned her to follow. "It smells better in a moment," he assured her. "But from here on we must be completely silent except for very urgent need, yes?"

She nodded, waving him on impatiently.

For all its unappealing qualities, this drainage tunnel had awakened an idea in her mind, though she would have to wait until he told her it was safe to speak again before finding out if it held any promise. *I'm sorry to keep judging you so hastily,* she silently informed whatever deity kept doing her these favors.

~

Escotte had done this to her. To them all. Her own cousin. Family. What did that word mean? Sian had assumed she knew once. Hadn't even thought to wonder. Then ...

Then there had been daughters who would not believe you even though you'd raised them from the very seed. Husbands who filed legal complaints against you just as soon as your misfortunes threatened to be bad for business. Cousins who did not think twice, it seemed, about handing you to murderers.

Family.

The god's young priest had told Sian that she was destined to heal what was broken. But, so far, it seemed that all she'd done was break whoever she came near — just as she'd been broken by the priest. Her family, scattered; Reikos and Pino wasting in a dungeon of their own; Maronne, abandoned to the mercies of Sian's monstrous cousin; and Arian des Chances, Factora-Consort of all Alizar ... hauled off to the temple executioner. All because they'd come too close to Sian. Did this new god do anything *but* butcher? When would the *healing* begin? Sian shook her head, wondering if even Konrad would be healed when the temple finally let her touch him — or just arch his back, cry out, and die. Was all this just some celestial joke? This Butchered God merely some sadistic comic?

The darkness of her cell was nothing to the darkness pooling in her heart. She sat staring down at where her *gifted* hands lay folded in her lap. Would she lose this gift at last when she had finally healed Konrad? And, if she did, would the temple still think it cost-effective to support a permanent guest with no useful skills they could exploit? *I'll be following you soon, I think, dear Arian,* she murmured to the empty air. Sian was not afraid. Just tired. And so very, very hungry. Death would solve both problems very handily — and a host of others. All at once.

Keys rattled — almost frantically — at the lock to her cell door. Sian looked up dully, hoping they'd decided just to kill her too. *Let's just get this over with*, she thought, waiting to see which face bad news would be wearing now.

There was no flood of light as the door swung open this time. The hallway seemed almost as dark as her cell. She could barely see her visitor.

"Sian Katté?" he whispered harshly. "Are you here?"

"What's happening?" she asked, wondering why he hadn't simply brought a light.

"Come! Quickly!" the man whispered urgently.

"Why?" Was it time to heal Konrad already? In such secrecy that even light could not be risked? "Are you —?"

"It is Het!" he whispered. "Hurry! Before someone comes!"

"Oh!" she exclaimed, leaping to her feet, her inner darkness instantly eclipsed. "*Oh, you've come!*" She rushed toward the door as quickly as she could with so little light to see by. "I have a friend here — somewhere —" she began, but Het shushed her fiercely into silence, fumbling for her hand, then dragging her behind him, out, and down the dimly illuminated hallway, around a corner, and through the open doorway of yet another darkened cell. He turned to close its door behind them just as soon as they were in. Only then did he pull out one of his little globes of pale light and start herding her before him toward one of its grimy corners.

"Are we —?" she tried to ask, but again he shushed her.

Not until they got there did she see the displaced stone grate lying beside the darkened gap. "Down," Het whispered, rushing past her to wriggle through first. When his head had vanished, Sian gathered her robes and did her best to follow. Halfway in, Het's hands found her dangling, unshod feet and guided them toward a rung ladder so offset that she might never have found it by herself. Moments later, her toes touched down inside some kind of wet, unpleasant tunnel. As Het brushed past her, climbing back up to replace the grate above them, Sian turned and peered into the darkness, trying to make out their surroundings.

"Sian?" someone whispered from not far behind her.

Sian spun, still unable to see. "Who's there?"

"It's Freda."

"Oh!" Sian cried. "Arian! Thank all the gods! He's —"

"*Shhhh!!!*" said both Arian and Het at once.

"Oh. I'm ..." Sian shut her mouth as she stumbled blindly toward her friend. Their outstretched hands found one another in the gloom, and they pulled each other into a fierce embrace. "You're safe!" Sian couldn't stop herself from whispering into Arian's ear as they held each other. "I was so afraid you might already —"

"Het came for me first," Arian whispered back. "But, please. He doesn't know. I'm still just Freda."

"Sorry. I'm so sorry. But I am so glad you are alive — and safe!"

"Not yet, we aren't," whispered Arian, "and Het has warned me that —"

"We must be silent still," Het finished for her, gruffly, coming from behind them with his pale light. "No whispering even, until I tell you it is safe, yes?"

They both nodded in the soft illumination and turned to follow as he passed them, heading further down the sopping tunnel.

They traveled on in silence for some time, through corroded, heavy iron gates, for which Het always managed to produce a key, up and down more narrow iron ladders, turning corner after corner, even doubling back on some occasions. Sian's heart stopped again each time someone stumbled or splashed too loudly, as they all paused to look up and listen apprehensively before continuing. Finally, they descended yet another set of iron rungs into a tunnel wider than the others, filled with the quiet rush of water coursing down a channel cut into its floor.

"Now," Het said just loudly enough to be heard above the water's murmur, "let us talk, yes?" He smiled at Sian. "Our Lady of the Islands is a powerful enchantress, is she not? To keep walking through our walls this way." Sian looked down, blushing at all she owed this man. "So then, there are several places in the temple where you might be safely hidden until —"

"Wait," said Arian. "I have a question first. Are you aware, by any chance, of the Ancients' web of inter-island tunnels, Het?"

Sian had heard such stories. Mostly in her youth — from other youth who'd been told by older siblings. Old wives' tales, she had been assured by elders. Tunnels running underneath the seabed itself? If such an engineering feat were even plausible, would they not just have been flooded anyway? Ridiculous tales, or so she had assumed.

Het's brows climbed slightly. "That *you* know of them surprises me."

Arian responded with a slight, if satisfied, smile. "I too have collected a few hidden and forgotten things, Father Het. What I want to know is whether these drainage tunnels join that network anywhere nearby. Do you know?"

He nodded. "But if you are thinking to escape that way, I would recommend against it. The entrance here is neither safe nor easy."

"What is, these days?" Arian asked. "We really do need to get out of here as quickly as we can, and not just to save ourselves."

He gave her a considering look. "The entrance I speak of is not far from here. Come. You may decide for yourselves." He turned to lead them.

The buried watercourse they walked through was soon joined by others, and others after that, until their drainage channels had become wider, deeper, much louder streams. In time they heard a roaring up ahead and, minutes later, walked out into a vast chamber many stories high, densely lined in twining roots, hanging vine, and lavish foliage much farther up where it was better lit — by morning sun, it seemed. Many other drainage tunnels met here, combining at the chamber's center where they emptied their contents into a giant shaft plunging straight down into darkness.

"There is your way into the greater tunnels!" Het had to shout, so deafening was the roar of falling water here. There was surely little risk they'd even hear each other now, from more than a few feet away, much less that they'd be overheard. "Ladders there, and there! Do you still wish to brave it?"

Sian looked where he was pointing, just able to make out two lines of slender metal rungs driven straight into the shaft's drenched rock walls. Each of these ladders descended at the center of a narrow strip of moss-slicked rock hemmed in by mere inches on either side by tons of crashing water. *Well, so much for that hope,* Sian thought.

Looking as discouraged as Sian felt, Arian yelled, "It is the only choice we have!"

"*What?*" Sian hollered back above the noise. "You can't be serious!"

"I don't suppose you know what we would find down there!" Arian asked Het, ignoring Sian.

Looking as surprised as Sian was, Het burst into laughter. "If you knew me better, Freda, you would have no need to ask!" He shot her a devilish grin, which Arian returned. "This shaft was among the first mysteries I felt compelled to plumb here as a boy!" He shrugged. "In my spare time, of course! We were not allowed to come here at all, much less try such reckless things as climbing down!"

"Is it flooded at the bottom?" Arian shouted.

He shook his head. "But it is darker and colder than night! Not like up here! You will be soaking wet before you reach the bottom — which is no short distance!" His smile vanished. "It will not be hard to fall!"

Sian could not believe they were even having such a conversation. "Freda, I don't think I'm fit to do this!"

Arian glanced warily at Het, then shook her head in obvious frustration and shouted back to Sian, "He's told me there's no other way to sneak us out of here right now! Who knows how long we'd have to hide inside the temple before some other chance arrives! My absence cannot be concealed forever! If we are to avoid calamity then we must get back now!" She turned back to Het. "Is there any other way at all?"

He shook his head, looking at her very strangely. "Please forgive me for prying, Freda," he yelled, "but I could not help hearing Sian call you Arian!" Arian's expression became stony. She looked down with hooded eyes. "Surely ... that could not be Arian des Chances, could it?"

Sian could feel herself blanch as Arian's eyes closed in resignation.

Het's brows climbed almost to his hairline. "Please, do not worry, my lady! I am not a man unskilled at keeping secrets, as you must surely know by now! While I would give most of my stolen keys to learn what the Factora-Consort is doing here, like this, inside the temple, I know better than to ask, yes?"

"I'm sorry, Father Het!" she yelled. "Both that you've guessed, and that

I cannot tell you more! There is just too much at stake! If you were caught before all this is over ..."

"You need not explain, my lady! I understand! But there is something you should know, I think! Your ... rather *spectacular* visit here not long ago —"

"I lost my head!" she cut in. "I regret that now! I have no desire to alienate the entire Mishrah-Khote! I just —"

Het held up his hands to interrupt her. "Many here agreed with you, my lady! There has been insurrection brewing for some time, in need of little but a spark to light its fuse, yes? Your very public altercation with Duon, it has provided that spark! There will be revolt inside the temple, very soon, I think!"

Sian gaped at him, as did Arian.

Het glanced again at the great shaft of falling water beside them. "It is, perhaps, better that you go, if you are willing to risk this way, my lady! What is coming will likely ignite sufficient chaos to assist in covering your departure, but such chaos is itself unsafe, yes? Especially for you, perhaps."

So, we may throw ourselves down this great dark hole, Sian thought, *or wait here to dash through the temple's own little civil war when it erupts.* It made her want to laugh, and sit down somewhere quickly before her legs gave way.

"Father Het ... I don't know what to say!" Arian replied. "I never meant to cause such trouble — everywhere I go, it seems!"

"You did not cause this trouble, my lady! *We* have caused it! Over many years now! You have only moved us to face the cost of cure! That is one of the first things an acolyte is taught to do here!" He looked down and shook his head. "But no one does! Least of all, our teachers!" He looked up at Arian again, and smiled. "The gods have heard your cry for Duon's fall, my lady! Their answer is already on its way!"

"Then I guess we should be too," said Arian, looking even paler now, as she gazed down the shaft they meant to climb. "I do not suppose you might want to come with us, Father Het? Might you not be safer elsewhere once our escape has been discovered?"

"I wish I could!" Het shouted. "It worries me deeply to send you and Sian down there alone! But there are many factions here vying to define our future once Duon's regime is past! I must stay to help make sure the right ones prevail! And there are treasures in this temple — not of gold, but of recorded wisdom and historical perspective — that some will wish conveniently destroyed during the coming conflict! That must not happen either, if we are to emerge from this rebellion any better than we have become! I and my *collection*," he patted his illicit ring of keys, "will be needed to see them kept out of harm's way!" He shook his head. "I am sorry, but I must remain here now!"

"I wish you well then, Father Het!" Arian replied.

"Do you have any food?" Sian asked Het, blushing yet again. She didn't know how long they might remain down in the depths, but she feared even trying to climb these ladders without something in her stomach to keep up her strength.

"Sadly, no!" Het called back. "I had just planned to take you a short ways into some hiding place! But I could go find something, and bring it back here!"

"No!" Arian replied before Sian could answer. "Too much time has already passed! Who knows what's happened out there since we disappeared? Or who's already searching for us right here in the temple? We have to go, while we still can!"

"You will need more clothing than those silks, I fear!" Het shouted. "And light!" He reached up to unfasten the clasp of his rough-spun cloak and hood, then shrugged out of them and held them out to Sian. "There are a few glow floats in one of its pockets! You remember how they work, yes?"

"I do! But give the cloak to Arian! My gift may help protect me from the cold as well! She has no such power to rely on!"

Arian shook her head. "I'm sure that I can handle cold as well as hunger if I must, but won't the absence of your cloak seem suspicious to someone, Father Het?"

Het shook his head, grinning at Sian. "I have a reputation for irresponsibility, and am known to misplace my clothing every now and then!"

"Stop arguing, and take the cloak!" Sian called crossly, forgetting altogether whom it was she yelled at for a moment. "I tried to refuse his gifts last time, and was very glad I hadn't later."

She saw Arian heave an impatient sigh and reach to take the cloak and hood from Het.

"You appear to be in need of sandals as well!" Het said to Sian. "Unfortunately I have none to offer you except my own! Would you like them?"

Sian looked down at his feet, and shook her head. "They are far too big!" She glanced toward the roaring shaft. "I can't imagine climbing down that wearing those. Thank you, but if we're doing this, we'd just better go!"

"You know how to find your way, when you are down there?" Het asked Arian.

"I do!" she called, already turning to go. "Goodbye, Father Het, and good luck! If we all live through this, I will find some way to reward you adequately!"

"You already have, my lady!" Het pointed upward, toward the surface. "You have ended our long sleep! For that, I thank you!" He grinned at her, then turned to startle Sian with a fierce hug. "Take care of her," he said against her ear. "She is the bravest woman I have ever known, except for you, My Lady of the Islands. Do not let her fall." He pulled back, and looked her gravely in the eyes. "In any way."

TWENTY-THREE

*S*ian glanced over at Arian. The Factora-Consort met her eye across the span of raging water, gave her a brave smile, then started down.

They had decided to take separate ladders, without ever saying aloud what they both knew: that if one of them should fall, there would be nothing the other could do — except be knocked off in turn, if she were straight below. Here, at the chasm's edge, the roar of water was already too loud to permit even shouted conversation. Inside the shaft there would be no hope at all of further communication before they were reunited at the bottom. Their robes were knotted up around their waists now, lest their feet become entangled in the hems. Sian shuddered at the thought. Arian had removed her sandals too, agreeing that bare feet would be better on the ladder. She had secured them with the glow floats inside a pocket of Het's thick cape, now fastened tightly at her chest and throat.

Sian took a deep breath. There was nothing left to do but start.

Just swinging her bare feet over the huge shaft's lip onto that first wet rung was almost too frightening to manage. Sian waited, immobilized with fear, for what seemed many minutes before moving further in. Both hands clenched around the sopping rung before her face. One foot lowered to the rung below. Footing checked and checked again. One hand pried loose and lowered down a rung. Her second foot brought down beside the first. Her second hand. Her first foot down another rung. Then another hand. The second foot. The second hand. A foot. A hand. A foot. A hand. The roar became ubiquitous. The world closed in to one rung at a time. A foot. A hand. A foot. The rungs, at first sharp with corrosion, soon grew slick with slime and dangling moss. For all her distaste at the feel of slime against her soles, she could well imagine how impossible Maronne's stiff sandals would have been here.

With knuckles white around their dripping bar, one foot scraped carefully against a rung too slippery to trust, struggling for some credible purchase. Then more scraping with her second foot. By now the constant rain of spray was so thick that Sian's hair and dress hung straight and limp around her like wet laundry, cold and heavy. She risked a glance across the cataract that separated herself from Arian, and saw, as she had feared, Het's cloak and hood hanging from the other woman's shoulders, dark and weighted now with moisture too. A moment's sympathy, and guilt, as Sian realized how much heavier that cloak must be than her own sopping dress. Nonetheless, Arian was further down already than Sian, moving faster, looking far more self-assured.

Another foot. Another hand. A foot. A hand. A foot. Scraping, always scraping now for purchase through the slime. Another foot, another hand. Was it getting darker? How far down had they already come? Sian looked up and saw the chasm's edge not quite ten feet above. Eyes closed in helpless desperation and disgust. *This will take forever — even if I don't die here.* If she fell, perhaps she'd simply heal at the bottom. *Should I just let go and get it over with?* Not thoughts to be having here. Or anywhere. *Stop thinking!* One foot down. One hand. Another foot, another hand …

~

Many lifetimes later it was getting truly dark. Sian's arms and legs had long ago begun to cramp and tremble with fatigue and cold. Just enough light still filtered down the cataracts to let her see her hands and feet, if only as ghostly forms against the darker ghosts of wall and ladder. But she worried now — vaguely, for her mind was numbing too — about how much longer there would be any light at all to see by. She dreaded the thought of having to feel her way in utter blindness down these sopping, slippery rungs into the void. She was not sure how much longer her trembling body would keep doing what she told it to. She glanced over yet again to check on Arian, but it was too dark. She could no longer spot her, which might just mean that Arian had descended too much faster to be seen anymore ... Or that she had fallen — her screams drowned with her in the constant roar. *Stop it. Stop.* By all the gods, she wished that she could, though she was not sure her arms and legs would heed even the call to stop now, so accustomed had they grown to their endless repetition. Down ...

～

Each step was her last. Each time a hand was lowered to the next rung down, she knew it would not move again. She stopped for many minutes, maybe hours, between every step now, trembling spastically. Her hunger was all but forgotten, buried underneath the blanket of weakness it had left behind. They were going to kill her anyway. If not today, then after she had healed Konrad, surely. At least this was an end *she* had chosen. She would die belonging to herself now, not to some arrogant shell of a man like Duon, composed of nothing but empty, billowing robes ...

The time had come to fall. To test her hypothesis. The thought filled her with relief. She looked down in preparation, and saw ...

A star.

Then a field of smaller stars twinkling around it.

She stared at these, uncomprehending. Had she become so disoriented here that even up and down are now confused? Could that be a patch of night sky above the shaft mouth? A sudden wave of vertigo clamped her hands convulsively around the rung they clung to. Her body didn't want to die, it seemed. Even now. The star began to move from side to side. *More vertigo*, she thought, until its movement became half frantic, as if the star were trying to draw her attention ...

And then the scene resolved. She recognized the blue glow float, and its twinkling reflections in ... was that standing water rippling underneath it? And the silhouette of Arian, alive! Standing on a solid ledge, waving her small light around to guide Sian the last short distance down to ...

Bottom!

Just a few more steps, and she would finally be allowed to stop!

Moving of their own volition now, Sian's hands and feet were still on the rungs when Arian reached up to wrap her arms around her. "Oh!" the other woman shouted. "You're as cold as ice! Come down here! Quickly!"

What do you think I'm doing? Sian silently complained, too relieved to feel much real umbrage at such ridiculous advisories. They were here. Alive. What an unexpected outcome.

An instant later, she felt solid ground beneath a foot. The other foot confirmed this diagnosis, and still her hands wouldn't release the bar until Arian pried her away from the ladder and pulled her close, wrapping Sian inside her drenched, but surprisingly warm, cape.

"Come over here!" Arian commanded, pulling her along some path, further from the falls. "Sit down!" she yelled above the water's roar. "We need to rest a while! That was ... Well, it's done now! Let's just rest before going any farther!"

Farther? Sian wondered, letting Arian pull her onto the stony ground. The very idea ... seemed absurd. Farther where? How? She lay back, their shared cape pulling Arian down to lie beside her. The woman was so warm. Het's cape ... must have helped. For all its extra weight.

Warm weight.

So warm.

So ...

~

Hungry! Sian groaned and clutched her stomach, rolling to one side and bumping into something large and soft, but much too heavy and substantial to be bedding. She opened her eyes, and still saw nothing but the dark. There was a roaring all around her. Was it wind? Where was this? What *was* she tangled in? She pushed again against the warm, soft bulk beside her — was that ... another person? *Oh!*

She bolted upright, wide awake now, wrenching her upper body free of the now hardly dampened cape. "Arian?" she called. Then louder to be heard above the water. *"Arian! Wake up!"* She shoved at Arian's inert form in the blackness, irrationally fearful that the other woman might have died while they were sleeping.

Arian rolled over, and groaned something inaudible.

Slumping in relief, Sian called, "Where have you put the light?"

"The *light!*" Arian shouted frantically, sitting up as well. "What's happened to the light?!"

"That's what I just asked," Sian shouted back. "Where have you put it?"

"It's right here, but it's gone out!" cried Arian.

"Just shake it!" Sian yelled. "It goes out if it's not shaken, but comes back, if—" She fell silent as the blue orb reignited, surprisingly bright to her very well-adjusted eyes. "Het says they're little luminescent creatures! They make light for a while after they're disturbed!"

"How long will this last?" Arian asked. Then, more urgently, "How long have we been asleep?"

"Do I look like a sundial? I feel quite rested, so it must have been some time."

"We must be going!" Arian yelled, already standing. "Are you well enough?"

"I'm better than I was, but Arian, I am so hungry! I've eaten nothing since we left Escotte's last night! Did they feed you ever?

Arian shook her head, rubbing her own stomach now. She shrugged out of Het's cape and held it out to Sian. "You take this. I'm fine for now. The cape's quite warm, even wet."

"Are you sure?" asked Sian.

"Yes. You were so cold. You must still need to build your warmth up."

"Thank you." Sian pulled the cape on. It was nearly dry, as was her dress. How long *had* they been asleep? What were they going to eat—and when? "How long do you think we'll be down here?"

"A few hours, at least!" Arian gave the small globe another shake. "These tunnels will not take us all the way to Home! But I think we should be able to reach Apricot!"

"From The Well?" Sian exclaimed. "But that could take us half the day!" Even on uncrowded streets—should Alizar ever have such things again—that would take several hours.

"That's why I want to go!" Arian yelled back, already holding her light out toward the tunnel walls around them, as if trying to find something. "Come on. Let's at least get far enough away from all this noise to hear ourselves!"

The rock shelf beneath them, Sian now saw, went from the bottoms of their ladders out onto a central platform in the middle of the shaft, then bent off at right angles, disappearing in both directions into a large tunnel intersecting the shaft's base. Happily, the smooth, dressed stone of which this path was made was easier on Sian's chafed and blistered feet than the corroded rungs had been.

Within moments they were headed down the tunnel to their left, along a wide path bordering the deep, but now placid, stream of water flowing from the falls. This new passage was lined in tiles cast as tiny faces, grimacing mouths with squared teeth and narrowed eyes. She could not be certain in the globe's blue light, but it looked as though the glazing had once been riotous with color, so that the tunnel walls resembled a stone garden of demon-faced flowers. The effect was both wondrous and terrifying, an aisle of blank stares watching over the two of them as they walked farther into this dank netherworld. "Where ... what *is* this place?"

"In the time of Ancients," Arian called back, "most of the islands were connected — below as well as above. We can only guess at whether these were used for moving water, or for transportation, or ... well, we just don't know." By now, they'd wandered far enough from the shaft to dim the sound considerably. "That's much better, isn't it?" Arian said, turning to Sian.

"I was always told that such tunnels were just a fable."

"I know," Arian smiled, her face ephemeral in the globe light. "They were only rediscovered a few decades before Alizar's uprising, I'm told, and they're deliberately kept secret now."

"But ... why? All this could be put to use in so many ways."

"Not so easily as it may seem. The system is riddled with leaks and collapsed sections. Some parts are even flooded. Yet, for all that damage, the materials these tunnels are built from seem as nearly indestructible as those from which the ruins up above are made, which makes repairs and modifications as impossible down here. Simply building over such a huge labyrinth of passages would be unthinkably costly, without even taking into consideration the huge new layers of bureaucracy required to supervise and maintain it all."

"Pardon me," Sian interjected, "but even if they can't be put to some profitable use, I still don't see why they've been kept so secret."

"Can't you? Really? Even now, as you and I make use of them to sneak out of the temple?" Arian turned and began to walk again. "These tunnels were instrumental in Alizar's defeat of the continental Factor. Their existence had been kept from him and nearly everyone except the Alizari loyalists who had been fortunate enough to rediscover them first. When the rebellion came, the rebels were able to move great numbers of people and virtually any supplies they wished more quickly and easily than they could have on the surface — and quite invisibly, of course. The occupying Factor faced an enemy who just kept coming up out of the very ground beneath him without warning." She shook her head. "That's why the war here was so brief, and so decisive — and a large part of why the continent was so willing to just let little Alizar go. If we've been as successful in suppressing knowledge of these tunnels as we hope, they still have no idea how Alizar routed their government with such ferocious ease."

"Amazing," Sian said, wondering how they'd buried what must have been such a widely known secret by the end of the rebellion.

"After the war, I'm told," said Arian, "there was some discussion about opening the tunnels for other uses, but it was quickly decided that their value as a weapon was both too valuable to the new Alizari Factorate, and too dangerous to them, too. It was decided then to conceal their existence and promote the belief that any stories told about them were just child-ish tales. All the entrances to Home have been blocked off, of course, lest someone do to us what we did to the continental government then. Other portions of these tunnels have doubtless been walled off as well as well, by other parties, for similar reasons. The few who do still know about them despite all our efforts, likely have good reasons of their own for not wanting their existence guessed at either. So they remain one of our nation's best-kept open secrets."

"Does Escotte know about these tunnels?" Sian asked.

"Yes. Unfortuantely, he is among the few who do."

Let's hope he doesn't tell the temple if he learns of our escape, she thought.

Sian followed Arian, still gaping at the weird beauty of this entirely hid-den place. To have lived in Alizar all her life, and never have suspected that the giant ruins above ground were barely half of the equation! She found herself wondering again who the Ancients had been, where they had gone, and what unimaginable force had it taken to ruin structures made of such seemingly indestructible materials. Might the Butchered God have been a harbinger of their return, after so much time? If so, might Alizar still learn what power had destroyed the Ancients' city? It was a frightening thought.

Among so many others, of course — some as mundane as starvation.

"I'm sorry, Arian," Sian said, coming to a halt. "But I don't know how much farther I can go without some food. I'm always so hungry after healing, and with all the rest of what we've been put through since last night ... I'm amazed I had the strength to make it down that shaft. Aren't you at least a little hungry too?"

Arian nodded. "Ravenous, actually. Which is strange, for me at least. We've missed nothing but breakfast. But ... maybe we can find something ..." She began to wave the globe around again, searching their surroundings as if she thought there might be a small tavern set into the tunnel's walls nearby.

"What are you looking for?" Sian asked.

"A map. Or some store of supplies. There should be powder flares cached down here somewhere. How long did you say this little ball of light will last?"

"I'm not sure. I've only ever used them once, the last time I escaped. But that took me no more than an hour or so. How many do we have?"

"Two more, I think." Arian reached inside her robe to check, then nodded.

"What kind of map do you expect to find down here?"

"There are markings carved into the walls that tell what lies ahead, how far away, and in what direction. When I find one, we'll be better able to orient ourselves."

"How do you know all this?" Sian asked. "Have you been down here before?"

"Not clear out on The Well, and not for many years, but yes. Viktor used to bring me down here. He liked hunting these tunnels for antiquities. He collects them, you know."

Sian thought of Escotte, wondering if this thirst for ancient artifacts was some inbred habit of the elite.

"We spent entire days down here sometimes, when we were first married." Arian smiled wistfully. "He was so adventurous then. So full of plans, such confidence and optimism. He wanted me to see every part of his ... his *kingdom*, I suppose. Whatever Alizar pretends it is." She grew quiet. Thoughtful. "Our first time here, he brought a picnic lunch along. We sat on a high ledge in a cavern underneath Viel and spat our plum-pits down into the water."

"I wish we had plums now," Sian sighed.

"Oh!" Arian exclaimed. "The water! Yes, of course. How silly of me!" She bent down beside the watercourse they followed, waving her light just above the surface, then reached in with her other hand to wrestle something loose and pluck it out. "Breakfast!" she said proudly, standing up and coming to show her harvest to Sian.

As she approached, Sian held out her hand, into which Arian dropped two small shells clamped tightly shut.

"Mussels?" Sian asked. "Down here?"

"They do not require light to live," said Arian. "Viktor often roasted them for me when we came down exploring. There are some very tasty snails in these channels too, as I recall."

"We have some way to make a fire then?" Sian asked, reawakened to the chilly temperature, even through her cape.

"Well... Not yet. Until we find a cache of powder flares, at least. But Escotte often serves raw shellfish at his dinner parties. It's considered quite a delicacy."

Sian looked at her askance, remembering the smell of sewage back up in those drainage tunnels they had snuck through to reach the shaft that fed this very stream. "My tastes are ... less refined, perhaps," she said, handing the mussels back to Arian. "I think we ought to wait until we have some fire, at least."

"Suit yourself," said Arian, though she made no effort to pry the creatures open and pop them into her mouth either. She just tossed them back into the water as she turned to carry on. "There should be plenty more around wherever we find the map and a supply cache. They were usually located together, as I recall."

Though Arian walked along with confidence, their footsteps echoed oddly in the tunnel, making it sound, at times, as if they were being followed.

Periodically they paused to listen, but decided that nothing followed them but their own noise, or at times, the scuttling swarms of tropical cockroaches that infested any of the islands' darker, damper places.

"I am glad for your company, healer," Arian said quietly after one such pause.

"I am glad for yours as well," said Sian, wondering if her refusal of those mussels had been hasty. "Can we rest another minute? Would you mind?"

"All right," Arian said, reluctantly.

Isn't she tired too? Sian wondered. Or did the drain of energy Sian experienced when she healed transfer into extra strength and energy for the recipient somehow?

Sian sank down against the tunnel's tiled wall, as Arian sat beside her, giving their little globe another shake. It felt unbelievably good to stop. Even if she weren't starving, Sian was too old for this kind of adventure: too old by far. She leaned back and closed her eyes, rubbing them with grubby fingers. If she caught some horrible infection from the grime and filth down here, she could just heal it, she supposed.

For some reason, these thoughts of infection brought Arouf to mind, his face red with incoherent anger after she had healed Bela. Then real rage — at their parting. Before that day, she had never imagined him quite so … unhinged. Though large and strong, he'd always seemed a gentle man.

"It must be something new husbands do," Sian said, "picnic lunches. My Arouf took me to the top of Little Loom Eyot when we first bought the island, before we'd built anything at all there. He pretended we were just going up to survey the site — deciding where to put the loom house and the dye works, where to build our home. But when we'd hacked our way through the jungle and reached the summit, he pulled out a white damask tablecloth and a whole delicious meal he'd hidden all the way up there beforehand; that morning, I suppose, while I'd still been sleeping. Even a jug of wine!"

"Viktor had the entire Factorate House rebuilt so that I would feel 'at home,'" said Arian, "though his ideas about what 'home' should look like were, perhaps, a bit more ostentatious, and a trifle less tasteful, than my father's had been." She laughed softly. "My husband is a good man, Sian, if not entirely practical, sometimes."

Sian thought about the Factor's *impractical* handling of that giant corpse now hailed as the Butchered God, but said nothing. She thought as well of the few times she'd visited the Factorate House. It had seemed a fairly nice palace to her, though she did not say this either. "Arouf is not managing things as well these days," she was startled to hear herself say instead.

Arian gave her a sober look. "To be honest, neither is Viktor." She looked away. "And I fear it is, at least in part, my fault."

"Your fault?" Sian asked hesitantly, wondering, suddenly, if it was quite safe to be sitting here with the Factora-Consort of Alizar, discussing the details of their marriages. Were the Factor and Factora-Consort's private troubles and uncertainties proper fodder for such conversation with a common anybody? Then again ... *She is a woman, just as I am,* Sian thought. *Flesh and blood. Love and loss. Wife and mother. Why should two women — relatives in fact — not discuss their men?* "How exactly, do you mean?"

"I have allowed him ... no, *encouraged* him to rely on me too much," said Arian. "I have *managed* him to the point where he is incapable of facing his own place as Factor here without me. And now, he is without me. At such a time." She gazed at the dark water. "Is he crumbling beneath the strain, I wonder? Or finding some inner strength at last, now that I am absent?" She released a quiet, bitter laugh. "And which of those do I most hope for, deep inside?"

Sian shivered as Arian's words struck home. "It is ... the same, I think, with Arouf and me." She felt astonished, having thought for all these years that he must be grateful for her part in their success! "For years, I have managed our business, our whole lives, and he just ... lets me." She turned to stare at Arian. "Our marriage too was so lively once. So full of passion. Now, we live as nothing more than acquaintances — or did, at least. Before all this. We have not even shared a bedroom since our younger daughter was born. Is this why? Have I ... put him to sleep somehow? By doing everything, and leaving him without anything of his own to strive for? Any sense of equal purpose?"

"Viktor's bedchamber and mine are not even in the same wing now," sighed Arian.

They sat in pensive melancholy for a while.

"I am rested enough," Sian said, climbing back up to her feet. The thoughts roiling through her mind now made her want to move. "Let's get you back to Viktor. Just in case he does still need your help." They smiled at one another as Arian stood too.

As they set off again, Sian struggled with this new frame Arian had given her through which to view her troubles with Arouf. Had she stifled him? Was she at fault for their waning relationship? The idea did seem somewhat compelling, and yet, she still felt very angry with him, though the reasons for that anger seemed more muddled now. She saw she'd likely had a part in their disintegration, but she certainly felt no new desire to go running back and apologize.

As focused as she was on this new line of questions, it became harder and harder to ignore her stomach. She found herself recalling every detail of that long-ago picnic on the unnamed island which had become Little Loom Eyot. Arouf had been so proud of his culinary prowess then, though he was a far more accomplished cook now. Not that she would ever taste his spicy sweetprawn stew again … A tear or two mingled with the dampness of the air on her face, though whether for the loss of her husband, or of his cooking, she was still unsure.

This reverie was broken by a quiet splash ahead, followed by a soft exclamation of dismay from Arian. Sian looked up to find her standing in an inch or two of water lying across their path.

Arian held up her globe of light, reaching as far forward as she could while peering into the gloom. "This is not welcome news," she said softly.

"What's wrong?"

"The path looks flooded up ahead." Arian looked back at Sian anxiously. "Either it's dipping down a bit — not for very long, I hope — or there is some obstruction damming up the waterway."

"Is there some other way around?"

"I have seen no other passages, have you?"

"No." Sian could not bring herself to ask aloud if this meant they must go back. She could not climb that ladder at the falls again. Not without a lot of food and much more rest, at least. Even then, she doubted she would make it. "What now?" was all she could manage.

"I think we had better just try pushing forward. It may not get that deep."

"So be it," Sian said, praying they would not be forced to turn around.

They sloshed through the grimy water for some time in silence. It was work just to concentrate on her footing now. A slippery carpet of some kind had formed across the submerged stone, sometimes pocked with small sinkholes of slimy mud. At least, Sian hoped that was what it was.

The water continued to deepen, gradually, until it came halfway up their shins.

Arian released a stifled scream, flailing her arms wildly. Sian cried out in sympathetic fright as Arian lurched toward the wall, both arms extended to fend off the impact as she splashed against it and regained her balance. "The edge!" she blurted. "Watch out for the channel edge! I almost fell into the stream!"

Sian pressed both hands against her heart, hoping to calm its fluttering beat.

"Stay well to your right," Arian cautioned, pressing forward once again. "There's no way to tell the streambed from the path through all this muck."

Before too long, to their relief, the water started to subside again. Had they crossed to Bayleaf yet, Sian wondered, or were they still somewhere underneath tiny Meaders? It was impossible to know. They might be underneath the open seabed, for all one could tell here. Though where all this water flowed to underneath an ocean, Sian could not begin to understand. Everything about the Ancients seemed impossibly mysterious.

"Oh no!" groaned Arian, splashing forward through the now just ankle-deep flood to press her hands against a brick wall someone had erected across the entire tunnel. Not recently either, judging by its age-blackened mortar and the seepage stains across its surface. As Sian arrived beside her, Arian waved her light in all directions, looking for a way around or through. The water passed beneath the blockage through a metal grating set along its base, but not through any space that they could hope to fit through also. "This is what I feared," said Arian. "Someone else who didn't want these tunnels left unblocked to cause them trouble."

"We could backtrack a bit …" Sian ventured.

"I guess we must." Arian gave her a grim smile. "Whatever Father Het's fanciful notions, I doubt there's any way for us to walk through brick walls."

"That's not a power I have acquired yet, no."

For a moment, Arian stared back into the gloomy distance they had come through, then sighed, "All right. Let's go."

Sian turned to follow, and saw something from the corner of her eye that they had missed while focused on the unanticipated wall. "Arian, wait! What's this?"

As Arian came splashing back, Sian pointed down at a small iron door, more a hatch, really, set low into the wall.

"Oh, Sian! What good work!" Arian reached down to grasp the corroded iron hook with which it was latched. Flecks of rust fell to the water as she tugged at it, but the latch held fast. As Sian leaned down to help, Arian simply pulled harder, and the door burst open with a muffled clatter and a gurgling swish.

Sian caught the scents of stagnation, rot, and mold. Happily, there would be just sufficient room to crouch through the opening without having to touch their faces to the shallow water — if the passage led to anywhere they wished to go, that was.

Arian looked back at Sian, then set her jaw, and stooped through the opening, taking the light with her. "I think we're saved!" her voice echoed from inside. "Come through. It's safe. There is a staircase here!"

Sian ducked through the hatch as well, if less gracefully than Arian had, and found herself in a small, brick-lined chamber more than high enough to stand in. A narrow masonry stair twisted upwards into darkness above them.

"Looks like they didn't want an army marching through here," Arian mused. "They left themselves a way, though, just big enough for one person at a time. What good luck! I bet this goes up around the wall and comes out on the other side. I'm *so* relieved. I can tell you now, I guess, how much I didn't want to climb back up that waterfall."

"Nor did I."

As they started up the stairs, Sian wondered why the dark itself seemed so much thicker here. Then she realized the truth. "The globe is running out, I think."

"Oh!" said Arian. "Oh dear, I think you're right. We have only two more left, and I don't think that will be enough if this is all the longer they last. We simply must find a cache of powder flares before much longer."

"That would be very nice," Sian said, thinking of those mussels she'd let Arian toss aside … how long ago? "How much longer do you think it might take to find one?"

"I'm surprised we haven't found one already. They seemed much more frequent when I came down here with Viktor. That was many years ago, of course, and a great ways from this part of the tunnel system. Still, that wall proves people have come down here too." She shook her head. "Let's just keep moving. I am sure we'll run across one soon."

Oh, I hope so, Sian thought, trusting Arian to know what she was doing here. She began to climb again behind her, willing dreams of roasting mussels to drive thoughts of endless darkness from her mind.

～

Reikos stood tensely beside Pino and Ennias, gazing up with them as yet another booming crash came rumbling through the dungeon ceiling. "What in hell is going on up there?"

Ennias shook his head, and went to peer out of their cage again. "Sarit!" he shouted. "Are you up there? *Sarit?*" For all their calling, they had neither seen nor heard any sign of their jailer since well before all the alarming noise upstairs had started.

"Where's he gone?" Pino asked anxiously. "It sounds like something's caving in up there." He turned to Ennias, eyes wide with fear. "Are they going to just bury us down here? Seal us in to keep us quiet?"

"Don't be crazy, boy," the sergeant said distractedly, his eyes back on the ceiling. "Why waste a building to do what any shovel would do just as well?"

"But what *are* they doing?" asked Reikos. "The lad is right. That sounded like a ton of rock being dropped. On what, though? Why?"

"Your guess is as good as mine." Ennias fell silent as another round of noise arrived, like heavy furniture being dragged around. "But, I'm thinking something … is going very —" A sudden swell of shouting was cut short by a deafening concussion from somewhere not far up the stairs.

All three men rushed to the bars.

"*Sarit!*" Ennias yelled again. "*Anyone!*"

"*Is anybody up there?*" Reikos shouted at his side.

Their calls were answered this time, by a clattering of feet inside the stairwell. "Sergeant Ennias!" came Sarit's frantic voice. "I'm coming!"

Thank all the gods! thought Reikos.

"What's happening?" Ennias demanded as Sarit came half-stumbling around the corner, and rushed toward their cell.

"The Hall has been attacked, sir!" Sarit gasped, fumbling for his keys as he arrived. "By troops from the *Factorate!* With cannon! *Cannon!* Half the building is in flames!"

"Gods!" Reikos blurted.

Pino simply gaped, first at Reikos, then at Ennias. "Is it the war?"

"It's started, then." For once, Ennias looked just as dismayed as anybody. "We've failed."

Sarit was already twisting his keys in the lock. "I was called away when the Factor's troops arrived. It's every man to save himself now, I'm afraid. But I'll not leave you men down here to starve, sir. Nor to burn. Got to live with myself, don't I. No matter how all this may end."

"Where's Domina Kattë?!" Pino exclaimed. "And the Factora-Consort?"

Sarit spared the boy a baffled glance at that. They'd not told him any of what Ennias had revealed last night. "The Consort's safe on Home, I would expect. Lord Alkattha's cousin, I cannot vouch for." He pulled their cell door open and stepped back. "Left with him, perhaps."

"Escotte's gone, then?" asked Ennias.

"No sign of him since late last night, sir." Sarit shrugged. "Quatama tells me he was headed for the Factorate, but maybe he knew this was coming, and has just escaped somewhere. Like him to run off without a word of warning to the rest of us. Or maybe he is dead already. Out of our hands now; that's all I know, and all I care. If the Factor is at war with his own cousin, then the world we knew is surely at an end." Another roaring crash came from above, more indicative of falling masonry than cannon fire this time. "If you're going, better get out now!" said Sarit, already running for the stairs again. "Best of luck, lads. The gods watch over you!"

They required no further prompting to be out and running upward after him, Reikos just behind the sergeant, with Pino at his back. At the top, they found Sarit trying with only partial success to wrench the upper door open. Ennias stepped forward to lend Sarit a hand, and the door swung in at last, now half blocked outside by fallen stone and broken timbers.

"Looks like I got the door shut just in time on that one, eh?" Sarit grunted, scrambling up and over the debris. "Such a pretty house to burn," he tisked.

Ennias climbed up and out just after Sarit. Reikos waved Pino on ahead of him, having come to feel protective of the boy by now. Then he climbed out as well.

Even now, they were still in the great house's vaulted basement, well below ground level, but evidence of just how savagely the Census Taker's residence had been punished lay all around them. With a wary glance and a hasty wave, Sarit took off running for the nearest stairwell, but Reikos and the others could do nothing for a moment but turn and gaze around them in astonishment. Two gaping patches of fallen ceiling hung into the basement at its farther end, trailing mangled streams of once-elegant furniture, chandeliers, draperies and carpet from the rooms above, onto the piles of rubble fallen through them. In the opposite direction, flames licked along roof beams as the room above them burned, presumably. Several of the house's huge foundation columns leaned askew now, fractured and sifting dust, staggered out of true by the violence done to upper floors. Shouts of conflict and continued crashing could be heard quite clearly now, without ten or fifteen feet of muffling stone to blunt them.

"I'll go up to see if I can find the ladies," Ennias said, breaking Reikos's trance of disbelief. He started for the stairwell Sarit had taken. "You two get as far away from this as —"

"Don't imagine we're not going with you," Reikos growled.

"That's right," said Pino, heading to the sergeant's side. "Domina Katthë is our friend, not yours."

"They were my friends too, however briefly." The sergeant's voice was surprisingly gentle, Reikos thought. "You two don't know the house. I do."

"And if you find them injured, or unconscious?" Reikos pressed, wincing at the scenes his mind was playing out. "You will carry them both out all by yourself?" Ennias gazed at him. "Which one will you leave to burn if you cannot return in time? Sian? Or your Factora-Consort?"

"All right," said Ennias. "Come then. We can spread out and search faster this way."

"Why are we still talking?" Pino asked, rushing for the stairs.

The sergeant turned to follow Pino. "We'll try Domina Kattë's guest room first. If it's still there."

TWENTY-FOUR

"Yes, this is it." Sian watched as Arian sat down and dipped her feet into the water, sliding them slowly forward. "Is this the floor, or ... aha! It is!" She stood up and took several cautious, plashing steps around the flooded chamber they'd descended into, twin to that in which they'd started, as far as Sian could tell, anyway.

Sian was no longer able to see much of anything clearly, so wan had their light become. They had not wanted to ignite a new globe until this one was entirely exhausted. "Is it all right then?"

"Yes, come down — it's not deep. Look, there's the door."

"I'll take your word for that."

Sian groped her way down the last few steps until she felt water on her toes, the stone grown slippery beneath them. She gripped the railing with one hand until she was sure she'd reached the bottom and her footing was secure.

"This way," came Arian's voice, from the left.

Sian moved slowly through ankle-deep water to where Arian crouched before another open metal hatch.

Arian bent even lower and slipped through. "It's just fine," she called from the other side.

After winding Het's cape around her shoulders, Sian followed, on her hands and knees, heedless of the muck and water. Better safe and stable than sorry, and things seemed to dry out again down here quickly enough. On the other side, Sian found the plash of Arian's footsteps almost easier to follow than her bobbing globe of dying light. "I can't see anything, can you?"

This wasn't entirely true; she could sense that the tunnel grew deeper in the middle; and she could sort of make out the curving edges of a wall beside her, the cavernous ceiling above, as well as Arian's dim figure before her. The mossy tunnel floor was more gentle on her feet again than the rough stone staircase had been, if far more treacherous to her balance.

"Not really," Arian replied. "But we're heading south again, I'm pretty sure."

"That's good, I guess. Should we perhaps take out that second glow float yet?"

"I can still see a little," said Arian. "Come take my hand if that will help, but I think we dare not waste a single drop of light."

As Sian was fumbling forward to accept her offer, Arian drew the failing light along the wall beside her, just inches from its surface, then paused. "Ah! There!"

Sian stopped where she was. "What's happened now?"

"Powder flares!" After a bit more splashing in the dark and the grating wrench of rusty metal, Sian heard a scraping sound, then a brilliant, smoky flash of light burst up before her, followed by the smell of sulfur as the flare subsided to a dull white-orange glow. Sian blinked and gasped, covering her face with a hand until the spots before her eyes had faded.

"I'm sorry!" Arian said. "I thought you knew what I was doing."

"I did — just not how bright it would be. I'll be fine." She blinked again and looked about. The powder flare burned low and steady now, not quite so bright as the globe had been when it was new, but far brighter than what they'd been making do with recently. It did seem they were back in the tunnel they had come from. Though its contours had changed: it was higher and more rounded than before. The tile faces were gone too. Near the spot where Arian had lit their flare, Sian could now see a tall metal locker mounted to the wall. "Is there food in there?"

"If there were, I doubt we'd want to eat it. Who knows how long ago these things were left here." Arian walked quickly further down the passage, stopping at the intersection of a smaller side-tunnel, to study something on the wall. "And here's a map at last!"

Sian waded after her to look. It just seemed a random jumble of hash marks to her. "If that's some language of the Ancients, it makes no sense to me."

"It's a simple shorthand, really. Not that hard, though I remember less of it than I had hoped." She scrutinized the marks a while longer. "All these are tunnels. And these dots denote the distance, while these angled shapes indicate directions of the compass, I believe. … I'm pretty certain this one means south, in which case, we're still headed in exactly the right direction!" She turned happily to Sian.

"That's wonderful," Sian replied. "And is there something in that closet of supplies that we can use to roast those mussels? I may lose consciousness from hunger soon."

"Well, I don't know. Let's go see."

As it happened, there was an empty wooden box just larger than Sian's hand, in which some other, long-vanished supply had been contained. It took them very little time to pry more of the omnipresent mussels from the channel rim, and when they pressed their powder flare against the wooden box, it produced just enough heat to set the wood ablaze — in a sullen, smoldering fashion. They piled their stash of mussels into it and let them cook as it burned down. When there was nothing left but charcoal underneath their stack of now-gaping shells, Sian reached down to nudge one up, tossing the hot little morsel back and forth between her hands until it cooled enough to pry further open. She scooped the bit of flesh inside it eagerly into her mouth, and made a face. "They can't have tasted this way at Escotte's."

Arian tried one next, and grimaced too. "Perhaps they're better raw. They were certainly more artfully seasoned when Viktor used to cook them for me. I'm … not sure these have been fully roasted, actually. That may be the problem. Sadly, we are out of wood." She looked thoughtfully around. "We could try holding our powder flare directly to the meat …"

"And add sulfur and who knows what else to this grim recipe?" Sian asked. Arouf would have known exactly how to cook these creatures. Alas. "Besides, I wouldn't want to put the flare out prematurely by shoving it into a wet shell. How long do they last, anyway?"

"Half an hour, perhaps. We have five more now, which should extend our light supply considerably. And there will surely be more such caches on our way."

Sian heaved a disappointed sigh. "Well, if it's these or starve ..." She took another mussel from the pile. If they died of poisoning here, well ... then they wouldn't have to worry any longer about running out of light.

"Think of them as an acquired taste," said Arian, reaching for another shell herself. "I hated caviar the first few times. Now I just adore it."

Sian scooped, and swallowed, trying not to taste at all, unable to imagine ever liking such rubbery little balls of fishy slime. Still, it was surely nourishment. Her body *needed* fuel.

When they had finished eating, they got up and started off again. Before long, the shallow water they'd been sloshing through for so long retreated back into its proper channel, to Sian's extreme relief. Her bare feet had started to both look and feel like days-dead fish.

As a third powder flare followed their second one, the tunnel began to turn more often, then to branch. At each such intersection, Arian found another of the inscrutable maps, and occasionally diverted them into some different passageway, to keep them traveling in the right direction. Twice her choices led them to dead ends. Blushing, Arian just led them back to the last intersection and took Sian the other way.

To Sian's relief, the mussels they had eaten did not make them sick. But they'd made a very modest meal, and her hunger began whispering again before much time had passed. Though the watercourses they followed were quite brackish, they'd found lots of freshwater seeps running down the tunnel walls along their way, so thirst, at least, had been no problem. Less happily, while there seemed no shortage of tunnel maps now, they all proved either unaccompanied by supply lockers, or the lockers had been raided and left empty. Arian had still not found another stash of powder flares when their last one began to sputter.

"I guess we'll have to use another glow float," Arian conceded. "We can't be that far from our goal now, I suppose."

This was fine with Sian. The glow float's light was better, and she breathed much easier without all that sulfur smoke the flares had cast behind them as she followed Arian.

On and on and on they slogged. In time, Sian followed Arian almost without thinking anymore, just trudging, trudging ... Her limbs grew ever heavier. Her eyes kept wanting to close. She wondered if perhaps it was already evening in the world above, though she didn't think it very likely. She could walk almost the length of Alizar in less than a day up on the surface, and these under-ways seemed much straighter than the winding streets and patchwork bridges she relied on there. Still, she wondered where they were, and when, if ever, they would finally reach their destination, whatever that might be, and how Arian would know it when they did.

The second glow float had begun to wane when Arian paused suddenly ahead of Sian, blinking in surprise at a side tunnel angled steeply upwards. "I ... think this is it," she said.

"This is what?" asked Sian.

"Our exit."

"From the tunnel?" Sian felt sure she must be misunderstanding.

"I think so!" said Arian. "As you see, it's very different from the others. I could hardly be mistaking it, could I?"

"You're not asking me, are you? I have no idea what we're looking for."

"Well, let's go up and find out!" She turned to Sian. "Have you got the last glow float?"

Sian reached into the pocket of Het's cape and pulled it out. "Should we light it yet? The other one's still got a little life in it, I think."

"If I am right," said Arian, "we should have more than enough light now. If not ... Well, I'm tired of living in the dark, aren't you? We'll just exit wherever this comes out, and make the rest of our way to Home across the surface. Very carefully, of course. But I'm quite certain this is Apricot, at last."

Sian's budding excitement was extinguished all at once by a dreadful thought. "Are we going to have climb another waterfall?"

"Oh, of course not. I have never seen another entrance like the one on The Well. The egress here is concealed in an abandoned warehouse, if I'm not mistaken."

Sian sighed with relief. "Then why are we standing here?" She handed their last glow float to Arian, who shook it as she turned to light their way.

This tunnel contained no water at all. But it was not an easy climb either, or a short one. Hours, it took, or seemed to. They had resorted to their hands and knees well before their last glow float began to dim. Sian watched it nervously, hoping desperately that Arian had not miscalculated, or mistaken some tunnel to nowhere at all for the exit she'd intended. When they came at last to a square, vertical shaft lined in solid stone, and Sian saw the iron rung ladder ascending its side, she buried her face in both sandpapered hands and groaned.

"Sian? This is the end," said Arian.

"I knew it," Sian murmured. "I knew we would get lost and die down here."

"What? No, I mean, we're here! Just raise your head and look."

Sian raised her eyes, and realized that Arian had put the float away. The pale light around them came from up above now. She shuffled forward and stood inside the shaft, gazing up at dazzling light streaming through a grate not twenty feet above their heads. She had to look away, so painful was the glare. Had her eyes become so accustomed to the darkness that even the dim light inside a warehouse was this blinding?

"It's just a little climb this time," said Arian. "Shall I go first, or would you prefer to?"

"You're the leader here." Sian smiled at her, abashed now at her lack of faith in Arian.

Arian virtually scrambled up the rungs, then paused at the top, looking through the grate. "That's odd."

"Is everything all right?" Sian asked, a few rungs beneath her.

"I'm not sure." She fumbled at the edges of the grate. "As I said before, it has been a long, long while since I was here … Aha!" Having found a latch, it seemed, she released it and swung the grate open on rusty hinges, then clambered out.

Sian climbed after her, and emerged, wincing, not into a warehouse, but into an alley that debouched onto a set of docks. It was late afternoon at least, or later, judging by the sunlight's low slant. The air was warm and heavy with fish odors, people smells and smoke. A fair amount of it. Someone must be burning refuse — or there was a lot more industry on Apricot than she remembered. She heard shouting in the distance, and the ever-present prayer lines. "Out at last," she sighed. "But where's your warehouse?"

"Well, it's likely been torn down." Arian looked around. "I was a fool to think the world would not have changed much in two decades."

Sian still blinked painfully as she joined Arian in gazing about, trying to reconcile what she was seeing with her own knowledge of the island of Apricot. It seemed bigger than she remembered, and far more crowded. "Where exactly are we?"

"East shore," Arian said, pointing at a little island further east. "That's Toad."

Sian tried to adjust her perspective, but … "Arian … This isn't Apricot. We're on Malençon. The *eastern edge* of Malençon!"

"Don't be absurd!"

But Sian knew she was right. Beyond the row of tumbledown shacks they stood beside, people milled about on crowded docks. Very familiar docks. "My daughter lives not far from here, Arian. That's not Toad, it's Crux. See, there's the curving roof of the Suba estate."

"It *can't* be! We can't …" Arian looked near tears. "We've gone entirely the wrong way!"

"It … seems so," said Sian.

"But — I followed all the markings! We should have crossed The Well, gone under Meaders and Bayleaf and Toad, then come up on Apricot!"

"Well, I'm afraid we haven't …" Sian said gently.

"We're *needed* at the Factorate House! We should have been there *yesterday!*"

Sian glanced nervously around. This alleyway was somewhat concealing. No one was paying them any attention yet, but if Arian kept on this way, they would be noticed very soon. "Arian. Calm down. We'll fix this."

As Arian began to cry, Sian pulled her into an embrace. "It's all right," she whispered, stroking Arian's hair. The faintest breath of ginger rode the sultry air as Sian's fingers grazed the back of her friend's neck; a small cloud of despair filled Sian's heart, then dissipated.

The Factora-Consort's weeping slowed and stopped a minute later. She disentangled from Sian, and took a small step back to gaze at her with mixed embarrassment and gratitude. "I'm all right now." She wiped quickly at her eyes.

"Good." Sian smiled at her. "So …"

"So, we are on the wrong side of Alizar, entirely." Arian shook her head. "We couldn't have gone farther astray if we'd tried."

"We must not have been oriented right. From the start."

"Or I didn't understand the maps as well as I imagined."

"Well, at least no one should be looking for us *here*."

Arian gazed down at herself. Freda's filthy, ragged, water-ruined dress, her hair bedraggled, dried mud and rock dust instead of cosmetics. "Indeed. They would not see *me* even if they were." She looked up and grinned at Sian. "And you're no prize yourself, Our Lady of the Bare Feet."

"I imagine not. And if we're staying up here, I must find some sandals. The streets are going to be far less gentle than the tunnels were."

Arian looked down at the docks. "We should just go find a boat and … oh."

"What?"

"The streets are not gentle here at all." Her tone had darkened; Sian followed her gaze.

A band of heavily armed soldiers marched along the waterfront, scattering people before them. Sian noticed more shouting from a few streets away, and … "Was that … cannon-fire?"

"Hide," Arian whispered.

Sian rushed into the shadows of a stand of trumpetvines growing between two nearby shacks. Arian gave the soldiers another quick look, then fled to join her.

"They wear no family colors that I recognize — including ours," Arian whispered. "They could be Lord Colara's, but if they bear insignias, I can't see them from up here. And … I can think of no reason that anyone's guard should be patrolling Malençon."

"Are they looking for us?"

"I don't want to find out. Do you?"

"So … back to the tunnels after all?" Sian asked, her heart sinking.

"No. We can't. It took us most of a day just to get here; it would be double that to backtrack all the way to Apricot — assuming that we didn't just get lost again. We have no light left, and no food still." Arian sat thinking a moment, as the soldiers passed the end of the wharf, then turned onto a street and marched away. "We must go see if the streets are all so heavily patrolled, or if those men just happened to be passing by."

"All right." Sian was dubious. Both she and Arian looked up as yet another *boom* sounded in the distance. Why would anyone be firing cannon here on Malençon — or anywhere in Alizar, for that matter? Perhaps that wasn't what it was at all. She glanced down at what seemed a little market of some kind down near the end of the wharf. "Wait here. I'll be right back."

Arian reached out and grabbed her arm. "What are you doing? We mustn't separate."

"My lady, I cannot put you in danger too ..."

"Danger? You say this to me now — after all we've been through? Have you some power to keep me *out* of danger, cousin?"

Sian shook her head.

"And please do not revert to all that 'my lady' nonsense. I must be Freda here at least as badly as anywhere before. Besides, I think we're very far past all that by now — in private anyway. Now tell me, what do you intend to do?"

Sian looked miserably at her feet. "I didn't really want to steal sandals in front of the Factor's wife, *Freda*. Even if we are *past all that*."

"Oh, for all the ..." Arian muttered. "Are you experienced at thievery?"

"No," Sian admitted.

"What if you're caught? Then all of this has been for nothing. Do you have some reason to believe you'll even find sandals down there somewhere? All I see are docks and a tavern and a fishmonger's storefront."

Sian took another glance at that supposed market, and realized that Arian was right. "I was just going to check."

Arian looked down at Sian's feet, and sighed. Dry mud coated them, nearly to her knees. "I see no need to risk it," she said, leaning down to unbuckle one of her own quite ruined sandals. "Here. One is better than none."

"What?"

The Factora-Consort held out her sandal. "We can lean on each other if we have to. I'd rather wear one of my feet down than risk either of us being jailed for stealing just now. Especially in a port crawling with armed men."

"You can't be serious."

"I can and am." She shoved the sandal into Sian's hand. "Put it on."

"I ... thank you." At least one of her feet might not be cut to ribbons now by the time they got to Home.

It was awkward going, but as they left the alley and started down the street, they saw no more patrols, though other signs of discord seemed disturbingly abundant — shops and taverns boarded up, quite hastily, it appeared; no children playing in the streets; a gang of grim young men moving furtively ahead of them, as if expecting something, or someone, unpleasant to show up at any moment. Arian shook her head. "Something has gone very wrong, I fear."

Within mere minutes, Arian hobbled to a stop, and gave Sian an exasperated look. "This was not a good idea." She reached down to remove her remaining sandal. "We look ridiculous, which is hardly safe if we are trying to avoid attention, and we'll just both go lame as quickly this way." She handed the second sandal to Sian. "Just for a little while," she rushed to clarify as Sian opened her mouth to object. "We can trade them back and forth at intervals. That way, both our feet will get to rest from time to time. Until we find some sandals that seem safe to steal, anyway," she added with a crooked grin.

Sian did not bother arguing this time.

As they crossed the narrow edge of Malençon to the southwestern waterfront, Sian gazed out across the bay at what she first took for a rising column of cloud in the orange evening light. Then she stopped walking. "Is that smoke?"

"Yes."

They both stood, staring, in the shadow of a tall mangosteen tree.

"It's Home," Arian said miserably. She resumed walking even faster — as if she might be able to run straight there.

"You can't know that," Sian protested, following. "It could be coming from any of the islands in the channel. We can't even *see* past Cutter's. Not from here."

Arian stumbled, clearly even less accustomed to bare feet than Sian was by now, then put a hand to her belly. "I'm so hungry, I can't think straight anymore."

"Listen, Arian. My daughter lives here, just past that peninsula. She and her husband will know what's going on, and we can get a meal there. There's no point rushing back across all the islands fainting from hunger without any notion of what we're even heading into."

"No! No more delays! Can't you see? We have to get there!"

"They have a boat."

Arian turned to look at her. "How large?"

"More than large enough. They'll loan it to me."

Arian stared out across the water at the rising column of smoke again. "All right."

～

"What else should I have done, Maleen? She's completely run amok. You haven't been there to see. You don't know." Arouf fell silent, tired of speaking to his daughter's back as she stared out the window at her son and husband in their yard, guarding the house from *looters*. He shook his head, unable to believe any of the things happening around him now. When Maleen just went on staring out the window, he asked, "Are you even listening?"

"Yes, I'm listening." She turned impatiently to face him again, shifting the sleeping baby to her other shoulder. "I'm just not believing anything I hear. You filed a *legal complaint*? Against *Mother*?" She gestured crossly at the window behind her. "Has someone tampered with the islands' food supply? Is that why the whole world has suddenly gone crazy?"

"You're calling *me* crazy? Your mother is the crazy one! That's what I'm telling you!"

He stopped talking as the front door banged open and his little grandson, Biri, came trotting in to tug at Maleen's dress. "Mommy, Papa said to tell you that some men who just came by say Lord Colara has sent soldiers to Three Cats to —"

"Yes, dear. Go tell your father thank you for me, but your grandpa and I are having an important conversation now, all right? Go back out and help your papa guard the house, okay?"

Little Jila stirred, and brought a thumb up to her mouth, but didn't waken.

"Okay." Biri pouted, but did as he was told.

If only everybody in this family were so obedient, thought Arouf. "All I did was ask her to be accountable for her behavior," he said when Biri was gone. "Was that so unreasonable? After she'd run off to march around with that Butchered God cult, and gotten herself infected with this ... obviously *demonic*, and completely *illegal* —"

"She didn't *march around* with anybody," Maleen cut him off. "She was attacked on her way to meet with —"

"There *was* no Hanchu trade delegation, Maleen! Do you think I didn't check? I don't think you understand how much trouble she's gotten us into. For a *week* now, I have been harassed — at home — by temple priests, Factorate security officials, trade associates, even bill collectors — all looking for your mother! If that's not abandonment, what is it? Some strange oaf even showed up claiming that Sian had hired him. It's been like a circus! If you ever came to see us anymore, you would know what she's been —"

"I've seen!" she cut him off again. His daughter had grown very rude, it seemed, since having children of her own. "She was here just a few weeks ago, remember? And yes, she said some ... strange things. But *abandonment* and *infidelity*? How could you?"

"I told you, she ran off with *Pino!* That was weeks ago!" He raised his arms helplessly. Had he not explained this several times already?

"And you call *her* crazy? Pino is a *boy*, Father! She's old enough to be *his* mother too!"

"That's what makes it so indecent! Can't you see that? And he's not the only one, Maleen. Oh no. These people who keep coming to harass me: they've been asking about some man named Reikos too. A sea captain! Who knows how many other men there are? She's turning our townhouse on Viel into some kind of brothel! Just imagine what our clients —"

"*Listen to you!*" Maleen screeched. Jila woke up and started to whine.

Maleen's eyes were round as coins now. She still wasn't getting it. What more would it take, he wondered, to make her understand how bad Sian had gotten?

Before either of them could say any more, the front door banged open once again as Biri ran inside. "Mommy! Come look, Mommy!" he exclaimed. "There's a fire on Three Cats now too!"

Maleen whirled around and went back to the window. Arouf came to see as well. Sure enough, a new column of smoke was rising there, just across the water. The insanity was coming closer. Maleen was right about one thing. Sian was not the only one who'd lost her mind all of a sudden. Maybe it *was* some kind of plague. Would they all be crazy like this by morning?

Maleen looked down at Biri anxiously, jiggling the baby. "I'm sorry, honey; what did Papa say those men told him — about the soldiers Lord Colara sent?"

"They went to fight Lord Orlan," Biri said, his eyes bright with excitement. "On Three Cats."

Arouf drew a startled breath. If the great houses were fighting each other now, then this was no longer just an Alkattha family quarrel. *What a disaster.* To think that he should live to see this … It hardly mattered what Sian did now, he thought. Nobody's business would survive this — except the Mishrah-Khote's. And the undertakers. Monde & Kattë was ruined now for sure.

Maleen looked back out across the water, shaking her head. "She could be anywhere out there … in all of this." She reached down to gather her son close, snuggling both her children as they gazed out at the new fire, then looked over her shoulder at Arouf, in tears now. "Did you even *try* to find out where she really is before you did this?"

"I sent her letters!" he protested. "I even went to the townhouse — it's clearly abandoned. I came here hoping you might know where she could be — as soon as I found out about the Factor's absurd war against the Census Taker."

"You should have let me know about this sooner, Father." Maleen turned back to the window. "She told me we were all in danger … I did not believe her." She looked down at her son. "Maybe you should stay in here now, Biri. Would you like to play with Grandpa for awhile before you go to bed?"

He shook his head. "I want to keep helping Papa."

She sighed, and smiled anxiously. "All right then. But if he tells you to come in, you do it right away. You hear me?"

Biri nodded, as if this were foolishly obvious, and turned to dash back out the door.

When he was gone again, Maleen turned back to Arouf, looking haunted. "Do you think she knew? That this was coming?"

"Your mother?" The idea seemed ridiculous at first, but, on second thought… "It would not surprise me anymore if she turned out to be responsible for all of this somehow."

Maleen inhaled sharply, glaring at him with such outrage that he took an involuntary step backward. "Go!" she hissed, launching one arm up to point rigidly at the door. "Go out and help my husband guard this house! Or go clear back to Little Loom Eyot! I don't care. But I won't hear another word of your insanity tonight. Is that clear? We all have too much to cope with at the moment!" She turned away as Jila started crying in earnest. "Even *she* is tired of your madness!"

Arouf knew how to pick his fights, and this one was clearly not a winner for him at the moment. He nodded, already sidling carefully around her toward the door. Perhaps Haron would be more reasonable to talk with.

"I'm so sure that *Mother* made the Factor burn the Census Hall!" Maleen yelled as he escaped into the yard. "I'll bet *Pino* was there too! And this Captain Reikos! I can see now why she left you!"

Arouf winced as he stepped out onto the landing and pulled the door closed, then turned to find both Haron and his grandson staring at him from beside the vine-covered gate. He offered them a sheepish smile as he descended the stairs.

Haron leaned against a hefty pike, brand new, it appeared, and considerably taller than himself. For all Haron's muscular physique, Arouf had always thought him rather short for a blacksmith.

"Do you find, sometimes, that women can be … difficult to live with?" Arouf asked, grinning at this time-honored little joke between two world-weary men.

"I do indeed. Sometimes." Haron turned back to look across the water at Three Cats. "Especially when I'm screwing up at something."

Arouf's grin faltered as Biri turned away as well, to look up at his father, then across at Three Cats too. No hope of support here either, then. Ah well. Arouf understood what it was like to be henpecked. Likely best to change the subject. "So …" he said, hesitantly, walking out to join them at the fence, "what do you suppose that is, burning over there?"

"Lord Orlon's estate, I'd guess, from what we heard a while ago about Colara's house guard. It's in about the right place for it."

"But why are they fighting each other like this at all?" Arouf asked with resurging irritation. "Where did this come from? Just a week ago, everything was fine."

"Was it?" Haron asked, still staring at the distant fire. "Work's been busier than ever for the last few months." He looked back at Arouf. "You know what I've been forging?"

"I can't begin to guess." Arouf knew, of course, that Haron's specialty was fine ornamental copper, brass, and silverplate, but he didn't see how months of brisk business could be anything but yet another indication that things had been going fine, just as he'd said.

"I've been forging weapons." Haron nodded at the pike he held. "Like this one." He turned to thrust his chin across the channel at the fire. "Not my normal stock in trade, but that's all anybody seemed to want. Lord Orlon's been among my biggest customers, though I've had large orders from three other major houses too. I have it on good authority from friends down at the guild hall that Orlon had a couple cannons made this year as well." He shrugged. "This hasn't all blown up since just last week, Arouf. I'm pretty sure of that much."

"Too much time on their hands," Arouf grumbled. "Too much money, and no idea what to do with it. That's what I think. And a damn poor Factor up on Home, of course."

Haron raised a brow at this. "That's our family you're speaking of."

"*Sian's* family, not mine." Arouf frowned at the memory of his last conversation with her. *They are targeting my family* … "Launching cannon at his own cousin. Insanely rash. I don't know or care what they were quarreling about, but *that's* what started this. The man has always been erratic. This whole Butchered God nonsense that's swallowed up my wife; he started that as well. Ordering that … *thing* that washed up, hacked to bits and *fed* to people? How mad was that? If he'd just had the sense to let the creature rot there, as it should have, our whole workforce wouldn't be out marching pointlessly around now while the nation's business goes to hell."

Haron shrugged again. "If so many people hadn't been so hungry, he'd not likely have come up with the idea."

"You *approve* of what he did?"

Haron sighed and looked back at Three Cats. The island had turned orange and purple in the evening light. "I'm just saying things were plenty bad for quite a while before that corpse arrived. If *it* hadn't snapped the twig, likely something else would have." He reached down absently to tousle his son's hair. "The question now is what to do about all this."

"About a *war*?" Arouf asked bitterly. "Too late to do much of anything, it seems to me. For us, at least. *They* have to figure out what's to be done now. It's their mess."

"Papa," Biri said.

"It's our mess," Haron told Arouf. "It may be their fault, or it may not. But the only person I can trust to make my life work is —"

"Papa!" Biri said again, tugging at his arm. "Who is that?"

Arouf and Haron both turned to squint into the sunset at whatever Biri was interrupting them about. Two haggard-looking women — aged vagrants by the look of them — were hobbling up the street.

"Is it looters?" Biri asked. "Should I go get Mommy?"

"No, son. They're just old ladies. They won't hurt us."

"Is it Grandma?"

Haron smiled down at his boy. "No, Biri. Grandma's somewhere else right now."

Biri looked back at the women uncertainly. "Why are they coming here then, Papa?"

"They're not coming here. They're just walking by to somewhere else."

Biri looked again, and shook his head. "No. Look! They're waving at us!"

To Arouf's surprise, they were — and one of them was calling Biri's name!

"It's Grandma!" Biri cheered, smiling broadly and waving back at them. "Hi, Grandma! We thought you were looters!"

TWENTY-FIVE

Footsore and parched, Arian followed Sian up the dust and gravel lane toward a modest but attractive teak-gabled house, raised on poles above the vegetation, with lovely wrought-iron grillwork over all its windows.

"Oh, there's Haron now," said Sian, "and my grandson, Biri!"

In the yard, before a large outbuilding, two men and a wiry, dark-haired little moppet stood beneath a jasmine-covered gate, watching them come, hands held up to shield their eyes against the evening sun. The handsome, coal-haired man beside the little boy was of medium height, but quite well muscled, holding up a tall, gleaming new brass pike, of all things. The larger man behind him was too obscured by flowers and shadows to make out well.

Sian raised her hand to wave at the little boy, who said something to his father, then grinned and started waving back.

The second man leaned out from behind Sian's son-in-law to peer at them in apparent surprise. "Who is that?" Arian asked Sian.

Sian stopped abruptly. "Arouf! What is *he* doing here?"

How cozy, Arian thought uncomfortably. "Should we modify our story then?"

"No." Sian frowned. "Let my husband hear what his stupidity has cost. Let them all hear."

They had realized while walking here how difficult it would be to explain Sian's 'maid' without touching on their time with Escotte — especially in their current, ragged condition. Arian did not want herself connected with any of the past few days' events — at Census Hall or temple. So they had built a new cover story around the abandonment complaint filed by Sian's husband. Which would doubtless be even more interesting to relate now, with him standing there to listen.

"Are you sure?" asked Arian.

"Yes." A grim smile curved Sian's lips. "This is even better, in its way."

The little boy had run back into their house by the time they reached the gate.

"*Sian?*" said Haron, coming out to meet them, astonishment and dismay written plainly on his face. "By all the gods, what has happened to you?"

Arouf came up behind him. "Where have you been?"

"Arouf," Sian said, her voice cold. "We need to talk."

"Indeed we do. I've been looking for you. For two *weeks* now! Who is this woman?"

"My name is Freda," Arian said, not liking this man any better for having met him in the flesh. What kind of greeting was this to give a lost wife in such obvious distress?

"What have you done now?" Sian's obnoxious husband demanded. "You both look like tramps."

"Arouf!" said Haron, turning to him in amazement.

"Mother? *Oh!*" Sian's daughter came running from the house with Biri at her heels. "What has happened to you?" the woman cried as she and Sian threw their arms around each other. "Are you hurt?"

"I cannot be hurt very easily anymore," Sian reminded her as they pulled back from one another. "But I'm much better than I've been, now that I am here with you. Where is baby Jila?"

"I've already put her down. Mother, where have you been?" Maleen asked, wiping tears from her eyes. "We've been so worried, what with everything that's happening." She waved an arm at the columns of smoke rising above and beyond Three Cats.

And what has *been happening, exactly?* Arian wondered yet again, hoping desperately that these people would be able to tell her.

"Well, I'm very sorry to say," Sian began, frowning back up at Arouf, "that until this afternoon, I have been held in the dungeons of the Factorate Justiciary. Thanks to *you*, husband."

"Me!" Arouf gasped. "How am I possibly —"

"Your ridiculous complaint!" she cut him off. "*Abandonment*, Arouf? After, what, two days? Had I been gone even that long when you sent your vile document after me?"

"Oh, *Father!*" Maleen exclaimed, turning to him angrily. "Look at what you've done!"

Arouf gaped from daughter to wife in disbelief. "No one is arrested for a marital complaint!"

"Not in ordinary times, perhaps," said Sian. They had prepared for this. "But these are clearly not such times, and they weren't feeling as lenient as usual. I have had much time to think about how angry I am with you, Arouf. Am I a child now, that I can't even leave home for a few days without permission? If not for all this sudden chaos, I might never have escaped."

"Why don't we all go inside," Haron said with studied calm. "Clearly, you two ladies need a moment to refresh yourselves. When that is done we can —"

"Oh no. No indeed," Arouf sputtered, shaking his head fiercely. "You are lying to us, woman. Again! I have been tormented all week long by temple priests and Factorate officials who seemed desperate to know where you might be. I told them about my complaint. I asked them why they hadn't found you yet. Are you telling us it did not occur to them to check in their own prisons?" He turned to Maleen. "Did I not tell you how she is now? This is all more lies!"

Seeing that a patch was needed quickly, Arian spoke up. "Have you ever been inside the Justiciary's prison, Domni Kattë?"

"Monde!" he snapped. "She is the Kattë here! I am *Monde!*"

Arian raised a brow at this. "Well then, *Domni Monde*, have you, or have you not?"

"Of course I haven't," he grated. "*I* am not a criminal."

"Then you don't understand what a madhouse it is," Arian said calmly, though the admission made her cringe inside. "There are dozens to a cell sometimes, and hundreds of cells. Sadly, it would not be very hard, I think, to lose someone there for years. You're lucky that your wife escaped at all. These officials you speak of might not have rediscovered her themselves until your grandson here was grown with children of his own."

"Who is this?" Arouf sneered. "One of your fellow *inmates*, Sian?"

"*Father!*" Maleen shouted. "You're frightening your grandchild." Everyone looked down to find Biri now hiding in his mother's skirts. Maleen reached down to stroke her anxious child's head. She shook her own, and turned to take the boy inside.

"We should go in now," Haron insisted. "Sian, Freda, please accept whatever refreshment we can offer you. Then perhaps we can discuss things more civilly." He shot Arouf another warning glance, and waved Sian and Arian toward the house behind Maleen and Biri.

Sian's repugnant husband lingered behind, shaking his head as if for some other, invisible audience, before following them. Arian could not imagine what had possessed Sian to stay with him long enough to bear children. Then again, she reminded herself, she was likely not seeing them at the best point in their long relationship — or at the least stressful time for anyone. Which reminded her …

"I am sorry," Arian said to Haron as they climbed the stairs and stepped into the family's comfortably appointed little dwelling. "Sian and I have only recently met, thrown together on the road as we fled all this … all those fires …" It took no acting ability to look distressed and confused.

"I have been imprisoned, of course," Sian added. "And Freda here was on her way to do some business on Three Cats when all the fighting there broke out. We've been afraid to approach anyone under such dangerous conditions, so we still aren't sure what's going on."

"Godsdamned civil war!" Sian's husband growled, just then coming in the door himself. "That's what's going on, wife. Our mad Factor took his cannons to the Census Taker's Hall this morning, and now all the greater houses are at each other's throats, if you've been too busy with your lovers to have heard. Your *cousins* have destroyed us all."

Arian had both hands against her face without thinking, no longer even breathing for fear of bursting into tears. *Oh Viktor.* She had failed him. She had failed the entire country. She had already guessed, of course, deep down, as they had seen fire bloom on Three Cats too. But she had hoped … somehow … to be wrong. Unable to contain her grief, she started sobbing as Sian came swiftly to embrace her. *Anyone might cry at such news, mightn't they?* Arian told herself as Sian's arms encircled her. This was a tragedy for all of Alizar now. Not just hers and Viktor's.

Arouf looked something like ashamed, at last, not that Arian much cared now.

"I'm so sorry," said Maleen, coming to stand helplessly beside them. "What island are you from, Freda?"

Arian found herself unable to reply, unsure of what to say.

"Home," Sian answered for her. "Freda's family lives on Home."

"Oh," Maleen said quietly, looking back at Haron in clear distress.

Maleen's expression told Arian that she was far from finished coping with bad news. But Sian's strong embrace was greatly fortifying. Truly, the woman's tenderness and compassion seemed almost as miraculous as her healing gift was. Arian felt her composure returning with surprising swiftness. The same inexplicable fearlessness she had discovered on that dreadful night of their initial capture seemed to reassert itself — almost physically — as it had also done after they'd emerged from the cisterns to find themselves so lost. She drew a deep, shuddering breath, then another, and pulled back from her cousin's arms. "Have you … any news of Home?" she asked without looking at Maleen, or anybody else.

"Where on Home does your family live?" Haron asked.

Arian thought quickly. It mustn't be anywhere too close to the Factorate. "Near the bridge to Apricot."

"Well, they should be fine then," Haron reassured her. "From what we've heard — out here at the edge of the world, of course — all the real fighting there has been in or near the Factorate."

The new wave of panic this news brought her must have shown quite plainly, because Maleen asked, "Do you have friends near there?"

She shook her head. "Not really. I was … just wondering if there's been any news about the Factor … or his family." She glanced at Maleen, then at Sian, worried that she was being too transparent, but no one looked as if they found the question strange. Who might not be curious about Alizar's rulers at such a time?

"Oh, there's been all kinds of news on that front," Haron sighed. "The Factor is holed up inside his house, fighting off the Census Taker's forces. The Factor's fled the country with a fleet of his family's ships. The Factor's been imprisoned in his own dungeons by the Census Taker. I've even heard people saying that the Factorate has fallen to some foreign invader, and that both the Census Taker and the Factor have been killed." He shook his head. "Pick the answer you least want to hear, and someone will confirm it on the best authority."

"Of course," said Arian. "As might be expected." There was one more question that she had to ask. "Any word at all about their son?"

"None that I've heard," Haron sighed. "Or the Factora-Consort either. The boy's been quite sick, of course. So maybe no one's bothering with him right now. Alkattha's consort …" He shrugged. "Her fate will be determined by his, I guess. So probably no one's wasting time or effort on her either. I imagine both she and her son have been taken somewhere safe for now."

"Well … That's very reassuring." Arian gave him a smile. "Thank you, Haron." He was clearly a good man. An optimistic one. As Viktor had been once.

"If you'd like," Maleen asked Arian, "I can show you to the bath out back?"

"Oh, thank you, dear," said Sian. "That would be lovely. You have no idea."

Maleen gave their disheveled conditions a pointed looking-over. "I have *some* idea, I think. I'll find you both some new clothes too, while you're bathing."

"How generous of you," said Arian. "Anything would be fine."

Maleen smiled at her mother. "I'll find something it's okay to ruin this time." Sian grinned back, ruefully. "Are you ready, Freda?"

"Yes, thank you."

The family's bath behind the house was walled for privacy, but roofless. Arian had never bathed beneath the open air before. It was a lovely feeling, staring up into the twilit sky. She wished they'd had such baths built at the Factorate House. An academic pipe dream now, of course. Only minutes after she had lowered herself into the lukewarm water, Maleen was back with a simple shift of auburn silk. Clean, unassuming clothing that would render her far less conspicuous than Freda's prim attire had done — especially in its current state. She and Sian would both have sandals now, she realized.

It had been right to stop here. She saw that now. Still, she was anxious to be off again as soon as possible. She still had no idea what might be happening right now to her son or husband. *Please let there be some way to find them,* she begged silently, in case any of Alizar's shy gods might still be listening. She thought Sian's god might be. The woman was a literal godsend. That had become clearer with every passing hour. *Please let her heal Konrad, even now,* she added, lying back until just her face remained above the water, still trying to absorb all she had learned.

The Census Taker's palace, burned … It seemed impossible to imagine. She wondered how enraged Escotte must be — and why Viktor had done such a thing. Perhaps when she had failed to reappear … But how could he have been sure that she was not still held within it? Her husband was impractical at times, and even paranoid, but he had never been so rash. Quite the opposite. He was timid to a fault, particularly these days. Had the apparent loss of her left him that badly carried off by anger? Or had Escotte realized that he was exposed somehow, after betraying them, and made some preemptive move on Viktor that had forced his hand? Whatever had occurred, the act had clearly not strengthened Viktor's image in the popular mind. *Our mad Factor… has destroyed us all…* Was that what everybody thought now? That this had all been Viktor's fault?

And what had come of poor Maronne? *Please let her have escaped somehow,* she thought, then shook her head. There would be no answers until they reached Home again, if then.

She sat up and scrubbed the worst dirt from her limbs, then filled her hands with the soft, scented soap and washed her hair. Some of the dark dye left it, staining the water. Arian hoped enough dye had remained to keep up her disguise. Well, if some of her pale hair leached through, perhaps people would just take it for gray.

After rinsing her hair, she reached over the copper basin's side to open the little tap that drained it, admiring Haron's work. She'd have hired him to make any number of things for her, if she were still Factora-Consort. She grimaced, hearing her own thought. "Don't *you* give up yet either, Arian," she murmured to herself, standing to use the towel Maleen had provided. She didn't know how this would end yet, after all — or what had happened since those first rumors had been generated. "If your arms are tied," she told herself, "that still leaves your feet."

When she had donned Maleen's pretty shift, a bit too tight for her, and a bit too short, but far better than what she had come in, she stepped into the plain but sturdy sandals Maleen had left as well, and went back into the house to tell Sian her turn had come.

She found Sian sitting at a table spread with food, gorging herself in a state of indecent bliss. With a faint groan of desire, Arian sat down immediately to follow her example. Maleen and Haron sat across from them, watching in bemusement, and nibbling at the corners of their feast. Biri had been put to bed, it seemed, while Arouf stood off by himself, leaning against the wall and scowling at Sian's back.

"*Pino* must not feed you very well," Arouf muttered, half swallowing the remark.

Everyone seemed to freeze, then went back to eating as if he hadn't spoken. Arian could make little sense of the oblique reference. Pino, she vaguely recalled, was one of two men Ennias had told her about. Sian's imprisoned friends. She had forgotten all about them, and worried for them too now, hoping they weren't still buried underneath the smoldering wreckage of the Census Hall. "The bath was lovely," she said to Maleen. "And this dress is perfect. Thank you so much. I have no way to repay you now, but just as soon as —"

Maleen waved her words off like annoying insects. "It's old, and of no use to me." She smiled at her mother again. "This time. Thank you for accompanying my mother here. You owe us nothing."

"You will stay with us tonight, of course," Haron added. "Or longer if you need to, while some of this dust settles."

"Oh!" said Arian. "Has Sian not told you? We must both be going. Very soon, in fact."

"Both?" Maleen asked, giving her mother a startled look.

Sian looked just as startled, turning to Arian with panic in her eyes.

Oh no! thought Arian. They'd planned to tell Sian's daughter that they were rushing back to Little Loom Eyot to deal with Arouf. But here he was now, so ... She should have thought.

"Why must you leave, Mother?" Maleen asked.

"I ... Freda is expected ... elsewhere on Malençon." She glanced at Arian, still clearly at a loss. "I promised I would accompany her. She's done the same for me, after all."

Genius, Arian thought, washed in relief. *The woman is a genius on her feet.*

"Oh, surely not," Haron said to Arian. "It's almost full dark out there now. That's no time to be wandering — even with a friend — given everything that's happening. You must stay here until morning, at least."

"Thank you, but ... You've been so much more than kind already. And my ... friends must already be quite frantic, wondering where I am. I cannot just leave them that way all night."

"Where on the island are they?" asked Maleen.

"Not far," said Sian. "I, uh, was hoping you might lend us your boat, actually." Haron and Maleen both looked startled. "Her friends are just across the bay," Sian pressed on. "And ... well, I thought sailing there would be much safer than walking. Just as you were saying, Haron."

Maleen and Haron exchanged a look. Then Haron said, "Well, then I will sail you there."

"Oh, no need!" said Arian. "I'm ... quite an experienced sailor myself, actually. You've already gone to so much trouble. We can manage fine."

"Can't *Captain Reikos* take you there?" Arouf growled from his corner. "Or is he the one you're really going to see, Sian?"

"*Father!*" Maleen snapped. "If I hear one more word of that nonsense — one — more — it will be you sailing home in the dark tonight. You hear me? We are all extremely tired of this."

Sian stood up, stone-faced, and set down her napkin. "I am going to take my bath now. We can decide what makes most sense when I get back." She gave Arian a look that clearly meant, *I will decide how to handle this, and you will play along.* Which was fine with Arian. Sian was clearly better at this sort of improvisation — lately, anyway.

With a final warning glare at her father, Maleen got up and left the room

behind her mother, presumably to help her reset the bath. For a while afterwards, no one spoke, or looked at anybody else. Arian and Haron ate, while
Arouf went out the front door, whether to cool off, or to sail home as Maleen
had suggested, Arian couldn't guess. What an unpleasant man. His mention
of the other fellow they had left in Escotte's dungeon left her worrying for
them again, but equally puzzled. What did *he* have against these friends of
Sian's? And, what had she been doing with them when Ennias had captured
her? It had not occurred to Arian to wonder before.

"Thank you for the lovely meal, Haron," she said, wiping her mouth
lightly and pushing back her chair. "I think I will go see if there is any help
I can provide Maleen and Sian." It had just occurred to her that she and
Sian might have a minute to talk privately, if they could convince Maleen
to come rejoin her husband.

Haron nodded as she stood. "You're very welcome, Freda. I'm sorry
about Maleen's father. These times have been hard on everyone. I'm sure
you understand."

"Oh yes." She offered him a reassuring smile. "Any marriage has its ups
and downs. I'm sure you know that, just as I do, from experience."

He smiled gratefully as she turned to go.

In the yard, Arian found Sian toweling off as Maleen stood by with her
new dress.

"Your father has gone out to ... cool himself, I assume," Arian told Maleen.
"I hope it wasn't rude of me to leave your husband at the table all alone, but ..."

"Why don't you go to him, dear," Sian told Maleen, rubbing the towel
through her long hair. She reached out to take the dress from her daughter.
"He might appreciate a private moment with you before your father comes
back in."

Maleen nodded and left them as Sian pulled on the dress.

"If necessary, *Freda* can go on alone tonight," Arian said, as soon as
she was gone. "There may be no point in dragging you into further danger
anyway, until I've been to see what's left to save."

"And then what?" Sian asked. "You'll come all the way back here for me?
Don't be ridiculous. Perhaps we should just tell them that —"

She fell silent as some new ruckus bloomed inside. They both looked toward the house as voices there grew louder. Men's voices, not all of them familiar.

"Now what?" Sian said, stepping quickly into her new sandals and rushing toward the house.

Arian followed, wondering if Biri's *looters* had arrived at last — and whether she and Sian would be more help or hindrance if they went inside now.

As they reached the door, Arian heard one of the unfamiliar voices speak Sian's name. She looked at Sian in alarm, fearing something worse than looters now, only to find the other woman wide-eyed and open-mouthed in … not fear, exactly.

"No, no. Please. I am just a longtime friend of your mother's," said the unfamiliar voice, more loudly, "with some cause to be concerned for her."

"*Reikos!*" Sian gasped, rushing inside.

Arian ran after her, relieved to think the man had escaped somehow, hoping this meant Maronne might have as well. But how had he known to find Sian here?

When they reached the front room, Sian rushed past Maleen and Haron and threw herself into the arms of a pale, compact, lightly bearded man covered in even more soot and grime than they had been that afternoon. Behind him stood a much younger man, watching their embrace with … very mixed emotions, it appeared. Arian glanced quickly at the others to find Haron looking troubled, Maleen gaping in confusion, and Arouf glaring almost happily at everyone around him.

"Have I not been telling you all afternoon, Maleen?" Arouf cried. "And now here's your mother's mob of lovers, come to save her from her cuckolded husband!"

What was going on here? Arian looked back at Sian and her friend. They weren't kissing, exactly … But that was no *sisterly* embrace Sian was giving him. A second glance around told her that no one else seemed much fooled either. And that grimy boy behind the captain … She recognized the look in his eyes too, or she was not a woman.

Oh dear, Arian thought. Might Sian have been less than entirely forthcoming with her, about the full nature of Arouf's complaint?

TWENTY-SIX

"Oh, Konstantin, thank all the gods you're safe!" Sian wept into his shoulder as they clung to one another. She leaned back to look into his pale eyes. "But how did you escape?"

"It is … a complicated story," he said, looking askance at those around them.

"Mother, who is this man?" Maleen asked quietly.

Remembering suddenly where she was and who was watching, Sian jerked free of Reikos, and turned to face her daughter. "I'm so sorry. Where are my manners? Please allow me to introduce my friend and business associate, Captain Konstantin Reikos of Lost Port." Only then did she truly register Pino's presence behind Reikos. "And Pino!" she cried, going to hug him too. "Whom you all know, I think," she added quickly. "Oh, dear Pino, I am just … so relieved to see you both alive!"

"Why shouldn't Pino be alive?" asked Haron, looking at her strangely.

Oh dear, she thought. What a fool she was being suddenly.

"Why should he be *allowed* to *live*, you mean," growled Arouf before Sian could think of what to say. "You wretched little scoundrel! I fed and housed you! I trusted you with my wife's safety all these years! This *foreign seaman*, I might understand, but *you!* How could you betray my trust this way?"

As Pino backed away, round-eyed with fright, Sian whirled at Arouf in disbelief. "How dare you speak to him like that? If this is still about the night I was beaten, I believe I told you he was not —"

"This is about *all* your nights together!" Arouf bellowed. "Not just that one."

"Father —" Maleen said uncertainly.

"No!" he snapped at her. "I'm tired of being scolded just for speaking the truth. Here's the proof — before your eyes now. Don't you *Father* me, girl."

"What is wrong with you?" Sian gasped.

"Wrong with *me*?" Arouf glared at her. "Nothing's wrong with *me*, Sian. I'm not the one who's run off with some teenage boy!"

"Run off with … With *Pino*?" Sian wasn't sure whether to laugh at him or scream. "*That* is what you think? You are truly mad!"

"I'm not just mad; I'm furious!" Arouf launched himself from the wall with balled fists, shoving Sian aside to get at Pino in the doorway. But Reikos snaked a hand out to grab Arouf around the arm before he got there, at which point Sian's husband turned with murder in his eyes to head-butt Reikos in the chest, while she shrieked and jumped out of the way.

"Stop it! Now!" yelled Haron, lunging forward to knock both men through the doorway into Pino, who went tumbling backward with them, out onto the moonlit landing. Haron moved to fill the doorjamb, followed by Sian, who peered past him. "I'll have no brawling here! If you can't behave like men instead of children, you can leave now." He glared down at Arouf. "Your grandchildren are asleep in here, old man. I don't know or care what may have happened elsewhere, but you *will* respect my home and family, or you will not be welcomed here again."

Arouf looked … not sorry, Sian thought. But cornered, anyway. And possibly embarrassed. As she was feeling too now. She sensed Arian's arrival just behind herself and Haron, and turned to find her looking out between them onto the landing as well.

Pino scrambled to his feet and backed away from both the other men. "Domni Monde, I have had nothing … *nothing* to do … *that way*, with Domina Kat#ë," he stammered, clearly as shocked as Sian was that her husband could have imagined such a thing.

Arouf stared daggers at him for a time before his fierce expression faltered, and uncertainty began to register instead.

Hopeful that this madness might be done at last, Sian allowed herself an impatient huff, which just reignited Arouf's ire. He turned to glare at Reikos next. "I am *possibly* mistaken about my runaway employee," he said a bit more quietly. "But I don't think I am mistaken about you."

"I am a shipper and importer, Domni Monde," Reikos said with icy calm. "A business associate of your wife's — and of *yours*, actually, for many years now — as you'd have known, if you had ever come to Alizar Main to negotiate with me yourself."

Sian watched them, careful to keep anything at all out of her face.

"My wife seems awfully fond of her *business associates* tonight," said Arouf, straining to imitate the captain's calm now, it seemed.

"And again, if you and I had seen more of each other all these years," Reikos answered, "we might have become such good friends ourselves by now."

Her husband shook his head and turned away. "You are a *snake*," he murmured.

"Arouf," Sian said, feeling responsible for this spectacle. "This is not the time or place. We'll work these things out at home."

He turned to her in mock astonishment. "Oh. You're finally coming home, then?"

Sian glanced back at Arian, wincing at the knowing expression on her face. She had not wished to tell her about the captain, or about the rest of Arouf's marital complaint. Now she wished she had. She looked back at Maleen and Haron as well, seeing very clearly that it was too late to have handled this more wisely with anyone.

"I'm sorry, husband. Truly," she said quietly. "I cannot come home just yet. I have ... unfinished business I must tend to."

He gazed at her, without any sign of the new outburst she'd been braced for. He just emitted a tiny *humph*. "You don't care at all what a fool you're making of me, do you," he said softly. "You never have."

That wasn't fair. "Whatever you've assumed, Arouf, I have not been off dallying with lovers all this time — or at all! I have been running for my life, imprisoned, tortured —"

"You're still clinging to that story?" he cut her off crossly, then jerked a thumb at Reikos. "With him standing here in front of us?"

"She's telling you the truth," said Pino. "The Census Taker had us all imprisoned!"

Sian heard Arian's soft gasp behind her in the doorway, and shook her head at the boy as slightly as she could and still have hope he'd notice.

"The *Census Taker*?" Arouf's brows climbed in comic parody of shock. "My dear wife's lofty cousin? Has he gone to war with *all* his family members now?" Arouf turned back to Sian. "I thought you'd been arrested by the Justiciary. Let's get our stories straight now, shall we? Which one was it?"

Sian had no idea what to say. Arian had gone still as porcelain. Even Pino looked around uncomfortably, seeming to realize that perhaps he'd said something wrong. Reikos had seemed turned to stone for some time now, while Haron and her daughter just wore sad, confused expressions. With Reikos and Pino here ... What a disaster.

"Cat got all your tongues?" Arouf glanced almost happily around. His eyes fell on Arian, and lingered. "And where do you fit into all of this, Freda? *Truthfully*, I mean. Do my wife's appetites these days run even more broadly than I had supposed?"

Arian's lips parted in offended astonishment.

"That's enough!" Sian shouted. "You're acting like a pig, Arouf!"

"You're acting like a whore!" he shouted back.

Haron moved to shut the door, but Sian stopped him. "There will be no more hitting here," she told him quietly. "But it is long past time Arouf and I spoke truth to one another. It cannot wait, apparently, and I am tired of waiting anyway." She'd done quite a bit of thinking since she and Arian had talked back in the tunnels. Whatever mistakes she'd made with her husband, he had not just been some passive object on which she had acted. He'd had as much power as she to see that things were going wrong, and try to fix it. He just hadn't tried.

"Well, this should be entertaining," Arouf said, folding his arms across his chest. "Which new *truth* will you tell us now, I wonder?"

"The truth about why we are finished," Sian said, feeling all her insides fall into her knees. "And about when our marriage really ended."

Her husband's face went very still. Maleen gasped, and put a hand across her mouth, her eyes wide and reddening. Haron looked back at his wife, then set his jaw and left the doorway to go take her hand.

"I did not leave you for any lover, Arouf," Sian said, slamming her heart shut to drown the frantic voices there all begging her to stop. "I never wanted to. It is you who have abandoned me. Many years ago, I think."

"What are you talking about?" He was still angry, but quiet now. "I've been right there making dinner for you every time you've bothered to come home from that townhouse you're so fond of. I've spent every day for years right there at the looms and dye works that provide our livelihood. I spend more time in any single month with all the people we employ than you've done in the past three years. I'm the one who's been at *home* the whole time you were *gone*! What have *I* abandoned?"

"Me," she said. "You have abandoned *me* to handle the whole frightening world for you, while you hide at home, puttering around the kitchen, and tinkering with machines *I've hired* people to maintain, enjoying your sleepy little home day after day without ever having to look up at all the paper I must wade through, reading 'til my eyes burn late each night, writing 'til my fingers knot. Or all the scheming people I must chase and charm and wheedle for concessions while you cook stew at home; the hiring, the management of supply and distribution, licenses and fees. You never have to leave your snug cocoon, Arouf — not even to come see your grandchildren. Not that I've been much better at that, anyway." She looked back at Maleen, wondering if that would be too broken now to fix as well. "You're right, Arouf. That's where I always find you, safe and sound, whenever I come back from all the precarious uncertainties and punishing expectations *you* have abdicated to your *absent wife*."

"I thought you *enjoyed* your work!" he protested.

"I thought you appreciated my help," she replied.

"If you've been so overwhelmed, why didn't you just ask my help?"

"Two weeks ago I begged for help! I told you I had been assaulted and … and changed into something frightening! I *proved* it to you, by healing Bela! All you did was clutch your precious *business* — the business I was out there trying to build when this was done to me — and call me a wicked, irresponsible threat to your cocoon!" She swiped away tears. "And told me you were *no part* of *my* troublesome family, of course," she added quietly. "I begged your help, and you just cast me straight into the sea. It's been my job all these years to protect you from trouble, hasn't it? Not to ask for help."

"Did you ever love me?" he asked, just above a whisper, looking only hurt, not sorry or concerned.

"We loved each other once, I think." She thought again about that picnic lunch atop their new island, many years before, and tears leaked out once again. "But we went to sleep somewhere along the way. I ... don't blame just you for that. Maybe I left you ... too little, when I agreed to go out and manage the world for us. Maybe I just *managed* you instead of paying attention to what was really best for *us*. But, Arouf, you were as capable as I of speaking up if you weren't satisfied — of struggling after answers. *I* did not force you from my bed, or from my life. You could have done something to try fixing all this too. Long ago." She shrugged miserably. "You don't though. You don't want to. You just keep sleeping, hiding, expecting *me* to fix what's wrong with *us*. Alone."

She saw something moving, finally, there behind his eyes. "So ... you're just going to leave me now?" He seemed genuinely astonished. "I'm sorry if ... if the complaint I filed caused you trouble." He looked at Haron, Pino, even Reikos, as if expecting them to take his side. Then his eyes wandered back to hers. "I just thought they'd bring you home."

"I hoped once ... that you would come after me."

"I have. I'm here, aren't I? Come home," he pled.

"I will," she said, "when I have finished dealing with the trouble I've been handed."

"And when will that be?" he asked. "I need you there. The business ..."

She closed her eyes. For just a minute, she had thought ... had hoped ... "You can hire someone to take care of that." She dared look, finally, at Reikos, who was gazing back at her with all the sadness in his sea-blue eyes that she had hoped for from Arouf. "We have the money to buy you a business manager, Arouf." She wished she dared go to Reikos right this minute and let him hold her as she cried into his shoulder once more. "We left each other long ago. We sleep alone now. We live separate lives." She looked back sadly at her onetime husband. "You make a very tasty stew. But I've eaten many lovely dinners with a lot of people I have never married, and will never love. I'm sorry."

Arouf looked down at the dark landing, seeming as bewildered as a child. Had he really thought she would just be bullied back in line, and come home to resume their long, sad, farce? *If you even wanted to wake up …* she thought. But no. He didn't. Even now. His expression became stony as he turned to walk slowly down the front stairs and into the yard. "If you've decided to divorce me, then you'll have to file the papers by yourself. I'm not going to do it. This wasn't my idea."

"I know," she said numbly. "I'll take care of everything. As soon as I have time."

~

I came here trying to save her, Reikos thought, watching Sian's husband leave the yard, head down, humiliated.

When they'd found no one left but fleeing servants and distracted soldiers in the Census Taker's burning mansion, Ennias had suggested they head for the Factorate on Home, since that was where the women had been bound if all had gone as planned. On Home, Ennias had learned from soldiers he knew there that the Factora-Consort was still missing and that no one even knew who Sian Kattë was. That's when Pino had suggested looking for them here. He'd known where Sian's daughter Maleen lived, of course. They'd left the sergeant at the Factorate to serve the embattled Factor there, and made their way back up through all the madness breaking out on Cutter's and Three Cats. … Only to destroy her marriage, and disgrace Sian before her family.

Reikos had come intending to tell Sian that he understood, at last, how blindly he'd been treating her — for years now. How much better he would be henceforth … He had intended to tell her that he loved her as he had never loved, nor ever wished to love, any other woman.

But one could hardly speak of love at such a moment. Especially when that moment was his fault. Always charging to the rescue. Always landing her in even greater trouble than he'd found her in. He looked up at her, standing sphinx-faced in the doorway, watching Arouf go. Did she need saving? It did not seem so.

So, what were they doing here?

"Will you come in, then?" Sian asked, looking first at him, then at Pino.

"Are we ... wanted?" Reikos replied.

Sian looked back into the house, toward her son-in-law and daughter, then turned back to him. "Have you somewhere else to be?

He shook his head.

"Then come inside," she said wearily, turning to go in herself.

Reikos looked at Pino, who shrugged at him. They started for the doorway.

"Mother, you're not really leaving him. Are you?" Reikos heard the daughter say.

"I'm ... so sorry," Sian said to her. "For everything that's happened here tonight."

"But, *are you?*" Maleen pressed.

Sian nodded, clearly struggling not to cry again. "Yes, Maleen, I'm sorry. But there's really nothing left there to go back to now."

Sian's son-in-law gazed stolidly at Sian, then turned to hug his weeping wife.

"I've been scolding him all afternoon," Maleen said wretchedly. "Yelling at him for making such ridiculous accusations." She looked at Reikos, who wished with all his heart now that he'd just refused Sian's invitation to come back in. "How much of what he said is true?"

The other woman there had retired to a latticed, teakwood bench across the room, as far away as possible from everyone by now, though she still watched with clear concern. Reikos wondered who *she* was, and wished he'd had the sense to plant himself much further off as well, but was afraid even to move now.

"I have never thought of touching Pino," Sian told Maleen. Reikos saw the look on Pino's face as this was said. Had Sian seen it too? No, of course not. She was clearly blind to all of Pino's looks. Perhaps the boy was luckier than he knew. Just now, at least. Or maybe not. "But your father and I ... have not been lovers either, for a long, long time, Maleen." Sian turned almost fearfully to Reikos, who just managed not to drop his head into his hands. "We had a kind of understanding about all of that. At least, I thought we did. It was one of those things ... as many things become when you've been married long enough. ... Or even too long, it appears."

Maleen shook her head, and looked away. "I can't believe this. It's like I have been living in some other world."

"You were living here. In your world, where you belong," Sian said. "With Haron and Biri and Jila. It is Arouf and I who have been ... out of touch. I don't know how to tell you — now — how sorry that makes me. How determined I am to change that much, at least. If ... you can forgive me, and allow it."

"I'm still not even sure what all I'm supposed to be forgiving you for." Maleen's eyes darted skittishly around the room. "Who are these people, really? Where have you been? What is really going on?" She gazed at the other woman. "Please, tell me who you are, and why you and my mother need to leave again tonight."

Reikos looked back at the other woman too now, more sharply, understanding only then that she was not just some friend of Maleen's family, some stray neighbor. If she and Sian were together ... and had to leave *tonight* — "*Oh, by all the bloody gods,*" he murmured.

Seeming to have just then reached the same conclusion, Pino looked at Reikos with round eyes, then, staring at the woman, went half-spastically onto one knee. Everybody stared at Pino, as Reikos wondered if he ought to do the same. He was no bloody Alizari. He'd never even seen the local royalty. Was he supposed to bow?

"Get up!" the woman said in obvious alarm. "What are you doing?"

"Aren't you ..." said Pino. Sian shook her head, too late. "The Factora-Consort?"

The woman's brows shot up. "How can you ... think such a ridiculous thing?" she backpedaled bravely.

Maleen's eyes darted back and forth between the woman and Pino, who got uncertainly back onto his feet. *The lad has all the sophistication of a newborn puppy*, Reikos thought. Of course they had told Maleen and her husband some concealing story.

"She's right," Maleen said to Pino. "What a ridiculous thing to ..." She looked back at the woman, who was still gazing at Pino, trying very hard to make distress seem irritation. "I've only ever seen the Factora-Consort from a distance," Maleen said. "But she looked not at all like you."

"Of course not!" the woman said, as if offended at the very thought. "I don't know what this boy's been drinking, but —"

"Why did you tell us you'd been imprisoned by the Census Taker?" Haron asked, looking at the boy with an expression that told Reikos all their masks were off, or just about to be. The man was clearly no one's fool.

Far too late, Pino looked uncertainly to Sian for guidance.

"Oh ... oh ... *no*," Maleen murmured, shaking her head as if she feared for her own sanity. "Don't tell me this." She spun to face her mother. "It can't be true! You *weren't there*." She glanced in panic back at Pino, then at Reikos. "Not *all* of you! I laughed at him! He said you were behind this, and I laughed!"

"Who — said I was behind what?" Sian asked.

"Father said this whole war was your fault!"

"That's absurd!" Sian protested.

"That's what I said," said Maleen.

"The war is my fault," said the strange woman, looking weary and resigned now. "And my husband's, and Escotte Alkattha's ... and the gods only know who else's, but not your mother's."

Maleen simply stared at her, incredulous. "You ... are clearly not ... in any way the —"

"She is without her usual cosmetics," Sian said quietly. "And her hair is dyed. As you will see now, if you look. We should do something about that if we can before we go, my lady."

Maleen just went on staring at them both and shaking her head.

Reikos had watched Haron watch the rest of this exchange with less surprise than calculation on his face, seeming already to have accepted what his wife could not. "My lady," Haron said calmly to the Factora-Consort, "may I ask why the Census Taker had imprisoned you and my wife's mother to begin with, and whether that is why the Factor burned his hall this morning?"

What a sensible man, Reikos thought. *I'd hire him as crew in a heartbeat. Hell. He'd probably do a better job as captain than I do.*

"The Census Taker never knew he had me," the Factora-Consort answered, just as calmly now, having clearly given up whatever pretense they'd been trying to perpetrate. "I was only there pretending to be Sian's maid."

"Her *maid*?" Maleen squeaked.

Still watching the Factora-Consort, Haron put a reassuring arm around his wife.

"He was holding your mother prisoner because he didn't want her to heal my son," the lady told Maleen. "I was there trying to get your mother out without his knowing, to avoid the very war it seems we've started now." She glanced at Reikos and poor Pino. "These two men have been in the Census Taker's dungeon for several weeks for trying to protect Sian. Whatever else you may think of them, you have that to thank them for."

And now I owe you a debt, my lady, Reikos thought gratefully.

"But, my lady," Haron said, "why did your husband —"

"I wish I knew," she cut him off with a sympathetic look. "I'm sure that all of this must make even less sense to you now than it did before, but I'm afraid we really haven't time to explain further. And I am counting on you all," she glanced pointedly at Pino, "not to breathe a word of what I've said here, or even of our presence tonight, to anyone, for any reason, until I or Sian have given you clear permission — if ever. Can I ask that of you all?"

"Yes, of course, my lady," Haron answered.

"I'm … yes, if you're …" Maleen ducked her head and started wiping at her eyes. "I'm so sorry. This is just so much more than I … was prepared to … to know tonight."

"Or ever, I am sure," Sian said sadly. She went hesitantly to her daughter, who raised her arms in a clear invitation. When they had held each other for a while, Sian said, "I will explain everything as soon as it is safe to, dear. I promise. May I come back to see you when we're done with all of this?"

"You're still my mother. Aren't you?" Maleen asked with a brave little grin.

"Oh, yes, my love." Sian gave her another hug. "That part was always true. More than ever, now, I think." She looked up at Haron. "Thank you both for being so tolerant and … understanding. We will fix as much of this as can be fixed."

"Sian," said Haron. "I think there must be so much we have yet to understand. But I suspect we must thank you as well." He turned to Reikos, who forced himself to meet the man's eyes, then to Pino. "And even both of you?"

"I care about your mother deeply," Reikos said to Maleen. "I have never wanted anything to hurt her. If I have failed in this, then not even she will ever close that wound." He looked at Sian, begging her to see what he could not say here or now. If ever.

Pino looked at no one anymore, Reikos noticed, feeling the lad's desolation like another pin pressed through his heart.

"And I am sorry to intrude again at such a time," the Factora-Consort said, "but I am led to understand you own a boat. Might we borrow it?" She glanced at Reikos. "Unless your vessel is docked here on Malençon somewhere?"

"Sadly, no, my lady," Reikos replied. "The *Fair Passage* is still in her berth on Cutter's. At least, I hope it is."

The Factora-Consort looked back at Haron, who said, "My lady, how could I refuse you anything you need?"

"You can, though," she replied. "I feel bound to be quite clear about this. I may already be no one's Factora-Consort." *What a brave woman*, Reikos thought, feeling suddenly more surrounded by his betters than he had since boyhood. "If my husband and I lose this fight, as we might have done already, for all I know, I may be in no position to return your boat at all — or even to replace it. So, you see, you can refuse me, if you'd rather."

"I'll sail you to wherever you are bound, myself," said Haron, drawing looks of alarm from both Maleen and Sian.

"Thank you." The Factora-Consort smiled at him gratefully. "That will not be necessary, though. Sian and I have two brave and clearly very capable men to escort us. Your wife and children need you here." She turned to Maleen, who seemed, at last, to have accepted the impossibilities surrounding her. "Whatever happens next, I wish you and your family well, dear. I will always remember your gracious hospitality at such a trying time. Your mother and I have had much time to become acquainted, and I must tell you, I have never known a more remarkable woman in my life. Not here in Alizar, or in any of the continental courts that I once frequented. I owe her more already than anyone will ever likely know. Far more than I can hope to repay, whether ... she is able still to heal my son or not."

Reikos watched Maleen gazing at her mother, clearly seeing much there she had never guessed before. "Someday," she said, "you must tell me. All of it. Even the parts you think might hurt me."

Sian nodded. "I love you, daughter. I will love you better from now on."

As I will love you better too, Reikos thought. *Whether you can love me anymore or not.*

PART III

TWENTY-SEVEN

Sian leaned beside Arian against the gunwale of *Coppersmith*, Haron and Maleen's deep-hulled sloop, peering out from under the tarp that covered them. They'd been underway for perhaps an hour. Silent running mostly, since they'd finished laying plans back on Malençon's docks. She could see Reikos and Pino now, working efficiently together in the moonlit darkness, but little else as they sailed toward Home.

"Thank the gods for a fair breeze tonight," she heard Reikos say to Pino. "There's Cutter's off to port already."

The Factora-Consort reached out and squeezed her hand; Sian squeezed back and sighed. She had not enough strength left even to feel the grief and heartbreak that must surely be there.

"Are you all right?" Arian whispered.

"I feel like my skin has been cut off and put back in the wrong place." Sian paused. "And I'm embarrassed. That was poorly done, back at Maleen's, I'm afraid. But otherwise, I'm fine."

"Otherwise." Arian smiled sadly.

All those years of marriage without arguments ... had not meant there weren't differences after all. She and Arouf had just saved up all their disagreements for the end, when everything had finally broken underneath the strain.

"I do mean to divorce him. That wasn't just a threat."

"I didn't think it was." Arian studied Sian's face in the dimness. "I think you generally mean what you say."

When I know what I mean, Sian thought, quietly astonished at how much she hadn't known — consciously, at least — just weeks earlier. *I'd have told you then that I was happy. I'd have said my marriage was sound and comfortable — if perhaps a little cooled with age. I'd have said my biggest problem was managing all the paperwork ... And I'd have meant it all.* "I should be asking how you are," Sian said aloud. "You seem so calm. I'm sure I would be half out of my mind by now."

"I am. Half out of my mind." Arian turned from their tiny slit of view to gaze at nothing in the gloom. "Respond to crisis with an outward show of calm ... That was perhaps the first thing my father taught me as a child. In the cradle even, I suspect." She shook her head. "But you've changed something in me too."

"Me?" Sian asked, half fearful to learn what.

Arian nodded. "Last night; you or whatever works through you now. I had no idea how afraid I've always been — of everything — until this power of yours swept through me, upending so much more than just bones and sinews, I think. Now ..." She sighed. "There is some much greater, clearer distance within me between what is actually happening and all the dreadful things that *might* happen later. Right now, I am in a boat, heading toward my family at last. When we get there ... We will see then whether I have cause to panic."

It was not me, Sian thought, recalling that haunted child on the beach. *There is something working through us all, I think.* "How will we get back into the Factorate?" she asked. "If there's still fighting ..."

"There is a passage to my rooms that no one knows of. I assume it is still secret. It opens well outside the Factorate grounds. If we can get even that close, it should take us safely inside. As for what we may find there ..." She shrugged. "As I said, we'll deal with that then. I am sorry to place you yet again into such danger."

"Danger?" Sian grinned at her. "You say this to me now?"

Arian smiled back, wearily.

Pino came to tuck their small window on the world closed. "We are being approached by another boat, my ladies," he whispered. "From ahead. You must keep very still until we find out what is happening."

They nodded together, and hunkered lower into the hull, feeling the sloop veer and slow beneath them. It seemed Reikos was making no effort to avoid the other craft. *Wise,* Sian thought. *Nothing gained by seeming frightened.*

"Ahoy, friends!" she heard Reikos shout. "What island do you hale from?"

"Viel!" came a more distant shout. "And yourselves?"

"Meaders!" Reikos lied, cleverly choosing a small island of little probable significance. "Have you any news of events on Home?"

"If that's where you're headed, turn back!" the other boat replied. "It's the heart of hell tonight! We're bound for Malençon — or farther, if we must — until this madness blows over!"

"Sadly, my young mate here has family on Home!" Reikos called. "Aged parents — too frail to flee alone! We hope to get them out of harm's way! Is there any part of the island where a small boat might still land more safely?"

"Not a chance!" the other voice replied. "The whole shore's ringed in gunboats and swarming with house troops and bands of armed civilians! All fighting willy-nilly, from what we saw as we sailed by!"

"Any news about who's winning?" Reikos called.

"Not sure who's even fighting anymore! Factor's dead! A couple hours back, we heard!" Sian felt Arian's sudden intake of breath in the dark beside her. "And every last man, woman and child seems to be looking for the Consort now! That's about the only two things everybody there seemed to agree on when we left!"

There was a pause, filled only with the sound of Arian's increasingly ragged breathing. Sian groped for her hand and squeezed it hard.

"Any news at all about the Factor's heir?" Reikos called less avidly — doubtless for Arian's sake.

"None we've heard! By all accounts the boy's been half dead for weeks already! Maybe he's gone too now, or nobody's just troubling to check with all the rest of this! I'm telling you, man, turn around! If one side don't blow your little craft to smithereens before it gets a hundred feet from shore, the other will! It's mindless chaos there!"

"I thank you for the warning!" Reikos called. "But this lad's folks are likely trapped, and we may still go have a look — from a safe distance, at least! Good luck to you and yours!"

"And to you!" The other voice had already grown dimmer as *Coppersmith* heeled over under re-trimmed sails, and began regaining speed.

"Oh, Arian, I'm so sorry," Sian said, gathering the other woman into her arms. "Maybe it's just another rumor. It doesn't sound like anything is very clear there yet."

Arian wept quietly against her shoulder, saying nothing at all. There were clearly limits to this new calm she'd spoken of — a fact Sian found re-assuring. Whatever her hands did to people now, they were left human still.

A few minutes later, the boat lost speed again and Sian heard hands fumbling at the tarp above their heads as Pino peeled it back. "Captain says we need to talk." Behind him, the sails flapped loosely in the wind.

Arian drew a shuddering breath, nodding as she pulled away from Sian and wiped her eyes. "If we cannot take a boat ashore on Home, then ... I suppose we have no choice but to go back into the tunnels." By now, they'd all told each other of their earlier adventures.

Sian looked askance at this. "Did you not tell me they were sealed up around the Factorate?"

"I said blocked, not sealed. There are still ways for one person at a time to get through. That's how Viktor and I went in, and Hivat still uses them quite often. They are gated, of course, but I know where the keys to most of those grates are hidden, and the others —"

"Yes," Sian cut in, "but you also told me Escotte knows about them."

"I did."

"Then, I'm sorry to say it, but if he's taken over the Factorate House, or even just some significant part of the island, wouldn't he be watching them?"

"If not using them for his own purposes already," said Reikos, having secured the tiller and come to stand behind Pino as their boat bobbed in the moonlit darkness. "If both your husband and the Census Taker knew about these tunnels, my lady, I would fly this boat into your palace through the sky before assuming that they aren't already swarming with forces from all sides." He shook his head. "I fear we would simply be walking into an even more confining trap without any ready exits."

"Then how are Sian and I to get ashore?" Arian asked.

"If it is true that everyone there is looking for you, my lady, getting you ashore without being shot out of the water seems but the first of many difficulties," Reikos observed. "Surmounting all this attention to yourself will be our biggest problem, I fear."

"Well, Sian and I must get into the Factorate somehow. If Viktor is dead ... My son is Viktor's heir, and the rightful Factor of Alizar, until the people legally dictate otherwise. If Escotte and his compatriots are allowed to triumph this way unopposed, then Alizar as we have known it — as its citizens fought so hard to make it — is over. I owe it to Viktor as well as to the nation not to allow that, if I can."

"With all due respect, my lady," Reikos pressed, "what would you have us do then, just sail to Home and hand you to the first armed band we encounter there?"

"Can we not divert their attention somehow?" Sian asked. "Just long enough to get Arian and myself to land and past the waterfront?"

"Have you some suggestion as to how?" Reikos asked patiently.

"Maybe I could do something," Pino said uncertainly. "Swim ashore ... Create some kind of disturbance, while the rest of you —"

"What kind of disturbance can any single man produce, sufficient to draw off an entire army? Don't be reckless, boy," Reikos added with surprising gentleness. "What they're all looking for is the Factora-Consort. Nothing we can do is likely to draw enough attention to distract everyone from that search."

"Then, maybe I could spread a rumor that she had been seen across the island somewhere else," Pino tried.

"A rumor that would spread all across the waterfront fast enough to do us any good?" Reikos parried.

A frustrated silence descended over all of them.

"But if it's me they're looking for," Arian murmured, "couldn't we just find an Alizari gunboat flying my husband's colors, and hand me and Sian over to its crew? They would take us to the Factorate surely — if I asked them to."

"If the Factorate is still under their control at all, my lady," Reikos said, "and if they were allowed to do so without being attacked from all sides just as soon as your husband's enemies realized what was happening. From what that fellow said, I doubt this little sloop would even reach such a gunboat before it or some other craft turned their cannons on us and sent us to the bottom." He grew thoughtful for a moment. "What we would need," he said pensively, "is some way to make them think you were aboard *this* boat, and get everyone to chase us, while you were actually being put ashore somehow..." He shook his head. "If only this poor dingy were large enough to carry a lifeboat of its own ..."

"Your ship!" Sian blurted. "It has lots of lifeboats."

Reikos smiled sadly. "My ship would certainly be large enough to attract everyone's attention — and slow and cumbersome enough at such close quarters to die a fiery death in Home's harbor before we had even gotten close enough to lower you ladies into the water behind her."

"Not if ..." Arian looked up at Reikos in excitement. "Is your ship equipped with cannon, Captain?"

Reikos gave her a skeptical look. "A few guns, yes, sufficient to repel a single pirate craft at sea, perhaps. But not half sufficient to repel a harbor full of hostile gunboats, my lady."

"You might not need to repel them, Captain; just convince them to chase you out into the open sea where I am sure a large craft would quickly outdistance their pursuit. I think I know how we can give them the Factora-Consort to chase — at quite a distance. I did it, in a way, just a week ago, at the temple's harbor. We would need your cannons, and some Alizari flags — preferably with Factorate insignia. But perhaps that would not be necessary, if ... if we had a decoy dressed to look like me from a great distance. It could be anyone in a fancy dress — with blond hair, or anything that looked like it."

"So, you are suggesting that I do what, exactly, with my ship?" Reikos asked quietly.

"I think, perhaps, that if a large ship bearing Factorate flags, with the 'Factora-Consort' herself standing at the prow — well lit by some means, of course — came just close enough to Home's waterfront to fire its cannons toward the harbor, everyone looking for me might give chase."

"And, meanwhile, you would be where — getting ashore how?" Reikos asked even more carefully.

"She and Domina Kattë would be with me," said Pino, catching on, "waiting in this boat as close to shore as we could get without being noticed. As soon as everyone was chasing you, we could sail ashore somewhere. It's a good plan, I think."

"And if my ship does not succeed in outrunning your nation's entire fleet of gunboats?" Reikos asked miserably.

"If we were in position before your ship arrived, you could just sail past the harbor at full speed, Captain, firing to draw them off without even slowing to let us down into the water, could you not? I expect they would have to pursue you from dead stop."

"Possibly …" He nodded, still looking very dubious. "And, I am sorry, my lady, but it is my ship we speak of risking here. Though I have no wish to hurt you further, I feel I must ask it. If your son is no longer at the Factorate House, or no longer … savable …"

"I say to you what I said to Sian's son-in-law. As I am no longer in any position to guarantee anything after the fact, the decision must, of course, be entirely yours."

Reikos looked at Sian, who felt awful now for having thrust such a decision upon him. "Is this what you wish, Sian?"

Ah, she thought with chagrin, *so it is to be my decision after all.* What did he owe her? Nothing that she could see. What did she owe him? More, perhaps. He had suffered much for her already — after she had cut him loose. He still cared for her. That much was obvious by now. Did she still care for him? She'd had no real chance to think any of this through yet. But she did care for him, clearly. More than she had thought — a week or two ago. Was she to let him suffer for her again? His ship … "I wish …" She struggled to find some anchor point inside. Some clear compass to guide her. "I have come to believe that I am … like this now so that I can heal Arian's son. I wish to have the chance to try."

Reikos gave her a soulful look, and a sad smile. Then he looked away and sighed. "We will sail to the port at Cutter's then, and hope my ship is even there. If she is, well, she's got a belly full of fine cloth. What are your colors, My Lady Consort?"

"White, light blue and green. The Factorate insignia is basically just a large gold star."

Reikos nodded, still not meeting anyone's eyes. "That can be arranged, I believe. My men are good at mending sails quickly in a storm. They can probably stitch together a crude flag of that description in less than half an hour." He turned to face them again, his eyes straying to Sian. "And we've a few nice dresses aboard as well. As soon as I'm aboard *Free Passage*, Pino will take you on to Home." He looked at Pino now. "Be careful, lad — for once. When we've parted, I'll have no way of knowing how you fare, much less of helping, should things go wrong." He looked back to Sian. "If things go right, I'm sure you'll know when it is time to sail ashore."

"Thank you," Sian said quietly, her heart breaking at the certain knowledge that it was for her he had agreed to risk his ship. "You will come back for me, I hope, when all of this is over?"

He smiled at last. "I'd like to see even a fleet of gunboats try to stop me."

"Captain," said Arian. "If I am still in any position to pay debts when this is over, you will have far more than my undying gratitude in reward."

He smiled at her as well, if strangely. "I dreamed once, not long ago, in fact, of a life more meaningful than the one I have been living all these years, my lady. Of doing things that mattered more — even to myself." He gave her an almost playful shrug. "Perhaps my dream is coming true." He gazed back at Sian. "I'm told it costs us everything to make the world new."

Sian climbed clumsily to her feet then, pushing the tarp aside as she lurched awkwardly from hiding on the swaying boat, and went to put her arms around him. An instant later, their lips touched, and she did not care who saw them kiss, or what they thought of it.

∼

Not half an hour later, Sian peered once again from underneath their concealing tarp, Arian beside her, as Cutter's shoreline ghosted past them off the starboard side now.

"My ladies," came Reikos's voice from above them, "we approach the harbor. I can see my ship from here, thank the gods of war, so it is not sunk or stolen since I left — but for a while now, you must again be cargo."

"All right," Sian said softly. Arian and she tucked the canvas closed around them, and crouched down to listen and wait.

As they drew near the port, Sian's ears told her that it was aswarm with activity — shouts and splashes, banging timber, the flap and boom of canvas being raised or lowered, the creaks and susurrations of many vessels, large and small, getting underway at once. From this collage emerged the sound of some much closer boat approaching them.

"Ahoy the *Coppersmith*!" came a voice from over the water. "I am the Cutter's Port Authority! You must turn back! The port is closed by order of the Factorate!"

"Ahoy the *Cutter's Queen*!" Reikos's voice boomed back. "I am Captain Konstantin Reikos of the *Fair Passage*, berthed just yonder! You know me, I believe! I am trying to return to my ship!"

Sian strained to hear but detected only mutters on the other boat. Then, "I recognize you, Captain! Where have you been? Your crew's been quite concerned — as have I!"

"Detained by unexpected business up on Malençon!" called Reikos. "All this took me by surprise! I've had the devil's own time getting back here!"

There was another pause, more half-obscured voices conversing on the *Cutter's Queen*.

"You may re-board your ship, Captain!" they finally responded. "But you may not go ashore for any reason, and must set sail at once! All foreign ships are to be evacuated from Alizari waters by Factorate decree until the current conflict is resolved!"

"I thank you — and will do so, sir!" Reikos called back, without hesitation.

"See to it quickly, Captain!" came the official's voice, already moving farther away as the *Coppersmith* eased forward. "Or I cannot vouch for the continued safety of your vessel!"

"Yes, yes," Reikos muttered. "Now to see if I've sufficient crew left to weigh anchor."

The *Coppersmith* tacked this way and that, doubtless avoiding heavy traffic in the narrow channel leading to the docks. Then Sian felt the sloop come sharply around to stall just before it bumped and recoiled gently as it slid against ... a dock perhaps? The *Fair Passage's* hull? She wasn't sure.

"Well, there's *someone* up there making ready to steal my ship," Reikos growled to Pino. "Here's hoping it's my crew. Ahoy the *Fair Passage!*" he called out. "Ahoy, *my* ship!"

"Captain? Oh, thank the gods! You be-n't dead then!"

"Kyrios!" Sian whispered, flooded with relief. *Fair Passage's* first mate, a wiry blond Smagadine with a quick smile and a stronger accent even than Reikos's.

"Sorry to disappoint you!" Reikos called back. Sian could hear the relief in his voice. "You'll not be taking her from me just yet after all!"

"Sir, the orders!" Kyrios protested. "I had no —"

"Yes, I know! You've done right, and thank you for it! How many of you have I left up there?"

"Only seven, sir! And a time I had getting some of them to stay, what with this war is going now. Most the others signed on with Kenners' boat when we're two weeks passing without word of you. What happened, Captain?"

"I'll explain it when we're under way! Lower a boat, will you? Off this side!"

"We already got them battened, Captain. But I can be having gangway down, sir, in a —"

"A boat, Kyrios! The port side, please! Right here beside us!"

"Aye-aye, Captain!"

A minute later, Sian heard Reikos tell Pino quietly, "As soon as I'm into the other boat, you set sail, lad. Take the channel between Cutter's and Montchattaran and Toad. It'll take you longer, but we'll be a while here yet, and that route will keep you farther out of harm's way between here and Home. When you get there, wait off the north face of the island, as close to the Factorate harbor as you can without being notice. And I'm serious, lad: none of your recklessness this time. Try thinking like a timid old man, will you?"

"I'll guard them with my life, Captain. It's what I'm sworn to do."

"If you're guarding them well, your life should not enter into it." There was a pause. "Sworn by whom?"

"The priest, sir. You were there. He charged me to guard her, and I don't mean to fail him — or the god."

"Hm," Reikos grunted. "That still stinks a bit much of heroics for my tastes, and I don't much care one way or another just now for the priest or his god. Don't you fail *me*. That's what matters — if you still wish to join my crew."

"Aye, aye, Captain," Sian heard Pino say with what seemed a touch of pride. "I won't fail any of you, sir."

"No heroics!" Reikos said again. "Heroics are dangerous! Are you hearing me?"

"No heroics, Captain. Think like an old man. I heard you, sir."

"Good. Here comes my boat. If I can't come myself when this is over, I'll send someone to fetch you. You've a bunk on *Fair Passage*, son. With my gratitude and respect. Now get out of here — and keep them hidden 'til you're safely ashore."

"Aye, aye, sir."

Sian heard a great splash, and the sloop rocked and scraped beneath her as the lifeboat landed beside them. Then she heard the scrape of boots against the gunwale, and a grunt or two as Reikos moved from one boat to the other. As she heard the winches start to lift Reikos to *Fair Passage*, she felt Pino fending them off and pushing them out far enough to trim the sails and get their small sloop moving.

"I hope," Arian murmured beside her, "I am not putting all of you through this for nothing."

"If this god gave me such a gift for nothing," Sian said, "then he's not much of a god. I think I'd know, if it were too late."

"By your god and any others listening," said Arian, "I hope with all my heart you're right."

"My ladies," Pino called to them, quietly, "there will likely be much heavier traffic on the waters around us from here on. It may be best to make no noise at all."

"Understood," Sian whispered.

Arian nodded, and silence settled in, filled only with the distant sounds of harried seamanship around the port.

From there the trip seemed uneventful. Even tedious. Darkness and silence. An occasional shout or mysterious boom from far across the water. Time stretched, and Sian's eyelids grew heavy. She put her chin down on her chest. Just for a moment ...

"By the gods and all their weeping mothers!"

Sian wakened with a start at Pino's exclamation.

Arian was already scrambling against her to peel back the tarp above them, just far enough to see out. "Oh!" she whispered in distress. "Oh, what have we done?"

Sian twisted and crawled to peer out beside her, all sleepiness forgotten as she gaped over the boat's rim.

Raging fires leapt high above the smoke-shrouded city in at least five places, casting a red and golden sheen across the water as *Coppersmith* crept ever closer. On its lofty perch, parts of the Factorate House were ablaze as well. In the darkness, it was impossible to tell whether the remaining portions of the structure were as yet untouched by fire, or had just already burned. All along the shoreline before them, gunboats flying the devices of half a dozen leading families in Alizar moved ponderously amidst dozens of other, smaller craft, often fitted out with ad hoc cannons of their own, it seemed — or just sat dead in the water, staking out some little patch of maritime territory, if not already sunk or burning. As they watched, several vessels along two different stretches of waterfront fired their cannons at who knew what targets. The shore itself seemed to writhe with troops and mobs of who knew what civilian contingencies, like swarms of fighting fire ants.

"How will we get through that?" Sian wondered aloud.

"It has grown much worse since we were here this morning," Pino told them in hushed wonder, still staring at the spectacle. "You two had better stay hidden, while I —"

He was cut short by a rapid volley of loud concussions from one of the nearer gunboats, still far ahead of them. Seconds later, all three of them looked up as something tore audibly through the sky above them, then hit the surface not a hundred feet away, sending gouts of foam and water up into the air. Pino wrenched the *Coppersmith's* tiller around, nearly jibing the mainsail, before letting it out to snap taut as they ran before the wind, away from shore. "That was just to warn us away — I think!" Pino shouted up to them. "I hope," he added, more quietly. "We will wait farther out. But get back under the tarp, please. We don't want to give them any new reason to take interest in our little boat."

Sian and Arian immediately crouched down again, and pulled the tarp back over their heads.

"I should not have asked this of your captain," Arian said. Her voice was shaky in the darkness, more frightened than Sian had ever heard her sound — even on the night they'd been attacked by Lod's temple thugs. "He cannot hope to draw all of that off. I had no idea. I've just lured him to his doom."

TWENTY-EIGHT

"**C**aptain, with respect, sir," Kyrios sputtered, despite the comfort of being free to speak his native tongue again, "this is ... Could we not just stand some kind of manikin upon the prow?"

"Their reason for chasing us must be convincing," Reikos said, just managing not to laugh as he turned from the charts he was studying to find his first mate wiping long, windblown blond hair out of his eyes while struggling to keep the elaborate silk dress he wore from blowing up into his face. "The Factora-Consort must shake her fist believably as we fire our cannons, and if they should decide to fire back at her, she must run away as well, or else the whole effect is spoiled. A manikin can do none of that, can it?" He went to hand Kyrios the charts. "Here. Take your mind off your elegant garb by keeping me from wrecking us on this godsforsaken minefield in the dark."

Off to port, the island of Toad was all that blocked their view of Home now. Just a few more minutes, and they'd be able to see what they were getting into. Reikos climbed to the helm and took up his spyglass in anticipation. Given the number of things he felt unwilling or forbidden to reveal even now about the exact nature of his entanglements these past few weeks, it had not been easy to explain to his scant remaining crew exactly where he'd been, or why they were headed now into the very center of a civil war to antagonize a whole fleet of Alizari gunboats.

All of that, however, had been easier than talking Kyrios into a dress. Reikos had been forced to some severity to keep the other crewmen from heckling the poor man mercilessly. The *Fair Passage* was a fairly honest trading ship, and his men were, for the most part, respectable sailors — not pirates used to such shenanigans as they were bound for now. Reikos hoped they wouldn't all just leap overboard the minute things got really scary — as he had no doubt they would before this ill-advised adventure had run its course.

As they started round Toad's westernmost promontory, Reikos did not need his spyglass to see the ominous glow of firelit smoke filling the sultry air over distant Home. A second later, the island itself began coming into view, and Reikos lifted his glass to have a closer look. "By the ghosts of all my fallen fathers," he murmured in disbelief, lowering the glass again as he struggled to absorb the sight. Fighting had erupted around the Factorate House before their brief visit to the island with Ennias that morning had ended. There had been a few exchanges of naval hostility as well ... But nothing like what he saw now. The heart of hell indeed. This was madness. Sheer hopeless madness.

As *Fair Passage* came further out of Toad's shadow, Reikos heard his small crew start to murmur and exclaim on the deck below him as they too began to understand what lay ahead.

"Kyrios, are those flags ready?" Reikos called down.

"Aye, Captain," Kyrios called back. "Rigged and ready to hoist, but, well, sir ... should we not, perhaps, go take a closer look before we raise them?"

"Indeed we should, man," Reikos growled in reply. "Rest assured, our suicide will be as cautiously navigated as anyone could ask. Douse all our lights. We'll fly no colors, and come around to full stop half a league off the island to adjust our plans as necessary. You have twenty minutes to memorize those charts. Use the time. The rest of you, come here and listen up."

Reikos climbed down from the helm and went to stand among his little remnant as they gathered around him in clear uncertainty. Propriety be damned. He was not going to ask them to sail into such an inferno without knowing better why. "You six men waited out my absence after all the others gave me up for lost and left. As I said before, I am both grateful and honored by that trust. Now, I fear, your trust is to be rewarded with even more danger than I had realized when we left Cutter's not an hour ago. So I'm going to tell you what I couldn't before. When you have heard it all, you must tell me whether you will do it. I cannot — and will not — attempt to order you against your will into what we all see yonder now." One or two of his men nodded, but none spoke. "I told you back at port that I had agreed to assist the besieged Alizari government by creating this small tactical diversion on our way out of the islands. But here's the rest, lads."

He pointed past them at the distant conflagration. "Right now, somewhere at the edge of that, the Factora-Consort of Alizar herself is waiting in a little boat for our arrival. Our diversion will, I hope, make it possible for her to get ashore and return to her husband and son." No need to tell them, he supposed, that at least one of those was likely dead already. "There are two others with her. One is Pino, who you met right before all this … trouble started. He is to be your fellow crewman, and a braver, more good-hearted lad there never was. The other …" How to handle this so that it would not sound as if he were asking them to risk their lives to save his girlfriend? "In your time ashore here these past few weeks, has any of you heard of a woman they're calling Our Lady of the Islands?"

The men glanced at one another. Dannos and Molian raised hands.

"She's a healer, is she not, sir?" said Dannos. "Touched by the gods, they say."

"She brought a dead man back to life, is what I heard, Captain," said Molian. "Right there on Cutter's somewhere."

Reikos nodded, seeing that Kyrios had come to join them, charts or no. "She did indeed. And I was there to see it. That dead man was Pino. He and I were imprisoned together after that, by the man now attacking Alizar's rightful Factor. The Census Taker of Alizar held Our Lady of the Islands prisoner as well, to prevent her from healing his own cousin's gravely ill son, the Factor's heir. The healer's escape from him is, in part, what set off this war. And she is the third person waiting in that little boat we go to rescue now."

At this, his men grew wide-eyed, looking at each other in astonishment.

"Then you have been … *involved* in all of this?" Kyrios asked him.

"I have, and am, though I never intended to be. So now you understand. We go to save the Factora-Consort, Our Lady of the Islands, the young man she brought back from death, and, if we succeed in helping them get ashore and back to the Factorate House in time, the life of the Alizari Factor's rightful heir as well. If we choose not to do this, it seems likely all of them will die. Tonight. That is what's at stake here."

He fell silent, awaiting their response.

"Well, *this* will make one hell of a tale to tell our grandkids, won't it, lads!" blurted Sellas, happily.

"My mum'll be right proud of her black-sheep salt dog now, I wager," said young Eagent, nodding in satisfaction, "once I go home and tell her how I saved the king and queen of Alizar."

Reikos allowed himself the merest smile, seeing no need to correct the fellow's political misapprehensions.

"If this Lady of the Islands is truly god-touched," said Dannos, "I figure it can't hurt to help her out and earn the favor of her god, right? Luck's no laughing matter for a sailor. And who's to say we don't end up cursed for *not* saving her? I say let's do it."

"I sure ain't just sailin' off and lettin' some puffed up gooney murder his own cousin's kid and steal his throne that way," Molian put in. "No sir, Captain. I ain't the sort." He turned to his fellows. "What about the rest of you?"

There was hearty assent from everyone then, including poor Kyrios, who seemed at last unconscious of his humiliating attire. Reikos loosed a quiet breath in relief. Perhaps he should not have doubted them. These were the ones who'd stayed, after all.

"All right then," Reikos said. "I hardly need to tell you this is likely to get hairy. With so few of us, I need every one of you to look sharp and keep your heads no matter what may happen." Having told them this much, he saw no reason not to sweeten the pot a bit — against likely second thoughts when they got in the thick of it. "The Factora-Consort has told me personally that if she and her husband win this fight, I'm to be richly rewarded. There can be no guarantee who'll win, of course, or even who will live, but I swear to each of you right now that if any such reward is given, it will be split evenly between us all. No Captain's portion in this venture. Tonight, we are brothers without rank to separate us. Agreed?"

A cheer went up all around. They clearly felt — just as he did, for once — that they were doing something momentous now. And their blood was stirred, as his was. *Here's hoping that's still how it seems come morning,* he thought, turning to head back up to the helm. "Now make this boat up neater than the Factor's bed, men! We can afford no tangled sheets or luffing canvas in the pinch tonight! Every one of you will need to be worth three!"

As they scurried to their tasks, he stood beside the wheel and retrieved his spyglass, shaking his head again at what he beheld through it. Brave speeches were not going to get them out of this unscathed. *Just don't any of you die tonight,* he thought. *I don't want your blood on my conscience, any more than Sian's or Pino's.*

Dark and silent, the *Fair Passage* ghosted closer to the burning island with its ring of angry gunboats and smaller, makeshift sniper-craft. As Kyrios stood beside him, burning holes through the charts with his eyes, Reikos scanned the water ahead with his glass for any sign of Pino's little sloop. They should have reached the island at least half an hour ahead of him. But there were so many craft around Home now, and so much glare and smoke from all the fires, both ashore and afloat as ruined vessels burned and sank, that he began to despair of ever finding them, if they were there at all still. What if they'd been sunk or captured already? Or just had the sense to go farther around the island in search of safer access? It's what Reikos would have done as soon as he'd seen this mad waterfront with his own eyes; what he'd have told Pino to do if he had understood in time what they were headed off to. If they weren't even there, this whole maneuver would just be pointless, if potentially very costly, theater.

And then he found them! Bobbing in the darkness, right where he had told the boy to wait. Reikos lowered the glass, and damned himself aloud.

"What is it?" Kyrios asked, looking up from his charts in concern.

"I've already sunk us all." Reikos brought a hand up to cover his eyes, as if that might make the scene before him go away.

"How?" said Kyrios. "We are not even —"

"I told him to wait just north of the island. So he wouldn't barrel too far ahead and get them killed before we even got here. The lad tends to be impetuous." He shook his head and let his hand fall. "Now, there he sits, just as instructed, right between the godsdamned harbor full of gunboats and our only path past them and out to sea. If we come straight in at speed, as

I'd intended, and veer off to starboard toward open water, all those armed boats will be drawn right through the sloop as they come after me. Even if they aren't seen and fired upon, they'll likely just be cut to bits and sunk beneath some rushing gunboat's prow."

"Then what are we to do?"

"I don't know! I never do these days, it seems." Reikos paced the little space around them. "If it were still mine to choose, now that I've seen this mess, I'd just sail past them without any fanfare whatsoever and continue out to sea. Abort this entire ridiculous affair. If the lad had any sense, he'd see me leave, and understand that he must give it up for now as well. But he hasn't any sense. He'll learn some, if he lives that long — he's not stupid. But right now he's just young and reckless and convinced that he is under some divine mandate. If I leave them to flee without our aid, he'll take it upon himself to do something heroic instead, and I will spend the rest of my days … mourning the results." *Alone,* he added silently. *I cannot leave Sian waiting in that boat, abandoned and betrayed by me.* "I have no choice."

"No choice but what, sir?" Kyrios asked fearfully.

"That's what I'm trying to figure out, man. Feel free to chime in with suggestions."

"So, the gunboats are to port of us, and the sea's to starboard, and the sloop we're here to save is in between?"

"That's a more concise summation, yes, though I derive no new insight from it."

"Then, can we not sail in just to port of them, between the sloop and gunboats, shout down as we pass that they must flee northward, then draw the gunboats southward out to sea?"

"Here," said Reikos, handing Kyrios the glass. "Look at where they sit." He pointed as Kyrios peered through the glass, then reached up to guide it with his hand. "The little sloop, its bow all covered up in tarp. The women hide beneath that. Do you see it?"

"Aye, Captain. I've got them now." Kyrios lowered the glass, looking sour.

"You see the problem then. Run so much as fifteen feet east of them, and we'll have no path back out to sea without turning this great tub at least ninety degrees to starboard before ramming into shore. Even if there's room for that — which I doubt — we'd have to surrender nearly all our speed to make the turn. They'd be on us like a pod of killer whales before we'd reached the point there." He shook his head. "We are left two choices now, old friend. Either we draw all those gunboats to the east instead, or … we save ourselves and leave the people in that sloop to die."

"But Captain," Kyrios said, pale and disbelieving. "To draw them east, we'd be sailing straight into the islands. Through the city's very heart."

"That's right."

Kyrios held up the charts he had been studying, as if Reikos might not understand what they foretold. "The channels aren't deep or wide enough between them. We'd just run aground."

Reikos nodded, already too lost in grief for his beautiful ship to attempt speech.

"How would that serve anyone, sir?" Kyrios asked desperately.

Reikos drew a long, deep breath. "That would depend on how long we could draw them off before we ran aground, I suppose. If we bought them time to get ashore, then we would not have sacrificed my ship in vain."

"Sir … you can't be serious. Are you?"

"Never more, I fear," Reikos said quietly. He looked back toward the firelit island. "Though we'd likely have outrun their ships the other way, there was never any surety that we'd have outrun all their cannon balls." He turned back to Kyrios, committed now, inside and out. "If they're going to sink us, better in shallow water with land close by on either side to swim to, eh? Than well out to sea where there's nothing for us to do but drown." He gave his first mate a companionable slap on the arm. "If we do manage to help the Factor and Factora-Consort win this fight, I'm sure she'll buy me another ship. Almost as nice," he added, with a catch in his throat. "Better go down and explain our new objective to the crew, I guess. I can count on you to help convince them, I hope?"

Kyrios looked at him with, to Reikos's consternation, the gleam of unshed tears in his eyes. "It's been an honor serving with you, Captain. All these years. I've no intention of abandoning you now."

"Don't start speaking of us in the past tense that way, will you?" Reikos dragged a pale grin from somewhere inside. "It'll just spook the others."

～

Is my Viktor really dead? Can this be true? The question circled endlessly, vanishing into the murky waters of Arian's mind, only to resurface moments later. If he was … it was her fault. Or was it? Could this have been avoided? Or was it all but started anyway before she'd even left the Factorate to free Sian? Arian could not imagine her husband dead. However pessimistic he had seemed at times, he had been too much alive last time she'd seen him. Only days ago.

Only days ago this war had seemed no more than an academic possibility to her. Only weeks ago they'd had no greater worries than the vicissitudes of Alizar's economic turmoil, and deflecting some inconvenient trade delegation from Copper Downs. Or so it had seemed.

And Konrad's illness, of course. Was her son, at least, still living? Where was he now? Not still lying in their burning house, surely. Where would they have taken him? And who would *they* have been? Was Lucia with him still? Was she even alive — or Maronne? What of her poor repentant brother, Aros? Was anyone she'd cared for here still living? She wondered if Viktor's pernicious cousin was happy with where his self-serving schemes had brought them all, or whether he too was hiding somewhere now, wishing as desperately as Arian did that he could take so many blunders back and wake up from this nightmare.

"Arian," Sian whispered, peeping through a crack between the gunwale and their tarp, "is that not another of Viktor's ships? I think … yes! It flies the banner of House Alkattha!"

"As do any ships Escotte has hired, I'm sure," said Arian, unable to prevent herself from raining pessimism even on Sian. "I'm sorry. That was …"

Sian shook her head. "I understand. This waiting … is not easy."

No, thought Arian. *It leaves too much time for thought.*

Rationally, she knew that they could not have been here for much more than half an hour, but it seemed they'd waited half the night. Was the captain still coming? She hoped, almost, that he was not; that something had prevented him from even leaving port on Cutter's. That she might yet avoid having his death and those of his crew on her conscience as well by morning.

"I see at least a few ships flying Factorate flags," Sian pressed. "If they're still fighting, then … we cannot have lost yet, can we?"

Perhaps not, thought Arian, *if they haven't just been captured or stolen during battle, and our flags left flying just to catch other members of my husband's fleet off guard.* She managed to keep her mouth shut this time, anyway. Was this what it had been like for Viktor, she wondered, drowning in despair while she had badgered him to be less pessimistic? "I've seen half a dozen all too recognizable warships tonight," Arian sighed. "I ordered them equipped with cannon myself, hardly more than a week ago, for that ridiculous parade to beard Duon in his own den." A wretched little laugh escaped her. "I can hope, I guess, that they're still under the command of captains loyal to my husband's government."

"My ladies!" Pino's urgent voice came muffled through the tarp. "I see him! Reikos is coming — fast!"

Heedless of the risk, Arian reached up to shove their tarp aside and stuck her head up. "Where is he?"

"My lady," Pino said, "please, stay hidden until —"

"No!" She had to see. Had to watch — praying that Reikos would realize the futility of what she'd asked of him, and turn around. "Please, I …"

"There, my lady," Pino said, abashed. He pointed into the darkness north of them, where it still took some time for her to find and recognize the hulking silhouette of his darkened ship. Heading straight at them, it seemed.

"I cannot see him," Sian murmured beside her.

"There," said Arian, just as lamps bloomed suddenly at the ship's prow. One, then three, then many more, lighting up … a figure, waving from the deck. No, shaking its fist. Long, pale hair and flowing lengths of amethyst silk lifted on the wind. Arian groaned and hid her eyes. "All my fault," she whispered.

"None of it," said Sian. "Escotte is to blame for this, and whoever put him up to it. If anybody did. I can see now that his greed alone may have been sufficient to cause all this."

Arian shook her head, not remotely willing to let herself off so easily. "They all warned me —"

"That you mustn't try to save your son. I know," Sian cut her off. "But if I wasn't given this terrible gift to heal Konrad, then why was I made to suffer it? And if a god cares enough to save your son, how could you have been wrong to care as well?"

Arian had once believed there were no gods in Alizar, then thought Sian's new god might save her son. Now she only wondered how they'd all allowed themselves to read whatever they most wished for in the tea leaves of this catastrophe. Even if there *was* some new god in Alizar again, how had she imagined that a deity her husband had ordered *butchered* might re-order the world just to help them save their son, much less their little kingdom? Why should a god care for any tiny clot of islands, much less three miniscule lives on one small hilltop?

"My ladies, we must make ready to sail now," Pino pled. "As soon as Reikos draws these ships away, we must start for shore. It will be very important then that you are not seen. *Please.*"

"I'm sorry," Arian said, knowing he would not suspect how deeply or for how much. "And Pino, please, do not endanger yourself either, if it can be helped at all." She and Sian ducked down again and pulled the tarp back into place above them, leaving a gap to see through.

Reikos's ship was fully lit now. Like a ballroom on the night of someone's coronation. Not one, but two fair sketches of the Factorate's banner had been raised upon its masts as well. Arian had not realized how close they were when they had been a shadow still. She glanced again at the ridiculous figure she had called for at its prow, then looked back at the harbor, realizing what felt wrong.

"He'll draw them here!" she hissed to Sian. "When he turns out to sea, the chase will bring all those other boats right past us! He must not realize where we are! Pino!" she shouted, "Pino, can you wave a light, or something? He must see us and change direction or we're —"

"My lady, no!" begged Pino. "They will see us too! On shore! You must stay down!"

"But don't you see? He's —" She glanced back at the looming ship, and fell silent, unable to make sense of what she saw. "What's he doing?" she gasped. "Why is he turning *east*?"

Sian put a hand to her mouth. "There is no escape for him that way!"

"My lady ..." Pino said, staring at *Fair Passage* in equal dismay as it thundered past them at full speed, not five hundred feet off their port side, "the other boats have seen him too. They are moving ... away from us, but ..." His eyes grew round. "*Hang on!*" he shouted as the great ship's foaming wake crashed toward them. Seconds later, the port side of their little boat was shoved into the air as Arian and Sian cried out and grabbed for any purchase they could find. Just as it seemed the boat would roll, the port side fell away again, more violently than it had risen, and the starboard side heaved up to roll them in the opposite direction, as water poured across the gunwales. There was barely time to gasp and grab once more at the sloop's bare ribs before the port side rose again, though not as swiftly or as far, followed by the starboard side, and then, as suddenly, the little craft grew still, bobbing quietly, as if to catch its breath.

"*Blackblood's balls!*" Pino gasped, unwrapping his arms from around the mast, and climbing to his feet again. "Did he not see us here, or —"

Whatever else he might have said was drowned out by a deafening roar as *Fair Passage* fired all its cannons at the passing shoreline, running due east now, without seeming to have slowed at all. As if the sound itself had torn them free, boats of every size and apparent faction began turning on the wind to follow Reikos toward the island channel.

"Now!" Pino shouted, yanking on the main sheet and the tiller simultaneously. "Get below the tarp, my ladies, and stay hidden 'til I call you out!" As Arian and Sian scrambled through six inches of standing water to gather the now-sopping tarp and drag it back across themselves, the sloop's luffing sails snapped taut, causing the boat to heel sharply as it started speeding toward the coast. Arian let out a yelp, stumbling into Sian again, and bringing both of them into a splashing tangle on the deck.

"Just stay down! Forget the tarp!" called Pino, his eyes riveted ahead of them. "Lean against the windward side! I've got to point her hard if we're to reach the shore before they all start running out of water and turn back! I need ballast portside!"

"Here!" Sian called out to Arian as she scurried to press herself against the portside gunwale. "Help me weigh the boat against the wind!"

"I know," said Arian, feeling embarrassed at her helpless behavior. "I'm married to a shipping magnate, after all." *Or, I was, at least,* she thought. *Oh Viktor, please, please don't be dead. Or Konrad either. I'm coming now, my loves. I'm finally coming home.*

TWENTY-NINE

"All right, boys," Reikos called down from his place at the helm, "let's go wreck my ship! Are the cannon ready, Molian?"

"Aye, sir! Powder only, as you ordered, sir, with shot and shrapnel standing ready."

"Thank you!" Reikos had seen no point in wasting good ordnance until they knew who or what actually needed shooting at. As they doubtless would at any moment now. "On my signal then!" He saw Pino's little boat coming up to starboard and hoped the boy would think to turn into his wake. With apologies, either way, he needed to leave himself as much room portside as he could for this doubtless already too-brief little chase.

"Stand ready!" he shouted to his crew. "Coming 30 degrees to port!"

He cranked the wheel hard, his tiny crew scrambling to re-trim so many sails as *Fair Passage* veered east just in time to avoid both Pino's craft and two of the half-submerged wrecks already littering Home's chaotic waterfront. "Kyrios! This'll likely be their only good look! Make them believe you!"

In his pool of lamplight at the prow, Kyrios rushed the starboard rail, shouting in falsetto and shaking his fists higher than ever at a cluster of gunboats flying the Orlon family crest. Rumors had been rife back at port on Cutter's that House Orlon had sided with the usurpers.

Having traded luxury goods for many years in Alizar, Reikos and his men knew who the islands' leading families were — and all their house devices at sight. A quick sweep of the shoreline made it plain that everyone had shown up for this party. In addition to a few Factorate ships, and a handful flying Alkattha colors — which might be the Factor's, or might be the Census Taker's, he realized — Reikos saw banners aloft for Houses Orlan, Sark, Suba-Tien, Colara, Phaero, and half a dozen others. Almost certainly *Fair Passage* would have friends as well as foes somewhere in this tangle. But, with the exception of those Factorate boats, and possibly those of House Orlon, he had no way of guessing — yet — who fought for which side here. Another reason to load only powder at this point.

"Ready cannons!" Reikos shouted as *Fair Passage* came broadside to the waterfront, still moving at a frightening speed. "Fire!"

The roar set his teeth rattling, but he felt sure that anyone distracted from their passage must be paying attention now. "Kyrios! You're done! Get up here, and man these charts!"

At the prow, his first mate gathered up his skirts and came running for the helm.

"Here they come, Captain!" shouted Dannos. "All of them, I think — gods help us!"

"Man your posts and pay attention to your work!" Reikos shouted down. "Molian, you and Eagent get those cannons loaded up again — with shot this time! But move 'em sternward first! That's where we'll need to fire 'em from now on!"

"Aye, aye!" Molian scrambled down the hatch to where Eagent was likely already at work on this very task.

"Sellas, get those jib sails trimmed!"

"Aye, Captain!" Sellas ran forward from the main mast where he'd been helping Jak.

"Dolous!" Reikos shouted to his seventh man, beneath the mizzen mast, struggling, like everyone else, with too many sheets at once. "We're on a reach now, not a tack!"

"Sorry, Captain!" Dolous called, rushing to correct the mizzen's top gallant sail.

They had already lost a lot of speed coming through the turn, which was good in one sense, as they were rushing toward their doom, but not so good in another. Reikos glanced back to find at least five well-armed craft already pulling ahead of the pack behind them.

Kyrios arrived at last, breathing hard, and grabbed up one of the charts clipped to the binnacle box. "The deepest channel's over there, sir." He thrust an arm out forty-five degrees to port. "But it won't take us much past the bridge to Apricot." His eyes raced up and down the parchment. "There's another, ten degrees starboard, that'll bring us to the bridge at a rough angle; but once we're under, it grows deeper as the other channel fails."

"Just what I wanted," Reikos growled, turning the wheel. "Sailing closer to shore."

Kyrios pointed ahead. "When we've come abreast of that burning wharf up there, resume your previous heading, and maintain your distance. That should keep us in the channel."

The boom of cannons came from well behind them, causing them both to turn.

Three great jets of water leapt into the air too far off their stern to matter much. Yet.

"One of Orlon's." Reikos shook his head, watching the roil of gunsmoke drift away behind their attacker. "Not just a rumor then."

"Traitorous bastard," Kyrios muttered, returning to his charts.

"Well, that's two less cannon balls to worry about." Reikos turned forward to peruse the course ahead of them. "Let's hope the vessel's captain is an impatient man who doesn't want to wait 'til we're in range to keep on firing."

"Here, sir. Ten degrees port, and we should be fine until we reach the bridge."

As Reikos turned the wheel, he glanced down at Jak, who was just tying things off beside the main mast. "Jak! Go get a saw, then climb up and cut halfway through the main mast, just below the gallant! Only *halfway!* Got that? And from the front — mind you — not the back!"

"Aye ...?" the man called, looking confused. "The *mast*, Captain?"

"Now, man! Do it before I need you down here trimming sail again!"

"Aye!" He went running to the carpentry locker.

"May I ask what you're doing, sir?" Kyrios inquired. "If the gallant falls, it'll take out gods know how much other rigging — which it does seem we could use just now."

"The solid half'll hold against one sail in airs like these," said Reikos.

"I'm *nearly* certain the bridge to Apricot is high enough to let us under; but if we're lucky enough to reach any of the others, I'd rather lose the top of my main mast than the whole thing. Wouldn't you agree?"

"Aye, Captain. I suppose I would."

"If there's time, I'll send him up to shave the mizzen as well."

Kyrios gazed up at the sails, then out across the darkened channel at the distant bridge to Apricot. "So we're truly going to wreck her?" he asked, as if still unable to believe it.

"I think that's a given at this point, old friend. Let's see how far we can take her first though, shall we? What do those charts say? Should we just go 'round Home toward Shingle Beach, or keep on between Montchattaran and Viel?"

"The channel between Home and Viel is wider, Captain, but too shallow. If the sea were just a little lower, they'd be a single island at low tide. We'll have to try our luck north of Viel — if we manage to get even half that far."

Reikos nodded. "And north of Viel even the main bridge is a good deal lower than Apricot's. I wonder how many of our followers ride low enough to fare any better than ourselves. Look back and tell me who we've got there."

Kyrios turned to gaze behind them. "Out in front, there's Orlon's two, of course. The big one that fired on us will be out of luck as soon as we are, likely. Might be why he's so impatient to be firing. The smaller one may get farther, and it's more maneuverable. That'll be a problem. Right behind him looks to be one of Colara's — heavily armed, it looks from here, but also too big to be trouble for us long if we can manage not to run aground too soon ... Behind them, I see two ships flying House Phaero's flag. His and hers, you think?"

Reikos grinned darkly. Lord and Lady Phaero were contentious siblings, their twin estates crowded onto one small island.

"They're small enough to make it quite a ways, perhaps," Kyrios continued. "Good or bad for us, depending on who they serve at present. Well back of those, I see two Factorate ships, and one Alkattha banner, I believe."

"Damn shame they were all so far west when we came through," Reikos said. "We sure could've used 'em up here between us and all these others."

"Aye, Captain. If wishes were dingies, as they say ... Well off to port back there, we've also got what seems a bunch of fishing boats with light guns tacked to their backs — all flying banners of House Sark, if I am not mistaken. Nimble as wasps, I wager. If they can catch us at all, and dare to risk our superior guns and height, they could cause us real trouble. Not that the bottom still isn't likelier to take us down first." He raised a hand to block the glare of firelight from shore. "I see one of Suba-Tien's trading clippers too, trailing quite a ways behind the rest. Can't tell from here if they're even armed, but I doubt they'll make it even this far anyway."

Reikos shook his head. "As in business, so in war, eh? Lady Suba-Tien does like to play things close to her vest. I wonder which side she's come down on — or if she's just here to straddle the plank and keep score. What about the shoreline? Are there troops following us as well, or is it only boats we've drawn away from Pino?"

Kyrios turned to peer into the firelight. "It's hard to tell, Captain. There's too much commotion in the streets, but the swarm does seem to flow this way a bit. Either way, Pino should be able to get ashore without being shot out of the water now." He turned to look back at the craft pursuing them, and frowned. "Speaking of which, Orlon's and Colara's gunboats have both gathered quite a bit of speed. Looks like a race to see who ends us first."

The words had barely passed his lips when a second volley of cannon fire made Reikos duck and spin around to see if this would be all the further they got. To his amazement, it was not his ship from which the crash and crackle of splintering wood issued. As clouds of smoke billowed just starboard of Colara's gunboat, Orlon's foremost ship shuddered and swayed as a gout of dust and shrapnel boiled from the sudden gaping hole in its port side. Seconds later, its main mast cracked audibly and slumped over. Though it didn't fall completely, a portion of the deck around it seemed to collapse. Reikos could hear the uproar of frightened shouts and screams across the distance as the ship began to lean, and fell swiftly away behind them.

"And now we know who at least one of our friends is." Reikos grinned, washed with relief, however ill-founded. One friendly gunboat wasn't likely to get them out of these straits, but with all the Factorate ships he could have counted on so far behind, it was a great encouragement. "If only we had the real Factora-Consort on board, I could just haul over and hand her off to Colara's men right now. We might even make it out of here."

"You think they'd notice if you gave them me, then?" Kyrios batted his eyes at Reikos.

"I think they'd sink us on the spot. Please don't do that with your eyes again. Things are frightening enough here." Reikos turned to peer ahead. The bridge to Apricot loomed closer in the darkness, pale and gracefully attenuated. Among the first built of Alizar's modern bridges, it had been styled by its grandiose designers to resemble the ancient ruins scattered so mysteriously throughout the island chain. They'd built it high enough to allow for some degree of maritime traffic back and forth between the inner city and the open sea — though nothing as large as *Fair Passage*, of course. As Kyrios kept pointing out, channel depths had been left shallow around the city's core — for good reason. Reikos was pretty sure *Fair Passage* would fit under it, however. Almost certain ... Looking upward, he saw Jak already up the main mast, busy with the saw. "No time to shave the mizzen mast, I guess. But if I have to lose one, it's the better choice."

～

Coppersmith fairly bounced across the bay's light chop now, leaning hard to starboard as they raced for shore. They had achieved a sort of balance, all leaning out against the portside gunwales, and Sian's ability to think beyond the instant was returning.

"I apologize," said Pino. "I should have turned the boat into that wake, but I was so surprised to see him ... go that way. I didn't think in time."

They all turned to stare at the astonishing flotilla behind them, still heading east into the city center where no vessels of such size could hope to sail safely, if at all.

"Why did he *do* this?" Sian asked.

"To save us, I'm afraid," Arian answered bleakly. "From drawing all those boats our way instead. What he means to do about it now, though, is beyond me."

"Shouldn't he be slowing down, at least?" asked Pino. "Soon there won't be room to turn at such a speed. He's nearly halfway to the bridge already. Doesn't he know —"

"Reikos has sailed these waters for many years," Sian cut in, shaking her head. "He could not have done this by mistake."

Pino turned to gaze shoreward again. "Well, whatever he's doing, it's bought us this chance to sidestep their blockade. That much, at least, has gone according to plan."

Sian and Arian both turned forward too. "But only the blockade, it seems," said Arian. "Does one of you see anyplace up there that looks remotely safe for us to come ashore?"

Sian scoured the waterfront. The Factorate's once posh marina was, unsurprisingly, just smoldering wreckage now. All else along the shoreline not engulfed in flames was teeming with people — mostly men, and armed — either actively engaged in combat, or looking primed for trouble. *Coppersmith's* fixed keel would prevent them from just sailing up onto some beach, even if they found one not already inundated with this conflict; and she could see few docks still fit even to tie a boat to, let alone safe for them to come ashore from without being immediately surrounded by potential enemies.

Pino shook his head as well. "We'll have to sail west, I think, until we find some bit of shoreline not so full of trouble. The whole island can't be in this state, can it?"

In the distance, cannon fire erupted briefly, and they all turned back to watch the mad parade following Reikos — still headed east toward the bridge to Apricot.

"Doesn't look as though they hit him," Pino said.

"Surely he cannot intend to sail underneath the bridge," said Arian.

"That would be suicidal," Sian murmured.

"I'm falling off the wind to turn now," Pino said, already pulling at the tiller. "Lean in, my ladies, please." The boat veered gently westward as Pino played its sails out, and it ceased leaning so severely.

This new trajectory put their backs to Reikos, as if they were just running from sight of whatever happened next. Sian could not believe he meant to smash his ship into the islands somewhere. No one had asked *that* of him, had they? *Had they?*

As they headed further toward the open sea, the surface chop grew rougher, and the wind began to rise. Soon the bow was bucking up over whitecaps and thudding jarringly into the troughs. Drenching spray flew over the gunwales to join the pool already sloshing at their feet. Arian grew quieter, looking, perhaps, a little green, though that might just have been the moonlight. Sian reached over to wrap Arian's hand in hers, and yes ... There was the scent of ginger, and a queasiness in Sian's throat and bowels as well. She closed her eyes and breathed more deeply while it passed.

A moment later, Arian looked over at her sharply. "Did you just ...?"

Sian shrugged, and looked away. "Why let you suffer, and waste the gift?"

"If only we had gotten you to Konrad earlier," Arian sighed.

Her words seemed echoed by the young priest's voice in Sian's memory: *If you had made any effort to deliver it, you would likely have found out by now.* How much might have happened differently, Sian wondered, if she'd just gone straight off to the ruling family as ordered to, and told them ... what? That she was suddenly a healer? Could the god really have expected her to understand so quickly that her *message* was the gift itself?

She had known about Konrad's illness, certainly. She had figured out by the next day that she was able now to heal with a touch, and yet ...

Would they reach the Factorate at last, only to discover that her earlier resistance had cost them their chance? She thought again of that poor child's dark gaze on Pembo's Beach. Had it been the god's reproach she'd seen peering from those eyes — for having failed him already?

In the distance, they heard another round of cannon fire, but they'd already come too far around the western point of Home to see the channel now. If they'd known before that they would need to sail around the island anyway, Sian realized, Reikos need never have placed his ship in danger to begin with. They could just have sailed where they were sailing without his help — as they were doing now — though she had no doubt that he'd still have been here in the boat with them. *How much else have those few days of my delay cost?*

"Domina Kattë," said Pino, "may I give you the tiller for a moment? These seas are getting high — with so much water in the boat. I'd better bail her out some." He was already reaching underneath his bench to grab the bucket stowed there.

"I can bail as well as you," Sian said, reaching out to take the pail.

"My lady, you should not have —"

"I cannot *sail* as well as you, however," she cut his protest short. "I won't capsize us out here while you're sparing me the need to bail."

"Is there another bucket?" Arian asked.

Pino stared at her, clearly scandalized at the mere idea of allowing the Factora-Consort of Alizar to bail his boat.

"Were you not listening to what she just said, young man?" Arian asked with something very like a smile. "Even ladies as pampered as we are not completely *un-armed*."

Pino looked queasy now himself — though not with sea sickness, Sian thought. "There is another, I believe, under the forward bench."

Sian offered him a reassuring smile, wondering just how much he felt sworn to 'protect' her from. They would need to talk about this, sometime very soon, she thought, bending to start scooping water from their boat.

To everyone's quiet dismay, the shore passing to their port side continued to be either without safe landing, or too crowded with potential trouble to risk. Clearly, all attention in this sudden war was focused here, on Home — and they were not the first to seek out any uncontested patch of access to or from the sea.

When the bailing had been done, and the buckets were re-stowed, a restive silence fell across them as they scanned the passing shore in vain.

"Domina Kattë," Pino said at last, with obvious unease. "There is ... I ..." He fell silent again.

"Say whatever you wish, Pino," she encouraged him. "What do you imagine can upset me after all we've been through just tonight?"

"I ... am not sure it is my place to tell you this, but ..." She saw him swallow, clearly on the verge of reconsidering, even now.

"You've started," she said with a smile, far too intrigued to let him off the hook. "Just finish. I promise, you won't break me."

The boy looked pained, then cross — with himself, clearly — then resigned. It was really rather comical. "Captain Reikos, and I ... We ... discussed you, some, when we were in the Census Taker's jail all that time. More than once ... A lot, I guess."

Oh marvelous, she thought wearily. What had Konstantin told him? Nothing too lurid, she hoped, despite the evening's very public revelations.

Her wariness must have shown, for he added quickly, "Neither of us thought we would come out of there alive, my lady. And ... I did trick him into telling me. That you two were ..."

"Lovers, yes," she said, desperate now just to help him get this over with, wherever it was headed. "You are allowed to say it, Pino. It's no secret anymore."

He looked relieved. "Well, all I mean to say then, is, I'm pretty sure he meant to tell you things, tonight, before ... all that happened at your daughter's house. He did a lot of thinking in that cell, and felt quite bad, I guess, about how he had ... mishandled things with you before."

"And what?" she said, damning herself silently for having pressed him.

Pino drew a deep breath and looked her squarely in the eyes. "He's really a very good man, Domina, and loves you even more than you may guess. He came to know that very clearly while we were down there, and has truly forsaken all the others." He seemed to start, even blanch a little. "You ... did know that there were others ... Didn't you?"

She just managed not to roll her eyes. "I did. Yes. Captain Reikos has a broad appreciation for all kinds of beauty. And ...?"

"And ... now that you have ... that you are ... parting with your husband, I'm certain that he hopes to marry you," Pino rushed to finish, looking as frightened as if he had just proposed to her himself.

Sian stared back at him, aware that Arian was staring now as well.

"I ... It seems ... so unsure now, what may happen. Now. I thought ..." Pino stammered to a halt at last, seeming, finally, to realize that it had been at best presumptuous to make any such announcement on another man's behalf — whether it was true or not.

But Sian was more than old enough to understand that boys learned some things about boundaries late in life. Some, like poor Arouf, never learned at all. And she had known Pino more than long enough to recognize the innocence — the bravery, even — behind what he had just tried to tell her — probably, in case ... She wanted very badly not to hurt this poor, guileless boy, and so, as she suddenly understood why he had taken this upon himself, she tried very hard not to burst into tears. She had all but promised him she wouldn't, hadn't she? How presumptuous had that been? He was not the only fool here. Not by any measure.

"He told you this?" she managed very quietly.

Pino shook his head. "But I know, my lady. The dungeon changed him. Deeply. And what the priest said to us all that night. He is no longer the same man he was. I guess that's what I wanted you … what I thought *he* might want you to know."

"Because you don't think he will live to tell me," she said, feeling herself harden inside against the sudden discovery that there were still things left to break there after all. Things she wasn't sure her new gift would have any power to cure.

Pino looked away, clearly distraught. "I am sorry, Domina. I should not …"

"Thank you," Sian said, loosing tears despite herself. "For being you, Pino. If just a tenth of us were half so good-hearted, so well-intentioned … maybe none of us would be in such trouble here tonight." Her tears were falling harder now. There was nothing she could do to stop them. "You have nothing to apologize for. Not to me. Not to anyone, I'm certain."

He nodded, without looking at her. Then turned his attention awkwardly to the further adjustment of their sails. Doubting she could heal this for him either, Sian left him to his own devices, and looked back toward the shadowed point of land receding behind them, somewhere beyond which, Reikos would survive this night or not.

Arian scooted close enough to wrap an arm around her and lay her head on Sian's shoulder. "What a night for all of us," she whispered.

Sian nodded. *Yes. For all of us. Who in these islands is not suffering tonight? I am not alone, nor anything like worst off here. Not by any measure.*

THIRTY

As the lofty bridge drew near at last, Reikos quickly understood what Kyrios had meant by 'a rough angle.' There were only three great arches underneath it wide enough to offer any hope of fitting through, and the channel they were following went only through the center one, but not at a straight angle. They'd have to turn more than forty-five degrees into the passage. More lost speed, and if Reikos didn't manage their momentum carefully, a rather swift ending on the portside bridge piling.

"Where's the tide?" he asked Kyrios.

"High, Captain, and still in flood — for another couple hours yet."

"Naturally," he sighed. "Stand ready to come about forty-eight degrees starboard!" Reikos shouted down to his crew. "On my mark ... Now!"

Reikos began tugging at the wheel as everyone below scurried to trim *Fair Passage's* sails from beam reach to close hauled. He aimed well starboard of the channel's center, anticipating some side-slippage at this speed. Their sturdy keel held the turn more closely than expected, though, which necessitated some very sloppy extra turns as they nosed into the arch.

As soon as he felt sure they'd make it, he and Kyrios both looked up to watch the main mast, and were startled to find a great crowd of astonished onlookers gawking down at them from atop the bridge itself, open-mouthed and pointing at yet another spectacle they'd likely never thought to see. Reikos shook his head, and pulled his eyes back to the main topgallant, praying he'd been right about the bridge's height. "'Ware the chance of falling rigging!" he yelled needlessly to his crew, their eyes all pointed just where his were as the mast glided up ... and ... under by an onion skin!

A rowdy cheer erupted from the crew, as Reikos bowed his head in relief — cut short by the jolting boom of cannon fire, just behind them.

There was only time to whirl and gape at Orlon's remaining gunboat before two great chunks of the bridge piling to their port side blossomed in an earsplitting chrysanthemum of dust and flying stone — most of which fell harmlessly into the water, though several smaller chunks tore little holes through a few mainmast sails, taking out a minor stay or two — though, happily, the weakened topgallant was not dislodged. From high above them came a din of panic as bridge-top gawkers cried out in terror, running for either end of the long span.

"Molian!" Reikos yelled, relieved to find the man right where he ought to be, head and shoulders thrust up through the aft hatch just behind him. "Fire at will!"

"Aye-aye, Captain! Eagent," he yelled down, "fire at —"

His compliance was cut short by the roar of their own cannons — one — two — three in quick succession — as Eagent must have had punk to powder down there even before the order had been given — a serious offense in ordinary times, perhaps, but godsdamned welcome now. If any of them lived to see the morning, Reikos would have a word with him about it.

Two of their three cannon balls flew wide. The third took Orlon's smaller gunboat straight through the foredeck's starboard side. Split-seconds later, a roar erupted from inside the injured craft, and a fireball blew their foredeck to confetti. Perhaps they'd had punk already set to powder in there too. Another known opponent was dispatched. That was all Reikos cared.

"Captain!" Kyrios shouted, lunging past him to grab the momentarily forgotten wheel.

Reikos spun to find his own neglected ship headed for a glancing blow against the starboard bridge piling as it exited the arch. "Gods!" he shouted, silently berating himself for a useless fool as his silk-clad first mate skillfully avoided the collision without over-correcting and taking their stern out on the bridge instead. "If we live through this," he said as Kyrios surrendered the wheel to him again, "I may just retire and hand this ship over to you after all."

"You mean the wreckage, sir? To what do I owe such a magnificent boon?"

"Of course," said Reikos, now twice embarrassed. "I did not mean to wreck her here, though. I'll find some way to reward you. Right now, however, would you tell me what is happening behind us — while I keep my eyes forward?"

Kyrios turned, but had no time to answer before a second burst of cannon fire made Reikos duck and cringe, braced for a rain of shrapnel through his back — though he did manage to stay looking straight ahead this time, with both hands on the wheel.

"*Hell's teeth!*" Kyrios spat. "That was Colara again. He's come full stop on the other side — smart man — and just took out one of the Phaeros' boats."

Reikos sagged in relief. "Then Lord and Lady Phaero must have chosen the usurper too."

"Did someone promise them a larger island, do you think?" Kyrios mused.

"That's two debts we now owe Colara in the morning."

"The Phaeros' other boat got through, though. They're not far behind us, sir, and gaining. Their draft's far shallower than ours. They must not have had to turn as we did."

"Molian!" Reikos shouted, turning for a quick glance back. "Can you hear me?"

"Aye, sir!" Molian's voice echoed from the hatch. "We've only got one gun reloaded, sir!"

"Fire it at the little schooner just behind us! Now!"

"Aye, Captain! Firing now!"

There was a breathless pause. Eagent must not have jumped the gun this time. Then came the roar Reikos had been waiting for. He glanced back again in time to see their cannon ball punch uselessly into the water just to starboard of the Phaeros' pretty little boat. Nonetheless, this seemed sufficient persuasion to make them drop back quickly out of range, which put *Fair Passage* out of their range too, as any cannon on a boat so small would have to be of lesser caliber.

"Should we fire the others, Captain?" Molian hollered up.

"Not yet!" called Reikos. He turned to Kyrios. "Look back there. Do they seem armed to fire from the bow?"

"I see gun hatches at the fore, Captain, but they're closed, I think. It's hard to tell. We're mostly out of firelight on this side of the bridge." Reikos realized then that there was very little burning on the shore to starboard, and nothing at all afire to port on Apricot. In fact, the island back here past the bridge seemed almost deserted. "Damn it," he muttered. If they'd only known, he and Pino could just have brought the ladies ashore here in *Coppersmith*, and left his ship somewhere out of harm's way.

"If I may take the wheel again, sir," said Kyrios, "you might wish to have a look?"

"Of course, thank you," Reikos said, surrendering the wheel.

Kyrios was right. It was much darker now. The Phaeros' remaining dollhouse schooner seemed little more than a shadow under its ghostly sails. From beyond the receding bridge came yet another volley of cannon fire, clearly not directed at *Fair Passage* this time either. Colara clearly knew a tactical advantage when he saw one. As long as the Phaeros' lone little boat kept its safe distance, things ought to get pretty quiet for a while now.

"Right," said Reikos, turning to retrieve the wheel from Kyrios. "Now I need to know how much longer we'll have this channel, and what I must do to keep us in it."

Kyrios gave his chart a glance or two, in between nervous glances back at the Phaeros' little schooner. "Just keep on as you are, sir. It stays along the starboard shoreline at about this distance all the way to that great old column rising from the bay ahead." He scrutinized his chart more carefully, and frowned. "After that, things will get very dicey, I'm afraid."

"*Abandon ship* dicey?" Reikos asked. "Or just … Look—what I really need to know is if there's even the remotest possibility of getting us out the other side of this somewhere. If not, we might as well just blow the Phaeros' schooner from the water to be safe, then drop anchor here and take one of the lifeboats in to shore. If Colara's going to sit there playing gatekeeper for us, I imagine we've left most of the larger boats behind now, which means any help we had to offer the Factora-Consort is exhausted."

"Well …" Kyrios said dubiously. "As the tide *is* high right now … if we're very, very clever … and don't have to waste too much more time on further skirmishes …" He turned the chart this way and that, seeming to follow some very convoluted line of movement. "There may be a tiny chance of getting all the way out — between Cutter's and Phaero, as it happens. It's hard to tell, though — especially in this light."

The binnacle lamp was flickering; out of oil, Reikos thought with irritation. They'd had a lot to think about as they'd rushed out of Cutter's. "Dolous!" he shouted. "Get two of those lamps up here from the bow, immediately! The brightest ones!"

"That should help, though maybe just to see why I was wrong," said Kyrios.

"Let's stay optimistic." Reikos grinned, not really having thought they'd get even this far.

"Wait … Captain?" Kyrios had turned to look back again at the Phaeros' schooner. "They're falling off to port. Fast and wide. Are they leaving us, or …"

"Are my eyes deceiving me, Kyrios," Reikos asked, peering at the shifting moonlit water up ahead of them, "or do you see something lying on the surface there?"

"Oh! Captain, it's a pier, I think!"

"Across *the channel*?" Reikos blurted, wrenching at the wheel.

"To port, sir! Hard to port!"

"I'm trying!" Reikos yelled, already knowing that, given their size and speed, they weren't going to miss it. "Oh to hell with it!" he spat, turning the wheel back to straighten their course.

"What are you —"

"I'm praying it is not a sturdy pier!" he shouted, seeing no point in ordering the sails emptied either. The more speed now, the better. "We stand a better chance of punching through it head-on than broadside! *All hands brace for impact!*" he shouted to his crew. "*Leave the sails — and 'ware that mainmast topgallant!*"

~

It had been half an hour, at least, since anyone had spoken. Arian, Sian and Pino were all lost in their own thoughts — or licking their own wounds, having sailed all the way down Home's western shore, and still found no safe landing. As *Coppersmith* veered east around the island's southwestern corner, the wind and rougher waters finally started to abate, at least. Though her embarrassing motion sickness had not returned since Sian had taken it away, Arian's aging spine was well past putting up politely with the constant jouncing up and down. From this side of the island, the burning Factorate House upon its hilltop could no longer be seen either, for which she was deeply grateful.

Sian and she had long since abandoned any attempt to stay hidden. If they'd not been seen already, hiking off the port side of the boat while racing out of Home's great harbor, there seemed little cause for concern now, out here alone, lit by nothing but the moon.

"Pino, have you noticed those lights back there?" Sian pointed off their stern at a cluster of small boats almost too far behind them to be seen but for their lanterns.

Pino turned to look. "Lots of boats off Home tonight, my lady."

"Yes, but they've been following us for some time — and getting closer, I believe."

He looked again, then shrugged. "Maybe they're looking for safe portage too. They're too far away to cause us any trouble, though — or even see us here, most likely."

"If we don't find someplace soon," said Arian, "we may just have to try dropping anchor out here somewhere and swimming in to shore. There can't be that many hours left before dawn arrives and robs us even of whatever cover darkness might provide."

"The tide is high, my lady," Pino said apologetically. "Most of the beaches here are under water, leaving only cliff face — likely why the few landings we've passed were all so crowded."

"The cliffs should end soon," she replied. "The island slopes more gently to the south."

"Are you a sturdy swimmer, my lady?" Pino asked dubiously. "Your dresses ..."

"Our silks are light and long," Arian answered. "Easily tied around our waists or shoulders, if necessary." She looked inquisitively at Sian, who nodded her agreement. "My husband told me when I came here that I would be spending half my life on boats now, and must learn to swim. I have found it quite an enjoyable activity, actually. Let's stop looking for a landing and just find an empty patch of shore with any kind of access to the land above."

"She's right," Sian said. "We can't just sail clear around the island to where we began."

"Very well, my ladies, but …" He glanced at them uncomfortably. "Won't you mind … the exposure?"

For the first time that day, Arian was moved, despite herself, to laugh. "Oh, dear boy, you've got nothing under there we have not both already seen many times by now."

"I did not mean … My pants are short," he sputtered. "I will keep them on, of course. I just meant … I don't know what the two of you are … wearing under …"

By now both she and Sian were laughing openly. Even in the moonlight, Arian could see Pino blush. What an innocent he was. She wondered how Arouf had ever entertained such ridiculous suspicions — about *this* boy, anyway.

"Then, let us look for someplace safe to swim to," Pino said, turning sullenly away.

"I'm sorry," said Arian. "I should not have teased you. Your concern is very sweet, and were the world still sane, entirely appropriate. This is war, however, in which even unclad bathing may be briefly necessary."

At this, Sian put a hand to her mouth to hold back further laughter.

Even Pino grinned now, if still in obvious embarrassment.

"Pino?" Sian said a moment later, no longer laughing. "Are you sure we shouldn't be concerned about those boats?"

Everyone turned to find the three mid-sized ketches, that had been little more than distant lanterns only moments ago, now sailing close enough behind them that Arian could see crew moving — very purposefully — about their decks.

"My ladies … there may be some cause for concern after all. Let's hope they haven't seen us yet. Please get back under the tarp."

With sudden tension in her belly, Arian helped Sian stretch the canvas over them as they lay back against the deck.

"Roll as far to starboard as you can, please," Pino asked them quietly. "I'm going to take the sails in and see if we can build some extra speed."

They fumbled awkwardly against each other underneath the tarp until they were as far up the starboard gunwale as they could get and still be covered. Arian felt the small boat heel into the wind, bouncing unpleasantly on the chop again.

Everyone was silent for a while. Perhaps fifteen minutes later, their bouncing lessened slightly as the boat slowed to veer further eastward, around the point, Arian supposed.

"You were right, my lady," Pino told them a moment later, sounding almost anguished. "I am sorry. They are following. They have far more sail than we do. I doubt I will be able to outrun them too much longer."

"Can you see if they are flying any colors or insignia?" Arian called softly.

There was a pause, then, "Yes, my lady. Orlon, I think."

"I fear we are in trouble," Arian whispered to Sian.

"Do you wish me to keep running?" Pino asked. "Or to pull toward shore? There is some large harbor up ahead of us, I think. Almost completely dark for some reason. Or ... wait. No, it's one of the raft slums." He paused again. "Not a safe place at any time, but ... Orlon's ships are not far behind, my ladies."

Arian closed her eyes and groaned. *The raft warrens. What predictably perfect luck. ... Or poetic justice.*

"Arian?" Sian whispered. "What should he do?"

"If I just come to and wait for them," said Pino, "I could tell them I'm going to help my parents, as we did before. Perhaps if they see no one else aboard, they'll just —"

He was cut short by a sickeningly familiar boom not far behind them, quickly followed by another.

"*Oh, the gods!*" Pino just had time to gasp before Arian heard first one, and then a second mighty splash, as cannon balls plunged into water somewhere not too far away.

"How far are we from the warrens?" she shouted.

"Too far to swim, my ladies!" Pino shouted back. "I don't think they meant to hit us — or their aim is very poor. They probably just want me to stop. But I think they must have seen you back there, or I don't know why they'd waste their cannons on a little boat like this. Should I come around, or run?"

"Run!" Arian replied. "Please, just try to get us to the warrens, Pino! We can leave the boat and swim there if we have to, but if I am captured here, we'll never see the Factorate until this war is long finished — if even then."

"I will try, my lady!" Pino cried. The boat heeled further as he pulled the sails recklessly into the wind and veered again. The jarring bounce from wave to wave increased, so whatever he had done must be helping them gain speed, she thought.

For several minutes she heard only water rushing past the gunwales and the bow's dull thud from trough to trough, Then came a second set of booms — much louder than the first — followed almost instantly by the roar of water shooting skyward near enough to rock the boat.

"I think they meant to hit me that time!" Pino shouted fearfully. "Thank the gods I'm a small target!"

"Stop then, Pino!" Arian called back. "Just come around, and tell them you were simply frightened by their cannons into running!" She could not ask him to die just to keep her out of Orlon's hands. There might be nothing left for them to do back at the Factorate by now, even if they got there. "Maybe you were right, and they'll let you go!"

"No, my lady! We're almost there. Get your dresses off or tied up, please. You will have to leave me very quickly in a minute!"

"What does he mean, *leave me*?" Sian asked as they squirmed about to gather up their silks and knot them as close and short as they were able to under the tarp.

"Tie your sandals in the silk as well," Arian told her, remembering what an issue that had been — for both of them.

"Pino!" Sian shouted as she went on tying up her clothes. "What do you mean? You're coming with us!"

"When I tell you, slip from underneath the tarp and over the port side as low and quiet as you can, my ladies!" Pino told them. "We'll be leaning away from them, and they may not see you, if you're quick and careful!"

"What about you?" Sian demanded again.

"Listen for my signal!" Pino called. "Are you ready? We are almost there!" There was a pause, then he hissed, "Damn them!" The boat veered sharply up into the wind, and heeled alarmingly to port, seconds before they heard the roar of cannons once again. The sounds of impact came from water just behind them this time. The sloop swerved again beneath them, its sails snapping back into a reach as they resumed their earlier direction.

"He must have seen them light the punk," Arian said to Sian, too frightened now to feel fear anymore. *So clever for such an innocent boy.*

"*Now, my ladies!*" Pino yelled. "*NOW!*"

Arian swept away the canvas above her with one hand, and grabbed Sian's arm with the other, tugging her into motion as they rolled across the deck and up the boat's port gunwale. Their added weight brought the boat's leeward side very low to water, so that getting over the edge took very little effort. The shock was bracing as her knotted silks began to drag — but not too badly, and the water wasn't all that cold. As she surfaced, treading and sputtering, she heard a second splash behind her, a surprising distance off, and turned again, only to find herself alone in the low chop. It took a moment more to find the *Coppersmith*, already at least fifty feet away, up into the wind again and slicing through the water at tremendous speed. She could not find Sian at all, but feared that calling out for her would draw attention from their pursuers. She started swimming toward where she had heard the second splash, and soon spotted Sian's dark head bobbing in the chop before her.

As she swam closer, Sian lifted one hand from the water to point urgently at something. Arian spun around, feeling the knotted silk brush and bump between her thighs, afraid that she would find one of Orlon's ketches coming for them. What she saw was just the tops of woven reed-thatch huts and hovels — not that far away. She had not even figured out precisely which way shore might be yet. She started swimming toward the warren — breast stroke, to make them as invisible as possible to anyone who might have seen them splash off of the boat. Sian was quickly swimming at her side.

"What of Pino?" Arian asked, glancing back but seeing no further sign of either *Coppersmith* or the boats that had been chasing it.

"He's gone to draw them off, the stupid boy!" Sian hissed angrily. "He should just have tied the tiller down and let the boat go on without him."

"Perhaps he will," said Arian. "It was smart of him to take it farther off from us, though."

In the distance, they heard cannon fire again.

Sian looked behind them, then shook her head miserably, and continued swimming shoreward. "*Smart* comes and goes with him, if you haven't noticed yet. But I pray you're right."

THIRTY-ONE

Molian and Eagent scrambled up out of the hatch behind Reikos, looking pale as death, and sat down to brace themselves against the coaming. For several sickening moments, there was nothing else to do but watch the long, low pier rush ever faster toward their bow.

Kyrios dropped as well to brace himself against the binnacle box. "Sorry, Captain, but it wasn't on the charts."

"What's it doing there?" Reikos asked helplessly. "Who builds a pier across a channel?"

"What are *we* doing here?" Kyrios replied tensely. "That's the question, Captain. I'm sure whoever put it here was not expecting us."

"*Here it comes!*" Reikos shouted, white-knuckled on the wheel. "*Hold tight, lads!*"

He watched the plank-and-post contraption disappear beneath his bowsprit, and … With a strangely muffled crash, the deck beneath him shuddered, shoving him hard against the wheel. Nearly everyone still standing was thrown violently forward across the decks, along with piles of loose tackle, as the boat hung up and started twisting round to starboard on the following current. The two unsecured lanterns that Dannos had not quite gotten to at the helm skidded across the planking and shattered, trailing burning oil as they went. *Well, I knew this was coming*, Reikos thought bleakly, still clinging to the wheel. *But on a godsforsaken pier?*

From beneath their prow came the awful wrench and crackle of splitting timber, which, even now, Reikos prayed was from the pier and not his ship. A second, even louder cavalcade of ghastly grinding sounds was followed by a sudden forward lurch, as the broken structure finally gave way beneath them to scrape horribly along the edge of their long keel.

Looking up, Reikos saw the Phaeros' little schooner come abreast of them, no more than two or three cables off to port. *Well, this would be the time to let us have it,* he thought sadly. To his surprise, however, they just trimmed their sails and raced eastward, on ahead of them. Did they fear he'd fire on them, even now? He had no leisure to wonder further as *Fair Passage* came free at last, trailing splintered beams and planking in its wake to either side.

"Kyrios, take the wheel," Reikos ordered grimly, as his crew climbed to their feet and raced to stamp down and smother the small oil fires those broken lamps had started. "Molian and Eagent, check down the hatch back there. If all seems well, go have a look into the hold. If we're taking any water, come tell me immediately."

Reikos hurried down the poop deck ladder and headed for the forward hatch, where all the real damage ought to be. As others fell in around him, he looked up, realizing that the main topgallant was *still* where it belonged. He wondered if perhaps Jak had not cut quite far enough through the mast. Fortunate, if so. *Never the disaster you're prepared for,* he thought.

Arriving at the hatchway, Reikos peered down and saw lamplight still shining dimly below deck — at least, he hoped that was what it was. Rushing down the ladder, he looked quickly about, but to his relief, all the hanging lanterns seemed intact. No fires to put out here, thank the gods. As others came down behind him, Reikos took one from its hook, and snaked further in to go peer down into the hold. To his astonishment, there was neither sight nor sound of so much as a trickle.

There was a lot of cargo in his way, of course — all tumbled forward, which made it even harder to get much of a look. But other than what might have been a couple hairline fractures in a bit of frame plank here and a length of hawse piece there, nothing seemed amiss. All the structural beams and posts — that he could see, at least — looked sound. All that awful noise must have been coming from the pier after all.

"Well…" he murmured to himself. Or maybe not just to himself, if Sian's god was listening. He wondered … "Perhaps you do like me just a little."

He stood up and handed the lantern back to Dannos. "Go down and take a closer look. Move the cargo around. Check the keel. But I think we may just have witnessed yet another miracle."

He left them staring after him and climbed back up onto deck, where he saw Molian in conversation with Kyrios at the helm. "What's it look like at the stern?" he called.

Molian grinned down at him. "Dry as a burlap flour sack, Captain! Eagent is still down there searching all the corners, but I've just been telling Kyrios, it seems the back end's still afloat! What news up there?"

"Seems fit as well, amazingly." He started up the ladder to join them. "And how's she steering, Kyrios?"

"I haven't put her through anything too stressful, Captain, 'til I got the word about what's happened down below, but from what little I have tried, she still seems responsive."

Reikos shook his head in disbelief. They'd even regained some speed since he'd gone down to check things out. They were already more than halfway to the ruined pillar which was *supposed* to have marked the spot where things got dicey. "And what of our little schooner?" He glanced around the moonlit bay, but saw no sign of any craft at all.

"Just up and gone, it seems," Kyrios confirmed.

"Run back to Phaero, do you think?"

"Who can say? They disappeared around that point there on Viel. That's all I know."

"Well, if you still think there might be some way to get us out of here too, it seems a shame to wreck such a sturdy ship now, doesn't it? Molian, would you bring us a new lantern? Then come take the wheel while Kyrios and I have another look at those charts, and see what *dicey* really means, exactly." He and Kyrios exchanged a grin.

"Aye, Captain."

As Molian left them, Kyrios handed the wheel back to Reikos and took up his chart again. "Once we reach that pillar, sir, we'll need a man out on the bowsprit to sound for us the rest of the way. Eagent maybe, if we've no further need of cannon for a while."

"Here's hoping," Reikos said, gazing out at the still empty bay around them.

"It'll be very slow going," Kyrios said, bringing the parchment up to point at things hardly visible in the guttering light of the binnacle's all but failed lantern. "A cable or two this side of the pillar, there's this bowl-shaped depression in the bottom. While the tide stays high, we may just be able to squeak across it to this long divot over here."

Reikos glanced down to where he pointed at the chart. "That … takes us back this way almost, doesn't it?"

"Aye, sir. But it connects right here with another underwater valley of sorts that, if we're careful with our sounding, may get us most of the way to this zig-zagging rut of water over here. For that, we may need two men sounding out on planks to either side." He looked and shrugged at Reikos. "This is only going to happen if we aren't chased again. There'll be no racing through this, sir. And we've at most three hours of flood tide left to keep us off the bottom."

Molian arrived with their new lanterns, hanging one up each side of the binnacle box, then gave Reikos a nod as he took the wheel in turn.

"Let's hope we've fallen out of everybody's interest, then." Reikos took the chart from Kyrios and held it up to the new lamps. "So if we make it through this zig-zag … we just have Viel's three bridges to get past," he sighed.

"If the tide's still high enough to see us through to Cutter's," Kyrios reiterated.

"Guess I'd better go up and take a look at Jak's saw-through, then," said Reikos. "And have him shave the upper mizzen now as well. Let's take the canvas down up there, and whatever boom and tackle we can lose as well. No point in making the fall worse."

"Then we'd best get them to it, sir."

Reikos nodded. "We have, what, fifteen minutes still, until we reach the pillar? Why don't you go slip out of that dress?" he grinned. "It'll be easier to swim without it, if we need to."

"I thought you'd never ask, sir." Kyrios wasted no time heading down to his bunk.

As soon as he was gone, Reikos retrieved the wheel from Molian and sent him down to gather up the other crew. When their orders regarding the masts and higher rigging had been issued, there was nothing left for him to do but hold a straight line across the empty, moonlit water. The night seemed almost preternaturally peaceful now. Hard to believe that just around the point behind them, war still raged on Home.

Kyrios soon returned, in normal clothing with his pale hair bound back as usual, just in time to call Eagent down off of the mizzenmast and send him to the prow to start sounding bottom. Minutes later, they came ninety degrees to port, and let the sails spill wind until they'd slowed to a crawl — almost literally, as the bottom wasn't even a fathom below their keel half the time now. From there on, everyone except for Eagent went about their work in silence — all listening as the soundings were called out, fearful of the scrape and shudder that would mean a long hard swim to shore.

Not fifteen minutes into their tiptoe across these shallows, Dolous called out from his station just below the mizzenmast. "Three ships off the stern, Captain! Closing fast, I think!"

Reikos and his first mate spun to see yet another nightmare realized. Running toward them, straight before the wind off of Viel, Lord and Lady Phaeros' lowly little schooner now trailed two massive, ocean-going catamarans, their pontoons freeing them from any fear of bottom. They were all still quite a distance off, but wouldn't be for long, if the combs of spray at their bows were any indication.

Reikos thrust the spyglass at Kyrios before turning back to steer his ship. "Tell me what we've got."

Kyrios raised the glass to his eye. "The cats fly Alkattha banners, Captain. Looks like they've got a cannon each. Swivel-mounted, at their prows."

"Are those cannons aimed at the Phaeros' boat?"

Kyrios shook his head. "They aren't even manned at present, Captain."

"Then we're screwed. They serve the wrong Alkattha."

"That's odd," said Kyrios, still gazing through the glass. "They've got some fellow in a dress on their boat too."

"*What?*" Reikos turned to stare. "Give me the glass — and take the wheel, please."

As Kyrios did so, Reikos raised the glass to look. "By all the meddling gods, it's the Census Taker himself!" He lowered the glass and looked back at Kyrios. "What's he doing out here on a boat? He's not the sort to do his own fighting. I'd have wagered both my nuts on that."

Kyrios shrugged. "It was a good run, Captain. Longer than I ever hoped for."

"Oh, it's not over yet, friend. You know this route we're taking far better than I do. Just keep the wheel."

"But ... why? The cats can sail anywhere in here at unencumbered speed, while we can only crawl." He glanced up at the masts, where all their top-gallant rigging was now absent. "With two sails gone? The game is up, sir."

"All hands!" Reikos shouted. "Prepare for immediate trim to full speed! Eagent, come down off that sprit and resume your station at the guns! Molian — the same!"

"*Full speed, sir?*" Kyrios blurted. "*Blind?*"

Reikos spun to face him. "Do you know the course or not?"

"I know where it should lie — in general, sir. But without careful sounding —"

"If we run aground, we run aground. But if we just sit here, we are had for certain. That's Escotte Alkattha coming for us, in whose dungeon I was buried until just last morning when the Factor blew its roof off. I have no intention of suffering his hospitality again — and certainly not passively!"

"Aye, Captain," Kyrios said, no longer meeting his eyes.

"I'm sorry," Reikos said. "I'm not ..." *I'm not capable of being rational*, he conceded silently. *Not with Sian, and now Alkattha, in my head. What* is *he doing out here himself?* "Kyrios, you've saved this ship more times tonight than I have," he pled quietly. "Please, just try to do it one more time, all right? The tide is high. Steer us where we'd hoped to go, and ... maybe we'll ..." He threw his hands up, knowing Kyrios was almost certainly correct, but still seeing no better options. "What bearing must we take?"

"Straight ahead about halfway to Montchattaran there, sir. Then port at least one hundred ten degrees — for which we'll have to slow almost to stop, even in a hundred fathoms."

"All hands! Trim for full speed, straight before the wind! Do it now!" Reikos shouted to his crew, who leapt to their tasks with nervous looks, but without question. "Then stand ready to change course at Kyrios's order!" He turned back to his first mate. "You have full command of my ship, old friend, just as I promised back there at the bridge." He smiled apologetically. "You may order them to full stop at any time, if you think it best."

Kyrios gazed at him, then nodded soberly as they felt the ship begin to surge beneath them.

Molian and Eagent came scrambling up the ladder, nodding warily to Reikos on their way to the aft hatch.

"I've given Kyrios command for now," Reikos told them. "If he orders you to fire, do so. Until then, *Eagent*, don't anticipate him."

Eagent looked down self-consciously. "Aye, sir."

With that, Reikos headed off to help Jak at the mainmast — until their pursuers got closer anyway. There'd be some tricky maneuvers to perform soon, he'd no doubt, and it had been far too long since he'd done any of the real sailing himself anyway.

～

Sian's silks had begun to come unbound, dragging at the water. And the tossing, moonlit surface was disorienting in the darkness. She was deeply spent, but very grateful when they finally reached something solid to grab hold of.

The islands' raft warrens were the sort of place everybody knew existed, but no one ever went to. Sian had never even seen one from less than a great distance away. As they'd swum here, she had anticipated a great cluster of ragged little boats, tied to some tawdry lattice of loosely tethered planks: a floating version of the beachside shantytown near port on Cutter's. What they now found, however, seemed more a floating island, made entirely of densely packed, woven and wire-bundled reeds. Its bristled sides were steep and firm, extending several feet, both down into the darkened water and up above the surface. Though it was not too hard to secure a grip on this strange, thatched shore, it proved too high for them to climb after such a swim. It took a while to find someplace gently sloped enough to allow them up and out at last.

For a moment, they just lay on the rough surface of the 'island', catching their breaths, then rose to gaze around at what seemed an entire village made of coarse, dry grass — and utterly abandoned. They heard no voices, saw not a single lamp or lighted window, or even any drifting smoke. To Sian's surprise, however, the moonlight revealed not only narrow streets and little gabled huts, but cane-fenced yards — and even gardens full of growing plants — all floating on this giant raft of reeds.

"Where has everybody gone?" Arian whispered.

There were little boats — most made of woven reed as well — moored here and there along thin canals bisecting the false, thatch 'ground' like a second set of streets. Sian had seen such boats quite often, all around the city, rowed by humble fishermen or messengers. The water taxis were all made of bundled reeds as well. She had never wondered where such boats came from — or went back to at night. If any of their owners were here, however, they were well hidden.

"Have they fled the fighting?" Arian wondered aloud.

"But ... there is no fighting here to flee," Sian replied. Perhaps this place simply held no interest or value for any of the factions raging across the rest of Home. Or maybe everyone had just forgotten, even now, that it existed.

From somewhere farther east came another round of cannon fire. She and Arian turned anxiously to look. But if it came from Orlon's ships, they'd gone too far around the bending coast to be seen anymore. Sian silently begged her new god to protect poor, brave, stupid, gentle Pino.

As she thought of him, it dawned on her that she and Arian might both as well be naked, for all the coverage their sopping silks afforded now. "We should at least unknot our dresses in case somebody comes," she told Arian, reaching down to finish unbinding her own shift.

"Oh. Yes. Oh dear," said Arian, looking down at her own bare limbs and sheer skin of silk. "If we're lucky, maybe no one's here, and we'll be dried a bit before we reach land."

As they began to 'dress', Sian saw Arian unbind her sandals from a length of knotted silk at her side, and grimaced. "I've lost my shoes again," she sighed.

Arian glanced at Sian's feet, then rolled her eyes.

"I was so busy worrying about Pino. I didn't even get them off before we had to leave the boat like that. They were gone as soon as I hit the water."

"Well, walk carefully until we're out of here," said Arian. "These dried reeds feel smooth enough right now, but their edges will be sharp as knives, I imagine. If you cut your feet up, I can hardly carry you across the island."

Thanks for the warning, Mother, Sian thought, trying to wring out the unbound silk around her legs. Her feet were getting tough by now — and would heal, gods knew, no matter what she did to them.

When they'd done their best, and bound up their wet hair, they moved warily into the eerie little village. The packed-reed streets had been stomped into a straw tea of sorts, almost as soft as stiff cloth against her skin. No danger of cut feet here. *All this might be sort of cheerful by day,* Sian thought, noticing fanciful little reed-woven garden sculptures in one small yard. Bougainvillea grew around someone's porch from woven baskets. A mobile of straw stars and crescent moons swayed gently from the gable of another tiny hut. She saw no sign of any real wealth, of course, yet it all seemed so ... tidy. Not what she'd expected. Not what she'd been told.

"Who are you?" said a piping high, but stern, voice from behind them.

Sian and Arian spun in unison to find a girl — a woman — something in between — melted straight out of the darkness. Her drab, loose, home-spun clothing only made her age even more ambiguous. Her skin and hair were very dark, her expression sober, and unafraid. "What you want here?"

"We ... are refugees," Arian said uncertainly. "From the fighting ... You do know about the fighting on the other side of Home?"

The girl-woman's look conveyed with embarrassing eloquence what she thought of being called stupid.

"We seek your help," Arian added meekly.

"*My* help?" The girl laughed. It was a girl. Her laughter made that clear — neither quite mocking, nor exactly kind. Only children had the knack of laughing that way.

"We were ... cast from a boat out there," said Sian.

"We know," said the girl. "We hear the cannons." She paused, staring at Sian as if expecting some further explanation.

"We just want permission to pass through your village," Arian said. "And perhaps to beg a pair of sandals for my friend here? She lost hers when we ... were thrown from the boat."

"Oh. Well then, you come talk to Rothkin." She walked past them, beckoning them to follow her further into the warren.

"Who is Rothkin?" asked Arian.

"My brother," said the girl. "He in charge of things like permission now. He know about the sandals too."

Arian looked at Sian, who shrugged, and turned to go with her. Acting frightened wasn't going to help them any; she was fairly sure of that much.

As they moved down the miniature street, Sian quickly realized that they were not — had never been — alone at all. Here and there, lamps bloomed in windows as they passed. A weathered old man appeared to watch them from his darkened doorway. Between or behind some of the huts, she saw shadows moving in the shadows now. A soft splash made her turn to see a man in silhouette, silently poling his tiny reed boat through a canal toward the moonlit sea beyond. It felt like a village full of ghosts now. Only the girl ahead of them seemed quite solid.

They were led further down the lane, around a corner, down another hut or two, and underneath a reed-latticed gateway into a yard filled with woven baskets, from which pea vines twined up tall reed-stalk cages, guarded by little bowl-hatted men, also woven from reeds.

Ahead of them, the girl pushed the hut's wired-cane door open without a word or knock, and beckoned them into the dimly lamp-lit interior.

Sian followed Arian in, surprised again to find a room much larger than she would have guessed outside, though with just a single window that seemed to provide little ventilation. The stifling air here carried traces of something... rotten. Barely detectable, but foul. The hut was hardly illuminated by the orange light of a single oil lantern, its walls reed-thatched like the hut's exterior, and furnished only with a cane-made table and some weathered wooden stools, cane shelving along one wall, and a host of rough crates and buckets filled with everything from vegetables to clothing scattered around its dim perimeter. A single darkened doorway, without any door, pierced the room's back wall. Leaning against its jamb, a dark-skinned young man with cropped black hair, hardly older than Pino, gazed at them with lazy insolence as they took in his home. Sweat stained his sleeveless shirt, and beaded on his forehead and bare arms.

"Would you be Rothkin?" asked Arian.

"Yes, Factora Lady," he said smiling, then turned to Sian. "Welcome to our humble house, Our Lady of the Islands. We very pleased to give you refuge here, if that what you want."

Sian and Arian shot each other a look of alarm. "How do you know us?" Arian asked.

"My cousin's child tell me," Rothkin said. "She know *many* things nobody else do now." He glanced down at the door behind him, and Sian nearly yelped aloud to see another, even smaller girl melt out of darkness there — her haunted gaze unmistakable.

"*You!*" Sian breathed.

The girl said nothing, only gazed at her again with those same dark, penetrating eyes. But Rothkin nodded, as if Sian had confirmed something.

"I thought you know her," Rothkin said. "You do this to her, no?"

"Do what to her?" Sian asked, nearly as helpless before the child's gaze as she had been on Pembo's beach that morning. "What is she doing here?"

"We come to Rothkin after you witch my little girl," said the child's mother almost timidly, appearing in the darkened doorway behind her daughter. "The world's not safe for us, since they start finding out what we can do. Everybody makes us tell them … what they don't want to hear." She glanced oddly at Rothkin. "Then they punish us."

"I don't understand," Sian said, dragging her eyes forcibly from the child's gaze to look up, bewildered, at her mother. "I did nothing to your girl."

"I saw the way you look at her," she said. "I remember. Then she start to talk to me." She put a hand to her head. "In here. She start to tell me things she cannot know. Why you gave her this, my lady? Why you witch my girl?"

To Sian's further confusion, the woman sounded more … *reverent* than accusing. "Truly, I did nothing. Nothing that I …" She thought back on that strange moment. The gaze she couldn't break. She'd thought it was the girl who'd held her there, but … Had it been the god? Had he done this to the child that morning? Through Sian? The idea horrified her. Could she change people just by looking at them now? She shook her head. Impossible. There were too many people she'd have given anything to change with just a glance since then. "What does she do now?" Sian asked fearfully.

"I don't just tell you?" Rothkin asked. "She a seer, now, *Our Lady*. God-touched, just like you." He smiled at the child proudly. "She tell us all about this war is gonna come. She tell us the Factor gonna die." He glanced dispassionately at Arian, who only paled and cast her eyes down at the floor. "She warn us when somebody come who mean us harm, so we can make them have a little accident in time." His smile turned sharp-edged. "A lot of little accidents today. Nobody come here now so much. Fight pass us by. When the cannons shoot out there, she tell us you come too." He studied Sian in the lamplight. "You don't give her this?"

Sian shook her head. "I think … her gift is from the god, perhaps. Like mine."

Rothkin gazed at her, then nodded without asking her which god she meant. Had he been in some prayer line she had passed, she wondered, or there on the night that she was beaten? *Little accidents*. Yes, this young man might have watched that night — and given it no second thought. Just another *little accident* in a life full of them, she suspected. He was frightening.

"So then … you two just … recognize each other? That what happen on the beach?" He asked as if her answer might be part of some private calculation. Whether to help them, maybe.

"Perhaps." Sian turned to look down at the little girl, then went to crouch before her. "I'm sorry, dear. The world isn't safe for me anymore either. It isn't easy, helping gods, is it."

The girl just stared back, her gaze more sad than frightening now.

"What's your name, child?" Sian asked.

"She don't talk," said the girl's mother. "She never talk, even to me, before …" The woman touched her head again. "She tell me what she know now. Up here. I'm the one who tell out loud." She looked down sadly at her little girl. "I'm the one who made us trouble, with my big mouth. Back there on the beach."

"She want sandals, Rothkin," announced the girl who'd brought them here, evidently tired of waiting to get down to business. "And permission to pass. That why I bring them here." She looked to Sian, as if for confirmation.

"My son … is very ill," said Arian, looking up again for the first time since

Rothkin's careless reference to her husband's death. "We are trying to get Our Lady of the Islands back to the Factorate in time to —"

"Yes, I have no doubt you do. We get to that, Factora Lady." Rothkin waved her off as if she were just some intrusive barmaid, and looked back to Sian. "If you don't do this to my cousin's girl, maybe you wanna heal her then, yes? Give her a voice, so she don't have to talk inside her momma's head no more?"

Sian's stared at him. "I'm not sure ... that I should even try to heal what the god has done."

"The god don't make her mute, Our Lady. The god just make her see these secrets — and fill her momma's head with things she got no power to shut out. If the girl have a voice, maybe my cousin get some peace, yes?" He shrugged, as if to ask, *What's the harm in trying?*

Sian looked back at the little girl. "Do you want to talk, dear?" The question came from nowhere, surprising Sian as much as anyone. But, to her further surprise, the child shook her head — quite emphatically. Sian looked up at Rothkin, who looked down at his cousin's daughter as if she had displeased him. Sian turned back to the little girl. "Are you sure?"

The girl nodded, just as firmly.

"She does not want a voice, it seems," Sian told Rothkin.

He rolled his eyes, and turned to his cousin, throwing his arms up as if to say, *I tried. What more can I do?* Then he looked back at Sian. "I just ask one more favor, then, Our Lady, and we talk about the sandals, yes?"

"What is it?" Sian asked, hoping he did not want her to help arrange somebody else's *little accident.*

"You come back and see my mother now." He waved toward the lightless door. "I know *she* wanna be healed. You do this, we talk. I promise." He glanced at his younger sister. "Bring the light, Faya." He started for the darkened doorway, beckoning Sian, but still ignoring Arian.

Sian held back, reluctant to go near the door — until Faya had brought the lamp, at least.

"Mamma," Rothkin cooed. "You got a visitor. Someone gonna help you heal, okay?"

As Faya reached the doorway with her lamp, Sian and Arian were left standing in near darkness. Rothkin turned to Sian, and beckoned her again, impatiently. A few steps from the doorway, Sian realized that whatever she'd been smelling since they'd entered was back there. Everything inside her balked. What was she being asked to heal this time — to experience in her own flesh, however briefly? If this was the price of freedom for herself and Arian... She forced her legs to take her forward, and stepped through the doorway struggling not to retch.

The floor was all but covered with straw pallets in various states of disrepair. This must be where they all slept — in this stench. A rough hole had been cut into one wall; an ad hoc window, she supposed, to ventilate the room a little. Faya stood in the farthest corner now, beside the thickest of these pallets, holding out her lantern over a pile of tangled, rough hemp bedding, which, a second later, moved. An aged woman, almost indistinguishable from her soiled sheets, more skeleton than flesh, turned to look at them, and began to cough convulsively into a blood-soaked towel clutched in her hand.

"*Ohh...*" Sian groaned, backing to the wall to keep from falling, in tears before the word *bloodpox* had finished resounding through her mind. She threw her hands across her eyes but couldn't keep from sobbing as her mother's long and dreadful death of this disease came back in every searing detail. An instant later, it *was* her mother lying on that blood-soaked pallet; a lifetime, or was it just a day or two ago. Part of Sian wanted just to rush to her. Make it stop, immediately. The other part was terrified of taking that into herself.

With a sob so deep it nearly choked her, Sian launched herself from the wall and ran across the room to plunge her hands across the woman's jutting collar bones. "Mother!" she cried, shaken by the force of her own sobbing. She dropped her cheek onto the woman's chest, above her heart, no longer aware of anyone inside the room but the woman and herself, as her own lungs filled with the agony of thickened blood. "Mother... no!" she gasped as she began to be smothered in it, literally drowning in the sickness. Rotten ginger filled her nostrils — a relief against the even worse putridity of the disease itself. Sian writhed involuntarily, and gasped for air, as the woman she now lay across coughed and writhed and moaned. Sian willed the life back into this woman — into her mother — into herself. She willed all of them — all of her — to hold on, not to fall over … Not to lose consciousness before …

She came back to herself on the floor, still coughing and gasping, to find everyone from Rothkin to Arian, who now leaned wide-eyed with horror against the doorjamb, gaping down at her in shock. Only the mute child and her mother smiled — as if they shared some happy secret that the others hadn't learned yet.

Struggling to rise off the floor and put her hands back on the woman, Sian could only turn her head, just far enough to see Rothkin's mother, still and silent, slumped half off the pallet.

"What … did you done to her?" Rothkin breathed in horror, lunging forward to grasp his mother's body gently, and hoist it back onto her bed. As he set her down the woman took a gasping breath, like a drowning swimmer reaching surface just in time. Rothkin let her go and jerked upright, clearly startled as her eyes flew open, and another gasp was followed by a couple of drier coughs, then another gasp. "Mamma?" Rothkin's voice was filled with quiet fear.

"Oh … my son," she whispered. Her voice was filled with wonder. "I can breathe."

"Mamma?" Rothkin croaked, tears leaking from his eyes as well now, to Sian's dull amazement. He dropped to his knees beside Sian and lifted his mother's body into his arms again, crying almost as hard as Sian had done before. "Mamma … are you really well?"

"I … think I may be," she murmured, sounding at least as surprised.

Rothkin rocked her in his arms and wept like a small child, as Sian felt the horrid darkness she'd been drowning in begin to dissipate within herself as well. Even the air seemed to smell better now — unless her nose had simply become inured to it already. *Thank you*, she thought. She closed her eyes again, and let her strength return, listening to the sound of deep, unencumbered breathing from the straw pallet behind her, between Rothkin's quiet sobs. *Thank you … thank you*, Sian kept repeating in her mind. For the life given, and for what had been taken. There was something missing now, deep inside herself. Something sharp, and dark, and heavy that she'd never been aware of. And always wanted gone. *Thank you.* She felt so much lighter. Almost light enough to drift up off the floor, and stand again.

"Our Lady of the Islands ..." she heard Rothkin moan, opening her eyes to find him kneeling at her feet now, bent to kiss the long-dry hem of her soiled silk shift. He looked up at her, still leaking tears. Just minutes earlier, she would not have thought him capable of any such emotion. "When you come into my door tonight ... I don't think you'll do this ..." His face began to cave in on itself again. "For any man ... like me." He shook with a new effort to rein in his tears, and lost again. "It no mistake the god bring you here," he wept. "I see that now. Real clear." He nodded, to her or to himself, she couldn't tell, then turned back to Faya who still held the lamp, trying to stare at everyone and everything at once. "Set that light down, girl, and go get them all. Tell 'em to get any kind of weapon they can get, and bring them here."

Faya stared at him a moment, then set the lantern down and ran out of the room as Arian stared after her. Sian heard the front door thud closed as she left the house.

Rothkin turned to her again. "I give you all the sandals in this village now, and fill them with an army."

"An ... army?"

Instead of answering her, Rothkin turned to look at Arian. "We chase away all kind of armies here today, Factora Lady. We can get you and Our Lady of the Islands to the Factor House to heal your son. Without any trouble. You see now, what the reed people can do."

THIRTY-TWO

As Reikos worked beside Jak beneath the mainmast, half his mind kept straying to the reckless speed at which he'd ordered them to dance across these shallows, while the other half could not quit wondering what on earth Escotte Alkattha was doing out here himself. Powerful, self-important men of the Census Taker's sort did not risk themselves this way. More importantly, perhaps: what should Reikos do about it? If they blew Alkattha out of the water here, would it end this war? Or just get Reikos and his crew all hung?

Alkattha *was* still the Census Taker of Alizar. And for all most people knew, the Factor had initiated these hostilities. The Factor was now most likely dead, and thus no longer able to rebut whatever stories the Census Taker's camp spread afterward. History was written by the victors, after all. Everybody knew that. And Alkattha's conspiracy wouldn't need Alkattha himself to win this, any more than a Factorate victory was dependent on a living Factor. No. While Reikos would have been all too happy to repay Alkattha's recent *hospitality* right here, with a cannon, he could not risk making fugitives of all his men — should the conspiracy go on to win this war, and declare Alizar's second-highest official a martyr to their cause.

So, yes. They ought to run. If there were any hope of doing so. As he hauled on the main topsail sheet, Reikos glanced back to see how much the catamarans had gained on them, only to remember that from down here, he couldn't see past the poop deck to know what might be happening to stern. That was a captain's privilege.

Up at the helm, he saw Kyrios in animated conversation with Molian and Eagent. They were clearly planning something, and Reikos itched to know what. But that too was a captain's privilege, and he had given Kyrios command. It had been perhaps his only good decision that night. The man had proven smarter than himself — or more clear-headed anyway — many times since leaving Cutter's. Perhaps a week in someone's dungeon followed by a day with neither food nor sleep to speak of was not the best of preparations for such a ... challenging voyage.

"Er, Captain?" Jak broke tentatively into his reverie. "Are we still runnin', sir? Or ... preparin' to come about?"

Reikos glanced up the mast to find that he'd been hauling at the topsail sheet for far too long now. He grinned sheepishly, and began to play it out again. "Thank you, Jak. I am distracted, I fear. After ordering you all night not to be. If you see me doing it again, don't be polite about it. Just give me a good cuffing, will you?"

"Sir?"

"I'm joking, lad. I'll keep my head about me now."

"You don't just want to go back up to the helm, sir?"

"Not while we're racing my ship across this wading pool, no. Let's tie this off and tighten up that course sail, shall we?"

"Cats now lead the schooner!" Reikos heard Dolous shout from back at the mizzen. "Closing to no more than fifty cables!"

Fifty cables! By the gods, those boats were flying.

Kyrios called out from the helm, "All hands, prepare to come about, one hundred fifteen degrees to port!"

Damn it, Alkattha will have us as we stall into the turn, Reikos thought wearily, bending to the mainmast winches beside Jak. *Right back into the bastard's hands — or to the bottom, more likely.* He could see no way around it now.

"On my mark, boys!" Kyrios shouted.

"Cats at twenty cables!" yelled Dolous.

Reickos closed his eyes. He'd tried.

"Come about!" Kyrios called down. "Now!"

Everyone set to at the winches, hauling the sails above them into close reach. Within seconds, the boat began to slow as it veered hard to port.

They were not even through the turn, however, before Reikos saw the prow and pontoons of one of Alkattha's cats surge abreast of them to starboard. He shook his head and continued hauling at the winch, wondering if Alkattha would just sink them now, or play with them a bit first. The latter did seem more his style, from what little Reikos had been able to observe back at the Census Hall.

"All hands, prepare to come around, full stop into the wind!" called Kyrios.

Reikos turned back to stare at his first mate, astonished that he hadn't at least a little more spine than this, then looked back across the prow, and understood. The cat that had just passed them had come about as well, directly in their path, its swivel-mounted cannon manned now and pointed dead on at *Fair Passage*.

"You're on your own here, Jak," he sighed, turning to pick up his jacket and go back up to the bridge. He had vainly hoped that Kyrios might pull some further miracle out of his sleeve, but he wasn't going to ask the man to negotiate their surrender now. That really was a captain's burden. He climbed up the companion ladder and walked to the wheel to clap a companionable hand on Kyrios's shoulder. "Thank you for trying, friend. And for everything you've accomplished here tonight. I'll navigate this part."

"Thank you, Captain," Kyrios said very quietly, neither looking at him, nor even moving his lips much. "But, the outcome here may still be less clear than it seems. If you wouldn't mind trying to keep Lord Alkattha talking for a moment, we might see what we see."

Reikos raised his brows, then quickly lowered them again, seeing the Census Taker's other cat just off their port side now, Alkattha on its deck in a pool of lamplight, watching him and Kyrios with interest through a spyglass. "Very well," he said as quietly, wondering exactly what his first mate and his gunmen had been discussing so earnestly up here a short while ago. "Think twice before you kill the Census Taker, though," he murmured through tight lips. "We could be hung for that, if the Factorate should lose this war."

Kyrios nodded very slightly. "I'm aware of it, sir."

Reikos went to the portside railing and raised a hand to greet Alkattha, who lowered his glass and grinned up at him — with ... was that a *monkey* on his shoulder?

"Captain Reikos!" Alkattha called across the water with something rather like delight. "How surprising! I had not expected to see you again! Least of all here."

"I might say the same, Lord Census Taker! Whatever are you doing out here on a boat?"

"Sparing you catastrophe, it seems! Had I not ordered my captain over there to block your way, I'm fairly certain you'd have run your ship into the bottom any minute now! Are you unaware of how much shallower the waters are here?"

"Are you aware that there's a rat crawling on your shoulder?" Reikos asked. *Sparing them catastrophe, indeed.* "Perhaps you ought to order your captain to keep a cleaner ship, my lord!"

Alkattha frowned at him, reaching up to stroke his monkey's back, as if concerned about its feelings. "I have heard the most astonishing rumors about your antics tonight, Captain! Can there be any truth to tales that you've the Factora-Consort aboard somewhere?"

Reikos saw the Phaeros' little schooner arriving off the stern, finally caught up again to its larger, faster companions. *Tattletales.* "What an absurd idea, my Lord Census Taker! I am only here executing my *secret mission* for you, of course!"

"So my erstwhile sergeant told you about that, did he? I am aware of his escape as well! He's been quite the thorn in my side all day long, actually! Is your little friend here too, then? The boy? Sadly, I cannot recall his name!"

If he didn't know where Pino was, better that he have no reason to keep looking. "*Sadly,* Pino did not survive the destruction of your palace!" he called back flatly.

"A shame," Alkattha tutted, reaching up to pet his monkey again. "I hate to see my cousin's talents wasted so!"

"Is that why you handed her to the temple, my lord?"

"What a lot you seem to know, Captain! Is she perhaps aboard your craft as well? What a harem you've collected in so short a time! Your reputation does not begin to do you service!"

"I have no idea what you mean, sir! There's no one on this ship except me and my crew!"

"Don't waste time being coy, Captain." Alkattha waved negligently toward the little schooner, now just heading toward *Fair Passage's* starboard side, hemming him in quite effectively. "I was all but gone when they informed me you were hung up on a pier nearby, in your haste to bring me the Factora-Consort as a parting gift. It would be even kinder if you've brought my cousin too, so that I might convey them both safely out of this dreadful conflict!"

"All but gone, my Lord Alkattha?" Reikos said, genuinely surprised. "You're going somewhere?"

The monkey bared its teeth and hissed at a member of Alkattha's crew who'd come too close on his way to keep the cat's huge sails trimmed — drawing Reikos's attention to the fact that they were maintaining careful readiness to sail again at any moment. Hardly the stance of a man confident of victory. Fleeing! That's what Alkattha was doing on this boat! Reikos — or more accurately, his imaginary passenger — were just a last-minute afterthought. He glanced back at Kyrios, whose raised brows signaled that the significance of this was not lost on him either.

Alkattha grabbed the irate monkey from his shoulder, and cradled it against his chest — rather more in restraint than in affection. "Though it's clear by now that I am to be blamed for all of this, I've been but a pawn in someone else's game — as were so many of us here. Now that my poor cousin Viktor has expired, there will be no one who can clear my name, however, so, as you can see, I must be off to join my lovely Violethé on the continent."

"The continent! Then why your interest in the Factora-Consort?" Reikos asked, no longer bothering with seemingly outmoded honorifics.

"In games like these, scapegoats need bargaining chips at least as badly as real villains do, Captain. If I have someone the real culprit wants, a lot of stupid things may not be done to me that surely will be otherwise. Now, if you'll send me the Factora-Consort — and Sian Kattë as well, if she's aboard — without any further trouble, I will not order your ship sunk right here." With another languid gesture, he indicated the gunman now manning his own craft's swivel-mounted cannon.

"You're ready to send your bargaining chip to the bottom with us, are you?" Reikos asked, far from sure a man desperate enough to flee would truly be that cavalier. Time to gamble. Big. "What if your first shot misses — and mine does not?"

"My sources tell me that your guns are all to stern this evening, Captain. You will notice that none of us are there to shoot at, while my ships are positioned to all three of your remaining sides. There seems very little chance that we will miss."

If he'd really meant to shoot, Reikos thought, he'd almost certainly have fired as soon as he'd received threats instead of compliance. Time to gamble even bigger, then ... "Kyrios, I think it's time we carried on," he said just loudly enough to feel sure that it would carry. "Ram his cat, if necessary. It can't be anything like as sturdy as that dock we just knifed through."

"Don't be stupid, Captain!" Alkattha shouted. "Carry on to where? You'll run aground here within minutes — any way you turn!"

Yup. Bluffing — or they'd definitely have been dead by now. Just as he'd assumed, Alkattha was a midnight backstabber, not a fighting man. Probably didn't want to be accused of murdering the Factora-Consort too as he ran off. What would he do, Reikos wondered, if *Fair Passage* simply started creeping forward again? Alkattha must feel some pressure to be on his way before someone came 'round to stop him, too. Did he have time to risk a real fight? He'd clearly come expecting *Fair Passage* to be hung up on that pier. Had he just been reaching for low-hanging fruit on his way out of town? Reikos was about to test his luck again, and find out, when the sudden roar of cannon came from port and bow at the same instant, sending him twisting away to throw himself down in shock, along with the rest of his crew. *The bastard! I was wrong!* A third cannon fired from somewhere just to starboard. There wouldn't even be time to apologize to anyone, he thought.

And yet ... The deck beneath him hardly swayed. All the shouting and the sounds of wrecking came from ... much too far away. He raised his head, and looked about at other faces as nonplussed as his. He and Kyrios had just started scrambling to their feet when yet another cannon sounded, sending everyone to deck again.

This time, *Fair Passage* bucked fiercely as a crackling spray of shattered planking flew from her forward port side and a chunk of quarterdeck leapt up to fly in pieces just above the heads of crew nearby.

There was a moment of stunned silence then, broken only by continued cries of fear and anger from the other ships around them. Reikos leapt up again, scanning his deck for casualties. Everyone seemed there and up already, rushing to and fro to check for further damage, or staring around themselves in stunned confusion. No one had been lying on that patch of deck, thank all the gods. Both masts were up still, and their rigging seemed intact. It didn't look as if the cannon ball had taken out anything structural on its way through. Shot from such a short distance away, it had probably punched through fairly cleanly. Reikos spun next to scan the sea around him, unable to make any sense at all of what he found there.

To port, Alkattha's catamaran, which must have fired the ball that hit them, was already racing off. Beyond *Fair Passage's* bow, Alkattha's second cat was foundering, its crew and a great deal of expensive-looking furniture and other cargo already bobbing or flailing in the water as it sank. To starboard, the Phaeros' schooner leaned heavily to port, trailing its snapped-off mizzenmast in the water.

"I … had Molian and Eagent move our guns, sir," Kyrios said, pale and shaking as he scanned their own damaged deck and the carnage all around *Fair Passage*. "One to starboard, one to port, and one positioned to be pointed at wherever our third pursuer might decide to park. Then …" He turned to Reikos looking frightened. "I gave them permission to load and fire at their own discretion. If we were fired on, or seriously threatened." He shook his head apologetically. "I didn't think that there was likely to be time for orders, sir. Not with three cannons stationed all around the boat, and just two men to fire them."

Reikos stared at him, still struggling to put everything together, then felt himself begin to grin. "You raving madman!" he laughed. "*You god-humping genius!*" He threw his arms around the half-stunned man, who only then began to laugh as well. Abruptly Kyrios stopped and wrenched himself from Reikos's grasp.

"Molian! And Eagent! They were below when —" Kyrios spun to sprint for the aft hatch. Reikos followed.

They had just gotten down the ladder when Molian staggered into their path, looking crazed but whole. "Captain! Eagent's stuck, sir! I need help to get him out!"

"Take us!" Reikos exclaimed. "How badly is he hurt?"

"Not hurt, sir," Molian said as they continued running toward the starboard bow. "'Least he says he ain't. But when that ball went through the deck behind him, he got buried in a pile of plank and timber. They're wedged against each other pretty tight. I couldn't lift 'em, and he's on his stomach, sir. Pinned too tight to turn much but his head. Says he's only stuck, though."

Reikos feared the boy might just be putting up a brave front, or too injured to feel any pain. He'd seen such injuries — to back or neck. They almost always proved the death of anyone who suffered them, within days or weeks at most. There was no more glow of triumph shining in his gut now. Only dread.

As they arrived and saw the mess, however, Eagent's color did seem good, though his expression was fearful as he turned to peer at them from underneath the drift of shattered wood that covered him from calves to shoulders. By the light of a lamp that Molian must have left there, it looked as if the buried cannon beside him held up half the pile, which had doubtless saved the boy, if saved he was.

"I'm sorry, Captain!" Eagent rushed to say. "I know you told me not to, but Kyrios —"

"I know! Calm down, lad. You're a flaming hero with no cause to apologize. Now, are you injured? Tell me straight, boy. I'll just hold bravery against you at the moment."

"Honestly, I'm fine, sir. Nothin' I'd call pain except it isn't very comfortable where some of these planks press on me."

"Can you feel your arms and legs then?" Reikos asked as he began to test the pile, wondering how best to disassemble it without risking further injury to Eagent.

"Oh yes, sir. I just ain't got room to move 'em much."

Reikos allowed himself a sigh of relief. "Then don't try, lad. We'll have all that off of you in just a minute."

They set to with a will, careful about the order in which things were pried away. As promised, they soon had him out and on his feet, where, to everyone's relief, he proved as well as he had claimed, but for some ugly cuts and bruises.

"Let's get you stitched up and bandaged, then." The ship's doctor had been kind enough to leave them some of his medicinal spirits and healing gum when he'd abandoned the *Fair Passage* after Reikos had gone missing. "Did he leave us any cat gut, Kyrios?"

"Aye, Captain, and some clean needles too."

"Very well, I'll leave his care to you then while I —"

He fell silent as they all turned to the clamber of someone running toward them, and saw Sellas rush in, looking frantic. "More boats comin', Captain! A bunch this time — and headed right our way!"

A mob of astonishing size had coalesced in eerie silence around Rothkin's hut by the time Arian followed him and Sian outside. Men and women. Even children. She could not believe there were so many of them; hundreds easily, where only a short while before, the village had seemed all but empty. They stretched off into the moonlit darkness, gripping everything from clubs, gaffing poles or pitchforks to machetes and stiletto knives, and stood nearly motionless as Rothkin climbed onto an overturned wooden box beside his garden gate.

"We take these ladies to the Factor House now," he said, his voice carrying with startling clarity on the still night air. "Nobody get close enough to see them the whole way." He looked down at Sian uncertainly, then back out at his army. "Hurt nobody you don't have to, yes? The world hang on this. You understand? This is Our Lady of the Islands here."

All faces turned to Sian in the darkness. Without a sound. A shiver ran down Arian's body as, here and there, people dropped onto their knees. Not a word about the *Factora-Consort*. Nor a look her way. This was Sian's army. Sian's night. Arian knew that now as well as anybody present. It felt strange … freeing even, to be so … *inconsequential*.

The only serious affliction Sian had ever healed in Arian's presence before had been her own injuries the previous night, and Arian had been lost inside her own experience of that event. Only as she'd watched Sian heal Rothkin's mother had she really come to understand what it must cost Sian every time she did this. What it might cost her to heal Konrad. If there was still time. Arian would gladly have gone down on her knees too now, if the look on Sian's face had not revealed so clearly how much discomfort such veneration caused her. Arian understood that dismay all too well. Having to inhabit someone else's dream of who you were. So many someone elses. It was a dreadful thing. A smothering responsibility. Arian pitied Sian in ways she'd never thought to — but she still wanted her son healed.

"You know what to do," Rothkin told his people, stepping from the crate. He beckoned Sian and Arian with a jerk of his chin as he stepped into the street. "Stay by me," he told them quietly. "Don't leave my side. For any reason, yes?"

As they left the yard behind, the crowd fell in around them like some enormous cloak of shadows — moving almost as silently as they had stood. An army of ghosts. Arian wondered how many of these *reed people* there might be in Alizar. This was only one of many such raft warrens in the islands. What a powder keg they'd all been sitting on, for gods knew how many years, up on their hilltop, fretting at their petty politics and intrigues …

What a farce their lives had been, she thought.

And yet, Sian had been commissioned by a god, it seemed, to heal her son. Arian agreed with Rothkin about one thing. It seemed very strange that mere coincidence had tossed them up on this small raft of reeds tonight, where so many things they needed, and so many people who seemed to need Sian, had all been waiting ready. If Sian and her god cared so much about reaching Konrad, then perhaps their lives weren't *just* farce after all.

I will try to take the world more seriously. To matter more. If I ever get an-other chance, Arian promised Sian's god in the silence of her heart. *That is not a bargain, sir. Just … a vow.*

In very little time, they reached the floating island's northern edge, and started, three or four abreast, across the relatively narrow bridge of float-ing reed pontoons and weathered wooden planks that separated it from Home. Even now, Arian heard so little sound behind them that she had to turn and look to be sure their army was still following. An endless stream of shadows silhouetted by the moon, yet hardly any footfall or ripple did they make. They moved like the breeze-born reeds for which they named themselves — or even like the breeze itself.

Ahead of them lay the streets and rooftops of the *other* island, Home; caught up in fear and chaos. Like the floating village, it seemed dark, if less abandoned than furtive and afraid. Small figures in the distance dashed from door to doorway, or hurried down the street, hugging walls or glanc-ing nervously back over shoulders. Light burned in scattered windows and atop infrequent lampposts, but the brightest illumination up ahead, by far, was the orange glow of fire cast from beyond the ridge top.

As they reached the bridge's other side, Rothkin stopped Sian and Arian with an upraised hand, while some of those behind them streamed past and fanned out to dissolve into the all but vacant waterfront — emptied by a long day of *little accidents,* perhaps? When a little less than half of Rothkin's force had passed them, he waved Sian and Arian back into their stream.

"Remember," Rothkin murmured back across his shoulder. "Do not leave my side."

As they got closer, Arian began to see smashed market stalls and the half-submerged wreckage of small boats littering the waterfront. Climbing up into the empty, winding streets above it, shattered windows and burned-out shopfronts trailing wraiths of smoke and reeking with the smell of char, gave mute testimony to the fighting that had passed there earlier that day.

Those who'd come across the bridge with them were gone now, vanished back into the darkened streets around them. Only Rothkin and two of his henchmen, an older man he called Stoke and a boy even younger than himself named Bartolo, remained to lead Sian and Arian up the hill, at an almost leisurely pace, surreally alone.

As they passed the demolished entrance of a dark and empty tavern, a nearly inaudible groan drew everyone's eyes toward a table overturned within its street-side courtyard. Bartolo drew the knife from his belt, then vaulted on one hand across the courtyard's bamboo railing, moving toward the fallen table with the grace of a hunting cat. Once there, however, he stuck his knife back in his belt and shrugged. "Good as dead," he muttered, turning to rejoin them.

Sian moved instantly through the small courtyard's gate and started for the table.

"Lady, no," Rothkin said.

She raised a hand to silence him, neither looking back nor slowing, and shoved the bamboo table to one side as Bartolo looked uncertainly to Rothkin for guidance about what to do. "Let her," Rothkin told the other boy.

Sian bent down and pushed a hand against the fallen man's torso, then inhaled sharply, threw her head up, eyes half closed as if in pain, and seemed to freeze that way. Arian stared, with all the others, wondering if one could ever get used to seeing miracles like this performed, as the man's whole body seemed to flex, going rigid as a board before falling limp again. Sian's chin fell too, her long hair tumbling down to hide the fellow's chest and face, slumped in exhaustion, or maybe just in shared relief.

As she stood again, breathing deeply, and turned to go, the man she'd healed brought both hands to his stomach, then raised his head and stared at her. "What ... did you do?"

She neither answered, nor looked back as she came out the gate. "Can you ... Is there any way that I might get a bite to eat?" Sian asked Rothkin. "Healing makes me very hungry."

"Our Lady, why you not say something sooner? We can feed you at the house, if you just ask us." He turned to Bartolo, and jerked his chin at the darkened tavern door.

The boy dashed inside, and was out again a minute later with a loaf of bread and a bowl of passion fruit. "This enough to fill you, lady?" the boy asked.

Sian nodded gratefully and tore the loaf in two, handing half to Arian.

"Thank you, my lady," Arian said, not thinking the words strange until they'd left her mouth. Were they, though? So strange? Sian was … something more than Arian could ever hope to be. She looked back to find the man Sian had healed standing now, staring at them.

Rothkin saw it too. "You go now, if you wish to live," he told the man, almost gently.

"Let him come with us, if he wants," Sian said, without looking up from the fruit she peeled with trembling fingers.

"Lady. Who know what folk he side with? What he do to you, if he get close enough."

"We've already been much closer than you can imagine, Rothkin," Sian said. "There is a *person* inside everyone I heal." She looked up at him, at last. Intently. "You taught me that. Back in your mother's room."

Rothkin looked down in … was that shame? *Miracles on top of miracles,* thought Arian.

Sian turned to face the newly healed man. "Are you my enemy?"

He shook his head. "No, my lady. I am … whatever you wish me to be. But, who are you?"

"She is Our Lady of the Islands," Rothkin said before Sian could answer. "And you owe her your life. Do not forget this."

No longer looking at any of them, Sian started walking up the street again, bringing the partially peeled fruit up to tear at with her teeth. Seeming almost horrified, Bartolo ran to take it gently from her, and started peeling and cutting it in slices with his knife, handing each piece to her tenderly as everyone resumed their walk. Behind them, the newest member of their entourage followed uncertainly, keeping his distance.

As they got further up the hill, Arian began to notice new sounds in the night. Disturbing sounds. An angry shout cut short from perhaps a street away. A strangled cry just minutes later, from the opposite direction. They followed Rothkin up the street alone, still seeing not a single person but themselves. Around a corner up ahead, Arian heard running feet, a wooden thump, and brief, almost inaudible scuffling sounds. When they reached the intersection, a young man — one of the reed people, clearly — smiled reverently at Sian as she walked by, then faded back into the darkened alleyway that they were passing.

What was Rothkin's army *doing* out there in the darkness?

Two blocks later, they found a man facedown in the street, moaning softly. His knife wounds were very fresh. Had this *accident* befallen him just for being in their way, Arian wondered queasily, or had he done something worse to earn his wounds? How many innocent people were suffering along their route tonight just because she and Sian happened to be passing by? Rothkin rolled his eyes as Sian bent to lay hands upon the body. Minutes later, they moved on again with yet another dazed but grateful servant of *Our Lady of the Islands* in their train.

The next fallen man they found had clearly been there for considerable time. He was still breathing, raggedly, but his left leg was bent forward at a wincingly unnatural angle. The dusty remnants of his armor — what looters had left him, Arian suspected — indicated that he'd been a member of House Orlon's guard. His injuries, at least, had likely been well earned, she thought.

Nonetheless, Sian reached down to put her hands upon him.

"Our Lady," Rothkin said, his face and voice filled with conflicting impatience, reverence, and shame, "we walkeen through a war zone here. It get worse as we get closer to the Factor House. You stop for everyone, we don't get there before dinnertime tomorrow."

"He wears Orlon's colors, Sian," Arian agreed. "The same people firing at Pino when we saw him last."

"I … don't think that matters," Sian said wearily, thrusting her hands onto the fellow's leg.

This time, they both screamed very loudly for quite a while, as the soldier's broken leg performed maneuvers that made even Rothkin look away almost at once. When the screaming had died down to whimpers, Arian turned back to find the man's leg straight, a look of astonished wonder on his face as he stared at Sian, who lay beside him, still gasping for breath.

Arian went to crouch beside Sian, and took her hand. "You cannot do this. It's taking too much from you, and we have so far to go."

"I … I can't *not* do it, Arian," Sian panted. "The gift … wants to be used. It … hurts to …"

"Sian, I think …" Arian glanced warily up at Rothkin. "I think the longer it takes us to pass through the city, the more people will be injured."

At first, Sian just looked confused. Then she turned to Rothkin, startled. "Is this true?"

"Is what true, Our Lady?" Rothkin wouldn't meet her eyes.

"I won't have people hurt just because they're in my way."

"Bartolo!" Rothkin snapped, looking frustrated. "Go tell them be more careful."

Not to hurt people, Arian wondered, *or not to leave them where Sian will find them?*

The boy ran off into the dark, as Rothkin looked apologetically back at Sian, now rising from the ground beside her latest beneficiary.

Stoke came immediately to place a supportive hand under her shoulder. "Now what we do with him?" he asked Rothkin, nodding at the guardsman who still lay upon the ground, perhaps not yet quite trusting his leg — or his luck.

"His house fighteen the Factor all day, Our Lady," Rothkin told Sian. "He an enemy of yours for certain."

"But I'm not, my lady!" said the soldier, crawling hesitantly up onto his knees at last. "I did serve Orlon's guard. It's true. But Orlon never gave me … what I have received from you. I serve you, my lady! Only you now. Truly."

"He say that to save his life," Rothkin sneered. "I say the same if I am him."

"I don't think that matters either … anymore," said Sian, turning almost vacantly to continue walking, with Stoke's assistance, toward the hilltop just ahead of them. She hardly seemed to care where she was now; who was watching, or what they thought.

What are we doing to her? Arian wondered anxiously. *What will this world do to her?*

Rothkin shrugged unhappily, and turned to Orlon's one-time guardsman. "You go ahead of us, and stay where I can see. Do exactly what I tell you, or I put you back where Our Lady find you, only both legs this time, yes?"

The man nodded, hurrying to get ahead of them as he'd been ordered.

Just shy of the crest, they came upon a fourth man lying in the street. His swollen face and hands were red, raw and blistered by fire. He too wore armor — this time of House Alkattha. Some member of the Factorate's contingent, Arian saw, not the Census Taker's. He keened pitifully as they approached, staring blindly at the sky, seeming unaware of them entirely.

"Please, Our Lady, no," groaned Rothkin as Sian walked stolidly toward the man. "Let … let *me* take away this misery from him." To Arian's alarm, he drew the machete from his belt. "He don't wanna be here anymore, Our Lady. I can promise you. He don't." He walked toward her, crooning, as if to a small child too innocent to understand such evil in the world.

You still don't see, thought Arian. *She already knows far better than you or I ever will.*

"He been gone a long time now already," Rothkin went on, placing himself in Sian's path just steps away from where the burned man lay. "His body just too dumb to know it yet."

"Your mother didn't know that I was there when I first touched her." Sian walked around him as his eyes began to glimmer in the pale light. With tears again, unshed this time.

A moment later, Sian lay atop the burned man, keening just as he had keened when they'd first arrived. Arian forced herself to watch now. It seemed the one brave thing that she could do. The only way not to abandon Sian as they writhed together, dancing horribly upon the ground. The soldier's face began to blur and soften as the angry welts and swollen, waxy mats of burned skin vanished. Sian grimaced as if suffering every burn, though her skin remained unblemished.

Arian looked back at the guardsman's nearly healed face, and gasped. "Oh! … Oh no, *Joreth!*" She ran to kneel beside him, and took his healed hands, blurred again, by tears this time. Joreth was a member of her husband's personal guard — a trusted friend of many years. She had not recognized him behind such awful scars, but the face before her was now more familiar than Sian's. "Oh, my dear Joreth, I'm so sorry. I'm sorry we have done this to you!" She laid her head down on his chest and cried.

"My ... Lady Consort?" he whispered. "Am I dreaming? ... Am I dead?"

She looked up, startled that he could have recognized her, given both their states.

"No, no," she wept. "You're fine now, Joreth. You've been healed."

"How?" He looked back over at Sian, and Arian saw understanding dawn across his recovered face. He was likely to have been among the very few told where Viktor's consort had disappeared to, and whom she'd gone to rescue. "Thank the gods," he murmured. "My lady ..." He looked back at Arian. "The Factor is half mad with grief. He's feared you dead for days."

For a moment, she could find no voice to answer him, so great was her own grief at what she must have put her husband through, before ... "Is he ... Have you seen him?"

"Just this morning, my lady, before I ..." Joreth looked confused. "What night is this?"

"Factora Lady," Rothkin said. "I don't like to break this talk up, but if you want to see the Factor House before dawn come ..."

"Yes. Of course. I'm sorry." She wiped quickly at her eyes, and stood.

Stoke now sat with Sian's head cradled against his chest, a stoic sadness on his weathered face. With a long, unsteady breath, Sian let him help her to her feet as well.

"Our Lady," Rothkin told Sian softly. "This gonna kill you soon, I worry. Please." His eyes drifted up the street ahead. "If we find any ..." He seemed to freeze, staring at something.

Arian followed his gaze, but saw only more rubble and ruined shopfronts.

Rothkin blinked and turned back to stare curiously at Sian, then down at Joreth. "You can stand now?" he asked brusquely.

Joreth climbed unsteadily to his feet. "What do you need of me, sir?"

Rothkin turned to the other three men Sian had healed, huddled together like skittish ponies now. "You three, go with this one. Bring Our Lady *that*." Rothkin pointed up the street, and only then did Arian realize what he'd been staring at amidst the wreckage there.

The bedraggled remains of a once-elegant curtained litter lay on its side, where some wealthy merchant had likely abandoned it when overtaken by the fighting.

The three men glanced at one another, then went as ordered, with Joreth right behind them, to turn the litter over, lift its poles onto their shoulders, and bring it back to set beside the woman who had given each of them their lives back.

"Nothing the god do get wasted," Rothkin said, grinning strangely at Sian. "I have to learn this many times." He gestured grandly at the litter. "The way to take you, Lady, and four men to carry it. The god provides."

She looked mortified at the conveyance, and shook her head. "That's not why I healed them. I can walk as well as anyone. Why else have you given me these sandals?"

Rothkin shook his head. "No, Our Lady. You are weak from all these things you do. We get you there to heal the Factora Lady's son much faster this way. That is best, no?"

"He's right, Sian," said Arian. "Reikos and Pino have given so much to help us get there. Please, just listen to him."

"Thank you, Factora Lady." Rothkin gave Arian an almost courtly little bow. "I think there room for two in there. You keep Our Lady company, please."

His tone was not that of a man just trying to be nice. She bowed her head in acquiescence and went to help Sian into the litter's dusty, silk-lined interior. When they had been lifted back onto the four men's shoulders, Rothkin came to pull the curtains closed around them.

Sian raised a hand to stop him. "I wish to see."

"No, Our Lady. It not safe. The curtain make sure others don't see who we got here." He swept the last one closed. "And you don't see them either," he added through the gauzy fabric.

Clever, Arian conceded silently. "He's right, again, I fear. We're wanted women, Sian. It's not fair of us to put these men in extra danger either. Let it go."

Sian closed her eyes, and leaned back into the cushions sewn onto their bench, clearly far too tired to argue anymore. And just as well.

The trip went much more quickly after that. The litter's creaking frame and swishing curtains made just enough noise to hide the sounds of any other *little accidents* that might be happening in the distance — though Arian dared hope there wouldn't be as many of them now. One could not control the world. That much, she had always known — if not as vividly as the past few days had taught her to.

She was nearly asleep herself when something at the edges of her awareness roused her. She startled awake to the sounds of many voices lifted up in … distant chanting. "What is happening out there?" she asked. When no one answered, she asked again more loudly, reaching to pull one of the curtains back. The streets ahead of them were filled with firelight, she thought at first. But then, she realized that it was cast by candles, carried by a streaming crowd.

"It's a prayer line, my lady," came Joreth's voice from his position at the pole just behind her. "The second one we've seen."

Rothkin came to close her curtain. "Now, for certain, you stay hidden, Factora Lady. My people say these prayer lines everywhere tonight. They go all up to the Factor House, like us. We got to join one soon, I think. No other way left open, and we maybe even safer in a crowd with them. I hear they very happy about something. But we want nobody see you, yes?"

"Yes," she said. "We don't. Sian's asleep, but if she wakens, I'll explain to her."

"Thank you, Factora Lady. You not so bad as I think once. I hope your son get well."

"Thank you, Rothkin. I am very grateful for all you've done tonight. If my husband's government should win this war, I hope we'll have the chance to talk again, perhaps. About a lot of things that should have been discussed a great deal earlier, I think. Agreed?"

"Oh yes, Factora Lady." Though she could not see his face now, she was certain she could hear him grin. "I think we talk about a lot of things when this is over. Right now, keep the curtains shut. You do that, and *we* keep Our Lady safe."

THIRTY-THREE

"Is Alkattha with them?" Reikos asked, already heading past Sellas toward the ladder.

"No, sir. He's long gone. They're small boats, mostly. Nothing half as fast. Sloop-rigged fishing boats, I think, and a yacht or two."

"Whose colors do they fly?"

"Too far away to tell yet, Captain."

"Eagent, I'm afraid those stitches will have to wait. The starboard cannon is a loss for now, but you and Molian go move the other two back sternward, please."

"Aye, sir." They went trotting off.

"Kyrios, let's go see if we're still fit to sail."

His first mate groaned. "We're at full stop, sir. They'll be on us before we get *Fair Passage* moving."

"How far back did you say they are, Sellas?"

"Clear back on the other side still, Captain. With a lot less canvas, once we're underway."

"There, Kyrios. It sounds worth a try. What better option have we got? The tide's still high, and we seemed to be doing pretty well before those cats showed up."

They arrived on deck to find the crew already scurrying in preparation — carefully avoiding the big hole in *Fair Passage's* quarter deck, of course. Reikos and Kyrios went straight there to stare down into the raggedly latticed gap, perhaps ten feet across. "Deck beams still seem fairly sound. Must have come up straight between them."

"Damn lucky shot," Kyrios agreed. "For us, at least."

"See anything else down there that looks like it should stop us?"

"All of this should stop us, Captain. But we came out here to wreck your ship, I guess."

"That's the spirit. Go up and take command again then, will you? You've still got those charts far better mapped out in your head than I do. I'll continue helping Jak out at the main."

Moments later, Kyrios called out from the helm, "All hands prepare to fall off the wind, fifty degrees to starboard! On my mark... Now!"

The winches ratcheted away, the sails turned into the wind again, and *Fair Passage* started moving ponderously to starboard. A few minutes more, and the ship had gained some real speed. The pursuing flotilla of fishing boats was still quite a ways away, off the port side now, allowing Reikos a clear look. They'd closed the gap enough for him to see that, as he'd feared, they were the same small swarm of lightly armed House Sark vessels he'd spotted trailing them beyond the bridge to Apricot. Where in this fight had House Sark come down? Not that there was room to wait and find out now.

"Prepare to come about!" Kyrios called down. "Ninety degrees from starboard!"

That was going to slow them down, Reikos thought sadly, hoping there wouldn't be a lot of turns like this before they'd put some extra distance between themselves and Sark.

There was no warning when they ran aground. Not the briefest scrape along their keel to let them find a grip on something. The ship simply slammed to a full stop, sending nearly everyone and everything not nailed down flying forward with terrific force. Watching the deck sweep past below him, Reikos had sufficient time to think, *This is really going to hurt.* Then his shoulder hit the breastwork, and he bounced perhaps six feet onto the forward hatch's grating, still too numb with shock to feel the impact very clearly.

Above him, the top halves of both masts bounced forward and broke off, leaving him just time to roll out of the way as the main topgallant mast careened toward him, taking out at least half the stays and other tackle as it came crashing down. Toward the stern, he heard the mizzen crack, and men cry out in terror as the rest of that mast fell — across the starboard rail, by some good fortune. The deck slid into a lean, weighed down now by the dragging mizzen.

Others were crying out in pain now, as the lancing knives in Reikos's own shoulder began to register. For a while, he was too faint to do much more than lie there, waiting for his thoughts to catch up with his body. Then he struggled, moaning, to his feet to gaze back at his ruined ship. At least three of his seven men still lay where they had fallen, though none so still as to be dead yet, groaning and clutching at sprained or broken limbs. Kyrios was one of these. He'd been thrown from the helm, over the rail onto the deck below, and now lay twisting in some agony underneath a tangle of fallen rope and tackle draped across his torso. Reikos staggered toward him across the slanting deck, clutching his left shoulder, fearful it was broken, but too concerned for his first mate to care. "Kyrios!" he yelled. "I'm coming!"

He reached the man, and bent to lift the tackle with his good hand, gasping an obscenity at what this small effort did to his bad shoulder. Happily, the two fallen blocks seemed to have missed Kyrios by inches. What lay on top of him was only rope and small shards of wood.

"Sorry, Captain. Sorry, sorry, sorry …" Kyrios moaned, his eyes still barely open.

"Shhhh now … This was my fault, none of yours." *Oh, the gods. It is. It is. We could have just surrendered.* "How badly are you hurt?"

"My ribs … sir," Kyrios groaned. "A few of 'em … did not much like … goin' through the rail."

"Blood and ashes. I am sorry, Kyrios. I've been so much a fool. Can you breathe?"

"Hurts, sir … Pretty bad. … But … I don't think there's … any fluid in 'em …" A bit more light and focus seemed to reach his eyes. "We're listing, sir."

"We are. The mizzen's hanging in the water off our starboard rail."

"Captain!" Eagent called from somewhere near the aft hatchway. "We're taking water, sir! Molian and me can hear it below decks! I think the bow's gone this time."

"The boats," moaned Kyrios. "The lifeboats. … Better get them … in the water …"

"Yes," said Reikos, standing. "Or they'll get too fouled to launch." He stood and shouted, "All able crew, report to me, right now!"

He was relieved to see everyone coming but Jak, who still lay moaning near the starboard breastwork, and Dannos, who leaned against the poop deck railing above them clutching at what looked to be a badly broken arm.

"We need two lifeboats launched!" he said. "My shoulder's broken, I'm afraid, or I'd be on it. Sellas, get Kyrios here strapped to a board, and careful of his broken ribs. We don't need a punctured lung to go with them. Molian, get Jak strapped to another. Eagent, help him not to twist Jak any more than we can help it 'til we know what's broken in him. Get them and Dannos into the boats first, then … we go." He turned to Molian and Eagent. "How bad is it down there?"

"Sounds like a river in the holds, sir. Pretty bad, I think."

"Then let's hop to it, lads. Dolous, cut me off some rope and a big patch of that netting there. Then help me bind this arm up. I'm useless with it hanging here."

"Aye, sir!" All his men rushed off to start their tasks.

As Dolous sawed at the indicated rigging, Reikos struggled up the slanting deck toward the port rail, to see how far away Sark's fishing boats might be. Still a good twenty minutes off, he guessed — for all that mattered anymore. They'd likely all be seeing dawn inside a prison somewhere now — if they were that lucky. *What an ass I was to run*, he thought miserably. *We'd not be going to jail with broken bones if I'd just had the sense a captain ought to … What's happened to my brain?* Too much. That was what. He knew it. Far too much had happened to keep up with in there these past weeks. Not that he'd forgive himself the sooner for having this or any other excuse so handy. He had failed his crew, and badly. What he'd not have given now to go back and change it all. He could feel the deck list further underneath him. They might not have much longer to get off this boat.

"Captain?" said Dolous behind him. "I've got what you asked for, sir."

"Let's get this over with then, shall we?"

Reikos tried very hard not to cry out while Dolous bound the arm against his side and chest, and failed at that as well. By the time the deed was finished, the rest of his crew were ready at the lifeboats on the starboard side. Thank the gods they only needed two for such a tiny crew. The portside boats were nigh on useless now already.

Reikos thanked Dolous and started down the inclined deck, but stopped and looked back at the aft companionway, remembering Matilda with a shock. "Wait! My parrot!"

He started toward the ladder, but Dolous was there before him. "I can get her faster, Captain! You get in the boat!"

This was only sense. Reikos nodded at the man's retreating back and continued toward the lifeboats. By the time they had him in and situated for the drop, Dolous was back, holding the cockatiel's cage at arm's length as the agitated parrot shrieked, *"Damn bird! Damn bird!"*

Reikos saw a grim smile or two as Molian called, "Lower away!"

For all their effort to be gentle, Reikos embarrassed himself by crying out again, along with Kyrios, as their boat hit the water. Then they started heading from *Fair Passage's* side, two able men to row per boat. As they departed, Reikos gazed back sorrowfully at his lovely brig, already riding almost to the cheek in water at her bow. *You were a quite a beauty,* Reikos whispered to her in his mind. *I failed you too. I'm sorry.*

It was predictably slow going, of course, and they'd hardly gotten up to speed before House Sark's little fleet was all but on them. Reikos looked down at Matilda, who stared up at him as if to ask exactly what all this was for. *"Kiss me, beauty,"* she croaked softly.

Reikos shook his head. "No reason you should go to jail too, my dear," he said, lifting her cage with his good hand. "They'd probably just eat you. Savages." He turned to Dolous. "Help me with the latch, will you?"

The man did easily what Reikos couldn't do at all with just one hand, then leaned away, clearly nervous of the bird as Reikos swung the cage door open, and shook Matilda out of it. She plopped onto the deck, ruffling her feathers at such rude treatment. "You're free now, dear," said Reikos. "Go find a real boy bird somewhere. I'm no good for you."

She only waddled about across the swaying planks at their feet. *"Damn bird! Damn bird!"* Reikos took a gentle swat at her with his foot, which just made her flap up onto the bench. *"DAMN BIRD!"* she screeched in outrage.

"Dolous, throw her over the side, please," Reikos said.

"Sir? ... She bites, sir!"

Rolling his eyes, Reikos stuck his hand down to pick up the bird himself, and sure enough, she stretched her neck and bit down on the skin between his thumb and forefinger as if trying to crack a nut there.

"Gods!" Reikos yelled, flinging her spastically aloft, spattering Dolous beside him with drops of blood in the process.

The bird fluttered in the air, then spread her wings and glided off across the surface — only to return a moment later, flying round and round the lifeboat squawking incoherently. Until the first of House Sark's sloops arrived, whereupon she lit out for the distant shoreline, screeching, *"Damn bird! Damn bird! Damn bird! ..."*

"I no doubt deserved that," Reikos said, proffering his bloodied hand to Dolous as the sloop luffed its sails and came around to pull up beside their boat. "Could you tear a strip off of that shirt, and plug this as best you can, lad?"

"Captain Reikos?" asked a voice that he was startled to recognize. "What in hell were you trying to accomplish back there? Are you gone mad?"

Gaping, Reikos peered up through the darkness to see Sergeant Ennias gazing down at him from the other boat. "Oh ..." he groaned, hanging his head, and struggling not to cry. "All of this. For nothing."

"Captain ...?" Sellas asked. "Do you know this man?"

"I thought ... Everyone who's chased us here tonight wanted us dead," Reikos said, not just to Ennias, but to anyone who'd listen as he struggled to explain it to himself. "Alkattha just took off the way you came from, after trying to sink us."

"I know," said Ennias. "We saw him."

"Then ..." Reikos looked up in confusion. "You didn't try to stop him?"

"He's not really that important anymore. It's the Factora-Consort we must have. Is she in the other boat?"

"No. She's not here at all, obviously."

"Then what's happened to her?" Ennias looked back in obvious concern at *Fair Passage*, which had already rolled onto her side, almost half submerged. "You didn't leave her on —"

"We never had her, Sergeant! That was just my first mate — in a dress."

Now it was the sergeant's turn to gape. "Why in the name of every wayward —"

"We were trying to draw enough attention from Home's shoreline so that Pino could get the Factora-Consort and Sian ashore! They'll be somewhere back on Home by now, I hope. Maybe even at the Factorate already."

With an incoherent growl of frustration, the sergeant slapped a hand to each side of his head. "I've been chasing you the whole damned night, Captain! For nothing!"

"Well, aren't we the pair then," Reikos sighed. "I have three badly injured men on these two lifeboats, Sergeant. And a broken shoulder of my own, I believe. If you're sailing back to Home now, might we catch a ride?"

∼

Reikos watched as portions of the Factorate House still smoldered atop the hill above them. The streets not blocked by fire were strewn with injured soldiers and civilians, not to mention wreck and rubble. But the fighting itself seemed finally to have ended.

"As you can see, it's mostly mop-up now," said Ennias as he and Reikos left the wharves behind in one of the two-man runner-carts House Sark's officers had generously arranged for after they'd come ashore. "I'd be quite surprised if the former Census Taker isn't far to sea already. The tide turned decisively against his forces well before I went running after you."

Ennias had caught Reikos up on the course of his own day as they'd sped back to Home. Reikos's injured crewmen had been brought to Apricot for medical attention in a quayside treatment camp set up there earlier that day, though it appeared they might be forced to wait there quite a while for it. Apparently, the Temple Mishrah-Khote had suffered an extremely ill-timed internal uprising of its own that morning, precipitating a serious shortage of priests to tend the brief war's countless wounded.

Soon after Reikos and Pino had left Ennias on Home, to go look for Sian on Malençon, the sergeant and Hivat had followed a rumor of her recent arrest and gone to seek her and the Factora-Consort on The Well — only to find the massive temple compound sealed against outsiders as its own small civil war raged on inside. *Very ugly, from what we've heard,* Ennias had informed him. *Alizar was just one great pile of dry tinder, eh? Who'd have guessed it?*

Fortunately, a number of the priestly healers had been spread throughout the island chain on other business when their temple had imploded that morning. Enough to assemble a small force to triage and treat the mounting number of wounded as the day had progressed. There were clearly nowhere near enough of them to keep up with demand, though.

Happily for Reikos, one of the Sark fleet's captains had happened to possess a quantity of marvelous powder to kill pain, which was making Reikos rather sleepy now, but had him not all that bothered by his wounded shoulder anymore. Given this temporary relief, and the dreadful shortage of physicians now, he had elected to forestall further treatment of his shoulder until after they'd found Sian. Of course, if they found her, he'd likely need no temple physician at all ... The thought seemed self-serving — every time he thought it. So he kept dismissing it. His shoulder really didn't seem so bad anymore. Perhaps it was just a bad sprain, after all.

Having spent the remainder of this punishing day fighting first beside the Factor himself, and then beside his chief of security, Hivat, Ennias was by now a veritable font of fascinating information. He'd confirmed the death of Viktor Alkattha, though his government had won the day, it seemed. Reikos had thought immediately of the Factora-Consort. Not to have been there, or even aware at the last. No chance to say goodbye ... There was too much pain to deal with here, and very little of it truly his. He was a foreign seaman who hadn't even known most of these people even weeks ago — excepting Sian, of course. He'd had to keep reminding himself of that, though the pain powder helped him set things down as well ...

Perhaps most interesting of all was another fact, uncovered by Hivat that afternoon, according to Ennias, as some of Escotte Alkattha's more reluctant co-conspirators had begun to get cold feet. It seemed the Census

Taker had dressed Lord Orlon's house troops up as Factorate guard the night before, and ordered them to blow up his own Census Hall that morning! When Ennias had first informed him of it, Reikos had responded with an uncertain laugh — assuming that his powder had prevented him from understanding some kind of joke. Only once the sergeant had explained that it'd been done so that Viktor would be blamed for starting these hostilities while Escotte Alkattha cultivated public support as the innocent victim, did Reikos understand what a truly sick man they'd been dealing with. If Escotte had won, the sergeant had conceded, it might have worked. But as the war had gone against him, and the truth leaked out, that strategy had apparently come to backfire quite spectacularly. The Census Taker's name seemed destined now to become a new obscenity in Alizar's rich lexicon — or so the sergeant claimed.

"So ... you don't think there's any truth to his claim that he was just a pawn of some other usurper?" Reikos asked as their cart runners struggled uphill through all the chaos.

The sergeant shook his head. "Just another of his endless lies, I'm sure. From what Hivat could determine, by the time I left to chase you down, at least, of all the houses who opposed the Factor, only Orlon did so willingly. The others were apparently coerced against their will by the Census Taker — which likely has a lot to do with why he lost. Escotte had threatened to expose things that I guess they thought too ruinous to survive — last night, at least." The sergeant shrugged. "I'm betting things will look pretty different to a lot of them this morning."

"Why did Orlon go along with this?"

"He's been an angry man with big ambitions for some time. He probably kept on fighting so long after others had surrendered because he knows his head will fall first and hardest."

Reikos sighed and looked up at the choking crowds ahead of them. They were going to have to leave this cart soon, he expected. There'd be no getting past whatever all of that was up there. "If only we had known this ... Any of it, just a couple hours earlier," he murmured, as much to himself as to the sergeant. "My crew would never have been injured. I'd still have my ship. And … I just hope the Factora-Consort and Sian have gotten here as safely by now." *Oh please, please, please* … he begged Sian's god through the fog of his new medication.

"We'll know soon enough," said Ennias. "We're almost to the top." He leaned forward to call up to their runners. "Gentlemen, I thank you, but we'll just get out and walk from here, I think. Do you know what all those people are about?"

"Oh, they prayer lines, General," said one of them, clearly mistaking his rank. "Come from everywhere tonight. They say Our Lady of the Islands at the Factor House!"

"By all the gods, I hope so!" Reikos said, rising to step carefully down from the cart, assisted by the other runner, who came rushing up to help him. "Let's go, Sergeant."

In less than optimum condition to be elbowing anyone aside himself tonight — or this morning, rather; he saw the horizon beginning to lighten — Reikos followed Ennias uphill, through the press. It took them almost fifteen minutes to wade just another street or two up through the chanting, cheering throng, all waving candles and exclaiming jubilantly about the Factor's victory. The *dead* Factor's victory, of course. Reikos doubted Arian was celebrating much tonight. Though, if Sian had healed her son by now …

"*By all the gods …*" Ennias gasped ahead of him. "Reikos, look at this!"

Reikos pushed his way carefully to the sergeant's side, and gaped as well. Filling every inch of ground for at least five hundred yards ahead of them, a solid mass of people stood all but motionless, bathed in candlelight, fanned out in all directions, every face turned toward the island nation's tortured house of government. There was no cheering here. Just the mighty, rumbling chant of countless voices raised in … prayer, he supposed, though he could not make out a single word of what they said — if they said words at all. Their chanting was a massive, rumbling sea of sound that swelled against the house's walls, and slid away again. "What is this?" Reikos said in awe, too softly to be heard even by Ennias. *Are you in there, somewhere, Sian?* he wondered. *Is it you they sing to? Or to something larger?*

～

She swam through waves of light ... lakes of fire. Carried on a rushing, lumi-nous current that compelled her ever forward, neither eager for, nor frightened of, whatever waited at its end. She was meant to go there. Quickly though.

She spread her arms, trying to swim faster. Or to fly. Faster than the river flowed. 'Don't fight the current,' something told her. 'Ride it. There is time. You always try too hard.'

She thought she knew what was meant, though not from whom these thoughts were coming. It did not occur to her to ask. She just listened, with understanding, and fell still, allowing herself to be carried on the moaning, rumbling song this fire sang. Such sad music. So much suffering. So much hope. So filled with —

We're here.

Where?

Wake up. We're —

"... here, Sian. Wake up, my dear."

Sian opened her eyes to find Arian leaning close with an apologetic smile. They were in some small room ... Or, no. Curtains. They were closed inside a litter; she remembered now, and knew something else as well. Something she had learned — or remembered — inside the dream already fading. "Trying too hard ..." she murmured, more to herself than to Arian.

"Trying ... what?" asked Arian.

Sian pushed herself upright. "Where are we?"

"At the Factorate, finally." Arian looked at her curiously. "Or nearly there, at least. I just peeked through the curtains, and saw it up ahead. But there are too many people now to move at all. They're shouting that the war is over, and that ... the Factor has won. They ... don't seem to know he's ... Do you think the rumors could be wrong, Sian? Could Viktor be alive still?"

Before Sian could answer, Rothkin's cautious voice came through the curtain next to her. "Our Lady, you awake? ... Can you hear me, Our Lady?"

"Yes. Can we get out of here, please?"

"Our Lady, we all but there. I can throw a rock and hit it. But I don't know how we get you to the building. There a swarm of marchers like the beehive out here now. The litter already make everybody look, but they don't let us through. ... Unless maybe I tell them who inside."

"Well, if you're going to tell them that, then we should just get out and walk," Sian sighed. "Arian thinks her husband's won the war already. Is that what you're hearing out there?"

"That what we hear, yes," he said uncertainly. "But ..."

"Then, who's going to try hurting us right here at the Factorate — in front of all these witnesses? Do these people seem angry at me or Arian for some reason?"

"No, Our Lady. No. They seem ... They wait for you, I think. If one of my folk tell them, I cut the bastard's tongue out, but I don't think so, Our Lady." There was a lengthy pause. "I think ... maybe ..." He sounded almost frightened. "Can the god tell them, you think?"

"I don't know what the god might do any more than you do, Rothkin, but if these people don't seem to want us harmed, then it's time you let us out."

The curtain beside her slid open just an inch or two. "Look out here," Rothkin said just loudly enough to be heard. "Tell me you sure about this first."

Sian leaned to peer through the crack.

For a second, she recalled the lake of fire from her dream, and sucked in a startled breath. But then she saw that it was only candles, thousands of them, and a sea of marchers, just as she'd been told. *Don't fight the current.* "I think it's time," she said — sure neither of what it was time for, exactly, or to whom she spoke anymore. She swept the curtain open. "Thank you for all you've done, Rothkin. I'm very grateful, but we'll just walk from here. You're free to go, or stay, as you prefer."

"I go nowhere, Our Lady!" Rothkin said, reaching up to lift her down. "I guard you 'til you inside the Factor House, at least."

A number of those around them had been watching for some time, it seemed. Before Rothkin had Sian's feet on the ground, someone nearby gasped, "It's her!"

"He called her Our Lady!" Sian heard someone exclaim. "She's come!"

From all directions, faces turned.

"She's over here!" shouted someone else. "Our Lady of the Islands!"

Rothkin put his back to Sian, a hand falling to his machete as Bartolo and Stoke rushed to flank Sian. "Stay back!" he shouted.

Worried by the fear in his voice, and what it might portend, Sian leaned up and said into his ear, "It's all right. The god didn't bring us this far just to let his own followers stop me now."

In truth, she had no idea what would happen, or whether they might hurt her. But though she recognized the thrill of fear within herself as well, it was being held down, kept far away, by some much closer, stronger … not quite compulsion, or just resignation either, but … *surrender.* To what she was now. What she had become. And to the certainty that all she'd been through since that young priest had seized her life and beaten it into this inscrutable new shape would finally come to some resolution here. She just wanted this thing done, whatever it was. How it happened, or what was done to her now, no longer seemed to warrant her attention.

"Make a path, you all!" cried Rothkin, still sounding fearful, but letting his hand fall. "Our Lady of the Islands got to get inside the Factor House! That why she here! In the god's name, let her through!"

As the four men she'd healed on her way set the litter down and gathered around her as well, the nearest watchers seemed unsure of what to do. The cries still rippled outward through the crowd, growing louder as they went. *Our Lady of the Islands! The Lady's come! …*

All at once, the ring of bystanders nearest them parted. "Let her through!" a man barked to those behind him. "Make way, for Our Lady of the Islands!" others called to those further out.

Move back! Make way! Let the Lady through!

The call spread, knifing through the crowd like the prow of some great ship, until there was a clear path before her, all the way to the Factorate's massive marble stairway. There, before the doorway, she saw the Butchered God's young priest looking back across the distance, as if he too were only mildly surprised to find her here.

"See them …" Rothkin breathed, gazing in awe at the path her mere presence had opened. "How they know you, Our Lady." He went forward first, followed by Bartolo and Arian, all virtually unnoticed by the crowd, who stared only at Sian.

As she stepped into the now almost silent gauntlet, followed by Stoke and her erstwhile litter-bearers, voices to either side began to murmur. *Our*

Lady... Heal us. Help us, Our Lady. Oh, Our Lady... A hand reached out timidly to brush her as she passed. Then another.

Stoke tried to bat the reaching hands away. Then Rothkin realized what was happening, and whirled angrily to shout, "Leave her be! You kill her, fools!"

"Rothkin! Don't," Sian said firmly. "It doesn't hurt me anymore." *Or not as much, at least.* "The god has ... shown me something I was doing wrong. Let them be. It's why I'm here."

He gazed at her as if she'd wounded *him*, then turned away to continue walking toward the Factorate steps.

Soon many arms stretched out to touch her arm, her sleeve, her hair. Each time, she felt the prick of pain, the illness or the wounds they carried, physical or emotional, and the healing flow from her. She knew what to do now, though. How not to try too hard.

She had remembered, in the dream, or after waking maybe, the night she'd healed so many people after temple thugs attacked their prayer line. One after another, she had touched them, hardly stopping, yet been left no more than tired and a little hungry afterward. Wondering why, Sian had realized that she'd not stayed with any of them long enough to suffer much that night. And still, they'd all recovered. Only since she had come to accept her gift, and learned to anticipate the pain, to feel *responsible* for taking every drop of what they suffered on herself — as if her own suffering were some required cost of being allowed to work such miracles — had these ordeals become so punishing. *You always try too hard.*

Though she'd surely paid as much as anyone by now, these had never been her miracles to pay for. Or even to do, really. She saw that now. She was, at most, a conduit through which the god's power flowed. She let them touch her now, and moved on, trusting the god to complete *his* work whether she remained to watch or not. The *god* was not Arouf, needing to be managed by Sian. This thought almost made her laugh. Almost. She was too tired, even for laughter.

Our Lady of the Islands, heal me! Please, Our Lady! Heal our Factor! Heal Alizar, Our Lady! Please, Our Lady, please! She let them reach. She let their fingers find her. She let the god's power flow, and suffered very little now, but for an aching weariness that grew inside her as she inched closer to the Factorate House. For all she knew, the god's power might be infinite. But his conduit was made of silk, it seemed. And she could feel threads breaking. Should she save herself for Konrad? Was she *still* trying too hard?

Rothkin turned to look at her again, clearly concerned. She gave him a reassuring nod, and kept walking down the corridor they'd made for her.

Our Lady! Oh, Our Lady, touch me! Please, Our Lady, I'm in pain! Our Lady!

When they reached the steps at last, lifting her feet to climb out of the crowd took surprising effort. She was … so tired now. The Butchered God's young priest rushed down to put his shoulder underneath her arm, his arm around her waist — the arm with which he had once wielded a bone against her — and began half-carrying her up toward the building's once-grand, now doorless, charred and shrapnel-pitted entrance. An instant later, Rothkin was there too, supporting her from the other side as Arian turned to watch them in concern, casting dubious glances at the priest. Did she even know who he was? Sian wondered.

"I tell you not to let them touch you," Rothkin reproached her quietly. "Now look how weak they make you. Why you say nothing to me sooner?"

"I'll be fine," she told him. "I just need a moment's rest once we're inside."

"I am relieved to see you," the priest murmured in her other ear as they ascended.

"Did you bring all these people?" Sian asked.

"I sent out the call. They came of their own will." He looked at her. "If you still have enemies in Alizar tonight, my lady, they will not penetrate this wall, I think — or even try to."

She nodded. "Thank you." She could never have imagined on the night they'd first encountered one another that someday he would be worried for her safety, or that she would thank him for it. As they topped the final step, and stood before the ruined entrance, she looked up into his schoolboy's face, and smiled. A schoolboy's eyes. A face so young. Too lean. Too full of grim resolve. *What happened to you?* she wondered again. *How were you beaten into the shape you bear now?* When this was finally over, she meant to make him tell her.

"May I come inside with you?" he asked.

Sian's brows rose in surprise at the idea that he could think he needed her permission. "Do you know what's going to happen? Has the god ..."

He shook his head and smiled. "I have no idea. But whatever you are going to do now ... I've waited a long time to see this, I believe. That's why I want to come."

"I suppose that is for the Factora-Consort to decide. This is not my home." She turned to Arian uncertainly, careful to set aside the familiarities to which they had become accustomed. They were no longer alone. What happened before so many witnesses would matter now, she realized. "My Lady Consort, this is the priest of the Butchered God, to whom I owe my gift of healing. He wishes to accompany us."

The Factora-Consort and the fugitive priest gazed at one another, each likely waiting for the other to erupt. They had hardly been allies, after all, before all this had changed the landscape so. "Do you wish me to admit him?" asked Arian.

"He is ... not as he has been portrayed, I think, my lady," Sian said. "I have come to recognize and value his wisdom. And his followers do seem to be ... supportive of us." She glanced out at the immense crowd surrounding them, fairly sure that Arian would not need the remaining implications of this decision explained to her.

"Then let us go and see what we will find." Arian turned to lead them all inside.

As Sian followed her toward the massive, empty jambs into the darkened Factorate House, the crowd behind her cheered and cried out more loudly than before: *Our Lady of the Islands! Save us, Lady! Heal our Factor! Save the islands! Help us, Lady! Cure us! Sian!*

At the sound of her name, her own, *real* name, she turned back, as did the rest of her protective entourage, searching the crowd to see who had called to *her*.

"*Sian! Wait! I'm here! I'm coming!*"

Then she saw him, near the bottom of the stairs, just behind someone else she recognized, shoving through the crowd to make a way for him, and for the first time since she'd left Rothkin's hut, her eyes began to well with tears.

THIRTY-FOUR

"We'll never find them in all this," Reikos muttered as he and Ennias struggled to make headway through the massive vigil surrounding the Factorate House. His anxiety was building quickly, despite the powder's muffling cloud. Had Sian and Arian ever gotten here at all? He did not allow his mind to wander toward the darkest possibilities — or refused to listen when it did, at least — but with Pino watching over them, he wasn't very hopeful they'd stayed out of trouble.

"If the Factora-Consort is here, she'll be inside by now anyway," said Ennias. "We just need to reach the door. Whoever's guarding it will likely know me, or …" He fell silent, stretching his tall frame to look across the heads of those around them. "What's happening over there?"

Reikos went onto his toes and tried to crane his neck as well, but pain powder or no, his shoulder wasn't having any. "What is it? I can't see."

"Everybody's moving up ahead. And shouting about something."

Reikos followed as Ennias pushed forward toward the disturbance.

"She's here!" someone ahead of them exclaimed. "Our Lady of the Islands!"

Sian! Reikos thought, washed in relief. "Can you see them, Sergeant?"

"No, but something's cut a swath through the crowd up there."

"Our Lady, heal us!" someone else cried out. "Heal our broken nation!"

"Let's try to head them off!" Ennias called over his shoulder, elbowing even more fiercely through the increasing crush. "Stay with me, Captain!"

Reikos grabbed the sergeant's shoulder with his good hand for fear of being knocked aside by others seemingly as frantic as himself to reach Sian.

"I see her!" Ennias shouted. "Just behind the Factora-Consort! They're both here!"

"Sian!" Reikos shoved around beside the sergeant as they neared the Factorate stairs, and finally saw her, with a small crowd of people at the building's ruined doorway. She had turned to stare out at the crowd. "Sian! Wait! I'm here! I'm coming!"

He saw her find him, and her face begin to pucker. She was going to cry, damn it all. "Sian!" he called again, shoving through the last wall of onlookers, heedless of his shoulder.

"Konstantin!" Sian cried out, as he ran up the stairs, a step ahead of Ennias, for once.

As her arms closed tight around him, Reikos was unable to prevent a shout of pain. Sian flinched back, gasping as if wounded too, and one of her companions — a tough-looking boy in a sleeveless shirt — lunged between them with murder in his eyes, drawing a machete, of all things. Behind him, Reikos saw two knives materialize in the hands of an even younger lad. At the bottom of the stairs, onlookers cried out in alarm.

"Rothkin, Bartolo! Stop!" Sian shouted. "He's injured! I just hurt him! We are fine!"

The fire in young *Rothkin's* eyes gave way to flustered chagrin, as his companion's knives vanished, and Sian reached up to wipe her tears away. The belligerent boy stepped back as quickly as he'd jumped in. "Thought you try to hurt her," he said, half accusingly, as if the whole misunderstanding were still Reikos's fault somehow. "I sworn to protect Our Lady."

"You too, eh?" Reikos looked around for Pino, massaging the renewed pain in his shoulder, which, oddly, seemed to be receding fairly quickly. He looked sharply at Sian. "Did you just — *oh, balls!*" he yelled, as the fractured bones seemed to leap and stretch. He cried out a second time, more loudly, grappling at the injury with his good hand, as if to swat out a fire there, then tearing at the burlap sling in which his arm had been re-dressed. The muscles around his shoulder convulsed again, then seemed to deflate before slumping all at once into position. The relief came just as swiftly and intensely, not only to his shoulder, but all through him. The cloud around his mind cleared as well. He felt well rested and alert now, and … realized the crowd below them had grown almost silent.

The boy called Rothkin gazed at him with naked envy now. The young priest studied him with avid interest. Even Ennias's eyes were fastened on him as he reached up calmly to unbind his sling, then lowered his uninjured arm.

"Well … That smashed thumb a while back was not a tiny patch on this," he told Sian.

The crowd began to murmur, then to cheer again, realizing they'd just seen her work another miracle. A few of them seemed about to start heading up the steps.

"We go in now, Our Lady," Rothkin said, giving Reikos an unhappy look, "or maybe you don't reach the door before they mob you here."

I do believe she's claimed another victim, Reikos thought, alert to jealousy in young men around Sian by now. As everyone rushed her toward the entrance, Reikos glanced around once more for Pino. He'd noticed Arian on his way up the stairs, of course, then recognized the young priest as well. Who all these other people might be, he had no idea, but Pino's absence worried him. Surprisingly, there seemed to be no guards inside the entrance either, which worried him as well. Was the building empty after all of this? "Where's Pino?" he asked Sian.

"Oh, Konstantin, I'm frightened for him." Rothkin went to right an overturned chair, as the priest led Sian to it. "Our boat was fired on by two of Orlon's ships —"

"What?" said Reikos. "Was Pino hurt?"

"He cast us into the water near shore, and led the ships away in *Copper-smith*," said Arian. "I believe we are alive and here at all now because of what he did."

"But, oh, I wish I knew that he was safe." Sian's face was filled with distress.

Heroics, Reikos thought sourly. *I knew it. Damn boy.* From what they'd said, it had likely been the right thing to do. *But if you've gone and gotten yourself hurt, I'll wring your neck, lad.*

"I would very much like him found, Sergeant," said Arian. "Is there anyone who might arrange a search?"

"My Lady Consort, as I see you have a guardsman with you," Ennias nodded at Joreth, "and this fellow who's so handy with the machete, I will go, with your permission, and look for Hivat. He'll know how to find Pino, if anyone in Alizar can."

"Hivat is alive then?" she asked with obvious relief.

"Yes, My Lady Consort." Ennias fell uncomfortably silent, then said gravely, "My lady, you are surely aware ... Has anybody told you yet about the Factor?"

"That he is dead?" When Ennias said nothing, she nodded palely. "I had hoped ... that these were only rumors, but ... Yes. I have known for some time. Thank you, Sergeant. For making sure. Have you ... any news about my son?"

Reikos watched Sian climb wearily to her feet, and go to take the Factora-Consort's hand.

"When I left to pursue ... what we thought was you, my lady," Ennias replied, "your son was hidden under guard with other members of the household in the Factorate cellars, and, to my knowledge, unconscious but alive. I know nothing more, having just returned myself; but, since hostilities ceased some time ago, they may all have been moved elsewhere now." He looked around the expansive chamber. "It does seem odd that there aren't any guards here. Perhaps the building's been evacuated. But, to my knowledge, your family's wing wasn't damaged very badly, and I doubt they would have moved your son farther than was necessary. So you might wish to check up there. I'll be back to let you know as soon as I learn anything, of course."

"Thank you, Sergeant. We have much else to discuss, but it can wait until we know that Pino is safe. When you find Hivat ..." She shook her head. "Never mind. Just go. And thank you."

"Yes, my lady. We are all more glad than you can know to see you back and well."

With that, he turned and headed out into the first, pale light of dawn.

"I go search for this man, Pino, too, Factora Lady," Rothkin said to Arian.

"He disappear outside our village, we know how to find him best of all, maybe. You and Our Lady safe now, like we promise." He thrust his chin at Joreth. "You got a guard and these other men to watch over you here, yes?" He shot Reikos the kind of frown he imagined a father might give his daughter's dubious new suitor. Reikos suppressed a doubtless impolitic urge to grin.

Arian nodded her consent. "Thank you, Rothkin. I will not forget what you have done for us. And I meant what I said before. We will speak again, I hope."

Rothkin nodded without smiling, gave Reikos another baleful look, and beckoned his two henchmen to follow as he left. This seemed a rather fractious little group. Reikos wondered how they'd come together as one of the remaining men, whose partial armor seemed to bear the colors of the now-infamous House Orlon if Reikos was not mistaken, spoke up next.

"My ladies ..." he said awkwardly. "I'm not sure I will be ... welcome here, given the current circumstances. Might I leave as well? I ... have a family who will be worried."

Sian nodded at him, in the lead, it seemed, though the Factora-Consort stood right beside her. "All three of you are free to go, of course. Thank you for your assistance."

The three men she'd spoken to nodded wordless, somehow uncertain farewells, like departing strangers — and to Sian again, not to the Factora-Consort, he noticed with interest — then left as well. Looking after them, Reikos realized the crowd outside had started chanting once again. 'Our Lady' were the only words he could make out clearly. Sian's status had clearly grown since she had come to him a few weeks before. Neither alone, nor helpless anymore, it seemed.

Arian turned to Sian. "Well then. Are you ready?"

Sian nodded. "It's long past time."

The five of them remaining moved toward the winding, marble staircase that led to the Factorate's upper stories. All but one of the leaded stained-glass windows lining it were smashed. Though the sun itself had still not risen, enough light came through them now to see how fierce the fighting must have been here. Nearly everything, right up to the blackened ceiling several floors above them, seemed marred beyond repair. Where the hall's grand masonry and plaster had not just been blown away in chunks, it was streaked and smeared with soot. Where not covered in rubble, the marble floor tiles were cracked and pitted. Once-elegant tapestries hung in ashy tatters now. Nearly all the entrance hall's fine furnishings and sculpture had been shattered or overturned. As they climbed farther up the staircase, they were able to look out and see the long wing of bureaucratic offices stretching south of them, just a blackened scaffold now against the paling sky. Smoke rose like incense from their charred skeletons.

Reikos thought again of his once-lovely ship, now lying with its costly cargo on the bottom of the bay somewhere between here and Montchattaran. *It costs us everything to make the world new.* He turned to gaze at the priest who'd told them that, now helping Sian ascend the steps just behind Arian. But what new world had they purchased here, Reikos wondered silently. Would they have anything more than ruin to show for all they'd lost?

Not until they'd reached the fifth and highest floor, and turned north toward the ruling family's private wing, did the destruction all around them dissipate — and the guards show up.

One minute they were walking through a smoke-stained ruin. Down a hallway, round a corner, and suddenly the marble floors gleamed freshly waxed again. Clean pastel walls were framed in delicate, undamaged plaster reliefs as white as snow. But for an occasional shattered windowpane, the relatively faint scent of smoke, and the darkened palace's utter emptiness, of course, there might never have been any war at all.

Then they turned another corner and came face to face with half a dozen armored guardsmen, pikes raised and ready in the ghostly light. "Halt, and state your business!" one of them demanded.

The dead Factor's guardsman, Joreth, immediately stepped forward. "Quino? Bartiem? Is the light so poor that you don't know me?"

"Joreth?" one of the guardsmen murmured in clear disbelief. "But … I saw you burn."

"Have you not heard of Our Lady of the Islands, Quino?" Joreth gestured toward Sian. "This is she, and everything they say is true. I did burn. But I hadn't died yet when she came along, and healed me." The guardsmen's faces slackened as they turned in unison to stare at Sian. "And though you will not likely recognize her any more than I did at first, this is the Factora-Consort, whom you are sworn to serve, if I'm not mistaken."

Now all the guardsmen stared at Arian.

"You ... do not look like her," said one of them, hesitantly.

"I have been traveling in disguise," she answered wearily. "Has no one told you anything about where I'd gone?"

He shook his head.

"The Factor told only myself and Castahn, my lady," Joreth said, "who perished ... with the Factor."

She sighed. "My hair is dyed, gentlemen, and this is surely the first time you've ever seen my face without its normal mask of paint and powder, but I assure you, if my ladies, Lucia ... or Maronne, are here perhaps somewhere, they will vouch for what I say."

The guardsman in charge came a few feet closer, still peering nervously at all of them. "With apologies, my lady, Joreth," he nodded at the Factora-Consort, the resurrected guardsman, and, belatedly, Sian as well, "Our ... Lady of the Islands, this has been a day to make me mistrust my own mother. Who are all these other people?"

"They are the ones who have gotten me back here safely," Arian said, beginning to sound a bit impatient, Reikos thought. "Do you know Sergeant Ennias, by any chance?"

"Yes. Of course." The guard came further forward, giving them an even closer looking-over. "But I don't see him here."

"He's gone to find Hivat," she said. "Before he left us, downstairs just now, he said that Konrad and ... and my husband's body had been under guard down in the cellars, with other members of the household. Are they here still somewhere? Do you know where I can find them?" Her voice had begin to tremble. Reikos wondered if she might be going to cry.

Perhaps that was what convinced them. First the one Joreth had called Quino, then each of the others dropped onto one knee. "Welcome home, my lady," said Quino, a gratifying tremble in his voice as well now. "It has been a day of miracles as well, it seems."

"Please, where are my son and husband?" Arian asked stolidly.

They looked uncomfortably at one another. "My lady," said the guard in charge. "There was nothing we could do. We couldn't leave him where he was once there was fighting in the house. We moved him as carefully as possible, but there were no priests to help us. I don't know if anyone has told you about what's happened at the temple, but —"

"I blame none of you for my husband's death, if that is what you fear," Arian cut in. "I just ... wish to see him, and my son. ... Now, please, if that's possible."

"We will escort you to them, then, of course," said the guard. "But ... my lady, I am sorry, but I wanted to be sure you understood, my lady, that ... they are *both* dead."

Reikos felt his mouth fall open. *All of this. Everything we've done, and lost ...*

"Both ... who?" asked the Factora-Consort as if the guardsman hadn't made himself quite clear, and she weren't already blinking away tears.

"The Factor, and your son, my lady," the guard said very quietly. "Your son died not quite an hour ago, just after we'd returned him to his rooms. I ... I am very sorry."

THIRTY-FIVE

*D*ead.

Sian's very thoughts seemed frozen in mid-turn. The young guards-man who had said the word stared miserably at Arian, clearly awaiting some response. But she no longer seemed to have a voice either. Even the god's young priest looked blank with shock.

Dead? It ... wasn't possible. What had all of this been for? What was *she* for now? The god ... The *GOD* had done these things to her — to all of them — just to *save this child!* ... Hadn't he? And now ... The child was *dead?* ... An *hour* ago?

"It can't be," the young priest whispered.

Sian wanted to whirl at him and demand some explanation. *What's happened to this god of yours? Where has he gone, now that it counts? Was he ever there at all — or are you just some lunatic, as I supposed, out beating random women just because you think ... because you DREAM of some 'new world' where there are gods to make things come out as they ought to?* But Sian could still not make her body move, much less find breath with which to fill such words. And the gift she had ... That *was* real. But for what now?

"Take me to them," Arian said at last, without expression, or even much inflection.

Seeming relieved to turn away, the commanding guard and his detail fell into formation before them and started down the hallway.

As Arian followed, Sian discovered that her legs could move after all, if more of their own volition than at her behest. Steps later, Reikos was beside her, tucking his arm beneath hers, taking her cold hand. But she could barely feel him, could not even turn to look, so rigid was her body. So ... *dead.* An hour ago. While she'd been sleeping in the litter.

Anything at all could have made the difference. If she hadn't taken time to heal Rothkin's mother — or those injured men along their route. If she'd not had to have a bath at Maleen's house, or taken time to eat so much there. Or argued with Arouf.

They'd have been here in time.

Should she have known? Had she not tried hard enough to satisfy this god? After all?

Weeks to get here. *One ... hour ... late.*

Ahead of her, Arian walked straight-backed, taking measured strides. As fixed as a porcelain figurine. Unflinching, even as it shatters.

Down two more hallways, then up a short wide flight of stairs, into yet another hallway, this one carpeted, which made their passage even more surreally silent. It was lined in windows facing east, through which Sian could see the multitude below, chanting to their god. About their *Lady of the Islands ...*

They stood packed around a great sundial that she hadn't seen from down there in their midst, ringed in only slightly damaged flowers. No one had thought the sundial worth destroying, she supposed. Just then, the sun itself broke free of clouds on the horizon, flooding the hilltop with its radiance, and causing the sundial to cast a sharp-edged shadow on the hour.

Sian's eyes shied from blinding brightness, only to find the sundial's stark shadow everywhere she looked now — its ghost burned on her retinas, slow to fade.

What did you bring me here for, if not to heal her son? she pled silently. *To stand uselessly and grieve with her? To take away her pain? Have I been through all of this to be nothing but an elaborate anesthetic? Is that pain not all she has left of them now? Should she be deprived of even that?*

At the sunlit hallway's farther end, the guards lined up to flank a double doorway, three to either side. They stood at sharp attention, staring straight ahead as Arian walked between them, the doors pulled open for her by the guards beside it. She stopped there, though, and turned back to Sian, her face still all but empty. "Can you ..." she trailed off, as if afraid to finish.

It took just seconds for Sian to realize what she was trying to ask. "I don't know," she replied, thinking suddenly about the chicken from the dockmarket. "I've had no real cause to try ..."

"Will you ... now?" asked Arian.

Sian nodded. Trembling. Not just because she feared to learn what it was like to share someone else's death, but, even more, because she feared to fail. She turned back to face the priest. "Can you help me do this? Have you any kind of ... power?"

He stared at her in obvious distress. "I have no power but the god within me. And that only sometimes. What he might or might not do now, I have no way of knowing."

"Then, if you will both come with me ..." Arian said, trailing off again, as if afraid to voice this last, unlikely hope aloud.

"With permission, my lady, I will await you here," Joreth said quietly.

"As will I." Reikos glanced uncertainly at Sian. But she knew he was right. No matter the outcome, this would be ... intensely private, she suspected. For Arian, if not for her.

Arian turned and went inside now, followed by Sian, and then the priest.

Beyond the door, a high-ceilinged, brightly sunlit room was elegantly gilded, with warmly colored parquet floors, and exquisite floral murals on three of its walls. The fourth wall faced east, filled with large, elaborate windows that looked down on the same sundial and its attendant crowd. The room's delicately sculpted furnishings, tastefully arranged, were empty. There was no one there.

"They are in your private chamber, my lady," one of the guards outside said quietly.

Nodding, as if he'd see it, Arian walked toward an open threshold on their left, where a woman suddenly appeared, drawn by the guard's call, perhaps, in elegant black silks which exaggerated the paleness of her strawberry blonde complexion. Her eyes went wide when she saw Arian. "Oh, my lady!" she exclaimed, running to embrace the woman without any apparent confusion about who she was. "I am so sorry, my lady! But so glad you are alive!" She was in tears now, as was Arian. "I was afraid we'd lost you all."

Lucia, Sian thought. This must be Arian's other maid.

Arian, pulled back from her, wiping at her eyes. "Has there been any word of Maronne?"

Lucia shook her head. "What happened, my lady? You both just disappeared."

"I will tell you," said Arian. "But first…" She glanced back at Sian, turmoil in her eyes. "Lucia, this is Viktor's cousin, Sian Katté."

"Oh! The healer!" Lucia gasped quietly. "If only…" She fell abruptly silent, seeming to realize that she ought not to say what all of them must know too well already.

"And this gentleman is a priest," said Arian, not quite meeting anyone's eyes.

"From the temple?" Lucia frowned. "Is your… trouble there resolved then? We could certainly have used a few more of you earlier."

"I am not from the temple, my lady," the priest said awkwardly.

"Oh?" Lucia looked from him to Arian in clear confusion. "Then where… *Oh!*" She glanced toward the windows, wide-eyed again, then back at the priest. "You are… their leader?"

"Their… liaison, if anything," he answered, self-consciously. "The god sometimes speaks through me, but I do not speak for him. Nor am I anybody's leader."

Lucia's eyes grew even wider. "Are you here to…" She raised a hand to her breast, her gaze leaping to Sian. "Can you still… heal them?"

"I don't know. But I am here to try."

"Come then!" Lucia turned back to the doorway. "Quickly!"

They followed her into the next room, which seemed some kind of office, or parlor, with a desk and many bookshelves. Lucia passed through this without hesitation, toward another open doorway at its far side, calling softly to someone beyond that, "Aros, your sister has returned, and brought the healer with her!"

"Aros?" Arian called out, walking faster as they came around a corner. "You are safe!" As they entered what was obviously her bedchamber, she stopped as if against a wall of glass, her face crumpling as she brought both fists up to her mouth.

Before them, on a high, wide bed draped in coverlets of gold and purple silk brocade, lay two bodies, side by side. The first had belonged to an older man with bushy, salt-and-pepper eyebrows and short-cropped, steel-gray hair. It wore smudged and dented armor, bloodied at several of the torn joints across his torso, despite the effort someone had clearly made to clean most of the gore away. Beside him lay a young boy in a simple white silk nightgown. His head was all but without hair, his waxen, nearly colorless features, skeletal. Of the two, Sian would have assumed that he had been dead far longer. Days, if not weeks already.

At the bed's far side, a pale man of medium build with long blonde hair tied back in ribbons, wearing silks of blue so dark as to be nearly black as well, stood staring in something like horror at Arian. "Where have you been?" he asked her, sounding bewildered. Hurt.

"I have been trying to get back here, Aros."

"From where? They would tell me nothing. *Me.* Your *brother.*" He shook his head, looking wounded, as if they had no greater tragedy to deal with. "They lied to me for days. They all said you were in seclusion here, though clearly you were not. I thought we had come to some … better understanding. Were you lying to me — even then?"

"We were trying to avoid this war, Aros," Arian said. "There was no time, and it was crucial that no hint of my activities got out."

"To *me*?" he asked.

She stared at him in equal disbelief. "May I have a moment, please, to …" she looked back down at her dead son and husband, "to deal … with this?"

Her brother fell silent, still looking sullen and offended. Sian wondered if he'd already had time to absorb this tragedy, or was still in too much shock, perhaps, to fully register the fact, or … simply didn't care? Her own heart was breaking, and she had never even met either of these … "My lady, may I?" she asked.

"Please," Arian whispered without looking up from them. "Please, please, please …" she begged someone softly.

The Factor's body was closest. And looked … more salvageable. Sian went to it, surprised at how much fear she felt. Of death. Both his and her own, suddenly. What would *this* feel like? If she didn't do it now, she wasn't sure she wouldn't lose her courage altogether.

She drew a deep breath, released an even deeper sigh, then she thrust her hands onto his own, as there was no other bare skin but his face for her to touch. She shut her eyes and braced herself...

But nothing came.

It felt no different than laying hands upon a table, or a stone. There was simply ... nothing there. Nothing there to fear. Nothing there to heal. Nothing left. To do.

The chicken ... must not have been fully dead. Or dead for long enough, perhaps ...

She turned to Arian. The truth must already have been clearly visible, in Sian's eyes or body language. Arian's face collapsed altogether as she lost her struggle for control.

Sian stood aside as the Factora-Consort of Alizar ran to throw herself across her husband's body, sobbing without any pretense of restraint. "I'm so sorry, Viktor! That I wasn't here! That you had to fight alone! Oh ... my husband ... I will never ... never forgive myself ... for what ... I ..." Her sobbing became too convulsive to allow for speech. She wept and wept, utterly alone, it seemed, despite the other people in the room. There was no way for anyone to join her where she was. That much was immediately clear, though Sian cried too now, for Arian more than for the dead she'd never known.

Lucia wept as well, gazing helplessly at her mistress's suffering.

Tears streaked silently even from the priest's eyes.

Only Aros's eyes were dry. Though he once again looked horrified by what he saw, after a moment focused on his sister's display of grief, his gaze started darting elsewhere: to Lucia, to the priest, finally to Sian. "There were no priests," he told her. "Viktor had them all kicked out. While everyone was lying to me. So there was no one left to treat him. Do you see? There was nothing *I* could do. For either of them."

His breathing had become extremely rapid. He seemed ... *terrified*, Sian realized. Did he think he needed to explain all this to her? Who was she to judge him? Why should he care what she thought? Especially now. He reminded her of Arouf. So self-absorbed. At such a moment.

Aros's gaze darted to the Butchered God's priest next. "You're a priest, aren't you? Can't your gods do something?"

The priest seemed as bewildered as Sian was by his manner. He shrugged helplessly, looking desolate. "I can do no more than you. I am only human."

"You're not from the temple, are you?" Aros replied scornfully, almost as if he had forgotten his sister entirely. "Those bastards would never have said anything so modest. Whose priest are you then? What useless god do *you* serve?"

The young priest's face hardened suddenly. He seemed … to age. To change before Sian's eyes. She'd seen this face on him before. Just once. And suddenly she feared, both for herself, and for Aros, however repugnant he might seem. She backed away now, having suffered this god's attention one too many times already.

"**I am the god whom you call Butchered,**" the priest said gravely, in a voice both his own, and yet somehow not quite human anymore. Yes. Sian recalled that voice. The memory chilled her to the bone.

"You're … a *god* now?" Aros scoffed, seeming on the edge of laughter, unbelievably. "The one my sister's husband had cut up to feed the poor?"

"Aros. Don't," Arian said quietly, her voice filled with fearful warning. She was staring at the priest from where she lay, her crying vanished all at once.

She knows too, Sian realized in surprise. But then, Arian had been touched by the god as well. The night *she* had been beaten. Perhaps something in her recognized that voice as clearly.

"Well then," Aros scoffed, "you'd just be here to gloat, I guess, not to raise him from the dead. Do you plan to have him cut up too? To feed … the temple maybe?"

"**He is gone beyond Me now, and wants no raising anyway,**" said the priest, advancing toward Aros. "**But *you* are still within My power to *assist*, poor little spider. Why keep trembling in the dark like this? The world is full of light this morning. Come out and join the dance.**"

"*Spider*? Trembling in the …" Aros's amusement seemed replaced by something tight — a little frantic even. "Whatever are you babbling about? Stay where you are." He backed toward the wall, only seeming then to realize that he was cornered by the bed. "Come no closer, or I'll call the guards and have you expelled."

"Six guards." The priest surprised Sian by stopping as requested. "To protect the last living member of the ruling family, for all they knew. Left alone in this great building. At such a troubled time, with just six guards. Why so undervalued, spider? Can you be that little loved?"

"You ... *presume* to come in here at such a time, and ... and *lecture* me?" Aros sputtered.

Arian crawled off the bed, and stood up, backing toward Sian. "May I ask who we're addressing now?" she asked the priest, almost convincingly calm.

The priest ignored her, still gazing at Aros. "Even now, one of your sister's loyal subjects rushes back here, bringing a little army to protect her. Yet for you, just one poor woman," he glanced briefly at Lucia, "and ... six ... guards. Do you wish to know why, little spider?"

"I wish for you to leave now," Aros said, seeming caught between fear and fury.

The priest took another step in his direction. "Those six guards were only left to honor and protect the bodies of your victims. The one who left them here, would have left none at all for you alone. Could it be that he's already sensed the truth?" Aros shied back reflexively, though there was still a bed between them. "Might he have run against the strands of your web in the darkness somewhere, do you think, and left ... suspecting?"

"Guards!" Aros shouted. "*Guards!*"

The priest just smiled, even as the sound of running, armored feet echoed through the doors behind them. He turned to Arian. "Daughter, your people need you now, to give them hope and help them to repair what you and yours have broken. Heed them. Do not settle for despair."

The guards arrived then, rushing in with pikes half-lowered.

"Seize him!" Aros pointed at the priest. "Kill him! Now!"

"Don't!" yelled Arian. "Stay where you are!"

The guards looked back and forth between them, clearly unsure of what to do, as Sian saw first Joreth, then Reikos appear in the next room, gazing through the door uncertainly.

"Am I not still Factora-Consort?" Arian asked the guardsmen.

"She is! I swear it!" said Lucia. "I helped dye her hair myself!"

"Stand down," the commanding guard told his fellows.

"Arian! What are you doing?" Aros exclaimed. "Can't you see that he's —"

"Silence!" she hissed. "Or I will have them arrest *you!*"

He complied. As a volcano might be silent in between eruptions, Sian thought.

Arian turned back to the priest. "Can you cure them? Either of them? I'll do anything. I'll trade my life for theirs. My husband meant well — when your body ... I know we ... I ... haven't trusted you at times, but —"

"Child, your husband is beyond your reach as well now, and would thank neither of us for changing that."

"My son?" she asked. "Can you ... Will you return him to me, at least? Is there anything —"

" — that you can pay Me with for such a favor?" The priest smiled at her, pityingly. **"You told Me it was not a bargain you were making, but a vow. Is this no longer so?"**

Her mouth fell open in surprise. Then she looked down, the very image of surrender. "And I will do my best to keep that vow, sir," she said quietly. "If that is what you wish of me."

Sian had no idea what this meant. Had Arian ... talked with this god before somewhere?

"Do you care, then, what I wish?" the priest, or what he hosted, asked.

"What does a god wish?" she said sadly. "It would interest me to know."

The priest turned to Sian, who backed still farther toward the windows.

"You've no cause to fear Me now," the priest said — so apologetically that for a moment, Sian thought perhaps the god had left him. **"I wish only that you do what you have come for."**

Sian looked at the bed, then back at him, confused. "But ... they're dead. I tried. And —"

"You came to heal, did you not?"

"Yes ... But how am I to —"

"Then start with him," the priest said softly, pointing back at Aros.

"Don't come near me," Aros quavered.

"What ... does he need to be healed of?" she asked.

"Does it matter? Put your hand upon his heart, Sian Katrë. You will see."

"Don't touch me!" Aros looked in desperation at his sister, then at the guards. "You're supposed to guard me, aren't you? Don't just stand there! Stop her!"

"Leave her be," Arian commanded them. "She is a *healer*. She won't hurt him any." She glanced back at Sian. "Will you?"

"Why would I hurt him? I ..." Sian looked back at the priest, utterly confused. "I don't understand what you want. I will not hurt him if I do this?"

"**Did I not just say you'd come to *heal*?**" the priest asked patiently.

We mean you no harm either, though we must harm you anyway, I fear. This voice had said that to her also, once. She wondered what would happen if she attempted to refuse now.

"**I will not compel you,**" said the priest, answering her thought with an almost amiable shrug. "**Nor punish you, or anybody else here later. You punish yourselves and each other much more than sufficiently already. Heal him, or not, *Our Lady*. The choice is yours.**"

"Arian ... *Sister*," Aros pled. "Will you really give me to her? Do you hate me that much?"

"What are you so afraid of, Aros?" Arian replied. "She's laid her hands on me, and I have only cause for thanks because of it."

"*I don't require healing!* Can't any of you see that?" He turned to the guards again, then to Lucia, even to Sian. "There's nothing wrong with me. I've done *nothing!*"

"Who said you had?" asked Arian. "Why has he been calling you a spider, brother?"

"Why does he do anything? *He's mad!*" cried Aros. "You're *all* mad, or you'd see that!"

"What exactly is it that you *haven't* done?" Arian pressed, walking toward him now, without a shred of sympathy.

"What are you doing?" he asked, cringing back from her. "Stay away from me!"

"You fear *me* now, *brother*? Your own *sister*? Answer my questions!"

"Guards!" he pled. "Protect me!"

"From the Factora-Consort, sir?" The commander no longer sounded sympathetic either.

"Sian," said Arian, her eyes still fastened coldly on her brother. "Come here and do as the god asked, please. I fear my brother may be unwell after all."

Hardly able to believe, much less understand, any of what she witnessed, Sian came hesitantly forward.

"You've always hated me!" Aros rasped at Arian. "Ever since I came here, you've done all you could to shame me — just like Father, and the rest of them. Kept me throttled like a lap dog on your jeweled leash! I did *nothing wrong!* He was dying anyway! He was only *suffering!*"

"Who?" Arian demanded angrily. "Who was dying, Aros?"

Her brother only shook his head, trying to press himself into the wall. "You deserved this. It was not my fault. It was *yours. And his!*" He thrust an arm toward Viktor's body. "He was destroying his whole family's future — killing all of Alizar! His own cousin told me so!"

"*What have you done?*" Arian shouted at him.

"I never asked them to ... I had no idea!" Aros looked in wide-eyed terror at the priest. "You have to know I never wanted any of this to happen! I just wanted ... I just —" He grabbed a small bronze candlestand from the bedside table and swung it wildly at his sister.

As Arian threw herself against the wall to avoid the blow, Aros shoved past her and fled around the bed — straight into Sian's path. Without any conscious thought, she thrust her hand out, hard and firm against the bare skin at his open collar.

Sian felt something even worse than fire coursing through his mind for just an instant before he collapsed. As she stared down at him, aghast, Aros clutched his head between his hands and started screaming — as if his skin were being peeled away. Horrified, she bent to put her hands on him again, desperate to heal whatever had just happened to him. But his eyes grew round, and he began to writhe and squirm away from her, screaming more hysterically than ever.

"What have I ..." She rose and whirled toward the priest. "What have you done to him? You promised me that he would not be —"

Arian and Lucia both shouted in alarm, and Sian spun again to find Aros on his feet behind her. She stumbled backward, sure he meant to strike her, but he just ran off toward the windows, past the guards, who stared at him in shock as he threw himself against the glass. Several panes shattered, sending a cascade of sparkling shards into the plaza, but their frames were strong enough to hold him. He backed up to charge again, but was tackled and brought down by all six guards this time before he got the chance.

Everyone stood frozen, watching as they wrestled Aros into submission. "Someone ... get me anything to bind him with!" one of them shouted. Two men leapt up, one grabbing at a braided curtain-pull, slashed free by the other with his belt knife. Moments later, they had Aros trussed up and comparatively quiescent on the floor, unaware of anybody now except himself, it seemed. He babbled quietly; an endless stream of barely audible excuses and accusations.

Sian turned on the priest again, her rage eclipsing both wisdom and fear. "You lied to me!" she spat. "You said I wouldn't hurt him. Do you call this *healing*?"

"**Some things must be broken to be healed,**" the priest said, sadly — as he had done once before, on the beach that night. "**Who should understand this better than yourself by now?**"

It was all she could do not to rush at him and pound his head and shoulders with her fists. She wanted a great bone to beat him with. A way to make him understand what it was like to be so used. "You make accomplices of us!" she yelled.

"**I but awaken what already sleeps within you,**" he replied. Unmoved. Unashamed. Un-offended. Insufferable. "**Do you suppose the gift you bear was My work?**"

"If not yours, then whose?" she scoffed.

"**Miracles lie slumbering in all of you.**" He glanced from face to watching face around the room. "**Beaten into that forgetfulness. Until they are needed ... with ... sufficient urgency.**"

"You're saying that this power was ... my work?" Sian asked in disbelief.

"**I did not say that. I did say, you have choice.**" He fell silent for a moment. "**I am not your enemy, Sian Kattë. Or his.**" The priest's eyes traveled back to Aros. "**And you have better things to do right now than rail at Me. Your work here is unfinished, healer.**"

"Oh, really." She still felt far from mollified. "Is there some further torture I'm required to inflict for you? If I'm supposed to exercise some *choice* in all of this, should I not have a hint, at least, of what my choices are? Speak plainly for once." She waited, but the priest just stared at her, looking … oddly confused. "Can a god not do that?" she asked.

Still, the priest just stared. Then looked around, seeming weak and pale. "He's gone."

"What?" Sian asked.

"The god," murmured the young priest. "I'm sorry … I have no power to keep him."

"Oh fine." Sian looked into the air above her. "Just run away then. How god-like." She turned to look at those around her. "Is someone else here in need of healing?" she asked wearily, abandoned, suddenly, by all the anger and adrenaline that had made her so recklessly fierce just moments before. Some shook their heads. No one spoke. She looked down at the bodies, lying just as they had been when she'd arrived. … Except … "Were his eyes open when we got here?" The words came out of her almost too quietly to carry. She was sure they hadn't been. And sure they must have been, or else …

Everyone now looked where she was looking.

"*Oh!*" cried Arian. "Konrad?"

The boy reacted not at all as Sian rushed to the bed, his face and body as inert as ever, his deathly pallor unimproved. His eyes might simply have been opened by some reflex of stiffening muscles. She'd heard tales of corpses sitting up — or coughing. But she had never put her hands upon him. After trying with the Factor, there had seemed no point. And then Arian had broken down … Without further thought, or any fear at all this time, Sian yanked the nightgown's collar open, and thrust her hands onto his chest.

"Oh! *Ohhhh*," she groaned, leaning forward so that when she fell she'd still be pressed against him. For she knew that she would fall. What climbed up her arms into herself now was … not survivable. She knew this, in no rational way, as she slumped down to cover him. Already feeling like a third corpse on the bed.

Her mind — and something more, something visceral — crawled through the ruined body, half pushing, half dragged along through organs reduced to clotted cheese, by poison. Someone had poisoned him, slowly over time, though she was too far gone herself now to reveal the fact aloud. There was scarcely any tissue left inside him not half disintegrated, by the toxins he'd been fed, or by those his body's failing parts themselves had emptied into him as they'd begun to rot. Oddly, there was very little pain. He had almost no sense of feeling left, anywhere inside him, thus, neither did Sian. Yet he wasn't dead. Still. Sian had heard other tales of people who woke up inside their tombs and coffins. After having been in what they called a deathsleep for too long, easily mistaken for death itself.

She felt the boy's deathsleep disturbed now, sensed him being pried, against his will, back into consciousness. He had been ready, long ago, to set life down. Had navigated that surrender once, and wanted to go through none of it a second time. This felt … like a violation of some kind, as he began to breathe. And choke. As feeling started to return before the pain had fully vanished. Now she heard him crying out, somewhere far away, and would have moaned along with him, if she'd had any strength or voice for it. She had gone too deeply down into the well from which she'd drawn him. They had barely felt each other as they'd passed, in opposite directions.

She heard Konrad scream, more faintly still, as she began to fray. Into a thousand shards of light and memory. There had been daughters. Going. Lovers. Past. Parents. Places. All becoming flat now. Paintings. Icons. Mere … ideas.

Nothing to fear. Nothing to feel.

Nothing.

Sian Kattë.

She knew the name. And didn't want it anymore.

Sian Kattë. I'm sorry.

No. NO. I don't want to go.

The time will come. But this is not that day. Too many need you still.

Please. She would have wept if she'd known how to anymore. She would have begged. But there was none of that here either. Though there was much more here to be. So much more to know. Everything. Ahead of her. And she was not to be allowed it. Please.

There is one choice, before you go, but not that one, child. I'm sorry.

But ... I am done with choices. PLEASE.

This is the moment, if you wish it. Choose.

The question was implacable. The choice inevitable. When this moment passed — here, where she was finally to have been free of moments too — it would be made. One way or the other.

Very well. She chose. And felt the tug. The dull cement of time and being. And remembered what it was to grieve.

THIRTY-SIX

The air smelled of flowers.

The scent had a name.

The same name as the flowers. But she could not remember it.

There were other scents as well.

Clean linen.

Salt air.

… Beeswax. On teakwood.

Curry … very faintly, and … onions … cooking …

Lavender. That was what the flower — and the scent — were called.

She heard something piping in the distance, high and shrill. A bird. She could see it in her mind. White and slender against the sunlit blue. Small and lean and graceful.

Tern.

The names of so many things were coming back. Hibiscus. Egret. Palm frond. Sail … Boat. Dragonfly. Plumeria … Sand. Seashell. Coral … Gecko … Ocean …

Silk.

Her eyes opened to find dark, slender fingers. On white linen dappled with sunlight. Beyond them, gauzy curtains billowed languidly before a bank of open windows. Framed in teak. Filled with turquoise light. She heard the sea somewhere. Foliage rustling in the breeze.

The fingers moved. Her fingers. She'd known that, but … it still seemed strange somehow. Not to be assumed. She wanted them to wiggle — and they did. It was … amusing.

"Did I just see her move?"

"Let's see if she is waking finally, yes?"

She wished to see who'd spoken. And her body turned. As slowly as ... *molasses*. Sweet and dark. *Molasses*.

She found a kindly face above her, not young, but smiling slightly. Thatched in thinning, light brown hair. His robe was rough and dark. Not *silk*. She knew what the robe was made of, but couldn't pull the word into focus. Yet. This face had a name she did know. "Het."

The word made so little sound, she wasn't sure she'd really said it until his smile widened with his eyes. "Ah! You *are* awake, Sian! How are you feeling?"

Sian. Yes. She knew that name too; reclaimed it, almost without effort. How was she feeling?

That was far too large a question. Much too hard to parse. She set it down again.

In a chair, well behind Het, by a table set with cups of ... *kava* — that name made her smile inside — sat another man, much younger. Lean and, somehow sad, though he smiled too as he got up to come join Het. His robe was just as rough and plain, but if there was a name for his face too, she couldn't find it.

"Welcome back, Our Lady," said this younger face as it arrived beside her bed.

No. *A* bed. But not *hers*. She felt quite certain of this, though she could not recall *her* bed, exactly. If there'd ever been one. This bed was where the smell of lavender came from. There was ... lavender inside it somewhere. And in ... *vases* ... set on tables at its sides. "Where is this?" Her voice seemed far less easily commanded than her fingers had been.

"You are in the summer house of Korlan Alkattha, the late Factor's father," Het said. "On the eastern shore of Home. Does that ... make any sense to you?"

She gazed up at him, and shook her head, understanding *summer*, and *house*, and ...*father*. But little of the rest. "What is a *late factor*?"

The smiles above her faltered slightly. Het drew a breath and sighed. "I have had to give you medicines that may dull your memory a bit, but it will all come back to you in time, my dear. You are safe, and loved here. Just relax and let us care for you. Do you want something to eat? Something light, yes? A bowl of fish broth?

Fish ... She knew that name as well. The faint scents of curry and cooking onion recaptured her attention. "May I have ..." There was a name. A delicious word. "*Bouillabaisse*?"

The smiles above her flared back into being.

"I suspect Korlan's kitchen is equipped to supply that too," said Het. "Though I must caution you to reconsider, yes? You have eaten nothing solid for four days now. Your stomach may not know quite what to do with bouillabaisse just yet."

"Days?" Sian knew what the word meant. The number, though, seemed ... strangely out of focus. What was *four* days? How long was that? "Four days?" she asked again.

"Yes, Sian," said Het, no longer smiling. "You nearly died when you healed Konrad. The Factora summoned me, and had you brought here to recover." Het paused, as if expecting some response, but his words were tugging at something still without names, deep inside her. Not very pleasantly. Her attention had all shifted there.

The kindly man glanced back at his younger companion, who leaned forward and asked, "Do you remember healing Konrad?"

Healing Konrad ... These words meant ... something ... urgent. *Healing Konrad.*

HEALING KONRAD! Everything came back at once. She sat up — or tried to, but collapsed again immediately, exhausted, and *sore*. In so many places. She felt faint. She'd been in Arian's bedchamber at the Factorate — only minutes earlier. How had she ... "*Four days?*" she said again. "Did Konrad ... Is he —"

"Quite alive, and recovering with *unnatural* speed, my lady," Het informed her. "You are remembering, yes? I did not mean to shock you."

"I remember. But ..." Four days. She had missed four days. The summer house ... of Viktor's father. "Where is the Factora-Consort? Is she here as well?"

"She is. And Konrad too. This house is functioning as temporary quarters for her new government. She is the Factora now, by unanimous consent of all the other ruling families — even House Orlon — and confirmed by popular demand of Alizar's electorate."

"Factora?" Sian asked, astonished. She had never heard the term without its suffix.

Het nodded. "She was understandably reluctant, at first. Not just unimaginably weary, I am sure, of all this nation's woes have already cost her, but worried too that no one would support a woman as Factor, much less a foreign-born one. But … there has never been so much support for any ruler here. Not since the rebellion, anyway. And I believe her connection to you may have something to do with that — though by no means all."

"To me?"

"You are quite a hero now, Our Lady," said the younger man, whom she knew as well now. The priest of the Butchered God. "Though you may have stretched even the god's power a bit thin back at the Factorate."

"House Alkattha is, of course, extremely grateful to you," said Het. "For reviving their heir to the Factorate, and restoring their place in the nation's political future. You may ask them — or a great many other people of importance here in Alizar — for nearly anything you wish now, and count on them to listen, I believe."

"What of Arian's brother?" Hero or not, the memory of what she'd done to him came back with a chill of shame. "Is he … recovered?"

"He is safely in our care at the temple," Het replied. "Under lock and key, of course, though in far nicer quarters than you were accorded there. Due to his condition, it is still unclear whether he or the former Census Taker was more at fault for this national calamity. But we will help him find himself again, and doubtless have it sorted out in time."

"Aros … was part of the conspiracy too?" Sian could hardly believe that Arian and Viktor had been betrayed by so many members of their own family.

"One of its architects, it seems," said Het. "Hivat has uncovered a great deal of unpleasantness since their coup attempt disintegrated. But the Factora's brother seems to have been under the impression that if the Factor's sole heir died without hope of replacement, he would be next in line for ascension to the Factor's seat, once Viktor and Arian were also dead."

"But ... that's ridiculous," said Sian. "The people would never have affirmed his claim. He's not even Alizari. The other houses would just have installed some new Factor of their own. Can he have failed to understand that?"

"Not if he could count on their support," Het interjected. "He made a lot of shockingly generous promises, it seems, to a lot of sadly ambitious and receptive people — some of them in my own temple. Which is how he came to the attention of the Census Taker. After that, it's anybody's guess, at this point, which of them was really in control."

At his mention of the temple, she had gone cold inside. "I am a hero now?" she asked.

"To say the least," said Het. "A national treasure, I would say."

"Then ... I have no further need to fear arrest?"

Het laughed, as did the young priest at his side. It was so strange, she realized, to see them standing there — together. "My dear!" Het beamed at her. "The world has changed a great deal since you left us. You would have no cause for worry now, even if the Mishrah-Khote's new Father Superior were not so favorably disposed toward you."

"Duon ... is no longer in power?"

Het's smile vanished. "He now enjoys the very same hospitality to which you were treated — though we have no intention of trying to starve him. If he can stomach skate fin soup."

"Duon has been *arrested*?" Sian said, incredulous.

"And Lod, and all the other toadies who supported what he stood for. If their so-called leadership these many years had not been sufficient to condemn them, their conduct in response to our very civil request for changes most certainly proved the criminal nature of their characters. I am profoundly sorry that it cost the rest of Alizar so many lives. We didn't know that someone was about to overthrow the Factorate as well, or we'd have delayed our own uprising for another week or two."

"In just four days." Sian shook her head. "I've ... missed so much."

"Ha!" Het looked more amused than ever. "My dear, you were at the very center of most of it. And hardly eager for any extra helpings, as I recall."

"So who is the new Father Superior?"

"Well … I am." Het offered her a small, self-deprecating smile. "I too have benefitted from my now quite open connection to you."

"That was hardly the only reason," said the younger priest. "With all respect to you, Our Lady," he added hastily.

"You … rule the Mishrah-Khote now?" she asked, beginning to wonder if she'd really woken yet at all. "You told me you were regarded as a disgrace there."

"By all the right people," Het answered. "Or the wrong ones, depending on the frame one chooses, yes? Let's just say, their disapproval was another of my stronger qualifications. And, no. The Mishrah-Khote is done with rulers, I believe. If I have any say, at least. I *guide* the temple now. As they will doubtless guide me in *our* pursuit of truth. No one rules it but the gods."

"So … no one at the temple minds now, that you're here rubbing shoulders with a notorious spiritual fraud and the Butchered God's fugitive priest?" she pressed.

"Sian," Het said soberly. "Events have rather settled all those accusations in your favor. Yours, and this courageous young man's. The temple clearly has much to learn from both of you, and many others on these islands, disregarded or suppressed by the previous regime. I don't suppose you might be interested in … being anointed as a healer, would you?"

"You're … offering to make me a *priest*?" She was almost certain she was meant to laugh. Even now. But he only nodded, without so much as a grin. "A *female* priest. The temple would stand for that?"

He nodded yet again. Quite soberly. "Now, at last, they would, I think."

After gaping at him for a moment, she shook her head. "I'm sorry. But I really cannot see myself…" She trailed off, disturbed by some … half-formed fragment of a memory. Which vanished instantly upon pursuit. "I cannot imagine being happy as some temple mystic, Father Het. Though I am … honored — and utterly astonished — by the invitation."

Het sighed. "I did not think so, but … I had to ask."

"The world I left is gone indeed." Sian looked up at the Butchered God's young priest. "Will *you* join the Mishrah-Khote now?"

"Oh no," he said, as if she must be teasing him. "I am hardly any kind of healer — as you would know better than most. Nor have I any real calling as a priest. I've just been a tool, however willing or unwilling in the moment."

"What makes that different from a priest?" Het asked. "I could say the same of myself."

"Well, it hardly matters now," the young priest sighed. "This god I've served has come for just one reason I'm aware of: to make the world new. And now ... it is. Or seems to be." He shrugged, not so much at them as to himself. "I'm not sure he'll stay now. I'm not sure he hasn't left already." He look up from his private reverie. "I may be in need of some whole new identity. But not as a priest. The Butchered God has no interest in religions, I don't think." He shook his head. "Not that he ever said as much to me. But I have ... carried him inside me now for long enough; been shaped enough by the visions he dispensed, that I cannot imagine he'd be pleased by any temple, or any list of rules to which his followers were all coerced. His nature seems ... entirely about movement. Change. Breaking and renewal. Even those would become rigid expectations once they were codified. How does one *establish* a religion around that?"

"Your followers will try," said Het. "As all followers do."

"You're doubtless right," the young man said. "But they will have no help from me. Or from the god they claim to worship, I don't think. If I understand anything he's compelled me to say or do these past few years, he only wants them awakened to what they were meant to be, and to start being it again. Not to settle on some clump of stone here and lord it over anybody."

"But ... why now?" Sian asked. "Why us? ... After all these ages."

The young man shrugged. "We were ... sufficiently ready to break, perhaps? I'm convinced we called to him somehow — knowingly or not. Not the other way around. Every nuance of his presence I have ever known conveyed this."

"So ... you think it's done, then," Sian said, feeling the tug again. Of something half-forgotten. She flexed her back, her arms and legs, and felt them complain. Yes, of course she'd lain in bed for four days now. Some stiffness in her joints and muscles was to be expected. Except that she'd been spared precisely this ever since the gift's arrival. Normal aches and pains. Now back, it seemed.

The niggling tug increased. For just an instant, she recalled … a choice. Made somewhere. At some time … "Were you hurt in any way during this revolt inside the temple, Father Het?"

"Fortunately no." He held up a bandaged finger, grinning. "Unless you count this little scratch I gave myself, shutting a tunnel grating on my own hand as I was smuggling documents to safety from the library."

"May I touch that hand, please?" Sian asked.

"Oh, my dear, no. You've just awakened. You don't need to start dispensing—"

"I would like to, Father Het. If you don't mind? I owe you quite a bit, as I recall. It would make me feel much better to make some small installment on repayment."

He rolled his eyes with an indulgent smile, and unwound the narrow bandage to reveal a finger darkly bruised from nail to knuckle.

"A scratch?" she asked. "You do tend to exaggerate the insignificance of your wounds. Reach down, please. I'm still a bit too stiff to sit."

He stretched his hand down, and she took it gently in her fingers.

No pain.

No ginger.

His bruise remained. She waited for a moment to be sure, but she had known. Before she'd even asked if he was injured.

She nodded, and let go, looking up at the Butchered God's ex-priest. "I too sometimes wondered if the gift would vanish once I'd healed Konrad. Whether all of this is done or not, it seems my part is finished." She gave them both a wistful smile, still unsure of how she felt about it. Was this loss, or liberation? "Am I still a hero, do you think?"

"Oh, yes! Of course," said Het. "You have done what you have done." But he gazed in perplexed surprise between Sian and his unhealed finger, obviously dismayed.

The younger priest nodded his agreement, though he too looked troubled.

You have choice, the god had told her. Sian felt certain she had made a choice of some kind here. She could not remember when, exactly. But it was there, inside her. Still tugging, very softly. For the most part, though, she felt relieved. She would be able to go walking in the streets now without being some kind of traveling sideshow. She could just throw her hands up again, like everybody else, and say, *The world's pain is endless, but what can I do?* She could safely buy a chicken at the market.

Still, she could not help wondering who she'd overlooked while there was time. Who she would wish later she could heal.

"Oh!" She tried to sit again, and fared no better than before. "Where is Pino?"

The two men nearly glanced at one another, aborting even that response almost in time. "My dear, all this conversation will exhaust you," Het said gently. "You've too much to absorb already. Why don't we —"

"No. Tell me. Have they found him?"

"I'm sorry, dear," said Het, stone-faced. "They did."

"Oh no," she whispered. "How bad ..." She felt her face begin to crumple. "Is he ..." Her eyes grew hot. If he were alive, they'd have said so first. She knew this. "Where?" she asked, already weeping.

"His body washed ashore amidst the wreckage of his boat," said Het.

She turned away and pressed her face into the pillows, crying harder. *Oh, Pino ... Pino ... I did not want this ... I did not ask this of you ...*

They had the grace to let her cry undisturbed by words of shallow comfort. They didn't leave her, though. Their simple presence helped as much as anything was likely to.

When she had no more crying left in her — for the moment, anyway — she rolled onto her back, and stared up at the ceiling. "Have they already burned him?"

Het shook his head. "He is not to be burned. The Factora has commanded that he have a full state funeral, and be interred beside her husband's body in the Factorate Hall of Ancestors. I am to officiate. We have begun the preparation of his body for preservation, but although the Factor's funeral was two days ago, she ordered that Pino's be postponed until you were sufficiently recovered to attend."

"I don't want him buried with the Factor," Sian said. It was a great honor. She understood that. But she didn't want him to be ... that alone. He had never known the Factor. Or any of the kind of people buried there. "I want his shrine on Little Loom Eyot. There is a hilltop there ... where he belongs."

"I cannot see why the Factora would refuse you," said Het. "I will speak with her, unless you'd rather do so."

"Thank you. She must be very busy now. I won't ask her to come here. I would be grateful if you'd convey my congratulations, and my condolences, along with my request."

"I will do so. In the meantime, I know of someone else who will want to know you are awake. With your permission, dear, I will go let him know?"

"Who?" Though she knew. She hoped, at least.

His smile returned. "Would you rather not just be surprised?" The smile faded. "Pleasantly, this time."

"Well. You'd better go then." She dredged up a smile from somewhere too, and waved him toward the door. When he'd gone, she turned to look up at the young man whose given name she still had never learned. "If I'm not even supposed to call you the Butchered God's priest now, what name should I use?"

He looked surprised. Nonplussed, in fact. As if he didn't know, himself.

"What do your guards call you?" she asked.

"Sir," he said, sheepishly.

"Oh, don't be ridiculous. You must have a name."

He shook his head, slowly, as if just realizing now how strange it was. "I left my name behind when I was taken by the god."

"Well then, what name *was* that?" she asked impatiently.

"I ... would rather not ..."

"You're really going to go through life now as *that man without a name*? If you're no longer a fugitive, what's the danger in telling me what you were called before all this began?"

"I guess ... you're right," he said. "I'll have to choose a name now."

She could not believe he was so thick. In fact, she was quite sure he wasn't. "You're avoiding my question. I asked what you *were* called. After all we've been through, may I not know where you're really from? How all this happened to you?"

"My lady, I know how this will sound, and I apologize. You are literally the last person in the world I would wish to offend, but ... I'm not sure it would be helpful to tell *you*. Specifically."

Sian gaped at him. "Well, now I really must know why." She was too surprised to feel offended. "You said that night out on the beach that you had grown up in the slums, but that's obviously not true. I have spent some time with people from the raft warrens, as you know, and you are not remotely like them."

"Are you certain?" he replied. "Het is from the warrens. His father was a foreign sailor. Left his mother in the warrens before Het was even born."

She had thought there could be no surprises left. "How would you know that?"

"We've spent a lot of time together here, these last few days. With little to do but talk. The temple took him as a child. For charity. They've educated him very well, but you can hear it in his speech still, if you listen."

"But not in yours," she said, moved nonetheless. "You've been here? All this time?"

"Where else had I to go?" He shrugged uncomfortably. "My task seems done as well, as I just told you. And ... I do feel ... both grateful, and a bit ... responsible still. To you."

"Then why won't you —"

"Because I fear that it might cause you pain," he cut her off in agitation. "And I have caused enough of that. To you especially." He took a breath to calm himself, and turned to go back to his doubtless stone-cold kava at the table. "Some stories are best left behind."

His past would cause *her* pain? How could he think she'd just sit still for that? "Have I ever told you how I was awakened to my gift of healing, *sir*?"

He looked up from his kava, as if she'd slapped him. "If you feel the need to mock me now ... I guess you'd be entitled." He looked away again, and raised his cup to drink.

"I have no desire to mock you," Sian said. "But I'm wondering what you think could possibly cause me too much pain to deal with after all I've been through. And forgiven you for."

His shoulders slumped. He set the kava down, staring at the table.

"I *have* forgiven you," she said. "I understand now what it's like to be used by a god. I harbor nothing but respect for you, young man. And the best of hopes for your relief from ... whatever haunts you so. But it would be ... gratifying to know that you trust me some as well. At least a little. You told me on the beach that night that you'd been beaten too. Harder and longer than I was. If you can't tell me where you're from, then may I know, at least, what was done to *you*?"

He released a bitter little laugh, and shook his head. "They are the same story, my lady."

A story clearly eating him alive, whatever it was. "Then tell me," she said softly. "And be free of it."

He looked at her at last. "I swear to you, my lady. This had no bearing on why you were chosen. That was the god's choice. Not my own. I swear it ... on my father's shrine. But ... it made nothing easier for me that night."

Her lips parted in surprise. Was there some reason after all that *she* had been chosen?

"To arouse your gift, the god used one of his own bones. And me." Though he still stared at Sian, the priest was clearly seeing something else now. "To awaken me, he used your family."

Sian felt her face slacken.

"My father was once a very highly placed employee in the household of Escotte Alkattha. Lord Alkattha had not yet been installed as Census Taker, but he was already an important man, and my father's position was high enough that we too lived in relative luxury on Alkattha's largess." His eyes flickered toward her again. "You are right, in part, my lady. I enjoyed a very fine education growing up, and learned how to conduct myself in one of the finest homes in Alizar. Until I was fourteen." His gaze softened again, once more focused on the past.

"My father did his job extremely well. He wasn't just hard-working. He was intelligent, creative, and honest to a fault. He was also just naïve enough to think that these things had won him at least the begrudging respect of his employer. Foolishly presuming on that assumption, he dared to question, politely, a fairly petty household policy injurious to many of the servants, which resulted in excessively high turnover among them, as well as reduced morale and productivity, and to no recognizable gain for Alkattha. My father may have dared to press the point a bit too hard, believing that a man of such apparently high character would be persuaded by reason and elevated moral vision to listen."

Sian closed her eyes, dreading to hear what her monstrous cousin had done to them. "What was this policy?" she asked.

"Something to do with household chain of command, I believe. Which positions were subservient to which others, how daily household questions and permissions were to be submitted, and to whom. I can't remember more than that. I was very young, and not involved in any of it but the aftermath." He sighed, and looked away again.

"Lord Alkattha was a rising star, of course, extremely conscious of his image in those days. To be corrected by an employee, however circumspectly ... There were precedents at stake here. People watching. Evidently, he felt some example must be made. To prevent such subversive instincts from infecting others, not just of his household, but of our family's class in general. Firing my father wasn't near enough to serve ..."

The priest fell silent, lost in what he was remembering for a time, then drew a deep breath and went on. "Your cousin used all his influence to make absolutely certain we were ruined. After we'd been kicked out of the house without a moment's notice, allowed nothing but the clothes we wore, he had us spied upon. Every time my father — or my mother — tried to get a job of any kind, however lowly, Alkattha sent someone to inform the prospective employer how they would be punished if they hired us. Others in your family assisted him in this. That much I know.

"When my family had been reduced to living in a bamboo lean-to down in Hell's Arch, he finally called his spies away. But even then, if he happened to hear that my father had found employment as a charcoal hauler, or a boat scraper, he made whatever effort was required to see him dismissed, even from that." The priest's eyes flickered toward Sian again. "He didn't live five years, my lady. My mother made it eight. She died four years ago, just after my sister, of grief as much as anything, I think. I am all that's left." He shrugged. "And then the god washed up. I was among the first to rush down to the beach that day, and beg my portion of the meat."

He drew another very long, deep breath, and stood to go look out a window at the sunlit sea. "There are many ways one may be beaten. I was beaten physically on any number of occasions during those years. Sometimes into stupor. That's how life is lived in such places. Such beatings were the *least* injurious of my torments.

"There is a great deal more, that I beg you not to make me recite, my lady." He turned to gaze at her again. "I do not attempt to justify — with this tale, or by any other means — what I *agreed* to do to you that night. I was convinced, not compelled, to do as the god asked. I still am not sure what I should have done. Not in my heart. I know that you've forgiven me. I know that in my body, as you will remember, I believe. That was a very great gift, my lady. I will never know how to tell you all you changed in me that night. For that, I am forever grateful. But your forgiveness does not make it all right to have been the one wielding the whip. Even for that hour. Not for me. This, I still hold against the god. And perhaps, against myself.

"That is why I've told you what you wished to know. If there is more that I can do, just name it, and I will. But I beg you, do not share this tale with anyone. Whatever I may become now, let me be it free of the shadow that was cast over my family. The man who cast it is gone at last, it seems. At least, I pray so. Let the memory be gone as well."

"I will tell no one," said Sian. "I ... am sorry, for whatever that is worth."

"You have nothing to be sorry for. That's why I didn't wish to tell you. I don't want you feeling blamed." He looked down, pale and drawn. "Or further used. By me. I knew you were related to the Alkatthas. But the god who urged that act upon me had already taught me to loath the self-consuming hunger for revenge. Through *several years* of beatings. Mostly self-inflicted as I tried, over and over, to satisfy my anger, rather than to set it down."

"I know," she told him. "And I believe you. Can you set it down now? Now that I know?"

He gazed at her a long time before saying, "Perhaps ..."

"I will keep your secret, but I will not forget," she said. "I am your witness now."

"Thank you, my lady ... For this as well. You have not lost your wisdom."

There was a knock upon the door behind him. The priest smiled sadly at Sian. "That will be the happier surprise Het promised, I imagine. At long last."

He went to pull the door open, and Reikos stuck his head inside, grinning as he saw her looking back. "Am I interrupting anything of import?" he asked in his stilted, foreign way, though his accent had diminished greatly these past few weeks.

"No. I was just leaving," said the priest. "Rest well, Our Lady. I will try to do the same now." He clapped Reikos on the shoulder as they passed each other. "Make her happy."

"Konstantin," she sighed, relieved that she'd been right. "Come here. I need you. I need someone to hold. Someone without painful secrets to reveal."

He closed the door, and came to sit down on the edge of her broad mattress, looking at her in concern. "Have these fools been telling you unhappy things?"

"They aren't fools, but yes, they have. You don't have painful secrets, do you? Are your crew all right? Your ship? I never even got to ask you, before I left."

"All my secrets are happy ones," he assured her with a smile. "But what have all these men who aren't fools been telling you?"

"Pino," she said, feeling her eyes grow hot and moist again.

"Ah. Yes. Pino." Reikos nodded. "I am sorry, Sian. I … I should have —"

"No. You *shouldn't have*," she said fiercely. "Not everything is yours to fix — or to command, Captain." She sighed. "None of us can keep the world from happening. Whatever way it wants to. You might have been dead now too, if you'd been anywhere except … wherever it was you ended up. Where was that?" She patted the mattress at her side, raising a fresh cloud of lavender scent. "Get in here, and tell me all these happy secrets."

"In there?" He managed to look both intrigued and scandalized. "What if someone should come in?"

"The Factora knows about us. And I'm sure Arouf's complained to everybody else in Alizar by now, so who is left to be dismayed by the discovery that we are lovers?" She gave him a sly smile. "And I said nothing about taking off your clothes."

"No?" Reikos offered her a tragic look. "Then, what is the —"

"Don't," she warned him, giving him the sort of look she'd used to give him all the time. Before the war. "Don't say something stupid like that. I wish to be *held*, Reikos. Just held. You must have run across this sort of thing before. Somewhere."

He smiled at her, and climbed under the covers in his clothes.

"Now, tell me," she said, as he put his arms around her, and she snuggled close. "What happened that night?"

"Well, to be as brief as it is possible, we wrecked *Fair Passage* on a reef. She's lying on the bottom somewhere not too far northeast of here. Three of my crew were injured rather badly, including Kyrios, who broke half a dozen ribs."

"These are your *happy secrets*?" Sian exclaimed, then realized she wasn't being very sympathetic. He'd only been there trying to help her, after all. "I'm very sorry, Konstantin. How did she get wrecked?"

"Running from Sergeant Ennias, as it turned out."

"Why were you running from the sergeant?"

"A very good question, to which I still have not any very good answer, I'm afraid."

None of this was at all what she'd been hoping for. "Are your men recovering, I hope?"

"Oh, they'll be a while healing," he said. "Unless you wish to come, when you're feeling better, of course, and speed things for them — not that I would ask you to. Not after all you've been through."

"Well, that's for the best," she said a little sadly. "Because my gift is gone, love. I cannot heal a cockroach now."

"Why is that a problem? Who wants a cockroach healed?" She was not sure, but he … seemed to think the question serious. "What do you mean, your gift is gone?"

"I mean, I can no longer heal. At all. After I healed Konrad … The gift did not come back with me from … wherever I have been."

He stared at her. "Oh, Sian … I am so sorry. No one told me."

"No one knew until just now. And don't be, Reikos. I am sorry I can't heal Kyrios and the others, but … I do not want to be a saint." She gazed into his eyes, and leaned up just far enough to kiss him, lightly on the cheek. "I hope that is all right with you?"

"Oh ... yes," he said, then smiled lasciviously. "I am not wanting you to be a saint, my love. Or — and I hope this is not too honest — to share you with the world that way."

She smiled back. "Your men *will* heal, though. Won't they?"

"Oh yes, I'm sure they will. And they are very happy anyway. I doubt they mind such broken bones at all."

"Why not?"

"They are all captains now, my love." His grin was like a little sunrise. "Each with his own ship! I think those who did not wait for me are much sorrier men today."

"They're all getting ships?" she asked, struggling up onto one arm to better see if he was joking. "Of their own?" He nodded happily. "From whom?"

"From me. And from the new Factora's father-in-law, of course. The Alkatthas are all shipping moguls, Sian. Surely, you must know this. And very happy with me, at the moment."

Sian gaped in delight. "The Factora's giving them all ships? Oh, Konstantin! That is ... wonderful news! What has she given you?"

"The ships I gave my men," said Reikos. "They are from her, really, I suppose, more than from me or Lord Alkattha. It is hard to say. Everybody is so happy and is wanting to say thank you." He shrugged. "The ships are from them all, I guess."

"So, you have a new ship too?"

He shook his head, still smiling at her.

"Then ..." She wondered when he had become ... quite this generous. He was a very good man, of course. She would not have loved him otherwise. But he had always been more than shrewd enough at business too. "How ... will *you* get a new ship? Or a new crew, for that matter?"

"My love, don't you see? The owner of an entire shipping fleet does not need to go to sea himself. Look at how these cousins of yours live. You do not see them swabbing decks or out cleaning brine off of the sheets in miserable weather for months on end. They stay here. In grand houses like this!"

"You own a *fleet*?"

"My crew still work for me," he said, looking so pleased with himself that she could not help but giggle. "Did I not make that clear? Finding crews for all my ships will be their problem now, not mine. I have had enough of life on the sea, Sian. I am going to stay ashore now. Here. With you, if you will have me. That is *my* new world."

THIRTY-SEVEN

She arrived this time, not with a flotilla of armed and decorated ships, but in a small sloop shared by no one but Ennias and the boatman who had sailed them here. There were no fierce paints and gleaming gold regalia now. Her hair had been restored to its natural blonde and gray, and she wore no cosmetic mask at all. She was done with faces not her own. Alizar would know her real face from now on. Her dress today was just a simple black silk robe. Not the blazing sun. Not the might of Alizar. She was a slender shadow now, a sliver of the night, passing unnoticed through a world dreaming its own dreams, oblivious, around her.

The contrast might have been laughable, if there'd been any laughter left inside her. She had her son back, and was deeply grateful. Every day. But there was no laughter even there. Someday, she hoped. But not yet. He had come back to her a sweet but strangely silent boy, to find his father dead, his home destroyed. His uncle … mad, and in a prison. For attempting to poison him, among other crimes. Very little laughter there at all.

Arian had made every effort to help Konrad absorb these truths as gently and as sensitively as possible. But there'd been no way to keep them from him without lying altogether. Which she found she could no longer do — to him, or anybody else now. There had been so many lies. They had poisoned so much more than just her son. She could not abide deception now. Neither in herself, nor in others. The truth. She hungered for it, desperately. Would not — *could* not feel secure until she felt she had it. Which was, in part, why she had come this morning, to see Aros.

Only two men met her at the nearly empty docks this time. Het helped her from the boat, while his secretary, Linget, helped Ennias and the boat-man to secure the little craft. Then, all but the boatmen turned and headed for a temple entrance carved into the cliff nearby.

"Have you seen him yet this morning?" Arian asked as they walked up and up a torch-lit stairway, carved out deep inside the living stone, Ennias and Het's secretary close behind.

"I have," said Het. "He seems calm. The medications we've administered appear to be effective. His state of agitation diminishes daily. There is almost never any screaming anymore."

"Did you tell him I was coming?"

Het nodded. "He took the news indifferently."

She nodded back. "I am glad to hear it." They climbed on in silence for a while. Somewhere far below them, Duon sat in a prison cell as well, likely pondering how *he* had come to such a pass. Arian wished that she were able to find more satisfaction in his demise. But it seemed fairly certain now that Duon had had no inkling her son was being poisoned. Lies upon lies. Had any of them been left undeceived? Not that Duon was undeserving of his fate, of course. He had created quite a large patch of the soil in which such lies had thrived. "Does he seem any more capable of understanding ques-tions, or answering them coherently?" she asked Het. "Is it permissible for me to ask them yet?"

Het shrugged. "He often seems as rational as you or I now. Ask what you wish, my lady. What he gives you in response may or may not make any sense, of course. If he becomes agitated, it is likely best to stop. Otherwise ... Learn what you may." He turned to look at her. "We *will* have the answers someday, my lady. The truth emerges. Sooner or later. The events we've just been through confirm that, yes?"

The events we've just been through ... she thought. *Already in past tense. Lucky man, able to set all of this aside so quickly.* She liked Het, as much as she'd despised Duon, and doubted that his frame of mind could be dis-honest or delusional. Perhaps his apparent confidence that all of this was over, somehow, came of having a clean conscience. Would she have such a conscience someday? Could such a thing be acquired, belatedly? "The events we've just been through confirm the need for truth, at least," she answered him.

"I wholeheartedly agree," said Het.

"For which, I thank you, Father Superior. The Factorate's relationship with your order will be ever so much more productive now because of that."

"Here we are," said Het, waving toward a heavy wooden door set in the wall ahead of them. "Linget? You have the keys, yes?"

"Of course, sir." The man hurried past them, fishing the key ring from his robes, and jingling up the one he needed, turning it in the lock as they approached.

"The cell is divided, of course, as are all our treatment cells, my lady," said Het. "There will be bars between you, but I'd advise against coming close to them. By no means should you attempt to touch him, even in affection. You'll have your guard, of course. Shall I stay as well?"

"No, Father Het. Thank you, but … Ennias will make him uncomfortable enough, I fear. I am hoping he will speak more freely if there is no one else of importance to him present."

Het nodded. "You may be right. Are you ready then, my lady?"

"I suppose."

Het turned to Linget. "You may open it."

Linget yanked upon the heavy door, and stepped aside as Ennias passed through.

Arian gave Het a nod, and followed her guard inside.

The cell was not as terrible as she'd anticipated. It was full of light, for one thing, and fresh air, unlike the stairs and hallway by which they had come here. The far wall, in Aros's side of the compartment, was pierced by two large windows — barred, of course, but with views of sunlit sky and water. The entire space was finished in clean white plaster, sparsely but comfortably furnished with a bed, a table and a chair for Aros. All very sturdy, and bolted to the floor, she noticed. Aros himself sat on the bed's edge, gazing at her, wearing a clean cream-colored shift of raw silk, his hair tied back with two very short white ribbons. The attire gave him an air of innocence that Arian found both disturbing and somehow heartbreaking.

Ennias had moved to stand off in one corner of the 'reception bay,' as Arian now thought of it, an alcove on their side of the bars with two chairs *not* bolted to the floor. She took one of them and sat, wondering how to start; what would happen when she spoke. … Who she would find, now, behind that oddly innocent gaze.

"They tell me you're made queen," Aros drawled. "Congratulations, sister. No more need to hide behind some man."

Well. Still himself, clearly. Or the self he had become somehow. "They have no queens in Alizar, Aros. We've been through all that, I think. Any number of times." As for *no more hiding behind some man*, she knew better than to take the bait, however hurtful.

The silence resettled as they gazed at one another. He certainly showed no evidence of remorse. That hurt her, even now, but also freed her to do or say whatever she had cause to. No point in niceties, or delay. "I wish to understand a great many things, brother. To understand *you* better." He just continued looking at her. Quizzically. "May I ask some … difficult questions?"

"You're the queen now," he said, deadpan. "What power have I to stop you?"

She took a breath, cultivating calm. "All right. To begin with, then, I wish to know, simply and plainly, whether it was your idea, or the Census Taker's, to overthrow Viktor's government?" This had been the fundamental question burning inside her almost since she'd realized that her own brother had been part of the conspiracy. Just as Viktor had so often warned her, and she had never for a second believed possible. Had Aros really been that villainous, or had her feckless brother just been used? It might not matter to the courts, or to the state, but it made all the difference in the world to her.

"Really?" Aros asked. "That's your question?" He seemed astonished, as if she'd asked why beans were green. "It was no one's idea at all. I would think that should be obvious by now."

"What … do you mean? Are you trying to deny there was a plot to —"

"Arian, it was over in *a day*! Have you seriously not wondered why? If anyone had been *plotting* civil war here … Well, it was certainly a half-assed effort, don't you think?"

"Then …"

"No one had planned on using force for anything. That's why it failed." Aros seemed surprised that Arian should prove so dull. "Escotte just panicked. That's what really happened. When he realized he'd been exposed, he ran around threatening everybody into solving *his little problem* this way. Even me! Stupid man." Aros turned away to gaze out the window. "And now he's run away, I'm told. After throwing all the rest of us into the fire. How like him."

Stupid? … Escotte? Not the Escotte she had ever known. "But, if no one had intended to overthrow the government, then what was this conspiracy about?"

"Succession." Aros shrugged. "Someone's surely told you that by now. It was all supposed to have been politics. Nothing more." He turned back to look at her. "Are these questions ever going to get interesting? Because, as you can see, I am a very busy man. A queen should be equipped to figure out such simple things without her *younger brother's* help."

Yes, she had been told by Hivat that Aros had imagined himself next in line for the Factor's seat, if Konrad died. "But why would Escotte have been involved in such maneuvers at all?" she asked. "He was in power already. Arguably more powerful than Viktor himself, given the state things had fallen into here."

"He would not have been for long. Not once your son died. As he seemed so certain to — before this god arrived to save him. We'd all have been quite quickly set aside then, wouldn't we? Escotte included. Why wait around for an unpopular Factor without an heir to die, when some other house, with a future, could just march right in and get the nation sailing in the right direction again? That's how Escotte saw things, anyway. That's why he agreed to support my bid for the throne, after Konrad died. I promised to keep him on."

"We don't *have* a throne here," Arian said severely. "This is not a continental court, Aros. Not since Alizar won their independence — more than a century ago! Your stubborn failure to accept that has cost … everybody everything."

"It's as good as any continental court, whatever they may wish to call it here. The rules are all the same. The rules that matter anyway. Escotte knew that, and so do you, *my lady*." Aros drew a breath, and sighed, his sullen frown becoming sad instead. "I'd have kept you and Viktor on as well. I would have needed you. I'm not an idiot, whatever you believe. And we *are* family, after all. I never wanted anybody dead. You have to know that."

"Except my son," she said coldly. "Who arranged to have him poisoned? Was it you?"

"*I asked nothing of the kind!*" he shouted suddenly, rising to his feet. "I never told those idiotic priests to …" He'd begun to tremble. "I just … I told them they need not … prolong his *suffering*. That was all I ever said!"

"Was this before or after he had started to recover?" Arian was trembling now as well. "You're his *uncle*! He trusted you. I *trusted you*! I *defended* you to Viktor! Time and time again!"

"*I didn't do it!*" he all but shrieked, breathing like a bellows now. "*He was dying anyway! Slowly! Terribly!* Were you not there? Did you not see?" He sank back onto the bed, his face fallen, his gaze turned inward. "I love my nephew. I just told them not to make him suffer."

"Politics is all conveyed in nuance, Aros," Arian snapped. "You know that at least as well as I do — with all your continental airs and ambitions. Did you really think, even for a moment, that those priests would not understand what was meant between the lines? What was *wanted*? By the Factor's self-proposed *successor*? Did you imagine they wouldn't think about how best to curry favor with their potential future ruler?" She wished there were no bars between them. It was not *her* those bars protected at that moment. "I do not think so, *brother*."

"I am not a murderer," he moaned, clutching at his head again, his inward gaze still fastened on the floor. "I am not. … I am not. I am —"

"How could you have done this?" Arian demanded. "To *me*, much less to Konrad? You were so sweet once. Timid even. Who taught you to be such a snake? When did this happen?"

He looked up at her, his eyes almost as soulful, suddenly, as Konrad's. "You do not know what it is like to be *surrounded* … and *ignored* … by people who all *matter*.

"Father, always off advising kings and councilmen. Alexandros, with his aspirations to the House of Guilds, if not the royal council of advisors;

Father's pride and joy. You, the gem of Copper Downs, constantly courted by Factors and princes. And me ... a little afterthought. The last-minute by-blow of some final flare of lust before Mother died. Trotting about that giant house all but unnoticed by anyone — except when I was in the way. Held in abeyance by the army of governesses and tutors our father hired to *suppress* me while he tended to *important* tasks, like grooming you and Alexandros to become the ones who *mattered*."

Arian gazed at him, taken by surprise. "Aros ... that's not how any of us —"

"*Yes it was!*" He shouted as if she'd just held something hot against his skin. "You just didn't *notice!* No one noticed! ... No one. I didn't matter enough to be noticed. I have never mattered."

Was it true? She looked down, thinking back. He had come along so late. And been so sweet. But so much younger. Very little of his world and hers had overlapped. That much was true. Even truer of their older brother, she supposed, and of her father. Aros's father. Had none of them noticed he was ... miserable? "Why have you not said something bef —"

"I did!" he cut her off, more pleading now than shouting. "I have been screaming it for years! Help me *matter*, sister! Help *me* matter, *too*! You just ignored me, except for all the times you laughed, or scoffed. Or shamed me ... just for wanting what you've *always had*."

She was horrified. Had she helped forge this monster that her once-charming little brother had become? Was she at fault for this as well?

"How long before I am to be executed?" Aros asked her, flatly now, gazing out the window once again.

"What makes you think you will be executed?"

"Is conspiring against the throne not a capital offense here?" he asked, distractedly. "I confess, I've never thought to ask. I just assumed it was."

She was on the verge of telling him, yet again, that Alizar had no *throne*, but checked herself in time. This obsession with aristocratic trappings was either part of his delusion or another pointless game. It was *still* not clear to her who had really orchestrated this affair. And right now, what mattered was that he get well enough to stand public trial at all. "I have no expectation that you will be hanged, Aros."

He turned to look at her, dead-eyed. "It will be no mercy, sister, if you let me live." She had never seen him look so tired before. He seemed to have aged ten years, just since glancing out the window. "It's so dark in here."

"So dark?" This was just self-pity now. "Look at all this light. How many prison cells do you suppose have such a view?"

He stared at her, seeming sapped of strength. "I mean … in *here*." His eyes emptied as she watched. "The dark goes on forever, in here … sister. … I will never find my way out now."

Though the words had been addressed to her, she didn't think it was herself that he was talking to. Not anymore. Grief suddenly replaced her anger.

"Make them kill me. Please." Only his lips moved now. Woodenly. Like those of a puppet. "You're the queen now. They will have to listen to you … If you ever loved me … do not let me live."

THIRTY-EIGHT

Pino's funeral was a relatively small affair, as formal state occasions
went. The Factora and her son had invited only the most important
people: Sian, of course, and her lover, Konstantin Reikos; the Mishrah-
Khote's new Father Superior, there to officiate; the Butchered God's once-
renegade priest, now in retirement according to the rumor mill; the de
facto leader of a humble raft warren on Home's southern shore, his unwed
cousin and her mute daughter; Pino's bewildered parents, a poor old fisherman and his wife, from an island north of Malençon too tiny to be named;
and, last but not *entirely* least, a small host of foreign dignitaries, important
government officials, and senior representatives from all of Alizar's most
illustrious families.

To accommodate even such a modest gathering, it had been necessary
to enlarge the hilltop meadow on Little Loom Eyot. With astonishing speed,
an army of Factorate-supplied laborers had removed half its trees and brush,
and leveled or terraced its irregular contours. An elegant stone crypt and
monument had been constructed, surrounded by beautifully landscaped
lawns and walks, pergolas, and gazebos. This place would henceforth be
a site of national significance. Little Loom Eyot — at Alizar's outermost
fringe — would never be anonymous again, or truly private. Not that Sian
cared. She wanted Pino close. But not forgotten. Ever.

The crowd on that sunny, breeze-swept afternoon was itself perhaps the
clearest tangible manifestation yet of how *new* the world truly was in Alizar.
Rothkin and his family had been given many gifts in appreciation of their
help that dreadful night — including some simple but elegant formal silk

attire, from Sian. Now she watched the young man moving like a peacock through the crowd of cordial and respectful, if not entirely comfortable, aristocrats, doubtless wondering how to work this windfall to his advantage. Rothkin had already been appointed to the new Factora's council of advisers, and was thus not to be lightly dismissed, even by them, however dubious his pedigree.

Earlier that morning, Het had quietly informed Sian that Rothkin's cousin, Hilara, and her daughter Paola had accepted his invitation to become the Mishrah-Khote's first anointed female acolytes. *The girl will be greater than any of us,* he'd told her, *if she is not already. Her rapport with the otherworld is generating awe within the temple. It is my hope that her poor mother too will find real refuge and some greater purpose of her own among us now. I fear she has been more needed than wanted since the girl's gift appeared — by many, including her cousin.* Upon hearing this, Sian had found herself recalling Paola's refusal of a voice that night in Rothkin's hut, and wondered if that refusal had been for her mother's sake. How quickly might Hilara have been cast away again — or worse — if she had ceased to be the only gateway to her daughter's secret knowledge? Could such a young child have understood this — more clearly than even her mother had perhaps?

Pino's distraught parents seemed most lost here. They had known nothing at all of their son's involvement in the short-lived war, much less of his death, having assumed him well out of harm's way, working at some little textiles firm on the world's other edge. It had taken weeks just to locate them. Now they sat beside the Factora and Konrad, under a small pavilion tent erected for Arian and her most honored guests, gazing about, often tearfully, at all the lofty people who suddenly seemed so grateful for their son's life. Sian had tried to tell them what a fine employee and dear friend he had become, how sorry she was for their loss. They had been very polite, very honored by her words — and clearly not that much consoled. Such fine compliments would obviously have meant so much more had they been delivered while Pino was still alive. But who ever thought of such things while there was still time to act on them?

Still, Sian meant to try harder from here on.

There were brighter events to note, of course. Also in the Factora's pavilion, just behind Arian and her son, sat Commander Ennias, the new head of her personal guard, beside his new affair of the heart, Maronne.

Having awakened that next morning to find Escotte Alkattha gone and his house under attack, it seemed Maronne had simply fled the house, impeded by no one in all the chaos. She had remained in hiding on Cutter's until the fighting seemed done, then reappeared at the Factorate only a day after Sian's long sleep had started.

Maronne's brief liaison with then-Sergeant Ennias during the 'dress-maker plot,' as they now called it, had apparently proven unexpectedly enjoy-able — for both of them, regardless of the fact that Ennias was nearly fifteen years her junior. From what Sian had heard, their affair had the Factora's whole-hearted approval. And Lucia had quietly informed Sian that the new commander's skill as a poet was proving quite surprising too — according to Maronne, at least, who was, to date, the sole inspiration and recipient of these unanticipated artistic endeavors.

When the guests had all arrived, and been given time to greet others before getting settled, the long ironwood horns were blown at last, toward the east and west, day's rising and its setting. Great carved onyx bowls of incense were lit, and the islands' dissonant, many-layered ritual music was sung with moving solemnity by a temple choir, as Pino's richly carved teak and copper sarcophagus was borne into the center of the meadow and laid upon its flower-strewn bier before the shrine.

Het's eulogy was focused on the impact one humble boat boy's bravery and sacrifice could have on an entire nation. Though heartfelt, it was brief. Like most there, he had never met Pino, or even heard of him before that week. When his own remarks were finished, Het invited the Butchered God's onetime priest forward to speak as well, to the quiet satisfaction or discomfort of the Factora's extremely varied guests. The controversial young man had known Pino better than most in attendance there, after the boy's parents and Sian, who had all declined to speak publicly. The former fugitive stepped onto the speaker's platform, dressed in a clean, plain robe of white silk. He nodded his respect, first to Pino's parents, then to the Factora and her son, and finally, Sian, then turned soberly to address the assembled gathering.

"Not quite a year ago, Pino came to me out of a crowd one day, like so many others, speaking of a hole he felt inside himself. A call, he said, a thirst, a vision, endlessly persistent, but never clear enough to name, much less to satisfy, though he claimed that it had been there all his life. I had heard such claims before. The sense of something missing, something imminent but elusive, was what drew all of us to the Butchered God. But Pino had what I can only call pure spirit. He seemed made of it entirely. And that was nothing I had ever seen before — or have seen since.

"There seemed no shadows in him. He did not envy those who had what he did not. He was not ruled by fear, or by ambition, or shame, or greed, or anger, or any of the darker things that shape and drive so many of us. He was honest to a fault, never defensive or more concerned for himself than for others. His one quiet but abiding passion was an endless search for the very light he seemed not to see burning inside himself, though so many others saw it there. When he could not find that light, he did little else but look for it. Whenever he found it, though, even for a moment, he threw himself into its service without hesitation or counting costs." The young priest paused, seeming lost in some sudden, private reflection. "Even on the night he died, I doubt he was much afraid. I cannot know, of course, but I suspect that even as his boat was struck, his full attention was still fixed entirely upon the light he followed at that moment. For all I know, he may be following that light still." He turned to Pino's parents, at the Factora's side. "I thank you for the love and wisdom it must have taken to nurture and permit such a pure, remarkable boy, such a singular life, such an example for each of us and for this nation, as so many of us look up and around at last to find and follow the light we had lost track of for so long. It has cost you more dearly than most to help make our world new. We are forever in your debt, and in your son's."

With that, the Butchered God's enigmatic priest stepped back off the speaker's platform and out of his 'priesthood' forever, Sian felt sure.

There was further pomp and ceremony after that, but Sian was rarely more than partially aware of it, lost now in recollection of that final night in Pino's life. Her mind kept returning to his awkward little profession of love on Reikos's behalf. For fear that Konstantin might not survive to tell her. She had thought him only young and somewhat foolish then, failing to see how selfless it had been to think of Reikos rather than himself at such a moment. Reikos had thought him reckless, but perhaps that too had just been purity in action. *Oh, Pino. Why did this light you sought so earnestly not watch over you more carefully?*

When the last words of ritual had been sounded, and Pino's body committed to its solitary rest inside the crypt, and the long horns blown one more time — in all six of the sacred directions — Het came to take Pino's parents aside and speak with them more privately. There were more explicit, if less public, expressions of thanks and concern to be conveyed, more tangible privileges and reassurances to be explained now, in compensation for all their son had done for the Factora, her heir, and the nation. It had been agreed that Het was best equipped to express all this to people so clearly overawed and discomfited by those of high station. Despite his own new title, Het knew how to put humble people at ease. He had always been, and would always be, one of them.

As the other guests began to mingle and dissipate, Sian and Reikos were invited to join Arian, Konrad, Lucia, Maronne, and Ennias for some light refreshment in a private section of the pavilion tent. Once there, however, conversation faltered. After hours of such gravity, neither further gravity nor frivolous small talk seemed quite … apropos. Sian was not the only one to glance at young Konrad, and look away again without speaking. He had returned to them such a strangely grave and quiet boy.

"So, a great deal of rebuilding now, I must assume," Reikos said at last, breaking their awkward silence as perhaps only an outsider of sorts could be allowed to.

"Oh … well, yes," said Arian. "We've already started with the most essential sites, of course: bridges, docks, marinas, businesses … But there will be much more, eventually. I intend to see the new Factorate House and Census Hall rebuilt of local materials, and in the architectural styles of Alizar, not those of the continent. It seems time the nation left its colonial past entirely behind."

That foreign bride of his … Sian thought, as she and the others nodded their approval of her plan. How many times had she heard Escotte dismiss

Arian that way? And yet, she doubted *he* would have approved this plan to abandon foreign pomp and make the nation's architectural monuments truly Alizari. It seemed just, if ironic, that her dreadful cousin should end up exiled to the continent he had pretended to despise, while Viktor's *foreign bride* should be here, leading Alizar into its own, at last.

"Unfortunately, we now require a new Census Taker too." Arian sighed. "I dread the task of finding someone to fill that post. The office is supposed to be impartial, though that pretense has always been a farce. After all we've just been through, however, I think it really must be filled this time by someone Alizar's people can genuinely trust to serve them first. Sadly, I am having trouble thinking of any candidate who quite answers that description." She shook her head. "In the current atmosphere, I will be accused of political pandering anyway, no matter whom I choose."

As Sian listened, the solution occurred to her with such force and clarity that she wondered if the Butchered God wasn't in her mind again, still meddling in Alizar's affairs after all. "My Lady Factora, if I may be so bold, I believe I may have someone to suggest."

"Really?" Arian's smile betrayed the slightest hint of wry amusement. "Are *you* interested in the job, my dear?"

"The gods forbid! No ... I'm sure this will sound crazy, but ... I think the Butchered God's former priest would be perfect for the job, in more ways than may seem apparent."

The astonished silence around her was embarrassingly profound. Only young Konrad appeared to watch her with something less than surprise on his grave face.

Wishing she had not promised to keep the priest's tale secret, Sian saw no choice now but to soldier on. "I've come to know him somewhat better during these past few weeks. He is a far more educated man than anyone assumes, and clearly a forceful and effective organizer. It must have taken considerable political and logistical skill to lead a massive popular movement capable of bringing down Alizar's whole economy, while managing to remain not only free of capture, but of any formal criminal charges."

"All of which recommends him how?" Arian asked, not quite concealing her incredulity. "I cannot imagine any leading house supporting such a nomination."

"They might not wish to," Sian said, "but you can't have forgotten that huge crowd assembled, *peaceably*, outside the Factorate. And neither will they. He has the unqualified support of Alizar's people, my lady. Nearly all of them. I would be surprised to see any of the leading houses risk opposing such a massive bloc of popular opinion. Not overtly anyway. And no one could accuse you of political pandering. Allegations of allegiance between himself and *any* of the leading houses would be absurd."

"For obvious reasons," Arian all but laughed. "The Census Taker must be someone the houses can work with, at least. And he must bring something of more value to the post than mere charisma."

"But I think he does," Sian pressed. "Despite decades of angry resentment among Alizar's workforce, the violence we've all just endured was inflicted by the country's rulers in the end, not by its people. I believe this young man had a lot to do with that. I once heard him speak to a great crowd of his god's followers, during which he very skillfully discouraged them from violent rebellion even as he encouraged them to abandon their employers. I have little doubt that he could lead them back to work as readily as anyone else can now, and without betraying them in any way. Surely that capacity alone would be of value to both the nation and its leading families."

To Sian's relief, Reikos finally broke the polite silence everyone had maintained through this awkward exchange. "My Lady Factora, I too heard the young man speak that night, and must admit to having found his insights both surprisingly wise and inspiring. And I know many of the common folk were heeding him ... even when others were seeking violence. If I may be allowed to say so, I am in agreement with Sian's assertions."

Arian took a deep breath, and crossed her arms. "Does he have the slightest idea what the job entails? The Census Taker isn't some religious leader; he's a bureaucrat. The most important bureaucrat in Alizar."

"I suspect he knows a great deal more about the post — and about Escotte Alkattha — than one might expect," said Sian.

"Really." Arian's eyes narrowed. "And why might that be?"

"I ... am not free to tell you," Sian conceded. "He has entrusted me with certain confidences which I have promised to protect."

"So you have reasons for this ... surprising suggestion which you aren't telling me. I thought as much." Arian turned to Ennias. "Would you go find this priest for me, please, and ask if he would come to speak with us?"

"Of course, my lady." Ennias turned and headed for the door.

"We'll look for him too," said Maronne, tugging at Lucia's sleeve. "Three will find him faster than one." They hastened after the commander.

"Then five will do better than that." Reikos turned to Konrad. "Shall we help them hunt, young man?"

"Oh yes!" Konrad broke into a rare grin and quickly followed Reikos from the tent. Since regaining his health, he had latched on to the sea captain almost hungrily, demanding to know everything about all the foreign places he had never expected to live to see.

When everyone was gone, Arian turned to Sian. "I know you are no fool. But now that we are alone, can you truly offer me no clue of what these confidences are?"

She shook her head. "But I'm hoping he'll agree to tell you."

"Very well. Shall we have some tea then, while we await him?"

"Yes, please."

They sat. Arian poured. They sipped. After a minute, Arian said, "Has your captain proposed marriage yet?"

Sian glanced over at her sharply, searching for the light of humor in her friend's eyes. But Arian appeared quite serious. "Ah, it seems a bit ... soon for that, I think." Then she smiled. "I am still becoming accustomed to having him so much around." She looked away. "And the divorce papers have only just been sent off to the Justiciary, of course."

"Well, yes. I guess a proposal might seem rather hasty, then." She smiled. "He is a good man. I am happy for you."

"Thank you. Indeed he is." Sian gazed down into her tea a minute. "I think we are all doing a great deal of rebuilding. It may take some time to understand the full shape of things, in this new world we've inherited."

"Yes." Now it was Arian's turn to study her teacup. "I always imagined that I ran this country before, behind the scenes. And that I worked twice as hard to do so, having to hide behind paint and courtesies and subtle in-fluence and intrigue." She gave a quiet snort of laughter. "But now ... Now that it's just me, it's ... no easier at all."

"I understand," Sian said, and she did. Monde & Kattë was a textile firm, not a nation; but without Arouf here to manage the daily operations, Sian was discovering all manner of unsuspected gaps in her own knowledge. "But you'll do fine," she told Arian. "You're strong, you're wise — and you're honest. Alizar trusts you."

Arian smiled at her; Sian could see the sadness in her eyes. "I hope their trust is well placed."

Sian reached over and patted her hand. "You might not always know the way through the tunnels, but you're willing to admit when you make a mistake. I can't think of a better quality in a leader."

"We've learned a lot about ourselves, haven't we. And what will you do now? You can't just go back now either, can you?"

The doorway curtain rustled; Ennias poked his head in. "My Lady Factora? We've found him."

"Good — send him in."

Sian was happy not to have to answer such a question, as the young priest stepped inside the tent.

"Thank you very much for coming," Arian said.

"Of course, My Lady Factora," he replied cautiously.

"I have a rather odd question to ask you, I'm afraid," Arian told the priest.

"I am not entirely unaccustomed to strange questions," he replied, smil-ing slightly.

"Hm." She smiled back. "How would you describe the Census Taker's job, young man?"

"The ... Census Taker's job? ... I am not certain I understand the ques-tion, my lady."

"I'm just asking you to describe the Census Taker's job to me — as you understand it."

"In general?" he asked, clearly nonplussed, for all his wry assurances. "Or as it was done specifically by the previous Census Taker?"

"In general, please."

"Well ... In theory, I suppose, the Census Taker exists to manage both the nation's wealth and much of its electoral process."

Arian's brows climbed slightly. "Elaborate, please?"

The priest's brows climbed a bit as well. "The Census Taker is a national power broker, my lady. His office, as I understand it, is responsible for collecting and reporting all manner of census data, on which countless decisions are based in regard to the implementation and regulation of public elections and referendums, and the allocation of national funds, public or private, in response to identified needs. Not that our most recent Census Taker ever did these jobs very well or honestly, from what I have observed. Is that ... sufficient?"

"I told you," Sian murmured.

The priest glanced at Sian, then back at Arian. "At the risk of seeming forward, My Lady Factora, may I ask why I am being given this exam?"

"Well," said Arian, "I wished to learn whether you knew anything about the job before bothering to decide whether or not I should consider offering it to you."

The priest's brows climbed a few more notches. "To ... *me?*"

"I have made no such decision yet," she added, "but I confess to wondering how a largely self-made religious leader has come to understand such a subject so ... concisely."

The priest shrugged, looking more and more confused. "To be perhaps foolishly candid, my lady, and with all due respect to you and your late husband, of course, neither I nor the god I served were ... all that happy about how the nation was being run. It is difficult to be so focused on the results of such poor governance without paying considerable attention to ... how the nation is being run. Does that seem so strange?"

"Only its unvarnished frankness," Arian replied. "Of which I approve. My cousin tells me there's a tale which I ought to hear, but which she is not free to tell me. Might I persuade you to trust me with it?"

"What tale is that?" The young man directed a bruised look at Sian.

"I have told her nothing," Sian assured him. "But I wish you would. Please?"

"Young man," said Arian, "I am in desperate need of a new Census

Taker, one nothing like the last one. My cousin seems to think you may be that man, but I have just watched my life, and the life of this whole nation, disastrously undone by layers of deception. I cannot even think of considering you for such a post while knowing there are things of significance being hidden from me."

"My lady ..." He shook his head, seeming dazed. "While I am ... honored, I suppose, by your consideration, the very idea ... seems ... I'm sorry, but this is absurd! I'd sooner be a temple priest than Alizar's top bureaucrat."

"A man I trusted told me once that it costs us everything to make the world new," Sian replied defiantly. "You could make the Census Taker's office new. You could change the politics of Alizar forever. You just praised Pino for being unafraid."

He looked at her as if she'd stabbed him.

"I can think of few things I would like more than to see the Census Taker's job done as it should be, rather than as it has been," Arian said quietly. "But you have still not answered my question, sir. Why does the thought of telling me your tale frighten you so badly?"

"Because the telling drags me back through all the pain I've ever known," he told her raggedly. "And because ... because it makes all I've been ... all I've done ... seem just another tale of revenge. Though it was not. I swear it. It was not."

"Oh," Sian whispered, seeing it at last. "Your whole life has been shaped by someone else's lies," she told him. "All those people who turned you and your family away. You kept telling them the truth, all those years, and yet, the lies prevailed. You still don't trust anyone to believe you, do you. Not even me. Not even now."

He stared at her like a cornered mouse.

"Revenge against whom?" Arian asked him gently.

"The Census Taker." His whole body sagged. Broken, once again. "And his family, my lady." He looked up at the Factora, seeming more sad than frightened now. "Yes. You can be certain, I have followed Escotte Alkattha's career quite carefully. I know better than most what his job was, and how he betrayed his mandate at every turn. I despised him. And hatred sharpens focus. But the god ... finally took that hatred from me. Brutally and effectively, my lady. I did not choose Sian Kattë that night because of her connection to House Alkattha. The god did." He turned back to Sian. "Nor was anything I did in service of the god meant to bring down the Alkattha family. Not by me, at least. I wished only to serve the vision shown me. To see Alizar awakened. And healed — your family included."

"As it has been," Sian told him. "Do you still think I cannot see that?"

"I grieve my husband's death, young man," said Arian. "But neither have you or your god done anything to bring down House Alkattha. Instead, it has been cleansed. Escotte is disgraced and gone, and whatever role you played in … transforming Sian led to the healing of my son. He's the future of House Alkatthas. My future. Where is there revenge in this? I see only proof, not negation, of all you've been, and done, in service of the god who healed me as well one night, through Sian's hands." She gazed at him, and shook her head. "There is only one thing I am still unsure of. Do you believe your own story, young man? … Can you?" She smiled at him, almost maternally. "I must know your answer, before I'll dare ask you to consider such a demanding new calling."

He gazed back at her, and drew a long, shuddering breath. "May I sit down?"

"Of course." Arian waved him toward the canvas chair beside her own.

He came to lower himself into it, rubbing at his face, and staring at something only he could see. "How much do you wish to know, my lady?"

"Everything," she said. "As much as you trust me to hear."

He nodded. "Very well, then. My name was … is Kalesh Salmian." He gave Sian a sad and weary smile. "My father once served Escotte Alkattha, very well, and was ruined by him for it …"

EPILOGUE

*S*ian awoke to moonlight, streaming through the open shutters and the
gauzy curtains around her bed, across the smooth back of her lover,
not gone back to his ship. Never to go back there now.

Arouf now lived in Monde & Kattë's townhouse on Viel; he'd surrendered Little Loom Eyot, and this home, with no real struggle. He'd
misplayed his cards quite badly. Even he could see that now. Sian had not
turned out to be the social disgrace or the threat to their business he had
once imagined. But what was done, was done. They had agreed to continue
their business partnership. That was what he really cared about, and, in
all fairness, what he had worked at hard enough for all these years to have
some right to still. Sian would need a business partner anyway, more badly
than before, in fact, with so many new distractions to be managing. With
his new shipping fleet to run, Reikos had no more need of, or interest in,
Monde & Kattë than Arouf did of or in their onetime marriage. It would
be good for him, Sian suspected, to be forced out of his kitchen-puttering
and back into the world. To do some real business once again. It might even
be empowering.

So Arouf was gone, and Little Loom Eyot belonged to herself and Reikos
now — who had told her just that evening of his grand plans for their *garden*.
The world was new.

As they'd sat together quietly, after the delicious dinner that Bela had
cooked for them, she had told Konstantin about what Pino had tried to do
for him the night he'd died, and been dismayed when Reikos had responded
by telling Sian about the true extent of Pino's own affection for her. These

men and their strange courtesies to one another. Such news had only further salted her grief, but, deep down, she understood. It could be hard to carry such secrets alone. Justice to the dead. Acknowledgement, however belated. Yes. She understood.

She lay now, thinking, listening to the soft music of night sounds outside the house, and to Reikos's quiet snoring at her side. It had been a long time since she had regularly shared a bed with a man. She watched the moonlight shift across their covers onto the floor, and finally rose, as stealthily as possible, to don her silk nightgown and go find a glass of something warm to help her back to sleep.

In the kitchen, moonlight poured as thick as cream through all the windows, and Sian went to stare out at the gilded sea. It felt as if the light were calling her. *A thirst. A vision not quite clear enough to name.* She found herself outside a moment later, in pursuit of … something.

Twenty minutes later, she sat on the newly planted lawn atop her island's highest hill, beside Pino's burial shrine. To the west, Little Loom Eyot stretched out before her, moon-burnished in the fragrant, luminescent darkness. To the east, the hilltop plunged severely down into the quicksilver sea, whispering and sighing up at her. *A call. A thirst. A vision not quite clear enough to name … much less to satisfy …*

"Are you at peace?" she whispered over her shoulder to Pino. "Have you finally caught up with the light you chased?"

She listened to the crickets and cicadas humming their night-songs in the forest far below her. To the wind. The distant water. The air smelled of dew, and soil, of night-blooming flowers and moist tree bark. Was Pino's answer somewhere in this quiet chorus?

She recalled his sunlit smile, his eager attention rowing or sailing her to and from the central island cluster. How had she been so blind? But what could she have said to him, even if she hadn't been? Had he sacrificed himself that night to prove his love somehow, or in despair of its futility? *He's really a very good man, Domina, and loves you even more than you may guess …* How much had that cost him?

"That priest you led me to is going to be the country's Census Taker now. The Factora you saved has made that possible. Do you know, wherever you are now, how much you changed the world?" The grief welled up again inside her. All at once, from wherever it had been hiding since she'd first heard the news of Pino's death. "I hope you know," she said as she began to weep. "You should be here to see it, Pino." She lay back on the grass and surrendered to the desolation she felt. "If I could change just one thing," she pled. "If I could choose one power. For just one moment ..." She broke down completely then, her grief, her helplessness, too great for words. He had loved her. This sweet, pure, darling boy. And all she'd had to give him in return — all she had to give him now — was death.

Now, my lady! NOW!

The memory of his voice came out of nowhere, like a shout within her mind. Telling her to leave the boat that night.

Yes! Leave the boat! His voice again — almost audibly, so forceful was the thought.

She sat up, and looked back at the crypt, a darkened silhouette against the moonlight. There was a new sound on the night air. A grumbling. Almost too low to hear, though it began to grow. For a startled instant, Sian thought it was coming from inside of Pino's shrine, then realized it came from everywhere at once, just as the stones of Pino's shrine began to grate against each other, and the ground began to sway beneath her.

"Oh!" She tried to scramble to her feet, but could not keep her balance, as if the very island had become a boat at sea. "OH! OH NO!" she gasped more loudly, understanding that it was an earthquake only as the ground began to buck and fracture all around her.

SWIM, MY LADY! WEST!

East of her, a great slab of hilltop vanished suddenly, plunging down into the sea with hardly any sound above the quake's own mighty rumble. As more ground split open and the collapse surged toward her, Sian scrambled on her hands and knees in abject terror past Pino's tomb, half running, half crawling toward the moonlight, while more hilltop fell away behind her. Only once did she glance back to find great chunks of ground thrusting up into the air now as others continued tumbling from the hill. She had no thoughts left beyond a deafening, wordless reflex to flee. She flailed across the gelid lawn, the fractured, grinding walks, until there was hardly any hilltop left in front of her to flee toward.

And all the motion ceased. As suddenly as it had begun.

For a moment, she just lay upon her patch of lawn, breathing hard, still gripping the ground itself with hands and feet, waiting for her mind to clear, for thought to reassert itself. For some further reassurance that the quake was truly over.

Finally, she looked behind her. Everything there was gone — including Pino's shrine and crypt. Hardly any of the hilltop remained except the patch she clung to. But that was not what made her turn and sit to gape in disbelieving terror.

Looming high above her, dark against the night, was a giant, even taller than her island — made of earth and rock, it seemed. It stood, motionless and silent, gazing down at her.

I am dreaming, she thought. *I am in my bed still. Lying beside Reikos.* She willed herself awake, but nothing happened. *I am dreaming. Or I'm dead?*

"**Sian Kattë**," the monster rumbled softly, its voice composed not just of the earthquake's rumble, but of the sea, the wind, the nocturnal insects even, all woven into those two words. The monster nodded at her, gravely. "**Not badly done.**"

Despite the voice's massive scale, its impossible composition, its terrifying source, Sian thought she heard something wry in this second utterance, and a little of her terror slid away. "Who are you?" she hardly more than breathed. "*What* are you?"

"**You know,**" it rumbled. "**Who else can I be?**"

"But … he said you'd gone," she whispered in a daze. "They cut your body up. On Cutter's."

"**A god is not His body.**" He turned, ponderously, to gaze across the moonlit ocean, east of Alizar. "**You were told this. Fare well.**" One of his massive earthen legs pulled forward, and Sian heard the water's distant roar as his first step dragged through the roiled surf into which half of her hill had fallen.

Sian realized that he was leaving. Just like that, without any further explanation. "Wait!" she called. "Why have you done this to my island? What was all this for?" When he just continued walking, out into the ocean, she stood up at last, becoming angry, against all sense. "Look at what you've done to Pino's grave!" she shouted. "It's completely gone now! Tumbled into the sea! Have you no respect for anything? He was devoted to you!"

The monstrous figure swayed to a halt, and slowly turned his head to look back at her across one enormous shoulder. "**To make the world new, even bodies may be taken up again, if necessary. Was this not what you requested?**" His gaze swung away once more, and he resumed his slow course out to sea.

It was then that Sian's eyes caught some small movement on the giant's other shoulder. Something tiny sat there in the darkness. Something she'd not seen when the god's great new body had still loomed above her. It looked for all the world like a person. Looking back at her, perhaps. The giant was already so far off that it was difficult to be certain, until the little figure raised an arm. Just once. As if to wave goodbye.

Sian's mouth fell open as she stared after them in silence, watching the god walk ever farther out to sea, until the moon was covered by a bank of fog rising in the west behind her, and she lost sight of them completely.

ABOUT THE AUTHORS

SHANNON PAGE was born on Halloween night and grew up on a commune in northern California's backwoods, where a childhood without television gave her a great love of the written word. Her work has appeared in numerous venues including *Clarkesworld*, *Interzone*, Tor.com, and the award-winning anthology *Grants Pass*. Her first novel, *Eel River*, was published by Morrigan Books in 2013; in 2015 Per Aspera Press will release *The Queen and The Tower*, the first book in The Nightcraft Quartet. Shannon is a long-time yoga practitioner and an avid gardener, and lives with her husband, Mark Ferrari, in Portland, Oregon. Visit her at www.shannonpage.net.

JAY LAKE was a prolific writer of science fiction and fantasy, an award-winning editor, a popular raconteur and toastmaster, and an excellent teacher at many writers' workshops. Jay won the John W. Campbell Award for best new writer in 2004, and was nominated multiple times for the Hugo, Nebula, and World Fantasy Awards. His other recent books include *Kalimpura* — the final novel in his *Green* cycle — and *Last Plane to Heaven* from Tor, and *Love in the Time of Metal and Flesh* from Prime Books. Following his diagnosis of colon cancer in 2008, Jay became known outside the sf genre for his powerful and brutally honest blogging about the progression of his disease. Jay Lake died on June 1, 2014.

Get an ebook of this novel bundled with purchase.

(visit bitlit.com)

~

Other Novels of the Fantastic
from Per Aspera Press

Being Small by Chaz Brenchley
(August 2014)

A Ragged Magic by Lindsey Johnson
(November 2014)

Waking Up Naked In Strange Places
by Julie McGalliard
(March 2015)

www.perasperapress.com

35396458R00300

Made in the USA
Charleston, SC
07 November 2014